C000143626

50p

EVERYMAN, I will go with thee,

and be thy guide,

In thy most need to go by thy side

EDMUND SPENSER

Born about 1552 in East Smithfield, London. M.A. Cambridge in 1576. Obtained place in Leicester's household. Went to Ireland, 1580, with Lord Grey de Wilton on the latter's appointment as Lord Deputy to that country, and lived there until 1598. Died in Westminster in 1599, and buried in Westminster Abbey.

EDMUND SPENSER

The Faerie Queene

A SELECTION

INTRODUCTION BY
DOUGLAS BROOKS-DAVIES,
M.A., PH.D.
*Lecturer in English Literature,
University of Manchester*

DENT: LONDON
EVERYMAN'S LIBRARY
DUTTON: NEW YORK

© Introduction and selection, J. M. Dent & Sons Ltd, 1976

All rights reserved
Made in Great Britain
at the
Aldine Press · Letchworth · Herts
for
J. M. DENT & SONS LTD
Aldine House · Albemarle Street · London
This selection first published in
Everyman's Library in 1976

Published in the U.S.A. by arrangement
with J. M. Dent & Sons Ltd

No. 443   Hardback ISBN 0 460 00443 3
No. 1443   Paperback ISBN 0 460 01443 9

CONTENTS

To Stevie, the first fruits, with my love

INTRODUCTION

In the April eclogue of his *Shepheardes Calender* (1579),
Spenser sings a beautiful song in praise of Elisa. It is a
simple song, in accordance with decorum, for it has been
composed by the shepherd-poet Colin Clout, but alongside
its rustic simplicity—the association of Elisa, the 'maiden
queen', with 'daffadowndillies, / And cowslips, and king-
cups, and lovéd lilies'—there are allusions to classical
mythology: Elisa's 'angelic face' is 'like Phœbe fair'; she is
the offspring of Syrinx and Pan; and the emblems at the end
of the eclogue, taken from Book I of Vergil's *Aeneid*,
identify her as the goddess Venus who appeared to her son
Aeneas disguised as a nymph of Diana. Elisa is Queen
Elizabeth. And here, in one of Spenser's earliest poems, we
have, recognizably, the Faerie Queene of his great epic, the
Faerie Queene who appears directly only in Arthur's fleeting
vision of her at I. ix. 13–14, but indirectly (or, rather, frag-
mented into different characters who represent Elizabeth in
her various roles) several times in the poem: in Book I as
Una, or Elizabeth as the one head of the Anglican church; in
Books II and III as Belphœbe, Elizabeth as the Virgin
Queen, follower of Phœbe/Diana/Cynthia, goddess of
chastity; and, also in Book III, as Britomart, Elizabeth as
the more militant armed patron of chastity, Minerva, and as
the ideal heroic woman, the British Mars.

The descriptions of Una and Belphœbe are especially
close to that of Colin's Elisa. Una is 'a goodly maiden
Queene' (I. xii. 8) and, in the previous stanza, is compared
to Diana; at stanza 21 she is 'as bright as . . . the morning
starre'. In other words, she is both virginal (like Diana) and
Venerean; for the morning star is the planet Venus. Simi-
larly, Belphœbe, on her appearance in II. iii, is dressed as a
hunter and compared to Diana (stanza 31)—Diana is god-
dess of the hunt as well as of chastity. But she has 'upon her
eyelids' the 'many Graces' which link her with Venus
(stanza 25), and 'yellow lockes' (stanza 30), again a detail

vii

that would associate her with Venus, since yellow was one of Venus's colours. Spenser doubtless got some guidance for this portrayal of Elizabeth as a composite figure incorporating Diana and Venus from Chaucer's *Knight's Tale*, in which the virginal Emelye, who prays to Diana, is portrayed with 'yelow heer' and described as going out to do her May observances to Venus. But the real origin of his conception lies in Vergil, as we have already seen: with that mysterious appearance of Venus as her own opposite, a nymph of Diana, which provoked much speculation among the neo-Platonic allegorists of the Renaissance, and became for them, and for Spenser following them, an emblem of chaste love.

At this point several questions have been raised: the relationship between *The Shepheardes Calender* and *The Faerie Queene*; the relationship between Spenser and Vergil; the nature of Spenser's myth-making; and his relationship with Renaissance neo-Platonism.

The first two are essentially the same question. Spenser was writing at a time when the influence of Continental humanism—the disciplined study of ancient, that is, Graeco-Roman, culture, and the belief that its glories in architecture, the visual arts, literature, and politics, were being cyclically renewed and superseded after the darkness of the Middle Ages—had reached England. But with the Renaissance had come increasing nationalism; and a corollary of that among literary theorists and writers was a concern with establishing vernacular, as opposed to Latin, literature. Ancient culture—the achievements of Greece and Rome, and especially Rome under Augustus—provided models for imitation; but the imitations were to be accomplished in the vernacular. Spenser offers particularly interesting examples of the fusion of the classical with native traditions, for with Chaucer as his native inspiration he modelled his whole career as a poet on that of Vergil.

The Renaissance inherited from the ancients a hierarchy of literary genres which, as far as poetry was concerned, began with the eclogue (a word misinterpreted as meaning 'goat-herd's tale') and ended with epic. There was a fit style as well as subject for each genre, and in all respects Vergil's career was regarded as exemplary, opening as it had with the *Eclogues*, moving then to the 'middle style' *Georgics*, and reaching its apogee with the *Aeneid*. Following Vergil, then,

Spenser wrote his *Shepheardes Calender* at the beginning of
his career, and finished it with *The Faerie Queene*, seeing
himself, despite spending much of his writing life in Ireland
in various government posts, as Elizabeth's court poet,
seeking her patronage as Vergil had enjoyed the interest of
the Emperor Augustus, and singing the growth of England
to nationhood in his epic as Vergil had sung the birth of
Rome in the *Aeneid*. Aeneas sees the panorama of Roman
history, culminating in the reign of Augustus, in his visit to
the underworld in Book VI; equivalent panoramas of
British history are found in *The Faerie Queene*, II. x, III. iii
and III. ix; Elizabeth is the English Augustus. We must not
forget an important historical parallel, either: Octavius
(crowned Augustus) had brought peace to Rome after civil
war; the Tudors had brought peace to England after civil
war. In the April eclogue of *The Shepheardes Calender*,
Elisa's cheeks are described as mingling the red rose with
the white. E.K., in his comment on this line, writes: 'By the
mingling of the red rose and the white is meant the uniting
of the two principal houses of Lancaster and York: by whose
long discord and deadly debate this realm many years was
sore travailed, and almost clean decayed.' This union is now
summed up in Elizabeth.

The view of British history adopted by Spenser for *The
Faerie Queene* is that recounted by Geoffrey of Monmouth in
his twelfth-century history of Britain in which we are told
how Brutus, great-grandson of Aeneas, arrived in Albion
(which he then called Britain to perpetuate his name), over-
came the native giants, divided up the kingdom, and
founded a capital city which, in honour of his lineage, he
named New Troy (see *The Faerie Queene*, II. x. 4 ff., and
III. ix. 44 ff.). And yet history is not merely dull chronology
and pedigrees to Spenser. It becomes part of his moral
argument when, for example, in the historical account in
II. x, Brutus's overcoming of the 'hideous Giaunts, and
halfe beastly men' (stanza 7) symbolizes the victory of
reason over the passions that Book II is specifically about,
and is the general concern of *The Faerie Queene* as a whole.
Conversely, when Britomart encounters Paridell and
Hellenore in Book III she, exemplifying chastity, is con-
fronting examples of lust and, simultaneously, as the British
Mars, she is Elizabeth confronting the origins of her own
race, since the Paridell who abducts Hellenore in canto x is

Paris, whose abduction of Helen initiated the Trojan war
(the identification is made explicit at III. x. 13).

There is a very real sense, then, in which Roman history
was, to the Elizabethans, British history; though the Tudors
regarded themselves more particularly as bringing again to
Britain the greatness of King Arthur. Hence Henry VII's
eldest son was named Arthur, and hence, too, Prince Arthur
is the questing hero of *The Faerie Queene*, searching for
Gloriana, the Faerie Queene, herself (I. ix. 15): that Gloriana
who is Elizabeth, the historical fulfilment of his own promise,
and also Glory, as Spenser tells us in his prefatory letter to
Raleigh. Here we have a hint of Spenser's neo-Platonism.
For Arthur's vision has been a glimpse not only of the ideal
kingdom foreshadowed in the England of Elizabeth but of
the Platonic One, which in Christian Platonism is God,
and/or (for we are reaching the realm where distinctions are
irrelevant) that 'Sapience . . . clad like a queen' of Spenser's
Hymne of Heavenly Beautie. Glory is at once the goal of the
knight errant or the warrior-courtier (at the end of his quest
the Red Crosse Knight has won a 'glorious name': II. i. 32)
and 'glory' in the sense of halo of light; so that Arthur's
glimpse of the 'royall Mayd' who appeared to him so
fleetingly in his vision is parallel to the Red Crosse Knight's
glimpse of the Heavenly Jerusalem in I. x, and to Spenser's
own plea at the end of the *Hymne of Heavenly Beautie* that
his 'hungry soul', which has sought after 'vain deceitful
shadows', might 'look at last up to that Sovereign Light,/
From whose pure beams all perfect beauty springs'. God's
light is infinite beauty to the neo-Platonists. It shines above
all. On earth it is parodied, perverted, distorted, darkened.
There were, traditionally, scales by which one could measure
the movement of one's soul to contemplation of God, the
One. Technicalities of this sort need not bother the reader
of *The Faerie Queene*, though. All he needs to feel is the
symbolic difference between darkness and light, and to see
Gloriana as a vision of the ultimate light which on earth is
shadowed forth in the person of the historical Elizabeth,
ordained by God to rule over England and her church, to
order her realm through wisdom, temperance, justice, and
mercy, and bind it together, too, through love, just as to
Plato and the neo-Platonists the universe itself was bound
together by love (for Spenser's version of this, see the *Hymne
in Honour of Love* and the *Hymne of Heavenly Love*). This is

why, in Spenser's mythology, Elizabeth is symbolized,
through Una and Belphœbe, as Diana-Venus, the embodi-
ment of that chaste love which is at once a moral state and,
much more than that, the informing principle of the cosmos.
But, since we live on earth, ideals are glimpsed and pursued
only rarely. The shadows predominate. In the realm of
politics Elizabeth is opposed by Mary Queen of Scots, the
false queen parading as the true. Seen in the terms of
Spenser's poem, Archimago holds sway—Archimago, who
is Satan, that dark figure who stands for our fallen condition,
our predisposition to succumb to vice and to follow the
illusion rather than the reality, the shadow rather than the
light. From this results the essentially simple structure of
The Faerie Queene, in which evil parodies good, trying by
illusion to seduce the knights as they go about their quests.
There is Florimell, there is false Florimell; Duessa parodies
Una; as Fidessa she parodies Fidelia; Acrasia is one of
several false Venuses in the poem; the true Venus is seen,
among other places, in IV. x and in the Garden of Adonis
in III. vi. In the poem as in life the problem is to distin-
guish false from true, and to distinguish degrees of falseness.

Ultimately, then, even under Elizabeth, whose quasi-
divinity Spenser, like many of his contemporaries, fervently
believed in, the ideal kingdom does not exist. Like the herb
haemony in Milton's *Comus* it flowers 'in another country',
above this earth. And yet it was on earth once, before Satan/
Archimago took over: in the Garden of Eden and the classical
Golden Age. It is here that eclogue—that lowest of poetical
forms—and epic meet. For pastoral poetry, in the form of
the eclogue, traditionally portrays the country life as an
ideal, Golden Age, existence, in which man is in harmony
with nature and shepherd-poets sing as an extension of that
harmony. Of course, death and winter are present, because
we aren't actually *in* the Golden Age any more. And yet the
poet, through the power of his imagination, has re-created it.
In Vergil's fourth eclogue the Golden Age itself *is* going to
return. And this vision is very close to that in Book VI of the
Aeneid, where it is prophesied that Augustus will restore
the Golden Age to Rome.

Similarly, Spenser's *Shepheardes Calender* depicts, in
spite of the pains of love and other dissonances, an ideal
rustic world far removed from sophisticated corruptions. It
is the heroic (or epic) version of this world that we are

shown in *The Faerie Queene*. And yet Spenser cannot believe in a completely cyclical history, in which Elizabeth-Augustus will in fact restore the Golden Age to England. Here his Christian Platonism intervenes, to tell him that the ideal belongs to the past and to the future (the after life), and to the present only through contemplation and the power of the creative imagination. *The Faerie Queene* is about the England of Elizabeth, certainly: historical allegory is present in most books, and particularly Books I and V; it is also about morality—temperance, chastity, justice, the education of the courtier into true courtesy. To that extent it is a practical instructive treatise, a courtesy book, like Castiglione's *Courtier* and Sir Thomas Elyot's *Boke named the governour*. But above all it is a poet's vision of the Golden Age which lies beyond history. The world of *The Faerie Queene* is the world of an idealized Arthurian England, of idealized chivalric romance. Its language, following on from that devised by Spenser for *The Shepheardes Calender*, is consciously archaic, an experiment in creating a vernacular language for poetry that is very successful in that it so beautifully creates a linguistic world that is just beyond reality. We are aware of this, and so were Spenser's contemporaries. It is also one in which symbols abound. The world of the poem is, therefore, the world of the mind, that part of us allegorized in II. ix. 45 ff. which is nearest to God. Symbols, for Spenser, are intermediaries between earth and the world beyond, concrete objects, physical phenomena, that have taken on a meaning greater than themselves, so that they become shadows of ultimate Truth.

And so, like *The Shepheardes Calender*, *The Faerie Queene* is about the poet and the world that the poet creates. To the poet (and the notion goes back through Plato into the dimmest past) belongs the power to sing the world into harmony, and man into harmony with it. The poet is Orpheus. Inspired by a vision of another world—the 'Sovereign Light' of the *Hymne of Heavenly Beautie*—the poet embodies that vision in verse whose music ravishes the souls of its hearers and readers. Arthur has his glimpse of Gloriana in a dream only. The Red Crosse Knight sees for a moment the Heavenly Jerusalem. But it is the poet himself who has imagined these visions. And so that the reader will not forget or underestimate the power of the poet as seer, Spenser introduces himself into Book VI in his familiar guise as the poet Colin Clout. This is of course—as it had to be for the poet to appear in it—the most pastoral of the books of *The Faerie Queene*. And the vision occurs in canto x, looking back to Red Crosse's vision of the Heavenly Jerusalem in I. x, and the mysteries of the Temple of Venus in IV. x. Here, in VI. x, Spenser as Colin Clout pipes a tune to which the three Graces, 'daughters of delight,/ Hand-maides of Venus', dance. The Graces represent love, civility, liberality, the harmonious centre of a well-ordered society. This is the climactic vision in the sixth book which is dedicated to the courtly virtue of Courtesy, that virtue which makes (in Chaucer's words) the 'verray, parfit gentil knyght'. Yet their dance also symbolizes the cosmic dance. They and the goddess whom they accompany are that love which, to the Christian Platonist, holds the universe together; and it is the poet Colin Clout who is accompanying them. Sir Calidore, the titular knight of Book VI, sees this dance only by accident; he is the outsider looking in, like Actaeon spying on Diana: 'soone as he appeared to their vew,/ They vanisht all away out of his sight,/ And cleane were gone . . .' The courtier, representative of the court, 'break[s] . . . their daunce' because he is clumsy and physical and has tried to climb into a dream of the ideal which the court—and civilization as a whole—longs to live by. Amid the Graces had been a fourth maiden, excelling the rest in beauty and 'crownd with a rosie girlond that right well/ Did her beseeme'. She takes the place of, but is not, Venus. She is 'a countrey lasse' who 'well deserves to be' another Grace, and a type of Gloriana, 'Sunne of the world, great glory of the sky' (VI. x. 28). Colin—the poet—has to explain all this to Sir Calidore. The poet mediates between the ideal and the real (Vergil, we recall, guides Dante through Hell and Purgatory). He was *in* the vision; Sir Calidore was outside it. This pastoral interlude has in it a hint of satire: the ideals by which the sophisticated court lives are to be found not in the court but in its extreme opposite, a rustic idyll. Pastoral is nearer perfection than epic. The simpler we are, the nearer we are to truth: close to Una, far from Duessa. It is no accident that this episode takes us right back to the April eclogue of *The Shepheardes Calender* with which I began, in which Elisa is created 'a fourth Grace, to make the dance even'.

So pastoral and epic—the two extremes—become one

again. The pastoral world is as much at home in epic as the chivalric virtues. Vergil had included a pastoral interlude in Book VIII of the *Aeneid*, where Aeneas visits the Arcadian king, Evander. But Spenser goes further: there is not only more pastoral subject-matter in *The Faerie Queene*; the language of the poem, too, is pastoral as well as heroic, constantly reminding the reader of the language of *The Shepheardes Calender*. It is, in part, the language of Chaucer; and Spenser's pastoral is not classical pastoral—the pastoral of Theocritus, Bion, Moschus, Vergil, Sidney, and parts of Milton's *Lycidas*—but native pastoral: a fusion of England, Ireland (where Spenser lived from 1580, writing most of *The Faerie Queene* there), and the Chaucerian Middle Ages. Spenser's humanism shows nowhere more favourably than in his almost unique ability to imitate classical models and produce truly English poems. His ultimate model was Vergil, for *The Shepheardes Calender*, the projected twelve books of *The Faerie Queene*, and for many details. Vergil is addressed as Tityrus in his own sixth *Eclogue*; but the Tityrus who 'taught [Colin Clout] . . . to make', and whose death is lamented in the June eclogue of *The Shepheardes Calender*, is Chaucer, whom Spenser again compliments in Book IV of *The Faerie Queene* by echoing his *Squire's Tale* and referring to him as 'Dan Chaucer, well of English undefyled' (IV. ii. 32). At this point classical and native traditions fuse, as, indeed, they do in the Tudor adoption of the Brutus story, in which the great-grandson of Aeneas is the founder of Britain and (albeit indirect) progenitor of Arthur and the Tudors.

Spenser had other models, too, of course. He wasn't directly following the *Aeneid* so much as Italian romantic epic imitations of it, Ariosto's *Orlando Furioso* (1516–32) and Tasso's *Gerusalemme Liberata* (1580). That having been said, the Italian poets can be forgotten. If the reader of Spenser is familiar with them, he will notice the similarities; if he is not, then being told about them will make Spenser's poem more distant and forbidding than it need be.

The Faerie Queene contains all the great symbols. We enter it, with the Red Crosse Knight and Una, through the dark wood of Error (I. i), the labyrinth, symbol of life's moral perplexities (this is how Dante begins his *Divine Comedy*, too). There we encounter Error herself, a dragon, one of the most potent symbols of evil. The dragon recurs in canto xi, and is defeated by Red Crosse on the third day of battle: this time it is the dragon-serpent Satan who has been defeated (on the third day because Christ rose on the third day after the Crucifixion, having spent the three days harrowing hell). This defeat means the release of Una's parents and the re-establishment of the Garden of Eden: that is, the old Adam (the sin into which we are born through the fall of our first parents) has been purged through the acquisition of faith and true understanding of Christ's redemptive role—the subject of Red Crosse's quest in Book I. Nominally they are different dragons (we might add the seven-headed beast on which Duessa as Fidessa rides in I. vii and viii, and the Blatant Beast of Book VI), but essentially they are the same—nightmare monsters from the depths of the subconscious, and recognized by Spenser as such, since all these encounters are going on within the mind of each knight. Archimago is inside Red Crosse; Acrasia is inside Guyon; Malecasta and Busyrane are impulses within Britomart. And they are all impulses inside the poet and his reader, too. Spenser's images were, of course, sanctified by tradition, both classical and Christian. But I think the modern reader finds that although our language for describing psychological phenomena is different from Spenser's, the images retain their validity.

Similarly, we can feel (rather than apprehend intellectually) that Spenser's giants are symbols of evil—for example, Orgoglio in Book I, Ollyphant in Book III. Though we can go further than that if we are inclined to, and see these oppressive giants as re-embodiments of the native giants whom Brutus had to slay before he could order Britain, and as embodiments, too, of fundamental rebellious impulses, the Giants who rebelled against Jupiter in Book I of Ovid's *Metamorphoses*. Looking closer still, we find that, when he has been overcome by Arthur, Orgoglio falls like an undermined castle (I. viii. 23), and that on his first appearance 'with his tallnesse [he] seemd to threat the skye' (I. vii. 8). We are meant, therefore, to associate him with the Tower of Babel, traditional emblem of pride, as well as with the classical myth of Antaeus (the giant born of the earth, as Orgoglio is. We notice, too, that Maleger, another arch-symbol of sin, who besieges Alma's castle— the castle of the human body—is a son of the earth and, like Antaeus, regains his strength every time he lies on the ground: II. xi. 45). Moreover, Orgoglio—spiritual pride, which attacks Red Crosse when he has laid aside his armour (the 'whole armour of God' of Ephesians vi. 11)—harks back to his earlier counterpart in Book I, Lucifera, or worldly pride, a female Lucifer. For the image of Orgoglio as the undermined castle echoes the description of Lucifera's palace in I. iv. 5, which is built on a 'weake foundation' on 'a sandie hill' (the house built on sand of Matthew vii. 26–7).

In addition, Orgoglio, with his club which is 'a snaggy Oke, which he had torne/ Out of his mothers bowelles' (I. vii. 10), would have been recognized at the time as a Wild Man, symbol of lawlessness, who goes back at least to the giant Cyclops with his pine-trunk staff in *Aeneid* III. He is thus an antitype of Hercules, who slew monsters with his club, and was regarded as an exemplar of heroic virtue and type of Christ, to whom the Red Crosse Knight is compared in I. xi. 27. As the lawless Wild Man he also raises another question—one fundamental to Spenser's age, and an important theme in, for instance, *The Tempest*: how to define man's moral nature using civilization ('art') as one touchstone and pastoral ('nature') as another? The question has a complicated answer. Courteous Sir Calidore, we recall, has his climactic vision in a moment of pastoral escape, far from the court. But the pastoral convention is, after all, nature controlled by art. Orgoglio, Ollyphant, and the cannibals of VI. viii. 35 ff. are basic, lawless man, lawless because perverting that natural law which the satyrs of I. vi. live by—for they are savage but not lawless, natural man without the benefit of Christian revelation who nevertheless intuitively worship Una.

It is possible to enjoy and understand Spenser without instantly suspecting and searching for complex meanings. Even so, it should be said that his myth-making, like that of his sophisticated humanist contemporaries and predecessors, is syncretistic, a product of the humanist fusion of classical mythology with Christian truth and the current belief that classical mythology was a distorted version of Christian mythology. This inevitably leads to complexity. Hence Spenser would have expected his readers to see in Mammon (II. vii.) a Saturnian figure—for he is solitary, black, and covetous, all traditional attributes of the planetary god Saturn; and in Acrasia (whose name, from the

Greek, means 'unmixed', and so 'intemperate') lust embod-
ied in a false Venus, a Venus *luxuria*, who has Verdant as
her lover in the Bower of Bliss as one of the true Venuses
has her Adonis in the Garden of Adonis (III. vi). Spenser
has, in other words, several traditions to call upon: classical
mythology and astrology (which were intimately related),
and the Bible. He uses them all, and sometimes to describe
just one figure: Una is Venus-Diana in I. vi. 16; she is the
'woman clothed with the sun' of Revelation xii. 1 in I. xii.
23; in I. xii. 21 she is the morning star which—as Lucifer—
makes her an antitype of Lucifera, her parody, also Venus
again (the planetary morning star), and, finally, Christ, 'the
bright and morning star' of Revelation xxii. 16. On other
occasions the traditions are utilized separately. This variety
enables Spenser to be remarkably subtle in making moral
and psychological distinctions: for example, between Una,
as Venus-Diana, and Acrasia, Belphœbe, Amoret, the Venus
of Book III and the Venus of Book IV.

The important point for the reader to remember, I think,
is Spenser's intention to write a didactic heroic poem.
Although 'didactic' is a pejorative word today, implying
restrictions and heavy-footed instruction, Spenser's didac-
ticism is different from that: it is intended, with the 'Sover-
eign Light' beyond as its reference—to open the mind, not
stifle or close it. It asks questions and demands from the
reader the capacity for discrimination. To read the poem we
have to discriminate, distinguish, and judge, as we do in
life; and this applies to every level of the poem's structure.
On the large-scale level of the virtues dealt with book by
book we have temperance, chastity, friendship, justice, and
courtesy. Temperance implies, but is different from, chastity;
chastity includes love, but a love that is different from
friendship; and friendship is a reflection among men of that
quality which, according to Plato in his creation myth in the
Timaeus, holds the four elements together in balanced
harmony, and so is related to (but different from) the balance
and equity of justice. Everywhere we are confronted with
similarities and differences. On the level of character we
have to distinguish between Britomart and Belphœbe, and
distinguish both from Una and the Faerie Queene herself.
Acrasia is an aspect of Duessa, but by no means Duessa in
her entirety. And on the intermediate level of episodes the
same technique of parallelism and echo, in which differences

are as important as similarities, operates. It operates within
the individual books: Lucifera's palace, dedicated to the sin
of pride, is approached by 'a broad high way' (I. iv. 2). It is
answered by the House of Holiness in canto x, which is
reached by a 'narrow path' (stanza 10). Lucifera's coach is
pulled by the other six deadly sins; near the House of
Holiness there is a hospital in which are 'seven Bead-men,
that had vowed all/ Their life to service of high heavens
King' (stanza 36), the antitypes of the seven sins. Again,
within the House of Holiness there is Fidelia (Faith), who
'in her right hand bore a cup of gold,/ With wine and water
fild up to the hight,/ In which a Serpent did himselfe enfold,/
That horrour made to all that did behold' (stanza 13). The
cup recalls Holy Communion; the serpent alludes to Num-
bers xxi, the brazen serpent made by Moses and put on a
pole, the sight of which gave life to those bitten by serpents,
which was interpreted by St John (iii. 14–15) as representing
Christ: 'And as Moses lifted up the serpent in the wilderness,
even so must the Son of man be lifted up: That whosoever
believeth in him should not perish, but have eternal life.'
This serpent looks back to the dragon on Arthur's helmet
(I. vii. 31), cancels out the dragon Error in canto i, Lucifera's
dragon (I. iv. 10), Fidessa's monster, and looks forward to
Red Crosse's victory over the dragon in canto xi. While the
picture of Fidelia holding the gold cup harks back to Fidessa
(the parody of true faith) holding her gold cup aloft as she
rides on her seven-headed beast (I. viii. 14). Similarly, in
Book III, Castle Joyous in canto i, with its tapestry of
Venus and Adonis (which, incidentally, announces the
controlling myth of this book), is answered by Busyrane's
house in cantos xi and xii, with its tapestries and masque of
Cupid. As a structural intermediary we have the description
of the Garden of Adonis itself in canto vi. The method
operates, too, from book to book: the Bower of Bliss in II.
xii can only be fully understood if we refer it to the Garden
of Adonis in the next book.

It needs an impossibly alert mind to seize on all these
parallels, and it is no help to be told that the Elizabethan
memory was far better trained than our own. As I hinted
earlier, simple reading and enjoyment should come first; the
difficulties can arrive in their own time. There is no need to
worry over levels of allegory—whether and at what point
Una is Truth, Queen Elizabeth, or the Anglican church,

when Duessa is Duplicity, Mary Queen of Scots, or the
Catholic church. Spenser did utilize medieval methods of
multiple allegory, it is true, even though Protestantism
discouraged them. But his allegory is always an attempt to
explain, to grasp at, the eternal and immutable. Beyond the
multiplicities of earthly phenomena is one Truth. Whatever
Una means to Spenser as allegorist and to the critic as
allegorist, her ultimate meaning is what her name suggests:
Oneness. Like Shelley in *Adonais*, Spenser's eye in *The
Faerie Queen* is firmly and hopefully on 'Heaven's light
[that] forever shines'; he, too, is aware that 'Earth's
shadows fly'. *The Faerie Queene* captures some of those
shadows and confronts us with them: fleeting images of our
moral selves. But it ends, in the 'unperfite' eighth canto
which follows the two mutability cantos, by transcending
those shadows, as we would expect. After Colin and the
Graces in Book VI where can we progress but to a vision of
eternity?

> But thence-forth all shall rest eternally
> With Him that is the God of Sabaoth hight:
> O! that great Sabaoth God, grant me that Sabaoths
>   sight.

1976   DOUGLAS BROOKS-DAVIES

The Text and Glossary here used are those of Dr R. Morris,
by kind permission of Messrs Macmillan & Co.

SELECT BIBLIOGRAPHY

WORKS: *The Shepheardes Calender*, 1579; *The Faerie Queene*, Books I to III, 1590; *Daphnaida*, 1591; *Complaints*, 1591; *Amoretti* and *Epithalamion*, 1595; *Colin Clouts Come Home Againe* and *Astrophel*, 1595; *The Faerie Queene*, Books I to VI inclusive, 1596; *Fowre Hymnes*, 1596; *Prothalamion*, 1596; *A Vewe of the present state of Irelande*, 1598; first folio edn of *The Faerie Queene*, including for the first time the *Two Cantos of Mutabilitie*, 1609.

EDITIONS: J. C. Smith (ed.), *Spenser's Faerie Queene*, 2 vols, 1909; E. de Selincourt (ed.), *Spenser's Minor Poems*, 1910; E. A. Greenlaw, F. M. Padelford, C. G. Osgood, *et al.* (eds), *The Works of Edmund Spenser: A Variorum Edition*, 10 vols, 1932–49.

FURTHER READING: Invaluable background material will be found in the works of Plato; Vergil's *Aeneid*; Ovid's *Metamorphoses*; the Bible, especially Genesis, the Song of Solomon, Isaiah, and Revelations; and Geoffrey of Monmouth's *History of the Kings of Britain*. Edgar Wind's *Pagan Mysteries in the Renaissance*, 1958 (revised 1967) is most helpful for Spenser's neo-Platonism and mythology.

SUGGESTED CRITICAL READING: Paul Alpers, *The Poetry of 'The Faerie Queene'*, 1967; Alpers has also edited the useful *Edmund Spenser: A Critical Anthology*, 1969; J. W. Bennett, *The Evolution of 'The Faerie Queen'*, 1942; Harry Berger Jr, *The Allegorical Temper*, 1957; Robert Ellrodt, *Neoplatonism in the Poetry of Spenser*, 1960; A. D. S. Fowler, *Spenser and the Numbers of Time*, 1964; Rosemary Freeman, *The Faerie Queene: A Companion for Readers*, 1970; A. C. Hamilton, *The Structure of Allegory in 'The Faerie Queene'*, 1961; J. E. Hankins, *Source and Meaning in Spenser's Allegory: A Study of 'The Faerie Queene'*, 1971; Graham Hough, *A Preface to 'The Faerie Queene'*, 1962; H. S. V. Jones, *A Spenser Handbook*, 1930 (out of date but still indispensable); A. C. Judson, *The Life of Edmund Spenser*, 1945; J. M. Kennedy and J. A. Reither (eds), *A Theatre for Spenserians*, 1973; C. S. Lewis, *The Allegory of Love*, 1936, *English Literature in the Sixteenth Century*, 1954, and *Spenser's Images of Life* (ed. Fowler),

1967; W. Nelson (ed.), *Form and Convention in the Poetry of Edmund Spenser*, 1961, and *The Poetry of Edmund Spenser*, 1963 (an excellent introduction); W. L. Renwick, *Edmund Spenser*, 1925; T. P. Roche Jr, *The Kindly Flame*, 1964; Mark Rose, *Spenser's Art: A Companion to Book One of 'The Faerie Queene'*, 1975; Roger Sale, *Reading Spenser: An Introduction to 'The Faerie Queene'*, 1968; Kathleen Williams, *Spenser's 'Faerie Queene'*, 1966; Frances A. Yates, *Astraea: The Imperial Theme in the Sixteenth Century*, 1975.

To

The most high, mightie, and magnificent

Empresse,

Renowmèd for pietie, vertue, and all gratious government,

ELIZABETH,

by the grace of God,

Queene of England, Fraunce, and Ireland,

and of Virginia,

Defendour of the Faith, etc.,

Her most humble servaunt

EDMUND SPENSER,

doth, in all humilitie,

dedicate, present, and consecrate

these his labours,

To live with the eternitie of her fame.

A LETTER OF THE AUTHORS,

*Expounding his whole intention in the course of this worke :
which, for that it giveth great light to the reader, for
the better understanding is hereunto annexed.*

To the Right Noble and Valorous

SIR WALTER RALEIGH, KNIGHT.

*Lord Wardein of the Stanneryes, and Her Maiesties
Liefetenaunt of the County of Cornewayll.*

*Sir, knowing how doubtfully all Allegories may be construed,
and this booke of mine, which I have entituled the Faery Queene,
being a continued Allegory, or darke conceit, I haue thought
good, as well for avoyding of gealous opinions and misconstruc-
tions, as also for your better light in reading thereof, (being so by
you commanded,) to discover unto you the general intention and
meaning, which in the whole course thereof I have fashioned,
without expressing of any particular purposes, or by accidents,
therein occasioned. The generall end therefore of all the booke
is to fashion a gentleman or noble person in vertuous and gentle
discipline : Which for that I conceived shoulde be most plausible
and pleasing, being coloured with an historicall fiction, the which
the most part of men delight to read, rather for variety of matter
then for profite of the ensample, I chose the historye of King
Arthure, as most fitte for the excellency of his person, being made
famous by many mens former workes, and also furthest from the
daunger of envy, and suspition of present time. In which I have
followed all the antique Poets historicall ; first Homere, who in
the Persons of Agamemnon and Ulysses hath ensampled a good
governour and a vertuous man, the one in his Ilias, the other in
his Odysseis : then Virgil, whose like intention was to doe in
the person of Aeneas : after him Ariosto comprised them both
in his Orlando : and lately Tasso dissevered them againe, and*

formed both parts in two persons, namely that part which they in Philosophy call Ethice, or vertues of a private man, coloured in his Rinaldo; the other named Politice in his Godfredo. By ensample of which excellente Poets, I labour to pourtraict in Arthure, before he was king, the image of a brave knight, perfected in the twelve private morall vertues, as Aristotle hath devised; the which is the purpose of these first twelve bookes: which if I finde to be well accepted, I may be perhaps encoraged to frame the other part of polliticke vertues in his person, after that hee came to be king.

To some, I know, this Methode will seeme displeasaunt, which had rather have good discipline delivered plainly in way of precepts, or sermoned at large, as they use, then thus clowdily enwrapped in Allegoricall devises. But such, me seeme, should be satisfide with the use of these dayes, seeing all things accounted by their showes, and nothing esteemed of, that is not delightfull and pleasing to commune sence. For this cause is Xenophon preferred before Plato, for that the one, in the exquisite depth of his judgement, formed a Commune welth, such as it should be; but the other in the person of Cyrus, and the Persians, fashioned a governement, such as might best be: So much more profitable and gratious is doctrine by ensample, then by rule. So haue I laboured to doe in the person of Arthure: whome I conceive, after his long education by Timon, to whom he was by Merlin delivered to be brought up, so soone as he was borne of the Lady Igrayne, to have seene in a dream or vision the Faery Queene, with whose excellent beauty ravished, he awaking resolved to seeke her out; and so being by Merlin armed, and by Timon throughly instructed, he went to seeke her forth in Faerye land. In that Faery Queene I meane glory in my generall intention, but in my particular I conceive the most excellent and glorious person of our soveraine the Queene, and her kingdome in Faery land. And yet, in some places els, I doe otherwise shadow her. For considering she beareth two persons, the one of a most royall Queene or Empresse, the other of a most vertuous and beautifull Lady, this latter part in some places I doe expresse in Belphœbe, fashioning her name according to your owne excellent conceipt of Cynthia, (Phœbe and Cynthia being both names of Diana). So in the person of Prince Arthure I sette forth magnificence in particular; which vertue, for that (according to Aristotle and the rest) it is the perfection of all the rest, and conteineth in it them all, therefore in the whole course I mention the deedes of Arthure applyable to that vertue, which I write of in that booke. But of the xii. other vertues, I make xii. other knights the patrones, for the more variety of the history : Of which these three bookes contayn three.

The first of the knight of the Redcrosse, in whome I expresse Holynes : The seconde of Sir Guyon, in whome I sette forth Temperaunce : The third of Britomartis, a Lady Knight, in whome I picture Chastity. But, because the beginning of the whole worke seemeth abrupte, and as depending upon other antecedents, it needs that ye know the occasion of these three knights seuerall adventures. For the Methode of a Poet historical is not such, as of an Historiographer. For an Historiographer discourseth of affayres orderly as they were donne, accounting as well the times as the actions ; but a Poet thrusteth into the middest, even where it most concerneth him, and there recoursing to the thinges fore-paste, and divining of thinges to come, maketh a pleasing Analysis of all.

The beginning therefore of my history, if it were to be told by an Historiographer should be the twelfth booke, which is the last ; where I devise that the Faery Queene kept her Annuall feaste xii. dayes ; uppon which xii. severall dayes, the occasions of the xii. severall adventures hapned, which, being undertaken by xii. severall knights, are in these xii. books severally handled and discoursed. The first was this. In the beginning of the feast, there presented him selfe a tall clownishe younge man, who falling before the Queene of Faeries desired a boone (as the manner then was) which during that feast she might not refuse : which was that hee might have the atchievement of any adventure, which during that feaste should happen : that being graunted, he rested him on the floore, unfitte through his rusticity for a better place. Soone after entred a faire Ladye in mourning weedes, riding on a white Asse, with a dwarfe behind her leading a warlike steed, that bore the Armes of a knight, and his speare in the dwarfes hand. Shee, falling before the Queene of Faeries, complayned that her father and mother, an ancient King and Queene, had bene by an huge dragon many years shut up in a brasen Castle, who then suffred them not to yssew ; and therefore besought the Faery Queene to assygne her some one of her knights to take on him that exployt. Presently that clownish person, upstarting, desired that adventure : whereat the Queene much wondering, and the Lady much gainesaying, yet he earnestly importuned his desire. In the end the Lady told him, that unlesse that armour which she brought, would serve him (that is, the armour of a Christian man specified by Saint Paul, vi. Ephes.) that he could not succeed in that enterprise ; which being forthwith put upon him, with dewe

furnitures thereunto, he seemed the goodliest man in al that company,
and was well liked of the Lady. And eftesoones taking on him
knighthood, and mounting on that straunge Courser, he went
forth with her on that adventure : where beginneth the first booke,
viz.

A gentle knight was pricking on the playne, etc.

The second day there came in a Palmer, bearing an Infant
with bloody hands, whose Parents he complained to have bene
slayn by an Enchaunteresse called Acrasia ; and therefore craved
of the Faery Queene, to appoint him some knight to performe that
adventure ; which being assigned to Sir Guyon, he presently went
forth with that same Palmer : which is the beginning of the second
booke, and the whole subject thereof. The third day there came in a
Groome, who complained before the Faery Queene, that a vile
Enchaunter, called Busirane, had in hand a most faire Lady,
called Amoretta, whom he kept in most grievous torment, because
she would not yield him the pleasure of her body. Whereupon
Sir Scudamour, the lover of that Lady, presently tooke on him
that adventure. But being unable to performe it by reason of the
hard Enchauntments, after long sorrow, in the end met with
Britomartis, who succoured him, and reskewed his loue.

But by occasion hereof many other adventures are intermedled ;
but rather as Accidents then intendments : As the love of Brito-
mart, the overthrow of Marinell, the misery of Florimell, the
vertuousnes of Belphœbe, the lasciviousnes of Hellenora, and many
the like.

Thus much, Sir, I have briefly overronne to direct your under-
standing to the wel-head of the History ; that from thence gathering
the whole intention of the conceit, ye may as in a handfull gripe
al the discourse, which otherwise may happily seeme tedious and
confused. So, humbly craving the continuance of your honorable
favour towards me, and th' eternall establishment of your happines,
I humbly take leave.

23. January 1589,
Yours most humbly affectionate,
Ed. Spenser.

THE FIRST BOOKE

CONTAYNING THE LEGEND OF THE KNIGHT OF THE RED
CROSSE, OR OF HOLINESSE

I. Lo! I, the man whose Muse whylome did maske,
    As time her taught, in lowly Shephards weeds,
    Am now enforst, a farre unfitter taske,
    For trumpets sterne to change mine Oaten reeds,
    And sing of Knights and Ladies gentle deeds;
    Whose praises having slept in silence long,
    Me, all too meane, the sacred Muse areeds
    To blazon broade emongst her learned throng:
Fierce warres and faithful loves shall moralize my song.

II. Helpe then, O holy virgin! chiefe of nyne,
    Thy weaker Novice to performe thy will;
    Lay forth out of thine everlasting scryne
    The antique rolles, which there lye hidden still,
    Of Faerie knights, and fayrest Tanaquill,
    Whom that most noble Briton Prince so long
    Sought through the world, and suffered so much ill,
    That I must rue his undeserved wrong:
O, helpe thou my weake wit, and sharpen my dull tong!

III. And thou, most dreaded impe of highest Jove,
    Faire Venus sonne, that with thy cruell dart
    At that good knight so cunningly didst rove,
    That glorious fire it kindled in his hart;
    Lay now thy deadly Heben bowe apart,
    And with thy mother mylde come to mine ayde;
    Come, both; and with you bring triumphant Mart,
    In loves and gentle jollities arraid,
After his murdrous spoyles and bloudie rage allayd.

iv. And with them eke, O Goddesse heavenly bright!
    Mirrour of grace and Majestie divine,
    Great Ladie of the greatest Isle, whose light
    Like Phœbus lampe throughout the world doth shine,
    Shed thy faire beames into my feeble eyne,
    And raise my thoughtes, too humble and too vile,
    To thinke of that true glorious type of thine,
    The argument of mine afflicted stile:
    The which to heare vouchsafe, O dearest dread, a-while!

CANTO I

The Patrone of true Holinesse
Foule Errour doth defeate:
Hypocrisie, him to entrappe,
Doth to his home entreate.

I. A gentle Knight was pricking on the plaine,
Ycladd in mightie armes and silver shielde,
Wherein old dints of deepe woundes did remaine,
The cruell markes of many' a bloody fielde;
Yet armes till that time did he never wield.
His angry steede did chide his foming bitt,
As much disdayning to the curbe to yield:
Full jolly knight he seemed, and faire did sitt,
As one for knightly giusts and fierce encounters fitt.

II. And on his brest a bloodie Crosse he bore,
The deare remembrance of his dying Lord,
For whose sweete sake that glorious badge he wore,
And dead, as living, ever him ador'd:
Upon his shield the like was also scor'd,
For soveraine hope which in his helpe he had.
Right faithfull true he was in deede and word,
But of his cheere did seeme too solemne sad;
Yet nothing did he dread, but ever was ydrad.

III. Upon a great adventure he was bond,
That greatest Gloriana to him gave,
(That greatest Glorious Queene of Faery lond)
To winne him worshippe, and her grace to have,
Which of all earthly thinges he most did crave:
And ever as he rode his hart did earne
To prove his puissance in battell brave
Upon his foe, and his new force to learne,
Upon his foe, a Dragon horrible and stearne.

IV. A lovely Ladie rode him faire beside,
Upon a lowly Asse more white then snow,
Yet she much whiter; but the same did hide

Under a vele, that wimpled was full low;
And over all a blacke stole shee did throw
As one that inly mournd, so was she sad,
And heavie sate upon her palfrey slow;
Seemed in heart some hidden care she had,
And by her, in a line, a milkewhite lambe she lad.

v. So pure and innocent, as that same lambe,
She was in life and every vertuous lore;
And by descent from Royall lynage came
Of ancient Kinges and Queenes, that had of yore
Their scepters stretcht from East to Westerne shore,
And all the world in their subjection held;
Till that infernall feend with foule uprore
Forwasted all their land, and them expeld;
Whom to avenge she had this Knight from far compeld.

vi. Behind her farre away a Dwarfe did lag,
That lasie seemd, in being ever last,
Or wearied with bearing of her bag
Of needments at his backe.   Thus as they past,
The day with cloudes was suddeine overcast,
And angry Jove an hideous storme of raine
Did poure into his Lemans lap so fast,
That everie wight to shrowd it did constrain;
And this faire couple eke to shroud themselves were fain.

vii. Enforst to seeke some covert nigh at hand,
A shadie grove not farr away they spide,
That promist ayde the tempest to withstand;
Whose loftie trees, yclad with sommers pride,
Did spred so broad, that heavens light did hide,
Not perceable with power of any starr:
And all within were pathes and alleies wide,
With footing worne, and leading inward farr.
Faire harbour that them seems, so in they entered ar.

viii. And foorth they passe, with pleasure forward led,
Joying to heare the birdes sweete harmony,
Which, therein shrouded from the tempest dred,
Seemd in their song to scorne the cruell sky.
Much can they praise the trees so straight and hy,
The sayling Pine; the Cedar proud and tall;

The vine-propp Elme; the Poplar never dry;
The builder Oake, sole king of forrests all;
The Aspine good for staves; the Cypresse funerall;

IX. The Laurell, meed of mightie Conquerours
And Poets sage; the Firre that weepeth still:
The Willow, worne of forlorne Paramours;
The Eugh, obedient to the benders will;
The Birch for shaftes; the Sallow for the mill;
The Mirrhe sweete-bleeding in the bitter wound;
The warlike Beech; the Ash for nothing ill;
The fruitfull Olive; and the Platane round;
The carver Holme; the Maple seeldom inward sound.

X. Led with delight, they thus beguile the way,
Untill the blustring storme is overblowne;
When, weening to returne whence they did stray,
They cannot finde that path, which first was showne,
But wander too and fro in waies unknowne,
Furthest from end then, when they neerest weene,
That makes them doubt their wits be not their owne:
So many pathes, so many turnings seene,
That which of them to take in diverse doubt they been.

XI. At last resolving forward still to fare,
Till that some end they finde, or in or out,
That path they take that beaten seemd most bare,
And like to lead the labyrinth about;
Which when by tract they hunted had throughout,
At length it brought them to a hollowe cave
Amid the thickest woods. The Champion stout
Eftsoones dismounted from his courser brave,
And to the Dwarfe a while his needlesse spere he gave.

XII. " Be well aware," quoth then that Ladie milde,
" Least suddaine mischiefe ye too rash provoke:
The danger hid, the place unknowne and wilde,
Breedes dreadfull doubts. Oft fire is without smoke,
And perill without show: therefore your stroke,
Sir Knight, with-hold, till further tryall made."
" Ah Ladie," (sayd he) " shame were to revoke
The forward footing for an hidden shade:
Vertue gives her selfe light through darknesse for to wade."

xiii. "Yea but" (quoth she) "the perill of this place
I better wot then you: though nowe too late
To wish you backe returne with foule disgrace,
Yet wisedome warnes, whilest foot is in the gate,
To stay the steppe, ere forced to retrate.
This is the wandring wood, this *Errours* den,
A monster vile, whom God and man does hate:
Therefore I read beware." "Fly, fly!" (quoth then
The fearefull Dwarfe) "this is no place for living men."

xiv. But, full of fire and greedy hardiment,
The youthfull Knight could not for aught be staide;
But forth unto the darksom hole he went,
And looked in: his glistring armor made
A litle glooming light, much like a shade;
By which he saw the ugly monster plaine,
Halfe like a serpent horribly displaide,
But th' other halfe did womans shape retaine,
Most lothsom, filthie, foule, and full of vile disdaine.

xv. And, as she lay upon the durtie ground,
Her huge long taile her den all overspred,
Yet was in knots and many boughtes upwound,
Pointed with mortall sting. Of her there bred
A thousand yong ones, which she dayly fed,
Sucking upon her poisnous dugs; each one
Of sundrie shapes, yet all ill-favored:
Soone as that uncouth light upon them shone,
Into her mouth they crept, and suddain all were gone.

xvi. Their dam upstart out of her den effraide,
And rushed forth, hurling her hideous taile
About her cursed head; whose folds displaid
Were stretcht now forth at length without entraile.
She lookt about, and seeing one in mayle,
Armed to point, sought backe to turne againe;
For light she hated as the deadly bale,
Ay wont in desert darknes to remaine,
Where plain none might her see, nor she see any plaine.

xvii. Which when the valiant Elfe perceiv'd, he lept
As Lyon fierce upon the flying pray,
And with his trenchand blade her boldly kept

From turning backe, and forced her to stay:
Therewith enrag'd she loudly gan to bray,
And turning fierce her speckled taile advaunst,
Threatning her angrie sting, him to dismay;
Who, nought aghast, his mightie hand enhaunst:
The stroke down from her head unto her shoulder glaunst

XVIII. Much daunted with that dint her sence was dazd;
Yet kindling rage her selfe she gathered round,
And all attonce her beastly bodie raizd
With doubled forces high above the ground:
Tho, wrapping up her wrethed sterne arownd,
Lept fierce upon his shield, and her huge traine
All suddenly about his body wound,
That hand or foot to stirr he strove in vaine.
God helpe the man so wrapt in Errours endlesse traine!

XIX. His Lady, sad to see his sore constraint,
Cride out, " Now, now, Sir knight, shew what ye bee;
Add faith unto your force, and be not faint;
Strangle her, els she sure will strangle thee."
That when he heard, in great perplexitie,
His gall did grate for griefe and high disdaine;
And, knitting all his force, got one hand free,
Wherewith he grypt her gorge with so great paine,
That soone to loose her wicked bands did her constraine.

XX. Therewith she spewd out of her filthie maw
A floud of poyson horrible and blacke,
Full of great lumps of flesh and gobbets raw,
Which stunck so vildly, that it forst him slacke
His grasping hold, and from her turne him backe.
Her vomit full of bookes and papers was,
With loathly frogs and toades, which eyes did lacke,
And creeping sought way in the weedy gras:
Her filthie parbreake all the place defiled has.

XXI. As when old father Nilus gins to swell
With timely pride above the Aegyptian vale
His fattie waves doe fertile slime outwell,
And overflow each plaine and lowly dale:
But, when his later spring gins to avale,
Huge heapes of mudd he leaves, wherein there breed

Ten thousand kindes of creatures, partly male
And partly femall, of his fruitful seed;
Such ugly monstrous shapes elswher may no man reed

XXII. The same so sore annoyed has the knight,
That, welnigh choked with the deadly stinke,
His forces faile, ne can no lenger fight:
Whose corage when the feend perceivd to shrinke,
She poured forth out of her hellish sinke
Her fruitfull cursed spawne of serpents small,
Deformed monsters, fowle, and blacke as inke,
Which swarming all about his legs did crall,
And him encombred sore, but could not hurt at all.

XXIII. As gentle shepheard in sweete eventide,
When ruddy Phebus gins to welke in west,
High on an hill, his flocke to vewen wide,
Markes which doe byte their hasty supper best;
A cloud of cumbrous gnattes doe him molest,
All striving to infixe their feeble stinges,
That from their noyance he no where can rest;
But with his clownish hands their tender wings
He brusheth oft, and oft doth mar their murmurings.

XXIV. Thus ill bestedd, and fearefull more of shame
Then of the certeine perill he stood in,
Halfe furious unto his foe he came,
Resolvd in minde all suddenly to win,
Or soone to lose, before he once would lin;
And stroke at her with more then manly force,
That from her body, full of filthie sin,
He raft her hatefull heade without remorse:
A streame of cole-black blood forth gushed from her corse.

XXV. Her scattered brood, soone as their Parent deare
They saw so rudely falling to the ground,
Groning full deadly, all with troublous feare
Gathred themselves about her body round,
Weening their wonted entrance to have found
At her wide mouth; but being there withstood,
They flocked all about her bleeding wound,
And sucked up their dying mothers bloud,
Making her death their life, and eke her hurt their good.

XXVI. That detestable sight him much amazde,
    To see th' unkindly Impes, of heaven accurst,
    Devoure their dam; on whom while so he gazd,
    Having all satisfide their bloudy thurst,
    Their bellies swolne he saw with fulnesse burst,
    And bowels gushing forth: well worthy end
    Of such as drunke her life the which them nurst!
    Now needeth him no lenger labour spend,
    His foes have slaine themselves, with whom he should
        contend.

XXVII. His Lady, seeing all that chaunst from farre,
    Approcht in hast to greet his victorie;
    And saide, " Faire knight, borne under happie starre,
    Who see your vanquisht foes before you lye,
    Well worthie be you of that Armory,
    Wherein ye have great glory wonne this day,
    And proov'd your strength on a strong enimie,
    Your first adventure: many such I pray,
    And henceforth ever wish that like succeed it may! "

XXVIII. Then mounted he upon his Steede againe,
    And with the Lady backward sought to wend.
    That path he kept which beaten was most plaine,
    Ne ever would to any byway bend,
    But still did follow one unto the end,
    The which at last out of the wood them brought.
    So forward on his way (with God to frend)
    He passed forth, and new adventure sought:
    Long way he traveiled before he heard of ought.

XXIX. At length they chaunst to meet upon the way
    An aged Sire, in long blacke weedes yclad,
    His feete all bare, his beard all hoarie gray,
    And by his belt his booke he hanging had:
    Sober he seemde, and very sagely sad,
    And to the ground his eyes were lowly bent,
    Simple in shew, and voide of malice bad;
    And all the way he prayed as he went,
    And often knockt his breast, as one that did repent.

XXX. He faire the knight saluted, louting low,
    Who faire him quited, as that courteous was;

And after asked him, if he did know
Of straunge adventures, which abroad did pas.
" Ah! my dear sonne," (quoth he) " how should, alas!
Silly old man, that lives in hidden cell,
Bidding his beades all day for his trespas,
Tydings of warre and worldly trouble tell?
With holy father sits not with such thinges to mell.

XXXI. " But if of daunger, which hereby doth dwell,
And homebredd evil ye desire to heare,
Of a straunge man I can you tidings tell,
That wasteth all this countrie, farre and neare."
" Of such," (saide he,) " I chiefly doe inquere,
And shall thee well rewarde to shew the place,
In which that wicked wight his dayes doth weare;
For to all knighthood it is foule disgrace,
That such a cursed creature lives so long a space."

XXXII. " Far hence " (quoth he) " in wastfull wildernesse
His dwelling is, by which no living wight
May ever passe, but thorough great distresse."
" Now," (saide the Ladie,) " draweth toward night,
And well I wote, that of your later fight
Y: all forwearied be; for what so strong,
But, wanting rest, will also want of might?
The Sunne, that measures heaven all day long,
At night doth baite his steedes the Ocean waves emong.

XXXIII. " Then with the Sunne take, Sir, your timely rest,
And with new day new worke at once begin:
Untroubled night, they say, gives counsell best."
" Right well, Sir knight, ye have advised bin,"
Quoth then that aged man: " the way to win
Is wisely to advise; now day is spent:
Therefore with me ye may take up your In
For this same night." The knight was well content;
So with that godly father to his home they went.

XXXIV. A litle lowly Hermitage it was,
Downe in a dale, hard by a forests side,
Far from resort of people that did pas
In traveill to and froe: a litle wyde
There was an holy chappell edifyde,

Wherein the Hermite dewly wont to say
His holy thinges each morne and eventyde:
Thereby a christall streame did gently play,
Which from a sacred fountaine welled forth alway.

XXXV. Arrived there, the litle house they fill,
Ne looke for entertainement where none was;
Rest is their feast, and all thinges at their will:
The noblest mind the best contentment has.
With faire discourse the evening so they pas;
For that olde man of pleasing wordes had store,
And well could file his tongue as smooth as glas:
He told of Saintes and Popes, and evermore
He strowd an *Ave-Mary* after and before.

XXXVI. The drouping night thus creepeth on them fast;
And the sad humor loading their eyeliddes,
As messenger of Morpheus, on them cast
Sweet slombring deaw, the which to sleep them biddes.
Unto their lodgings then his guestes he riddes:
Where when all drownd in deadly sleepe he findes,
He to his studie goes; and there amiddes
His magick bookes, and artes of sundrie kindes,
He seekes out mighty charmes to trouble sleepy minds.

XXXVII. Then choosing out few words most horrible,
(Let none them read) thereof did verses frame;
With which, and other spelles like terrible,
He bad awake blacke Plutoes griesly Dame;
And cursed heven; and spake reprochful shame
Of highest God, the Lord of life and light:
A bold bad man, that dar'd to call by name
Great Gorgon, prince of darkness and dead night;
At which Cocytus quakes, and Styx is put to flight.

XXXVIII. And forth he cald out of deepe darknes dredd
Legions of Sprights, the which, like litle flyes
Fluttring about his ever-damned hedd,
Awaite whereto their service he applyes,
To aide his friendes, or fray his enimies.
Of those he chose out two, the falsest twoo,
And fittest for to forge true-seeming lyes:
The one of them he gave a message too,
The other by him selfe staide, other worke to doo.

XXXIX. He, making speedy way through spersed ayre,
And through the world of waters wide and deepe,
To Morpheus house doth hastily repaire.
Amid the bowels of the earth full steepe,
And low, where dawning day doth never peepe,
His dwelling is; there Tethys his wet bed
Doth ever wash, and Cynthia still doth steepe
In silver deaw his ever-drouping hed,
Whiles sad Night over him her mantle black doth spred.

XL. Whose double gates he findeth locked fast,
The one faire fram'd of burnisht Yvory,
The other all with silver overcast;
And wakeful dogges before them farre doe lye,
Watching to banish Care their enimy,
Who oft is wont to trouble gentle Sleepe.
By them the Sprite doth passe in quietly,
And unto Morpheus comes, whom drowned deepe
In drowsie fit he findes: of nothing he takes keepe.

XLI. And more to lulle him in his slumber soft,
A trickling streame from high rock tumbling downe,
And ever-drizling raine upon the loft,
Mixt with a murmuring winde, much like the sowne
Of swarming Bees, did cast him in a swowne.
No other noyse, nor peoples troublous cryes,
As still are wont t' annoy the walled towne,
Might there be heard; but carelesse Quiet lyes
Wrapt in eternall silence farre from enimyes.

XLII. The Messenger approching to him spake;
But his waste wordes retournd to him in vaine:
So sound he slept, that nought mought him awake.
Then rudely he him thrust, and pusht with paine,
Whereat he gan to stretch; but he againe
Shooke him so hard, that forced him to speake.
As one then in a dreame, whose dryer braine
Is tost with troubled sights and fancies weake,
He mumbled soft, but would not all his silence breake.

XLIII. The Sprite then gan more boldly him to wake,
And threatned unto him the dreaded name
Of Hecate: whereat he gan to quake,

And, lifting up his lompish head, with blame
Halfe angrie asked him, for what he came.
" Hether " (quoth he,) " me Archimago sent,
He that the stubborne Sprites can wisely tame,
He bids thee to him send for his intent
A fit false dreame, that can delude the sleepers sent.

XLIV. The God obayde; and, calling forth straight way
A diverse Dreame out of his prison darke,
Delivered it to him, and downe did lay
His heavie head, devoide of carefull carke;
Whose sences all were straight benumbd and starke.
He, backe returning by the Yvorie dore,
Remounted up as light as chearefull Larke;
And on his litle winges the dreame he bore
In hast unto his Lord, where he him left afore.

XLV. Who all this while, with charmes and hidden artes,
Had made a Lady of that other Spright,
And fram'd of liquid ayre her tender partes,
So lively and so like in all mens sight,
That weaker sence it could have ravisht quight:
The maker selfe, for all his wondrous witt,
Was nigh beguiled with so goodly sight.
Her all in white he clad, and over it
Cast a black stole, most like to seeme for Una fit.

XLVI. Now, when that ydle dreame was to him brought,
Unto that Elfin knight he bad him fly,
Where he slept soundly void of evil thought,
And with false shewes abuse his fantasy,
In sort as he him schooled privily:
And that new creature, borne without her dew,
Full of the makers guyle, with usage sly
He taught to imitate that Lady trew,
Whose semblance she did carrie under feigned hew,

XLVII. Thus, well instructed, to their worke they haste;
And, comming where the knight in slomber lay,
The one upon his hardie head him plaste,
And made him dreame of loves and lustfull play,
That night his manly hart did melt away,
Bathed in wanton blis and wicked joy.

Then seemed him his Lady by him lay,
And to him playnd, how that false winged boy
Her chaste hart had subdewd to learne Dame Pleasures toy.

XLVIII. And she her selfe, of beautie soveraigne Queene,
Fayre Venus, seemde unto his bed to bring
Her, whom he, waking, evermore did weene
To bee the chastest flowre that aye did spring
On earthly braunch, the daughter of a king,
Now a loose Leman to vile service bound:
And eke the Graces seemed all to sing,
Hymen Iö Hymen! dauncing all around;
Whylst freshest Flora her with Yvie girlond crownd.

XLIX. In this great passion of unwonted lust,
Or wonted feare of doing ought amis,
He starteth up, as seeming to mistrust
Some secret ill, or hidden foe of his.
Lo! there before his face his Ladie is,
Under blacke stole hyding her bayted hooke;
And as halfe blushing offred him to kis,
With gentle blandishment and lovely looke,
Most like that virgin true which for her knight him took.

L. All cleane dismayd to see so uncouth sight,
And half enraged at her shameless guise,
He thought have slaine her in his fierce despight;
But hastie heat tempring with sufferance wise,
He stayde his hand; and gan himselfe advise
To prove his sense, and tempt her faigned truth.
Wringing her hands, in wemens pitteous wise,
Tho can she weepe, to stirre up gentle ruth
Both for her noble blood, and for her tender youth.

LI. And sayd, "Ah Sir, my liege Lord, and my love,
Shall I accuse the hidden cruell fate,
And mightie causes wrought in heaven above,
Or the blind God that doth me thus amate,
For hoped love to winne me certaine hate?
Yet thus perforce he bids me do, or die.
Die is my dew; yet rew my wretched state,
You, whom my hard avenging destinie
Hath made judge of my life or death indifferently.

LII. " Your owne deare sake forst me at first to leave
My fathers kingdom "—There she stopt with teares;
Her swollen hart her speech seemd to bereave,
And then againe begonne; " My weaker yeares,
Captiv'd to fortune and frayle worldly feares,
Fly to your fayth for succour and sure ayde:
Let me not die in languor and long teares."
" Why, Dame," (quoth he,) " what hath ye thus dismayd?
What frayes ye, that were wont to comfort me affrayd? "

LIII. " Love of your selfe," she saide, " and deare constraint,
Lets me not sleepe, but waste the wearie night
In secret anguish and unpittied plaint,
Whiles you in carelesse sleepe are drowned quight."
Her doubtfull words made that redoubted knight
Suspect her truth: yet since no' untruth he knew,
Her fawning love with foule disdainefull spight
He would not shend; but said, " Deare dame, I rew,
That for my sake unknowne such griefe unto you grew.

LIV. " Assure your selfe, it fell not all to ground;
For all so deare as life is to my hart,
I deeme your love, and hold me to you bound:
Ne let vaine feares procure your needlesse smart,
Where cause is none; but to your rest depart."
Not all content, yet seemd she to appease
Her mournefull plaintes, beguiled of her art,
And fed with words that could not chose but please:
So, slyding softly forth, she turnd as to her ease.

LV. Long after lay he musing at her mood,
Much griev'd to thinke that gentle Dame so light,
For whose defence he was to shed his blood.
At last, dull wearines of former fight
Having yrockt asleepe his irkesome spright,
That troublous dreame gan freshly tosse his braine
With bowres, and beds, and ladies deare delight:
But, when he saw his labour all was vaine,
With that misformed spright he backe returnd againe.

CANTO II

The guilefull great Enchaunter parts
The Redcrosse Knight from Truth:
Into whose stead faire falshood steps,
And workes him woefull ruth.

I. By this the Northerne wagoner had set
   His sevenfold teme behind the stedfast starre
   That was in Ocean waves yet never wet,
   But firme is fixt, and sendeth light from farre
   To al that in the wide deepe wandring arre;
   And chearefull Chaunticlere with his note shrill
   Had warned once, that Phœbus fiery carre
   In hast was climbing up the Easterne hill,
   Full envious that night so long his roome did fill:

II. When those accursed messengers of hell,
    That feigning dreame, and that faire-forged Spright,
    Came to their wicked maister, and gan tel
    Their bootelesse paines, and ill succeeding night:
    Who, all in rage to see his skilfull might
    Deluded so, gan threaten hellish paine,
    And sad Proserpines wrath, them to affright:
    But, when he saw his threatning was but vaine,
    He cast about, and searcht his baleful bokes againe.

III. Eftsoones he tooke that miscreated faire,
     And that false other Spright, on whom he spred
     A seeming body of the subtile aire,
     Like a young Squire, in loves and lusty-hed
     His wanton daies that ever loosely led,
     Without regard of armes and dreaded fight:
     Those twoo he tooke, and in a secrete bed,
     Covered with darkenes and misdeeming night,
     Them both together laid to joy in vaine delight.

IV. Forthwith he runnes with feigned faithfull hast
    Unto his guest, who, after troublous sights
    And dreames, gan now to take more sound repast;

Whom suddenly he wakes with fearful frights,
As one aghast with feends or damned sprights,
And to him cals; "Rise, rise! unhappy Swaine,
That here wex old in sleepe, whiles wicked wights
Have knit themselves in Venus shameful chaine:
Come, see where your false Lady doth her honor staine."

v. All in amaze he suddenly up start
With sword in hand, and with the old man went;
Who soone him brought into a secret part,
Where that false couple were full closely ment
In wanton lust and leud embracement:
Which when he saw, he burnt with gealous fire;
The eie of reason was with rage yblent,
And would have slaine them in his furious ire,
But hardly was restreined of that aged sire.

vi. Retourning to his bed in torment great,
And bitter anguish of his guilty sight,
He could not rest; but did his stout heart eat,
And wast his inward gall with deepe despight,
Yrkesome of life, and too long lingring night.
At last faire Hesperus in highest skie
Had spent his lampe, and brought forth dawning light;
Then up he rose, and clad him hastily:
The dwarfe him brought his steed; so both away do fly.

vii. Now when the rosy fingred Morning faire,
Weary of aged Tithones saffron bed,
Had spred her purple robe through deawy aire,
And the high hils Titan discovered,
The royall virgin shooke off drousy-hed;
And, rising forth out of her baser bowre,
Lookt for her knight, who far away was fled,
And for her dwarfe, that wont to wait each howre:
Then gan she wail and weepe to see that woeful stowre.

viii. And after him she rode, with so much speede
As her slowe beast could make; but all in vaine,
For him so far had borne his light-foot steede,
Pricked with wrath and fiery fierce disdaine,
That him to follow was but fruitlesse paine:
Yet she her weary limbes would never rest;

But every hil and dale, each wood and plaine,
Did search, sore grieved in her gentle brest,
He so ungently left her, whome she loved best.

IX. But subtill Archimago, when his guests
He saw divided into double parts,
And Una wandring in woods and forrests,
Th' end of his drift, he praisd his divelish arts,
That had such might over true meaning harts:
Yet rests not so, but other meanes doth make,
How he may worke unto her further smarts;
For her he hated as the hissing snake,
And in her many troubles did most pleasure take.

X. He then devisde himselfe how to disguise;
For by his mighty science he could take
As many formes and shapes in seeming wise,
As ever Proteus to himselfe could make:
Sometime a fowle, sometime a fish in lake,
Now like a foxe, now like a dragon fell;
That of himselfe he ofte for feare would quake,
And oft would flie away.   O! who can tell
The hidden powre of herbes, and might of Magick spel?

XI. But now seemde best the person to put on
Of that good knight, his late beguiled guest:
In mighty armes he was yclad anon,
And silver shield; upon his coward brest
A bloody crosse, and on his craven crest
A bounch of heares discolourd diversly.
Full jolly knight he seemde, and wel addrest;
And when he sate upon his courser free,
Saint George himselfe ye would have deemed him to be.

XII. But he, the knight whose semblaunt he did beare,
The true Saint George, was wandred far away,
Still flying from his thoughts and gealous feare:
Will was his guide, and griefe led him astray.
At last him chaunst to meete upon the way
A faithlesse Sarazin, all armde to point,
In whose great shield was writ with letters gay
Sans foy; full large of limbe and every joint
He was, and cared not for God or man a point.

XIII. Hee had a faire companion of his way,
    A goodly Lady clad in scarlot red,
    Purfled with gold and pearle of rich assay;
    And like a Persian mitre on her hed
    Shee wore, with crowns and owches garnished,
    The which her lavish lovers to her gave.
    Her wanton palfrey all was overspred
    With tinsell trappings, woven like a wave,
    Whose bridle rung with golden bels and bosses brave.

XIV. With faire disport, and courting dalliaunce,
    She intertainde her lover all the way;
    But, when she saw the knight his speare advaunce,
    She soone left off her mirth and wanton play,
    And bad her knight addresse him to the fray,
    His foe was nigh at hand.   He, prickte with pride
    And hope to winne his Ladies hearte that day,
    Forth spurred fast: adowne his coursers side
    The red bloud trickling staind the way, as he did ride.

XV. The knight of the Redcrosse, when him he spide
    Spurring so hote with rage dispiteous,
    Gan fairely couch his speare, and towards ride.
    Soone meete they both, both fell and furious,
    That, daunted with theyr forces hideous,
    Their steeds doe stagger, and amazed stand;
    And eke themselves, too rudely rigorous,
    Astonied with the stroke of their owne hand,
    Doe backe rebutte, and ech to other yealdeth land.

XVI. As when two rams, stird with ambitious pride,
    Fight for the rule of the rich fleeced flocke,
    Their horned fronts so fierce on either side
    Doe meete, that, with the terror of the shocke,
    Astonied, both stand sencelesse as a blocke,
    Forgetfull of the hanging victory:
    So stood these twaine, unmoved as a rocke,
    Both staring fierce, and holding idely
    The broken reliques of their former cruelty.

XVII. The Sarazin, sore daunted with the buffe,
    Snatched his sword, and fiercely to him flies;
    Who well it wards, and quyteth cuff with cuff:

Each others equall puissaunce envies,
And through their iron sides with cruell spies
Does seeke to perce; repining courage yields
No foote to foe: the flashing fier flies,
As from a forge, out of their burning shields;
And streams of purple bloud new die the verdant fields.

XVIII. " Curse on that Cross," (quoth then the Sarazin,)
" That keepes thy body from the bitter fitt!
Dead long ygoe, I wote, thou haddest bin,
Had not that charme from thee forwarned itt:
But yet I warne thee now assured sitt,
And hide thy head." Therewith upon his crest
With rigor so outrageous he smitt,
That a large share it hewd out of the rest,
And glauncing downe his shield from blame him fairly blest.

XIX. Who, thereat wondrous wroth, the sleeping spark
Of native vertue gan eftsoones revive;
And at his haughty helmet making mark,
So hugely stroke, that it the steele did rive,
And cleft his head. He, tumbling downe alive,
With bloudy mouth his mother earth did kis,
Greeting his grave: his grudging ghost did strive
With the fraile flesh; at last it flitted is,
Whither the soules doe fly of men that live amis.

XX. The Lady, when she saw her champion fall
Like the old ruines of a broken towre,
Staid not to waile his woefull funerall,
But from him fled away with all her powre;
Who after her as hastily gan scowre,
Bidding the dwarfe with him to bring away
The Sarazins shield, signe of the conqueroure.
Her soone he overtooke, and bad to stay;
For present cause was none of dread her to dismay.

XXI. Shee turning backe, with ruefull countenaunce,
Cride, " Mercy, mercy, Sir, vouchsafe to show
On silly Dame, subject to hard mischaunce,
And to your mighty wil!" Her humblesse low,
In so ritch weedes, and seeming glorious show,
Did much emmove his stout heroicke heart;

And said, " Deare dame, your sudden overthrow
    Much rueth me; but now put feare apart,
    And tel both who ye be, and who that tooke your part."

XXII. Melting in teares, then gan shee thus lament,
    " The wretched woman, whom unhappy howre
    Hath now made thrall to your commandement,
    Before that angry heavens list to lowre,
    And fortune false betraide me to thy powre,
    Was (O! what now availeth that I was?)
    Borne the sole daughter of an Emperour,
    He that the wide West under his rule has,
    And high hath set his throne where Tiberis doth pas.

XXIII. " He, in the first flowre of my freshest age,
    Betrothed me unto the onley haire
    Of a most mighty king, most rich and sage:
    Was never Prince so faithfull and so faire,
    Was never Prince so meeke and debonaire;
    But ere my hoped day of spousall shone,
    My dearest Lord fell from high honors staire
    Into the hands of hys accursed fone,
    And cruelly was slaine; that shall I ever mone.

XXIV. " His blessed body, spoild of lively breath,
    Was afterward, I know not how, convaid,
    And fro me hid: of whose most innocent death
    When tidings came to mee, unhappy maid,
    O, how great sorrow my sad soule assaid!
    Then forth I went his woefull corse to find,
    And many yeares throughout the world I straid,
    A virgin widow, whose deepe wounded mind
    With love long time did languish, as the striken hind.

XXV. " At last it chaunced this proud Sarazin
    To meete me wandring; who perforce me led
    With him away, but yet could never win
    The Fort, that Ladies hold in soveraigne dread.
    There lies he now with foule dishonour dead,
    Who, whiles he livde, was called proud Sans foy,
    The eldest of three brethren; all three bred
    Of one bad sire, whose youngest is Sans joy;
    And twixt them both was born the bloudy bold Sans loy.

XXVI. " In this sad plight, friendlesse, unfortunate,
        Now miserable I, Fidessa, dwell,
        Craving of you, in pitty of my state,
        To doe none ill, if please ye not doe well."
        He in great passion al this while did dwell,
        More busying his quicke eies her face to view,
        Then his dull eares to heare what shee did tell;
        And said, " faire lady, hart of flint would rew
        The undeserved woes and sorrowes, which ye shew.

XXVII. " Henceforth in safe assuraunce may ye rest,
        Having both found a new friend you to aid,
        And lost an old foe that did you molest;
        Better new friend then an old foe is said."
        With chaunge of chear the seeming simple maid
        Let fal her eien, as shamefast, to the earth,
        And yeelding soft, in that she nought gainsaid,
        So forth they rode, he feining seemely merth,
        And shee coy lookes: so dainty, they say, maketh derth.

XXVIII. Long time they thus together traveiled;
        Til, weary of their way, they came at last
        Where grew two goodly trees, that faire did spred
        Their armes abroad, with gray mosse overcast;
        And their greene leaves, trembling with every blast,
        Made a calme shadowe far in compasse round:
        The fearefull shepheard, often there aghast,
        Under them never sat, ne wont there sound
        His mery oaten pipe, but shund th' unlucky ground.

XXIX. But this good knight, soone as he them can spie,
        For the coole shade him thither hastly got:
        For golden Phœbus, now ymounted hie,
        From fiery wheeles of his faire chariot
        Hurled his beame so scorching cruell hot,
        That living creature mote it not abide;
        And his new Lady it endured not.
        There they alight, in hope themselves to hide
        From the fierce heat, and rest their weary limbs a tide.

XXX. Faire seemely pleasaunce each to other makes,
        With goodly purposes, there as they sit;
        And in his falsed fancy he her takes

To be the fairest wight that lived yit;
Which to expresse he bends his gentle wit:
And, thinking of those braunches greene to frame
A girlond for her dainty forehead fit,
He pluckt a bough; out of whose rifte there came
Smal drops of gory bloud, that trickled down the same

XXXI. Therewith a piteous yelling voice was heard,
Crying, " O! spare with guilty hands to teare
My tender sides in this rough rynd embard;
But fly, ah! fly far hence away, for feare
Least to you hap that happened to me heare,
And to this wretched Lady, my deare love;
O, too deare love, love bought with death too deare! "
Astond he stood, and up his heare did hove;
And with that suddein horror could no member move.

XXXII. At last whenas the dreadfull passion
Was overpast, and manhood well awake,
Yet musing at the straunge occasion,
And doubting much his sence, he thus bespake:
" What voice of damned Ghost from Limbo lake,
Or guilefull spright wandring in empty aire,
Both which fraile men doe oftentimes mistake,
Sends to my doubtful eares these speaches rare,
And ruefull plaints, me bidding guiltlesse blood to
spare? "

XXXIII. Then, groning deep; " Nor damned Ghost," (quoth he,)
" Nor guileful sprite to thee these words doth speake;
But once a man, Fradubio, now a tree;
Wretched man, wretched tree! whose nature weake
A cruell witch, her cursed will to wreake,
Hath thus transformd, and plast in open plaines,
Where Boreas doth blow full bitter bleake,
And scorching Sunne does dry my secret vaines;
For though a tree I seme, yet cold and heat me paines."

XXXIV. " Say on, Fradubio, then, or man or tree."
Quoth then the Knight; " by whose mischievous arts
Art thou misshaped thus, as now I see?
He oft finds med'cine who his griefe imparts,
But double griefs afflict concealing harts,

As raging flames who striveth to suppresse."
" The author then," (said he) " of all my smarts,
Is one Duessa, a false sorceresse,
That many errant knights hath broght to wretchednesse.

xxxv. " In prime of youthly yeares, when corage hott
The fire of love, and joy of chevalree,
First kindled in my brest, it was my lott
To love this gentle Lady, whome ye see
Now not a Lady, but a seeming tree;
With whome, as once I rode accompanyde,
Me chaunced of a knight encountred bee,
That had a like faire Lady by his syde;
Lyke a faire Lady, but did fowle Duessa hyde.

xxxvi. " Whose forged beauty he did take in hand
All other Dames to have exceeded farre:
I in defence of mine did likewise stand,
Mine, that did then shine as the Morning starre.
So both to batteill fierce arraunged arre,
In which his harder fortune was to fall
Under my speare: such is the dye of warre.
His Lady, left as a prise martiall,
Did yield her comely person to be at my call.

xxxvii. " So doubly lov'd of ladies, unlike faire,
Th' one seeming such, the other such indeede,
One day in doubt I cast for to compare
Whether in beauties glorie did exceede:
A Rosy girlond was the victors meede.
Both seemde to win, and both seemed won to bee,
So hard the discord was to be agreede.
Frælissa was as faire as faire mote bee,
And ever false Duessa seemde as faire as shee.

xxxviii. " The wicked witch, now seeing all this while
The doubtfull ballaunce equally to sway,
What not by right she cast to win by guile;
And by her hellish science raisd streight way
A foggy mist that overcast the day,
And a dull blast, that breathing on her face
Dimmed her former beauties shining ray,
And with foule ugly forme did her disgrace:
Then was she fayre alone, when none was faire in place.

XXXIX. " Then cride she out, ' Fye, fye! deformed wight,
Whose borrowed beautie now appeareth plaine
To have before bewitched all mens sight:
O! leave her soone, or let her soone be slaine.'
Her loathly visage viewing with disdaine,
Eftsoones I thought her such as she me told,
And would have kild her; but with faigned paine
The false witch did my wrathful hand withhold:
So left her, where she now is turnd to treen mould.

XL. " Thensforth I tooke Duessa for my Dame,
And in the witch unweeting joyd long time,
Ne ever wist but that she was the same;
Till on a day (that day is everie Prime,
When Witches wont do penance for their crime,)
I chaunst to see her in her proper hew,
Bathing her selfe in origane and thyme:
A filthy foule old woman I did vew,
That ever to have toucht her I did deadly rew.

XLI. " Her neather partes misshapen, monstruous,
Were hidd in water, that I could not see;
But they did seeme more foule and hideous,
Then womans shape man would beleeve to bee.
Thensforth from her most beastly companie
I gan refraine, in minde to slipp away,
Soone as appeard safe opportunitie:
For danger great, if not assured decay,
I saw before mine eyes, if I were knowne to stray.

XLII. " The divelish hag by chaunges of my cheare
Perceiv'd my thought; and, drownd in sleepie night,
With wicked herbes and oyntments did besmeare
My body all, through charmes and magicke might,
That all my senses were bereaved quight:
Then brought she me into this desert waste,
And by my wretched lovers side me pight;
Where now, enclosed in wooden wals full faste,
Banisht from living wights, our wearie daies we waste."

XLIII. " But how long time," said then the Elfin knight,
" Are you in this misformed hous to dwell? "
" We may not chaunge," (quoth he,) " this evill plight,

Till we be bathed in a living well:
That is the terme prescribed by the spell."
" O! how," sayd he, " mote I that well out find,
That may restore you to your wonted well? "
" Time and suffised fates to former kynd
Shall us restore; none else from hence may us unbynd."

XLIV. The false Duessa, now Fidessa hight,
Heard how in vaine Fradubio did lament,
And knew well all was true.   But the good knight,
Full of sad feare and ghastly dreriment,
When all this speech the living tree had spent,
The bleeding bough did thrust into the ground,
That from the blood he might be innocent,
And with fresh clay did close the wooden wound:
Then, turning to his Lady, dead with feare her fownd.

XLV. Her seeming dead he fownd with feigned feare,
As all unweeting of that well she knew;
And paynd himselfe with busie care to reare
Her out of carelesse swowne.   Her eyelids blew,
And dimmed sight, with pale and deadly hew,
At last she up gan lift: with trembling cheare
Her up he tooke, (too simple and too trew)
And oft her kist.   At length, all passed feare,
He set her on her steede, and forward forth did beare.

CANTO III

Forsaken Truth long seekes her love,
And makes the Lyon mylde;
Marres blind Devotions mart, and fals
In hand of leachour vylde.

I. NOUGHT is there under heav'ns wide hollownesse,
    That moves more deare compassion of mind,
    Then beautie brought t'unworthie wretchednesse
    Through envies snares, or fortunes freakes unkind.
    I, whether lately through her brightnes blynd,
    Or through alleageance, and fast fealty,
    Which I do owe unto all womankynd,
    Feele my hart perst with so great agony,
    When such I see, that all for pitty I could dy.

II. And now it is empassioned so deepe,
    For fairest Unaes sake, of whom I sing,
    That my frayle eies these lines with teares do steepe,
    To thinke how she through guylefull handeling,
    Though true as touch, though daughter of a king,
    Though faire as ever living wight was fayre,
    Though nor in word nor deede ill meriting,
    Is from her knight divorced in despayre,
    And her dew loves deryv'd to that vile witches shayre.

III. Yet she, most faithfull Ladie, all this while
    Forsaken, wofull, solitarie mayd,
    Far from all peoples preace, as in exile,
    In wildernesse and wastfull deserts strayd,
    To seeke her knight; who, subtily betrayd
    Through that late vision which th'Enchaunter wrought,
    Had her abandond.   She, of nought affrayd,
    Through woods and wastnes wide him daily sought;
    Yet wished tydinges none of him unto her brought.

IV. One day, nigh wearie of the yrkesome way,
    From her unhastie beast she did alight;
    And on the grasse her dainty limbs did lay

In secrete shadow, far from all mens sight:
From her fayre head her fillet she undight,
And layd her stole aside.   Her angels face,
As the great eye of heaven, shyned bright,
And made a sunshine in the shady place;
Did ever mortall eye behold such heavenly grace.

v. It fortuned, out of the thickest wood
A ramping Lyon rushed suddeinly,
Hunting full greedy after salvage blood.
Soone as the royall virgin he did spy,
With gaping mouth at her ran greedily,
To have attonce devourd her tender corse;
But to the pray when as he drew more ny,
His bloody rage aswaged with remorse,
And, with the sight amazd, forgat his furious forse.

vi. In stead thereof he kist her wearie feet,
And lickt her lilly hands with fawning tong,
As he her wronged innocence did weet.
O, how can beautie maister the most strong,
And simple truth subdue avenging wrong!
Whose yielded pryde and proud submission,
Still dreading death, when she had marked long,
Her hart gan melt in great compassion;
And drizling teares did shed for pure affection.

vii. " The Lyon, Lord of everie beast in field,"
Quoth she, " his princely puissance doth abate,
And mightie proud to humble weake does yield,
Forgetfull of the hungry rage, which late
Him prickt, in pittie of my sad estate:
But he, my Lyon, and my noble Lord,
How does he find in cruell hart to hate
Her, that him lov'd, and ever most adord
As the God of my life? why hath he me abhord? "

viii. Redounding teares did choke th' end of her plaint,
Which softly ecchoed from the neighbour wood;
And, sad to see her sorrowfull constraint,
The kingly beast upon her gazing stood:
With pittie calmd downe fell his angry mood.
At last, in close hart shutting up her payne,

Arose the virgin, borne of heavenly brood,
And to her snowy Palfrey got agayne,
To seeke her strayed Champion if she might attayne.

IX. The Lyon would not leave her desolate,
But with her went along, as a strong gard
Of her chast person, and a faythfull mate
Of her sad troubles and misfortunes hard:
Still, when she slept, he kept both watch and ward;
And, when she wakt, he wayted diligent,
With humble service to her will prepard:
From her fayre eyes he tooke commandement,
And ever by her lookes conceived her intent.

X. Long she thus traveiled through deserts wyde,
By which she thought her wandring knight shold pas,
Yet never shew of living wight espyde;
Till that at length she found the troden gras,
In which the tract of peoples footing was,
Under the steepe foot of a mountaine hore:
The same she followes, till at last she has
A damzel spyde, slow footing her before,
That on her shoulders sad a pot of water bore.

XI. To whom approching she to her gan call,
To weet if dwelling place were nigh at hand;
But the rude wench her answerd nought at all:
She could not heare, nor speake, nor understand;
Till, seeing by her side the Lyon stand,
With suddeine feare her pitcher downe she threw,
And fled away: for never in that land
Face of fayre Lady she before did vew,
And that dredd Lyons looke her cast in deadly hew.

XII. Full fast she fled, ne ever lookt behynd,
As if her life upon the wager lay;
And home she came, whereas her mother blynd
Sate in eternall night: nought could she say;
But, suddeine catching hold, did her dismay
With quaking hands, and other signes of feare:
Who, full of ghastly fright and cold affray,
Gan shut the dore.   By this arrived there
Dame Una, weary Dame, and entrance did requere:

XIII. Which when none yielded, her unruly Page
With his rude clawes the wicket open rent,
And let her in; where, of his cruell rage
Nigh dead with feare, and faint astonishment,
Shee found them both in darksome corner pent;
Where that old woman day and night did pray
Upon her beads, devoutly penitent:
Nine hundred *Pater nosters* every day,
And thrise nine hundred *Aves* she was wont to say.

XIV. And to augment her painefull penaunce more,
Thrise every weeke in ashes shee did sitt,
And next her wrinkled skin rough sackecloth wore,
And thrise three times did fast from any bitt:
But now, for feare her beads she did forgett:
Whose needlesse dread for to remove away,
Faire Una framed words and count'naunce fitt;
Which hardly doen, at length she gan them pray,
That in their cotage small that night she rest her may.

XV. The day is spent; and commeth drowsie night,
When every creature shrowded is in sleepe.
Sad Una downe her laies in weary plight,
And at her feete the Lyon watch doth keepe:
In stead of rest she does lament and weepe,
For the late losse of her deare loved knight,
And sighes, and grones, and evermore does steepe
Her tender brest in bitter teares all night;
All night she thinks too long, and often lookes for light.

XVI. Now when Aldeboran was mounted hye
Above the shinie Cassiopeias chaire,
And all in deadly sleepe did drowned lye
One knocked at the dore, and in would fare:
He knocked fast, and often curst, and sware,
That ready entraunce was not at his call;
For on his backe a heavy load he bare
Of nightly stelths, and pillage severall,
Which he had got abroad by purchas criminall.

XVII. He was, to weete, a stout and sturdy thiefe,
Wont to robbe churches of their ornaments,
And poore mens boxes of their due reliefe,

Which given was to them for good intents:
The holy Saints of their rich vestiments
He did disrobe, when all men carelesse slept,
And spoild the Priests of their habiliments;
Whiles none the holy things in safety kept,
Then he by conning sleights in at the window crept.

xviii. And all that he by right or wrong could find,
Unto this house he brought, and did bestow
Upon the daughter of this woman blind,
Abessa, daughter of Corceca slow,
With whom he whoredome usd, that few did know,
And fed her fatt with feast of offerings,
And plenty, which in all the land did grow:
Ne spared he to give her gold and rings;
And now he to her brought part of his stolen things.

xix. Thus, long the dore with rage and threats he bett,
Yet of those fearfull women none durst rize,
The Lyon frayed them, him in to lett.
He would no lenger stay him to advize,
But open breakes the dore in furious wize,
And entring is, when that disdainfull beast,
Encountring fierce, him suddein doth surprize;
And, seizing cruell clawes on trembling brest,
Under his Lordly foot him proudly hath supprest.

xx. Him booteth not resist, nor succour call,
His bleeding hart is in the vengers hand;
Who streight him rent in thousand peeces small,
And quite dismembred hath: the thirsty land
Dronke up his life; his corse left on the strand.
His fearefull freends weare out the wofull night,
Ne dare to weepe, nor seeme to understand
The heavie hap which on them is alight;
Affraid least to themselves the like mishappen might.

xxi. Now when broad day the world discovered has,
Up Una rose, up rose the lyon eke;
And on their former journey forward pas,
In waies unknowne, her wandring knight to seeke,
With paines far passing that long wandring Greeke,
That for his love refused deitye.

Such were the labours of this Lady meeke,
Still seeking him, that from her still did flye;
Then furthest from her hope, when most she weened nye.

XXII. Soone as she parted thence, the fearfull twayne,
That blind old woman, and her daughter dear,
Came forth; and, finding Kirkrapine there slayne,
For anguish great they gan to rend their heare,
And beat their brests, and naked flesh to teare:
And when they both had wept and wayld their fill,
Then forth they ran, like two amazed deare,
Halfe mad through malice and revenging will,
To follow her that was the causer of their ill.

XXIII. Whome overtaking, they gan loudly bray,
With hollow houling, and lamenting cry;
Shamefully at her rayling all the way,
And her accusing of dishonesty,
That was the flowre of faith and chastity:
And still, amidst her rayling, she did pray
That plagues, and mischiefes, and long misery,
Might fall on her, and follow all the way,
And that in endlesse error she might ever stray.

XXIV. But, when she saw her prayers nought prevaile,
Shee backe retourned with some labour lost;
And in the way, as shee did weepe and waile,
A knight her mett in mighty armes embost,
Yet knight was not for all his bragging bost;
But subtill Archimag, that Una sought
By traynes into new troubles to have toste:
Of that old woman tidings he besought,
If that of such a Lady shee could tellen ought.

XXV. Therewith she gan her passion to renew,
And cry, and curse, and raile, and rend her heare,
Saying, that harlott she too lately knew,
That causd her shed so many a bitter teare;
And so forth told the story of her feare.
Much seemed he to mone her haplesse chaunce,
And after for that Lady did inquere;
Which being taught, he forward gan advaunce
His fair enchaunted steed, and eke his charmed launce.

XXVI. Ere long he came where Una traveild slow,
    And that wilde champion wayting her besyde;
    Whome seeing such, for dread hee durst not show
    Him selfe too nigh at hand, but turned wyde
    Unto an hil; from whence when she him spyde,
    By his like seeming shield her knight by name
    She weend it was, and towards him gan ride:
    Approaching nigh she wist it was the same;
    And with faire fearefull humblesse towards him shee
        came:

XXVII. And weeping said, " Ah, my long lacked Lord,
    Where have ye bene thus long out of my sight?
    Much feared I to have bene quite abhord,
    Or ought have done, that ye displeasen might,
    That should as death unto my deare heart light:
    For since mine eie your joyous sight did mis,
    My chearefull day is turnd to chearelesse night,
    And eke my night of death the shadow is;
    But welcome now, my light, and shining lampe of blis!"

XXVIII. He thereto meeting said, " My dearest Dame,
    Far be it from your thought, and fro my wil,
    To thinke that knighthood I so much should shame,
    As you to leave that have me loved stil,
    And chose in Faery court, of meere goodwil,
    Where noblest knights were to be found on earth.
    The earth shall sooner leave her kindly skil
    To bring forth fruit, and make eternal derth,
    Then I leave you, my liefe, yborn of hevenly berth.

XXIX. " And sooth to say, why I lefte you so long,
    Was for to seeke adventure in straunge place;
    Where, Archimago said, a felon strong
    To many knights did daily worke disgrace;
    But knight he now shall never more deface:
    Good cause of mine excuse, that mote ye please
    Well to accept, and evermore embrace
    My faithfull service, that by land and seas
    Have vowd you to defend. Now then, your plaint
        appease."

XXX. His lovely words her seemd due recompence
    Of all her passed paines: one loving howre

For many yeares of sorrow can dispence;
A dram of sweete is worth a pound of sowre.
Shee has forgott how many a woeful stowre
For him she late endurd; she speakes no more
Of past: true is, that true love hath no powre
To looken backe; his eies be fixt before.
Before her stands her knight, for whom she toyld so sore.

XXXI. Much like, as when the beaten marinere,
That long hath wandred in the Ocean wide,
Ofte soust in swelling Tethys saltish teare;
And long time having tand his tawney hide
With blustring breath of Heaven, that none can bide,
And scorching flames of fierce Orions hound;
Soone as the port from far he has espide,
His chearfull whistle merily doth sound,
And Nereus crownes with cups; his mates him pledge
around.

XXXII. Such joy made Una, when her knight she found;
And eke th' enchaunter joyous seemde no lesse
Then the glad marchant, that does vew from ground
His ship far come from watrie wildernesse;
He hurles out vowes, and Neptune oft doth blesse.
So forth they past; and all the way they spent
Discoursing of her dreadful late distresse,
In which he askt her, what the Lyon ment;
Who told her all that fell, in journey as she went.

XXXIII. They had not ridden far, when they might see
One pricking towards them with hastie heat,
Full strongly armd, and on a courser free
That through his fiersnesse fomed all with sweat,
And the sharpe yron did for anger eat,
When his hot ryder spurd his chauffed side:
His looke was sterne, and seemed still to threat
Cruell revenge, which he in hart did hyde;
And on his shield *Sansloy* in bloody lines was dyde.

XXXIV. When nigh he drew unto this gentle payre,
And saw the Red-crosse which the knight did beare,
He burnt in fire; and gan eftsoones prepare
Himselfe to batteill with his couched speare.

Loth was that other, and did faint through feare,
To taste th' untryed dint of deadly steele:
But yet his Lady did so well him cheare,
That hope of new good hap he gan to feele;
So bent his speare, and spurd his horse with yron heele.

xxxv. But that proud Paynim forward came so ferce
And full of wrath, that, with his sharphead speare,
Through vainly crossed shield he quite did perce;
And, had his staggering steed not shronke for feare,
Through shield and body eke he should him beare:
Yet, so great was the puissance of his push,
That from his sadle quite he did him beare.
He, tombling rudely downe, to ground did rush,
And from his gored wound a well of bloud did gush.

xxxvi. Dismounting lightly from his loftie steed,
He to him lept, in minde to reave his life,
And proudly said; " Lo! there the worthie meed
Of him that slew Sansfoy with bloody knife:
Henceforth his ghost, freed from repining strife,
In peace may passen over Lethe lake;
When mourning altars, purged with enimies life,
The black infernall Furies doen aslake:
Life from Sansfoy thou tookst, Sansloy shall from thee
    take."

xxxvii. Therewith in haste his helmet gan unlace,
Till Una cride, " O! hold that heavie hand,
Deare Sir, what ever that thou be in place:
Enough is, that thy foe doth vanquisht stand
Now at thy mercy: Mercy not withstand;
For he is one the truest knight alive,
Though conquered now he lye on lowly land;
And, whilest him fortune favourd, fayre did thrive
In bloudy field; therefore, of life him not deprive."

xxxviii. Her piteous wordes might not abate his rage,
But, rudely rending up his helmet, would
Have slayne him streight; and when he sees his age,
And hoarie head of Archimago old,
His hasty hand he doth amased hold,
And halfe ashamed wondred at the sight:

For the old man well knew he, though untold,
In charmes and magick to have wondrous might,
Ne ever wont in field, ne in round lists, to fight:

XXXIX. And said, " Why Archimago, lucklesse syre,
What doe I see? what hard mishap is this,
That hath thee hether brought to taste mine yre?
Or thine the fault, or mine the error is,
In stead of foe to wound my friend amis? "
He answered nought, but in a traunce still lay,
And on those guilefull dazed eyes of his
The cloude of death did sit.   Which doen away,
He left him lying so, ne would no lenger stay:

XL. But to the virgin comes; who all this while
Amased stands, her selfe so mockt to see
By him, who has the guerdon of his guile,
For so misfeigning her true knight to bee:
Yet is she now in more perplexitie,
Left in the hand of that same Paynim bold,
From whom her booteth not at all to flie:
Who, by her cleanly garment catching hold,
Her from her Palfrey pluckt, her visage to behold.

XLI. But her fiers servant, full of kingly aw
And high disdaine, whenas his soveraine Dame
So rudely handled by her foe he saw,
With gaping jawes full greedy at him came,
And, ramping on his shield, did weene the same
Have reft away with his sharp rending clawes:
But he was stout, and lust did now inflame
His corage more, that from his griping pawes
He hath his shield redeemed, and forth his swerd he
drawes.

XLII. O! then, too weake and feeble was the forse
Of salvage beast his puissance to withstand;
For he was strong, and of so mightie corse,
As ever wielded speare in warlike hand,
And feates of armes did wisely understand.
Eft soones he perced through his chaufed chest
With thrilling point of deadly yron brand,
And launcht his Lordly hart: with death opprest
He ror'd aloud, whiles life forsooke his stubborne brest.

XLIII. Who now is left to keepe the forlorne maid
From raging spoile of lawlesse victors will?
Her faithfull gard remov'd, her hope dismaid,
Her selfe a yielded pray to save or spill:
He now, Lord of the field, his pride to fill,
With foule reproches and disdaineful spight
Her vildly entertaines; and, will or nill,
Beares her away upon his courser light:
Her prayers nought prevaile, his rage is more of might.

XLIV. And all the way, with great lamenting paine,
And piteous plaintes, she filleth his dull eares,
That stony hart could riven have in twaine;
And all the way she wetts with flowing teares;
But he, enrag'd with rancor, nothing heares.
Her servile beast yet would not leave her so,
But followes her far off, ne ought he feares
To be partaker of her wondring woe;
More mild in beastly kind then that her beastly foe.

CANTO IV

To sinfull hous of Pryde Duessa
Guydes the faithfull knight;
Where, brothers death to wreak, Sansjoy
Doth chaleng him to fight.

I. Young knight whatever, that dost armes professe,
And through long labours huntest after fame,
Beware of fraud, beware of ficklenesse,
In choice, and chaunge of thy deare-loved Dame;
Least thou of her believe too lightly blame,
And rash misweening doe thy hart remove:
For unto knight there is no greater shame
Then lightnesse and inconstancie in love:
That doth this Redcrosse knights ensample plainly prove.

II. Who, after that he had faire Una lorne,
Through light misdeeming of her loialtie;
And false Duessa in her sted had borne,
Called Fidess', and so suppos'd to be,
Long with her traveild; till at last they see
A goodly building bravely garnished;
The house of mightie Prince it seemd to be,
And towards it a broad high way that led,
All bare through peoples feet which thether traveiled.

III. Great troupes of people traveild thetherward
Both day and night, of each degree and place;
But few returned, having scaped hard,
With balefull beggery, or foule disgrace;
Which ever after in most wretched case,
Like loathsome lazars, by the hedges lay.
Thether Duessa badd him bend his pace,
For she is wearie of the toilsom way,
And also nigh consumed is the lingring day.

IV. A stately Pallace built of squared bricke,
Which cunningly was without morter laid,
Whose wals were high, but nothing strong nor thick

And golden foile all over them displaid,
That purest skye with brightnesse they dismaid:
High lifted up were many loftie towres,
And goodly galleries far over laid,
Full of faire windowes and delightful bowres:
And on the top a Diall told the timely howres.

v. It was a goodly heape for to behould,
And spake the praises of the workmans witt;
But full great pittie, that so faire a mould
Did on so weake foundation ever sitt:
For on a sandie hill, that still did flitt
And fall away, it mounted was full hie,
That every breath of heaven shaked itt:
And all the hinder partes, that few could spie,
Were ruinous and old, but painted cunningly.

vi. Arrived there, they passed in forth right;
For still to all the gates stood open wide:
Yet charge of them was to a Porter hight,
Cald Malvenú, who entrance none denide:
Thence to the hall, which was on every side
With rich array and costly arras dight.
Infinite sortes of people did abide
There waiting long, to win the wished sight
Of her, that was the Lady of that Pallace bright.

vii. By them they passe, all gazing on them round,
And to the Presence mount; whose glorious vew
Their frayle amazed senses did confound:
In living Princes court none ever knew
Such endlesse richesse, and so sumpteous shew;
Ne Persia selfe, the nourse of pompous pride,
Like ever saw.   And there a noble crew
Of Lords and Ladies stood on every side,
Which with their presence fayre the place much beautifide.

viii. High above all a cloth of State was spred,
And a rich throne, as bright as sunny day;
On which there sate, most brave embellished
With royall robes and gorgeous array,
A mayden Queene that shone as Titans ray,
In glistring gold and perelesse pretious stone;

Yet her bright blazing beautie did assay
To dim the brightnesse of her glorious throne,
As envying her selfe, that too exceeding shone:

IX. Exceeding shone, like Phœbus fayrest childe,
That did presume his fathers fyrie wayne,
And flaming mouthes of steedes, unwonted wilde,
Through highest heaven with weaker hand to rayr :
Proud of such glory and advancement vayne,
While flashing beames do daze his feeble eyen,
He leaves the welkin way most beaten playne,
And, rapt with whirling wheeles, inflames the skyen
With fire not made to burne, but fayrely for to shyne.

X. So proud she shyned in her princely state,
Looking to heaven, for earth she did disdayne,
And sitting high, for lowly she did hate:
Lo! underneath her scornefull feete was layne
A dreadfull Dragon with an hideous trayne;
And in her hand she held a mirrhour bright,
Wherein her face she often vewed fayne,
And in her selfe-lov'd semblance took delight;
For she was wondrous faire, as any living wight.

XI. Of griesly Pluto she the daughter was,
And sad Proserpina, the Queene of helle;
Yet did she thinke her pearelesse worth to pas
That parentage, with pride so did she swell;
And thundring Jove, that high in heaven doth dwell
And wield the world, she claymed for her syre,
Or if that any else did Jove excell;
For to the highest she did still aspyre,
Or, if ought higher were than that, did it desyre.

XII. And proud Lucifera men did her call,
That made her selfe a Queene, and crownd to be;
Yet rightfull kingdome she had none at all,
Ne heritage of native soveraintie;
But did usurpe with wrong and tyrannie
Upon the scepter which she now did hold:
Ne ruld her Realme with lawes, but pollicie,
And strong advizement of six wisards old,
That, with their counsels bad, her kingdome did uphold.

XIII. Soone as the Elfin knight in presence came,
And false Duessa, seeming Lady fayre,
A gentle Husher, Vanitie by name,
Made rowme, and passage for them did prepaire:
So goodly brought them to the lowest stayre
Of her high throne; where they, on humble knee
Making obeysaunce, did the cause declare,
Why they were come her roiall state to see,
To prove the wide report of her great Majestee.

XIV. With loftie eyes, halfe loth to looke so lowe,
She thancked them in her disdainefull wise:
Ne other grace vouchsafed them to showe
Of Princesse worthy; scarse them bad arise.
Her Lordes and Ladies all this while devise
Themselves to setten forth to straungers sight:
Some frounce their curled heare in courtly guise;
Some prancke their ruffes; and others trimly dight
Their gay attyre; each others greater pride does spight.

XV. Goodly they all that knight doe entertayne,
Right glad with him to have increast their crew;
But to Duess' each one himselfe did payne
All kindnesse and faire courtesie to shew,
For in that court whylome her well they knew:
Yet the stout Faery mongst the middest crowd
Thought all their glorie vaine in knightly vew,
And tha' great Princesse too exceeding prowd,
That to strange knight no better countenance allowd.

XVI. Suddein upriseth from her stately place
The roiall Dame, and for her coche doth call:
All hurtlen forth; and she, with princely pace,
As faire Aurora in her purple pall
Out of the East the dawning day doth call.
So forth she comes; her brightnes brode doth blaze.
The heapes of people, thronging in the hall,
Doe ride each other upon her to gaze:
Her glorious glitterand light doth all mens eies amaze.

XVII. So forth she comes, and to her coche does clyme,
Adorned all with gold and girlonds gay,
That seemed as fresh as Flora in her prime;

And strove to match, in roiall rich array,
Great Junoes golden chayre; the which, they say,
The gods stand gazing on, when she does ride
To Joves high hous through heavens bras-paved way,
Drawne of fayre Pecocks, that excell in pride,
And full of Argus eyes their tayles dispredden wide.

XVIII. But this was drawne of six unequall beasts,
On which her six sage Counsellours did ryde,
Taught to obay their bestiall beheasts,
With like conditions to their kindes applyde:
Of which the first, that all the rest did guyde,
Was sluggish Idlenesse, the nourse of sin;
Upon a slouthfull Asse he chose to ryde,
Arayd in habit blacke, and amis thin,
Like to an holy Monck, the service to begin.

XIX. And in his hand his Portesse still he bare,
That much was worne, but therein little redd;
For of devotion he had little care,
Still drownd in sleepe, and most of his daies dedd:
Scarse could he once uphold his heavie hedd,
To looken whether it were night or day.
May seeme the wayne was very evill ledd,
When such an one had guiding of the way,
That knew not whether right he went, or else astray.

XX. From worldly cares himselfe he did esloyne,
And greatly shunned manly exercise;
From everie worke he chalenged essoyne,
For contemplation sake: yet otherwise
His life he led in lawlesse riotise,
By which he grew to grievous malady;
For in his lustlesse limbs, through evill guise,
A shaking fever raignd continually.
Such one was Idlenesse, first of this company.

XXI. And by his side rode loathsome Gluttony,
Deformed creature, on a filthie swyne.
His belly was upblowne with luxury,
And eke with fatnesse swollen were his eyne;
And like a Crane his necke was long and fyne
With which he swallowed up excessive feast,

For want whereof poore people oft did pyne:
And all the way, most like a brutish beast,
He spued up his gorge, that all did him deteast.

XXII. In greene vine leaves he was right fitly clad,
For other clothes he could not ware for heate;
And on his head an yvie girland had,
From under which fast trickled downe the sweat.
Still as he rode he somewhat still did eat,
And in his hand did beare a bouzing can,
Of which he supt so oft, that on his seat
His dronken corse he scarse upholden can:
In shape and life more like a monster then a man.

XXIII. Unfit he was for any worldly thing,
And eke unhable once to stirre or go;
Not meet to be of counsell to a king,
Whose mind in meat and drinke was drowned so,
That from his frend he seeldome knew his fo.
Full of diseases was his carcas blew,
And a dry dropsie through his flesh did flow,
Which by misdiet daily greater grew.
Such one was Gluttony, the second of that crew.

XXIV. And next to him rode lustfull Lechery
Upon a bearded Gote, whose rugged heare,
And whally eies (the signe of gelosy,)
Was like the person selfe whom he did beare:
Who rough, and blacke, and filthy, did appeare,
Unseemely man to please faire Ladies eye;
Yet he of Ladies oft was loved deare,
When fairer faces were bid standen by:
O! who does know the bent of womens fantasy?

XXV. In a greene gowne he clothed was full faire,
Which underneath did hide his filthinesse;
And in his hand a burning hart he bare,
Full of vaine follies and new fanglenesse:
For he was false, and fraught with ficklenesse,
And learned had to love with secret lookes;
And well could daunce, and sing with ruefulnesse;
And fortunes tell, and read in loving bookes,
And thousand other waies to bait his fleshly hookes.

XXVI. Inconstant man, that loved all he saw,
And lusted after all that he did love;
Ne would his looser life be tide to law,
But joyd weake wemens hearts to tempt, and prove,
If from their loyall loves he might them move:
Which lewdnes fild him with reprochfull pain
Of that foule evill, which all men reprove,
That rotts the marrow, and consumes the braine.
Such one was Lechery, the third of all this traine.

XXVII. And greedy Avarice by him did ride,
Uppon a Camell loaden all with gold:
Two iron coffers hong on either side,
With precious metall full as they might hold;
And in his lap an heap of coine he told;
For of his wicked pelfe his God he made,
And unto hell him selfe for money sold:
Accursed usury was all his trade,
And right and wrong ylike in equall ballaunce waide.

XXVIII. His life was nigh unto deaths dore yplaste;
And thred-bare cote, and cobled shoes, hee ware;
Ne scarse good morsell all his life did taste,
But both from backe and belly still did spare,
To fill his bags, and richesse to compare:
Yet childe ne kinsman living had he none
To leave them to; but thorough daily care
To get, and nightly feare to lose his owne,
He led a wretched life, unto himselfe unknowne.

XXIX. Most wretched wight, whom nothing might suffise;
Whose greedy lust did lacke in greatest store;
Whose need had end, but no end covetise;
Whose welth was want, whose plenty made him pore;
Who had enough, yett wished ever more;
A vile disease: and eke in foote and hand
A grievous gout tormented him full sore,
That well he could not touch, nor goe, nor stand.
Such one was Avarice, the fourth of this faire band.

XXX. And next to him malicious Envy rode
Upon a ravenous wolfe, and still did chaw
Between his cankred teeth a venemous tode,

That all the poison ran about his chaw;
But inwardly he chawed his owne maw
At neighbours welth, that made him ever sad,
For death it was, when any good he saw;
And wept, that cause of weeping none he had;
But when he heard of harme he wexed wondrous glad.

XXXI. All in a kirtle of discolourd say
He clothed was, ypaynted full of eies;
And in his bosome secretly there lay
An hatefull Snake, the which his taile uptyes
In many folds, and mortall sting implyes.
Still as he rode he gnasht his teeth to see
Those heapes of gold with griple Covetyse;
And grudged at the great felicitee
Of proud Lucifera, and his owne companee.

XXXII. He hated all good workes and vertuous deeds,
And him no lesse, that any like did use;
And who with gratious bread the hungry feeds,
His almes for want of faith he doth accuse.
So every good to bad he doth abuse;
And eke the verse of famous Poets witt
He does backebite, and spightfull poison spues
From leprous mouth on all that ever writt.
Such one vile Envy was, that fifte in row did sitt.

XXXIII. And him beside rides fierce revenging Wrath,
Upon a Lion, loth for to be led;
And in his hand a burning brond he hath,
The which he brandisheth about his hed:
His eies did hurle forth sparcles fiery red,
And stared sterne on all that him beheld;
As ashes pale of hew, and seeming ded;
And on his dagger still his hand he held,
Trembling through hasty rage when choler in him sweld.

XXXIV. His ruffin raiment all was staind with blood
Which he had split, and all to rags yrent,
Through unadvized rashnes woxen wood;
For of his hands he had no governement,
Ne car'd for blood in his avengement:
But, when the furious fitt was overpast,

His cruel facts he often would repent;
Yet, wilfull man, he never would forecast
How many mischieves should ensue his heedlesse hast.

xxxv. Full many mischiefes follow cruell Wrath:
Abhorred bloodshed, and tumultuous strife,
Unmanly murder, and unthrifty scath,
Bitter despight, with rancours rusty knife,
And fretting griefe, the enemy of life:
All these, and many evils moe haunt ire,
The swelling Splene, and Frenzy raging rife,
The shaking Palsey, and Saint Fraunces fire.
Such one was Wrath, the last of this ungodly tire.

xxxvi. And, after all, upon the wagon beame,
Rode Sathan with a smarting whip in hand,
With which he forward lasht the laesy teme,
So oft as Slowth still in the mire did stand.
Huge routs of people did about them band,
Showting for joy; and still before their way
A foggy mist had covered all the land;
And, underneath their feet, all scattered lay
Dead sculls and bones of men whose life had gone astray.

xxxvii. So forth they marchen in this goodly sort,
To take the solace of the open aire,
And in fresh flowring fields themselves to sport:
Emongst the rest rode that false Lady faire,
The foule Duessa, next unto the chaire
Of proud Lucifer', as one of the traine:
But that good knight would not so nigh repaire,
Him selfe estraunging from their joyaunce vaine,
Whose fellowship seemd far unfitt for warlike swaine.

xxxviii. So, having solaced themselves a space
With pleasaunce of the breathing fields yfed,
They backe retourned to the princely Place;
Whereas an errant knight in armes ycled,
And heathnish shield, wherein with letters red,
Was writt *Sansjoy*, they new arrived find:
Enflam'd with fury and fiers hardy hed,
He seemd in hart to harbour thoughts unkind,
And nourish bloody vengeance in his bitter mind.

XXXIX. Who, when the shamed shield of slaine Sansfoy
    He spide with that same Faery champions page,
    Bewraying him that did of late destroy
    His eldest brother; burning all with rage,
    He to him lept, and that same envious gage
    Of victors glory from him snacht away:
    But th' Elfin knight, which ought that warlike wage,
    Disdaind to loose the meed he wonne in fray;
    And, him rencountring fierce, reskewd the noble pray.

XL. Therewith they gan to hurtlen greedily,
    Redoubted battaile ready to darrayne,
    And clash their shields, and shake their swerds on hy,
    That with their sturre they troubled all the traine;
    Till that great Queene, upon eternall paine
    Of high displeasure that ensewen might,
    Commaunded them their fury to refraine;
    And, if that either to that shield had right,
    In equall lists they should the morrow next it fight.

XLI. " Ah dearest Dame," quoth then the Paynim bold,
    " Pardon the error of enraged wight,
    Whome great griefe made forgett the raines to hold
    Of reasons rule, to see this recreaunt knight,
    No knight, but treachour full of false despight
    And shameful treason, who through guile hath slayn
    The prowest knight that ever field did fight,
    Even stout Sansfoy, (O who can then refrayn?)
    Whose shield he beares renverst, the more to heap disdayn.

XLII. " And, to augment the glorie of his guile,
    His dearest love, the faire Fidessa, loe!
    Is there possessed of the traytour vile;
    Who reapes the harvest sowen by his foe,
    Sowen in bloodie field, and bought with woe:
    That brothers hand shall dearely well requight,
    So be, O Queene! you equall favour showe."
    Him litle answerd th' angry Elfin knight;
    He never meant with words, but swords, to plead his right:

XLIII. But threw his gauntlet, as a sacred pledge
    His cause in combat the next day to try:
    So been they parted both, with harts on edge

To be aveng'd each on his enimy.
That night they pas in joy and jollity,
Feasting and courting both in bowre and hall;
For Steward was excessive Gluttony,
That of his plenty poured forth to all:
Which doen, the Chamberlain, Slowth, did to rest them call.

XLIV. Now when as darkesome night had all displayed
Her coleblacke curtein over brightest skye;
The warlike youthes, on dayntie couches layd,
Did chace away sweet sleepe from sluggish eye,
To muse on meanes of hoped victory.
But whenas Morpheus had with leaden mace
Arrested all that courtly company,
Uprose Duessa from her resting place,
And to the Paynims lodging comes with silent pace.

XLV. Whom broad awake she findes, in troublous fitt,
Fore-casting how his foe he might annoy;
And him amoves with speaches seeming fitt:
" Ah deare Sansjoy, next dearest to Sansfoy,
Cause of my new griefe, cause of my new joy;
Joyous to see his ymage in mine eye,
And greevd to thinke how foe did him destroy,
That was the flowre of grace and chevalrye;
Lo! his Fidessa, to thy secret faith I flye."

XLVI. With gentle wordes he can her fayrely greet,
And bad say on the secrete of her hart:
Then, sighing soft; " I learne that litle sweet
Oft tempred is," (quoth she,) " with muchell smart:
For since my brest was launcht with lovely dart
Of deare Sansfoy, I never joyed howre,
But in eternall woes my weaker hart
Have wasted, loving him with all my powre,
And for his sake have felt full many an heavie stowre.

XLVII. " At last, when perils all I weened past,
And hop'd to reape the crop of all my care,
Into new woes unweeting I was cast
By this false faytor, who unworthie ware
His worthie shield, whom he with guilefull snare
Entrapped slew, and brought to shamefull grave:

Me, silly maid, away with him he bare,
And ever since hath kept in darksom cave,
For that I would not yeeld that to Sansfoy I gave.

XLVIII. " But since faire Sunne hath sperst that lowring clowd,
And to my loathed life now shewes some light,
Under your beames I will me safely shrowd
From dreaded storme of his disdainfull spight:
To you th' inheritance belonges by right
Of brothers prayse, to you eke longes his love.
Let not his love, let not his restlesse spright,
Be unreveng'd, that calles to you above
From wandring Stygian shores, where it doth endlesse
       move."

XLIX. Thereto said he, " Faire Dame, be nought dismaid
For sorrowes past; their griefe is with them gone:
Ne yet of present perill be affraid,
For needlesse feare did never vantage none;
And helplesse hap it booteth not to mone.
Dead is Sansfoy, his vitall paines are past,
Though greeved ghost for vengeance deep do grone:
He lives that shall him pay his dewties last,
And guiltie Elfin blood shall sacrifice in hast."

  ? " O! but I feare the fickle freakes," (quoth shee)
" Of fortune false, and oddes of armes in field."
" Why, dame," (quoth he) " what oddes can ever bee,
Where both doe fight alike, to win or yield? "
" Yea, but," (quoth she) " he beares a charmed shield,
And eke enchaunted armes; that none can perce,
Ne none can wound the man that does them wield."
" Charmd or enchaunted," answered he then ferce,
" I no whitt reck; ne you the like need to reherce.

LI. " But, faire Fidessa sithens fortunes guile,
Or enimies powre, hath now captived you,
Returne from whence ye came, and rest a while,
Till morrow next that I the Elfe subdew,
And with Sansfoyes dead dowry you endew."
" Ah me! that is a double death," (she said)
" With proud foes sight my sorrow to renew,
Where ever yet I be, my secret aide
Shall follow you." So, passing forth, she him obaid.

CANTO V

The faithfull knight in equall field
Subdewes his faithlesse foe;
Whom false Duessa saves, and for
His cure to hell does goe.

I. THE noble hart that harbours vertuous thought,
   And is with childe of glorious great intent,
   Can never rest, untill it forth have brought
   Th' eternall brood of glorie excellent:
   Such restlesse passion did all night torment
   The flaming corage of that Faery knight,
   Devizing how that doughtie turnament
   With greatest honour he atchieven might:
   Still did he wake, and still did watch for dawning light.

II. At last, the golden Orientall gate
    Of greatest heaven gan to open fayre;
    And Phœbus, fresh as brydegrome to his mate,
    Came dauncing forth, shaking his deawie hayre,
    And hurld his glistring beams through gloomy ayre.
    Which when the wakeful Elfe perceiv'd, streight way,
    He started up, and did him selfe prepayre
    In sunbright armes, and battailous array;
    For with that Pagan proud he combatt will that day.

III. And forth he comes into the commune hall;
     Where earely waite him many a gazing eye,
     To weet what end to straunger knights may fall.
     There many Minstrales maken melody,
     To drive away the dull melancholy;
     And many Bardes, that to the trembling chord
     Can tune their timely voices cunningly;
     And many Chroniclers, that can record
     Old loves, and warres for Ladies doen by many a Lord.

IV. Soone after comes the cruell Sarazin,
    In woven maile all armed warily;
    And sternly lookes at him, who not a pin

Does care for looke of living creatures eye.
They bring them wines of Greece and Araby,
And daintie spices fetch from furthest Ynd,
To kindle heat of corage privily;
And in the wine a solemne oth thy bynd
T' observe the sacred lawes of armes that are assynd.

v. At last forth comes that far renowned Queene:
With royall pomp and princely majestie
She is ybrought unto a paled greene,
And placed under stately canapee,
The warlike feates of both those knights to see.
On th' other side in all mens open vew
Duessa placed is, and on a tree
Sansfoy his shield is hangd with bloody hew;
Both those the lawrell girlonds to the victor dew.

vi. A shrilling trompett sownded from on hye,
And unto battaill bad them selves addresse:
Their shining shieldes about their wrestes they tye,
And burning blades about their heades doe blesse,
The instruments of wrath and heavinesse.
With greedy force each other doth assayle,
And strike so fiercely, that they do impresse
Deepe dinted furrowes in the battred mayle:
The yron walles to ward their blowes are weak and fraile.

vii. The Sarazin was stout and wondrous strong,
And heaped blowes like yron hammers great;
For after blood and vengeance he did long:
The knight was fiers, and full of youthly heat,
And doubled strokes, like dreaded thunders threat;
For all for praise and honour he did fight.
Both stricken stryke, and beaten both doe beat,
That from their shields forth flyeth firie light,
And hewen helmets deepe shew marks of eithers might.

viii. So th' one for wrong, the other strives for right.
As when a Gryfon, seized of his pray,
A Dragon fiers encountreth in his flight,
Through widest ayre making his ydle way,
That would his rightfull ravine rend away:
With hideous horror both together smight,

And souce so sore that they the heavens affray;
The wise Southsayer, seeing so sad sight,
Th' amazed vulgar telles of warres and mortall fight.

IX. So th' one for wrong, the other strives for right,
And each to deadly shame would drive his foe:
The cruell steele so greedily doth bight
In tender flesh, that streames of blood down flow;
With which the armes, that earst so bright did show,
Into a pure vermillion now are dyde.
Great ruth in all the gazers harts did grow,
Seeing the gored woundes to gape so wyde,
That victory they dare not wish to either side.

X. At last the Paynim chaunst to cast his eye,
His suddein eye flaming with wrathfull fyre,
Upon his brothers shield, which hong thereby:
Therewith redoubled was his raging yre,
And said; "Ah! wretched sonne of wofull syre,
Doest thou sit wayling by blacke Stygian lake,
Whylest here thy shield is hangd for victors hyre?
And, sluggish german, doest thy forces slake
To after-send his foe, that him may overtake?

XI. "Goe, caytive Elfe, him quickly overtake,
And soone redeeme from his long-wandring woe:
Goe, guiltie ghost, to him my message make,
That I his shield have quit from dying foe."
Therewith upon his crest he stroke him so,
That twise he reeled, readie twise to fall:
End of the doubtfull battaile deemed tho
The lookers on; and lowd to him gan call
The false Duessa, "Thine the shield, and I, and all!"

XII. Soone as the Faerie heard his Ladie speake,
Out of his swowning dreame he gan awake;
And quickning faith, that earst was woxen weake,
The creeping deadly cold away did shake:
Tho mov'd with wrath, and shame, and Ladies sake,
Of all attonce he cast avengd to be,
And with so' exceeding furie at him strake,
That forced him to stoupe upon his knee:
Had he not stouped so, he should have cloven bee.

XIII. And to him said; " Goe now, proud Miscreant,
Thyselfe thy message do to german deare;
Alone he, wandring, thee too long doth want:
Goe say, his foe thy shield with his doth beare."
Therewith his heavie hand he high gan reare,
Him to have slaine; when lo! a darkesome clowd
Upon him fell: he no where doth appeare,
But vanisht is. The Elfe him calls alowd,
But answer none receives; the darknes him does shrowd.

XIV. In haste Duessa from her place arose,
And to him running said; " O! prowest knight,
That ever Ladie to her love did chose,
Let now abate the terrour of your might,
And quench the flame of furious despight,
And bloodie vengeance: lo! th' infernall powres,
Covering your foe with cloud of deadly night,
Have borne him hence to Plutoes balefull bowres:
The conquest yours; I yours; the shield, and glory yours."

XV. Not all so satisfide, with greedy eye
He sought all round about, his thristy blade
To bathe in blood of faithlesse enimy;
Who all that while lay hid in secret shade.
He standes amazed how he thence should fade:
At last the trumpets Triumph sound on hie;
And running Heralds humble homage made,
Greeting him goodly with new victorie,
And to him brought the shield, the cause of enmitie.

XVI. Wherewith he goeth to that soveraine Queene;
And falling her before on lowly knee,
To her makes present of his service seene:
Which she accepts with thankes and goodly gree,
Greatly advauncing his gay chevalree:
So marcheth home, and by her takes the knight,
Whom all the people followe with great glee,
Shouting, and clapping all their hands on hight,
That all the ayre it fills, and flyes to heaven bright.

XVII. Home is he brought, and layd in sumptous bed,
Where many skilfull leaches him abide
To salve his hurts, that yet still freshly bled.

In wine and oyle they wash his woundes wide,
And softly gan embalme on everie side:
And all the while most heavenly melody
About the bed sweet musicke did divide,
Him to beguile of griefe and agony;
And all the while Duessa wept full bitterly.

XVIII. As when a wearie traveiler, that strayes
By muddy shore of broad seven-mouthed Nile,
Unweeting of the perillous wandring wayes,
Doth meete a cruell craftie Crocodile,
Which, in false griefe hyding his harmefull guile,
Doth weepe full sore, and sheddeth tender teares;
The foolish man, that pities all this while
His mournefull plight, is swallowed up unwares,
Forgetfull of his owne that mindes an others cares.

XIX. So wept Duessa untill eventyde,
That shyning lampes in Joves high house were light;
Then forth she rose, ne lenger would abide,
But comes unto tl e place where th' Hethen knight,
In slombring swownd, nigh voyd of vitall spright,
Lay cover'd with inchaunted cloud all day:
Whom when she found, as she him left in plight,
To wayle his wofull case she would not stay,
But to the Easterne coast of heaven makes speedy way:

XX. Where griesly Night, with visage deadly sad,
That Phœbus chearefull face durst never vew,
And in a foule blacke pitchy mantle clad,
She findes forth comming from her darksome mew,
Where she all day did hide her hated hew.
Before the dore her yron charet stood,
Already harnessed for journey new,
And cole blacke steedes yborne of hellish brood,
That on their rusty bits did champ as they were wood.

XXI. Who when she saw Duessa, sunny bright,
Adornd with gold and jewels shining cleare,
She greatly grew amazed at the sight,
And th' unacquainted light began to feare,
For never did such brightnes there appeare;
And would have backe retyred to her cave,

Untill the witches speach she gan to heare,
Saying; " Yet, O thou dreaded Dame! I crave
Abyde, till I have told the message which I have."

XXII. She stayd; and foorth Duessa gan proceede:
" O! thou most auncient Grandmother of all,
More old then Jove, whom thou at first didst breede,
Or that great house of Gods cælestiall,
Which wast begot in Dæmogorgons hall,
And sawst the secrets of the world unmade,
Why suffredst thou thy Nephewes deare to fall,
With Elfin sword most shamefully betrade?
Lo! where the stout Sansjoy doth sleepe in deadly shade.

XXIII. " And him before, I saw with bitter eyes
The bold Sansfoy shrinck underneath his speare:
And now the pray of fowles in field he lyes,
Nor wayld of friends, nor layd on groning beare,
That whylome was to me too dearely deare.
O! what of gods then boots it to be borne,
If old Aveugles sonnes so evill heare?
Or who shall not great Nightes children scorne,
When two of three her Nephewes are so fowle forlorne?

XXIV. " Up, then! up, dreary Dame, of darknes Queene!,
Go, gather up the reliques of thy race;
Or else goe them avenge, and let be seene
That dreaded Night in brightest day hath place,
And can the children of fayre light deface."
Her feeling speaches some compassion mov'd
In hart, and chaunge in that great mothers face:
Yet pitty in her heart was never prov'd
Till then, for evermore she hated, never lov'd:

XXV. And said, " Deare daughter, rightly may I rew
The fall of famous children borne of mee,
And good successes which their foes ensew:
But who can turne the stream of destinee,
Or breake the chayne of strong necessitee,
Which fast is tyde to Joves eternall seat?
The sonnes of Day he favoureth, I see,
And by my ruines thinkes to make them great:
To make one great by others losse is bad excheat.

XXVI. " Yet shall they not escape so freely all,
　　　　For some shall pay the price of others guilt;
　　　　And he the man that made Sansfoy to fall,
　　　　Shall with his owne blood price that he hath spilt.
　　　　But what art thou, that telst of Nephews kilt? "
　　　　" I, that do seeme not I, Duessa ame,"
　　　　Quoth she, " how ever now, in garments gilt
　　　　And gorgeous gold arrayd, I to thee came,
　　　　Duessa I, the daughter of Deceipt and Shame."

XXVII. Then, bowing downe her aged backe, she kist
　　　　The wicked witch, saying, " In that fayre face
　　　　The false resemblaunce of Deceipt, I wist,
　　　　Did closely lurke; yet so true-seeming grace
　　　　It carried, that I scarse in darksome place
　　　　Could it discerne, though I the mother bee
　　　　Of falsehood, and roote of Duessaes race.
　　　　O welcome, child! whom I have longd to see,
　　　　And now have seene unwares. Lo! now I goe with thee."

XXVIII. Then to her yron wagon she betakes,
　　　　And with her beares the fowle welfavourd witch.
　　　　Through mirkesome aire her ready way she makes:
　　　　Her twyfold Teme, of which two blacke as pitch,
　　　　And two were browne, yet each to each unlich,
　　　　Did softly swim away, ne ever stamp
　　　　Unlesse she chaunst their stubborne mouths to twitch;
　　　　Then, foming tarre, their bridles they would champ,
　　　　And trampling the fine element would fiercely ramp.

XXIX. So well they sped, that they be come at length
　　　　Unto the place whereas the Paynim lay,
　　　　Devoid of outward sence and native strength,
　　　　Coverd with charmed cloud from vew of day,
　　　　And sight of men, since his late luckelesse fray.
　　　　His cruell wounds, with cruddy bloud congeald,
　　　　They binden up so wisely as they may,
　　　　And handle softly, till they can be heald:
　　　　So lay him in her charett, close in night conceald.

XXX. And, all the while she stood upon the ground,
　　　　The wakefull dogs did never cease to bay,
　　　　As giving warning of th' unwonted sound,

With which her yron wheeles did them affray,
And her darke griesly looke them much dismay:
The messenger of death, the ghastly owle,
With drery shriekes did also her bewray;
And hungry wolves continually did howle
At her abhorred face, so filthy and so fowle.

XXXI. Thence turning backe in silence softe they stole,
And brought the heavy corse with easy pace
To yawning gulfe of deepe Avernus hole.
By that same hole an entraunce, darke and bace,
With smoake and sulphur hiding all the place,
Descends to hell: there creature never past,
That backe retourned without heavenly grace;
But dreadfull Furies, which their chaines have brast,
And damned sprights sent forth to make ill men aghast.

XXXII. By that same way the direfull dames doe drive
Their mournefull charett, fild with rusty blood,
And downe to Plutoes house are come bilive:
Which passing through, on every side them stood
The trembling ghosts with sad amazed mood,
Chattring their iron teeth, and staring wide
With stony eies; and all the hellish brood
Of feends infernall flockt on every side,
To gaze on erthly wight that with the Night durst ride.

XXXIII. They pas the bitter waves of Acheron,
Where many soules sit wailing woefully,
And come to fiery flood of Phlegeton,
Whereas the damned ghosts in torments fry,
And with sharp shrilling shriekes doe bootlesse cry,
Cursing high Jove, the which them thither sent.
The house of endlesse paine is built thereby,
In which ten thousand sorts of punishment
The cursed creatures doe eternally torment.

XXXIV. Before the threshold dreadfull Cerberus
His three deformed heads did lay along,
Curled with thousand adders venemous,
And lilled forth his bloody flaming tong:
At them he gan to reare his bristles strong,
And felly gnarre, untill Dayes enemy

Did him appease; then downe his taile he hong,
And suffered them to passen quietly;
For she in hell and heaven had power equally.

XXXV. There was Ixion turned on a wheele,
For daring tempt the Queene of heaven to sin;
And Sisyphus an huge round stone did reele
Against an hill, ne might from labour lin;
There thristy Tantalus hong by the chin;
And Tityus fed a vulture on his maw;
Typhœus joynts were stretched on a gin;
Theseus condemned to endlesse slouth by law;
And fifty sisters water in leke vessels draw.

XXXVI. They all, beholding worldly wights in place,
Leave off their worke, unmindfull of their smart,
To gaze on them; who forth by them doe pace,
Till they be come unto the furthest part;
Where was a Cave ywrought by wondrous art
Deepe, darke, uneasy, doleful, comfortlesse.
In which sad Aesculapius far apart
Emprisond was in chaines remedilesse;
For that Hippolytus rent corse he did redresse.

XXXVII. Hippolytus a jolly huntsman was,
That wont in charett chace the foming bore:
He all his Peeres in beauty did surpas,
But Ladies love as losse of time forbore:
His wanton stepdame loved him the more;
But, when she saw her offred sweets refusd,
Her love she turnd to hate, and him before
His father fierce of treason false accusd,
And with her gealous termes his open eares abusd:

XXXVIII. Who, all in rage, his Sea-god syre besought
Some cursed vengeaunce on his sonne to cast.
From surging gulf two Monsters streight were brought,
With dread whereof his chacing steedes aghast
Both charett swifte and huntsman overcast:
His goodly corps, on ragged cliffs yrent,
Was quite dismembered, and his members chast
Scattered on every mountaine as he went,
That of Hippolytus was lefte no moniment.

XXXIX. His cruell step-dame, seeing what was donne,
Her wicked daies with wretched knife did end,
In death avowing th' innocence of her sonne.
Which hearing, his rash syre began to rend
His heare, and hasty tong that did offend:
Tho, gathering up the reliques of his smart,
By Dianes meanes, who was Hippolyts frend,
Them brought to Aesculape, that by his art
Did heale them all againe, and joyned every part.

XL. Such wondrous science in mans witt to rain
When Jove avizd, that could the dead revive,
And fates expired could renew again,
Of endlesse life he might him not deprive,
But unto hell did thrust him downe alive,
With flashing thunderbolt ywounded sore:
Where, long remaining, he did alwaies strive
Himselfe with salves to health for to restore,
And slake the heavenly fire that raged evermore.

XLI. There auncient Night arriving did alight
From her high weary wayne, and in her armes
To Aesculapius brought the wounded knight:
Whome having softly disaraid of armes,
Tho gan to him discover all his harmes,
Beseeching him with prayer and with praise,
If either salves, or oyles, or herbes, or charmes,
A fordonne wight from dore of death mote raise,
He would at her request prolong her nephews daies.

XLII. " Ah Dame," (quoth he) " thou temptest me in vaine,
To dare the thing, which daily yet I rew,
And the old cause of my continued paine
With like attempt to like end to renew.
Is not enough, that, thrust from heaven dew,
Here endlesse penaunce for one fault I pay,
But that redoubled crime with vengeaunce new
Thou biddest me to eeke?   Can Night defray
The wrath of thundring Jove, that rules both night and
            day ? "

XLIII. " Not so," (quoth she) " but, sith that heavens king
From hope of heaven hath thee excluded quight,

Why fearest thou, that canst not hope for thing;
And fearest not that more thee hurten might,
Now in the powre of everlasting Night?
Goe to then, O thou far renowmed sonne
Of great Apollo! shew thy famous might
In medicine, that els hath to thee wonne
Great pains, and greater praise, both never to be donne."

XLIV. Her words prevaild: And then the learned leach
His cunning hand gan to his wounds to lay,
And all things els the which his art did teach:
Which having seene, from thence arose away
The mother of dredd darknesse, and let stay
Aveugles sonne there in the leaches cure;
And, backe retourning, took her wonted way
To ronne her timely race, whilst Phœbus pure
In westerne waves his weary wagon did recure.

XLV. The false Duessa, leaving noyous Night,
Returned to stately pallace of Dame Pryde:
Where when she came, she found the Faery knight
Departed thence; albee his woundes wyde
Not throughly heald unready were to ryde.
Good cause he had to hasten thence away;
For on a day his wary Dwarfe had spyde
Where in a dungeon deepe huge nombers lay
Of caytive wretched thralls, that wayled night and day:

XLVI. A ruefull sight as could be seene with eie;
Of whom he learned had in secret wise
The hidden cause of their captivitie;
How mortgaging their lives to Covetise,
Through wastfull Pride and wanton Riotise,
They were by law of that proud Tyrannesse,
Provokt with Wrath and Envyes false surmise,
Condemned to that Dongeon mercilesse,
Where they should live in wo, and dye in wretchednesse.

XLVII. There was that great proud king of Babylon,
That would compell all nations to adore,
And him as onely God to call upon;
Till, through celestiall doome thrown out of dore,
Into an Oxe he was transformd of yore.

There also was king Crœsus, that enhaunst
His hart too high through his great richesse store;
And proud Antiochus, the which advaunst
His cursed hand gainst God, and on his altares daunst.

XLVIII. And them long time before, great Nimrod was,
That first the world with sword and fire warrayd;
And after him old Ninus far did pas
In princely pomp, of all the world obayd.
There also was that mightie Monarch layd
Low under all, yet above all in pride,
That name of native syre did fowle upbrayd,
And would as Ammons sonne be magnified,
Till, scornd of God and man, a shamefull death he dide.

XLIX. All these together in one heape were throwne,
Like carkases of beastes in butchers stall.
And in another corner wide were strowne
The Antique ruins of the Romanes fall:
Great Romulus, the Grandsyre of them all;
Proud Tarquin, and too lordly Lentulus;
Stout Scipio, and stubborne Hanniball;
Ambitious Sylla, and sterne Marius;
High Cæsar, great Pompey, and fiers Antonius.

L. Amongst these mightie men were wemen mixt,
Proud wemen, vaine, forgetfull of their yoke;
The bold Semiramis, whose sides transfixt
With sonnes own blade her fowle reproches spoke:
Fayre Sthenobœa, that her selfe did choke
With wilfull chord for wanting of her will;
High minded Cleopatra, that with stroke
Of Aspes sting her selfe did stoutly kill;
And thousands moe the like that did that dongeon fill.

LI. Besides the endlesse routes of wretched thralles,
Which thither were assembled day by day
From all the world, after their wofull falles,
Through wicked pride and wasted welthes decay.
But most of all, which in that dongeon lay,
Fell from high Princes courtes, or Ladies bowres,
Where they in ydle pomp, or wanton play,
Consumed had their goods and thriftlesse howres,
And lastly thrown themselves into these heavy stowres.

LII. Whose case whenas the careful Dwarfe had tould,
And made ensample of their mournfull sight
Unto his Maister, he no lenger would
There dwell in perill of like painefull plight,
But earely rose; and, ere that dawning light
Discovered had the world to heaven wyde,
He by a privy Posterne tooke his flight,
That of no envious eyes he mote be spyde;
For, doubtlesse, death ensewd if any him descryde.

LIII. Scarse could he footing find in that fowle way,
For many corses, like a great Lay-stall,
Of murdred men, which therein strowed lay
Without remorse or decent funerall;
Which al through that great Princesse pride did fall,
And came to shamefull end.   And them besyde,
Forth ryding underneath the castell wall,
A Donghill of dead carcases he spyde;
The dreadfull spectacle of that sad house of Pryde.

CANTO VI

From lawlesse lust by wondrous grace]
Fayre Una is releast:
Whom salvage nation does adore,
And learnes her wise beheast.

I. As when a ship, that flyes fayre under sayle,
   An hidden rocke escaped hath unwares,
   That lay in waite her wrack for to bewaile,
   The Marriner yet halfe amazed stares
   At perill past, and yet in doubt ne dares
   To joy at his foolhappie oversight:
   So doubly is distrest twixt joy and cares
   The dreadlesse corage of this Elfin knight,
   Having escapt so sad ensamples in his sight.

II. Yet sad he was, that his too hastie speed
    The fayre Duess' had forst him leave behind;
    And yet more sad, that Una, his deare dreed,
    Her truth hath staynd with treason so unkind:
    Yet cryme in her could never creature find;
    But for his love, and for her own selfe sake,
    She wandred had from one to other Ynd,
    Him for to seeke, ne ever would forsake,
    Till her unwares the fiers Sansloy did overtake:

III. Who, after Archimagoes fowle defeat,
     Led her away into a forest wilde;
     And, turning wrathfull fyre to lustfull heat,
     With beastly sin thought her to have defilde,
     And made the vassall of his pleasures vilde.
     Yet first he cast by treatie, and by traynes
     Her to persuade that stubborne fort to yilde:
     For greater conquest of hard love he gaynes,
     That workes it to his will, then he that it constraines.

IV. With fawning wordes he courted her a while;
    And, looking lovely and oft sighing sore,
    Her constant hart did tempt with diverse guile:

But wordes, and lookes, and sighes she did abhore;
As rock of Diamond stedfast evermore.
Yet for to feed his fyrie lustfull eye,
He snatcht the vele that hong her face before:
Then gan her beautie shyne as brightest skye,
And burnt his beastly hart t'efforce her chastitye.

v. So when he saw his flatt'ring artes to fayle,
And subtile engines bett from batteree;
With greedy force he gan the fort assayle,
Whereof he weend possessed soone to bee,
And win rich spoile of ransackt chastitee.
Ah heavens! that doe this hideous act behold,
And heavenly virgin thus outraged see,
How can ye vengeance just so long withhold,
And hurle not flashing flames upon that Paynim bold?

vi. The pitteous mayden, carefull, comfortlesse,
Does throw out thrilling shriekes, and shrieking cryes,
The last vaine helpe of womens great distresse,
And with loud plaintes importuneth the skyes,
That molten starres doe drop like weeping eyes;
And Phœbus, flying so most shamefull sight,
His blushing face in foggy cloud implyes,
And hydes for shame. What witt of mortal wight
Can now devise to quitt a thrall from such a plight?

vii. Eternall providence, exceeding thought,
Where none appeares can make her selfe a way.
A wondrous way it for this Lady wrought,
From Lyons clawes to pluck the gryped pray.
Her shrill outcryes and shrieks so loud did bray,
That all the woodes and forestes did resownd:
A troupe of Faunes and Satyres far away
Within the wood were dauncing in a rownd,
Whiles old Sylvanus slept in shady arber sownd:

viii. Who, when they heard that pitteous strained voice,
In haste forsooke their rurall meriment,
And ran towardes the far rebownded noyce,
To weet what wight so loudly did lament.
Unto the place they come incontinent:
Whom when the raging Sarazin espyde,

A rude, mishapen, monstrous rablement,
Whose like he never saw, he durst not byde,
But got his ready steed, and fast away gan ryde.

IX. The wyld woodgods, arrived in the place,
There find the virgin, doolfull, desolate,
With ruffled rayments, and fayre blubbred face,
As her outrageous foe had left her late;
And trembling yet through feare of former hate.
All stand amazed at so uncouth sight,
And gin to pittie her unhappie state:
All stand astonied at her beautie bright,
In their rude eyes unworthie of so wofull plight.

X. She, more amazd, in double dread doth dwell;
And every tender part for feare does shake.
As when a greedy Wolfe, through honger fell,
A seely Lamb far from the flock does take,
Of whom he meanes his bloody feast to make,
A Lyon spyes fast running towards him,
The innocent pray in hast he does forsake;
Which, quitt from death, yet quakes in every lim
With chaunge of feare, to see the Lyon looke so grim.

XI. Such fearefull fitt assaid her trembling hart,
Ne word to speake, ne joynt to move, she had;
The salvage nation feele her secret smart,
And read her sorrow in her count'nance sad;
Their frowning forheades, with rough hornes yclad,
And rustick horror, all asyde doe lay;
And, gently grenning, shew a semblance glad
To comfort her; and, feare to put away,
Their backward bent knees teach her humbly to obay.

XII. The doubtfull Damzell dare not yet committ
Her single person to their barbarous truth;
But still twixt feare and hope amazd does sitt,
Late learnd what harme to hasty trust ensu'th.
They, in compassion of her tender youth,
And wonder of her beautie soverayne,
Are wonne with pitty and unwonted ruth;
And, all prostrate upon the lowly playne,
Doe kisse her feete, and fawne on her with count'nance
    fayne.

XIII. Their harts she ghesseth by their humble guise,
      And yieldes her to extremitie of time:
      So from the ground she fearelesse doth arise,
      And walketh forth without suspect of crime.
      They, all as glad as birdes of joyous Pryme,
      Thence lead her forth, about her dauncing round,
      Shouting, and singing all a shepheards ryme;
      And with greene braunches strowing all the ground,
      Do worship her as Queene with olive girlond cround.

XIV. And all the way their merry pipes they sound,
     That all the woods with doubled Eccho ring;
     And with their horned feet doe weare the ground,
     Leaping like wanton kids in pleasant Spring.
     So towards old Sylvanus they her bring;
     Who, with the noyse awaked, commeth out
     To weet the cause, his weake steps governing
     And aged limbs on cypresse stadle stout;
     And with an yvie twyne his waste is girt about.

XV. Far off he wonders what them makes so glad;
    Or Bacchus merry fruit they did invent,
    Or Cybeles franticke rites have made them mad:
    They, drawing nigh, unto their God present
    That flowre of fayth and beautie excellent.
    The God himselfe, vewing that mirrhour rare,
    Stood long amazd, and burnt in his intent:
    His owne fayre Dryope now he thinkes not faire,
    And Pholoe fowle, when her to this he doth compaire.

XVI. The woodborne people fall before her flat,
     And worship her as Goddesse of the wood;
     And old Sylvanus selfe bethinkes not what
     To thinke of wight so fayre, but gazing stood
     In doubt to deeme her borne of earthly brood:
     Sometimes dame Venus selfe he seemes to see;
     But Venus never had so sober mood:
     Sometimes Diana he her takes to be,
     But misseth bow and shaftes, and buskins to her knee.

XVII. By vew of her he ginneth to revive
      His ancient love, and dearest Cyparisse;
      And calles to mind his pourtraiture alive,

How fayre he was, and yet not fayre to this;
And how he slew with glauncing dart amisse
A gentle Hynd, the which the lovely boy
Did love as life, above all worldly blisse;
For griefe whereof the lad n'ould after joy,
But pynd away in anguish and selfe-wild annoy.

XVIII. The wooddy nymphes, faire Hamadryades,
Her to behold do thither runne apace;
And all the troupe of light-foot Naiades
Flocke all about to see her lovely face;
But, when they vewed have her heavenly grace,
They envy her in their malitious mind,
And fly away for feare of fowle disgrace:
But all the Satyres scorne their woody kind,
And henceforth nothing faire but her on earth they find.

XIX. Glad of such lucke, the luckelesse lucky mayd
Did her content to please their feeble eyes,
And long time with that salvage people stayd,
To gather breath in many miseryes.
During which time her gentle wit she plyes
To teach them truth, which worshipt her in vaine,
And made her th' Image of Idolatryes;
But when their bootlesse zeale she did restrayne
From her own worship, they her Asse would worship fayn,

XX. It fortuned, a noble warlike knight
By just occasion to that forrest came
To seeke his kindred, and the lignage right
From whence he tooke his weldeserved name:
He had in armes abroad wonne muchell fame,
And fild far landes with glorie of his might:
Plaine, faithfull, true, and enimy of shame,
And ever lov'd to fight for Ladies right;
But in vaine glorious frayes he litle did delight.

XXI. A Satyres sonne, yborne in forrest wyld,
By straunge adventure as it did betyde,
And there begotten of a Lady myld,
Fayre Thyamis, the daughter of Labryde;
That was in sacred bandes of wedlocke tyde
To Therion, a loose unruly swayne,

Who had more joy to raunge the forrest wyde,
And chase the salvage beast with busie payne,
Then serve his Ladies love, and waste in pleasures vayne.

XXII. The forlorne mayd did with loves longing burne,
And could not lacke her lovers company;
But to the woods she goes, to serve her turne,
And seeke her spouse that from her still does fly,
And followes other game and venery:
A Satyre chaunst her wandring for to finde;
And, kindling coles of lust in brutish eye,
The loyall linkes of wedlocke did unbinde,
And made her person thrall unto his beastly kind.

XXIII. So long in secret cabin there he held
Her captive to his sensuall desyre,
Till that with timely fruit her belly sweld,
And bore a boy unto that salvage syre:
Then home he suffred her for to retyre,
For ransome leaving him the late-borne childe;
Whom, till to ryper yeares he gan aspyre,
He nousled up in life and manners wilde,
Emongst wilde beastes and woods, from lawes of men
exilde.

XXIV. For all he taught the tender ymp was but
To banish cowardize and bastard feare:
His trembling hand he would him force to put
Upon the Lyon and the rugged Beare;
And from the she Beares teats her whelps to teare;
And eke wyld roring Buls he would him make
To tame, and ryde their backes, not made to beare;
And the Robuckes in flight to overtake,
That everie beast for feare of him did fly, and quake.

XXV. Thereby so fearlessé and so fell he grew,
That his own syre, and maister of his guise,
Did often tremble at his horrid vew;
And oft, for dread of hurt, would him advise
The angry beastes not rashly to despise,
Nor too much to provoke; for he would learne
The Lyon stoup to him in lowly wise,
(A lesson hard) and make the Libbard sterne
Leave roaring, when in rage he for revenge did earne.

XXVI. And for to make his powre approved more,
Wyld beastes in yron yokes he would compell;
The spotted Panther, and the tusked Bore,
The Pardale swift, and the Tigre cruell,
The Antelope, and Wolfe both fiers and fell;
And them constraine in equall teme to draw.
Such joy he had their stubborne harts to quell,
And sturdie courage tame with dreadfull aw,
That his beheast they feared as a tyrans law.

XXVII. His loving mother came upon a day
Unto the woodes, to see her little sonne;
And chaunst unwares to meet him in the way,
After his sportes and cruell pastime donne;
When after him a Lyonesse did runne,
That roaring all with rage did lowd requere
Her children deare, whom he away had wonne:
The Lyon whelpes she saw how he did beare,
And lull in rugged armes withouten childish feare.

XXVIII. The fearefull Dame all quaked at the sight,
And turning backe gan fast to fly away;
Untill, with love revokt from vaine affright,
She hardly yet perswaded was to stay,
And then to him these womanish words gan say:
" Ah Satyrane, my dearling and my joy,
For love of me leave off this dreadfull play;
To dally thus with death is no fit toy:
Go, find some other play-fellowes, mine own sweet boy."

XXIX. In these and like delightes of bloody game
He trayned was, till ryper years he raught;
And there abode, whylst any beast of name
Walkt in that forrest, whom he had not taught
To feare his force: and then his courage haught
Desyrd of forreine foemen to be knowne,
And far abroad for strange adventures sought;
In which his might was never overthrowne;
But through al Faery lond his famous worth was blown.

XXX. Yet evermore it was his maner faire,
After long labours and adventures spent,
Unto those native woods for to repaire,

To see his syre and ofspring auncient.
And now he thither came for like intent;
Where he unwares the fairest Una found,
Straunge Lady in so straunge habiliment,
Teaching the Satyres, which her sat around,
Trew sacred lore, which from her sweet lips did redound.

XXXI. He wondred at her wisedome hevenly rare,
Whose like in womens witt he never knew;
And, when her curteous deeds he did compare,
Gan her admire, and her sad sorrowes rew,
Blaming of Fortune, which such troubles threw,
And joyd to make proofe of her cruelty
On gentle Dame, so hurtlesse and so trew:
Thenceforth he kept her goodly company,
And learnd her discipline of faith and verity.

XXXII. But she, all vowd unto the Redcrosse Knight,
His wandring perill closely did lament,
Ne in this new acquaintaunce could delight;
But her deare heart with anguish did torment,
And all her witt in secret counsels spent,
How to escape.   At last in privy wise
To Satyrane she shewed her intent;
Who, glad to gain such favour, gan devise,
How with that pensive Maid he best might thence arise

XXXIII. So on a day, when Satyres all were gone
To do their service to Sylvanus old,
The gentle virgin, left behinde alone,
He led away with corage stout and bold.
Too late it was to Satyres to be told,
Or ever hope recover her againe:
In vaine he seekes that having cannot hold.
So fast he carried her with carefull paine,
That they the woods are past, and come now to the
    plaine.

XXXIV. The better part now of the lingring day
They traveild had, whenas they far espide
A weary wight forwandring by the way;
And towards him they gan in haste to ride,
To weete of newes that did abroad betide,
Or tidings of her knight of the Redcrosse;

But he them spying gan to turne aside
For feare, as seemd, or for some feigned losse:
More greedy they of newes fast towards him do crosse.

XXXV. A silly man, in simple weeds forworne,
And soild with dust of the long dried way;
His sandales were with toilsome travell torne,
And face all tand with scorching sunny ray,
As he had traveild many a sommers day
Through boyling sands of Arabie and Ynde,
And in his hand a Jacobs staffe, to stay
His weary limbs upon; and eke behind
His scrip did hang, in which his needments he did bind.

XXXVI. The knight, approching nigh, of him inquerd
Tidings of warre, and of adventures new;
But warres, nor new adventures, none he herd.
Then Una gan to aske, if ought he knew,
Or heard abroad of that her champion trew,
That in his armour bare a croslet red?
" Ay me! Deare dame," (quoth he) " well may I rew
To tell the sad sight which mine eies have red;
These eies did see that knight both living and eke ded."

XXXVII. That cruell word her tender hart so thrild,
That suddein cold did ronne through every vaine,
And stony horrour all her sences fild
With dying fitt, that downe she fell for paine.
The knight her lightly reared up againe,
And comforted with curteous kind reliefe:
Then, wonne from death, she bad him tellen plaine
The further processe of her hidden griefe:
The lesser pangs can beare who had endur'd the chief.

XXXVIII. Then gan the Pilgrim thus: " I chaunst this day,
This fatall day that shall I ever rew,
To see two knights, in travell on my way,
(A sory sight) arraung'd in batteill new,
Both breathing vengeaunce, both of wrathfull hew.
My fearefull flesh did tremble at their strife,
To see their blades so greedily imbrew,
That, dronke with blood, yet thristed after life:
What more? the Redcrosse knight was slain with
Paynim knife."

XXXIX. " Ah! dearest Lord," (quoth she) " how might that bee,
And he the stoutest knight that ever wonne? "
" Ah! dearest dame," (quoth hee) " how might I see
The thing that might not be, and yet was donne? "
" Where is," (said Satyrane) " that Paynims sonne,
That him of life, and us of joy, hath refte? "
" Not far away," (quoth he) " he hence doth wonne,
Foreby a fountaine, where I late him lefte
    Washing his bloody wounds, that through the steel
      were cleft."

XL. Therewith the knight thence marched forth in hast,
Whiles Una, with huge heavinesse opprest,
Could not for sorrow follow him so fast;
And soone he came, as he the place had ghest,
Whereas that Pagan proud him selfe did rest
In secret shadow by a fountaine side:
Even he it was, that earst would have supprest
Faire Una; whom when Satyrane espide,
    With foule reprochfull words he boldly him defide.

XLI. And said; " Arise, thou cursed Miscreaunt,
That hast with knightlesse guile, and trecherous train,
Faire knighthood fowly shamed, and doest vaunt
That good knight of the Redcrosse to have slain:
Arise, and with like treason now maintain
The guilty wrong, or els thee guilty yield."
The Sarazin, this hearing, rose amain,
And, catching up in hast his three-square shield
    And shining helmet, soone him buckled to the field.

XLII. And, drawing nigh him, said; " Ah! misborn Elfe,
In evill houre thy foes thee hither sent
Anothers wrongs to wreak upon thy selfe:
Yet ill thou blamest me for having blent
My name with guile and traiterous intent:
That Redcrosse knight, perdie, I never slew;
But had he beene where earst his armes were lent,
Th' enchaunter vaine his errour should not rew:
    But thou his errour shalt, I hope, now proven trew."

XLIII. Therewith they gan, both furious and fell,
To thunder blowes, and fiersly to assaile

Each other, bent his enimy to quell,
That with their force they perst both plate and maile,
And made wide furrowes in their fleshes fraile,
That it would pitty any living eie.
Large floods of blood adowne their sides did raile,
But floods of blood could not them satisfie:
Both hongred after death; both chose to win, or die.

XLIV. So long they fight, and full revenge pursue,
That, fainting, each themselves to breathen lett,
And, ofte refreshed, battell oft renue.
As when two Bores, with rancling malice mett,
Their gory sides fresh bleeding fiercely frett;
Til breathlesse both themselves aside retire,
Where foming wrath their cruell tuskes they whett,
And trample th' earth, the whiles they may respire,
Then backe to fight againe, new breathed and entire.

XLV. So fiersly, when these knights had breathed once,
They gan to fight retourne, increasing more
Their puissant force, and cruell rage attonce,
With heaped strokes more hugely then before;
That with their drery wounds, and bloody gore,
They both, deformed, scarsely could bee known.
By this, sad Una fraught with anguish sore,
Led with their noise which through the aire was thrown,
Arriv'd wher they in erth their fruitles blood had sown.

XLVI. Whom all so soone as that proud Sarazin
Espide, he gan revive the memory
Of his leud lusts, and late attempted sin,
And lefte the doubtfull battell hastily,
To catch her, newly offred to his eie;
But Satyrane, with strokes him turning, staid,
And sternely bad him other businesse plie
Then hunt the steps of pure unspotted Maid:
Wherewith he al enrag'd these bitter speaches said.

XLVII. " O foolish faeries sonne! what fury mad
Hath thee incenst to hast thy dolefull fate?
Were it not better I that Lady had
Then that thou hadst repented it too late?
Most sencelesse man he, that himselfe doth hate,

To love another: Lo! then, for thine ayd,
Here take thy lovers token on thy pate."
So they to fight; the whiles the royall Mayd
Fledd farre away, of that proud Paynim sore afrayd.

XLVIII. But that false Pilgrim, which that leasing told,
Being in deed old Archimage, did stay
In secret shadow all this to behold;
And much rejoyced in their bloody fray:
But, when he saw the Damsell passe away,
He left his stond, and her pursewd apace,
In hope to bring her to her last decay.
But for to tell her lamentable cace,
And eke this battels end, will need another place.

CANTO VII

The Redcrosse knight is captive made
By Tyaunt proud opprest:
Prince Arthure meets with Una great-
ly with those newes distrest.

I. What man so wise, what earthly witt so ware,
As to discry the crafty cunning traine,
By which deceipt doth maske in visour faire,
And cast her coulours, died deepe in graine,
To seeme like truth, whose shape she well can faine,
And fitting gestures to her purpose frame,
The guiltlesse man with guile to entertaine?
Great maistresse of her art was that false Dame,
The false Duessa, cloked with Fidessaes name.

II. Who when, returning from the drery Night,
She fownd not in that perilous hous of Pryde,
Where she had left the noble Redcrosse knight,
Her hoped pray, she would no lenger byde,
But forth she went to seeke him far and wide.
Ere long she fownd, whereas he wearie sate
To reste him selfe foreby a fountaine syde,
Disarmed all of yron-coted Plate;
And by his side his steed the grassy forage ate.

III. Hee feedes upon the cooling shade, and bayes
His sweatie forehead in the breathing wynd,
Which through the trembling leaves full gently playes,
Wherein the chearefull birds of sundry kynd
Doe chaunt sweet musick to delight his mynd.
The witch approching gan him fayrely greet,
And with reproch of carelesnes unkynd
Upbrayd, for leaving her in place unmeet,
With fowle words tempring faire, soure gall with hony
    sweet.

IV. Unkindnesse past, they gan of solace treat,
And bathe in pleasaunce of the joyous shade,

Which shielded them against the boyling heat,
And with greene boughes decking a gloomy glade,
About the fountaine like a girlond made;
Whose bubbling wave did ever freshly well,
Ne ever would through fervent sommer fade:
The sacred Nymph, which therein wont to dwell,
Was out of Dianes favor, as it then befell.

v. The cause was this: one day, when Phœbe fayre
With all her band was following the chace,
This nymph, quite tyr'd with heat of scorching ayre,
Satt downe to rest in middest of the race:
The goddesse wroth gan fowly her disgrace,
And badd the waters, which from her did flow,
Be such as she her selfe was then in place.
Thenceforth her waters wexed dull and slow,
And all that drinke thereof do faint and feeble grow.

vi. Hereof this gentle knight unweeting was;
And lying downe upon the sandie graile,
Dronke of the streame, as cleare as christall glas:
Eftsoones his manly forces gan to fayle,
And mightie strong was turnd to feeble frayle.
His chaunged powres at first them selves not felt;
Till crudled cold his corage gan assayle,
And chearefull blood in fayntnes chill did melt,
Which like a fever fit through all his bodie swelt.

vii. Yet goodly court he made still to his Dame,
Pourd out in loosnesse on the grassy grownd,
Both careless of his health, and of his fame;
Till at the last he heard a dreadfull sownd,
Which through the wood loud bellowing did rebownd,
That all the earth for terror seemd to shake,
And trees did tremble.   Th' Elfe, therewith astownd,
Upstarted lightly from his looser make,
And his unready weapons gan in hand to take.

viii. But ere he could his armour on him dight,
Or gett his shield, his monstrous enimy
With sturdie steps came stalking in his sight,
An hideous Geaunt, horrible and hye,
That with his tallnesse seemd to threat the skye;

The ground eke groned under him for dreed:
His living like saw never living eye,
Ne durst behold: his stature did exceed
The hight of three the tallest sonnes of mortall seed.

IX. The greatest Earth his uncouth mother was,
And blustring Æolus his boasted syre;
Who with his breath. which through the world doth pas,
Her hollow womb did secretly inspyre,
And fild her hidden caves with stormie yre,
That she conceiv'd; and trebling the dew time
In which the wombes of wemen doe expyre,
Brought forth this monstrous masse of earthly slyme,
Puft up with emptie wynd, and fild with sinfull cryme.

X. So growen great, through arrogant delight
Of th' high descent whereof he was yborne,
And through presumption of his matchlesse might,
All other powres and knighthood he did scorne.
Such now he marcheth to this man forlorne,
And left to losse; his stalking steps are stayde
Upon a snaggy Oke, which he had torne
Out of his mothers bowelles, and it made
His mortall mace, wherewith his foemen he dismayde.

XI. That, when the knight he spyde, he gan advaunce
With huge force and insupportable mayne,
And towardes him with dreadfull fury praunce;
Who haplesse, and eke hopelesse, all in vaine
Did to him pace sad battaile to darrayne,
Disarmd, disgraste, and inwardly dismayde;
And eke so faint in every joynt and vayne,
Through that fraile fountain which him feeble made,
That scarsely could he weeld his bootlesse single blade.

XII. The Geaunt strooke so maynly mercilesse,
That could have overthrowne a stony towre;
And, were not hevenly grace that did him blesse,
He had beene pouldred all as thin as flowre:
But he was wary of that deadly stowre,
And lightly lept from underneath the blow:
Yet so exceeding was the villeins powre,
That with the winde it did him overthrow,
And all his sences stound that still he lay full low.

XIII. As when that divelish yron Engin, wrought
    In deepest Hell, and framd by Furies skill,
    With windy Nitre and quick Sulphur fraught,
    And ramd with bollet rownd, ordaind to kill,
    Conceiveth fyre, the heavens it doth fill
    With thundring noyse, and all the ayre doth choke,
    That none can breath, nor see, nor heare at will,
    Through smouldry cloud of duskish stincking smoke;
    That th' only breath him daunts, who hath escapt the
        stroke.

XIV. So daunted when the Geaunt saw the knight,
    His heavie hand he heaved up on hye,
    And him to dust thought to have battred quight,
    Untill Duessa loud to him gan crye,
    " O great Orgoglio! greatest under skye,
    O! hold thy mortall hand for Ladies sake;
    Hold for my sake, and doe him not to dye,
    But vanquisht thine eternall bondslave make,
    And me, thy worthy meed, unto thy Leman take."

XV. He hearkned, and did stay from further harmes,
    To gayne so goodly guerdon as she spake:
    So willingly she came into his armes,
    Who her as willingly to grace did take,
    And was possessed of his newfound make,
    Then up he tooke the slombred sencelesse corse,
    And, ere he could out of his swowne awake,
    Him to his castle brought with hastie forse,
    And in a Dongeon deepe him threw without remorse.

XVI. From that day forth Duessa was his deare,
    And highly honoured in his haughtie eye:
    He gave her gold and purple pall to weare,
    And triple crowne set on her head full hye,
    And her endowd with royall majestye.
    Then, for to make her dreaded more of men,
    And peoples hartes with awfull terror tye,
    A monstrous beast ybredd in filthy fen
    He chose, which he had kept long time in darksom den.

XVII. Such one it was, as that renowmed Snake
    Which great Alcides in Stremona slew,
    Long fostred in the filth of Lerna lake:

Whose many heades, out budding ever new,
Did breed him endlesse labor to subdew.
But this same Monster much more ugly was,
For seven great heads out of his body grew,
An yron brest, and back of scaly bras,
And all embrewd in blood his eyes did shine as glas.

XVIII. His tayle was stretched out in wondrous length,
That to the hous of hevenly gods it raught:
And with extorted powre, and borrow'd strength,
The everburning lamps from thence it braught,
And prowdly threw to ground, as things of naught;
And underneath his filthy feet did tread
The sacred thinges, and holy heastes foretaught.
Upon this dreadfull Beast with sevenfold head
He sett the false Duessa, for more aw and dread.

XIX. The wofull Dwarfe, which saw his maisters fall
Whiles he had keeping of his grasing steed,
And valiant knight become a caytive thrall,
When all was past, tooke up his forlorne weed;
His mightie Armour, missing most at need;
His silver shield, now idle, maisterlesse;
His poynant speare that many made to bleed,
The rueful moniments of heavinesse;
And with them all departes to tell his great distresse.

XX. He had not travaild long, when on the way
He wofull Lady, wofull Una, met,
Fast flying from that Paynims greedy pray,
Whilest Satyrane him from pursuit did let:
Who when her eyes she on the Dwarf had set,
And saw the signes that deadly tydings spake,
She fell to ground for sorrowfull regret,
And lively breath her sad brest did forsake;
Yet might her pitteous hart be seene to pant and quake.

XXI. The messenger of so unhappie newes
Would faine have dyde: dead was his hart within,
Yet outwardly some little comfort shewes.
At last, recovering hart, he does begin
To rubb her temples, and to chaufe her chin,
And everie tender part does tosse and turne:

So hardly he the flitted life does win
Unto her native prison to retourne;
Then gins her grieved ghost thus to lament and mourne:

XXII. " Ye dreary instruments of dolefull sight,
That doe this deadly spectacle behold,
Why doe ye lenger feed on loathed light,
Or liking find to gaze on earthly mould,
Sith cruell fates the carefull threds unfould,
The which my life and love together tyde?
Now let the stony dart of sencelesse cold
Perce to my hart, and pas through everie side,
And let eternall night so sad sight fro me hyde.

XXIII. " O lightsome day! the lampe of highest Jove,
First made by him mens wandring wayes to guyde,
When darknesse he in deepest dongeon drove,
Henceforth thy hated face for ever hyde,
And shut up heavens windowes shyning wyde;
For earthly sight can nought but sorrow breed,
And late repentance which shall long abyde:
Mine eyes no more on vanitie shall feed,
But seeled up with death shall have their deadly meed."

XXIV. Then downe againe she fell unto the ground,
But he her quickly reared up againe:
Thrise did she sinke adowne in deadly swownd,
And thrise he her reviv'd with busie paine.
At last when life recover'd had the raine,
And over-wrestled his strong enimy,
With foltring tong, and trembling everie vaine,
" Tell on," (quoth she) " the wofull Tragedy,
The which these reliques sad present unto mine eye.

XXV. " Tempestuous fortune hath spent all her spight,
And thrilling sorrow throwne his utmost dart:
Thy sad tong cannot tell more heavy plight
Then that I feele, and harbour in mine hart:
Who hath endur'd the whole can beare ech part.
If death it be, it is not the first wound
That launched hath my brest with bleeding smart.
Begin, and end the bitter balefull stound;
If lesse then that I feare, more favour I have found."

XXVI. Then gan the Dwarfe the whole discourse declare;
    The subtile traines of Archimago old;
    The wanton loves of false Fidessa fayre,
    Bought with the blood of vanquisht Paynim bold;
    The wretched payre transformd to treën mould;
    The house of Pryde, and perilles round about;
    The combat which he with Sansjoy did hould;
    The lucklesse conflict with the Gyaunt stout,
    Wherein captiv'd, of life or death he stood in doubt.

XXVII. She heard with patience all unto the end,
    And strove to maister sorrowfull assay,
    Which greater grew the more she did contend,
    And almost rent her tender hart in tway;
    And love fresh coles unto her fire did lay;
    For greater love, the greater is the losse.
    Was never Lady loved dearer day
    Then she did love the knight of the Redcrosse,
    For whose deare sake so many troubles her did tosse.

XXVIII. At last when fervent sorrow slaked was,
    She up arose, resolving him to find
    Alive or dead; and forward forth doth pas,
    All as the Dwarfe the way to her assynd;
    And evermore, in constant carefull mind,
    She fedd her wound with fresh renewed bale.
    Long tost with stormes, and bet with bitter wind,
    High over hills, and lowe adowne the dale,
    She wandred many a wood, and measurd many a vale.

XXIX. At last she chaunced by good hap to meet
    A goodly knight, faire marching by the way,
    Together with his Squyre, arayed meet:
    His glitterand armour shined far away,
    Like glauncing light of Phœbus brightest ray;
    From top to toe no place appeared bare,
    That deadly dint of steele endanger may.
    Athwart his brest a bauldrick brave he ware,
    That shind, like twinkling stars, with stones most
        pretious rare.

XXX. And in the midst thereof one pretious stone
    Of wondrous worth, and eke of wondrous mights,
    Shapt like a Ladies head, exceeding shone,

Like Hesperus emongst the lesser lights,
And strove for to amaze the weaker sights:
Thereby his mortall blade full comely hong
In yvory sheath, ycarv'd with curious slights,
Whose hilts were burnisht gold, and handle strong
Of mother perle; and buckled with a golden tong.

XXXI. His haughtie Helmet, horrid all with gold,
Both glorious brightnesse and great terrour bredd:
For all the crest a Dragon did enfold
With greedie pawes, and over all did spredd
His golden winges: his dreadfull hideous hedd,
Close couched on the bever, seemd to throw
From flaming mouth bright sparckles fiery redd,
That suddeine horrour to faint hartes did show;
And scaly tayle was stretcht adowne his back full low.

XXXII. Upon the top of all his loftie crest,
A bounch of heares discoloured diversly,
With sprincled pearle and gold full richly drest,
Did shake, and seemd to daunce for jollity,
Like to an almond tree ymounted hye
On top of greene Selinis all alone,
With blossoms brave bedecked daintily;
Whose tender locks do tremble every one
At everie little breath that under heaven is blowne.

XXXIII. His warlike shield all closely cover'd was,
Ne might of mortall eye be ever seene;
Not made of steele, nor of enduring bras,
Such earthly mettals soon consumed beene,
But all of Diamond perfect pure and cleene
It framed was, one massy entire mould,
Hewen out of Adamant rocke with engines keene,
That point of speare it never percen could,
Ne dint of direfull sword divide the substance would.

XXXIV. The same to wight he never wont disclose,
But whenas monsters huge he would dismay,
Or daunt unequall armies of his foes,
Or when the flying heavens he would affray;
For so exceeding shone his glistring ray,
That Phœbus golden face it did attaint,

As when a cloud his beames doth over-lay;
And silver Cynthia wexed pale and faynt,
As when her face is staynd with magicke arts constraint.

xxxv. No magicke arts hereof had any might,
Nor bloody wordes of bold Enchaunters call;
But all that was not such as seemd in sight
Before that shield did fade, and suddeine fall:
And when him list the raskall routes appall,
Men into stones therewith he could transmew,
And stones to dust, and dust to nought at all;
And, when him list the prouder lookes subdew,
He would them gazing blind, or turne to other hew.

xxxvi. Ne let it seeme that credence this exceedes;
For he that made the same was knowne right well
To have done much more admirable deedes.
It Merlin was, which whylome did excell
All living wightes in might of magicke spell:
Both shield and sword, and armour all he wrought
For this young Prince, when first to armes he fell;
But, when he dyde, the Faery Queene it brought
To Faerie lond, where yet it may be seene, if sought:

xxxvii. A gentle youth, his dearely loved Squire,
His speare of heben wood behind him bare,
Whose harmeful head, thrise heated in the fire,
Had riven many a brest with pikehead square:
A goodly person, and could menage faire
His stubborne steed with curbed canon bitt,
Who under him did trample as the aire,
And chauft that any on his backe should sitt:
The yron rowels into frothy fome he bitt.

xxxviii. Whenas this knight nigh to the Lady drew,
With lovely court he gan her entertaine;
But, when he heard her answers loth, he knew
Some secret sorrow did her heart distraine;
Which to allay, and calme her storming paine,
Faire feeling words he wisely gan display,
And for her humor fitting purpose faine,
To tempt the cause it selfe for to bewray,
Wherewith enmovd, these bleeding words she gan to say.

XXXIX. "What worlds delight, or joy of living speach,
    Can hart, so plungd in sea of sorrowes deep,
    And heaped with so huge misfortunes, reach?
    The carefull cold beginneth for to creep,
    And in my heart his yron arrow steep,
    Soone as I thinke upon my bitter bale.
    Such helplesse harmes yts better hidden keep,
    Then rip up griefe where it may not availe:
    My last left comfort is my woes to weepe and waile."

XL. "Ah Lady deare," quoth then the gentle knight,
    "Well may I ween your griefe is wondrous great;
    For wondrous great griefe groneth in my spright,
    Whiles thus I heare you of your sorrowes treat.
    But, woefull Lady, let me you intrete,
    For to unfold the anguish of your hart:
    Mishaps are maistred by advice discrete,
    And counsell mitigates the greatest smart:
    Found never help who never would his hurts impart."

XLI. "O but," (quoth she) "great greife will not be tould,
    And can more easily be thought then said."
    "Right so," (quoth he) "but he that never would
    Could never: will to might gives greatest aid."
    "But griefe," (quoth she) "does greater grow displaid,
    If then it find not helpe, and breeds despaire."
    "Despaire breeds not," (quoth he) "where faith is staid."
    "No faith so fast," (quoth she) "but flesh does paire."
    "Flesh may empaire," (quoth he) "but reason can repaire."

XLII. His goodly reason, and well guided speach,
    So deepe did settle in her gracious thought,
    That her perswaded to disclose the breach
    Which love and fortune in her heart had wrought;
    And said; "Faire Sir, I hope good hap hath brought
    You to inquere the secrets of my griefe,
    Or that your wisedome will direct my thought,
    Or that your prowesse can me yield reliefe:
    Then, heare the story sad, which I shall tell you briefe.

XLIII. "The forlorne Maiden, whom your eies have seene
    The laughing stocke of fortunes mockeries,
    Am th' onely daughter of a King and Queene,

Whose parents deare, whiles equal destinies
Did ronne about, and their felicities
The favourable heavens did not envy,
Did spred their rule through all the territories,
Which Phison and Euphrates floweth by,
And Gehons golden waves doe wash continually:

XLIV. " Till that their cruell cursed enemy,
An huge great Dragon, horrible in sight,
Bred in the loathly lakes of Tartary,
With murdrous ravine, and devouring might,
Their kingdome spoild, and countrey wasted quight:
Themselves, for feare into his jawes to fall,
He forst to castle strong to take their flight;
Where, fast embard in mighty brasen wall,
He has them now fowr years besieged to make them thrall.

XLV. " Full many knights, adventurous and stout,
Have enterpriz'd that Monster to subdew:
From every coast that heaven walks about
Have thither come the noble Martial crew.
That famous harde atchievements still pursew;
Yet never any could that girlond win,
But all still shronke, and still he greater grew:
All they, for want of faith, or guilt of sin,
The pitteous pray of his fiers cruelty have bin.

XLVI. " At last, yled with far reported praise,
Which flying fame throughout the world had spred,
Of doughty knights, whom Faery land did raise,
That noble order hight of maidenhed,
Forthwith to court of Gloriane I sped,
Of Gloriane, great Queene of glory bright,
Whose kingdomes seat Cleopolis is red;
There to obtaine some such redoubted knight,
That Parents deare from tyrants powre deliver might.

XLVII. " Yt was my chaunce (my chaunce was faire and good)
There for to find a fresh unproved knight;
Whose manly hands imbrewd in guilty blood
Had never beene, ne ever by his might
Had throwne to ground the unregarded right:
Yet of his prowesse proofe he since hath made

(I witnes am) in many a cruell fight;
The groning ghosts of many one dismaide
Have felt the bitter dint of his avenging blade.

XLVIII. "An ye, the forlorne reliques of his powre,
His biting sword, and his devouring speare,
Which have endured many a dreadful stowre,
Can speake his prowesse that did earst you beare,
And well could rule; now he hath left you heare
To be the record of his ruefull losse,
And of my dolefull disaventurous deare.
O! heavie record of the good Redcrosse,
Where have yee left your lord that could so well you
tosse?

XLIX. "Well hoped I, and faire beginnings had,
That he my captive langour should redeeme:
Till, all unweeting, an Enchaunter bad
His sence abused, and made him to misdeeme
My loyalty, not such as it did seeme,
That rather death desire then such despight.
Be judge, ye heavens, that all things right esteeme,
How I him lov'd, and love with all my might.
So thought I eke of him, and think I thought aright.

L. "Thenceforth me desolate he quite forsooke,
To wander where wilde fortune would me lead,
And other bywaies he himselfe betooke,
Where never foote of living wight did tread,
That brought not backe the balefull body dead:
In which him chaunced false Duessa meete,
Mine onely foe, mine onely deadly dread;
Who with her witchcraft, and misseeming sweete,
Inveigled him to follow her desires unmeete.

LI. "At last, by subtile sleights she him betraid
Unto his foe, a Gyaunt huge and tall;
Who him disarmed, dissolute, dismaid,
Unwares surprised, and with mighty mall
The monster mercilesse him made to fall,
Whose fall did never foe before behold:
And now in darkesome dungeon, wretched thrall,
Remedilesse for aie he doth him hold.
This is my cause of griefe, more great then may be told."

LII. Ere she had ended all she gan to faint:
But he her comforted, and faire bespake:
" Certes, Madame, ye have great cause of plaint;
That stoutest heart, I weene, could cause to quake:
But be of cheare, and comfort to you take;
For till I have acquitt your captive knight,
Assure your selfe I will you not forsake."
His chearefull words reviv'd her chearelesse spright,
So forth they went, the Dwarfe them guiding ever right.

CANTO VIII

Faire virgin, to redeeme her deare,
Brings Arthure to the fight:
Who slayes the Gyaunt, wounds the beast,
And strips Duessa quight.

I. Ay me! how many perils doe enfold
The righteous man, to make him daily fall,
Were not that heavenly grace doth him uphold,
And stedfast truth acquite him out of all.
Her love is firme, her care continuall,
So oft as he, through his own foolish pride
Or weakness, is to sinfull bands made thrall:
Els should this Redcrosse knight in bands have dyde,
For whose deliverance she this Prince doth thither guyd.

II. They sadly traveild thus, untill they came
Nigh to a castle builded strong and hye:
Then cryde the Dwarfe, " Lo! yonder is the same,
In which my Lord, my liege, doth lucklesse ly
Thrall to that Gyaunts hatefull tyranny:
Therefore, deare Sir, your mightie powres assay."
The noble knight alighted by and by
From loftie steed, and badd the Ladie stay,
To see what end of fight should him befall that day.

III. So with his Squire, th' admirer of his might,
He marched forth towardes that castle wall,
Whose gates he fownd fast shutt, ne living wight
To warde the same, nor answere commers call.
Then tooke that Squire an horne of bugle small,
Which hong adowne his side in twisted gold
And tasselles gay.   Wyde wonders over all
Of that same hornes great virtues weren told,
Which had approved bene in uses manifold.

IV. Was never wight that heard that shrilling sownd,
But trembling feare did feel in every vaine:
Three miles it might be easy heard arownd,

And Ecchoes three aunswer'd it selfe againe:
No false enchauntment, nor deceiptfull traine,
Might once abide the terror of that blast,
But presently was void and wholly vaine:
No gate so strong, no locke so firme and fast,
But with that percing noise flew open quite, or brast.

v. The same before the Geaunts gate he blew,
That all the castle quaked from the grownd,
And every dore of freewill open flew.
The Gyaunt selfe, dismaied with that sownd,
Where he with his Duessa dalliaunce fownd,
In hast came rushing forth from inner bowre,
With staring countenance sterne, as one astownd,
And staggering steps, to weet what suddein stowre
Had wrought that horror strange, and dar'd his dreaded
        powre.

vi. And after him the proud Duessa came,
High mounted on her many headed beast,
And every head with fyrie tongue did flame,
And every head was crowned on his creast,
And bloody mouthed with late cruell feast.
That when the knight beheld, his mightie shild
Upon his manly arme he soone addrest,
And at him fiersly flew, with corage fild,
And eger greedinesse through every member thrild.

vii. Therewith the Gyant buckled him to fight,
Inflamd with scornefull wrath and high disdaine,
And lifting up his dreadfull club on hight,
All armd with ragged snubbes and knottie graine,
Him thought at first encounter to have slaine.
But wise and wary was that noble Pere;
And, lightly leaping from so monstrous maine,
Did fayre avoide the violence him nere:
It booted nought to thinke such thunderbolts to beare.

viii. Ne shame he thought to shonne so hideous might:
The ydle stroke, enforcing furious way,
Missing the marke of his misaymed sight,
Did fall to ground, and with his heavy sway
So deepely dinted in the driven clay,
That three yardes deepe a furrow up did throw.

The sad earth, wounded with so sore assay,
Did grone full grievous underneath the blow,
And trembling with strange feare did like an erthquake
    show.

IX. As when almightie Jove, in wrathfull mood,
To wreake the guilt of mortall sins is bent,
Hurles forth his thundring dart with deadly food
Enrold in flames, and smouldring dreriment,
Through riven cloudes and molten firmament,
The fiers threeforked engin, making way,
Both loftie towres and highest trees hath rent,
And all that might his angry passage stay;
And, shooting in the earth, castes up a mount of clay.

X. His boystrous club, so buried in the grownd,
He could not rearen up againe so light,
But that the Knight him at advantage fownd;
And, whiles he strove his combred clubbe to quight
Out of the earth, with blade all burning bright
He smott off his left arme, which like a block
Did fall to ground, depriv'd of native might:
Large streames of blood out of the truncked stock
Forth gushed, like fresh water streame from riven rocke.

XI. Dismayed with so desperate deadly wound,
And eke impatient of unwonted payne,
He loudly brayd with beastly yelling sownd,
That all the fieldes rebellowed againe.
As great a noyse, as when in Cymbrian plaine
An heard of Bulles, whom kindly rage doth sting,
Doe for the milky mothers want complaine,
And fill the fieldes with troublous bellowing:
The neighbor woods arownd with hollow murmur ring.

XII. That when his deare Duessa heard, and saw
The evil stownd that daungerd her estate,
Unto his aide she hastily did draw
Her dreadfull beast; who, swolne with blood of late,
Came ramping forth with proud presumpteous gate,
And threatned all his heades like flaming brandes.
But him the Squire made quickly to retrate,
Encountring fiers with single sword in hand;
And twixt him and his Lord did like a bulwarke stand.

XIII. The proud Duessa, full of wrathfull spight,
And fiers disdaine to be affronted so,
Enforst her purple beast with all her might,
That stop out of the way to overthroe,
Scorning the let of so unequall foe:
But nathemore would that corageous swayne
To her yeeld passage gainst his Lord to goe,
But with outrageous strokes did him restraine,
And with his body bard the way atwixt them twaine.

XIV. Then tooke the angrie witch her golden cup,
Which still she bore, replete with magick artes;
Death and despeyre did many thereof sup,
And secret poyson through their inner partes,
Th' eternall bale of heavie wounded harts:
Which, after charmes and some enchauntments said,
She lightly sprinkled on his weaker partes:
Therewith his sturdie corage soon was quayd,
And all his sences were with suddein dread dismayd.

XV. So downe he fell before the cruell beast,
Who on his neck his bloody clawes did seize,
That life nigh crusht out of his panting brest:
No powre he had to stirre, nor will to rize.
That when the carefull knight gan well avise,
He lightly left the foe with whom he fought,
And to the beast gan turne his enterprise;
For wondrous anguish in his hart it wrought,
To see his loved Squyre into such thraldom brought:

XVI. And, high advauncing his blood-thirstie blade,
Stroke one of those deformed heades so sore,
That of his puissaunce proud ensample made:
His monstrous scalpe downe to his teeth it tore,
And that misformed shape misshaped more.
A sea of blood gusht from the gaping wownd,
That her gay garments staynd with filthy gore,
And overflowed all the field arownd,
That over shoes in blood he waded on the grownd.

XVII. Thereat he rored for exceeding paine,
That to have heard great horror would have bred;
And scourging th' emptie ayre with his long trayne,

Through great impatience of his grieved hed,
His gorgeous ryder from her loftie sted
Would have cast downe, and trodd in durty myre,
Had not the Gyaunt soone her succoured;
Who, all enrag'd with smart and frantick yre,
Came hurtling in full fiers, and forst the knight retyre.

XVIII. The force, which wont in two to be disperst,
In one alone left hand he now unites,
Which is through rage more strong then both were erst;
With which his hideous club aloft he dites,
And at his foe with furious rigor smites,
That strongest Oake might seeme to overthrow.
The stroke upon his shield so heavie lites,
That to the ground it doubleth him full low:
What mortall wight could ever beare so monstrous blow?

XIX. And in his fall his shield, that covered was,
Did loose his vele by chaunce, and open flew;
The light whereof, that hevens light did pas,
Such blazing brightnesse through the ayer threw,
That eye mote not the same endure to vew.
Which when the Gyaunt spyde with staring eye,
He downe let fall his arme, and soft withdrew
His weapon huge, that heaved was on hye
For to have slain the man, that on the ground did lye.

XX. And eke the fruitfull-headed beast, amazd
At flashing beames of that sunshiny shield,
Became stark blind, and all his sences dazd,
That downe he tumbled on the durtie field,
And seemd himselfe as conquered to yield.
Whom when his maistresse proud perceiv'd to fall,
Whiles yet his feeble feet for faintnesse reeld,
Unto the Gyaunt lowdly she gan call;
" O! helpe, Orgoglio; helpe! or els we perish all."

XXI. At her so pitteous cry was much amoov'd
Her champion stout; and for to ayde his frend,
Againe his wonted angry weapon proov'd,
But all in vaine, for he has redd his end
In that bright shield, and all their forces spend
Them selves in vaine: for, since that glauncing sight,

He hath no powre to hurt, nor to defend.
As where th' Almighties lightning brond does light,
It dimmes the dazed eyen, and daunts the sences quight.

XXII. Whom when the Prince, to batteill new addrest
And threatning high his dreadfull stroke, did see,
His sparkling blade about his head he blest,
And smote off quite his right leg by the knee,
That downe he tombled; as an aged tree,
High growing on the top of rocky clift,
Whose hartstrings with keene steele nigh hewen be;
The mightie trunck, halfe rent with ragged rift,
Doth roll adowne the rocks, and fall with fearefull drift.

XXIII. Or as a Castle, reared high and round,
By subtile engins and malitious slight
Is undermined from the lowest ground,
And her foundation forst, and feebled quight,
At last downe falles; and with her heaped hight
Her hastie ruine does more heavie make,
And yields it selfe unto the victours might:
Such was this Gyaunts fall, that seemd to shake
The stedfast globe of earth, as it for feare did quake.

XXIV. The knight, then lightly leaping to the pray,
With mortall steele him smot againe so sore,
That headlesse his unweldy bodie lay,
All wallowd in his owne fowle bloody gore,
Which flowed from his wounds in wondrous store.
But, soone as breath out of his brest did pas,
That huge great body, which the Gyaunt bore,
Was vanisht quite; and of that monstrous mas
Was nothing left, but like an emptie blader was.

XXV. Whose grievous fall when false Duessa spyde,
Her golden cup she cast unto the ground,
And crowned mitre rudely threw asyde:
Such percing griefe her stubborne hart did wound,
That she could not endure that dolefull stound
But leaving all behind her fled away:
The light-foot Squyre her quickly turnd around,
And, by hard meanes enforcing her to stay,
So brought unto his Lord as his deserved pray.

XXVI. The roiall Virgin which beheld from farre,
    In pensive plight and sad perplexitie,
    The whole atchievement of this doubtfull warre,
    Came running fast to greet his victorie,
    With sober gladnesse and myld modestie;
    And with sweet joyous cheare him thus bespake:
    " Fayre braunch of noblesse, flowre of chevalrie,
    That with your worth the world amazed make,
    How shall I quite the paynes ye suffer for my sake?

XXVII. " And you, fresh budd of vertue springing fast,
    Whom these sad eyes saw nigh unto deaths dore,
    What hath poore Virgin for such perill past
    Wherewith you to reward?   Accept therefore
    My simple selfe, and service evermore:
    And he that high does sit, and all things see
    With equall eye, their merites to restore,
    Behold what ye this day have done for mee,
    And what I cannot quite requite with usuree.

XXVIII. " But sith the heavens, and your faire handeling,
    Have made you master of the field this day,
    Your fortune maister eke with governing,
    And, well begonne, end all so well, I pray!
    Ne let that wicked woman scape away;
    For she it is, that did my Lord bethrall,
    My dearest Lord, and deepe in dongeon lay,
    Where he his better dayes hath wasted all:
    O heare, how piteous he to you for ayd does call! "

XXIX. Forthwith he gave in charge unto his Squyre,
    That scarlot whore to keepen carefully;
    Whyles he himselfe with greedie great desyre
    Into the Castle entred forcibly,
    Where living creature none he did espye.
    Then gan he lowdly through the house to call,
    But no man car'd to answere to his crye:
    There raignd a solemne silence over all:
    Nor voice was heard, nor wight was seene in bowre or hall.

XXX. At last, with creeping crooked pace forth came
    An old old man, with beard as white as snow,
    That on a staffe his feeble steps did frame,

And guyde his wearie gate both too and fro,
For his eye sight him fayled long ygo;
And on his arme a bounch of keyes he bore,
The which unused rust did overgrow:
Those were the keyes of every inner dore;
But he could not them use, but kept them still in store.

XXXI. But very uncouth sight was to behold,
How he did fashion his untoward pace;
For as he forward moovd his footing old,
So backward still was turnd his wrincled face:
Unlike to men, who ever, as they trace,
Both feet and face one way are wont to lead.
This was the auncient keeper of that place,
And foster father of the Gyaunt dead;
His name Ignaro did his nature right aread.

XXXII. His reverend heares and holy gravitee
The knight much honord, as beseemed well;
And gently askt, where all the people bee,
Which in that stately building wont to dwell:
Who answerd him full soft, *he could not tell.*
Again he askt, where that same knight was layd,
Whom great Orgoglio with his puissaunce fell
Had made his caytive thrall: againe he sayde,
He could not tell ; ne ever other answere made.

XXXIII. Then asked he, which way he in might pas?
He could not tell, againe he answered.
Thereat the courteous knight displeased was,
And said; " Old syre, it seemes thou hast not red
How ill it sits with that same silver hed,
In vaine to mocke, or mockt in vaine to bee:
But if thou be, as thou art pourtrahed
With natures pen, in ages grave degree,
Aread in graver wise what I demaund of thee."

XXXIV. His answere likewise was, *he could not tell :*
Whose sencelesse speach, and doted ignorance,
Whenas the noble Prince had marked well,
He ghest his nature by his countenance,
And calmd his wrath with goodly temperance.
Then, to him stepping, from his arme did reach
Those keyes, and made himselfe free enterance.

Each dore he opened without any breach,
There was no barre to stop, nor foe him to empeach.

XXXV. There all within full rich arayd he found,
With royall arras, and resplendent gold,
And did with store of every thing abound,
That greatest Princes presence might behold.
But all the floore (too filthy to be told)
With blood of guiltlesse babes, and innocents trew,
Which there were slaine as sheepe out of the fold,
Defiled was, that dreadfull was to vew;
And sacred ashes over it was strowed new.

XXXVI. And there beside of marble stone was built
An Altare, carv'd with cunning ymagery,
On which trew Christians blood was often spilt,
And holy Martyres often doen to dye
With cruell malice and strong tyranny:
Whose blessed sprites, from underneath the stone,
To God for vengeance cryde continually;
And with great griefe were often heard to grone,
That hardest heart would bleede to hear their piteous
     mone.

XXXVII. Through every rowme he sought, and everie bowr,
But no where could he find that wofull thrall:
At last he came unto an yron doore,
That fast was lockt, but key found not at all
Emongst that bounch to open it withall;
But in the same a little grate was pight,
Through which he sent his voyce, and lowd did call
With all his powre, to weet if living wight
Were housed therewithin, whom he enlargen might.

XXXVIII. Therewith an hollow, dreary, murmuring voyce
These pitteous plaintes and dolours did resound:
"O! who is that, which bringes me happy choyce
Of death, that here lye dying every stound,
Yet live perforce in balefull darkenesse bound?
For now three Moones have changed thrice their hew,
And have been thrice hid underneath the ground,
Since I the heavens chearefull face did vew.
O! welcome thou, that doest of death bring tydings
     trew."

XXXIX. Which when that Champion heard, with percing point
Of pitty deare his hart was thrilled sore;
And trembling horrour ran through every joynt,
For ruth of gentle knight so fowle forlore;
Which shaking off, he rent that yron dore
With furious force and indignation fell;
Where entred in, his foot could find no flore,
But all a deepe descent, as darke as hell,
That breathed ever forth a filthie banefull smell.

XL. But nether darkenesse fowle, nor filthy bands,
Nor noyous smell, his purpose could withhold,
(Entire affection hateth nicer hands)
But that with constant zele and corage bold,
After long paines and labors manifold,
He found the meanes that Prisoner up to reare;
Whose feeble thighes, unable to uphold
His pined corse, him scarse to light could beare;
A ruefull spectacle of death and ghastly drere.

XLI. His sad dull eies, deepe sunck in hollow pits,
Could not endure th' unwonted sunne to view;
His bare thin cheekes for want of better bits,
And empty sides deceived of their dew,
Could make a stony hart his hap to rew;
His rawbone armes, whose mighty brawned bowrs
Were wont to rive steele plates, and helmets hew,
Were clene consum'd; and all his vitall powres
Decayd, and all his flesh shronk up like withered flowers.

XLII. Whome when his Lady saw, to him she ran
With hasty joy: to see him made her glad,
And sad to view his visage pale and wan,
Who earst in flowres of freshest youth was clad.
Tho, when her well of teares she wasted had,
She said; " Ah dearest Lord! what evill starre
On you hath frownd, and pourd his influence bad,
That of your selfe ye thus berobbed arre,
And this misseeming hew your manly looks doth marre?

XLIII. " But welcome now, my Lord in wele or woe,
Whose presence I have lackt too long a day:
And fie on Fortune, mine avowed foe,

Whose wrathful wreakes them selves doe now alay;
And for these wronges shall treble penaunce pay
Of treble good: good growes of evils priefe."
The chearelesse man, whom sorrow did dismay,
Had no delight to treaten of his griefe;
His long endured famine needed more reliefe.

XLIV. "Faire Lady," then said that victorious knight,
    "The things, that grievous were to doe, or beare,
    Them to renew, I wrote, breeds no delight;
    Best musicke breeds delight in loathing eare:
    But th' only good that growes of passed feare
    Is to be wise, and ware of like agein.
    This daies ensample hath this lesson deare
    Deepe written in my heart with yron pen,
    That blisse may not abide in state of mortall men.

XLV. "Henceforth, Sir knight, take to you wonted strength,
    And maister these mishaps with patient might.
    Loe! where your foe lies stretcht in monstrous length;
    And loe! that wicked woman in your sight,
    The roote of all your care and wretched plight,
    Now in your powre, to let her live, or die."
    "To doe her die," (quoth Una) "were despight,
    And shame t'avenge so weake an enimy;
    But spoile her of her scarlet robe, and let her fly."

XLVI. So, as she bad, that witch they disaraid,
    And robd of roiall robes, and purple pall,
    And ornaments that richly were displaid;
    Ne spared they to strip her naked all.
    Then, when they had despoyld her tire and call,
    Such as she was their eies might her behold,
    That her misshaped parts did them appall:
    A loathly, wrinckled hag, ill favoured, old,
    Whose secret filth good manners biddeth not be told.

XLVII. Her crafty head was altogether bald,
    And, as in hate of honorable eld,
    Was overgrowne with scurfe and filthy scald;
    Her teeth out of her rotten gummes were feld,
    And her sowre breath abhominably smeld;
    Her dried dugs, lyke bladders lacking wind,

Hong downe, and filthy matter from them weld;
Her wrizled skin, as rough as maple rind,
So scabby was that would have loathd all womankind.

XLVIII. Her neather parts, the shame of all her kind,
My chaster Muse for shame doth blush to write;
But at her rompe she growing had behind
A foxes taile, with dong all fowly dight;
And eke her feete most monstrous were in sight;
For one of them was like an Eagles claw,
With griping talaunts armd to greedy fight;
The other like a beares uneven paw,
More ugly shape yet never living creature saw.

XLIX. Which when the knights beheld amazd they were,
And wondred at so fowle deformed wight.
" Such then," (said Una,) " as she seemeth here,
Such is the face of falshood: such the sight
Of fowle Duessa, when her borrowed light
Is laid away, and counterfesaunce knowne."
Thus when they had the witch disrobed quight,
And all her filthy feature open showne,
They let her goe at will, and wander waies unknowne.

L. Shee, flying fast from heavens hated face,
And from the world that her discovered wide,
Fled to the wastfull wildernesse apace,
From living eies her open shame to hide,
And lurkt in rocks and caves, long unespide.
But that faire crew of knights, and Una faire,
Did in that castle afterwards abide,
To rest them selves, and weary powres repaire;
Where store they fownd of al that dainty was and rare.

CANTO IX

His loves and lignage Arthure tells:
The knights knitt friendly hands:
Sir Trevisan flies from Despeyre,
Whom Redcros knight withstands.

I. O GOODLY golden chayne, wherewith yfere
　The vertues linked are in lovely wize;
　And noble mindes of yore allyed were,
　In brave poursuitt of chevalrous emprize,
　That none did others safety despize,
　Nor aid envy to him in need that stands;
　But friendly each did others praise devize,
　How to advaunce with favourable hands,
　As this good Prince redeemd the Redcrosse knight from
　　bands.

II. Who when their powres, empayrd through labor long,
　With dew repast they had recured well,
　And that weake captive wight now wexed strong,
　Them list no lenger there at leasure dwell,
　But forward fare as their adventures fell:
　But, ere they parted, Una faire besought
　That straunger knight his name and nation tell;
　Least so great good, as he for her had wrought,
　Should die unknown, and buried be in thankles thought.

III. " Faire virgin," (said the Prince,) " yee me require
　A thing without the compas of my witt;
　For both the lignage, and the certein Sire,
　From which I sprong, from mee are hidden yitt;
　For all so soone as life did me admitt
　Into this world, and shewed hevens light,
　From mothers pap I taken was unfitt,
　And streight deliver'd to a Fary knight,
　To be upbrought in gentle thewes and martiall might.

IV. " Unto Old Timon he me brought bylive;
　Old Timon, who in youthly yeares hath beene
　In warlike feates th' expertest man alive,

And is the wisest now on earth I weene:
His dwelling is low in a valley greene,
Under the foot of Rauran mossy hore,
From whence the river Dee, as silver cleene,
His tombling billowes rolls with gentle rore;
There all my daies he traind mee up in vertuous lore.

v. " Thither the great magicien Merlin came,
As was his use, ofttimes to visitt me;
For he had charge my discipline to frame,
And Tutors nouriture to oversee.
Him oft and oft I askt in privity,
Of what loines and what lignage I did spring;
Whose aunswere bad me still assured bee,
That I was sonne and heire unto a king,
As time in her just term the truth to light should bring."

vi. " Well worthy impe," said then the Lady gent,
" And Pupill fitt for such a Tutors hand!
But what adventure, or what high intent,
Hath brought you hither into Faery land,
Aread, Prince Arthure, crowne of Martiall band? "
" Full hard it is," (quoth he) " to read aright
The course of heavenly cause, or understand
The secret meaning of th' eternall might,
That rules mens waies, and rules the thoughts of living
       wight.

vii. " For whether he, through fatal deepe foresight,
Me hither sent for cause to me unghest;
Or that fresh bleeding wound, which day and night
Whilome doth rancle in my riven brest,
With forced fury following his behest,
Me hither brought by wayes yet never found,
You to have helpt I hold my selfe yet blest."
" Ah! courteous Knight," (quoth she) " what secret wound
Could ever find to grieve the gentlest hart on ground? "

viii. " Dear Dame," (quoth he) " you sleeping sparkes awake,
Which, troubled once, into huge flames will grow;
Ne ever will their fervent fury slake,
Till living moysture into smoke do flow,
And wasted life doe lye in ashes low:
Yet sithens silence lesseneth not my fire,

But, told, it flames; and, hidden, it does glow,
I will revele what ye so much desire.
Ah, Love! lay down thy bow, the whiles I may respyre.

IX. " It was in freshest flowre of youthly yeares,
When corage first does creepe in manly chest,
Then first the cole of kindly heat appeares
To kindle love in every living brest:
But me had warnd old Timons wise behest,
Those creeping flames by reason to subdew,
Before their rage grew to so great unrest,
As miserable lovers use to rew,
Which still wex old in woe, whiles wo stil wexeth new.

X. " That ydle name of love, and lovers life,
As losse of time, and vertues enimy,
I ever scornd, and joyd to stirre up strife,
In middest of their mournfull Tragedy;
Ay wont to laugh when them I heard to cry,
And blow the fire which them to ashes brent:
Their God himselfe, grieved at my libertie,
Shott many a dart at me with fiers intent;
But I them warded all with wary government.

XI. " But all in vaine: no fort can be so strong,
Ne fleshly brest can armed be so sownd,
But will at last be wonne with battrie long,
Or unawares at disavantage fownd.
Nothing is sure that growes on earthly grownd;
And who most trustes in arme of fleshly might,
And boastes in beauties chaine not to be bownd,
Doth soonest fall in disaventrous fight.
And yeeldes his caytive neck to victours most despight.

XII. " Ensample make of him your haplesse joy,
And of my selfe now mated, as ye see;
Whose prouder vaunt that proud avenging boy
Did soone pluck downe, and curbd my libertee.
For on a day, prickt forth with jollitee
Of looser life and heat of hardiment,
Raunging the forest wide on courser free,
The fields, the floods, the heavens, with one consent,
Did seeme to laugh on me, and favour mine intent.

XIII. " Forwearied with my sportes, I did alight
From loftie steed, and downe to sleepe me layd;
The verdant gras my couch did goodly dight,
And pillow was my helmett fayre displayd;
Whiles every sence the humour sweet embayd,
And slombring soft my hart did steale away,
Me seemed, by my side a royall Mayd
Her daintie limbes full softly down did lay:
So fayre a creature yet saw never sunny day.

XIV. " Most goodly glee and lovely blandishment
She to me made, and badd me love her deare;
For dearely sure her love was to me bent,
As, when just time expired, should appeare.
But whether dreames delude, or true it were,
Was never hart so ravisht with delight,
Ne living man like wordes did ever heare,
As she to me delivered all that night;
And at her parting said, She Queene of Faeries hight.

XV. " When I awoke, and found her place devoyd,
And nought but pressed gras where she had lyen,
I sorrowed all so much as earst I joyd,
And washed all her place with watry eyen.
From that day forth I lov'd that face divyne;
From that day forth I cast in carefull mynd,
To seek her out with labor and long tyne,
And never vowd to rest till her I fynd:
Nyne monethes I seek in vain, yet ni'll that vow unbynd."

XVI. Thus as he spake, his visage wexed pale,
And chaunge of hew great passion did bewray;
Yett still he strove to cloke his inward bale,
And hide the smoke that did his fire display,
Till gentle Una thus to him gan say:
" O happy Queene of Faeries! that hast fownd,
Mongst many, one that with his prowesse may
Defend thine honour, and thy foes confownd.
True loves are often sown, but seldom grow on grownd."

XVII. " Thine, O! then," said the gentle Redcrosse knight,
" Next to that Ladies love, shalbe the place,
O fayrest virgin! full of heavenly light,

Whose wondrous faith, exceeding earthly race,
Was firmest fixt in myne extremest case.
And you, my Lord, the Patrone of my life,
Of that great Queene may well gaine worthie grace,
For onely worthie you through prowes priefe,
Yf living man mote worthie be to be her liefe."

XVIII. So diversly discoursing of their loves,
The golden Sunne his glistring head gan shew,
And sad remembraunce now the Prince amoves
With fresh desire his voyage to pursew;
Als Una earnd her traveill to renew.
Then those two knights, fast friendship for to bynd,
And love establish each to other trew,
Gave goodly gifts, the signes of gratefull mynd,
And eke, as pledges firme, right hands together joynd

XIX. Prince Arthur gave a boxe of Diamond sure,
Embowd with gold and gorgeous ornament,
Wherein were closd few drops of liquor pure,
Of wondrous worth, and vertue excellent,
That any wownd could heale incontinent.
Which to requite, the Redcrosse knight him gave
A booke, wherein his Saveours testament
Was writt with golden letters rich and brave:
A worke of wondrous grace, and hable soules to save.

XX. Thus beene they parted; Arthur on his way
To seeke his love, and th' other for to fight
With Unaes foe, that all her realme did pray.
But she, now weighing the decayed plight
And shrunken synewes of her chosen knight,
Would not a while her forward course pursew,
Ne bring him forth in face of dreadfull fight,
Till he recovered had his former hew;
For him to be yet weake and wearie well she knew.

XXI. So as they traveild, lo! they gan espy
An armed knight towards them gallop fast,
That seemed from some feared foe to fly,
Or other griesly thing that him aghast.
Still as he fledd his eye was backward cast,
As if his feare still followed him behynd:

Als flew his steed as he his bandes had brast,
And with his winged heeles did tread the wynd,
As he had beene a fole of Pegasus his kynd.

XXII. Nigh as he drew, they might perceive his head
To bee unarmd, and curld uncombed heares
Upstaring stiffe, dismaid with uncouth dread:
Nor drop of blood in all his face appeares,
Nor life in limbe; and, to increase his feares,
In fowle reproch of knighthoodes fayre degree,
About his neck an hempen rope he weares,
That with his glistring armes does ill agree;
But he of rope or armes has now no memoree.

XXIII. The Redcrosse knight toward him crossed fast,
To weet what mister wight was so dismayd.
There him he findes all sencelesse and aghast,
That of him selfe he seemd to be afrayd;
Whom hardly he from flying forward stayd,
Till he these wordes to him deliver might:
" Sir knight, aread who hath ye thus arayd,
And eke from whom make ye this hasty flight?
For never knight I saw in such misseeming plight."

XXIV. He answerd nought at all; but adding new
Feare to his first amazement, staring wyde
With stony eyes and hartlesse hollow hew,
Astonisht stood, as one that had aspyde
Infernall furies with their chaines untyde.
Him yett againe, and yett againe, bespake
The gentle knight; who nought to him replyde;
But, trembling every joynt, did inly quake,
And foltring tongue, at last, these words seemd forth to
    shake;

XXV. " For Gods deare love, Sir knight, doe me not stay;
For loe! he comes, he comes fast after mee."
Eft looking back would faine have runne away;
But he him forst to stay, and tellen free
The secrete cause of his perplexitie:
Yet nathemore by his bold hartie speach
Could his blood frosen hart emboldened bee,
But through his boldnes rather feare did reach;
Yett, forst, at last he made through silence suddein breach.

XXVI. " And am I now in safetie sure," (quoth he)
 " From him that would have forced me to dye?
 And is the point of death now turnd fro mee,
 That I may tell this haplesse history? "
 " Fear nought," (quoth he) " no daunger now is nye."
 " Then shall I you recount a ruefull cace,"
 (Said he) " the which with this unlucky eye
 I late beheld; and, had not greater grace
 Me reft from it, had bene partaker of the place.

XXVII. " I lately chaunst (Would I had never chaunst!)
 With a fayre knight to keepen companee,
 Sir Terwin hight, that well himselfe advaunst
 In all affayres, and was both bold and free;
 But not so happy as mote happy bee:
 He lov'd, as was his lot, a Lady gent
 That him againe lov'd in the least degree;
 For she was proud, and of too high intent,
 And joyd to see her lover languish and lament:

XXVIII. " From whom retourning sad and comfortlesse,
 As on the way together we did fare,
 We met that villen, (God from him me blesse!)
 That cursed wight, from whom I scapt whyleare,
 A man of hell that calls himselfe Despayre:
 Who first us greets, and after fayre areedes
 Of tydinges straunge, and of adventures rare:
 So creeping close, as Snake in hidden weedes,
 Inquireth of our states, and of our knightly deedes.

XXIX. " Which when he knew, and felt our feeble harts
 Embost with bale, and bitter byting griefe,
 Which love had launched with his deadly darts,
 With wounding words, and termes of foule repriefe,
 He pluckt from us all hope of dew reliefe,
 That earst us held in love of lingring life;
 Then hopelesse, hartlesse, gan the cunning thiefe
 Perswade us dye, to stint all further strife:
 To me he lent this rope, to him a rusty knife.

XXX. " With which sad instrument of hasty death,
 That wofull lover, loathing lenger light,
 A wyde way made to let forth living breath:

But I, more fearefull or more lucky wight,
Dismayd with that deformed dismall sight,
Fledd fast away, halfe dead with dying feare;
Ne yet assur'd of life by you, Sir knight,
Whose like infirmity like chaunce may beare;
But God you never let his charmed speaches heare!"

XXXI. " How may a man," (said he) " with idle speach
Be wonne to spoyle the Castle of his health? "
" I wote," (quoth he) " whom tryall late did teach,
That like would not for all this worldes wealth.
His subtile tong like dropping honny mealt'h
Into the heart, and searcheth every vaine;
That, ere one be aware, by secret stealth
His powre is reft, and weaknes doth remaine.
O! never, Sir, desire to try his guilefull traine."

XXXII. " Certes," (sayd he) " hence shall I never rest,
Till I that treachours art have heard and tryde;
And you, Sir knight, whose name mote I request,
Of grace do me unto his cabin guyde."
" I, that hight Trevisan," (quoth he) " will ryde
Against my liking backe to doe you grace:
But nor for gold nor glee will I abyde
By you, when ye arrive in that same place;
For lever had I die then see his deadly face."

XXXIII. Ere long they come where that same wicked wight
His dwelling has, low in an hollow cave,
For underneath a craggy cliff ypight,
Darke, dolefull, dreary, like a greedy grave,
That still for carrion carcases doth crave:
On top whereof ay dwelt the ghastly Owle,
Shrieking his balefull note, which ever drave
Far from that haunt all other chearefull fowle;
And all about it wandring ghostes did wayle and howle.

XXXIV. And all about old stockes and stubs of trees,
Whereon nor fruit nor leafe was ever seene,
Did hang upon the ragged rocky knees;
On which had many wretches hanged beene,
Whose carcases were scattred on the greene,
And throwne about the cliffs.   Arrived there,

That bare-head knight, for dread and dolefull teene,
Would faine have fled, ne durst approchen neare;
But th' other forst him staye, and comforted in feare.

XXXV. That darkesome cave they enter, where they find
That cursed man, low sitting on the ground,
Musing full sadly in his sullein mind:
His griesie lockes, long growen and unbound,
Disordred hong about his shoulders round,
And hid his face, through which his hollow eyne
Lookt deadly dull, and stared as astound;
His raw-bone cheekes, through penurie and pine,
Were shronke into his jawes, as he did never dyne.

XXXVI. His garment, nought but many ragged clouts,
With thornes together pind and patched was,
The which his naked sides he wrapt abouts;
And him beside there lay upon the gras
A dreary corse, whose life away did pas,
All wallowd in his own yet luke-warme blood,
That from his wound yet welled fresh, alas!
In which a rusty knife fast fixed stood,
And made an open passage for the gushing flood.

XXXVII. Which piteous spectacle, approving trew
The wofull tale that Trevisan had told,
Whenas the gentle Redcrosse knight did vew,
With firie zeale he burnt in courage bold
Him to avenge before his blood were cold,
And to the villein sayd; " Thou damned wight,
The authour of this fact we here behold,
What justice can but judge against thee right,
With thine owne blood to price his blood, here shed in
    sight? "

XXXVIII. " What franticke fit," (quoth he) " hath thus distraught
Thee, foolish man, so rash a doome to give?
What justice ever other judgement taught,
But he should dye who merites not to live?
None els to death this man despayring drive
But his owne guiltie mind, deserving death.
Is then unjust to each his dew to give?
Or let him dye, that loatheth living breath,
Or let him die at ease, that liveth here uneath?

XXXIX. " Who travailes by the wearie wandring way,
To come unto his wished home in haste,
And meetes a flood that doth his passage stay,
Is not great grace to helpe him over past,
Or free his feet that in the myre sticke fast?
Most envious man, that grieves at neighbours good;
And fond, that joyest in the woe thou hast!
Why wilt not let him passe, that long hath stood
Upon the bancke, yet wilt thy selfe not pas the flood?

XL. " He there does now enjoy eternall rest
And happy ease, which thou doest want and crave,
And further from it daily wanderest:
What if some little payne the passage have,
That makes frayle flesh to feare the bitter wave,
Is not short payne well borne, that bringes long ease,
And layes the soule to sleepe in quiet grave?
Sleepe after toyle, port after stormie seas,
Ease after warre, death after life, does greatly please."

XLI. The knight much wondred at his suddeine wit,
And sayd; " The terme of life is limited,
Ne may a man prolong, nor shorten, it:
The souldier may not move from watchfull sted,
Nor leave his stand untill his Captaine bed."
" Who life did limit by almightie doome,"
(Quoth he) " knowes best the termes established;
And he, that points the Centonell his roome,
Doth license him depart at sound of morning droome."

XLII. " Is not his deed, what ever thing is donne
In heaven and earth? Did not he all create
To die againe? All ends that was begonne:
Their times in his eternall booke of fate
Are written sure, and have their certein date.
Who then can strive with strong necessitie,
That holds the world in his still chaunging state,
Or shunne the death ordaynd by destinie?
When houre of death is come, let none aske whence, nor
why.

XLIII. " The lenger life, I wote, the greater sin;
The greater sin, the greater punishment:
All those great battels, which thou boasts to win

Through strife, and blood-shed, and avengement,
Now praysd, hereafter deare thou shalt repent;
For life must life, and blood must blood, repay.
Is not enough thy evill life forespent?
For he that once hath missed the right way,
The further he doth goe, the further he doth stray.

XLIV. " Then doe no further goe, no further stray,
But here ly downe, and to thy rest betake,
Th' ill to prevent, that life ensewen may;
For what hath life that may it loved make,
And gives not rather cause it to forsake?
Feare, sicknesse, age, losse, labour, sorrow, strife,
Payne, hunger, cold that makes the hart to quake,
And ever fickle fortune rageth rife;
All which, and thousands mo, do make a loathsome life.

XLV. " Thou, wretched man, of death hast greatest need,
If in true ballaunce thou wilt weigh thy state;
For never knight, that dared warlike deed,
More luckless dissaventures did amate: ·
Witnes the dungeon deepe, wherein of late
Thy life shutt up for death so oft did call;
And though good lucke prolonged hath thy date,
Yet death then would the like mishaps forestall,
Into the which hereafter thou maist happen fall.

XLVI. " Why then doest thou, O man of sin! desire
To draw thy dayes forth to their last degree?
Is not the measure of thy sinfull hire
High heaped up with huge iniquitee,
Against the day of wrath to burden thee?
Is not enough, that to this Lady mild
Thou falsed hast thy faith with perjuree,
And sold thy selfe to serve Duessa vild,
With whom in al abuse thou hast thy selfe defild?

XLVII. " Is not he just, that all this doth behold
From highest heven, and beares an equall eie?
Shall he thy sins up in his knowledge fold,
And guilty be of thine impietie?
Is not his lawe, Let every sinner die;
Die shall all flesh?   What then must needs be donne,

Is it not better to doe willinglie,
Then linger till the glas be all out ronne?
Death is the end of woes: die soone, O faeries sonne!"

XLVIII. The knight was much enmoved with his speach,
That as a swords poynt through his hart did perse,
And in his conscience made a secrete breach,
Well knowing trew all that he did reherse,
And to his fresh remembraunce did reverse
The ugly vew of his deformed crimes;
That all his manly powres it did disperse,
As he were charmed with inchaunted rimes;
That oftentimes he quakt, and fainted oftentimes.

XLIX. In which amazement when the Miscreaunt
Perceived him to waver, weake and fraile,
Whiles trembling horror did his conscience daunt,
And hellish anguish did his soule assaile;
To drive him to despaire, and quite to quaile,
Hee shewd him, painted in a table plaine,
The damned ghosts that doe in torments waile,
And thousand feends that doe them endlesse paine
With fire and brimstone, which for ever shall remaine.

L. The sight whereof so throughly him dismaid,
That nought but death before his eies he saw,
And ever burning wrath before him laid,
By righteous sentence of th' Almighties law.
Then gan the villein him to overcraw,
And brought unto him swords, ropes, poison, fire,
And all that might him to perdition draw;
And bad him choose what death he would desire:
For death was dew to him that had provokt Gods ire.

LI. But, whenas none of them he saw him take,
He to him raught a dagger sharpe and keene,
And gave it him in hand: his hand did quake
And tremble like a leafe of Aspin greene,
And troubled blood through his pale face was seene
To come and goe with tidings from the heart,
As it a ronning messenger had beene.
At last, resolv'd to work his finall smart,
He lifted up his hand, that backe againe did start.

LII. Which whenas Una saw, through every vaine
The crudled cold ran to her well of life,
As in a swowne: but, soone reliv'd againe,
Out of his hand she snatcht the cursed knife,
And threw it to the ground, enraged rife,
And to him said; " Fie, fie, faint hearted Knight!
What meanest thou by this reprochfull strife?
Is this the battaile which thou vauntst to fight
With that fire-mouthed Dragon, horrible and bright?

LIII. " Come; come away, fraile, feeble, fleshly wight,
Ne let vaine words bewitch thy manly hart,
Ne divelish thoughts dismay thy constant spright:
In heavenly mercies hast thou not a part?
Why shouldst thou then despeire, that chosen art?
Where justice growes, there grows eke greater grace,
The which doth quench the brond of hellish smart,
And that accurst hand-writing doth deface.
Arise, sir Knight; arise, and leave this cursed place."

LIV. So up he rose, and thence amounted streight.
Which when the carle beheld, and saw his guest
Would safe depart, for all his subtile sleight,
He chose an halter from among the rest,
And with it hong him selfe, unbid, unblest.
But death he could not worke himselfe thereby;
For thousand times he so him selfe had drest,
Yet nathelesse it could not doe him die,
Till he should die his last, that is, eternally.

CANTO X

Her faithfull knight faire Una brings
To house of Holinesse;
Where he is taught repentaunce, and
The way to hevenly blesse.

I. WHAT man is he, that boasts of fleshly might
And vaine assuraunce of mortality,
Which, all so soone as it doth come to fight
Against spirituall foes, yields by and by,
Or from the fielde most cowardly doth fly!
Ne let the man ascribe it to his skill,
That thorough grace hath gained victory:
If any strength we have, it is to ill,
But all the good is Gods, both power and eke will.

II. By that which lately hapned Una saw
That this her knight was feeble, and too faint;
And all his sinewes woxen weake and raw,
Through long enprisonment, and hard constraint,
Which he endured in his late restraint,
That yet he was unfitt for bloody fight.
Therefore, to cherish him with diets daint,
She cast to bring him where he chearen might,
Till he recovered had his late decayed plight.

III. There was an auncient house nor far away,
Renowmd throughout the world for sacred lore
And pure unspotted life: so well, they say,
It governd was, and guided evermore,
Through wisedome of a matrone grave and hore;
Whose onely joy was to relieve the needes
Of wretched soules, and helpe the helpelesse pore:
All night she spent in bidding of her bedes,
And all the day in doing good and godly deedes.

IV. Dame Cælia men did her call, as thought
From heaven to come, or thither to arise;
The mother of three daughters, well upbrought

In goodly thewes, and godly exercise:
The eldest two, most sober, chast, and wise,
Fidelia and Speranza, virgins were;
Though spousd, yet wanting wedlocks solemnize;
But faire Charissa to a lovely fere
Was lincked, and by him had many pledges dere.

v. Arrived there, the dore they find fast lockt,
For it was warely watched night and day,
For feare of many foes; but, when they knockt,
The Porter opened unto them streight way.
He was an aged syre, all hory gray,
With lookes full lowly cast, and gate full slow,
Wont on a staffe his feeble steps to stay,
Hight Humiltá.   They passe in, stouping low;
For streight and narrow was the way which he did show.

vi. Each goodly thing is hardest to begin;
But, entred in, a spatious court they see,
Both plaine and pleasaunt to be walked in;
Where them does meete a francklin faire and free,
And entertaines with comely courteous glee;
His name was Zele, that him right well became:
For in his speaches and behaviour hee
Did labour lively to expresse the same,
And gladly did them guide, till to the Hall they came.

vii. There fayrely them receives a gentle Squyre,
Of myld demeanure and rare courtesee,
Right cleanly clad in comely sad attyre;
In word and deede that shewd great modestee,
And knew his good to all of each degree,
Hight Reverence.   He them with speaches meet
Does faire entreat; no courting nicetee,
But simple, trew, and eke unfained sweet,
As might become a Squyre so great persons to greet.

viii. And afterwardes them to his Dame he leades,
That aged Dame, the Lady of the place,
Who all this while was busy at her beades;
Which doen, she up arose with seemely grace,
And toward them full matronely did pace.
Where, when that fairest Una she beheld,

Whom well she knew to spring from hevenly race,
Her heart with joy unwonted inly sweld,
As feeling wondrous comfort in her weaker eld:

IX. And, her embracing, said; " O happy earth,
Whereon thy innocent feet doe ever tread!
Most vertuous virgin, borne of hevenly berth,
That, to redeeme thy woefull parents head
From tyrans rage and ever-dying dread,
Hast wandred through the world now long a day,
Yett ceassest not thy weary soles to lead;
What grace hath thee now hither brought this way?
Or doen thy feeble feet unweeting hither stray?

X. " Straunge thing it is an errant knight to see
Here in this place; or any other wight,
That hither turnes his steps.   So few there bee,
That chose the narrow path, or seeke the right:
All keepe the broad high way, and take delight
With many rather for to goe astray,
And be partakers of their evill plight,
Then with a few to walke the rightest way.
O foolish men! why hast ye to your own decay? "

XI. " Thy selfe to see, and tyred limbes to rest,
O matrone sage," (quoth she) " I hither came;
And this good knight his way with me addrest,
Ledd with thy prayses, and broad-blazed fame,
That up to heven is blowne."   The auncient Dame
Him goodly greeted in her modest guyse,
And enterteynd them both, as best became,
With all the court'sies that she could devyse,
Ne wanted ought to shew her bounteous or wise.

XII. Thus as they gan of sondrie thinges devise,
Loe! two most goodly virgins came in place,
Ylinked arme in arme in lovely wise:
With countenance demure, and modest grace,
They numbred even steps and equall pace;
Of which the eldest, that Fidelia hight,
Like sunny beames threw from her Christall face
That could have dazd the rash beholders sight,
And round about her head did shine like hevens light.

XIII. She was araied all in lilly white,
    And in her right hand bore a cup of gold,
    With wine and water fild up to the hight,
    In which a Serpent did himselfe enfold,
    That horrour made to all that did behold;
    But she no whitt did chaunge her constant mood:
    And in her other hand she fast did hold
    A booke, that was both signd and seald with blood;
    Wherein darke things were writt, hard to be understood.

XIV. Her younger sister, that Speranza hight,
    Was clad in blew, that her beseemed well;
    Not all so chearefull seemed she of sight,
    As was her sister: whether dread did dwell
    Or anguish in her hart, is hard to tell.
    Upon her arme a silver anchor lay,
    Whereon she leaned ever, as befell;
    And ever up to heven, as she did pray,
    Her stedfast eyes were bent, ne swarved other way.

XV. They, seeing Una, towardes her gan wend,
    Who them encounters with like courtesee;
    Many kind speeches they betweene them spend,
    And greatly joy each other for to see:
    Then to the knight with shamefast modestie
    They turne themselves, at Unaes meeke request,
    And him salute with well beseeming glee;
    Who faire them quites, as him beseemed best,
    And goodly gan discourse of many a noble gest.

XVI. Then Una thus: "But she, your sister deare,
    The deare Charissa, where is she become?
    Or wants she health, or busie is elsewhere?"
    "Ah! no," said they, "but forth she may not come;
    For she of late is lightned of her wombe,
    And hath encreast the world with one sonne more,
    That her to see should be but troublesome."
    "Indeed," (quoth she) "that should her trouble sore;
    But thankt be God, and her encrease so evermore!"

XVII. Then said the aged Cælia, "Deare dame,
    And you, good Sir, I wote that of youré toyle
    And labors long, through which ye hither came,

Ye both forwearied be: therefore, a whyle
I read you rest, and to your bowres recoyle."
Then called she a Groome, that forth him ledd
Into a goodly lodge, and gan despoile
Of puissant armes, and laid in easie bedd.
His name was meeke Obedience, rightfully aredd.

XVIII. Now when their wearie limbes with kindly rest,
And bodies were refresht with dew repast,
Fayre Una gan Fidelia fayre request,
To have her knight into her schoolehous plaste,
That of her heavenly learning he might taste,
And heare the wisdom of her wordes divine.
She graunted; and that knight so much agraste,
That she him taught celestiall discipline,
And opened his dull eyes, that light mote in them shine.

XIX. And that her sacred Booke, with blood ywritt,
That none could reade except she did them teach,
She unto him disclosed every whitt;
And heavenly documents thereout did preach,
That weaker witt of man could never reach;
Of God; of grace; of justice; of free-will;
That wonder was to heare her goodly speach:
For she was hable with her wordes to kill,
And rayse againe to life the hart that she did thrill.

XX. And, when she list poure out her larger spright,
She would commaund the hasty Sunne to stay,
Or backward turne his course from hevens hight:
Sometimes great hostes of men she could dismay;
Dry-shod to passe she parts the flouds in tway;
And eke huge mountaines from their native seat
She would commaund themselves to beare away,
And throw in raging sea with roaring threat.
Almightie God her gave such powre and puissaunce great.

XXI. The faithfull knight now grew in little space,
By hearing her, and by her sisters lore,
To such perfection of all hevenly grace,
That wretched world he gan for to abhore,
And mortall life gan loath as thing forlore,
Greevd with remembrance of his wicked wayes,

And prickt with anguish of his sinnes so sore,
That he desirde to end his wretched dayes:
So much the dart of sinfull guilt the soule dismayes.

XXII. But wise Speranza gave him comfort sweet,
And taught him how to take assured hold
Upon her silver anchor, as was meet;
Els had his sinnes, so great and manifold,
Made him forget all that Fidelia told.
In this distressed doubtfull agony,
When him his dearest Una did behold
Disdeining life, desiring leave to dye,
She found her selfe assayld with great perplexity;

XXIII. And came to Cælia to declare her smart;
Who, well acquainted with that commune plight,
Which sinfull horror workes in wounded hart,
Her wisely comforted all that she might,
With goodly counsell and advisement right;
And streightway sent with carefull diligence,
To fetch a Leach, the which had great insight
In that disease of grieved conscience,
And well could cure the same: His name was Patience.

XXIV. Who, comming to that sowle-diseased knight,
Could hardly him intreat to tell his grief:
Which knowne, and all that noyd his heavie spright
Well searcht, eftsoones he gan apply relief
Of salves and med'cines, which had passing prief;
And thereto added wordes of wondrous might.
By which to ease he him recured brief,
And much aswag'd the passion of his plight,
That he his paine endur'd, as seeming now more light.

XXV. But yet the cause and root of all his ill,
Inward corruption and infected sin,
Not purg'd nor heald, behind remained still,
And festring sore did ranckle yett within,
Close creeping twixt the marow and the skin:
Which to extirpe, he laid him privily
Downe in a darksome lowly place far in,
Whereas he meant his corrosives to apply,
And with streight diet tame his stubborne malady.

XXVI. In ashes and sackcloth he did array
　　　His daintie corse, proud humors to abate;
　　　And dieted with fasting every day,
　　　The swelling of his woundes to mitigate;
　　　And made him pray both earely and eke late:
　　　And ever, as superfluous flesh did rott,
　　　Amendment readie still at hand did wayt,
　　　To pluck it out with pincers fyrie whott,
　　　That soone in him was lefte no one corrupted jott.

XXVII. And bitter Penaunce, with an yron whip,
　　　Was wont him once to disple every day:
　　　And sharp Remorse his hart did prick and nip,
　　　That drops of blood thence like a well did play:
　　　And sad Repentance used to embay
　　　His blamefull body in salt water sore,
　　　The filthy blottes of sin to wash away.
　　　So in short space they did to health restore
　　　The man that would not live, but erst lay at deathes dore.

XXVIII. In which his torment often was so great,
　　　That like a Lyon he would cry and rore,
　　　And rend his flesh, and his owne synewes eat.
　　　His owne deare Una, hearing evermore
　　　His ruefull shriekes and gronings, often tore
　　　Her guiltlesse garments and her golden heare,
　　　For pitty of his payne and anguish sore:
　　　Yet all with patience wisely she did beare,
　　　For well she wist his cryme could els be never cleare.

XXIX. Whom, thus recover'd by wise Patience
　　　And trew Repentaunce, they to Una brought;
　　　Who, joyous of his cured conscience,
　　　Him dearely kist, and fayrely eke besought
　　　Himselfe to chearish, and consuming thought
　　　To put away out of his carefull brest.
　　　By this Charissa, late in child-bed brought,
　　　Was woxen strong, and left her fruitfull nest:
　　　To her fayre Una brought this unacquainted guest.

XXX. She was a woman in her freshest age,
　　　Of wondrous beauty, and of bounty rare,
　　　With goodly grace and comely personage,

That was on earth not easie to compare;
Full of great love, but Cupids wanton snare
As hell she hated; chaste in worke and will:
Her necke and brests were ever open bare,
That ay thereof her babes might sucke their fill;
The rest was all in yellow robes arayed still.

XXXI. A multitude of babes about her hong,
Playing their sportes, that joyd her to behold;
Whom still she fed whiles they were weake and young,
But thrust them forth still as they wexed old:
And on her head she wore a tyre of gold,
Adornd with gemmes and owches wondrous fayre,
Whose passing price uneath was to be told:
And by her syde there sate a gentle payre,
Of turtle doves, she sitting in an yvory chayre.

XXXII. The knight and Una entring fayre her greet,
And bid her joy of that her happy brood;
Who them requites with court'sies seeming meet,
And entertaynes with friendly chearefull mood.
Then Una her besought, to be so good
As in her vertuous rules to schoole her knight,
Now after all his torment well withstood
In that sad house of Penaunce, where his spright
Had past the paines of hell and long-enduring night.

XXXIII. She was right joyous of her just request;
And taking by the hand that Faeries sonne,
Gan him instruct in everie good behest,
Of love, and righteousness, and well to donne;
And wrath and hatred warely to shonne,
That drew on men Gods hatred and his wrath,
And many soules in dolours had fordonne:
In which when him she well instructed hath,
From thence to heaven she teacheth him the ready path.

XXXIV. Wherein his weaker wandring steps to guyde,
An auncient matrone she to her does call,
Whose sober lookes her wisedome well descryde:
Her name was Mercy; well knowne over-all
To be both gratious and eke liberall:
To whom the carefull charge of him she gave,

To leade aright, that he should never fall
In all his waies through this wide worldes wave;
That Mercy in the end his righteous soule might save.

xxxv. The godly Matrone by the hand him beares
Forth from her presence, by a narrow way,
Scattred with bushy thornes and ragged breares,
Which still before him she remov'd away,
That nothing might his ready passage stay:
And ever, when his feet encombred were,
Or gan to shrinke, or from the right to stray,
She held him fast, and firmely did upbeare,
As carefull Nourse her child from falling oft does reare.

xxxvi. Eftsoones unto an holy Hospitall,
That was foreby the way, she did him bring;
In which seven Bead-men, that had vowed all
Their life to service of high heavens King,
Did spend their daies in doing godly thing.
Their gates to all were open evermore,
That by the wearie way were traveiling;
And one sate wayting ever them before,
To call in commers-by that needy were and pore.

xxxvii. The first of them, that eldest was and best,
Of all the house had charge and government,
As Guardian and Steward of the rest.
His office was to give entertainement
And lodging unto all that came and went;
Not unto such as could him feast againe,
And double quite for that he on them spent;
But such as want of harbour did constraine:
Those for Gods sake his dewty was to entertaine.

xxxviii. The second was as Almner of the place:
His office was the hungry for to feed,
And thristy give to drinke; a worke of grace.
He feard not once himselfe to be in need,
Ne car'd to hoord for those whom he did breede:
The grace of God he layd up still in store,
Which as a stocke he left unto his seede.
He had enough; what need him care for more?
And had he lesse, yet some he would give to the pore.

XXXIX. The third had of their wardrobe custody,
In which were not rich tyres, nor garments gay,
The plumes of pride, and winges of vanity,
But clothes meet to keepe keene cold away,
And naked nature seemely to aray;
With which bare wretched wights he dayly clad,
The images of God in earthly clay;
And, if that no spare clothes to give he had,
His owne cote he would cut, and it distribute glad.

XL. The fourth appointed by his office was
Poore prisoners to relieve with gratious ayd,
And captives to redeeme with price of bras
From Turkes and Sarazins, which them had stayd:
And though they faulty were, yet well he wayd,
That God to us forgiveth every howre
Much more then that why they in bands were layd;
And he, that harrowd hell with heavie stowre,
The faulty soules from thence brought to his heavenly
bowre.

XLI. The fift had charge sick persons to attend,
And comfort those in point of death which lay;
For them most needeth comfort in the end,
When sin, and hell, and death, doe most dismay
The feeble soule departing hence away.
All is but lost, that living we bestow,
If not well ended at our dying day.
O man! have mind of that last bitter throw;
For as the tree does fall, so lyes it ever low.

XLII. The sixt had charge of them now being dead,
In seemely sort their corses to engrave,
And deck with dainty flowres their brydall bed,
That to their heavenly spouse both sweet and brave
They might appeare, when he their soules shall save.
The wondrous workmanship of Gods owne mould,
Whose face he made all beastes to feare, and gave
All in his hand, even dead we honour should.
Ah, dearest God, me graunt, I dead be not defould!

XLIII. The seventh, now after death and buriall done,
Had charge the tender Orphans of the dead
And wydowes ayd, least they should be undone:

In face of judgement he their right would plead,
Ne ought the powre of mighty men did dread
In their defence; nor would for gold or fee
Be wonne their rightfull causes downe to tread;
And, when they stood in most necessitee,
He did supply their want, and gave them ever free.

XLIV. There when the Elfin knight arrived was,
The first and chiefest of the seven, whose care
Was guests to welcome, towardes him did pas;
Where seeing Mercie, that his steps upbare
And alwaies led, to her with reverence rare
He humbly louted in meeke lowlinesse,
And seemely welcome for her did prepare:
For of their order she was Patronesse,
Albe Charissa were their chiefest founderesse.

XLV. There she awhile him stayes, himselfe to rest,
That to the rest more hable he might bee;
During which time, in every good behest,
And godly worke of Almes and charitee,
Shee him instructed with great industree.
Shortly therein so perfect he became,
That, from the first unto the last degree,
His mortall life he learned had to frame
In holy righteousnesse, without rebuke or blame.

XLVI. Thence forward by that painfull way they pas
Forth to an hill that was both steepe and hy,
On top whereof a sacred chappell was,
And eke a litle Hermitage thereby,
Wherein an aged holy man did lie,
That day and night said his devotion,
Ne other worldly business did apply:
His name was hevenly Contemplation;
Of God and goodnes was his meditation.

XLVII. Great grace that old man to him given had;
For God he often saw from heavens hight:
All were his earthly eien both blunt and bad,
And through great age had lost their kindly sight,
Yet wondrous quick and persaunt was his spright,
As Eagles eie that can behold the Sunne.

That hill they scale with all their powre and might,
That his fraile thighes, nigh weary and fordonne,
Gan faile; but by her helpe the top at last he wonne.

XLVIII. There they doe finde that godly aged Sire,
With snowy lockes adowne his shoulders shed;
As hoary frost with spangles doth attire
The mossy braunches of an Oke halfe ded.
Each bone might through his body well be red
And every sinew seene, through his long fast:
For nought he car'd his carcas long unfed;
His mind was full of spirituall repast,
And pyn'd his flesh to keepe his body low and chast.

XLIX. Who, when these two approching he aspide,
At their first presence grew agrieved sore,
That forst him lay his hevenly thoughts aside;
And had he not that Dame respected more,
Whom highly he did reverence and adore,
He would not once have moved for the knight.
They him saluted, standing far afore,
Who, well them greeting, humbly did requight,
And asked to what end they clomb that tedious hight?

L. " What end," (quoth she) "should cause us take such paine,
But that same end, which every living wight
Should make his marke high heaven to attaine?
Is not from hence the way, that leadeth right
To that most glorious house, that glistreth bright
With burning starres and everliving fire,
Whereof the keies are to thy hand behight
By wise Fidelia?   Shee doth thee require,
To shew it to this knight, according his desire."

LI. " Thrise happy man," said then the father grave,
" Whose staggering steps thy steady hand doth lead,
And shewes the way his sinfull soule to save!
Who better can the way to heaven aread
Then thou thyselfe, that was both borne and bred
In hevenly throne, where thousand Angels shine?
Thou doest the praiers of the righteous sead
Present before the majesty divine,
And his avenging wrath to clemency incline.

LII. " Yet, since thou bidst, thy pleasure shalbe donne.
    Then come, thou man of earth, and see the way,
    That never yet was seene of Faeries sonne;
    That never leads the traveiler astray,
    But after labors long and sad delay,
    Brings them to joyous rest and endlesse blis.
    But first thou must a season fast and pray,
    Till from her hands the spright assoiled is,
    And have her strength recur'd from fraile infirmitis.

LIII. " That done, he leads him to the highest Mount,
    Such one as that same mighty man of God,
    That blood-red billowes, like a walled front,
    On either side disparted with his rod,
    Till that his army dry-foot through them yod,
    Dwelt forty daies upon; where, writt in stone
    With bloody letters by the hand of God,
    The bitter doome of death and balefull mone
    He did receive, whiles flashing fire about him shone:

LIV. Or like that sacred hill, whose head full hie,
    Adornd with fruitfull Olives all arownd,
    Is, as it were for endlesse memory
    Of that deare Lord who oft thereon was fownd,
    For ever with a flowring girlond crownd:
    Or like that pleasaunt Mount, that is for ay
    Through famous Poets verse each where renownd,
    On which the thrise three learned Ladies play
    Their hevenly notes, and make full many a lovely lay.

LV. From thence, far off he unto him did shew
    A little path that was both steepe and long,
    Which to a goodly Citty led his vew,
    Whose wals and towres were builded high and strong
    Of perle and precious stone, that earthly tong
    Cannot describe, nor wit of man can tell;
    Too high a ditty for my simple song.
    The Citty of the greate king hight it well,
    Wherein eternall peace and happinesse doth dwell.

LVI. As he thereon stood gazing, he might see
    The blessed Angels to and fro descend
    From highest heven in gladsome companee,

And with great joy into that Citty wend,
As commonly as frend does with his friend.
Whereat he wondred much, and gan enquere,
What stately building durst so high extend
Her lofty towres unto the starry sphere,
And what unknowen nation there empeopled were?

LVII. " Faire Knight," (quoth he) " Hierusalem that is,
The new Hierusalem, that God has built
For those to dwell in that are chosen his,
His chosen people, purg'd from sinful guilt
With pretious blood, which cruelly was spilt
On cursed tree, of that unspotted lam,
That for the sinnes of al the world was kilt:
Now are they Saints all in that Citty sam,
More dear unto their God then younglings to their dam."

LVIII. " Till now," said then the knight, " I weened well,
That great Cleopolis, where I have beene,
In which that fairest Faery Queene doth dwell,
The fairest city was that might be seene;
And that bright towre, all built of christall clene,
Panthea, seemd the brightest thing that was;
But now by proofe all otherwise I weene,
For this great Citty that does far surpas,
And this bright Angels towre quite dims that towre of glas."

LIX. " Most trew," then said the holy aged man;
" Yet is Cleopolis, for earthly frame,
The fairest peece that eie beholden can;
And well beseemes all knights of noble name,
That covett in th' immortall booke of fame
To be eternized, that same to haunt,
And doen their service to that soveraigne Dame,
That glory does to them for guerdon graunt:
For she is hevenly borne, and heaven may justly vaunt.

LX. " And thou, faire ymp, sprong out from English race,
How ever now accompted Elfins sonne,
Well worthy doest thy service for her grace,
To aide a virgin desolate, foredonne;
But when thou famous victory hast wonne,
And high emongst all knights hast hong thy shield,

Thenceforth the suitt of earthly conquest shonne,
And wash thy hands from guilt of bloody field:
For blood can nought but sin, and wars but sorrows yield.

LXI. " Then seek this path that I to thee presage,
Which after all to heaven shall thee send;
Then peaceably thy painefull pilgrimage
To yonder same Hierusalem doe bend,
Where is for thee ordaind a blessed end:
For thou, emongst those Saints whom thou doest see,
Shalt be a Saint, and thine owne nations frend
And Patrone: thou *Saint George* shalt called bee,
Saint George of mery *England*, the signe of victoree."

LXII. " Unworthy wretch," (quoth he) " of so great grace,
How dare I thinke such glory to attaine? "
" These, that have it attaynd, were in like cace,
As wretched men, and lived in like paine."
" But deeds of armes must I at last be faine
And Ladies love to leave, so dearely bought? "
" What need of armes, where peace doth ay remaine,"
(Said he) " and bitter battailes all are fought?
As for loose loves, they'are vaine, and vanish into nought."

LXIII. " O! let me not," (quoth he) " then turne againe
Backe to the world, whose joyes so fruitlesse are;
But let me heare for aie in peace remaine,
Or streightway on that last long voiage fare,
That nothing may my present hope empare."
" That may not be," (said he) " ne maist thou yitt
Forgoe that royal maides bequeathed care,
Who did her cause into thy hand committ,
Till from her cursed foe thou have her freely quitt."

LXIV. " Then shall I soone," (quoth he) " so God me grace,
Abett that virgins cause disconsolate,
And shortly back returne unto this place,
To walke this way in Pilgrims poore estate.
But now aread, old father, why of late
Didst thou behight me borne of English blood,
Whom all a Faeries sonne doen nominate? "
" That word shall I," (said he) " avouchen good,
Sith to thee is unknowne the cradle of thy brood.

LXV. " For, well I wote, thou springst from ancient race
Of Saxon kinges, that have with mightie hand,
And many bloody battailes fought in face,
High reard their royall throne in Britans land,
And vanquisht them, unable to withstand:
From thence a Faery thee unweeting reft,
There as thou slepst in tender swadling band,
And her base Elfin brood there for thee left:
Such, men do Chaungelings call, so chaung'd by Faeries
theft.

LXVI. " Thence she thee brought into this Faery lond,
And in an heaped furrow did thee hyde;
Where thee a Ploughman all unweeting fond,
As he his toylesome teme that way did guyde,
And brought thee up in ploughmans state to byde,
Whereof Georgos he thee gave to name;
Till prickt with courage, and thy forces pryde,
To Faery court thou cam'st to seek for fame,
And prove thy puissant armes, as seemes thee best became."

LXVII. " O holy Sire! " (quoth he) " how shall I quight
The many favours I with thee have fownd,
That hast my name and nation redd aright,
And taught the way that does to heaven bownd! "
This saide, adowne he looked to the grownd
To have returnd; but dazed were his eyne
Through passing brightnes, which did quite confound
His feeble sence, and too exceeding shyne.
So darke are earthly thinges compard to things divine.

LXVIII. At last, whenas himselfe he gan to fynd,
To Una back he cast him to retyre,
Who him awaited still with pensive mynd.
Great thankes, and goodly meed, to that good syre
He thens departing gave for his paynes hyre
So came to Una, who him joyd to see;
And, after litle rest, gan him desyre
Of her adventure myndfull for to bee.
So leave they take of Cælia and her daughters three.

CANTO XI

The knight with that old Dragon fights
Two days incessantly:
The third him overthrowes, and gayns
Most glorious victory.

I. HIGH time now gan it wex for Una fayre
  To thinke of those her captive Parents deare,
  And their forwasted kingdom to repayre:
  Whereto whenas they now approched neare,
  With hartie wordes her knight she gan to cheare,
  And in her modest maner thus bespake:
  " Deare knight, as deare as ever knight was deare,
  That all these sorrowes suffer for my sake,
  High heven behold the tedious toyle ye for me take!

II. " Now are we come unto my native soyle,
  And to the place where all our perilles dwell;
  Here hauntes that feend, and does his dayly spoyle;
  Therefore, henceforth, bee at your keeping well,
  And ever ready for your foeman fell:
  The sparke of noble corage now awake,
  And strive your excellent selfe to excell:
  That shall ye evermore renowmed make
  Above all knights on earth, that batteill undertake."

III. And pointing forth, " Lo! yonder is," (said she)
  " The brasen towre, in which my parents deare
  For dread of that huge feend emprisond be;
  Whom I from far see on the walles appeare,
  Whose sight my feeble soule doth greatly cheare:
  And on the top of all I do espye
  The watchman wayting tydings glad to heare;
  That, (O my Parents!) might I happily
  Unto you bring, to ease you of your misery."

IV. With that they heard a roaring hideous sownd,
  That all the ayre with terror filled wyde,
  And seemd uneath to shake the stedfast ground.

Eftsoones that dreadful Dragon they espyde,
Where stretcht he lay upon the sunny side
Of a great hill, himselfe like a great hill:
But, all so soone as he from far descryde
Those glistring armes that heven with light did fill,
He rousd himselfe full blyth, and hastned them untill.

v. Then badd the knight his Lady yede aloof,
And to an hill herselfe withdraw asyde;
From whence she might behold that battailles proof,
And eke be safe from daunger far descryde.
She him obayd, and turned a little wyde.—
Now, O thou sacred Muse! most learned Dame,
Fayre ympe of Phœbus and his aged bryde,
The Nourse of time and everlasting fame,
That warlike handes ennoblest with immortall name;

vi. O! gently come into my feeble brest;
Come gently, but not with that mightie rage,
Wherewith the martiall troupes thou doest infest,
And hartes of great Heroës doest enrage,
That nought their kindled corage may aswage:
Soone as thy dreadfull trompe begins to sownd,
The God of warre with his fiers equipage
Thou doest awake, sleepe never he so sownd;
And scared nations doest with horror sterne astownd.

vii. Fayre Goddesse, lay that furious fitt asyde,
Till I of warres and bloody Mars doe sing,
And Bryton fieldes with Sarazin blood bedyde,
Twixt that great faery Queene and Paynim king,
That with their horror heven and earth did ring;
A worke of labour long, and endlesse prayse:
But now a while lett downe that haughtie string,
And to my tunes thy second tenor rayse,
That I this man of God his godly armes may blaze.

viii. By this, the dreadful Beast drew nigh to hand,
Halfe flying and halfe footing in his haste,
That with his largenesse measured much land,
And made wide shadow under his huge waste,
As mountaine doth the valley overcaste.
Approching nigh, he reared high afore

His body monstrous, horrible, and vaste;
Which, to increase his wondrous greatnes more,
Was swoln with wrath and poyson, and with bloody gore;

IX. And over all with brasen scales was armd,
  Like plated cote of steele, so couched neare
  That nought mote perce; ne might his corse bee harmd
  With dint of swerd, nor push of pointed speare:
  Which as an Eagle, seeing pray appeare,
  His aery plumes doth rouze, full rudely dight;
  So shaked he, that horror was to heare:
  For as the clashing of an Armor bright,
  Such noyse his rouzed scales did send unto the knight.

X. His flaggy winges, when forth he did display,
  Were like two sayles, in which the hollow wynd
  Is gathered full, and worketh speedy way:
  And eke the pennes, that did his pineons bynd,
  Were like mayne-yardes with flying canvas lynd;
  With which whenas him list the ayre to beat,
  And there by force unwonted passage fynd,
  The cloudes before him fledd for terror great,
  And all the hevens stood still amazed with his threat.

XI. His huge long tayle, wownd up in hundred foldes,
  Does overspred his long bras-scaly back,
  Whose wreathed boughtes when ever he unfoldes,
  And thick entangled knots adown does slack,
  Bespotted as with shieldes of red and blacke,
  It sweepeth all the land behind him farre,
  And of three furlongs does but litle lacke;
  And at the point two stinges in fixed arre,
  Both deadly sharp, that sharpest steele exceeden farre.

XII. But stinges and sharpest steele did far exceed
  The sharpnesse of his cruel rending clawes:
  Dead was it sure, as sure as death in deed,
  What ever thing does touch his ravenous pawes,
  Or what within his reach he ever drawes.
  But his most hideous head my tongue to tell
  Does tremble; for his deepe devouring jawes
  Wyde gaped, like the griesly mouth of hell.
  Through which into his darke abysse all ravin fell.

XIII. And, that more wondrous was, in either jaw
Threeranckes of yron teeth enraunged were,
In which yett trickling blood, and gobbets raw,
Of late devoured bodies did appeare,
That sight thereof bredd cold congealed feare;
Which to increase, and all atonce to kill,
A cloud of smoothering smoke, and sulphure seare,
Out of his stinking gorge forth steemed still,
That all the ayre about with smoke and stench did fill.

XIV. His blazing eyes, like two bright shining shieldes,
Did burne with wrath, and sparkled living fyre:
As two broad Beacons, sett in open fieldes,
Send forth their flames far off to every shyre,
And warning give that enimies conspyre
With fire and sword the region to invade:
So flam'd his eyne with rage and rancorous yre;
But far within, as in a hollow glade,
Those glaring lampes were sett that made a dreadfull shade.

XV. So dreadfully he towardes him did pas,
Forelifting up a-loft his speckled brest,
And often bounding on the brused gras,
As for great joyance of his newcome guest.
Eftsoones he gan advance his haughty crest,
As chauffed Bore his bristles doth upreare;
And shoke his scales to battaile ready drest,
That made the Redcrosse knight nigh quake for feare,
As bidding bold defyaunce to his foeman neare.

XVI. The knight gan fayrely couch his steady speare,
And fiersely ran at him with rigorous might:
The pointed steele, arriving rudely theare,
His harder hyde would nether perce nor bight,
But, glauncing by, foorth passed forward right.
Yet sore amoved with so puissaunt push,
The wrathfull beast about him turned light,
And him so rudely, passing by, did brush
With his long tayle, that horse and man to ground did rush.

XVII. Both horse and man up lightly rose againe,
And fresh encounter towardes him addrest;
But th' ydle stroke yet backe recoyld in vaine,

And found no place his deadly point to rest.
Exceeding rage enflam'd the furious Beast,
To be avenged of so great despight;
For never felt his imperceable brest
So wondrous force from hand of living wight;
Yet had he prov'd the powre of many a puissant knight.

XVIII. Then, with his waving wings displayed wyde,
Himselfe up high he lifted from the ground,
And with strong flight did forcibly divyde
The yielding ayre, which nigh too feeble found
Her flitting parts, and element unsound,
To beare so great a weight: he, cutting way
With his broad sayles, about him soared round;
At last, low stouping with unweldy sway,
Snatcht up both horse and man, to beare them quite away.

XIX. Long he them bore above the subject plaine,
So far as Ewghen bow a shaft may send,
Till struggling strong did him at last constraine
To let them downe before his flightes end:
As hagard hauke, presuming to contend
With hardy fowle above his hable might,
His wearie pounces all in vaine doth spend
To trusse the pray too heavy for his flight;
Which, comming down to ground, does free it selfe by fight.

XX. He so disseized of his gryping grosse,
The knight his thrillant speare againe assayd
In his bras-plated body to embosse,
And three mens strength unto the stroake he layd;
Wherewith the stiffe beame quaked as affrayd,
And glauncing from his scaly necke did glyde
Close under his left wing, then broad displayd:
The percing steele there wrought a wound full wyde,
That with the uncouth smart the Monster lowdly cryde.

XXI. He cryde, as raging seas are wont to rore
When wintry storme his wrathful wreck does threat;
The rolling billowes beate the ragged shore,
As they the earth would shoulder from her seat;
And greedy gulfe does gape, as he would eat
His neighbour element in his revenge:

Then gin the blustring brethren boldly threat
To move the world from off his stedfast henge,
And boystrous battaile make, each other to avenge.

XXII. The steely head stuck fast still in his flesh,
Till with his cruell clawes he snatcht the wood,
And quite a sunder broke.   Forth flowed fresh
A gushing river of blacke gory blood,
That drowned all the land whereon he stood;
The streame thereof would drive a water-mill:
Trebly augmented was his furious mood
With bitter sence of his deepe rooted ill,
That flames of fire he threw forth from his large nosethril

XXIII. His hideous tayle then hurled he about,
And therewith all enwrapt the nimble thyes
Of his froth-fomy steed, whose courage stout
Striving to loose the knott that fast him tyes,
Himselfe in streighter bandes too rash implyes,
That to the ground he is perforce constraynd
To throw his ryder; who can quickly ryse
From off the earth, with durty blood distaynd,
For that reprochfull fall right fowly he disdaynd;

XXIV. And fercely tooke his trenchand blade in hand,
With which he stroke so furious and so fell,
That nothing seemd the puissaunce could withstand:
Upon his crest the hardned yron fell,
But his more hardned crest was armd so well,
That deeper dint therein it would not make;
Yet so extremely did the buffe him quell,
That from thenceforth he shund the like to take,
But when he saw them come he did them still forsake.

XXV. The knight was wroth to see his stroke beguyld,
And smot againe with more outrageous might;
But backe againe the sparcling steele recoyld,
And left not any marke where it did light,
As if in Adamant rocke it had beene pight.
The beast, impatient of his smarting wound
And of so fierce and forcible despight,
Thought with his winges to stye above the ground;
But his late wounded wing unserviceable found.

XXVI. Then full of griefe and anguish vehement,
       He lowdly brayd, that like was never heard;
       And from his wide devouring oven sent
       A flake of fire, that flashing in his beard
       Him all amazd, and almost made afeard:
       The scorching flame sore swinged all his face,
       And through his armour all his body seard,
       That he could not endure so cruell cace,
       But thought his armes to leave, and helmet to unlace.

XXVII. Not that great Champion of the antique world,
       Whom famous Poetes verse so much doth vaunt,
       And hath for twelve huge labours high extold,
       So many furies and sharpe fits did haunt,
       When him the poysoned garment did enchaunt,
       When Centaures blood and bloody verses charmd;
       As did this knight twelve thousand dolours daunt,
       Whom fyrie steele now burnt, that erst him armd;
       That erst him goodly armd, now most of all him harmd.

XXVIII. Faynt, wearie, sore, emboyled, grieved, brent,
       With heat, toyle, wounds, armes, smart, and inward fire,
       That never man such mischiefes did torment:
       Death better were; death did he oft desire,
       But death will never come when needes require.
       Whom so dismayd when that his foe beheld,
       He cast to suffer him no more respire,
       But gan his sturdy sterne about to weld,
       And him so strongly stroke, that to the ground him feld.

XXIX. It fortuned, (as fayre it then befell)
       Behynd his backe, unweeting, where he stood,
       Of auncient time there was a springing well,
       From which fast trickled forth a silver flood,
       Full of great vertues, and for med'cine good:
       Whylome, before that cursed Dragon got
       That happy land, and all with innocent blood
       Defyld those sacred waves, it rightly hot
       The well of life, ne yet his vertues had forgot:

XXX.   For unto life the dead it could restore,
       And guilt of sinfull crimes cleane wash away;
       Those that with sicknesse were infected sore

It could recure; and aged long decay
Renew, as one were borne that very day.
Both Silo this, and Jordan, did excell,
And th' English Bath, and eke the German Spau;
Ne can Cephise, nor Hebrus, match this well:
Into the same the knight back overthrowen fell.

XXXI. Now gan the golden Phœbus for to steepe
His fierie face in billowes of the west,
And his faint steedes watred in Ocean deepe,
Whiles from their journall labours they did rest;
When that infernall Monster, having kest
His wearie foe into that living well,
Gan high advaunce his broad discoloured brest
Above his wonted pitch, with countenance fell,
And clapt his yron wings as victor he did dwell.

XXXII. Which when his pensive Lady saw from farre,
Great woe and sorrow did her soule assay,
As weening that the sad end of the warre;
And gan to highest God entirely pray
That feared chaunce from her to turne away:
With folded hands, and knees full lowly bent,
All night shee watcht, ne once adowne would lay
Her dainty limbs in her sad dreriment,
But praying still did wake, and waking did lament.

XXXIII. The morrow next gan earely to appeare,
That Titan rose to runne his daily race;
But earely, ere the morrow next gan reare
Out of the sea faire Titans deawy face,
Up rose the gentle virgin from her place,
And looked all about, if she might spy
Her loved knight to move his manly pace:
For she had great doubt of his safety,
Since late she saw him fall before his enimy.

XXXIV. At last she saw where he upstarted brave
Out of the well, wherein he drenched lay:
As Eagle, fresh out of the ocean wave,
Where he hath lefte his plumes all hory gray,
And deckt himselfe with fethers youthly gay,
Like Eyas hauke up mounts unto the skies,

His newly-budded pineons to assay,
And marveiles at himselfe stil as he flies:
So new this new-borne knight to battell new did rise.

xxxv. Whom when the damned feend so fresh did spy
No wonder if he wondred at the sight,
And doubted whether his late enimy
It were, or other new supplied knight.
He now, to prove his late-renewed might,
High brandishing his bright deaw-burning blade,
Upon his crested scalp so sore did smite,
That to the scull a yawning wound it made:
The deadly dint his dulled sences all dismaid.

xxxvi. I wote not whether the revenging steele
Were hardned with that holy water dew
Wherein he fell, or sharper edge did feele,
Or his baptized hands now greater grew,
Or other secret vertue did ensew;
Els never could the force of fleshly arme,
Ne molten mettall, in his blood embrew;
For till that stownd could never wight him harme
By subtilty, nor slight, nor might, nor mighty charme.

xxxvii. The cruell wound enraged him so sore,
That loud he yelled for exceeding paine;
As hundred ramping Lions seemd to rore,
Whom ravenous hunger did thereto constraine:
Then gan he tosse aloft his stretched traine,
And therewith scourge the buxome aire so sore,
That to his force to yielden it was faine;
Ne ought his sturdy strokes might stand afore,
That high trees overthrew, and rocks in peeces tore.

xxxviii. The same advauncing high above his head,
With sharpe intended sting so rude him smott,
That to the earth him drove, as stricken dead;
Ne living wight would have him life behott:
The mortall sting his angry needle shott
Quite through his shield, and in his shoulder seasd,
Where fast it stucke, ne would thereout be gott:
The griefe thereof him wondrous sore diseasd,
Ne might his rancling paine with patience be appeasd.

XXXIX. But yet, more mindfull of his honour deare
Then of the grievous smart which him did wring,
From loathed soile he can him lightly reare,
And strove to loose the far infixed sting:
Which when in vaine he tryde with struggeling,
Inflam'd with wrath, his raging blade he hefte,
And strooke so strongly, that the knotty string
Of his huge taile he quite a sonder clefte;
Five joints thereof he hewd, and but the stump him lefte.

XL. Hart cannot thinke what outrage and what cries,
With fowle enfouldred smoake and flashing fire,
The hell-bred beast threw forth unto the skies,
That all was covered with darknesse dire:
Then, fraught with rancour and engorged yre,
He cast at once him to avenge for all,
And, gathering up himselfe out of the mire
With his uneven wings, did fiercely fall
Upon his sunne-bright shield, and grypt it fast withall.

XLI. Much was the man encombred with his hold,
In feare to lose his weapon in his paw,
Ne wist yett how his talaunts to unfold;
Nor harder was from Cerberus greedy jaw
To plucke a bone, then from his cruell claw
To reave by strength the griped gage away:
Thrise he assayd it from his foote to draw,
And thrise in vaine to draw it did assay;
It booted nought to thinke to robbe him of his pray.

XLII. Tho, when he saw no power might prevaile,
His trusty sword he cald to his last aid,
Wherewith he fiersly did his foe assaile,
And double blowes about him stoutly laid,
That glauncing fire out of the yron plaid,
As sparkles from the Andvile use to fly,
When heavy hammers on the wedge are swaid:
Therewith at last he forst him to unty
One of his grasping feete, him to defend thereby,

XLIII. The other foote, fast fixed on his shield,
Whenas no strength nor stroks mote him constraine
To loose, ne yet the warlike pledge to yield,

He smott thereat with all his might and maine,
That nought so wondrous puissance might sustaine:
Upon the joint the lucky steele did light,
And made such way that hewd it quite in twaine;
The paw yett missed not his minisht might,
But hong still on the shield, as it at first was pight.

XLIV. For griefe thereof and divelish despight,
From his infernall fournace forth he threw
Huge flames that dimmed all the hevens light,
Enrold in duskish smoke and brimstone blew:
As burning Aetna from his boyling stew
Doth belch out flames, and rockes in peeces broke,
And ragged ribs of mountaines molten new,
Enwrapt in coleblacke clowds and filthy smoke,
That al the land with stench and heven with horror choke.

XLV. The heate whereof, and harmefull pestilence,
So sore him noyd, that forst him to retire
A little backeward for his best defence,
To save his body from the scorching fire,
Which he from hellish entrailes did expire.
It chaunst, (eternall God that chaunce did guide)
As he recoiled backeward, in the mire
His nigh foreweried feeble feet did slide,
And downe he fell, with dread of shame sore terrifide.

XLVI. There grew a goodly tree him faire beside,
Loaden with fruit and apples rosy redd,
As they in pure vermilion had been dide,
Whereof great vertues over-all were redd;
For happy life to all which thereon fedd,
And life eke everlasting did befall:
Great God it planted in that blessed stedd
With his Almighty hand, and did it call
The tree of life, the crime of our first fathers fall.

XLVII. In all the world like was not to be fownd,
Save in that soile, where all good things did grow,
And freely sprong out of the fruitfull grownd,
As incorrupted Nature did them sow,
Till that dredd Dragon all did overthrow.
Another like faire tree eke grew thereby,

Whereof whoso did eat, eftsoones did know
Both good and ill. O mournfull memory!
That tree through one mans fault hath doen us all to dy.

XLVIII. From that first tree forth flowd, as from a well,
A trickling streame of Balme, most soveraine
And dainty deare, which on the ground still fell,
And overflowed all the fertile plaine,
As it had deawed bene with timely raine:
Life and long health that gracious ointment gave,
And deadly wounds could heale, and reare againe
The sencelesse corse appointed for the grave:
Into that same he fell, which did from death him save.

XLIX. For nigh thereto the ever damned Beast
Durst not approch, for he was deadly made,
And al that life preserved did detest;
Yet he it oft adventur'd to invade.
By this the drouping day-light gan to fade,
And yield his rowme to sad succeeding night,
Who with her sable mantle gan to shade
The face of earth and wayes of living wight,
And high her burning torch set up in heaven bright.

L. When gentle Una saw the second fall
Of her deare knight, who, weary of long fight
And faint through losse of blood, moov'd not at all,
But lay, as in a dreame of deepe delight,
Besmeard with pretious Balme, whose vertuous might
Did heale his woundes, and scorching heat alay;
Againe she stricken was with sore affright,
And for his safetie gan devoutly pray,
And watch the noyous night, and wait for joyous day.

LI. The joyous day gan early to appeare;
And fayre Aurora from the deawy bed
Of aged Tithone gan herselfe to reare
With rosy cheekes, for shame as blushing red:
Her golden locks for hast were loosely shed
About her eares, when Una her did marke
Clymbe to her charet, all with flowers spred,
From heven high to chace the chearelesse darke;
With mery note her lowd salutes the mounting larke.

LII. Then freshly up arose the doughty knight,
All healed of his hurts and woundes wide,
And did himselfe to battaile ready dight;
Whose early foe awaiting him beside
To have devourd, so soone as day he spyde,
When now he saw himselfe so freshly reare,
As if late fight had nought him damnifyde,
He woxe dismaid, and gan his fate to feare:
Nathlesse with wonted rage he him advaunced neare.

LIII. And in his first encounter, gaping wyde,
He thought attonce him to have swallowd quight,
And rusht upon him with outragious pryde;
Who him rencountring fierce, as hauke in flight,
Perforce rebutted backe.   The weapon bright,
Taking advantage of his open jaw,
Ran through his mouth with so importune might,
That deepe emperst his darksom hollow maw,
And, back retyrd, his life blood forth with all did draw.

LIV. So downe he fell, and forth his life did breath,
That vanisht into smoke and cloudes swift;
So downe he fell, that th' earth him underneath
Did grone, as feeble so great load to lift;
So downe he fell, as an huge rocky clift,
Whose false foundacion waves have washt away,
With dreadfull poyse is from the mayneland rift,
And rolling downe great Neptune doth dismay:
So downe he fell, and like an heaped mountaine lay.

LV. The knight him selfe even trembled at his fall,
So huge and horrible a masse it seemd;
And his deare Lady, that beheld it all,
Durst not approch for dread which she misdeemd;
But yet at last, whenas the direfull feend
She saw not stirre, off-shaking vaine affright
She nigher drew, and saw that joyous end:
Then God she praysd, and thankt her faithfull knight,
That had atchievde so great a conquest by his might.

CANTO XII

Fayre Una to the Redcrosse Knight
Betrouthed is with joy:
Though false Duessa, it to barre,
Her false sleightes doe imploy.

I. Behold! I see the haven nigh at hand
To which I meane my wearie course to bend;
Vere the maine shete, and beare up with the land,
To which afore is fayrly to be kend,
And seemeth safe from storms that may offend;
There this fayre virgin wearie of her way
Must landed bee, now at her journeyes end;
There eke my feeble barke a while may stay,
Till mery wynd and weather call her thence away.

II. Scarsely had Phœbus in the glooming East
Yett harnessed his fyrie-footed teeme,
Ne reard above the earth his flaming creast,
When the last deadly smoke aloft did steeme,
That signe of last outbreathed life did seeme
Unto the watchman on the castle-wall;
Who thereby dead that balefull Beast did deeme,
And to his Lord and Lady lowd gan call,
To tell how he had seene the Dragons fatall fall.

III. Uprose with hasty joy, and feeble speed,
That aged Syre, the Lord of all that land,
And looked forth, to weet if trew indeed
Those tydinges were, as he did understand:
Which whenas trew by tryall he out fond,
He badd to open wyde his brasen gate,
Which long time had beene shut, and out of hond
Proclaymed joy and peace through all his state;
For dead now was their foe, which them forrayed late.

IV. Then gan triumphant Trompets sownd on hye,
That sent to heven the ecchoed report
Of their new joy, and happie victory

Gainst him, that had them long opprest with tort,
And fast imprisoned in sieged fort.
Then all the people, as in solemne feast,
To him assembled with one full consort,
Rejoycing at the fall of that great beast,
From whose eternall bondage now thy were releast.

v. Forth came that auncient Lord, and aged Queene,
Arayd in antique robes downe to the grownd,
And sad habiliments right well beseene:
A noble crew about them waited rownd
Of sage and sober peres, all gravely gownd;
Whom far before did march a goodly band
Of tall young men, all hable armes to sownd;
But now they laurell braunches bore in hand,
Glad signe of victory and peace in all their land.

vi. Unto that doughtie Conquerour they came,
And him before themselves prostrating low,
Their Lord and Patrone loud did him proclame,
And at his feet their lawrell boughes did throw.
Soone after them, all dauncing on a row,
The comely virgins came, with girlands dight,
As fresh as flowres in medow greene doe grow
When morning deaw upon their leaves doth light;
And in their handes sweet Timbrels all upheld on hight.

vii. And them before the fry of children yong
Their wanton sportes and childish mirth did play,
And to the Maydens sownding tymbrels song
In well attuned notes a joyous lay,
And made delightfull musick all the way,
Untill they came where that faire virgin stood:
As fayre Diana in fresh sommers day
Beholdes her nymphes enraung'd in shady wood,
Some wrestle, some do run, some bathe in christall flood.

viii. So she beheld those maydens meriment
With chearefull vew; who, when to her they came,
Themselves to ground with gracious humblesse bent,
And her ador'd by honorable name,
Lifting to heven her everlasting fame:
Then on her head they sett a girlond greene,

And crowned her twixt earnest and twixt game:
Who, in her self-resemblance well beseene,
Did seeme, such as she was, a goodly maiden Queene.

IX. And after all the raskall many ran,
Heaped together in rude rablement,
To see the face of that victorious man,
Whom all admired as from heaven sent,
And gazd upon with gaping wonderment;
But when they came where that dead Dragon lay,
Stretcht on the ground in monstrous large extent,
The sight with ydle feare did them dismay,
Ne durst approch him nigh to touch, or once assay.

X. Some feard, and fledd; some feard, and well it faynd;
One, that would wiser seeme then all the rest,
Warnd him not touch, for yet perhaps remaynd
Some lingring life within his hollow brest,
Or in his wombe might lurke some hidden nest
Of many Dragonettes, his fruitfull seede:
Another saide, that in his eyes did rest
Yet sparckling fyre, and badd thereof take heed;
Another said, he saw him move his eyes indeed.

XI. One mother, whenas her foolehardy chyld
Did come too neare, and with his talants play,
Halfe dead through feare, her litle babe revyld,
And to her gossibs gan in counsell say;
"How can I tell, but that his talants may
Yet scratch my sonne, or rend his tender hand?"
So diversly them selves in vaine they fray;
Whiles some more bold to measure him nigh stand,
To prove how many acres he did spred of land.

XII. Thus flocked all the folke him rownd about;
The whiles that hoarie king, with all his traine,
Being arrived where that champion stout
After his foes defeasaunce did remaine,
Him goodly greetes, and fayre does entertayne
With princely gifts of yvory and gold,
And thousand thankes him yeeldes for all his paine.
Then when his daughter deare he does behold,
Her dearely doth imbrace, and kisseth manifold.

xiii. And after to his Pallace he them bringes,
With shaumes, and trompets, and with Clarions sweet;
And all the way the joyous people singes,
And with their garments strowes the paved street;
Whence mounting up, they fynd purveyaunce meet
Of all, that royall Princes court became;
And all the floore was underneath their feet
Bespredd with costly scarlott of great name,
On which they lowly sitt, and fitting purpose frame.

xiv. What needes me tell their feast and goodly guize,
In which was nothing riotous nor vaine?
What needes of dainty dishes to devize,
Of comely services, or courtly trayne?
My narrow leaves cannot in them contayne
The large discourse of roiall Princes state.
Yet was their manner then but bare and playne;
For th' antique world excesse and pryde did hate:
Such proud luxurious pompe is swollen up but late.

xv. Then, when with meates and drinkes of every kinde
Their fervent appetites they quenched had,
That auncient Lord gan fit occasion finde,
Of straunge adventures, and of perils sad
Which in his travell him befallen had,
For to demaund of his renowmed guest:
Who then with utt'rance grave, and count'nance sad,
From poynt to poynt, as is before exprest,
Discourst his voyage long, according his request.

xvi. Great pleasure, mixt with pittiful regard,
That godly King and Queene did passionate,
Whyles they his pittifull adventures heard;
That oft they did lament his lucklesse state,
And often blame the too importune fate
That heapd on him so many wrathfull wreakes;
For never gentle knight, as he of late,
So tossed was in fortunes cruell freakes:
And all the while salt teares bedeawd the hearers cheaks.

xvii. Then sayd that royall Pere in sober wise;
" Deare Sonne, great beene the evils which ye bore
From first to last in your late enterprise,

That I note whether praise or pitty more;
For never living man, I weene, so sore
In sea of deadly daungers was distrest:
But since now safe ye seised have the shore,
And well arrived are, (high God be blest!)
Let us devize of ease and everlasting rest."

XVIII. "Ah dearest Lord!" said then that doughty knight,
"Of ease or rest I may not yet devize;
For by the faith which I to armes have plight,
I bownden am streight after this emprize,
As that your daughter can ye well advize,
Backe to retourne to that great Faery Queene,
And her to serve six yeares in warlike wize,
Gainst that proud Paynim king that works her teene:
Therefore I ought crave pardon, till I there have beene."

XIX. "Unhappy falls that hard necessity,"
(Quoth he) "the troubler of my happy peace,
And vowed foe of my felicity;
Ne I against the same can justly preace:
But since that band ye cannot now release,
Nor doen undo, (for vowes may not be vayne)
Soone as the terme of those six yeares shall cease,
Ye then shall hither backe retourne agayne,
The marriage to accomplish vowd betwixt you twayn.

XX. "Which, for my part, I covet to performe
In sort as through the world I did proclame,
That who-so kild that monster most deforme,
And him in hardy battyle overcame,
Should have mine onely daughter to his Dame,
And of my kingdome heyre apparaunt bee:
Therefore, since now to thee perteynes the same
By dew desert of noble chevalree,
Both daughter and eke kingdome lo! I yield to thee."

XXI. Then forth he called that his daughter fayre,
The fairest Un', his onely daughter deare,
His onely daughter and his only hayre;
Who forth proceeding with sad sober cheare,
As bright as doth the morning starre appeare
Out of the East, with flaming lockes bedight,

To tell that dawning day is drawing neare,
And to the world does bring long-wished light:
So faire and fresh that Lady shewd herselfe in sight.

XXII. So faire and fresh, as freshest flowre in May;
For she had layd her mournefull stole aside,
And widow-like sad wimple throwne away,
Wherewith her heavenly beautie she did hide,
Whiles on her wearie journey she did ride;
And on her now a garment she did weare
All lilly white, withoutten spot or pride,
That seemd like silke and silver woven neare:
But neither silke nor silver therein did appeare.

XXIII. The blazing brightnesse of her beauties beame,
And glorious light of her sunshyny face,
To tell were as to strive against the streame:
My ragged rimes are all too rude and bace
Her heavenly lineaments for to enchace.
Ne wonder; for her own deare loved knight,
All were she daily with himselfe in place,
Did wonder much at her celestiall sight:
Oft had he seene her faire, but never so faire dight.

XXIV. So fairely dight when she in presence came,
She to her Syre made humble reverence,
And bowed low, that her right well became,
And added grace unto her excellence:
Who with great wisedome and grave eloquence
Thus gan to say—But, eare he thus had sayd,
With flying speede, and seeming great pretence,
Came running in, much like a man dismayd,
A Messenger with letters, which his message sayd.

XXV. All in the open hall amazed stood
At suddeinnesse of that unwary sight,
And wondred at his breathlesse hasty mood:
But he for nought would stay his passage right,
Till fast before the king he did alight;
Where falling flat great humblesse he did make,
And kist the ground whereon his foot was pight;
Then to his handes that writt he did betake,
Which he disclosing read thus, as the paper spake:

XXVI. " To thee, most mighty king of Eden fayré,
　　　Her greeting sends in these sad lines addrest
　　　The wofull daughter and forsaken heyre
　　　Of that great Emperour of all the West;
　　　And bids thee be advized for the best,
　　　Ere thou thy daughter linck, in holy band
　　　Of wedlocke, to that new unknowen guest:
　　　For he already plighted his right hand
　　　Unto another love, and to another land.

XXVII. " To me, sad mayd, or rather widow sad,
　　　He was affyaunced long time before,
　　　And sacred pledges he both gave, and had,
　　　False erraunt knight, infamous, and forswore!
　　　Witnesse the burning Altars, which he swore,
　　　And guilty heavens of his bold perjury;
　　　Which though he hath polluted oft of yore,
　　　Yet I to them for judgement just doe fly,
　　　And them conjure t'avenge this shamefull injury.

XXVIII. " Therefore, since mine he is, or free or bond,
　　　Or false, or trew, or living or else dead,
　　　Withhold, O soverayne Prince! your hasty hond
　　　From knitting league with him, I you aread;
　　　Ne weene my right with strength adowne to tread,
　　　Through weaknesse of my widowhed or woe;
　　　For truth is strong her rightfull cause to plead,
　　　And shall finde friends, if need requireth soe.
　　　So bids thee well to fare, Thy neither friend nor foe,
　　　　　Fidessa."

XXIX. When he these bitter byting wordes had red,
　　　The tydings straunge did him abashed make,
　　　That still he sate long time astonished,
　　　As in great muse, ne word to creature spake.
　　　At last his solemn silence thus he brake,
　　　With doubtfull eyes fast fixed on his guest:
　　　" Redoubted knight, that for myne only sake
　　　Thy life and honor late adventurest,
　　　Let nought be hid from me that ought to be exprest.

XXX. " What meane these bloody vowes and idle threats,
　　　Throwne out from womanish impatient mynd?
　　　What hevens? what altars? what enraged heates,

Here heaped up with termes of love unkynd,
My conscience cleare with guilty bands would bynd?
High God be witnesse that I guiltlesse ame;
But if yourselfe, Sir knight, ye faulty fynd,
Or wrapped be in loves of former Dame,
With cryme doe not it cover, but disclose the same."

XXXI. To whom the Redcrosse knight this answere sent:
" My Lord, my king, be nought hereat dismayd,
Till well ye wote by grave intendiment,
What woman, and wherefore, doth me upbrayd
With breach of love and loialty betrayd.
It was in my mishaps, as hitherward
I lately traveild, that unwares I strayd
Out of my way, through perils straunge and hard,
That day should faile me ere I had them all declard.

XXXII. " There did I find, or rather I was fownd
Of this false woman that Fidessa hight,
Fidessa hight the falsest Dame on grownd,
Most false Duessa, royall richly dight,
That easy was t' inveigle weaker sight:
Who by her wicked arts and wylie skill,
Too false and strong for earthly skill or might,
Unwares me wrought unto her wicked will,
And to my foe betrayd when least I feared ill."

XXXIII. Then stepped forth the goodly royall Mayd,
And on the ground herselfe prostrating low,
With sober countenance thus to him sayd:
" O! pardon me, my soveraine Lord, to sheow
The secret treasons, which of late I know
To have bene wrought by that false sorceresse:
Shee, onely she, it is, that earst did throw
This gentle knight into so great distresse,
That death him did awaite in daily wretchednesse.

XXXIV. " And now it seemes, that she suborned hath
This crafty messenger with letters vaine,
To worke new woe and improvided scath,
By breaking of the band betwixt us twaine;
Wherein she used hath the practicke paine
Of this false footman, clokt with simplenesse,

Whome if ye please for to discover plaine,
Ye shall him Archimago find, I ghesse,
The falsest man alive: who tries, shall find no lesse."

xxxv. The king was greatly moved at her speach;
And, all with sudden indignation fraight,
Bad on that Messenger rude hands to reach.
Eftsoones the Gard, which on his state did wait,
Attacht that faytor false, and bound him strait,
Who seeming sorely chauffed at his band,
As chained beare whom cruell dogs doe bait,
With ydle force did faine them to withstand,
And often semblaunce made to scape out of their hand.

xxxvi. But they him layd low in dungeon deepe,
And bound him hand and foote with yron chaines;
And with continual watch did warely keepe.
Who then would thinke that by his subtile traines
He could escape fowle death or deadly pains?
Thus, when that Princes wrath was pacifide,
He gan renew the late forbidden bains,
And to the knight his daughter deare he tyde
With sacred rites and vowes for ever to abyde.

xxxvii. His owne two hands the holy knotts did knitt,
That none but death for ever can divide;
His owne two hands, for such a turne most fitt,
The housling fire did kindle and provide,
And holy water thereon sprinckled wide;
At which the bushy Teade a groome did light,
And sacred lamp in secret chamber hide,
Where it should not be quenched day nor night,
For feare of evil fates, but burnen ever bright.

xxxviii. Then gan they sprinckle all the posts with wine,
And made great feast to solemnize that day:
They all perfumde with frankincense divine,
And precious odours fetcht from far away,
That all the house did sweat with great aray:
And all the while sweete Musicke did apply
Her curious skill the warbling notes to play,
To drive away the dull Melancholy;
The whiles one sung a song of love and jollity.

XXXIX. During the which there was an heavenly noise
  Heard sownd through all the Pallace pleasantly,
  Like as it had bene many an Angels voice
  Singing before th' eternall majesty,
  In their trinall triplicities on hye:
  Yett wist no creature whence that hevenly sweet
  Proceeded, yet each one felt secretly
  Himselfe thereby refte of his sences meet,
  And ravished with rare impression in his sprite.

XL. Great joy was made that day of young and old,
  And solemne feast proclaymd throughout the land,
  That their exceeding merth may not be told:
  Suffice it heare by signes to understand
  The usuall joyes at knitting of loves band.
  Thrise happy man the knight himselfe did hold,
  Possessed of his Ladies hart and hand;
  And ever, when his eie did her behold,
  His heart did seeme to melt in pleasures manifold.

XLI. Her joyous presence, and sweet company,
  In full content he there did long enjoy;
  Ne wicked envy, ne vile gealosy,
  His deare delights were hable to annoy:
  Yet, swimming in that sea of blisfull joy,
  He nought forgott how he whilome had sworne,
  In case he could that monstrous beast destroy,
  Unto his Faery Queene backe to retourne;
  The which he shortly did, and Una left to mourn.

XLII. Now, strike your sailes, yee jolly Mariners,
  For we be come unto a quiet rode,
  Where we must land some of our passengers,
  And light this weary vessell of her lode:
  Here she a while may make her safe abode,
  Till she repaired have her tackles spent,
  And wants supplide; And then againe abroad
  On the long voiage whereto she is bent:
  Well may she speede, and fairely finish her intent!

THE SECOND BOOK

I. RIGHT well I wote, most mighty Soveraine,
   That all this famous antique history
   Of some th' aboundance of an ydle braine
   Will judged be, and painted forgery,
   Rather then matter of just memory;
   Sith none that breatheth living aire does know
   Where is that happy land of Faery,
   Which I so much doe vaunt, yet no where show,
   But vouch antiquities, which no body can know.

II. But let that man with better sence advize,
   That of the world least part to us is red;
   And daily how through hardy enterprize
   Many great Regions are discovered,
   Which to late age were never mentioned.
   Who ever heard of th' Indian Peru?
   Or who in venturous vessell measured
   The Amazon huge river, now found trew?
   Or fruitfullest Virginia who did ever vew?

III. Yet all these were, when no man did them know,
   Yet have from wisest ages hidden beene;
   And later times thinges more unknowne shall show.
   Why then should witlesse man so much misweene,
   That nothing is but that which he hath seene?
   What if within the Moones fayre shining spheare,
   What if in every other starre unseene
   Of other worldes he happily should heare,
   He wonder would much more; yet such to some appeare.

IV. Of faery lond yet if he more inquyre,
   By certain signes, here sett in sondrie place,
   He may it fynd; ne let him then admyre,

But yield his sence to bee too blunt and bace,
That no'te without an hound fine footing trace,
And thou, O fayrest Princesse under sky!
In this fayre mirrhour maist behold thy face,
And thine owne realmes in lond of Faery,
And in this antique ymage thy great auncestry,

v. The which O! pardon me thus to enfold
In covert vele, and wrap in shadowes light,
That feeble eyes your glory may behold,
Which ells could not endure those beames bright,
But would bee dazled with exceeding light.
O! pardon, and vouchsafe with patient eare
The brave adventures of this faery knight,
The good Sir Guyon, gratiously to heare;
In whom great rule of Temp'raunce goodly doth appeare.

CANTO I

Guyon, by Archimage abusd,
The Redcrosse knight awaytes;
Fyndes Mordant and Amavia slaine
With pleasures poisoned haytes.

I. THAT conning Architect of cancred guyle,
    Whom Princes late displeasure left in bands,
    For falsed letters and suborned wyle,
    Soone as the Redcrosse knight he understands
    To beene departed out of Eden landes,
    To serve againe his soveraine Elfin Queene,
    His artes he moves, and out of caytives handes
    Himselfe he frees by secret meanes unseene;
    His shackles emptie lefte, himselfe escaped cleene.

II. And forth he fares, full of malicious mynd,
    To worken mischiefe, and avenging woe,
    Where ever he that godly knight may fynd,
    His onely hart-sore, and his onely foe;
    Sith Una now he algates must forgoe,
    Whom his victorious handes did earst restore
    To native crowne and kingdom late ygoe;
    Where she enjoyes sure peace for evermore,
    As wetherbeaten ship arryv'd on happie shore.

III. Him therefore now the object of his spight
    And deadly food he makes: him to offend,
    By forged treason or by open fight,
    He seekes, of all his drifte the aymed end:
    Thereto his subtile engins he does bend,
    His practick witt and his fayre fyled tonge,
    With thousand other sleightes; for well he kend
    His credit now in doubtfull ballaunce hong:
    For hardly could bee hurt who was already stong.

IV. Still as he went he craftie stales did lay,
    With cunning traynes him to entrap unwares,
    And privy spyals plast in all his way,

To weete what course he takes, and how he fares,
To ketch him at a vauntage in his snares.
But now so wise and wary was the knight
By tryall of his former harmes and cares,
That he descryde and shonned still his slight:
The fish that once was caught new bait wil hardly byte.

v. Nath'lesse th' Enchaunter would not spare his payne,
In hope to win occasion to his will;
Which when he long awaited had in vayne,
He chaungd his mynd from one to other ill;
For to all good he enimy was still.
Upon the way him fortuned to meete,
Fayre marching underneath a shady hill,
A goodly knight, all armd in harnesse meete,
That from his head no place appeared to his feete.

vi. His carriage was full comely and upright;
His countenance demure and temperate;
But yett so sterne and terrible in sight,
That cheard his friendes, and did his foes amate:
He was an Elfin borne of noble state
And mickle worship in his native land;
Well could he tourney, and in lists debate,
And knighthood tooke of good Sir Huons hand,
When with king Oberon he came to Faery land.

vii. Him als accompanyd upon the way
A comely Palmer, clad in black attyre,
Of rypest yeares, and heares all hoarie gray,
That with a staffe his feeble steps did stire,
Least his long way his aged limbes should tire:
And, if by lookes one may the mind aread,
He seemd to be a sage and sober syre;
And ever with slow pace the knight did lead,
Who taught his trampling steed with equall steps to tread.

viii. Such whenas Archimago them did view,
He weened well to worke some uncouth wyle:
Eftsoones untwisting his deceiptfull clew,
He gan to weave a web of wicked guyle,
And, with faire countenance and flattering style
To them approaching, thus the knight bespake;

" Fayre sonne of Mars, that seeke with warlike spoyle,
And great atchiev'ments, great your selfe to make,
Vouchsafe to stay your steed for humble misers sake."

IX. He stayd his steed for humble misers sake,
And badd tell on the tenor of his playnt:
Who feigning then in every limb to quake
Through inward feare, and seeming pale and faynt,
With piteous mone his percing speach gan paynt:
" Deare Lady! how shall I declare thy cace,
Whom late I left in languorous constraynt?
Would God! thy selfe now present were in place
To tell this ruefull tale: thy sight could win thee grace.

X. " Or rather would, O! would it so had chaunst,
That you, most noble Sir, had present beene
When that lewd rybauld, with vyle lust advaunst,
Laid first his filthie hands on virgin cleene,
To spoyle her dainty corps, so faire and sheene
As on the earth, great mother of us all,
With living eye more fayre was never seene
Of chastity and honour virginall:
Witnes, ye heavens, whom she in vaine to help did call."

XI. " How may it be," sayd then the knight halfe wroth,
" That knight should knighthood ever so have shent? "
" None but that saw," (quoth he) " would weene for troth,
How shamefully that Mayd he did torment:
Her looser golden lockes he rudely rent,
And drew her on the ground; and his sharpe sword
Against her snowy brest he fiercely bent,
And threatned death with many a bloodie word:
Tounge hates to tell the rest that eye to see abhord."

XII. Therewith amoved from his sober mood,
" And lives he yet," (said he) " that wrought this act?
And doen the heavens afford him vitall food? "
" He lives," (quoth he) " and boasteth of the fact,
Ne yet hath any knight his courage crackt."
" Where may that treachour then," (sayd he) " be found,
Or by what meanes may I his footing tract? "
" That shall I shew," (sayd he) " as sure as hound
The stricken Deare doth chalenge by the bleeding wound."

XIII. He stayd not lenger talke, but with fierce yre
And zealous haste away is quickly gone
To seeke that knight, where him that crafty Squyre
Supposd to be.   They do arrive anone
Where sate a gentle Lady all alone,
With garments rent, and heare discheveled,
Wringing her handes, and making piteous mone:
Her swollen eyes were much disfigured,
And her faire face with teares was fowly blubbered.

XIV. The knight, approching nigh, thus to her said:
" Fayre Lady, through fowle sorrow ill bedight,
Great pitty is to see you thus dismayd,
And marre the blossom of your beauty bright:
For-thy appease your griefe and heavy plight,
And tell the cause of your conceived payne;
For, if he live that hath you doen despight,
He shall you doe dew recompence agayne,
Or els his wrong with greater puissance maintaine."

XV. Which when she heard, as in despightfull wise
She wilfully her sorrow did augment,
And offred hope of comfort did despise:
Her golden lockes most cruelly she rent,
And scratcht her face with ghastly dreriment;
Ne would she speake, ne see, ne yet be seene,
But hid her visage, and her head downe bent,
Either for grievous shame, or for great teene,
As if her hart with sorrow had transfixed beene:

XVI. Till her that Squyre bespake: " Madame, my liefe,
For Gods deare love be not so wilfull bent,
But doe vouchsafe now to receive reliefe,
The which good fortune doth to you present.
For what bootes it to weepe and to wayment
When ill is chaunst, but doth the ill increase,
And the weake minde with double woe torment? "
When she her Squyre heard speake, she gan appease
Her voluntarie paine, and feele some secret ease.

XVII. Eftsoone she said; " Ah! gentle trustie Squyre,
What comfort can I, wofull wretch, conceave?
Or why should ever I henceforth desyre

To see faire heavens face, and life not leave,
Sith that false Traytour did my honour reave?"
"False traytour certes," (saide the Faerie knight)
"I read the man, that ever would deceave
A gentle Lady, or her wrong through might:
Death were too litle paine for such a fowle despight.

XVIII. "But now, fayre Lady, comfort to you make,
And read who hath ye wrought this shamefull plight,
That short revenge the man may overtake,
Where-so he be, and soone upon him light."
"Certes," (saide she) "I wote not how he hight,
But under him a gray steede he did wield,
Whose sides with dapled circles weren dight;
Upright he rode, and in his silver shield
He bore a bloodie Crosse that quartred all the field."

XIX. "Now by my head," (saide Guyon) "much I muse,
How that same knight should doe so fowle amis,
Or ever gentle Damzell so abuse:
For, may I boldly say, he surely is
A right good knight, and trew of word ywis:
I present was, and can it witnesse well,
When armes he swore, and streight did enterpris
Th' adventure of the Errant damozell;
In which he hath great glory wonne, as I heare tell.

XX. "Nathlesse he shortly shall againe be tryde,
And fairely quit him of th' imputed blame;
Els, be ye sure, he dearely shall abyde,
Or make you good amendment for the same:
All wrongs have mendes, but no amendes of shame.
Now therefore, Lady, rise out of your paine,
And see the salving of your blotted name."
Full loth she seemd thereto, but yet did faine,
For she was inly glad her purpose so to gaine.

XXI. Her purpose was not such as she did faine,
Ne yet her person such as it was seene;
But under simple shew, and semblant plaine,
Lurkt false Duessa secretly unseene,
As a chaste Virgin that had wronged beene:
So had false Archimago her disguysd,

To cloke her guile with sorrow and sad teene;
And eke himselfe had craftily devisd
To be her Squire, and do her service well aguisd.

XXII. Her, late forlorne and naked, he had found
Where she did wander in waste wildernesse,
Lurking in rockes and caves far under ground,
And with greene mosse cov'ring her nakednesse
To hide her shame and loathly filthinesse,
Sith her Prince Arthur of proud ornaments
And borrowed beauty spoyld.   Her nathelesse
Th' enchaunter finding fit for his intents
Did thus revest, and deckt with dew habiliments.

XXIII. For all he did was to deceive good knights,
And draw them from pursuit of praise and fame
To slug in slouth and sensuall delights,
And end their daies with irrenowmed shame.
And now exceeding griefe him overcame,
To see the Redcrosse thus advaunced hye;
Therefore this craftie engine he did frame,
Against his praise to stirre up enmitye
Of such, as vertues like mote unto him allye.

XXIV. So now he Guyon guydes an uncouth way
Through woods and mountaines, till they came at last
Into a pleasant dale that lowly lay
Betwixt two hils, whose high heads overplast
The valley did with coole shade overcast:
Through midst thereof a little river rold,
By which there sate a knight with helme unlaste,
Himselfe refreshing with the liquid cold,
After his travell long and labours manifold.

XXV. "Lo! yonder he," cryde Archimage alowd,
"That wrought the shamefull fact which I did shew;
And now he doth himselfe in secret shrowd,
To fly the vengeaunce for his outrage dew:
But vaine; for ye shall dearely do him rev,
So God ye speed and send you good successe,
Which we far off will here abide to vew,"
So they him left inflam'd with wrathfulnesse,
That streight against that knight his speare he did addresse.

XXVI. Who, seeing him from far so fierce to pricke,
    His warlike armes about him gan embrace,
    And in the rest his ready speare did sticke:
    Tho, when as still he saw him towards pace,
    He gan rencounter him in equall race.
    They bene ymett, both ready to affrap,
    When suddeinly that warriour gan abace
    His threatned speare, as if some new mishap,
    Had him betide, or hidden danger did entrap;

XXVII. And cryde, " Mercie, Sir knight! and mercie, Lord,
    For mine offence and heedelesse hardiment,
    That had almost committed crime abhord,
    And with reprochfull shame mine honour shent,
    Whiles cursed steele against that badge I bent,
    The sacred badge of my Redeemers death,
    Which on your shield is set for ornament! "
    But his fierce foe his steed could stay uneath,
    Who, prickt with courage kene, did cruell battell breath.

XXVIII. But, when he heard him speake, streight way he knew
    His errour; and, himselfe inclyning, sayd;
    " Ah! deare Sir Guyon, well becommeth you,
    But me behoveth rather to upbrayd,
    Whose hastie hand so far from reason strayd,
    That almost it did haynous violence
    On that fayre ymage of that heavenly Mayd,
    That decks and armes your shield with faire defence:
    Your court'sie takes on you anothers dew offence."

XXIX. So beene they both at one, and doen upreare
    Their bevers bright each other for to greet;
    Goodly comportaunce each to other beare,
    And entertaine themselves with court'sies meet.
    Then said the Redcrosse knight; " Now mote I weet,
    Sir Guyon, why with so fierce saliaunce,
    And fell intent, ye did at earst me meet;
    For sith I know your goodly governaunce,
    Great cause, I weene, you guided, or some uncouth
      chaunce."

XXX. " Certes," (said he), " well mote I shame to tell
    The fond encheason that me hither led.
    A false infamous faitour late befell

Me for to meet, that seemed ill bested,
And playnd of grievous outrage, which he red
A knight had wrought against a Ladie gent;
Which to avenge he to this place me led,
Where you he made the marke of his intent,
And now is fled: foule shame him follow wher he went!"

XXXI. So can he turne his earnest unto game,
Through goodly handling and wise temperaunce,
By this his aged Guide in presence came;
Who, soone as on that knight his eye did glaunce,
Eftsoones of him had perfect cognizaunce,
Sith him in Faery court he late avizd;
And sayd; " Fayre sonne, God give you happy chaunce,
And that deare Crosse uppon your shield devizd,
Wherewith above all knights ye goodly seeme aguizd!

XXXII. " Joy may you have, and everlasting fame,
Of late most hard atchiev'ment by you donne,
For which enrolled is your glorious name
In heavenly Regesters above the Sunne,
Where you a Saint with Saints your seat have wonne:
But wretched we, where ye have left your marke,
Must now anew begin like race to ronne,
God guide thee, Guyon, well to end thy warke,
And to the wished haven bring thy weary barke!"

XXXIII. " Palmer," him answered the Redcrosse knight,
" His be the praise that this atchiev'ment wrought,
Who made my hand the organ of his might:
More then goodwill to me attribute nought;
For all I did, I did but as I ought.
But you, faire Sir, whose pageant next ensewes,
Well mote yee thee, as well can wish your thought,
That home ye may report thrise happy newes;
For well ye worthy bene for worth and gentle thewes."

XXXIV. So courteous conge both did give and take,
With right hands plighted, pledges of good will.
Then Guyon forward gan his voyage make
With his blacke Palmer, that him guided still:
Still he him guided over dale and hill,
And with his steedy staffe did point his way;

His race with reason, and with words his will,
From fowle intemperaunce he ofte did stay,
And suffred not in wrath his hasty steps to stray.

xxxv. In this faire wize they traveild long yfere,
Through many hard assayes which did betide;
Of which he honour still away did beare,
And spred his glory through all countryes wide.
At last, as chaunst them by a forest side
To passe, for succour from the scorching ray,
They heard a ruefull voice, that dearnly cride
With percing shriekes and many a dolefull lay;
Which to attend awhile their forward steps they stay.

xxxvi. " But if that carelesse hevens," (quoth she) " despise
The doome of just revenge, and take delight
To see sad pageaunts of mens miseries,
As bownd by them to live in lives despight;
Yet can they not warne death from wretched wight.
Come, then; come soone; come sweetest death, to me,
And take away this long lent loathed light:
Sharpe be thy wounds, but sweete the medicines be,
That long captived soules from weary thraldome free.

xxxvii. " But thou, sweete Babe, whom frowning froward fate
Hath made sad witnesse of thy fathers fall,
Sith heven thee deignes to hold in living state,
Long maist thou live, and better thrive withall
Then to thy lucklesse parents did befall.
Live thou; and to thy mother dead attest
That cleare she dide from blemish criminall:
Thy litle hands embrewd in bleeding brest
Loe! I for pledges leave. So give me leave to rest."

xxxviii. With that a deadly shrieke she forth did throw
That through the wood re-echoed againe;
And after gave a grone so deepe and low
That seemd her tender heart was rent in twaine,
Or thrild with point of thorough-piercing paine:
As gentle Hynd, whose sides with cruell steele
Through launched, forth her bleeding life does raine,
Whiles the sad pang approching shee does feele,
Braies out her latest breath, and up her eies doth seele.

XXXIX. Which when that warriour heard, dismounting straict
From his tall steed, he rusht into the thick,
And soone arrived where that sad pourtraict
Of death and dolour lay, halfe dead, halfe quick;
In whose white alabaster brest did stick
A cruell knife that made a griesly wownd,
From which forth gusht a stream of gore blood thick,
That all her goodly garments staind arownd,
And into a deepe sanguine dide the grassy grownd.

XL. Pitifull spectacle of deadly smart,
Beside a bubling fountaine low she lay,
Which shee increased with her bleeding hart,
And the cleane waves with purple gore did ray:
Als in her lap a lovely babe did play
His cruell sport, in stead of sorrow dew;
For in her streaming blood he did embay
His litle hands, and tender joints embrew:
Pitifull spectacle, as ever eie did vew!

XLI. Besides them both, upon the soiled gras
The dead corse of an armed knight was spred,
Whose armour all with blood besprincled was;
His ruddy lips did smyle, and rosy red
Did paint his chearefull cheekes, yett being ded;
Seemd to have beene a goodly personage,
Now in his freshest flowre of lusty-hed,
Fitt to inflame faire Lady with loves rage,
But that fiers fate did crop the blossome of his age.

XLII. Whom when the good Sir Guyon did behold,
His hart gan wexe as starke as marble stone,
And his fresh blood did frieze with fearefull cold,
That all his sences seemd berefte attone:
At last his mighty ghost gan deepe to grone,
As Lion, grudging in his great disdaine,
Mournes inwardly, and makes to him selfe mone;
Til ruth and fraile affection did constraine
His stout courage to stoupe, and shew his inward paine.

XLIII. Out of her gored wound the cruell steel
He lightly snatcht, and did the floodgate stop
With his faire garment; then gan softly feel

Her feeble pulse, to prove if any drop
Of living blood yet in her veynes did hop:
Which when he felt to move, he hoped faire
To call backe life to her forsaken shop.
So well he did her deadly wounds repaire,
That at the last shee gan to breath out living aire.

XLIV. Which he perceiving greatly gan rejoice,
And goodly counsell, that for wounded hart
Is meetest med'cine, tempred with sweete voice:
" Ay me ! deare Lady, which the ymage art
Of ruefull pitty and impatient smart,
What direfull chaunce, armd with avenging fate,
Or cursed hand, hath plaid this cruell part,
Thus fowle to hasten your untimely date?
Speake, O dear Lady, speake ! help never comes too late."

XLV. Therewith her dim eie-lids she up gan reare,
On which the drery death did sitt as sad
As lump of lead, and made darke clouds appeare:
But when as him, all in bright armour clad,
Before her standing she espied had,
As one out of a deadly dreame affright,
She weakely started, yet she nothing drad:
Streight downe againe herselfe, in great despight,
She groveling threw to ground, as hating life and light.

XLVI. The gentle knight her soone with carefull paine
Uplifted light, and softly did uphold:
Thrise he her reared, and thrise she sunck againe,
Till he his armes about her sides gan fold,
And to her said; " Yet, if the stony cold
Have not all seized on your frozen hart,
Let one word fall that may your grief unfold,
And tell the secrete of your mortall smart:
He oft finds present helpe who does his griefe impart."

XLVII. Then, casting up a deadly looke, full low
Shee sight from bottome of her wounded brest;
And after, many bitter throbs did throw,
With lips full pale and foltring tong opprest,
These words she breathed forth from riven chest:
" Leave, ah ! leave off, whatever wight thou bee,

To lett a weary wretch from her dew rest,
And trouble dying soules tranquilitee;
Take not away, now got, which none would give to me."

XLVIII. " Ah! far be it," (said he) " Deare dame, fro mee,
To hinder soule from her desired rest,
Or hold sad life in long captivitee;
For all I seeke is but to have redrest
The bitter pangs that doth your heart infest.
Tell then, O Lady! tell what fatall priefe
Hath with so huge misfortune you opprest;
That I may cast to compas your reliefe,
Or die with you in sorrow, and partake your griefe."

XLIX. With feeble hands then stretched forth on hye,
As heven accusing guilty of her death,
And with dry drops congealed in her eye,
In these sad wordes she spent her utmost breath:
" Heare then, O man! the sorrowes that uneath
My tong can tell, so far all sence they pas.
Loe! this dead corpse, that lies here underneath,
The gentlest knight, that ever on greene gras
Gay steed with spurs did pricke, the good Sir Mortdant was:

L. " Was, (ay the while, that he is not so now!)
My Lord, my love, my deare Lord, my deare love!
So long as hevens just with equall brow
Vouchsafed to behold us from above.
One day, when him high corage did emmove,
As wont ye knightes to seeke adventures wilde,
He pricked forth his puissant force to prove.
Me then he left enwombed of this childe,
This luckles childe, whom thus ye see with blood defild.

LI. " Him fortuned (hard fortune ye may ghesse)
To come, where vile Acrasia does wonne;
Acrasia, a false enchaunteresse,
That many errant knightes hath fowle fordonne;
Within a wandring Island, that doth ronne
And stray in perilous gulfe, her dwelling is.
Fayre Sir, if ever there ye travell, shonne
The cursed land where many wend amis,
And know it by the name: it hight the *Bowre of blis.*

LII. " Her blis is all in pleasure, and delight,
Wherewith she makes her lovers dronken mad;
And then with words, and weedes, of wondrous might,
On them she workes her will to uses bad:
My liefest Lord she thus beguiled had;
For he was flesh: (all flesh doth frayltie breed)
Whom when I heard to beene so ill bestad,
Weake wretch, I wrapt myselfe in Palmers weed,
And cast to seek him forth through danger and great dreed.

LIII. " Now had fayre Cynthia by even tournes
Full measured three quarters of her yeare,
And thrise three tymes had fild her crooked hornes,
Whenas my wombe her burdein would forbeare,
And bade me call Lucina to me neare.
Lucina came; a manchild forth I brought;
The woods, the nymphes, my bowres, my midwives, weare:
Hard help at need! So deare thee, babe, I bought;
Yet nought too dear I deemd, while so my deare I sought.

LIV. " Him so I sought; and so at last I fownd,
Where him that witch had thralled to her will,
In chaines of lust and lewde desyres ybownd,
And so transformed from his former skill,
That me he knew not, nether his owne ill;
Till, through wise handling and faire governaunce,
I him recured to a better will,
Purged from drugs of fowle intemperaunce:
Then meanes I gan devise for his deliveraunce.

LV. " Which when the vile Enchaunteresse perceiv'd,
How that my Lord from her I would reprive,
With cup thus charmd him parting she deceivd;
' Sad verse, give death to him that death does give,
And losse of love to her that loves to live,
So soone as Bacchus with the Nymphe does lincke!'
So parted we, and on our journey drive;
Till, coming to this well, he stoupt to drincke:
The charme fulfild, dead suddeinly he downe did sincke.

LVI. " Which when I, wretch "—Not one word more she sayd,
But breaking off the end for want of breath,
And slyding soft, as downe to sleepe her layd,

And ended all her woe in quiet death.
That seeing, good Sir Guyon could uneath
From teares abstayne; for griefe his hart did grate,
And from so heavie sight his head did wreath,
Accusing fortune, and too cruell fate,
Which plonged had faire Lady in so wretched state.

LVII. Then turning to his Palmer said; " Old syre,
Behold the ymage of mortalitie,
And feeble nature cloth'd with fleshly tyre.
When raging passion with fierce tyranny
Robs reason of her dew regalitie,
And makes it servaunt to her basest part,
The strong it weakens with infirmitie,
And with bold furie armes the weakest hart:
The strong through pleasure soonest falles, the weake
through smart."

LVIII. " But temperaunce " (said he) " with golden squire
Betwixt them both can measure out a meane;
Nether to melt in pleasures whott desyre,
Nor frye in hartlesse griefe and dolefull tene:
Thrise happy man, who fares them both atweene!
But sith this wretched woman overcome
Of anguish, rather then of crime, hath bene,
Reserve her cause to her eternall doome;
And, in the meane, vouchsafe her honorable toombe."

LIX. " Palmer," quoth he, " death is an equall doome
To good and bad, the common In of rest;
But after death the tryall is to come,
When best shall bee to them that lived best;
But both alike, when death hath both supprest,
Religious reverence doth buriall teene;
Which whoso wants, wants so much of his rest:
For all so great shame after death I weene,
As selfe to dyen bad, unburied bad to beene."

LX. So both agree their bodies to engrave:
The great earthes wombe they open to the sky,
And with sad Cypresse seemely it embrave;
Then, covering with a clod their closed eye,
They lay therein their corses tenderly,

And bid them sleepe in everlasting peace.
But, ere they did their utmost obsequy,
Sir Guyon, more affection to increace,
Bynempt a sacred vow, which none should ay releace,

LXI. The dead knights sword out of his sheath he drew,
With which he cutt a lock of all their heare,
Which medling with their blood and earth he threw
Into the grave, and gan devoutly sweare;
" Such and such evil God on Guyon reare,
And worse and worse, young Orphane, be thy payne,
If I, or thou, dew vengeaunce doe forbeare,
Till guiltie blood her guerdon doe obtayne! "
So shedding many teares they closd the earth agayne.

CANTO II

Babes bloody handes may not be clensd:
The face of golden Meane:
Her sisters, two Extremities,
Strive her to banish cleane.

I. THUS when Sir Guyon with his faithful guyde
Had with dew rites and dolorous lament
The end of their sad Tragedie uptyde,
The litle babe up in his armes he hent;
Who with sweet pleasaunce, and bold blandishment,
Gan smyle on them, that rather ought to weepe,
As carelesse of his woe, or innocent
Of that was doen; that ruth emperced deepe
In that knightes hart, and wordes with bitter teares
        did steepe:

II. " Ah! lucklesse babe, borne under cruell starre,
And in dead parents balefull ashes bred,
Full little weenest thou what sorrowes are
Left thee for porcion of thy livelyhed;
Poore Orphane! in the wild world scattered,
As budding braunch rent from the native tree,
And throwen forth, till it be withered.
Such is the state of men: Thus enter we
Into this life with woe, and end with miseree! "

III. Then, soft himselfe inclyning on his knee
Downe to that well, did in the water weene
(So love does loath disdainefull nicitee)
His guiltie handes from bloody gore to cleene.
He washt them oft and oft, yet nought they beene
For all his washing cleaner. Still he strove;
Yet still the litle hands were bloody seene:
The which him into great amaz'ment drove,
And into diverse doubt his wavering wonder clove.

IV. He wist not whether blott of fowle offence
Might not be purgd with water nor with bath;
Or that high God, in lieu of innocence,

Imprinted had that token of his wrath,
To shew how sore bloodguiltinesse he hat'th;
Or that the charme and veneme which they dronck,
Their blood with secret filth infected hath,
Being diffused through the senceless tronck,
That through the great contagion direful deadly stonck.

v. Whom thus at gaze the Palmer gan to bord
With goodly reason, and thus fayre bespake;
" Ye bene right hard amated, gratious Lord,
And of your ignorance great merveill make,
Whiles cause not well conceived ye mistake:
But know, that secret vertues are infusd
In every fountaine, and in everie lake,
Which who hath skill them rightly to have chusd,
To proofe of passing wonders hath full often usd:

vi. " Of those, some were so from their sourse indewd
By great Dame Nature, from whose fruitfull pap
Their welheads spring, and are with moisture deawd;
Which feedes each living plant with liquid sap,
And filles with flowres fayre Floraes painted lap:
But other some, by guifte of later grace,
Or by good prayers, or by other hap,
Had vertue pourd into their waters bace,
And thenceforth were renowmd, and sought from place
to place.

vii. " Such is this well, wrought by occasion straunge,
Which to her Nymph befell.   Upon a day,
As she the woodes with bow and shaftes did raunge,
The hartlesse Hynd and Robucke to dismay,
Dan Faunus chaunst to meet her by the way,
And, kindling fire at her faire-burning eye,
Inflamed was to follow beauties pray,
And chaced her that fast from him did fly;
As hynd from her, so she fled from her enimy.

viii. " At last, when fayling breath began to faint,
And saw no meanes to scape, of shame affrayd,
She set her downe to weepe for sore constraint;
And to Diana calling lowd for ayde,
Her deare besought to let her die a mayd.
The goddesse heard; and suddeine, where she sate

Welling out streames of teares, and quite dismayd
With stony feare of that rude rustick mate,
Transformd her to a stone from stedfast virgins state.

IX. " Lo! now she is that stone; from whose two heads,
As from two weeping eyes, fresh streames do flow,
Yet colde through feare and old conceived dreads;
And yet the stone her semblance seemes to show,
Shapt like a maide, that such ye may her know:
And yet her vertues in her water byde,
For it is chaste and pure as purest snow,
Ne lets her waves with any filth be dyde;
But ever, like herselfe, unstayned hath beene tryde.

X. " From thence it comes, that this babes bloody hand
May not be clensd with water of this well:
Ne certes, Sir, strive you it to withstand,
But let them still be bloody, as befell,
That they his mothers innocence may tell,
As she bequeathd in her last testament;
That, as a sacred Symbole, it may dwell
In her sonnes flesh, to mind revengement,
And be for all chaste Dames an endlesse moniment."

XI. He hearkned to his reason, and the childe
Uptaking, to the Palmer gave to beare;
But his sad fathers armes with blood defilde,
An heavie load, himselfe did lightly reare;
And turning to that place, in which whyleare
He left his loftie steed with golden sell
And goodly gorgeous barbes, him found not theare:
By other accident, that earst befell,
He is convaide; but how, or where, here fits not tell.

XII. Which when Sir Guyon saw, all were he wroth,
Yet algates mote he softe himselfe appease,
And fairely fare on foot, how ever loth:
His double burden did him sore disease.
So long they traveiled with litle ease,
Till that at last they to a Castle came,
Built on a rocke adjoyning to the seas:
It was an auncient worke of antique fame,
And wondrous strong by nature, and by skilful frame.

XIII. Therein three sisters dwelt of sundry sort,
The children of one syre by mothers three;
Who dying whylome did divide this fort
To them by equall shares in equall fee:
But stryfull mind and diverse qualitee
Drew them in partes, and each made others foe:
Still did they strive and daily disagree;
The eldest did against the youngest goe,
And both against the middest meant to worken woe.

XIV. Where when the knight arriv'd, he was right well
Receiv'd, as knight of so much worth became,
Of second sister, who did far excell
The other two: Medina was her name,
A sober sad and comely courteous Dame;
Who rich arayd, and yet in modest guize,
In goodly garments that her well became,
Fayre marching forth in honorable wize,
Him at the threshold mett, and well did enterprize.

XV. She led him up into a goodly bowre,
And comely courted with meet modestie;
Ne in her speach, ne in her haviour,
Was lightnesse seene or looser vanitie,
But gratious womanhood, and gravitie,
Above the reason of her youthly yeares.
Her golden lockes she roundly did uptye
In breaded tramels, that no looser heares
Did out of order stray about her daintie eares.

XVI. Whilest she her selfe thus busily did frame
Seemely to entertaine her new-come guest,
Newes hereof to her other sisters came,
Who all this while were at their wanton rest,
Accourting each her frend with lavish fest:
They were two knights of perelesse puissaunce,
And famous far abroad for warlike gest,
Which to these Ladies love did countenaunce,
And to his mistresse each himselfe strove to advaunce.

XVII. He that made love unto the eldest Dame,
Was hight Sir Huddibras, an hardy man;
Yet not so good of deedes as great of name,

Which he by many rash adventures wan,
Since errant armes to sew he first began:
More huge in strength then wise in workes he was,
And reason with foole-hardize over ran;
Sterne melancholy did his courage pas,
And was, for terrour more, all armd in shyning bras.

XVIII. But he that lov'd the youngest was Sansloy;
He, that faire Una late fowle outraged,
The most unruly and the boldest boy
That ever warlike weapons menaged,
And all to lawlesse lust encouraged
Through strong opinion of his matchlesse might;
Ne ought he car'd whom he endamaged
By tortious wrong, or whom bereav'd of right:
He, now this Ladies Champion, chose for love to fight.

XIX. These two gay knights, vowd to so diverse loves,
Each other does envy with deadly hate,
And daily warre against his foeman moves,
In hope to win more favour with his mate,
And th' others pleasing service to abate,
To magnifie his owne.   But when they heard
How in that place straunge knight arrived late,
Both knightes and ladies forth right angry far'd,
And fercely unto battell sterne themselves prepar'd.

XX. But ere they could proceede unto the place
Where he abode, themselves at discord fell,
And cruell combat joynd in middle space:
With horrible assault, and fury fell,
They heapt huge strokes the scorned life to quell,
That all on uprore from her settled seat,
The house was raysd, and all that in did dwell.
Seemd that lowde thunder with amazement great
Did rend the ratling skyes with flames of fouldring heat.

XXI. The noyse thereof cald forth that straunger knight,
To weet what dreadfull thing was there in hond;
Where whenas two brave knightes in bloody fight
With deadly rancour he enraunged fond,
His sunbroad shield about his wrest he bond,
And shyning blade unsheathd, with which he ran

Unto that stead, their strife to understond;
And at his first arrivall them began
With goodly meanes to pacifie, well as he can.

XXII. But they, him spying, both with greedy forse
Attonce upon him ran, and him beset
With strokes of mortall steele without remorse,
And on his shield like yron sledges bet:
As when a Beare and Tygre, being met
In cruell fight on Lybicke Ocean wide,
Espye a traveiler with feet surbet,
Whom they in equall pray hope to divide,
They stint their strife and him assayle on everie side.

XXIII. But he, not like a weary traveilere,
Their sharp assault right boldly did rebut,
And suffred not their blowes to byte him nere,
But with redoubled buffes them backe did put:
Whose grieved mindes, which choler did englut,
Against themselves turning their wrathfull spight,
Gan with new rage their shieldes to hew and cut;
But still, when Guyon came to part their fight,
With heavie load on him they freshly gan to smight.

XXIV. As a tall ship tossed in troublous seas,
Whom raging windes, threatning to make the pray
Of the rough rockes, doe diversly disease,
Meetes two contrarie billowes by the way,
That her on either side doe sore assay,
And boast to swallow her in greedy grave;
Shee, scorning both their spights, does make wide way,
And with her brest breaking the fomy wave,
Does ride on both their backs, and faire her self doth save.

XXV. So boldly he him beares, and rusheth forth
Betweene them both by conduct of his blade.
Wondrous great prowesse and heroick worth
He shewd that day, and rare ensample made,
When two so mighty warriours he dismade.
Attonce he wards and strikes; he takes and paies;
Now forst to yield, now forcing to invade;
Before, behind, and round about him laies;
So double was his paines, so double be his praise.

XXVI. Straunge sort of fight, three valiaunt knights to see
Three combates joine in one, and to darraine
A triple warre with triple enmitee,
All for their Ladies froward love to gaine,
Which gotten was but hate.   So love does raine
In stoutest minds, and maketh monstrous warre;
He maketh warre, he maketh peace againe,
And yett his peace is but continual jarre:
O miserable men that to him subject arre!

XXVII. Whilst thus they mingled were in furious armes,
The faire Medina, with her tresses torne
And naked brest, in pitty of their harmes,
Emongst them ran; and, falling them beforne,
Besought them by the womb which them had born,
And by the loves which were to them most deare,
And by the knighthood which they sure had sworn,
Their deadly cruell discord to forbeare,
And to her just conditions of faire peace to heare.

XXVIII. But her two other sisters, standing by,
Her lowd gainsaid, and both their champions bad
Pursew the end of their strong enmity,
As ever of their loves they would be glad:
Yet she with pitthy words, and counsell sad,
Still strove their stubborne rages to revoke;
That at the last, suppressing fury mad,
They gan abstaine from dint of direfull stroke,
And hearken to the sober speaches which she spoke.

XXIX. " Ah, puissaunt Lords! what cursed evil Spright,
Or fell Erinnys, in your noble harts
Her hellish brond hath kindled with despight,
And stird you up to worke your wilfull smarts?
Is this the joy of armes? be these the parts
Of glorious knighthood, after blood to thrust,
And not regard dew right and just desarts?
Vaine is the vaunt, and victory unjust,
That more to mighty hands then rightfull cause doth trust.

XXX. " And were there rightfull cause of difference,
Yet were not better fayre it to accord
Then with bloodguiltinesse to heape offence,

And mortal vengeaunce joyne to crime abhord?
O! fly from wrath; fly, O my liefest Lord!
Sad be the sights, and bitter fruites of warre,
And thousand furies wait on wrathfull sword;
Ne ought the praise of prowesse more doth marre
Then fowle revenging rage, and base contentious jarre

XXXI. " But lovely concord, and most sacred peace,
Doth nourish vertue, and fast friendship breeds,
Weake she makes strong, and strong thing does increace,
Till it the pitch of highest praise exceeds:
Brave be her warres, and honorable deeds,
By which she triumphes over yre and pride,
And winnes an Olive girlond for her meeds.
Be, therefore, O my deare Lords! pacifide,
And this misseeming discord meekely lay aside."

XXXII. Her gracious words their rancour did appall,
And suncke so deepe into their boyling brests,
That downe they lett their cruell weapons fall,
And lowly did abase their lofty crests
To her faire presence and discrete behests.
Then she began a treaty to procure,
And stablish terms betwixt both their requests,
That as a law forever should endure;
Which to observe in word of knights they did assure.

XXXIII. Which to confirme, and fast to bind their league,
After their weary sweat and bloody toile,
She them besought, during their quiet treague,
Into her lodging to repaire awhile,
To rest themselves, and grace to reconcile.
They soone consent: so forth with her they fare;
Where they are well receivd, and made to spoile
Themselves of soiled armes, and to prepare
Their minds to pleasure, and their mouths to dainty fare.

XXXIV. And those two froward sisters, their faire loves,
Came with them eke, all were they wondrous loth,
And fained cheare, as for the time behoves,
But could not colour yet so well the troth,
But that their natures bad appeard in both;
For both did at their second sister grutch

And inly grieve, as doth an hidden moth
The inner garment frett, not th' utter touch:
One thought her cheare too litle, th' other thought too
    mutch.

XXXV. Elissa (so the eldest hight) did deeme
    Such entertainment base, ne ought would eat,
    Ne ought would speake, but evermore did seeme
    As discontent for want of merth or meat:
    No solace could her Paramour intreat
    Her once to show, ne court, nor dalliaunce;
    But with bent lowring browes, as she would threat,
    She scould, and frownd with froward countenaunce;
    Unworthy of faire Ladies comely governaunce.

XXXVI. But young Perissa was of other mynd,
    Full of disport, still laughing, loosely light,
    And quite contrary to her sisters kynd;
    No measure in her mood, no rule of right,
    But poured out in pleasure and delight:
    In wine and meats she flowd above the banck,
    And in excesse exceeded her owne might;
    In sumptuous tire she joyd her selfe to pranck,
    But of her love too lavish: (litle have she thanck!)

XXXVII. Fast by her side did sitt the bold Sansloy,
    Fitt mate for such a mincing mineon,
    Who in her loosenesse tooke exceeding joy;
    Might not be found a francker franion,
    Of her leawd parts to make companion:
    But Huddibras, more like a Malecontent,
    Did see and grieve at his bold fashion;
    Hardly could he endure his hardiment,
    Yett still he satt, and inly did him selfe torment.

XXXVIII. Betwixt them both the faire Medina sate
    With sober grace and goodly carriage:
    With equall measure she did moderate
    The strong extremities of their outrage.
    That forward paire she ever would asswage,
    When they would strive dew reason to exceed,
    But that same froward twaine would accorage,
    And of her plenty adde unto their need:
    So kept she them in order, and her selfe in heed.

XXXIX. Thus fairely shee attempered her feast,
   And pleasd them all with meete satiety.
   At last, when lust of meat and drinke was ceast,
   She Guyon deare besought of curtesie
   To tell from whence he came through jeopardy,
   And whither now on new adventure bownd:
   Who with bold grace, and comely gravity,
   Drawing to him the eies of all arownd,
   From lofty siege began these words aloud to sownd.

XL. " This thy demaund, O Lady! doth revive
   Fresh memory in me of that great Queene,
   Great and most glorious virgin Queene alive,
   That with her soveraine power, and scepter shene,
   All Faery lond does peaceably sustene,
   In widest Ocean she her throne does reare,
   That over all the earth it may be seene;
   As morning Sunne her beames dispredden cleare,
   And in her face faire peace and mercy doth appeare.

XLI. " In her the richesse of all heavenly grace
   In chiefe degree are heaped up on hye:
   And all, that els this worlds enclosure bace
   Hath great or glorious in mortall eye,
   Adornes the person of her Majestye;
   That men, beholding so great excellence
   And rare perfection in mortalitye,
   Doe her adore with sacred reverence,
   As th' Idole of her makers great magnificence.

XLII. " To her I homage and my service owe,
   In number of the noblest knightes on ground;
   Mongst whom on me she deigned to bestowe
   Order of Maydenhead, the most renownd
   That may this day in all the world be found.
   An yearely solemne feast she wontes to hold,
   The day that first doth lead the yeare around,
   To which all knights of worth and courage bold
   Resort, to heare of straunge adventures to be told.

XLIII. " There this old Palmer shewd himselfe that day,
   And to that mighty Princesse did complaine
   Of grievous mischiefes which a wicked Fay

Had wrought, and many whelmd in deadly paine;
Whereof he crav'd redresse.   My Soveraine,
Whose glory is in gracious deeds, and joyes
Throughout the world her mercy to maintaine,
Eftsoones devised redresse for such annoyes:
Me, all unfitt for so great purpose, she employes.

XLIV. " Now hath faire Phebe with her silver face
Thrise seene the shadowes of the neather world,
Sith last I left that honorable place,
In which her roiall presence is enrold;
Ne ever shall I rest in house nor hold,
Till I that false Acrasia have wonne;
Of whose fowle deedes, too hideous to bee told,
I witnesse am, and this their wretched sonne,
Whose wofull parents she hath wickedly fordonne."

XLV. " Tell on, fayre Sir," said she, " that dolefull tale,
From which sad ruth does seeme you to restraine,
That we may pitty such unhappie bale,
And learne from pleasures poyson to abstaine:
Ill by ensample good doth often gayne."
Then forward he his purpose gan pursew,
And told the story of the mortall payne,
Which Mordant and Amavia did rew,
As with lamenting eyes him selfe did lately vew.

XLVI. Night was far spent; and now in Ocean deep
Orion, flying fast from hissing snake,
His flaming head did hasten for to steep,
When of his pitteous tale he end did make:
Whilst with delight of that he wisely spake
Those guestes, beguyled, did beguyle their eyes
Of kindly sleepe that did them overtake.
At last, when they had markt the chaunged skyes,
They wist their houre was spent; then each to rest him hyes.

CANTO III

Vaine Braggadocchio, getting Guy-
ons horse, is made the scorne
Of knighthood trew; and is of fayre
Belphœbe fowle forlorne.

I. Soone as the morrow fayre with purple beames
　　Disperst the shadowes of the misty night,
　　And Titan, playing on the eastern streames,
　　Gan cleare the deawy ayre with springing light,
　　Sir Guyon, mindfull of his vow yplight,
　　Uprose from drowsie couch, and him addrest
　　Unto the journey which he had behight:
　　His puissant armes about his noble brest,
　　And many-folded shield he bound about his wrest.

II. Then, taking Congé of that virgin pure,
　　The bloody-handed babe unto her truth
　　Did earnestly committ, and her conjure
　　In vertuous lore to traine his tender youth,
　　And all that gentle noriture ensu'th;
　　And that, so soone as ryper yeares he raught,
　　He might, for memory of that dayes ruth,
　　Be called Ruddymane; and thereby taught
　　T' avenge his Parents death on them that had it wrought.

III. So forth he far'd, as now befell, on foot,
　　Sith his good steed is lately from him gone;
　　Patience perforce: helplesse what may it boot
　　To frett for anger, or for griefe to mone?
　　His Palmer now shall foot no more alone.
　　So fortune wrought, as under greene woodes syde
　　He lately heard that dying Lady grone,
　　He left his steed without, and speare besyde,
　　And rushed in on foot to ayd her ere she dyde.

IV. The whyles a losell wandring by the way,
　　One that to bountie never cast his mynd,
　　Ne thought of honour ever did assay

His baser brest, but in his kestrell kynd
A pleasing vaine of glory he did fynd,
To which his flowing toung and troublous spright
Gave him great ayd, and made him more inclynd:
He, that brave steed there finding ready dight,
Purloynd both steed and speare, and ran away full light.

v. Now gan his hart all swell in jollity,
And of him selfe great hope and help conceiv'd,
That puffed up with smoke of vanity,
And with selfe-loved personage deceiv'd,
He gan to hope of men to be receiv'd
For such as he him thought, or faine would bee:
But for in court gay portaunce he perceiv'd,
And gallant shew to be in greatest gree,
Eftsoones to court he cast t' advaunce his first degree.

vi. And by the way he chaunced to espy
One sitting ydle on a sunny banck,
To him avaunting in great bravery,
As Peacocke that his painted plumes doth pranck,
He smote his courser in the trembling flanck,
And to him threatned his hart-thrilling speare:
The seely man, seeing him ryde so ranck,
And ayme at him, fell flatt to ground for feare,
And crying, " Mercy ! " loud, his pitious handes gan reare.

vii. Thereat the Scarcrow wexed wondrous prowd,
Through fortune of his first adventure fayre,
And with big thundring voice revyld him lowd:
" Vile Caytive, vassall of dread and despayre,
Unworthie of the commune breathed ayre,
Why livest thou, dead dog, a lenger day,
And doest not unto death thyselfe prepayre?
Dy, or thyselfe my captive yield for ay.
Great favour I thee graunt for aunswere thus to stay."

viii. " Hold, O deare Lord! hold your dead-doing hand,"
Then loud he cryde; " I am your humble thrall."
" Ay wretch," (quoth he) " thy destinies withstand
My wrathfull will, and doe for mercy call.
I give thee life: therefore prostrated fall,
And kisse my stirrup; that thy homage bee."

The Miser threw him selfe, as an Offall,
Streight at his foot in base humilitee,
And cleeped him his liege, to hold of him in fee.

IX. So happy peace they made and faire accord.
Eftsoones this liegeman gan to wexe more bold,
And when he felt the folly of his Lord,
In his owne kind he gan him selfe unfold;
For he was wylie witted, and growne old
In cunning sleightes and practick knavery.
From that day forth he cast for to uphold
His ydle humour with fine flattery,
And blow the bellowes to his swelling vanity.

X. Trompart, fitt man for Braggadochio,
To serve at court in view of vaunting eye;
Vaine-glorious man, when fluttring wind does blow
In his light winges, is lifted up to skye;
The scorne of knighthood and trew chevalrye,
To thinke, without desert of gentle deed
And noble worth, to be advaunced hye:
Such prayse is shame; but honour, vertues meed,
Doth beare the fayrest flowre in honourable seed.

XI. So forth they pas, a well consorted payre,
Till that at length with Archimage they meet:
Who seeing one, that shone in armour fayre,
On goodly courser thondring with his feet,
Eftsoones supposed him a person meet
Of his revenge to make the instrument;
For since the Redcrosse knight he erst did weet
To been with Guyon knitt in one consent,
The ill, which earst to him, he now to Guyon ment.

XII. And coming close to Trompart gan inquere
Of him, what mightie warriour that mote bee,
That rode in golden sell with single spere,
But wanted sword to wreake his enmitee?
" He is a great adventurer," (said he)
" That hath his sword through hard assay forgone,
And now hath vowd, till he avenged bee
Of that despight, never to wearen none:
That speare is him enough to doen a thousand grone."

XIII. Th' enchaunter greatly joyed in the vaunt,
And weened well ere long his will to win,
And both his foen with equall foyle to daunt.
Tho to him louting lowly did begin
To plaine of wronges, which had committed bin
By Guyon, and by that false Redcrosse knight;
Which two, through treason and deceiptfull gin,
Had slayne Sir Mordant and his Lady bright:
That mote him honour win to wreak so foule despight.

XIV. Therewith all suddeinly he seemd enragd,
And threatned death with dreadfull countenaunce,
As if their lives had in his hand beene gagd;
And with stiffe force shaking his mortall launce,
To let him weet his doughtie valiaunce,
Thus said: " Old man, great sure shal be thy meed,
If, where those knights for feare of dew vengeaunce
Doe lurke, thou certeinly to mee areed,
That I may wreake on them their hainous hatefull deed."

XV. " Certes, my Lord," (said he) " that shall I soone,
And give you eke good helpe to their decay.
But mote I wisely you advise to doon,
Give no ods to your foes, but doe purvay
Your selfe of sword before that bloody day;
For they be two the prowest knights on grownd,
And oft approv'd in many hard assay;
And eke of surest steele that may be fownd,
Do arme your self against that day, them to confownd."

XVI. " Dotard," (said he) " let be thy deepe advise:
Seemes that through many yeares thy wits thee faile,
And that weake eld hath left thee nothing wise;
Els never should thy judgement be so frayle
To measure manhood by the sword or mayle.
Is not enough fowre quarters of a man,
Withouten sword or shield, an hoste to quayle?
Thou litle wotest what this right-hand can:
Speake they which have beheld the battailes which it wan."

XVII. The man was much abashed at his boast;
Yet well he wist that whoso would contend
With either of those knightes on even coast,

    Should neede of all his armes him to defend,
    Yet feared least his boldnesse should offend,
    When Braggadocchio saide; " Once I did sweare,
    When with one sword seven knightes I brought to end,
    Thenceforth in battaile never sword to beare;
    But it were that which noblest knight on earth doth weare."

x VIII. " Perdy, Sir knight," saide then th' enchaunter blive,
    " That shall I shortly purchase to your hond;
    For now the best and noblest knight alive
    Prince Arthur is, that wonnes in Faerie lond:
    He hath a sword that flames like burning brond.
    The same by my device I undertake
    Shall by to morrow by thy side be fond."
    At which bold word that boaster gan to quake,
    And wondred in his minde what mote that Monster make.

XIX. He stayd not for more bidding, but away
    Was suddein vanished out of his sight:
    The Northerne winde his wings did broad display
    At his commaund, and reared him up light
    From off the earth to take his aerie flight.
    They lookt about, but nowhere could espye
    Tract of his foot: then dead through great affright
    They both nigh were, and each bad other flye:
    Both fled attonce, ne ever backe retourned eye;

XX. Till that they come unto a forrest greene,
    In which they shrowd themselves from causeles feare;
    Yet feare them followes still where so they beene.
    Each trembling leafe and whistling wind they heare,
    As ghastly bug, does greatly them affeare:
    Yet both doe strive their fearefulnesse to faine.
    At last they heard a horne that thrilled cleare
    Throughout the wood that ecchoed againe,
    And made the forrest ring, as it would rive in twaine.

XXI. Eft through the thicke they heard one rudely rush,
    With noyse whereof he from his loftie steed
    Downe fell to ground, and crept into a bush,
    To hide his coward head from dying dreed:
    But Trompart stoutly stayd to taken heed
    Of what might hap.   Eftsoone there stepped foorth

A goodly Ladie clad in hunters weed,
That seemd to be a woman of great worth,
And by her stately portance borne of heavenly birth.

XXII. Her face so faire as flesh it seemed not,
But hevenly pourtraict of bright Angels hew,
Cleare as the skye, withouten blame or blot,
Through goodly mixture of complexions dew;
And in her cheekes the vermeill red did shew
Like roses in a bed of lillies shed,
The which ambrosiall odours from them threw,
And gazers sence with double pleasure fed,
Hable to heale the sicke, and to revive the ded.

XXIII. In her faire eyes two living lamps did flame,
Kindled above at th' hevenly makers light,
And darted fyrie beames out of the same,
So passing persant, and so wondrous bright,
That quite bereav'd the rash beholders sight:
In them the blinded god his lustfull fyre
To kindle oft assayd, but had no might;
For, with dredd Majestie and awfull yre,
She broke his wanton darts, and quenched bace desyre.

XXIV. Her yvorie forhead, full of bountie brave,
Like a broad table did it selfe dispred,
For Love his loftie triumphes to engrave,
And write the battailes of his great godhed:
All good and honour might therein be red,
For there their dwelling was.   And, when she spake,
Sweete wordes like dropping honny she did shed;
And twixt the perles and rubins softly brake
A silver sound, that heavenly musicke seemd to make.

XXV. Upon her eyelids many Graces sate,
Under the shadow of her even browes,
Working belgardes and amorous retrate;
And everie one her with a grace endowes,
And everie one with meekenesse to her bowes.
So glorious mirrhour of celestiall grace,
And soveraine moniment of mortall vowes,
How shall frayle pen descrive her heavenly face,
For feare, through want of skill, her beauty to disgrace?

XXVI. So faire, and thousand thousand times more faire,
    She seemd, when she presented was to sight;
    And was yclad, for heat of scorching aire,
    All in a silken Camus lilly whight,
    Purfled upon with many a folded plight,
    Which all above besprinckled was throughout
    With golden aygulets, that glistred bright
    Like twinckling starres; and all the skirt about
    Was hemd with golden fringe.

XXVII. Below her ham her weed did somewhat trayne,
    And her streight legs most bravely were embayld
    In gilden buskins of costly Cordwayne,
    All bard with golden bendes, which were entayld
    With curious antickes, and full fayre aumayld:
    Before, they fastned were under her knee
    In a rich jewell, and therein entrayld
    The ends of all the knots, that none might see
    How they within their fouldings close enwrapped bee:

XXVIII. Like two faire marble pillours they were seene,
    Which doe the temple of the Gods support,
    Whom all the people decke with girlands greene,
    And honour in their festivall resort;
    Those same with stately grace and princely port
    She taught to tread, when she herselfe would grace;
    But with the woody Nymphes when she did play,
    Or when the flying Libbard she did chace,
    She could then nimbly move, and after fly apace.

XXIX. And in her hand a sharpe bore-speare she held,
    And at her backe a bow and quiver gay,
    Stuft with steele-headed dartes, wherewith she queld
    The salvage beastes in her victorious play,
    Knit with a golden bauldricke, which forelay
    Athwart her snowy brest, and did divide
    Her daintie paps; which, like young fruit in May,
    Now little gan to swell, and being tide
    Through her thin weed their places only signifide.

XXX. Her yellow lockes, crisped like golden wyre,
    About her shoulders weren loosely shed,
    And, when the winde emongst them did inspyre,

They waved like a penon wyde dispred,
And low behinde her backe were scattered:
And, whether art it were or heedlesse hap,
As through the flouring forrest rash she fled,
In her rude heares sweet flowres themselves did lap,
And flourishing fresh leaves and blossomes did enwrap.

XXXI. Such as Diana by the sandy shore
Of swift Eurotas, or on Cynthus greene,
Where all the Nymphes have her unwares forlore,
Wandreth alone with bow and arrowes keene,
To seeke her game: Or as that famous Queene
Of Amazons, whom Pyrrhus did destroy,
The day that first of Priame she was seene,
Did shew her selfe in great triumphant joy,
To succour the weake state of sad afflicted Troy.

XXXII. Such when as hartlesse Trompart her did vew,
He was dismayed in his coward minde,
And doubted whether he himselfe should shew,
Or fly away, or bide alone behinde;
Both feare and hope he in her face did finde:
When she at last him spying thus bespake:
" Hayle, Groome! didst not thou see a bleeding Hynde,
Whose right haunch earst my stedfast arrow strake?
If thou didst, tell me, that I may her overtake."

XXXIII. Wherewith reviv'd, this answere forth he threw:
" O Goddesse, (for such I thee take to bee)
For nether doth thy face terrestriall shew,
Nor voyce sound mortall; I avow to thee,
Such wounded beast as that I did not see,
Sith earst into this forrest wild I came.
But mote thy goodlyhed forgive it mee,
To weete which of the gods I shall thee name,
That unto thee dew worship I may rightly frame."

XXXIV. To whom she thus—but ere her words ensewd,
Unto the bush her eye did suldein glaunce,
In which vaine Braggadocchio was mewd,
And saw it stirre: she lefte her percing launce,
And towards gan a deadly shafte advaunce,
In mind to marke the beast.   At which sad stowre

Trompart forth stept to stay the mortall chaunce,
Out crying; " O! what ever hevenly powre,
Or earthly wight thou be, withhold this deadly howre.

xxxv. " O! stay thy hand; for yonder is no game
For thy fiers arrowes, them to exercize;
But loe! my Lord, my liege, whose warlike name
Is far renowmd through many bold emprize;
And now in shade he shrowded yonder lies."
She staid: with that he crauld out of his nest,
Forth creeping on his caitive hands and thies;
And, standing stoutly up, his lofty crest
Did fiercely shake, and rowze as comming late from rest,

xxxvi. As fearfull fowle, that long in secret cave
For dread of soring hauke her selfe hath hid,
Nor caring how, her silly life to save,
She her gay painted plumes disorderid;
Seeing at last her selfe from daunger rid,
Peepes forth, and soone renews her native pride:
She gins her feathers fowle disfigured
Prowdly to prune, and sett on every side;
She shakes off shame, ne thinks how erst she did her hide,

xxxvii. So when her goodly visage he beheld,
He gan himselfe to vaunt: but, when he vewd
Those deadly tooles which in her hand she held,
Soone into other fitts he was transmewd,
Till she to him her gracious speach renewd:
" All haile, Sir knight! and well may thee befall,
As all the like, which honor have pursewd
Through deeds of armes and prowesse martiall,
All vertue merits praise, but such the most of all."

xxxviii. To whom he thus: " O fairest under skie!
Trew be thy words, and worthy of thy praise,
That warlike feats doest highest glorifie.
Therein I have spent all my youthly daies,
And many battailes fought and many fraies
Throughout the world, wher-so they might be found,
Endevoring my dreaded name to raise
Above the Moone, that fame may it resound
In her eternall tromp, with laurell girlond cround,

XXXIX. " But what art thou, O Lady! which doest raunge
In this wildé forest, where no pleasure is,
And doest not it for joyous court exchaunge,
Emongst thine equall peres, where happy blis
And all delight does raigne, much more then this?
There thou maist love, and dearly loved be,
And swim in pleasure, which thou here doest mis:
There maist thou best be seene, and best maist see:
The wood is fit for beasts, the court is fitt for thee."

XL. " Who-so in pompe of prowd estate " (quoth she)
" Does swim, and bathes him selfe in courtly blis,
Does waste his dayes in darke obscuritee,
And in oblivion ever buried is;
Where ease abownds yt's eath to doe amis:
But who his limbs with labours, and his mynd
Behaves with cares, cannot so easy mis.
Abroad in armes, at home in studious kynd,
Who seekes with painfull toile shall honor soonest fynd:

XLI. " In woods, in waves, in warres, she wonts to dwell,
And wil be found with perill and with paine;
Ne can the man that moulds in ydle cell
Unto her happy mansion attaine:
Before her gate high God did Sweate ordaine,
And wakefull watches ever to abide;
But easy is the way and passage plaine
To pleasures pallace: it may soone be spide,
And day and night her dores to all stand open wide.

XLII. " In Princes court "—The rest she would have sayd,
But that the foolish man, fild with delight
Of her sweete words that all his sence dismayd,
And with her wondrous beauty ravisht quight,
Gan burne in filthy lust; and, leaping light,
Thought in his bastard armes her to embrace.
With that she, swarving backe, her Javelin bright
Against him bent, and fiercely did menace:
So turned her about, and fled away apace.

XLIII. Which when the Pesaunt saw, amazd he stood,
And grieved at her flight; yet durst he nott
Pursew her steps through wild unknowen wood:

Besides he feard her wrath, and threatned shott,
Whiles in the bush he lay, not yett forgott:
Ne car'd he greatly for her presence vayne,
But turning said to Trompart; " What fowle blott
Is this to knight, that Lady should agayne
Depart to woods untoucht, and leave so proud disdayne."

XLIV. " Perdy," (said Trompart) " lett her pas at will,
Least by her presence daunger mote befall;
For who can tell (and sure I feare it ill)
But that shee is some powre celestiall?
For whiles she spake her great words did appall
My feeble corage, and my heart oppresse,
That yet I quake and tremble over-all."
" And I," (said Braggadocchio) " thought no lesse,
When first I heard her horn sound with such ghastlinesse.

XLV. " For from my mothers wombe this grace I have
Me given by eternall destiny,
That earthly thing may not my corage brave
Dismay with feare, or cause one foot to flye,
But either hellish feends, or powres on hye:
Which was the cause, when earst that horne I heard,
Weening it had beene thunder in the skye,
I hid my selfe from it, as one affeard;
But, when I other knew, my self I boldly reard.

XLVI. " But now, for feare of worse that may betide,
Let us soone hence depart." They soone agree:
So to his steed he gott, and gan to ride
As one unfitt therefore, that all might see
He had not trayned bene in chevalree.
Which well that valiaunt courser did discerne;
For he despisd to tread in dew degree,
But chaufd and fom'd with corage fiers and sterne,
And to be easd of that base burden still did erne.

CANTO IV

Guyon does Furor bind in chaines,
And stops occasion:
Delivers Phaon, and therefore
By strife is rayld uppon.

I. In brave poursuitt of honorable deed,
There is I know not (what) great difference
Betweene the vulgar and the noble seed,
Which unto things of valorous pretence
Seemes to be borne by native influence;
As feates of armes, and love to entertaine:
But chiefly skill to ride seemes a science
Proper to gentle blood: some others faine
To menage steeds, as did this vaunter, but in vaine.

II. But he, the rightfull owner of that steede,
Who well could menage and subdew his pride,
The whiles on foot was forced for to yeed
With that blacke Palmer, his most trusty guide,
Who suffred not his wandring feete to slide;
But when strong passion, or weake fleshlinesse,
Would from the right way seeke to draw him wide,
He would, through temperaunce and stedfastnesse,
Teach him the weak to strengthen, and the strong suppresse.

III. It fortuned, forth faring on his way,
He saw from far, or seemed for to see,
Some troublous uprore or contentious fray,
Whereto he drew in hast it to agree.
A mad man, or that feigned mad to bee,
Drew by the heare along upon the grownd
A handsom stripling with great crueltee,
Whom sore he bett, and gor'd with many a wownd,
That cheekes with teares, and sydes with blood, did all
abownd.

IV. And him behynd a wicked Hag did stalke,
In ragged robes and filthy disaray;
Her other leg was lame, that she no'te walke,

But on a staffe her feeble steps did stay:
Her lockes, that loathly were and hoarie gray,
Grew all afore, and loosely hong unrold;
But all behinde was bald, and worne away,
That none thereof could ever taken hold;
And eke her face ill-favourd, full of wrinckles old.

v. And ever as she went her toung did walke
In fowle reproch, and termes of vile despight,
Provoking him, by her outrageous talke,
To heape more vengeance on that wretched wight:
Sometimes she raught him stones, wherwith to smite,
Sometimes her staffe, though it her one leg were,
Withouten which she could not goe upright;
Ne any evill meanes she did forbeare,
That might him move to wrath, and indignation reare.

vi. The noble Guyon, mov'd with great remorse,
Approching, first the Hag did thrust away;
And after, adding more impetuous forse,
His mighty hands did on the madman lay,
And pluckt him backe; who, all on fire streight way,
Against him turning all his fell intent,
With beastly brutish rage gan him assay,
And smott, and bitt, and kickt, and scratcht, and rent,
And did he wist not what in his avengement.

vii. And sure he was a man of mickle might,
Had he had governaunce it well to guyde;
But, when the frantick fitt inflamd his spright,
His force was vaine, and strooke more often wyde,
Then at the aymed marke which he had eyde:
And oft himselfe he chaunst to hurt unwares,
Whylest reason, blent through passion, nought descryde;
But, as a blindfold Bull, at randon fares,
And where he hits nought knowes, and whom he hurts
nought cares.

viii. His rude assault and rugged handeling
Straunge seemed to the knight, that aye with foe
In fayre defence and goodly menaging
Of armes was wont to fight; yet nathemoe
Was he abashed now, not fighting so;
But more enfierced through his currish play,

Him sternly grypt, and hailing to and fro,
To overthrow him strongly did assay,
But overthrew him selfe unwares, and lower lay:

IX. And being downe the villein sore did beate
And bruze with clownish fistes his manly face;
And eke the Hag, with many a bitter threat,
Still cald upon to kill him in the place.
With whose reproch, and odious menace,
The knight emboyling in his haughtie hart
Knitt all his forces, and gan soone unbrace
His grasping hold: so lightly did upstart,
And drew his deadly weapon to maintaine his part.

X. Which when the Palmer saw, he loudly cryde,
" Not so, O Guyon! never thinke that so
That Monster can be maistred or destroyd:
He is not, ah! he is not such a foe,
As steele can wound, or strength can overthroe.
That same is Furor, cursed cruel wight,
That unto knighthood workes much shame and woe;
And that same Hag, his aged mother, hight
Occasion; the roote of all wrath and despight.

XI. " With her, whoso will raging Furor tame,
Must first begin, and well her amenage:
First her restraine from her reprochfull blame
And evill meanes, with which she doth enrage
Her frantick sonne, and kindles his corage;
Then, when she is withdrawne or strong withstood,
It's eath his ydle fury to aswage,
And calme the tempest of his passion wood:
The bankes are overflowne when stopped is the flood."

XII. Therewith Sir Guyon left his first emprise,
And, turning to that woman, fast her hent
By the hoare lockes that hong before her eyes,
And to the ground her threw: yet n'ould she stent
Her bitter rayling and foule revilement,
But still provokt her sonne to wreake her wrong;
But nathelesse he did her still torment,
And, catching hold of her ungratious tonge
Thereon an yron lock did fasten firme and strong.

XIII. Then, whenas use of speach was from her reft,
     With her two crooked handes she signes did make,
     And beckned him, the last help she had left;
     But he that last left helpe away did take,
     And both her handes fast bound unto a stake,
     That she note stirre.   Then gan her sonne to flye
     Full fast away, and did her quite forsake;
     But Guyon after him in hast did hye,
     And soone him overtooke in sad perplexitye.

XIV. In his strong armes he stifly him embraste,
     Who him gainstriving nought at all prevaild;
     For all his power was utterly defaste,
     And furious fitts at earst quite weren quaild:
     Oft he re'nforst, and oft his forces fayld,
     Yet yield he would not, nor his rancor slack.
     Then him to ground he cast, and rudely hayld,
     And both his hands fast bound behind his backe,
     And both his feet in fetters to an yron racke.

XV. With hundred yron chaines he did him bind,
     And hundred knots, that did him sore constraine;
     Yet his great yron teeth he still did grind
     And grimly gnash, threatning revenge in vaine:
     His burning eyen, whom bloody strakes did staine,
     Stared full wide, and threw forth sparkes of fyre;
     And more for ranck despight then for great paine,
     Shakt his long locks colourd like copper-wyre,
     And bitt his tawny beard to shew his raging yre.

XVI. Thus when as Guyon Furor had captivd,
     Turning about he saw that wretched Squyre,
     Whom that mad man of life nigh late deprivd,
     Lying on ground, all soild with blood and myre:
     Whom whenas he perceived to respyre,
     He gan to comfort, and his woundes to dresse.
     Being at last recured, he gan inquyre
     What hard mishap him brought to such distresse,
     And made that caytives thrall, the thrall of wretchednesse.

XVII. With hart then throbbing, and with watry eyes,
     " Fayre Sir " (quoth he) " What man can shun the hap,
     That hidden lyes unwares him to surpryse?

Misfortune waites advantage to entrap
The man most wary in her whelming lap:
So me weake wretch, of many weakest one,
Unweeting and unware of such mishap,
She brought to mischiefe through Occasion,
Where this same wicked villein did me light upon.

XVIII. " It was a faithlesse Squire, that was the sourse
Of all my sorrow and of these sad teares,
With whom from tender dug of commune nourse
Attonce I was upbrought; and eft, when yeares
More rype us reason lent to chose our Peares,
Our selves in league of vowed love wee knitt;
In which we long time, without gealous feares
Or faultie thoughts, contynewd as was fitt;
And for my part, I vow, dissembled not a whitt.

XIX. " It was my fortune, commune to that age,
To love a Lady fayre of great degree,
The which was borne of noble parentage,
And set in highest seat of dignitee,
Yet seemd no lesse to love then lov'd to bee:
Long I her serv'd, and found her faithful still,
Ne ever thing could cause us disagree.
Love, that two harts makes one, makes eke one will;
Each strove to please, and others pleasure to fulfill.

XX. " My friend, hight Philemon, I did partake
Of all my love and all my privitie;
Who greatly joyous seemed for my sake,
And gratious to that Lady as to mee;
Ne ever wight that mote so welcome bee
As he to her, withouten blott or blame;
He ever thing that she could think or see,
But unto him she would impart the same.
O wretched man, that would abuse so gentle Dame!

XXI. " At last such grace I found, and meanes I wrought,
That I that Lady to my spouse had wonne;
Accord of friendes, consent of Parents sought,
Affyaunce made, my happinesse begonne,
There wanted nought but few rites to be donne,
Which mariage make: that day too farre did seeme.

Most joyous man, on whom the shining Sunne
Did shew his face, my selfe I did esteeme,
And that my falser friend did no less joyous deeme.

XXII. " But ear that wished day his beame disclosd,
He, either envying my toward good,
Or of him selfe to treason ill disposed,
One day unto me came in friendly mood,
And told for secret, how he understood
That Lady, whom I had to me assynd,
Had both distaind her honorable blood,
And eke the faith which she to me did bynd;
And therefore wisht me stay till I more truth should fynd.

XXIII. " The gnawing anguish, and sharp gelosy,
Which his sad speach infixed in my brest,
Ranckled so sore, and festred inwardly,
That my engreeved mind could find no rest,
Till that the truth thereof I did out wrest;
And him besought, by that same sacred band
Betwixt us both, to counsell me the best:
He then with solemne oath and plighted hand
Assurd, ere long the truth to let me understand.

XXIV. " Ere long with like againe he boorded mee,
Saying, he now had boulted all the floure,
And that it was a groome of base degree,
Which of my love was partener Paramoure:
Who used in a darkesome inner bowre
Her oft to meete: which better to approve,
He promised to bring me at that howre,
When I should see that would me nearer move,
And drive me to withdraw my blind abused love.

XXV. " This gracelesse man, for furtherance of his guile,
Did court the handmayd of my Lady deare,
Who, glad t' embosome his affection vile,
Did all she might more pleasing to appeare.
One day, to worke her to his will more neare,
He woo'd her thus: Pryene, (so she hight,)
What great despight doth fortune to thee beare,
Thus lowly to abase thy beautie bright,
That it should not deface all others lesser light?

XXVI. " But if she had her least helpe to thee lent,
T'adorne thy forme according thy desart,
Their blazing pride thou wouldest soone have blent,
And staynd their prayses with thy least good part;
Ne should faire Claribell with all her art,
Tho' she thy Lady be, approch thee neare:
For proofe thereof, this evening, as thou art,
Aray thyselfe in her most gorgeous geare,
That I may more delight in thy embracement deare.

XXVII. " The Mayden, proud through praise and mad through
love,
Him hearkned to, and soone her selfe arrayd,
The whiles to me the treachour did remove
His craftie engin; and, as he had sayd,
Me leading, in a secret corner layd,
The sad spectatour of my Tragedie:
Where left, he went, and his owne false part playd,
Disguised like that groome of base degree,
Whom he had feignd th' abuser of my love to bee.

XXVIII. " Eftsoones he came unto th' appointed place,
And with him brought Pryene, rich arayd,
In Claribellaes clothes.   Her proper face
I not descerned in that darkesome shade,
But weend it was my love with whom he playd.
Ah God! what horrour and tormenting griefe
My hart, my handes, mine eies, and all assayd!
Me liefer were ten thousand deathes priefe
Then wounde of gealous worme, and shame of such
repriefe.

XXIX. " I home retourning, fraught with fowle despight,
And chawing vengeaunce all the way I went,
Soone as my loathed love appeard in sight,
With wrathfull hand I slew her innocent,
That after soone I dearely did lament;
For, when the cause of that outrageous deede
Demaunded, I made plaine and evident,
Her faultie Handmayd, which that bale did breede,
Confest how Philemon her wrought to chaunge her
weede.

xxx. " Which when I heard, with horrible affright
And hellish fury all enragd, I sought
Upon myselfe that vengeable despight
To punish: yet it better first I thought
To wreake my wrath on him that first it wrought:
To Philemon, false faytour Philemon,
I cast to pay that I so dearely bought.
Of deadly drugs I gave him drinke anon,
And washt away his guilt with guilty potion.

xxxi. " Thus heaping crime on crime, and griefe on griefe,
To losse of love adjoyning losse of frend,
I meant to purge both with a third mischiefe,
And in my woes beginner it to end:
That was Pryene; she did first offend,
She last should smart: with which cruell intent,
When I at her my murdrous blade did bend,
She fled away with ghastly dreriment,
And I, poursewing my fell purpose, after went.

xxxii. " Feare gave her winges, and rage enforst my flight;
Through woods and plaines so long I did her chace,
Till this mad man, whom your victorious might
Hath now fast bound, me met in middle space.
As I her, so he me poursewd apace,
And shortly overtooke: I, breathing yre,
Sore chauffed at my stay in such a cace,
And with my heat kindled his cruell fyre;
Which kindled once, his mother did more rage inspyre.

xxxiii. " Betwixt them both they have me doen to dye,
Through wounds, and strokes, and stubborne handeling,
That death were better then such agony
As griefe and fury unto me did bring;
Of which in me yet stickes the mortall sting,
That during life will never be appeased!"
When he thus ended had his sorrowing,
Said Guyon; " Squyre, sore have ye beene diseasd,
But all your hurts may soone through temperance be
easd."

xxxiv. Then gan the Palmer thus; " Most wretched man,
That to affections does the bridle lend!
In their beginning they are weake and wan,

But soone through suff'rance growe to fearefull end:
Whiles they are weake, betimes with them contend;
For, when they once to perfect strength do grow,
Strong warres they make, and cruell battry bend
Gainst fort of Reason, it to overthrow:
Wrath, gelosy, griefe, love, this Squyre have laide thus
    low.

xxxv. " Wrath, gealosie, griefe, love, do thus expell:
Wrath is a fire; and gealosie a weede;
Griefe is a flood; and love a monster fell;
The fire of sparkes, the weede of little seede,
The flood of drops, the Monster filth did breede:
But sparks, seed, drops, and filth, do thus delay;
The sparks soone quench, the springing seed outweed,
The drops dry up, and filth wipe cleane away:
So shall wrath, gealosy, griefe, love, die and decay."

xxxvi. " Unlucky Squire," (saide Guyon) " sith thou hast
Falne into mischiefe through intemperaunce,
Henceforth take heede of that thou now hast past,
And guyde thy waies with warie governaunce,
Least worse betide thee by some later chaunce,
But read how art thou nam'd, and of what kin? "
" Phaon I hight," (quoth he) " and do advaunce
Mine auncestry from famous Coradin,
Who first to rayse our house to honour did begin."

xxxvii. Thus as he spake, lo! far away they spyde
A varlet ronning towardes hastily,
Whose flying feet so fast their way applyde,
That round about a cloud of dust did fly,
Which, mingled all with sweate, did dim his eye.
He soone approched, panting, breathlesse, whot,
And all so soyld that none could him descry:
His countenance was bold, and bashed not
For Guyons lookes, but scornefull eye glaunce at him shot.

xxxviii. Behind his backe he bore a brasen shield,
On which was drawen faire, in colours fit,
A flaming fire in midst of bloody field,
And round about the wreath this word was writ,
Burnt I doe burne.   Right well beseemed it
To be the shield of some redoubted knight;

And in his hand two dartes, exceeding flit
And deadly sharpe, he held, whose heads were dight
In poyson and in blood of malice and despight.

XXXIX. When he in presence came, to Guyon first
He boldly spake; " Sir knight, if knight thou bee,
Abandon this forestalled place at erst,
For feare of further harme, I counsell thee;
Or bide the chaunce at thine owne jeopardee."
The knight at his great boldnesse wondered;
And, though he scornd his ydle vanitee,
Yet mildly him to purpose answered;
For not to grow of nought he it conjectured.

XL. " Varlet, this place most dew to me I deeme,
Yielded by him that held it forcibly:
But whence should come that harme, which thou dost
      seeme
To threat to him that mindes his chaunce t' abye? "
" Perdy," (sayd he) " here comes, and is hard by,
A knight of wondrous powre and great assay,
That never yet encountred enemy
But did him deadly daunt, or fowle dismay;
Ne thou for better hope, if thou his presence stay."

XLI. " How hight he then," (said Guyon) " and from
      whence? "
" Pyrochles is his name, renowmed farre
For his bold feates and hardy confidence,
Full oft approvd in many a cruell warre;
The brother of Cymochles, both which arre
The sonnes of old Acrates and Despight;
Acrates, sonne of Phlegeton and Jarre;
But Phlegeton is sonne of Herebus and Night;
But Herebus sonne of Aeternitie is hight.

XLII. " So from immortall race he does proceede,
That mortall hands may not withstand his might,
Drad for his derring doe and bloody deed;
For all in blood and spoile is his delight.
His am I Atin, his in wrong and right,
That matter make for him to worke upon,
And stirre him up to strife and cruell fight.

Fly therefore, fly this fearefull stead anon,
Least thy foolhardize worke thy sad confusion."

XLIII. "His be that care, whom most it doth concerne,"
(Sayd he) " but whither with such hasty flight
Art thou now bownd? for well mote I discerne
Great cause, that carries thee so swifte and light."
" My Lord," (quoth he) " me sent, and streight behight
To seeke Occasion, where so she bee:
For he is all disposd to bloody fight,
And breathes out wrath and hainous crueltee:
Hard is his hap that first fals in his jeopardee."

XLIV. " Mad man," (said then the Palmer) " that does seeke
Occasion to wrath, and cause of strife:
Shee comes unsought, and shonned followes eke.
Happy! who can abstaine, when Rancor rife
Kindles Revenge, and threats his rusty knife.
Woe never wants where every cause is caught;
And rash Occasion makes unquiet life!"
" Then loe! wher bound she sits, whom thou hast
        sought,"
Said Guyon: " let that message to thy Lord be
        brought."

XLV. That when the varlett heard and saw, streight way
He wexed wondrous wroth, and said; " Vile knight,
That knights and knighthood doest with shame upbray,
And shewst th' ensample of thy childishe might,
With silly weake old woman that did fight!
Great glory and gay spoile, sure hast thou gott,
And stoutly prov'd thy puissaunce here in sight.
That shall Pyrochles well requite, I wott,
And with thy blood abolish so reprochfull blott."

XLVI. With that one of his thrillant darts he threw,
Headed with yre and vengeable despight.
The quivering steele his aymed end wel knew,
And to his brest it selfe intended right:
But he was wary, and, ere it empight
In the meant marke, advaunst his shield atweene,
On which it seizing no way enter might,
But backe rebownding left the forckhead keene:
Eftsoones he fled away, and might no where be seene.

CANTO V

Pyrochles does with Guyon fight,
And Furors chayne untyes,
Who him sore wounds: whiles Atin to
Cymochles for ayd flyes.

I. Who ever doth to temperaunce apply
His stedfast life, and all his actions frame,
Trust me, shal find no greater enimy
Then stubborne perturbation to the same;
To which right wel the wise doe give that name,
For it the goodly peace of staied mindes
Does overthrow, and troublous warre proclame:
His owne woes author, who so bound it findes,
As did Pyrochles, and it wilfully unbindes.

II. After that varlets flight, it was not long
Ere on the plaine fast pricking Guyon spide
One in bright armes embatteiled full strong,
That, as the Sunny beames do glaunce and glide
Upon the trembling wave, so shined bright,
And round about him threw forth sparkling fire,
That seemd him to enflame on every side:
His steed was bloody red, and fomed yre,
When with the maistring spur he did him roughly stire.

III. Approching nigh, he never staid to greete,
Ne chaffar words, prowd corage to provoke,
But prickt so fiers, that underneath his feete
The smouldring dust did rownd about him smoke,
Both horse and man nigh able for to choke;
And fayrly couching his steeleheaded speare,
Him first saluted with a sturdy stroke:
It booted nought Sir Guyon, comming neare,
To thincke such hideous puissaunce on foot to beare;

IV. But lightly shunned it; and, passing by,
With his bright blade did smite at him so fell,
That the sharpe steele, arriving forcibly

On his broad shield, bitt not, but glauncing fell
On his horse necke before the quilted sell,
And from the head the body sundred quight.
So him dismounted low he did compell
On foot with him to matchen equall fight:
The truncked beast fast bleeding did him fowly dight.

v. Sore bruzed with the fall he slow uprose,
And all enraged thus him loudly shent;
" Disleall Knight, whose coward corage chose
To wreake it selfe on beast all innocent,
And shund the marke at which it should be ment;
Therby thine armes seem strong, but manhood frayl:
So hast thou oft with guile thine honor blent;
But litle may such guile thee now avayl,
If wonted force and fortune doe me not much fayl."

vi. With that he drew his flaming sword, and strooke
At him so fiercely, that the upper marge
Of his sevenfolded shield away it tooke,
And, glauncing on his helmet, made a large
And open gash therein: were not his targe
That broke the violence of his intent,
The weary sowle from thence it would discharge;
Nathelesse so sore a buff to him it lent,
That made him reele, and to his brest his bever bent.

vii. Exceeding wroth was Guyon at that blow,
And much ashamd that stroke of living arme
Should him dismay, and make him stoup so low,
Though otherwise it did him litle harme:
Tho, hurling high his yron braced arme,
He smote so manly on his shoulder plate,
That all his left side it did quite disarme;
Yet there the steel stayd not, but inly bate
Deepe in his flesh, and opened wide a red floodgate.

viii. Deadly dismayd with horror of that dint
Pyrochles was, and grieved eke entyre;
Yet nathemore did it his fury stint,
But added flame unto his former fire,
That wel nigh molt his hart in raging yre:
Ne thenceforth his approved skill, to ward,

Or strike, or hurtle rownd in warlike gyre,
Remembred he, ne car'd for his saufgard,
But rudely rag'd, and like a cruell tygre far'd.

IX. He hewd, and lasht, and foynd, and thondred blowes,
And every way did seeke into his life;
Ne plate, ne male, could ward so mighty throwes,
But yielded passage to his cruell knife.
But Guyon, in the heat of all his strife,
Was wary wise, and closely did awayt
Avauntage, whilest his foe did rage most rife:
Sometimes athwart, sometimes he strook him strayt,
And falsed oft his blowes t' illude him with such bayt.

X. Like as a Lyon, whose imperiall powre
A prowd rebellious Unicorn defyes,
T' avoide the rash assault and wrathful stowre
Of his fiers foe, him to a tree applyes,
And when him ronning in full course he spyes,
He slips aside; the whiles that furious beast
His precious horne, sought of his enimyes,
Strikes in the stocke, ne thence can be releast,
But to the mighty victor yields a bounteous feast.

XI. With such faire sleight him Guyon often fayld,
Till at the last all breathlesse, weary, faint,
Him spying, with fresh onsett he assayld,
And kindling new his corage seeming queint,
Strooke him so hugely, that through great constraint
He made him stoup perforce unto his knee,
And doe unwilling worship to the Saint,
That on his shield depainted he did see:
Such homage till that instant never learned hee.

XII. Whom Guyon seeing stoup, poursewed fast
The present offer of faire victory,
And soone his dreadfull blade about he cast,
Wherewith he smote his haughty crest so hye,
That streight on grownd made him full low to lye;
Then on his brest his victor foote he thrust:
With that he cryde, " Mercy! doe me not dye,
Ne deeme thy force by fortunes doome unjust,
That hath (maugre her spight) thus low me laid in dust."

XIII. Eftsoones his cruel hand Sir Guyon stayd,
Tempring the passion with advizement slow,
And maistring might on enimy dismayd;
For th' equall die of warre he well did know:
Then to him said, " Live, and alleagaunce owe
To him that gives thee life and liberty;
And henceforth by this daies ensample trow,
That hasty wroth, and heedlesse hazardry,
Doe breede repentaunce late, and lasting infamy."

XIV. So up he let him rise; who, with grim looke
And count'naunce sterne, upstanding, gan to grind
His grated teeth for great disdeigne, and shooke
His sandy lockes, long hanging downe behind,
Knotted in blood and dust, for grief of mind
That he in ods of armes was conquered:
Yet in himselfe some comfort he did find,
That him so noble knight had maystered;
Whose bounty more then might, yet both, he wondered.

XV. Which Guyon marking said, " Be nought agriev'd,
Sir knight, that thus ye now subdewed arre:
Was never man, who most conquestes atchiev'd,
But sometimes had the worse, and lost by warre,
Yet shortly gaynd that losse exceeded farre.
Losse is no shame, nor to bee lesse then foe;
But to bee lesser than himselfe doth marre
Both loosers lott, and victours prayse alsoe:
Vaine others overthrowes who selfe doth overthrow.

XVI. " Fly, O Pyrochles! fly the dreadfull warre
That in thy selfe thy lesser partes do move;
Outrageous anger, and woe-working jarre,
Direfull impatience, and hart-murdring love:
Those, those thy foes, those warriours far remove,
Which thee to endlesse bale captived lead,
But sith in might thou didst my mercy prove,
Of courtesie to mee the cause aread
That thee against me drew with so impetuous dread."

XVII. " Dreadlesse," (said he) " that shall I soone declare.
It was complaind that thou hadst done great tort
Unto an aged woman, poore and bare,

And thralled her in chaines with strong effort,
Voide of all succour and needfull comfort;
That ill beseemes thee, such as I thee see,
To worke such shame.   Therefore, I thee exhort
To chaunce thy will, and set Occasion free,
And to her captive sonne yield his first libertee."

XVIII. Thereat Sir Guyon smylde, " And is that all,
(Said he) " that thee so sore displeased hath?
Great mercy, sure, for to enlarge a thrall,
Whose freedom shall thee turne to greatest scath!
Nath'lesse now quench thy whott emboyling wrath:
Loe! there they bee; to thee I yield them free."
Thereat he, wondrous glad, out of the path
Did lightly leape, where he them bound did see,
And gan to breake the bands of their captivitee.

XIX. Soone as Occasion felt her selfe untyde,
Before her sonne could well assoyled bee,
She to her use returnd, and streight defyde
Both Guyon and Pyrochles; th' one (said shee)
Bycause he wonne; the other, because hee
Was wonne.   So matter did she make of nought,
To stirre up strife, and garre them disagree:
But, soone as Furor was enlargd, she sought
To kindle his quencht fyre, and thousand causes wrought.

XX. It was not long ere she inflam'd him so,
That he would algates with Pyrochles fight,
And his redeemer chalengd for his foe,
Because he had not well mainteind his right,
But yielded had to that same straunger knight.
Now gan Pyrochles wex as wood as hee,
And him affronted with impatient might:
So both together fiers engrasped bee,
Whyles Guyon standing by their uncouth strife does see.

XXI. Him all that while Occasion did provoke
Against Pyrochles, and new matter fram'd
Upon the old, him stirring to bee wroke
Of his late wronges, in which she oft him blam'd
For suffering such abuse as knighthood sham'd,
And him dishabled quyte.   But he was wise,

Ne would with vaine occasions be inflam'd;
Yet others she more urgent did devise;
Yet nothing could him to impatience entise.

XXII. Their fell contention still increased more,
And more thereby increased Furors might,
That he his foe has hurt and wounded sore,
And him in blood and durt deformed quight.
His mother eke, more to augment his spight,
Now brought to him a flaming fyer brond,
Which she in Stygian lake, ay burning bright,
Had kindled: that she gave into his hond,
That armd with fire more hardly he mote him withstond

XXIII. Tho gan that villein wex so fiers and strong,
That nothing might sustaine his furious forse.
He cast him downe to ground, and all along
Drew him through durt and myre without remorse,
And fowly battered his comely corse,
That Guyon much disdeigned so loathly sight.
At last he was compeld to cry perforse,
" Help, O Sir Guyon! helpe, most noble knight,
To ridd a wretched man from handes of hellish wight! "

XXIV. The knight was greatly moved at his playnt,
And gan him dight to succour his distresse,
Till that the Palmer, by his grave restraynt,
Him stayd from yielding pitifull redresse,
And said; " Deare sonne, thy causelesse ruth represse,
Ne let thy stout hart melt in pitty vayne:
He that his sorrow sought through wilfulnesse,
And his foe fettred would release agayne,
Deserves to taste his follies fruit, repented payne."

XXV. Guyon obayd: So him away he drew
From needlesse trouble of renewing fight
Already fought, his voyage to poursew.
But rash Pyrochles varlett, Atin hight,
When late he saw his Lord in heavie plight
Under Sir Guyons puissaunt stroke to fall,
Him deeming dead, as then he seemd in sight,
Fledd fast away to tell his funerall
Unto his brother, whom Cymochles men did call.

XXVI. He was a man of rare redoubted might,
Famous throughout the world for warlike prayse,
And glorious spoiles, purchast in perilous fight:
Full many doughtie knightes he in his dayes
Had doen to death, subdewde in equall frayes
Whose carkases, for terrour of his name,
Of fowles and beastes he made the piteous prayes,
And hong their conquered armes, for more defame,
On gallow trees, in honour of his dearest Dame.

XXVII. His dearest Dame is that Enchaunteresse,
The vyle Acrasia, that with vaine delightes,
And ydle pleasures in her Bowre of Blisse,
Does charme her lovers, and the feeble sprightes
Can call out of the bodies of fraile wightes;
Whom then she does transforme to monstrous hewes,
And horribly misshapes with ugly sightes,
Captiv'd eternally in yron mewes
And darksom dens, where Titan his face never shewes.

XXVIII. There Atin fownd Cymochles sojourning,
To serve his Lemans love: for he by kynd
Was given all to lust and loose living,
When ever his fiers handes he free mote fynd:
And now he has pourd out his ydle mynd
In daintie delices, and lavish joyes,
Having his warlike weapons cast behynd,
And flowes in pleasures and vaine pleasing toyes,
Mingled emongst loose Ladies and lascivious boyes.

XXIX. And over him art, stryving to compayre
With nature, did an Arber greene dispred,
Framed of wanton Yvie, flouring fayre,
Through which the fragrant Eglantine did spred
His prickling armes, entrayld with roses red,
Which daintie odours round about them threw:
And all within with flowres was garnished,
That, when myld Zephyrus emongst them blew,
Did breath out bounteous smels, and painted colors shew.

XXX. And fast beside there trickled softly downe
A gentle streame, whose murmuring wave did play
Emongst the pumy stones, and made a sowne,

To lull him soft asleepe that by it lay:
The wearie Traveiler, wandring that way,
Therein did often quench his thristy heat,
And then by it his wearie limbes display,
Whiles creeping slomber made him to forget
His former payne, and wypt away his toilsom sweat.

XXXI. And on the other syde a pleasaunt grove
Was shott up high, full of the stately tree
That dedicated is t' Olympick Jove,
And to his sonne Alcides, whenas hee
In Nemus gayned goodly victoree:
Therein the mery birdes of every sorte
Chaunted alowd their chearefull harmonee,
And made emongst them selves a sweete consort,
That quickned the dull spright with musicall comfort.

XXXII. There he him found all carelessly displaid,
In secrete shadow from the sunny ray,
On a sweet bed of lillies softly laid,
Amidst a flock of Damzelles fresh and gay,
That rownd about him dissolute did play
Their wanton follies and light meriments:
Every of which did loosely disaray
Her upper partes of meet habiliments,
And shewd them naked, deckt with many ornaments.

XXXIII. And every of them strove with most delights
Him to aggrate, and greatest pleasures shew:
Some framd faire lookes, glancing like evening lights;
Others sweet wordes, dropping like honny dew;
Some bathed kisses, and did soft embrew
The sugred licour through his melting lips:
One boastes her beautie, and does yield to vew
Her dainty limbes above her tender hips;
Another her out boastes, and all for tryall strips.

XXXIV. He, like an Adder lurking in the weedes,
His wandring thought in deepe desire does steepe,
And his frayle eye with spoyle of beauty feedes:
Sometimes he falsely faines himselfe to sleepe,
Whiles through their lids his wanton eies do peepe
To steale a snatch of amorous conceipt,

Whereby close fire into his heart does creepe:
So he them deceives, deceivd in his deceipt,
Made dronke with drugs of deare voluptuous receipt.

XXXV. Atin, arriving there, when him he spyde
Thus in still waves of deepe delight to wade
Fiercely approaching to him lowdly cryde,
" Cymochles; oh! no, but Cymochles shade,
In which that manly person late did fade.
What is become of great Acrates sonne?
Or where hath he hong up his mortall blade,
That hath so many haughty conquests wonne?
Is all his force forlorne, and all his glory donne?

XXXVI. Then, pricking him with his sharp-pointed dart,
He saide; " Up, up! thou womanish weake knight,
That here in Ladies lap entombed art,
Unmindfull of thy praise and prowest might,
And weetlesse eke of lately wrought despight,
Whiles sad Pyrochles lies on sencelesse ground,
And groneth out his utmost grudging spright
Through many a stroke and many a streaming wound,
Calling thy helpe in vaine that here in joyes art dround."

XXXVII. Suddeinly out of his delightfull dreame
The man awoke, and would have questiond more;
But he would not endure that wofull theame
For to dilate at large, but urged sore,
With percing wordes and pittifull implore,
Him hasty to arise.   As one affright
With hellish feends, or Furies made uprore,
He then uprose, inflamd with fell despight,
And called for his armes, for he would algates fight:

XXXVIII. They bene ybrought; he quickly does him dight,
And lightly mounted passeth on his way;
Ne Ladies loves, ne sweete entreaties, might
Appease his heat, or hastie passage stay;
For he has vowd to beene avengd that day
(That day it selfe him seemed all too long)
On him, that did Pyrochles deare dismay:
So proudly pricketh on his courser strong,
And Atin ay him pricks with spurs of shame and wrong.

CANTO VI

Guyon is of immodest Merth
Led into loose desyre;
Fights with Cymochles, whiles his bro-
ther burns in furious fyre.

I. A HARDER lesson to learne Continence
In joyous pleasure then in grievous paine;
For sweetnesse doth allure the weaker sence
So strongly, that uneathes it can refraine
From that which feeble nature covets faine:
But griefe and wrath, that be her enemies
And foes of life, she better can abstaine:
Yet vertue vaunts in both her victories,
And Guyon in them all shewes goodly maysteries.

II. Whom bold Cymochles traveiling to finde,
With cruell purpose bent to wreake on him
The wrath which Atin kindled in his mind,
Came to a river, by whose utmost brim
Wayting to passe, he saw whereas did swim
Along the shore, as swift as glaunce of eye,
A litle Gondelay, bedecked trim
With boughes and arbours woven cunningly,
That like a litle forrest seemed outwardly.

III. And therein sate a Lady fresh and fayre,
Making sweet solace to herselfe alone:
Sometimes she song as lowd as larke in ayre,
Sometimes she laught, as merry as Pope Jone;
Yet was there not with her else any one,
That to her might move cause of meriment:
Matter of merth enough, though there were none,
She could devise; and thousand waies invent
To feede her foolish humour and vaine jolliment.

IV. Which when far off Cymochles heard and saw,
He lowdly cald to such as were abord
The little barke unto the shore to draw,

And him to ferry over that deepe ford.
The merry mariner unto his word
Soone hearkned, and her painted bote streightway
Turnd to the shore, where that same warlike Lord
She in receiv'd; but Atin by no way
She would admit, albe the knight her much did pray.

v. Eftsoones her shallow ship away did slide,
   More swift then swallow sheres the liquid skye,
   Withouten oare or Pilot it to guide,
   Or winged canvas with the wind to fly:
   Onely she turnd a pin, and by and by
   It cut away upon the yielding wave,
   Ne cared she her course for to apply;
   For it was taught the way which she would have,
   And both from rocks and flats it selfe could wisely save.

vi. And all the way the wanton Damsell found
   New merth her passenger to entertaine;
   For she in pleasaunt purpose did abound,
   And greatly joyed merry tales to faine,
   Of which a store-house did with her remaine:
   Yet seemed, nothing well they her became;
   For all her wordes she drownd with laughter vaine,
   And wanted grace in utt'ring of the same,
   That turnd all her pleasaunce to a scoffing game.

vii. And other whiles vaine toyes she would devize,
   As her fantasticke wit did most delight:
   Sometimes her head she fondly would aguize
   With gaudy girlonds, or fresh flowrets dight
   About her necke, or rings of rushes plight:
   Sometimes, to do him laugh, she would assay
   To laugh at shaking of the leaves light
   Or to behold the water worke and play
   About her little frigot, therein making way.

viii. Her light behaviour and loose dalliaunce
   Gave wondrous great contentment to the knight,
   That of his way he had no sovenaunce,
   Nor care of vow'd revenge and cruell fight,
   But to weake wench did yield his martiall might:
   So easie was to quench his flamed minde

With one sweete drop of sensuall delight.
So easie is t' appease the stormy winde
Of malice in the calme of pleasaunt womankind.

IX. Diverse discourses in their way they spent;
Mongst which Cymochles of her questioned
Both what she was, and what that usage ment,
Which in her cott she daily practized?
" Vaine man," (saide she) " that wouldest be reckoned
A straunger in thy home, and ignoraunt
Of Phædria, (for so my name is red)
Of Phædria, thine owne fellow servaunt;
For thou to serve Acrasia thy selfe doest vaunt.

X. " In this wide Inland sea, that hight by name
The Idle lake, my wandring ship I row,
That knowes her port, and thither sayles by ayme,
Ne care, ne feare I how the wind do blow,
Or whether swift I wend, or whether slow:
Both slow and swift alike do serve my tourne;
Ne swelling Neptune ne lowd thundring Jove
Can chaunge my cheare, or make me ever mourne:
My little boat can safely passe this perilous bourne."

XI. Whiles thus she talked, and whiles thus she toyd,
They were far past the passage which he spake,
And come unto an Island waste and voyd,
That floted in the midst of that great lake;
There her small Gondelay her port did make,
And that gay payre, issewing on the shore,
Disburdned her.   Their way they forward take
Into the land that lay them faire before,
Whose pleasaunce she him shewd, and plentifull great store.

XII. It was a chosen plott of fertile land,
Emongst wide waves sett, like a litle nest,
As if it had by Natures cunning hand
Bene choycely picked out from all the rest,
And laid forth for ensample of the best:
No daintie flowre or herbe that growes on grownd,
No arborett with painted blossomes drest
And smelling sweete, but there it might be fownd
To bud out faire, and throwe her sweete smels al arownd.

XIII. No tree whose braunches did not bravely spring;
　　No braunch whereon a fine bird did not sitt;
　　No bird but did her shrill notes sweetely sing;
　　No song but did containe a lovely ditt.
　　Trees, braunches, birds, and songs, were framed fitt
　　For to allure fraile mind to carelesse ease:
　　Carelesse the man soone woxe, and his weake witt
　　Was overcome of thing that did him please;
　　So pleased did his wrathfull purpose faire appease.

XIV. Thus when shee had his eyes and sences fed
　　With false delights, and fild with pleasures vayn,
　　Into a shady dale she soft him led,
　　And layd him downe upon a grassy playn;
　　And her sweete selfe without dread or disdayn
　　She sett beside, laying his head disarmd
　　In her loose lap, it softly to sustayn,
　　Where soone he slumbred fearing not be harmd:
　　The whiles with a love lay she thus him sweetely charmd.

XV. " Behold, O man! that toilesome paines doest take,
　　The flowrs, the fields, and all that pleasaunt growes,
　　How they them selves doe thine ensample make,
　　Whiles nothing envious nature them forth throwes
　　Out of her fruitfull lap; how no man knowes,
　　They spring, they bud, they blossome fresh and faire,
　　And decke the world with their rich pompous showes;
　　Yet no man for them taketh paines or care,
　　Yet no man to them can his carefull paines compare.

XVI. " The lilly, Lady of the flowring field,
　　The flowre-deluce, her lovely Paramoure,
　　Bid thee to them thy fruitlesse labors yield,
　　And soone leave off this toylsome weary stoure:
　　Loe, loe! how brave she decks her bounteous boure,
　　With silkin curtens and gold coverletts,
　　Therein to shrowd her sumptuous Belamoure;
　　Yet nether spinnes nor cardes, ne cares nor fretts,
　　But to her mother Nature all her care she letts.

XVII. " Why then doest thou, O man! that of them all
　　Art Lord, and eke of nature Soveraine,
　　Wilfully make thyselfe a wretched thrall,

And waste thy joyous howres in needlesse paine,
Seeking for daunger and adventures vaine?
What bootes it al to have, and nothing use?
Who shall him rew that swimming in the maine
Will die for thrist, and water doth refuse?
Refuse such fruitlesse toile, and present pleasures chuse."

XVIII. By this she had him lulled fast asleepe,
That of no worldly thing he care did take:
Then she with liquors strong his eies did steepe,
That nothing should him hastily awake.
So she him lefte, and did her selfe betake
Unto her boat again, with which she clefte
The slothfull wave of that great griesy lake:
Soone shee that Island far behind her lefte,
And now is come to that same place where first she wefte.

XIX. By this time was the worthy Guyon brought
Unto the other side of that wide strond
Where she was rowing, and for passage sought.
Him needed not long call; shee soone to hond
Her ferry brought, where him she byding fond
With his sad guide: him selfe she tooke aboord,
But the Blacke Palmer suffred still to stond,
Ne would for price or prayers once affoord
To ferry that old man over the perlous foord.

XX. Guyon was loath to leave his guide behind,
Yet being entred might not backe retyre;
For the flitt barke, obaying to her mind,
Forth launched quickly as she did desire,
Ne gave him leave to bid that aged sire
Adieu; but nimbly ran her wonted course
Through the dull billowes thicke as troubled mire,
Whom nether wind out of their seat could forse
Nor timely tides did drive out of their sluggish sourse.

XXI. And by the way, as was her wonted guize,
Her mery fitt shee freshly gan to reare,
And did of joy and jollity devize,
Her selfe to cherish, and her guest to cheare.
The knight was courteous, and did not forbeare
Her honest merth and pleasaunce to partake;

But when he saw her toy, and gibe, and geare,
And passe the bonds of modest merimake,
Her dalliaunce he despis'd, and follies did forsake.

XXII. Yet she still followed her former style,
And said and did all that mote him delight,
Till they arrived in that pleasaunt Ile,
Where sleeping late she lefte her other knight.
But whenas Guyon of that land had sight,
He wist him selfe amisse, and angry said;
" Ah, Dame! perdy ye have not doen me right,
Thus to mislead mee, whiles I you obaid:
Me litle needed from my right way to have straid."

XXIII. " Faire Sir," (quoth she) " be not displeased at all.
Who fares on sea may not commaund his way,
Ne wind and weather at his pleasure call:
The sea is wide, and easy for to stray;
The wind unstable, and doth never stay.
But here a while ye may in safety rest,
Till season serve new passage to assay:
Better safe port then be in seas distrest."
Therewith she laught, and did her earnest end in jest.

XXIV. But he, halfe discontent, mote nathelesse
Himselfe appease, and issewd forth on shore;
The joyes whereof and happy fruitfulnesse,
Such as he saw she gan him lay before,
And all, though pleasaunt, yet she made much more:
The fields did laugh, the flowres did freshly spring,
The trees did bud, and early blossomes bore;
And all the quire of birds did sweetly sing,
And told that gardins pleasures in their caroling.

XXV. And she, more sweete then any bird on bough,
Would oftentimes emongst them beare a part,
And strive to passe (as she could well enough)
Their native musicke by her skilful art:
So did she all that might his constant hart
Withdraw from thought of warlike enterprize,
And drowne in dissolute delights apart,
Where noise of armes, or vew of martiall guize,
Might not revive desire of knightly exercize.

XXVI. But he was wise, and wary of her will,
And ever held his hand upon his hart;
Yet would not seeme so rude, and thewed ill,
As to despise so curteous seeming part
That gentle Lady did to him impart:
But, fairly tempring, fond desire subdewd,
And ever her desired to depart.
She list not heare, but her disports poursewd,
And ever bad him stay till time the tide renewd.

XXVII. And now by this Cymochles howre was spent,
That he awoke out of his ydle dreme; /
And, shaking off his drowsy dreriment,
Gan him avize, howe ill did him beseme
In slouthfull sleepe his molten hart to steme,
And quench the brond of his conceived yre:
Tho up he started, stird with shame extreme,
Ne staied for his Damsell to inquire,
But marched to the Strond there passage to require.

XXVIII. And in the way he with Sir Guyon mett,
Accompanyde with Phædria the faire:
Eftsoones he gan to rage, and inly frett,
Crying; " Let be that Lady debonaire,
Thou recreaunt knight, and soone thyselfe prepaire
To batteile, if thou meane her love to gayn.
Loe, loe! already how the fowles in aire
Doe flocke, awaiting shortly to obtayn
Thy carcas for their pray, the guerdon of thy payn."

XXIX. And therewithall he fiersly at him flew,
And with importune outrage him assayld;
Who, soone prepard to field, his sword forth drew,
And him with equall valew countervayld:
Their mightie strokes their haberjeons dismayld,
And naked made each others manly spalles;
The mortall steele despiteously entayld
Deepe in their flesh, quite through the yron walles,
That a large purple streame adowne their giambeux
falles.

XXX. Cymochles, that had never mett before
So puissant foe, with envious despight
His prowd presumed force increased more,

Disdeigning to bee held so long in fight.
Sir Guyon, grudging not so much his might
As those unknightly raylinges which he spoke,
With wrathfull fire his corage kindled bright,
Thereof devising shortly to be wroke,
And doubling all his powers redoubled every stroke.

XXXI. Both of them high attonce their handes enhaunst,
And both attonce their huge blowes down did sway.
Cymochles sword on Guyons shield yglaunst,
And thereof nigh one quarter sheard away;
But Guyons angry blade so fiers did play
On th' others helmett, which as Titan shone,
That quite it clove his plumed crest in tway,
And bared all his head unto the bone;
Wherewith astonisht, still he stood as sencelesse stone.

XXXII. Still as he stood, fayre Phædria, that beheld
That deadly daunger, soone atweene them ran;
And at their feet her selfe most humbly feld,
Crying with pitteous voyce, and count'nance wan,
" Ah, well away! most noble Lords, how can
Your cruell eyes endure so pitteous sight,
To shed your lives on ground?   Wo worth the man,
That first did teach the cursed steele to bight
In his owne flesh, and make way to the living spright!

XXXIII. " If ever love of Lady did empierce
Your yron brestes, or pittie could find place,
Withhold your bloody handes from battaill fierce;
And, sith for me ye fight, to me this grace
Both yield, to stay your deadly stryfe a space."
They stayd a while, and forth she gan proceede:
" Most wretched woman and of wicked race,
That am the authour of this hainous deed,
And cause of death betweene two doughtie knights dѻ
breed!

XXXIV. " But, if for me ye fight, or me will serve,
Not this rude kynd of battaill, nor these armes
Are meet, the which doe men in bale to sterve,
And doolefull sorrow heape with deadly harmes:
Such cruell game my scarmoges disarmes.
Another warre, and other weapons, I

Doe love, where love does give his sweet Alarmes
Without bloodshed, and where the enimy
Does yield unto his foe a pleasaunt victory.

XXXV. " Debatefull strife, and cruell enmity,
The famous name of knighthood fowly shend;
But lovely peace, and gentle amity,
And in Amours the passing howres to spend,
The mightie martiall handes doe most commend:
Of love they ever greater glory bore
Then of their armes; Mars is Cupidoes frend,
And is for Venus loves renowmed more
Then all his wars and spoiles, the which he did of yore."

XXXVI. Therewith she sweetly smyld. They, though full bent
To prove extremities of bloody fight,
Yet at her speach their rages gan relent,
And calme the sea of their tempestuous spight.
Such powre have pleasing wordes: such is the might
Of courteous clemency in gentle hart.
Now after all was ceast, the Faery knight
Besought that Damzell suffer him depart,
And yield him ready passage to that other part.

XXXVII. She no lesse glad then he desirous was
Of his departure thence; for of her joy
And vaine delight she saw he light did pas,
A foe of folly and immodest toy,
Still solemne sad, or still disdainfull coy;
Delighting all in armes and cruell warre,
That her sweet peace and pleasures did annoy,
Troubled with terrour and unquiet jarre,
That she well pleased was thence to amove him farre

XXXVIII. Tho him she brought abord, and her swift bote
Forthwith directed to that further strand;
The which on the dull waves did lightly flote,
And soone arrived on the shallow sand,
Where gladsome Guyon salied forth to land,
And to that Damsell thankes gave for reward.
Upon that shore he spyed Atin stand,
There by his maister left, when late he far'd
In Phædrias flitt barck over that perlous shard.

XXXIX. Well could he him remember, sith of late
    He with Pyrochles sharp debatement made:
    Streight gan he him revyle, and bitter rate,
    As Shepheardes curre, that in darke eveninges shade
    Hath tracted forth some salvage beastes trade:
    " Vile Miscreaunt," (said he) " whither dost thou flye
    The shame and death, which will thee soone invade?
    What coward hand shall doe thee next to dye,
    That art thus fowly fledd from famous enimy? "

XL. With that he stifly shooke his steelhead dart:
    But sober Guyon, hearing him so rayle,
    Though somewhat moved in his mightie hart,
    Yet with strong reason maistred passion fraile,
    And passed fayrely forth.   He, turning taile,
    Back to the strond retyrd, and there still stayd,
    Awaiting passage which him late did faile;
    The whiles Cymochles with that wanton mayd
    The hasty heat of his avowd revenge delayd.

XLI. Whylest there the varlet stood, he saw from farre
    An armed knight that towardes him fast ran;
    He ran on foot, as if in lucklesse warre
    His forlorne steed from him the victour wan:
    He seemed breathlesse, hartlesse, faint, and wan;
    And all his armour sprinckled was with blood,
    And soyld with durtie gore, that no man can
    Discerne the hew thereof.   He never stood,
    But bent his hastie course towardes the ydle flood.

XLII. The varlett saw, when to the flood he came,
    How without stop or stay he fiersly lept,
    And deepe him selfe beducked in the same,
    That in the lake his loftie crest was stept,
    Ne of his safetie seemed care he kept;
    But with his raging armes he rudely flasht
    The waves about, and all his armour swept,
    That all the blood and filth away was washt;
    Yet still he bet the water, and the billowes dasht.

XLIII. Atin drew nigh to weet what it mote bee,
    For much he wondred at that uncouth sight:
    Whom should he but his owne deare Lord there see,

His owne deare Lord Pyrochles in sad plight,
Ready to drowne him selfe for fell despight:
" Harrow now out, and well away ! " he cryde,
" What dismall day hath lent this cursed light,
To see my Lord so deadly damnifyde?
Pyrochles, O Pyrochles! what is thee betyde? "

XLIV. " I burne, I burne, I burne ! " then lowd he cryde,
" O! how I burne with implacable fyre;
Yet nought can quench mine inly flaming syde,
Nor sea of licour cold, nor lake of myre:
Nothing but death can doe me to respyre."
" Ah! be it," (said he) " from Pyrochles farre
After pursewing death once to requyre,
Or think, that ought those puissant hands may marre:
Death is for wretches borne under unhappy starre."

XLV. " Perdye, then is it fitt for me," (said he)
" That am, I weene, most wretched man alive;
Burning in flames, yet no flames can I see,
And dying dayly, dayly yet revive.
O Atin! helpe to me last death to give."
The varlet at his plaint was grieved so sore,
That his deepe wounded hart in two did rive;
And, his owne health remembring now no more,
Did follow that ensample which he blam'd afore.

XLVI. Into the lake he lept his Lord to ayd,
(So Love the dread of daunger doth despise)
And of him catching hold him strongly stayd
From drowning.   But more happy he then wise,
Of that seas nature did him not avise:
The waves thereof so slow and sluggish were,
Engrost with mud which did them fowle agrise,
That every weighty thing they did upbeare,
Ne ought mote ever sinck downe to the bottom there.

XLVII. Whiles thus they strugled in that ydle wave,
And strove in vaine, the one him selfe to drowne,
The other both from drowning for to save,
Lo! to that shore one in an auncient gowne,
Whose hoary locks great gravitie did crowne,
Holding in hand a goodly arming sword,

By fortune came, ledd with the troublous sowne:
Where drenched deepe he fownd in that dull ford
The carefull servaunt stryving with his raging Lord.

XLVIII. Him Atin spying knew right well of yore,
And lowdly cald; " Helpe, helpe! O Archimage!
To save my Lord in wretched plight forlore;
Helpe with thy hand, or with thy counsell sage:
Weake handes, but counsell is most strong in age."
Him when the old man saw, he wondred sore
To see Pyrochles there so rudely rage;
Yet sithens helpe, he saw, he needed more
Then pitty, he in hast approched to the shore,

XLIX. And cald; " Pyrochles! what is this I see?
What hellish fury hath at earst thee hent?
Furious ever I thee knew to bee,
Yet never in this straunge astonishment."
" These flames, these flames " (he cryde) " doe me
torment."
" Wha flames," (quoth he), when I thee present see
In daunger rather to be drent then brent? "
" Harrow! the flames which me consume," (said hee)
" Ne can be quencht, within my secret bowelles bee.

L. " That cursed man, that cruel feend of hell,
Furor, oh! Furor hath me thus bedight:
His deadly woundes within my liver swell,
And his whott fyre burnes in mine entralles bright,
Kindled through his infernall brond of spight,
Sith late with him I batteill vaine would boste;
That now, I weene, Joves dreaded thunder light
Does scorch not halfe so sore, nor damned gh
In flaming Phlegeton does not so felly roste."

LI. Which when as Archimago heard, his griefe
He knew right well, and him attonce disarm'd;
Then searcht his secret woundes, and made a priefe
Of every place that was with bruzing harmd,
Or with the hidden fire too inly warmd.
Which doen, he balmes and herbes thereto applyde,
And evermore with mightie spels them charmd;
That in short space he has them qualifyde,
And him restor'd to helth that would have algates dyde.

CANTO VII

Guyon findes Mamon in a delve
Sunning his threasure hore;
Is by him tempted, and led downe
To see his secrete store.

ɪ. As Pilot well expert in perilous wave,
That to a stedfast starre his course hath bent,
When foggy mistes or cloudy tempests have
The faithful light of that faire lampe yblent,
And cover'd heaven with hideous dreriment,
Upon his card and compas firmes his eye,
The maysters of his long experiment,
And to them does the steddy helme apply,
Bidding his winged vessell fairely forward fly:

ɪɪ. So Guyon having lost his trustie guyde,
Late left beyond that Ydle lake, proceedes
Yet on his way, of none accompanyde;
And evermore himselfe with comfort feedes
Of his own vertues and praise-worthie deedes.
So, long he yode, yet no adventure found,
Which fame of her shrill trompet worthy reedes;
For still he traveild through wide wastfull ground,
That nought but desert wildernesse shewed all around.

ɪɪɪ. At last he came unto a gloomy glade,
Cover'd with boughes and shrubs from heavens light,
Whereas he sitting found in secret shade
An uncouth, salvage, and uncivile wight,
Of griesly hew and fowle ill favour'd sight;
His face with smoke was tand, and eies were bleard,
His head and beard with sout were ill bedight,
His cole-blacke hands did seeme to have ben seard
In smythes fire-spitting forge, and nayles like clawes
appeard.

ɪᴠ. His yron cote, all overgrowne with rust,
Was underneath enveloped with gold;
Whose glistring glosse, darkned with filthy dust,

Well yet appeared to have beene of old
A worke of rich entayle and curious mould,
Woven with antickes and wyld ymagery;
And in his lap a masse of coyne he told,
And turned upside downe, to feede his eye
And covetous desire with his huge threasury.

v. And round about him lay on every side
Great heapes of gold that never could be spent;
Of which some were rude owre, not purifide
Of Mulcibers devouring element;
Some others were new driven, and distent
Into great Ingowes and to wedges square;
Some in round plates withouten moniment;
But most were stampt, and in their metal bare
The antique shapes of kinges and kesars straunge and rare.

vi. Soone as he Guyon saw, in great affright
And haste he rose for to remove aside
Those pretious hils from straungers envious sight,
And downe them poured through an hole full wide
Into the hollow earth, them there to hide.
But Guyon, lightly to him leaping, stayd
His hand that trembled as one terrifyde;
And though himselfe were at the sight dismayd,
Yet him perforce restraynd, and to him doubtfull sayd:

vii. " What art thou, man, (if man at all thou art)
That here in desert hast thine habitaunce,
And these rich hils of welth doest hide apart
From the worldes eye, and from her right usaunce? "
Thereat, with staring eyes fixed askaunce,
In great disdaine he answerd: " Hardy Elfe,
That darest view my direfull countenaunce,
I read thee rash and heedelesse of thy selfe,
To trouble my still seate, and heapes of pretious pelfe.

viii. " God of the world and worldlings I me call,
Great Mammon, greatest god below the skye,
That of my plenty poure out unto all,
And unto none my graces do envye:
Riches, renowme, and principality,
Honour, estate, and all this worldes good,

For which men swinck and sweat incessantly,
Fro me do flow into an ample flood,
And in the hollow earth have their eternal brood.

IX. " Wherefore, if me thou deigne to serve and sew,
At thy commaund lo! all these mountaines bee:
Or if to thy great mind, or greedy vew,
All these may not suffise, there shall to thee
Ten times so much be nombred francke and free."
" Mammon," (said he) " thy godheads vaunt is vaine,
And idle offers of thy golden fee;
To them that covet such eye-glutting gaine
Proffer thy giftes, and fitter servaunts entertaine.

X. " Me ill besits, that in der-doing armes
And honours suit my vowed daies do spend,
Unto thy bounteous baytes and pleasing charmes,
With which weake men thou witchest, to attend;
Regard of worldly mucke doth fowly blend,
And low abase the high heroicke spright,
That joyes for crownes and kingdomes to contend:
Faire shields, gay steedes, bright armes be my delight;
Those be the riches fit for an advent'rous knight."

XI. " Vaine glorious Elfe," (saide he) " doest not thou weet,
That money can thy wantes at will supply?
Sheilds, steeds, and armes, and all things for thce meet,
It can purvay in twinckling of an eye;
And crownes and kingdomes to thee multiply.
Do not I kings create, and throw the crowne
Sometimes to him that low in dust doth ly,
And him that raignd into his rowme thrust downe,
And whom I lust do heape with glory and renowne? "

XII. " All otherwise " (saide he) " I riches read,
And deeme them roote of all disquietnesse;
First got with guile, and then preserv'd with dread,
And after spent with pride and lavishnesse,
Leaving behind them griefe and heavinesse:
Infinite mischiefes of them doe arize,
Strife and debate, bloodshed and bitternesse,
Outrageous wrong, and hellish covetize,
That noble heart as great dishonour doth despize.

XIII. " Ne thine be kingdomes, ne the scepters thine;
But realmes and rulers thou doest both confound,
And loyall truth to treason doest incline:
Witnesse the guiltlesse blood pourd oft on ground,
The crowned often slaine, the slayer cround;
The sacred Diademe in peeces rent,
And purple robe gored with many a wound,
Castles surprizd, great cities sackt and brent:
So mak'st thou kings, and gaynest wrongfull government.

XIV. " Long were to tell the troublous stormes that tosse
The private state, and make the life unsweet:
Who swelling sayles in Caspian sea doth crosse,
And in frayle wood on Adrian gulf doth fleet,
Doth not, I weene, so many evils meet."
Then Mammon wexing wroth; " And why then," sayd,
" Are mortall men so fond and undiscreet
So evill thing to seeke unto their ayd,
And having not complaine, and having it upbrayd? "

XV. " Indeede," (quoth he) " through fowle intemperaunce,
Frayle men are oft captiv'd to covetise;
But would they thinke with how small allowaunce
Untroubled Nature doth her selfe suffise,
Such superfluities they would despise,
Which with sad cares empeach our native joyes.
At the well-head the purest streames arise;
But mucky filth his braunching armes annoyes,
And with uncomely weedes the gentle wave accloyes.

XVI. " The antique world, in his first flowring youth,
Fownd no defect in his Creators grace;
But with glad thankes, and unreproved truth,
The guifts of soveraine bounty did embrace:
Like Angels life was then mens happy cace;
But later ages pride, like corn-fed steed,
Abusd her plenty and fat swolne encreace
To all licentious lust, and gan exceed
The measure of her meane and naturall first need.

XVII. " Then gan a cursed hand the quiet wombe
Of his great Grandmother with steele to wound,
And the hid treasures in her sacred tombe

With Sacriledge to dig.   Therein he fownd
Fountaines of gold and silver to abownd,
Of which the matter of his huge desire
And pompous pride eftsoones he did compownd;
Then avarice gan through his veines inspire
His greedy flames, and kindled life-devouring fire."

XVIII. " Sonne," (said he then) " lett be thy bitter scorne,
And leave the rudenesse of that antique age
To them that liv'd therein in state forlorne:
Thou, that doest live in later times, must wage
Thy workes for wealth, and life for gold engage.
If then thee list my offred grace to use,
Take what thou please of all this surplusage;
If thee list not, leave have thou to refuse:
But thing refused doe not afterward accuse."

XIX. " Me list not " (said the Elfin knight) " receave
Thing offred, till I know it well be gott;
Ne wote I but thou didst these goods bereave
From rightfull owner by unrighteous lott,
Or that bloodguiltinesse or guile them blott."
" Perdy," (quoth he) " yet never eie did vew,
Ne tong did tell, ne hand these handled not;
But safe I have them kept in secret mew
From hevens sight, and powre of al which them poursew."

XX. " What secret place " (quoth he) " can safely hold
So huge a masse, and hide from heavens eie?
Or where hast thou thy wonne, that so much gold
Thou canst preserve from wrong and robbery?"
" Come thou," (quoth he) " and see."   So by and by
Through that thick covert he him led, and fownd
A darkesome way, which no man could descry,
That deep descended through the hollow grownd,
And was with dread and horror compassed arownd.

XXI. At length they came into a larger space,
That stretcht itselfe into an ample playne;
Through which a beaten broad high way did trace,
That streight did lead to Plutoes griesly rayne.
By that wayes side there sate internall Payne,
And fast beside him sat tumultuous Strife:

The one in hand an yron whip did strayne,
The other brandished a bloody knife;
And both did gnash their teeth, and both did threten life.

XXII. On thother side in one consort there sate
Cruell Revenge, and rancorous Despight,
Disloyall Treason, and hart-burning Hate;
But gnawing Gealousy, out of their sight
Sitting alone, his bitter lips did bight;
And trembling Feare still to and fro did fly,
And found no place wher safe he shroud him might:
Lamenting Sorrow did in darknes lye,
And shame his ugly face did hide from living eye.

XXIII. And over them sad horror with grim hew
Did alwaies sore, beating his yron wings;
And after him Owles and Night-ravens flew,
The hatefull messengers of heavy things,
Of death and dolor telling sad tidings;
Whiles sad Celeno, sitting on a clifte,
A song of bale and bitter sorrow sings,
That hart of flint asonder could have rifte;
Which having ended after him she flyeth swifte.

XXIV. All these before the gates of Pluto lay,
By whom they passing spake unto them nought;
But th' Elfin knight with wonder all the way
Did feed his eyes, and fild his inner thought.
At last him to a litle dore he brought,
That to the gate of Hell, which gaped wide,
Was next adjoyning, ne them parted ought:
Betwixt them both was but a litle stride,
That did the house of Richesse from hell-mouth divide.

XXV. Before the dore sat selfe-consuming Care,
Day and night keeping wary watch and ward,
For feare least Force or Fraud should unaware
Breake in, and spoile the treasure there in gard:
Ne would he suffer Sleepe once thither-ward
Approch, albe his drowsy den were next;
For next to death is Sleepe to be compard;
Therefore his house is unto his annext:
Here Sleep, ther Richesse, and Hel-gate them both betwext.

XXVI. So soon as Mammon there arrivd, the dore
To him did open and affoorded way:
Him followed eke Sir Guyon evermore,
Ne darkenesse him, ne daunger might dismay.
Soone as he entred was, the dore streight way
Did shutt, and from behind it forth there lept
An ugly feend, more fowle then dismall day,
The which with monstrous stalke behind him stept,
And ever as he went dew watch upon him kept.

XXVII. Well hoped hee, ere long that hardy guest,
If ever covetous hand, or lustfull eye,
Or lips he layd on thing that likte him best,
Or ever sleepe his eie-strings did untye,
Should be his pray.   And therefore still on hye
He over him did hold his cruell clawes,
Threatning with greedy gripe to doe him dye,
And rend in peeces with his ravenous pawes,
If ever he transgrest the fatall Stygian lawes.

XXVIII. That houses forme within was rude and strong,
Lyke an huge cave hewne out of rocky clifte,
From whose rough vaut the ragged breaches hong
Embost with massy gold of glorious guifte,
And with rich metall loaded every rifte,
That heavy ruine they did seeme to threatt;
And over them Arachne did lifte
Her cunning web, and spred her subtile nett,
Enwrapped in fowle smoke and clouds more black
than Jett.

XXIX. Both roofe, and floore, and walls, were all of gold,
But overgrowne with dust and old decay,
And hid in darkenes, that none could behold
The hew thereof; for vew of cherefull day
Did never in that house it selfe display,
But a faint shadow of uncertein light:
Such as a lamp, whose life does fade away,
Or as the Moone, cloathed with clowdy night,
Does show to him that walkes in feare and sad affright.

XXX. In all that rowme was nothing to be seene
But huge great yron chests, and coffers strong,
All bard with double bends, that none could weene

Them to efforce by violence or wrong:
On every side they placed were along;
But all the grownd with sculs was scattered,
And dead mens bones, which round about were flong;
Whose lives, it seemed, whilome there were shed,
And their vile carcases now left unburied.

XXXI. They forward passe; ne Guyon yet spoke word,
Till that they came unto an yron dore,
Which to them opened of his owne accord,
And shewd of richesse such exceeding store,
As eie of man did never see before,
Ne ever could within one place be fownd,
Though all the wealth which is, or was of yore,
Could gathered be through all the world arownd,
And that above were added to that under grownd.

XXXII. The charge thereof unto a covetous Spright
Commaunded was, who thereby did attend,
And warily awaited day and night,
From other covetous feends it to defend,
Who it to rob and ransacke did intend.
Then Mammon, turning to that warriour, said;
" Loe! here the worldes blis: loe! here the end,
To which al men doe ayme, rich to be made:
Such grace now to be happy is before thee laid."

XXXIII. " Certes," (sayd he) " I n'ill thine offred grace,
Ne to be made so happy doe intend:
Another blis before mine eyes I place,
Another happines, another end.
To them that list these base regardes I lend;
But I in armes, and in atchievements brave,
Do rather choose my flitting houres to spend,
And to be Lord of those that riches have,
Then them to have my selfe, and be their servile sclave."

XXXIV. Thereat the feend his gnashing teeth did grate,
And griev'd so long to lacke his greedie pray;
For well he weened that so glorious bayte
Would tempt his guest to take thereof assay;
Had he so doen, he had him snatcht away,
More light then Culver in the Faulcons fist.

Eternall God thee save from such decay!
But, whenas Mammon saw his purpose mist,
Him to entrap unwares another way he wist.

xxxv. Thence forward he him ledd, and shortly brought
Unto another rowme, whose dore forthright
To him did open, as it had been taught.
Therein an hundred raunges weren pight,
And hundred fournaces all burning bright:
By every fournace many feendes did byde,
Deformed creatures, horrible in sight;
And every feend his busie paines applyde
To melt the golden metall, ready to be tryde.

xxxvi. One with great bellowes gathered filling ayre,
And with forst wind the fewell did inflame;
Another did the dying bronds repayre
With yron tongs, and sprinckled ofte the same
With liquid waves, fiers Vulcans rage to tame,
Who, maystring them, renewd his former heat:
Some scumd the drosse that from the metall came;
Some stird the molten owre with ladles great;
And every one did swincke, and every one did sweat.

xxxvii. But, when an earthly wight they present saw
Glistring in armes and battailous aray,
From their whot work they did themselves withdraw
To wonder at the sight; for till that day
They never creature saw that cam that way:
Their staring eyes sparckling with fervent fyre
And ugly shapes did nigh the man dismay,
That, were it not for shame, he would retyre;
Till that him thus bespake their soveraine Lord and
syre;

xxxviii. " Behold, thou Faeries sonne, with mortall eye,
That living eye before did never see.
The thing, that thou didst crave so earnestly,
To weet whence all the wealth late shewd by mee
Proceeded, lo! now is reveald to thee.
Here is the fountaine of the worldes good:
Now, therefore, if thou wilt enriched bee,
Avise thee well, and chaunge thy wilfull mood,
Least thou perhaps hereafter wish, and be withstood."

XXXIX. " Suffise it then, thou Money God," (quoth hee)
    " That all thine ydle offers I refuse.
    All that I need I have: what needeth mee
    To covet more then I have cause to use?
    With such vaine shewes thy worldlinges vyle abuse;
    But give me leave to follow mine emprise."
    Mammon was much displeasd, yet no'te he chuse
    But beare the rigour of his bold mesprise;
    And thence him forward ledd him further to entise.

XL. He brought him, through a darksom narrow strayt,
    To a broad gate all built of beaten gold:
    The gate was open; but therein did wayt
    A sturdie villein, stryding stiffe and bold,
    As if the highest God defy he would:
    In his right hand an yron club he held,
    But he himselfe was all of golden mould,
    Yet had both life and sence, and well could weld
    That cursed weapon, when his cruell foes he queld.

XLI. Disdayne he called was, and did disdayne
    To be so cald, and who so did him call:
    Sterne was his looke, and full of stomacke vayne;
    His portaunce terrible, and stature tall,
    Far passing th' hight of men terrestriall,
    Like an huge Gyant of the Titans race;
    That made him scorne all creatures great and small.
    And with his pride all others powre deface:
    More fitt emongst black fiendes then men to have his
        place.

XLII. Soone as those glitterand armes he did espye,
    That with their brightnesse made that darknes light,
    His harmefull club he gan to hurtle hye,
    And threaten batteill to the Faery knight;
    Who likewise gan himselfe to batteill dight,
    Till Mammon did his hasty hand withhold,
    And counseld him abstaine from perilous fight;
    For nothing might abash the villein bold,
    Ne mortall steele emperce his miscreated mould.

XLIII. So having him with reason pacifyde,
    And that fiers Carle commaunding to forbeare,

He brought him in.   The rowme was large and wyde,
As it some Gyeld or solemne Temple weare.
Many great golden pillours did upbeare
The massy roofe, and riches huge sustayne;
And every pillour decked was full deare
With crownes, and Diademes, and titles vaine,
Which mortall Princes wore whiles they on earth did
       rayne.

XLIV. A route of people there assembled were,
Of every sort and nation under skye,
Which with great uprore preaced to draw nere
To th' upper part, where was advaunced hye
A stately siege of soveraine majestye;
And thereon satt a woman, gorgeous gay
And richly cladd in robes of royaltye,
That never earthly Prince in such array
His glory did enhaunce, and pompous pryde display.

XLV. Her face right wondrous faire did seeme to bee,
That her broad beauties beam great brightnes threw
Through the dim shade, that all men might it see:
Yet was not that same her owne native hew,
But wrought by art and counterfetted shew,
Thereby more lovers unto her to call:
Nath'lesse most hevenly faire in deed and vew
She by creation was, till she did fall;
Thenceforth she sought for helps to cloke her crime
       withall.

XLVI. There, as in glistring glory she did sitt,
She held a great gold chaine ylincked well,
Whose upper end to highest heven was knitt,
And lower part did reach to lowest Hell;
And all that preace did rownd about her swell
To catchen hold of that long chaine, thereby
To climbe aloft, and others to excell:
That was Ambition, rash desire to sty,
And every linck thereof a step of dignity.

XLVII. Some thought to raise themselves to high degree
By riches and unrighteous reward;
Some by close shouldring; some by flatteree;

Others through friendes; others for base regard,
And all by wrong waies for themselves prepard:
Those that were up themselves kept others low;
Those that were low themselves held others hard,
Ne suffred them to ryse or greater grow;
But every one did strive his fellow downe to throw.

XLVIII. Which whenas Guyon saw, he gan inquire,
What meant that preace about that Ladies throne,
And what she was that did so high aspyre?
Him Mammon answered; " That goodly one,
Whom all that folke with such contention
Doe flock about, my deare, my daughter is:
Honour and dignitie from her alone
Derived are, and all this worldes blis,
For which ye men doe strive; few gett, but many mis:

XLIX. " And fayre Philotime she rightly hight,
The fairest wight that wonneth under skie,
But that this darksom neather world her light
Doth dim with horror and deformity;
Worthie of heven and hye felicitie,
From whence the gods have her for envy thrust:
But, sith thou hast found favour in mine eye,
Thy spouse I will her make, if that thou lust,
That she may thee advance for works and merits just."

L. " Gramercy, Mammon," (said the gentle knight)
" For so great grace and offred high estate;
But I, that am fraile flesh and earthly wight,
Unworthy match for such immortall mate
My selfe well wote, and mine unequall fate:
And were I not, yet is my trouth yplight,
And love avowd to other Lady late,
That to remove the same I have no might:
To chaunge love causelesse is reproch to warlike knight."

LI. Mammon emmoved was with inward wrath;
Yet, forcing it to fayne, him forth thence ledd,
Through griesly shadowes by a beaten path,
Into a gardin goodly garnished
With hearbs and fruits, whose kinds mote not be redd:
Not such as earth out of her fruitfull woomb

Throwes forth to men, sweet and well savored,
But direfull deadly black, both leafe and bloom,
Fitt to adorne the dead, and deck the drery toombe.

LII. There mournfull Cypresse grew in greatest store,
And trees of bitter Gall, and Heben sad;
Dead sleeping Poppy, and black Hellebore;
Cold Coloquintida, and Tetra mad;
Mortall Samnitis, and Cicuta bad,
With which th' unjust Atheniens made to dy
Wise Socrates; who, thereof quaffing glad,
Pourd out his life and last Philosophy
To the fayre Critias, his dearest Belamy!

LIII. The Gardin of Proserpina this hight;
And in the midst thereof a silver seat,
With a thick Arber goodly over-dight,
In which she often usd from open heat
Her selfe to shroud, and pleasures to entreat:
Next thereunto did grow a goodly tree,
With braunches broad dispredd and body great,
Clothed with leaves, that non the wood mote see,
And loaden all with fruit as thick as it might bee.

LIV. Their fruit were golden apples glistring bright,
That goodly was their glory to behold;
On earth like never grew, ne living wight
Like ever saw, but they from hence were sold;
For those which Hercules, with conquest bold
Got from great Atlas daughters, hence began,
And planted there did bring forth fruit of gold;
And those with which th' Eubœan young man wan
Swift Atalanta, when through craft he her out ran.

LV. Here also sprong that goodly golden fruit,
With which Acontius got his lover trew,
Whom he had long time sought with fruitlesse suit:
Here eke that famous golden Apple grew
The which emongst the gods false Ate threw;
For which th' Idæan Ladies disagreed,
Till partiall Paris dempt it Venus dew,
And had of her fayre Helen for his meed,
That many noble Greekes and Trojans made to bleed.

LVI. The warlike Elfe much wondred at this tree,
So fayre and great that shadowed all the ground,
And his broad braunches, laden with rich fee,
Did stretcht themselves without the utmost bound
Of this great gardin, compast with a mound;
Which over-hanging, they themselves did steepe
In a blacke flood, which flow'd about it round.
That is the river of Cocytus deepe,
In which full many soules do endlesse wayle and weepe.

LVII. Which to behold he clomb up to the bancke,
And looking downe saw many damned wightes
In those sad waves, which direfull deadly stancke,
Plonged continually of cruell Sprightes,
That with their piteous cryes, and yelling shrightes,
They made the further shore resounden wide.
Emongst the rest of those same ruefull sightes,
One cursed creature he by chaunce espide,
That drenched lay full deepe under the Garden si

LVIII. Deepe was he drenched to the upmost chin,
Yet gaped still as coveting to drinke
Of the cold liquor which he waded in;
And stretching forth his hand did often thinke
To reach the fruit which grew upon the brincke;
But both the fruit from hand, and flood from mouth,
Did fly abacke, and made him vainely swincke;
The whiles he sterv'd with hunger, and with drouth,
He daily dyde, yet never throughly dyen couth.

LIX. The knight, him seeing labour so in vaine,
Askt who he was, and what he ment thereby?
Who, groning deepe, thus answerd him againe;
" Most cursed of all creatures under skye,
Lo! Tantalus, I here tormented lye:
Of whom high Jove wont whylome feasted bee;
Lo! here I now for want of food doe dye:
But, if that thou be such as I thee see,
Of grace I pray thee, give to eat and drinke to mee!"

LX. " Nay, nay, thou greedy Tantalus," (quoth he)
" Abide the fortune of thy present fate;
And unto all that live in high degree,

Ensample be of mind intemperate,
To teach them how to use their present state."
Then gan the cursed wretch alowd to cry,
Accusing highest Jove and gods ingrate;
And eke blaspheming heaven bitterly,
As author of unjustice, there to let him dye,

LXI. He lookt a litle further, and espyde
Another wretch, whose carcas deepe was drent
Within the river, which the same did hyde;
But both his handes, most filthy feculent,
Above the water were on high extent,
And faynd to wash themselves incessantly,
Yet nothing cleaner were for such intent,
But rather fowler seemed to the eye;
So lost his labour vaine and ydle industry,

LXII. The knight him calling asked who he was?
Who, lifting up his head, him answered thus;
" I Pilate am, the falsest Judge, alas!
And most unjust; that, by unrighteous
And wicked doome, to Jewes despiteous
Delivered up the Lord of life to dye,
And did acquite a murdrer felonous;
The whiles my handes I washt in purity,
The whiles my soule was soyld with fowle iniquity."

LXIII. Infinite moe tormented in like paine
He there beheld, too long here to be told:
Ne Mammon would there let him long remayne,
For terrour of the tortures manifold,
In which the damned soules he did behold,
But roughly him bespake: " Thou fearefull foole,
Why takest not of that same fruite of gold?
Ne sittest downe on that same silver stoole,
To rest thy weary person in the shadow coole? "

LXIV. All which he did to do him deadly fall
In frayle intemperaunce through sinfull bayt;
To which if he inclyned had at all,
That dreadfull feend, which did behinde him wayt,
Would him have rent in thousand peeces strayt:
But he was wary wise in all his way,

And well perceived·his deceiptfull sleight,
Ne suffred lust his safety to betray.
So goodly did beguile the Guyler of his pray.

LXV. And now he has so long remained theare,
That vitall powres gan wexe both weake and wan
For want of food and sleepe, which two upbeare,
Like mightie pillours, this frayle life of man,
That none without the same enduren can:
For now three dayes of men were full out-wrought,
Since he this hardy enterprize began:
Forthy great Mammon fayrely he besought
Into the world to guyde him backe, as he him brought.

LXVI. The God, though loth, yet was constraynd t' obay;
For lenger time then that no living wight
Below the earth might suffred be to stay:
So backe againe him brought to living light.
But all so soone as his enfeebled spright
Gan sucke this vitall ayre into his brest,
As overcome with too exceeding might,
The life did flit away out of her nest,
And all his sences were with deadly fit opprest.

CANTO VIII

Sir Guyon, layd in swowne, is by
Acrates sonnes despoyld;
Whom Arthure soone hath reskewed,
And Paynim brethren foyld.

I. AND is there care in heaven?   And is there love
In heavenly spirits to these creatures bace,
That may compassion of their evilles move?
There is: else much more wretched were the cace
Of men then beasts.   But O! th' exceeding grace
Of highest God that loves his creatures so,
And all his workes with mercy doth embrace,
That blessed Angels he sends to and fro,
To serve to wicked man, to serve his wicked foe.

II. How oft do they their silver bowers leave,
To come to succour us that succour want!
How oft do they with golden pineons cleave
The flitting skyes, like flying Pursuivant,
Against fowle feendes to ayd us militant!
They for us fight, they watch and dewly ward,
And their bright Squadrons round about us plant;
And all for love, and nothing for reward.
O! why should hevenly God to men have such regard?

III. During the while that Guyon did abide
In Mamons house, the Palmer, whom whyleare
That wanton Mayd of passage had denide,
By further search had passage found elsewhere;
And, being on his way, approched neare
Where Guyon lay in traunce; when suddeinly
He heard a voyce that called lowd and cleare,
" Come hither! hither! O, come hastily! "
That all the fields resounded with the ruefull cry.

IV. The Palmer lent his eare unto the noyce,
To weet who called so importunely:
Againe he heard a more efforced voyce,

That bad him come in haste. He by and by
His feeble feet directed to the cry;
Which to that shady delve him brought at last,
Where Mammon earst did sunne his threasury;
There the good Guyon he found slumbring fast
In senceles dreame; which sight at first him sore aghast.

v. Beside his head there satt a faire young man,
Of wondrous beauty and of freshest yeares,
Whose tender bud to blossome new began,
And florish faire above his equall peares:
His snowy front, curled with golden heares,
Like Phœbus face adornd with sunny rayes,
Divinely shone; and two sharpe winged sheares,
Decked with diverse plumes, like painted Jayes,
Were fixed at his backe to cut his ayery wayes.

vi. Like as Cupido on Idæan hill,
When having laid his cruell bow away
And mortall arrowes, wherewith he doth fill
The world with murdrous spoiles and bloody pray,
With his faire mother he him dights to play,
And with his goodly sisters, Graces three:
The Goddesse, pleased with his wanton play,
Suffers her selfe through sleepe beguild to bee,
The whiles the other Ladies mind theyr mery glee.

vii. Whom when the Palmer saw, abasht he was
Through fear and wonder that he nought could say,
Till him the childe bespoke; " Long lackt, alas!
Hath bene thy faithfull aide in hard assay,
Whiles deadly fitt thy pupill doth dismay.
Behold this heavy sight, thou reverend Sire!
But dread of death and dolor doe away;
For life ere long shall to her home retire,
And he that breathlesse seems shal corage both respire.

viii. " The charge, which God doth unto me arrett,
Of his deare safety, I to thee commend;
Yet will I not forgoe, ne yet forgett
The care thereof my selfe unto the end,
But evermore him succour, and defend
Against his foe and mine: watch thou, I pray,

For evill is at hand him to offend."
So having said, eftsoones he gan display
His painted nimble wings, and vanisht quite away.

IX. The Palmer seeing his lefte empty place,
And his slow eies beguiled of their sight,
Woxe sore affraid, and standing still a space
Gaz'd after him, as fowle escapt by flight.
At last, him turning to his charge behight,
With trembling hand his troubled pulse gan try;
Where finding life not yet dislodged quight,
He much rejoyst, and courd it tenderly,
As chicken newly hatcht, from dreaded destiny.

X. At last he spide where towards him did pace
Two Paynim knights al armd as bright as skie,
And them beside an aged Sire did trace,
And far before a light-foote Page did flie,
That breathed strife and troublous enmitie,
Those were the two sonnes of Acrates old,
Who, meeting earst with Archimago slie
Foreby that idle strond, of him were told
That he which earst them combatted was Guyon bold.

XI. Which to avenge on him they dearly vowd,
Where ever that on ground they mote him find:
False Archimage provokte their corage prowd,
And stryful Atin in their stubborne mind
Coles of contention and whot vengeaunce tind.
Now bene they come whereas the Palmer sate,
Keeping that slombred corse to him assind:
Well knew they both his person, sith of late
With him in bloody armes they rashly did debate.

XII. Whom when Pyrochles saw, inflam'd with rage
That sire he fowl bespake: Thou dotard vile,
That with thy brutenesse shendst thy comely age,
Abandon soone, I read, the caytive spoile
Of that same outcast carcas, that erewhile
Made it selfe famous through false trechery,
And crownd his coward crest with knightly stile;
Loe! where he now inglorious doth lye,
To proove he lived il that did thus fowly dye.

xiii. To whom the Palmer fearlesse answered:
       " Certes, Sir knight, ye bene too much to blame,
       Thus for to blott the honor of the dead,
       And with fowle cowardize his carcas shame,
       Whose living handes immortalizd his name.
       Vile is the vengeaunce on the ashes cold,
       And envy base to barke at sleeping fame.
       Was never wight that treason of him told:
       Your self his prowesse prov'd, and found him fiers and
           bold."

xiv. Then sayd Cymochles: " Palmer, thou doest dote,
       Ne canst of prowesse ne of knighthood deeme,
       Save as thou seest or hearst.   But well I wote,
       That of his puissance tryall made extreeme:
       Yet gold al is not that doth golden seeme;
       Ne all good knights that shake well speare and shield.
       The worth of all men by their end esteeme,
       And then dew praise or dew reproch them yield;
       Bad therefore I him deeme that thus lies dead on field."

xv. " Good or bad," gan his brother fiers reply,
       " What doe I recke, sith that he dide entire?
       Or what doth his bad death now satisfy
       The greedy hunger of revenging yre,
       Sith wrathfull hand wrought not her owne desire?
       Yet since no way is lefte to wreake my spight,
       I will him reave of armes, the victors hire,
       And of that shield, more worthy of good knight;
       For why should a dead dog be deckt in armour bright? "

xvi. " Fayr Sir," said then the Palmer suppliaunt,
       " For knighthoods love doe not so fowle a deed,
       Ne blame your honor with so shamefull vaunt
       Of vile revenge.   To spoile the dead of weed
       Is sacrilege, and doth all sinnes exceed:
       But leave these relicks of his living might
       To decke his herce, and trap his tomb-blacke steed."
       " What herce or steed " (said he) " should he have dight,
       But be entombed in the raven or the kight? "

xvii. With that, rude hand upon his shield he laid,
       And th' other brother gan his helme unlace,
       Both fiercely bent to have him disaraid;

Till that they spyde where towards them did pace
An armed knight, of bold and bounteous grace,
Whose squire bore after him an heben launce
And covered shield.   Well kend him so far space
Th' enchaunter by his armes and amenaunce,
When under him he saw his Lybian steed to praunce;

XVIII. And to those brethren sayd; "Rise, rise bylive,
And unto batteil doe your selves addresse;
For yonder comes the prowest knight alive,
Prince Arthur, flowre of grace and nobilesse,
That hath to Paynim knights wrought gret distresse,
And thousand Sar'zins fowly donne to dye."
That word so deepe did in their harts impresse,
That both eftsoones upstarted furiously,
And gan themselves prepare to batteill greedily.

XIX. But fiers Pyrochles, lacking his owne sword,
The want thereof now greatly gan to plaine,
And Archimage besought, him that afford
Which he had brought for Braggadochio vaine.
"So would I," (said th' enchaunter) "glad and faine
Beteeme to you this sword, you to defend,
Or ought that els your honour might maintaine;
But that this weapons powre I well have kend
To be contrary to the worke which ye intend:

XX. "For that same knights owne sword that is, of yore
Which Merlin made by his almightie art
For that his noursling, when he knighthood swore,
Therewith to doen his foes eternall smart.
The metall first he mext with Medæwart,
That no enchauntment from his dint might save;
Then it in flames of Aetna wrought apart,
And seven times dipped in the bitter wave
Of hellish Styx, which hidden vertue to it gave.

XXI. "The vertue is, that nether steele nor stone
The stroke thereof from entraunce may defend;
Ne ever may be used by his fone,
Ne forst his rightful owner to offend;
Ne ever will it breake, ne ever bend:
Wherefore *Morddure* it rightfully is hight.

In vaine therefore, Pyrochles, should I lend
The same to thee, against his lord to fight;
For sure yt would deceive thy labor and thy might."

XXII. "Foolish old man," said then the Pagan wroth,
"That weenest words or charms may force withstond:
Soone shalt thou see, and then beleeve for troth,
That I can carve with this inchaunted brond
His Lords owne flesh."   Therewith out of his hond
That vertuous steele he rudely snatcht away,
And Guyons shield about his wrest he bond:
So ready dight fierce battaile to assay,
And match his brother proud in battailous aray.

XXIII. By this, that straunger knight in presence came,
And goodly salued them; who nought againe
Him answered, as courtesie became;
But with sterne lookes, and stomachous disdaine,
Gave signes of grudge and discontentment vaine.
Then, turning to the Palmer, he gan spy
Where at his feet, with sorrowfull demayne
And deadly hew, an armed corse did lye,
In whose dead face he redd great magnanimity.

XXIV. Sayd he then to the Palmer: "Reverend Syre,
What great misfortune hath betidd this knight?
Or did his life her fatall date expyre,
Or did he fall by treason, or by fight?
How ever, sure I rew his pitteous plight."
"Not one, nor other," sayd the Palmer grave,
"Hath him befalne; but cloudes of deadly night
A while his heavy eylids cover'd have,
And all his sences drowned in deep sencelesse wave:

XXV. "Which those his cruell foes, that stand hereby,
Making advauntage, to revenge their spight,
Would him disarme and treaten shamefully;
Unworthie usage of redoubted knight.
But you, faire Sir, whose honourable sight
Doth promise hope of helpe and timely grace,
Mote I beseech to succour his sad plight,
And by your powre protect his feeble cace?
First prayse of knighthood is fowle outrage to deface."

XXVI. " Palmer," (said he) " no knight so rude, I weene,
As to doen outrage to a sleeping ghost;
Ne was there ever noble corage seene,
That in advauntage would his puissaunce bost:
Honour is least where oddes appeareth most.
May bee, that better reason will aswage
The rash revengers heat.   Words, well dispost,
Have secrete powre t' appease inflamed rage:
If not, leave unto me thy knights last patronage."

XXVII. Tho, turning to those brethren, thus bespoke:
" Ye warlike payre, whose valorous great might,
It seemes, just wronges to vengeaunce doe provoke,
To wreake your wrath on this dead seeming knight,
Mote ought allay the storme of your despight,
And settle patience in so furious heat?
Not to debate the chalenge of your right,
But for his carkas pardon I entreat,
Whom fortune hath already laid in lowest seat."

XXVIII. To whom Cymochles said; " For what art thou,
That mak'st thy selfe his dayes-man, to prolong
The vengeaunce prest?   Or who shall let me now
On this vile body from to wreak my wrong,
And made his carkas as the outcast dong?
Why should not that dead carrion satisfye
The guilt which, if he lived had thus long,
His life for dew revenge should deare abye?
The trespass still doth live, albee the person dye."

XXIX. " Indeed," then said the Prince, " the evill donne
Dyes not, when breath the body first doth leave;
But from the grandsyre to the Nephewes sonne,
And all his seede the curse doth often cleave,
Till vengeaunce utterly the guilt bereave:
So streightly God doth judge.   But gentle Knight,
That doth against the dead his hand upheave,
His honour staines with rancour and despight,
And great disparagment makes to his former might."

XXX. Pyrochles gan reply the second tyme,
And to him said: " Now, felon, sure I read,
How that thou art partaker of his cryme:

Therefore, by Termagaunt thou shalt be dead."
With that his hand, more sad then lomp of lead,
Uplifting high, he weened with Morddure,
His owen good sword Morddure, to cleave his head.
The faithfull steele such treason no'uld endure,
But, swarving from the marke, his Lordes life did assure.

XXXI. Yet was the force so furious and so fell,
That horse and man it made to reele asyde:
Nath'lesse the Prince would not forsake his sell,
For well of yore he learned had to ryde,
But full of anger fiersly to him cryde;
" False traitour! miscreaunt! thou broken hast
The law of armes to strike foe undefide:
But thou thy treasons fruit, I hope, shalt taste
Right sowre, and feele the law the which thou hast
    defast."

XXXII. With that his balefull speare he fiercely bent
Against the Pagans brest, and therewith thought
His cursed life out of her lodge have rent;
But ere the point arrived where it ought,
That seven fold shield, which he from Guyon brought,
He cast between to ward the bitter stownd:
Through all those foldes the steelehead passage wrought,
And through his shoulder perst; wherwith to ground
He groveling fell, all gored in his gushing wound.

XXXIII. Which when his brother saw, fraught with great griefe
And wrath, he to him leaped furiously,
And fowly saide: " By Mahoune, cursed thiefe,
That direfull stroke thou dearely shalt aby: "
Then, hurling up his harmefull blade on hy,
Smote him so hugely on his haughtie crest,
That from his saddle forced him to fly;
Els mote it needes downe to his manly brest
Have cleft his head in twaine, and life thence dispossest.

XXXIV. Now was the Prince in daungerous distresse,
Wanting his sword when he on foot should fight:
His single speare could doe him small redresse
Against two foes of so exceeding might,
The least of which was match for any knight.
And now the other, whom he earst did daunt,

Had reard him selfe againe to cruel fight
Three times more furious and more puissaunt,
Unmindfull of his wound, of his fate ignoraunt.

XXXV. So both attonce him charge on either syde
With hideous strokes and importable powre,
That forced him his ground to traverse wyde,
And wisely watch to ward that deadly stowre;
For in his shield, as thicke as stormie showre,
Their strokes did raine: yet did he never quaile,
Ne backward shrinke, but as a stedfast towre,
Whom foe with double battry doth assaile,
Them on her bulwarke beares, and bids them nought
availe.

XXXVI. So stoutly he withstood their strong assay;
Till that at last, when he advantage spyde,
His poynant speare he thrust with puissant sway
At proud Cymochles, whiles his shield was wyde,
That through his thigh the mortall steele did gryde:
He, swarving with the force, within his flesh
Did breake the launce, and let the head abyde.
Out of the wound the red blood flowed fresh,
That underneath his feet soone made a purple plesh.

XXXVII. Horribly then he gan to rage and rayle,
Cursing his Gods, and him selfe damning deepe:
Als when his brother saw the red blood rayle
Adowne so fast, and all his armour steepe,
For very felnesse lowd he gan to weepe,
And said; " Caytive, curse on thy cruell hond,
That twise hath spedd; yet shall it not thee keepe
From the third brunt of this my fatall brond:
Lo! where the dreadfull Death behynd thy backe doth
stond."

XXXVIII. With that he strooke, and thother strooke withall,
That nothing seemd mote beare so monstrous might:
The one upon his covered shield did fall,
And glauncing downe would not his owner byte;
But thother did upon his troncheon smyte,
Which hewing quite asunder, further way
It made, and on his hacqueton did lyte,

The which dividing with importune sway,
It seized in his right side, and there the dint did stay.

XXXIX. Wyde was the wound, and a large lukewarme flood,
Red as the Rose, thence gushed grievously;
That when the Paynym spyde the streaming blood,
Gave him great hart and hope of victory.
On th' other side, in huge perplexity
The Prince now stood, having his weapon broke;
Nought could he hurt, but still at warde did ly:
Yet with his troncheon he so rudely stroke
Cymochles twise, that twise him forst his foot revoke.

XL. Whom when the Palmer saw in such distresse,
Sir Guyon's sword he lightly to him raught,
And said; "Fayre Sonne, great God thy right hand
     blesse,
To use that sword so well as he it ought!"
Glad was the knight, and with fresh courage fraught,
When as againe he armed felt his hond:
Then like a Lyon, which hath long time saught
His robbed whelpes, and at the last them fond
Emongst the shepeheard swaynes, then wexeth wood
     and yond:

XLI. So fierce he laid about him, and dealt blowes
On either side, that neither mayle could hold,
Ne shield defend the thunder of his throwes:
Now to Pyrochles many strokes he told;
Eft to Cymochles twise so many fold;
Then, backe againe turning his busie hond,
Them both atonce compeld with courage bold
To yield wide way to his hart-thrilling brond;
And though they both stood stiffe, yet could not both
     withstond.

XLII. As salvage Bull, whom two fierce mastives bayt,
When rancour doth with rage him once engore,
Forgets with wary warde them to awayt,
But with his dreadfull hornes them drives afore,
Or flings aloft, or treades downe in the flore,
Beathing out wrath, and bellowing disdaine,
That all the forest quakes to heare him rore:

So rag'd Prince Arthur twixt his foemen twaine,
That neither could his mightie puissaunce sustaine.

XLIII. But ever at Pyrochles when he smitt,
(Who Guyons shield cast ever him before,
Whereon the Faery Queenes pourtract was writt,)
His hand relented and the stroke forbore,
And his deare hart the picture gan adore;
Which oft the Paynim sav'd from deadly stowre:
But him henceforth the same can save no more;
For now arrived is his fatall howre,
That no'te avoyded be by earthly skill or powre.

XLIV. For when Cymochles saw the fowle reproch,
Which them appeached, prickt with guiltie shame
And inward griefe, he fiercely gan approch,
Resolv'd to put away that loathly blame,
Or dye with honour and desert of fame;
And on the haubergh stroke the Prince so sore,
That quite disparted all the linked frame,
And pierced to the skin, but bit no more;
Yet made him twise to reele, that never moov'd afore.

XLV. Whereat renfierst with wrath and sharp regret,
He stroke so hugely with his borrowd blade,
That it empierst the Pagans burganet;
And, cleaving the hard steele, did deepe invade
Into his head, and cruell passage made
Quite through his brayne. He, tombling downe on
    ground,
Breathd out his ghost, which, to th' infernall shade
Fast flying, there eternall torment found
For all the sinnes wherewith his lewd life did abound.

XLVI. Which when his german saw, the stony feare
Ran to his hart, and all his sence dismayd,
Ne thenceforth life ne corage did appeare;
But as a man whom hellish feendes have frayd,
Long trembling still he stoode: at last thus sayd;
" Traytour, what hast thou doen? How ever may
Thy cursed hand so cruelly have swayd
Against that knight! Harrow and well away!
After so wicked deede why liv'st thou lenger day? "

XLVII. With that all desperate, as loathing light,
    And with revenge desyring soone to dye,
    Assembling all his force and utmost might,
    With his owne swerd he fierce at him did flye,
    And strooke, and foynd, and lasht outrageously,
    Withouten reason or regard.   Well knew
    The Prince, with pacience and sufferaunce sly
    So hasty heat soone cooled to subdew:
    Tho, when this breathlesse woxe, that batteil gan renew.

XLVIII. As when a windy tempest bloweth hye,
    That nothing may withstand his stormy stowre,
    The clowdes, as thinges affrayd, before him flye;
    But all so soone as his outrageous powre
    Is layd, they fiercely then begin to showre;
    And, as in scorne of his spent stormy spight,
    Now all attonce their malice forth do poure:
    So did Prince Arthur beare himselfe in fight,
    And suffred rash Pyrochles waste his ydle might.

XLIX. At last, when as the Sarazin perceiv'd
    How that straunge sword refusd to serve his neede,
    But when he stroke most strong the dint deceiv'd,
    He flong it from him; and, devoyd of dreed,
    Upon him lightly leaping without heed
    Twixt his two mighty armes engrasped fast,
    Thinking to overthrowe and downe him tred:
    But him in strength and skill the Prince surpast,
    And through his nimble sleight did under him down cast.

L. Nought booted it the Paynim then to strive;
    For as a Bittur in the Eagles clawe,
    That may not hope by flight to scape alive,
    Still waytes for death with dread and trembling aw;
    So he, now subject to the victours law,
    Did not once move, nor upward cast his eye,
    For vile disdaine and rancour, which did gnaw
    His hart in twaine with sad melancholy;
    As one that loathed life, and yet despysd to dye.

LI. But full of princely bounty and great mind,
    The Conquerour nought cared him to slay;
    But casting wronges and all revenge behind,

More glory thought to give life then decay,
And sayd; "Paynim, this is thy dismall day;
Yet if thou wilt renounce thy miscreaunce,
And my trew liegeman yield thy selfe for ay,
Life will I graunt thee for thy valiaunce,
And all thy wronges will wipe out of my sovenaunce."

LII. "Foole!" (sayd the Pagan) "I thy gift defye
But use thy fortune as it doth befall;
And say, that I not overcome doe dye,
But in despight of life for death doe call."
Wroth was the Prince, and sory yet withall,
That he so wilfully refused grace;
Yet sith his fate so cruelly did fall,
His shining Helmet he gan soone unlace,
And left his headlesse body bleeding all the place.

LIII. By this Sir Guyon from his traunce awakt,
Life having maystered her sencelesse foe,
And looking up, whenas his shield he lakt
And sword saw not, he wexed wondrous woe;
But when the Palmer, whom he long ygoe
Had lost, he by him spyde, right glad he grew,
And saide; "Deare sir, whom wandring to and fro
I long have lackt, I joy thy face to vew:
Firme is thy faith, whom daunger never fro me drew.

LIV. "But read, what wicked hand hath robbed mee
Of my good sword and shield?" The Palmer, glad
With so fresh hew uprysing him to see,
Him answered: "Fayre sonne, be no whit sad
For want of weapons; they shall soone be had."
So gan he to discourse the whole debate,
Which that straunge knight for him sustained had,
And those two Sarazins confounded late,
Whose carcases on ground were horribly prostrate.

LV. Which when he heard, and saw the tokens trew,
His hart with great affection was embayd,
And to the Prince, bowing with reverence dew
As to the patrone of his life, thus sayd;
"My Lord, my liege, by whose most gratious ayd
I live this day, and see my foes subdewd,

What may suffice to be for meede repayd
Of so great graces as ye have me shewd,
But to be ever bound "——

LVI. To whom the Infant thus; " Fayre Sir, what need
Good turnes be counted as a servile bond
To bind their doers to receive their meed?
Are not all knightes by oath bound to withstond
Oppressours powre by armes and puissant hond?
Suffise that I have done my dew in place."
So goodly purpose they together fond
Of kindnesse and of courteous aggrace;
The whiles false Archimage and Atin fled apace.

CANTO IX

The house of Temperance, in which
Doth sober Alma dwell,
Besiegd of many foes, whom straung-
er knightes to flight compell.

I. Of all Gods workes which doe this worlde adorne,
There is no one more faire and excellent
Then is mans body, both for powre and forme,
Whiles it is kept in sober government;
But none then it more fowle and indecent,
Distempred through misrule and passions bace;
It growes a Monster, and incontinent
Doth loose his dignity and native grace:
Behold, who list, both one and other in this place.

II. After the Paynim brethren conquer'd were,
The Briton Prince recov'ring his stolne sword,
And Guyon his lost shield, they both yfere
Forth passed on their way in fayre accord,
Till him the Prince with gentle court did bord:
" Sir knight, mote I of you this court'sy read,
To weet why on your shield, so goodly scord,
Beare ye the picture of that Ladies head?
Full lively is the semblaunt, though the substance dead."

III. " Fayre Sir," (sayd he) " if in that picture dead
Such life ye read, and vertue in vaine shew;
What mote ye weene, if the trew lively-head
Of that most glorious visage ye did vew:
But yf the beauty of her mind ye knew,
That is, her bounty, and imperiall powre,
Thousand times fairer than her mortall hew,
O! how great wonder would your thoughts devoure,
And infinite desire into your spirite poure.

IV. " Shee is the mighty Queene of Faery,
Whose faire retraitt I in my shield doe beare;
Shee is the flowre of grace and chastity

Throughout the world, renowmed far and neare,
My liefe, my liege, my Soveraine, my deare,
Whose glory shineth as the morning starre,
And with her light the earth enlumines cleare:
Far reach her mercies, and her praises farre,
As well in state of peace, as puissaunce in warre."

v. " Thrise happy man," (said then the Briton knight)
    " Whom gracious lott and thy great valiaunce
    Have made thee soldier of that Princesse bright,
    Which with her bounty and glad countenaunce
    Doth blesse her servaunts, and them high advaunce,
    How may straunge knight hope ever to aspire,
    By faithfull service and meete amenaunce,
    Unto such blisse? sufficient were that hire
    For losse of thousand lives, to die at her desire."

vi. Said Guyon, " Noble Lord, what meed so great,
    Or grace of earthly Prince so soveraine,
    But by your wondrous worth and warlike feat
    Ye well may hope, and easely attaine?
    But were your will her sold to entertaine,
    And numbred be mongst knights of Maydenhed,
    Great guerdon, well I wote, should you remaine,
    And in her favor high bee reckoned,
    As Arthegall and Sophy now beene honored."

vii. " Certes," (then said the Prince) " I God avow,
     That sith I armes and knighthood first did plight,
     My whole desire hath beene, and yet is now,
     To serve that Queene with al my powre and might.
     Seven times the Sunne, with his lamp-burning light,
     Hath walkte about the world, and I no lesse,
     Sith of that Goddesse I have sought the sight,
     Yet no where can her find: such happinesse
     Heven doth to me envy, and fortune favourlesse."

viii. " Fortune, the foe of famous chevisaunce,
      " Seldom " (said Guyon) " yields to vertue aide,
      But in her way throwes mischiefe and mischaunce,
      Whereby her course is stopt and passage staid:
      But you, faire Sir, be not herewith dismaid,
      But constant keepe the way in which ye stand;

Which, were it not that I am els delaid
With hard adventure which I have in hand,
I labour would to guide you through al Faery land."

IX. "Gramercy Sir," said he; "but mote I weete
What straunge adventure doe ye now pursew?
Perhaps my succour or advizement meete
Mote stead you much your purpose to subdew."
Then gan Sir Guyon all the story shew
Of false Acrasia, and her wicked wiles;
Which to avenge the Palmer him forth drew
From Faery court.   So talked they, the whiles
They wasted had much way, and measurd many miles.

X. And now faire Phœbus gan decline in haste
His weary wagon to the Westerne vale,
Whenas they spide a goodly castle, plaste
Foreby a river in a pleasaunt dale;
Which choosing for that evenings hospitale,
They thither marcht: but when they came in sight,
And from their sweaty Coursers did avale,
They found the gates fast barred long ere night,
And every loup fast lockt, as fearing foes despight.

XI. Which when they saw, they weened fowle reproch
Was to them doen, their entraunce to forestall,
Till that the Squire gan nigher to approch,
And wind his horne under the castle wall,
That with the noise it shooke as it would fall.
Eftsoones forth looked from the highest spire
The watch, and lowd unto the knights did call,
To weete what they so rudely did require?
Who gently answered, They entraunce did desire.

XII. "Fly fly, good knights," (said he) "fly fast away,
If that your lives ye love, as meete ye should;
Fly fast, and save your selves from neare decay;
Here may ye not have entraunce, though we would:
We would, and would againe, if that we could;
But thousand enemies about us rave,
And with long siege us in the castle hould.
Seven yeares this wize they us besieged have,
And many good knights slaine that have us sought to save."

XIII. Thus as he spoke, loe! with outragious cry
    A thousand villeins rownd about them swarmd
    Out of the rockes and caves adjoyning nye;
    Vile caitive wretches, ragged, rude, deformd,
    All threatning death, all in straunge manner armd;
    Some with unweldy clubs, some with long speares,
    Some rusty knifes, some staves in fier warmd:
    Sterne was their looke; like wild amazed steares,
    Staring with hollow eies, and stiffe upstanding heares.

XIV. Fiersly at first those knights they did assayle,
    And drove them to recoile; but when againe
    They gave fresh charge, their forces gan to fayle,
    Unhable their encounter to sustaine;
    For with such puissaunce and impetuous maine
    Those Champions broke on them, that forst them fly,
    Like scattered Sheepe, whenas the Shepherds swaine
    A Lyon and a Tigre doth espye,
    With greedy pace forth rushing from the forest nye.

XV. A while they fled, but soone retournd againe
    With greater fury then before was fownd;
    And evermore their cruell Capitaine
    Sought with his raskall routs t' enclose them rownd,
    And, overronne, to tread them to the grownd:
    But soone the knights with their bright burning blades
    Broke their rude troupes, and orders did confownd,
    Hewing and slashing at their idle shades;
    For though they bodies seem, yet substaunce from
      them fades.

XVI. As when a swarme of Gnats at eventide
    Out of the fennes of Allan doe arise,
    Their murmuring small trompetts sownden wide,
    Whiles in the aire their clustring army flies,
    That as a cloud doth seeme to dim the skies;
    Ne man nor beast may rest, or take repast
    For their sharpe wounds and noyous injuries,
    Till the fierce Northerne wind with blustring blast
    Doth blow them quite away, and in the Ocean cast.

XVII. Thus when they had that troublous rout disperst,
    Unto the castle gate they come againe,
    And entraunce crav'd which was denied erst.

Now when report of that their perlous paine,
And combrous conflict which they did sustaine,
Came to the Ladies eare which there did dwell,
Shee forth issewed with a goodly traine
Of Squires and Ladies equipaged well,
And entertained them right fairely, as befell.

XVIII. Alma she called was; a virgin bright,
That had not yet felt Cupides wanton rage;
Yet was shee woo'd of many a gentle knight,
And many a Lord of noble parentage,
That sought with her to lincke in marriage:
For shee was faire as faire mote ever bee,
And in the flowre now of her freshest age;
Yet full of grace and goodly modestee,
That even heven rejoyced her sweete face to see.

XIX. In robe of lilly white she was arayd,
That from her shoulder to her heele downe raught;
The traine whereof loose far behind her strayd,
Braunched with gold and perle most richly wrought,
And borne of two faire Damsels which were taught
That service well.   Her yellow golden heare
Was trimly woven and in tresses wrought,
Ne other tire she on her head did weare,
But crowned with a garland of sweete Rosiere.

XX. Goodly shee entertaind those noble knights,
And brought them up into her castle hall;
Where gentle court and gracious delight
Shee to them made, with mildnesse virginall,
Shewing her selfe both wise and liberall.
Then, when they rested had a season dew,
They her besought of favour speciall
Of that faire Castle to affoord them vew:
Shee graunted; and, them leading forth, the same did shew.

XXI. First she them lead up to the Castle wall,
That was so high as foe might not it clime,
And all so faire and fensible withall;
Not built of bricke, ne yet of stone and lime,
But of thing like to that Ægyptian slime,
Whereof king Nine whilome built Babell towre.

But O great pitty! that no lenger time
So goodly workemanship should not endure:
Soone it must turne to earth; no earthly thing is sure.

XXII. The frame thereof seemd partly circulare,
And part triangulare; O worke divine!
Those two the first and last proportions are;
The one imperfect, mortall, fœminine,
Th' other immortall, perfect, masculine;
And twixt them both a quadrate was the base
Proportiond equally by seven and nine;
Nine was the circle sett in heavens place:
All which compacted made a goodly Diapase.

XXIII. Therein two gates were placed seemly well:
The one before, by which all in did pas,
Did th' other far in workmanship excell;
For not of wood, nor of enduring bras,
But of more worthy substance fram'd it was:
Doubly disparted, it did locke and close,
That when it locked none might thorough pas,
And when it opened, no man might it close,
Still open to their friendes, and closed to their foes.

XXIV. Of hewen stone the porch was fayrely wrought,
Stone more of valew, and more smooth and fine,
Then Jett or Marble far from Ireland brought;
Over the which was cast a wandring vine,
Enchaced with a wanton yvie twine;
And over it a fayre Portcullis hong,
Which to the gate directly did incline
With comely compasse and compacture strong,
Nether unseemly short, nor yet exceeding long.

XXV. Within the Barbican a Porter sate,
Day and night duely keeping watch and ward;
Nor wight nor word mote passe out of the gate,
But in good order, and with dew regard;
Utterers of secrets he from thence debard,
Bablers of folly, and blazers of cryme:
His larumbell might lowd and wyde be hard
When cause requyrd, but never out of time;
Early and late it rong, at evening and at prime.

XXVI. And rownd about the porch on every syde
Twise sixteene warders satt, all armed bright
In glistring steele, and strongly fortifyde:
Tall yeomen seemed they and of great might,
And were enraunged ready still for fight.
By them as Alma passed with her guestes,
They did obeysaunce, as beseemed right,
And then againe retourned to their restes:
The Porter eke to her did lout with humble gestes.

XXVII. Thence she them brought into a stately Hall,
Wherein were many tables fayre dispred,
And ready dight with drapets festivall,
Against the viaundes should be ministred.
At th' upper end there sate, yclad in red
Downe to the ground, a comely personage,
That in his hand a white rod menaged:
He Steward was, hight Diet; rype of age,
And in demeanure sober, and in counsell sage.

XXVIII. And through the Hall there walked to and fro
A jolly yeoman, Marshall of the same,
Whose name was Appetite: he did bestow
Both guestes and meate, when ever in they came,
And knew them how to order without blame,
As him the Steward badd.   They both attone
Did dewty to their Lady, as became;
Who, passing by, forth ledd her guestes anone
Into the kitchen rowme, ne spard for nicenesse none.

XXIX. It was a vaut ybuilt for great dispence,
With many raunges reard along the wall,
And one great chimney, whose long tonnell thence
The smoke forth threw.   And in the midst of all
There placed was a caudron wide and tall
Upon a mightie fornace, burning whott,
More whott then Aetn', or flaming Mongiball
For day and night it brent, ne ceased not,
So long as any thing it in the caudron gott. ·

XXX. But to delay the heat, least by mischaunce
It might breake out and sett the whole on fyre,
There added was by goodly ordinaunce

An huge great payre of bellowes, which did styre
Continually, and cooling breath inspyre.
About the Caudron many Cookes accoyld
With hookes and ladles, as need did requyre;
The whyles the viaundes in the vessell boyld
They did about their businesse sweat, and sorely toyld.

XXXI. The maister Cooke was cald Concoction;
A carefull man, and full of comely guyse.
The kitchin clerke, that hight Digestion,
Did order all th' Achates in seemely wise,
And set them forth, as well he could devise.
The rest had severall offices assynd;
Some to remove the scum as it did rise;
Others to beare the same away did mynd;
And others it to use according to his kynd.

XXXII. But all the liquour, which was fowle and waste,
Not good nor serviceable elles for ought,
They in another great rownd vessell plaste,
Till by a conduit pipe it thence were brought:
And all the rest, that noyous was and nought,
By secret wayes, that none might it espy,
Was close convaid, and to the backgate brought,
That cleped was Port Esquiline, whereby
It was avoided quite, and throwne out privily.

XXXIII. Which goodly order and great workmans skill
Whenas those knightes beheld, with rare delight
And gazing wonder they their mindes did fill;
For never had they seene so straunge a sight.
Thence backe againe faire Alma led them right,
And soone into a goodly Parlour brought,
That was with royall arras richly dight,
In which was nothing pourtrahed nor wrought;
Not wrought nor pourtrahed, but easie to be thought.

XXXIV. And in the midst thereof upon the floure
A lovely bevy of faire Ladies sate,
Courted of many a jolly Paramoure,
The which them did in modest wise amate,
And each one sought his Lady to aggrate:
And eke emongst them litle Cupid playd

His wanton sportes, being retourned late
From his fierce warres, and having from him layd
His cruel bow, wherewith he thousands hath dismayd.

xxxv. Diverse delights they fownd them selves to please;
Some song in sweet consort; some laught for joy;
Some plaid with strawes; some ydly satt at ease;
But other some could not abide to toy;
All pleasaunce was to them griefe and annoy:
This fround, that faund, the third for shame did blush,
Another seemd envious or coy,
Another in her teeth did gnaw a rush;
But at these straungers presence every one did hush.

xxxvi. Soone as the gracious Alma came in place,
They all attonce out of their seates arose,
And to her homage made with humble grace:
Whom when the knights beheld, they gan dispose
Themselves to court, and each a damzell chose.
The Prince by chaunce did on a Lady light,
That was right faire and fresh as morning rose,
But somwhat sad and solemne eke in sight,
As if some pensive thought constraind her gentle spright.

xxxvii. In a long purple pall, whose skirt with gold
Was fretted all about, she was arayd;
And in her hand a Poplar braunch did hold:
To whom the Prince in courteous maner sayd;
" Gentle Madame, why beene ye thus dismayd,
And your faire beautie doe with sadnes spill?
Lives any that you hath thus ill apayd?
Or doen you love? or doen you lack your will?
What ever bee the cause, it sure beseemes you ill."

xxxviii. " Fayre Sir," said she, halfe in disdaineful wise,
" How is it that this mood in me ye blame,
And in your selfe doe not the same advise?
Him ill beseemes anothers fault to name,
That may unwares bee blotted with the same:
Pensive I yeeld I am, and sad in mind,
Through great desire of glory and of fame;
Ne ought, I weene, are ye therein behynd,
That have three years sought one, yet no where can her
find."

XXXIX. The Prince was inly moved at her speach,
     Well weeting trew what she had rashly told;
     Yet with faire semblaunt sought to hyde the breach,
     Which chaunge of colour did perforce unfold,
     Now seeming flaming whott, now stony cold:
     Tho, turning soft aside, he did inquyre
     What wight she was that Poplar braunch did hold?
     It answered was, her name was Prays-desire,
     That by well doing sought to honour to aspyre.

XL. The whyles the Faery knight did entertayne
     Another Damsell of that gentle crew,
     That was right fayre and modest of demayne,
     But that too oft she chaung'd her native hew.
     Straunge was her tyre, and all her garment blew,
     Close rownd about her tuckt with many a plight:
     Upon her fist the bird, which shonneth vew,
     And keepes in coverts close from living wight,
     Did sitt, as yet ashamed how rude Pan did her dight.

XLI. So long as Guyon with her commoned,
     Unto the grownd she cast her modest eye,
     And ever and anone with rosy red
     The bashfull blood her snowy cheekes did dye,
     That her became, as polisht yvory
     Which cunning Craftesman hand hath overlayd
     With fayre vermilion or pure Castory.
     Great wonder had the knight to see the mayd
     So straungely passioned, and to her gently said:

XLII. " Fayre Damzell, seemeth by your troubled cheare,
     That either me too bold ye weene, this wise
     You to molest, or other ill to feare
     That in the secret of your hart close lyes,
     From whence it doth, as cloud from sea, aryse.
     If it be I, of pardon I you pray;
     But if ought else that I mote not devyse,
     I will, if please you it discure, assay
     To ease you of that ill, so wisely as I may."

XLIII. She answerd nought, but more abasht for shame
     Held downe her head, the whiles her lovely face
     The flashing blood with blushing did inflame,

And the strong passion mard her modest grace,
That Guyon mervayld at her uncouth cace;
Till Alma him bespake: "Why wonder yee,
Faire Sir, at that which ye so much embrace?
She is the fountaine of your modestee:
You shamefast are, but Shamefastnes it selfe is shee."

XLIV. Thereat the Elfe did blush in privitee,
And turned his face away, but she the same
Dissembled faire, and faynd to oversee.
Thus they awhile with court and goodly game
Themselves did solace each one with his Dame,
Till that great Lady thence away them sought
To vew her Castles other wondrous frame:
Up to a stately Turret she them brought,
Ascending by ten steps of Alabaster wrought.

XLV. That Turrets frame most admirable was,
Like highest heaven compassed around,
And lifted high above this earthly masse,
Which it survewd as hils doen lower ground;
But not on ground mote like to this be found:
Not that, which antique Cadmus whylome built
In Thebes, which Alexander did confound;
Nor that proud towre of Troy, though richly guilt,
From which young Hectors blood by cruell Greekes was
    spilt.

XLVI. The roofe hereof was arched over head,
And deckt with flowers and herbars daintily:
Two goodly Beacons, set in watches stead,
Therein gave light, and flamd continually;
For they of living fire most subtilly
Were made, and set in silver sockets bright,
Cover'd with lids deviz'd of substance sly,
That readily they shut and open might.
O! who can tell the prayses of that makers might?

XLVII. Ne can I tell, ne can I stay to tell,
This parts great workemanship and wondrous powre,
That all this other worldes worke doth excell,
And likest is unto that heavenly towre
That God hath built for his owne blessed bowre.
Therein were divers rowmes, and divers stages;

But three the chiefest and of greatest powre,
In which there dwelt three honorable sages,
The wisest men, I weene, that lived in their ages.

XLVIII. Not he, whom Greece, the Nourse of all good arts,
By Phœbus doome the wisest thought alive,
Might be compar'd to these by many parts:
Nor that sage Pylian syre, which did survive
Three ages, such as mortall men contrive,
By whose advise old Priams citie fell,
With these in praise of pollicies mote strive.
These three in these three rowmes did sondry dwell,
And counselled faire Alma how to governe well.

XLIX. The first of them could things to come foresee;
The next could of thinges present best advize;
The third things past could keep in memoree:
So that no time nor reason could arize,
But that the same could one of these comprize.
For-thy the first did in the forepart sit,
That nought mote hinder his quicke prejudize:
He had a sharpe foresight and working wit
That never idle was, ne once would rest a whit.

L. His chamber was dispainted all within
With sondry colours, in the which were writ
Infinite shapes of thinges dispersed thin;
Some such as in the world were never yit,
Ne can devized be of mortall wit;
Some daily seene and knowen by their names,
Such as in idle fantasies do flit;
Infernall Hags, Centaurs, feendes, Hippodames,
Apes, Lyons, Aegles, Owles, fooles, lovers, children, Dames.

LI. And all the chamber filled was with flyes
Which buzzed all about, and made such sound
That they encombred all mens eares and eyes;
Like many swarmes of Bees assembled round,
After their hives with honny do abound.
All those were idle thoughtes and fantasies,
Devices, dreames, opinions unsound,
Shewes, visions, sooth-sayes, and prophesies;
And all that fained is, as leasings, tales, and lies.

LII. Emongst them all sate he which wonned there,
That hight Phantastes by his nature trew;
A man of yeares yet fresh, as mote appere,
Of swarth complexion, and of crabbed hew,
That him full of melancholy did shew;
Bent hollow beetle browes, sharpe staring eyes,
That mad or foolish seemd: one by his vew
Mote deeme him borne with ill-disposed skyes,
When oblique Saturne sate in th' house of agonyes.

LIII. Whom Alma having shewed to her guestes,
Thence brought them to the second rowme, whose wals
Were painted faire with memorable gestes
Of famous Wisards; and with picturals
Of Magistrates, of courts, of tribunals,
Of commen-wealthes, of states, of pollicy,
Of lawes, of judgementes, and of decretals,
All artes, all science, all Philosophy,
And all that in the world was ay thought wittily.

LIV. Of those that rowme was full; and them among
There sate a man of ripe and perfect age,
Who did them meditate all his life long,
That through continuall practise and usage
He now was growne right wise and wondrous sage:
Great pleasure had those straunger knightes to see
His goodly reason and grave personage,
That his disciples both desyrd to bee;
But Alma thence them led to th' hindmost rowme of three.

LV. That chamber seemed ruinous and old,
And therefore was removed far behind,
Yet were the wals, that did the same uphold,
Right firme and strong, though somewhat they declind;
And therein sat an old old man, halfe blind,
And all decrepit in his feeble corse,
Yet lively vigour rested in his mind,
And recompenst them with a bitter scorse:
Weake body wel is chang'd for minds redoubled forse.

LVI. This man of infinite remembraunce was,
And things foregone through many ages held,
Which he recorded still as they did pas,
Ne suffred them to perish through long eld,

As all things els the which this world doth weld;
But laid them up in his immortall scrine,
Where they for ever incorrupted dweld:
The warres he well remembred of king Nine,
Of old Assaracus, and Inachus divine.

LVII. The yeares of Nestor nothing were to his,
Ne yet Mathusalem, though longest liv'd;
For he remembred both their infancis:
Ne wonder then, if that he were depriv'd
Of native strength now that he them surviv'd.
His chamber all was hangd about with rolls
And old records from auncient times derivd,
Some made in books, some in long parchment scrolls,
That were all worm-eaten and full of canker holes.

LVIII. Amidst them all he in a chaire was sett,
Tossing and turning them withouten end;
But for he was unhable them to fett,
A litle boy did on him still attend
To reach, when ever he for ought did send;
And oft when thinges were lost, or laid amis,
That boy them sought and unto him did lend:
Therefore he Anamnestes cleped is;
And that old man Eumnestes, by their propertis.

LIX. The knightes there entring did him reverence dew,
And wondred at his endlesse exercise:
Then as they gan his Library to vew,
And antique Regesters for to avise,
There chaunced to the Princes hand to rize
An auncient booke, hight *Briton moniments*,
That of this lands first conquest did devize,
And old division into Regiments,
Till it reduced was to one mans governements.

LX. Sir Guyon chaunst eke on another booke,
That hight *Antiquitee of Faery lond :*
In which whenas he greedily did looke,
Th' ofspring of Elves and Faeryes there he fond,
As it delivered was from hond to hond:
Whereat they, burning both with fervent fire
Their countreys auncestry to understond,
Crav'd leave of Alma and that aged sire
To read those bookes; who glady graunted their desire.

[In canto x Arthur reads in *Briton moniments* of Elizabeth's ancestry, beginning with Aeneas's descendant Brutus and finishing with Uther Pendragon (st. 68). In Stanzas 70–76 Guyon reads briefly about her elfin pedigree. The importance of this historical interlude is discussed in the Introduction.]

CANTO XI

The enimies of Temperaunce
Besiege her dwelling place:
Prince Arthure them repelles, and rowu
Maleger doth deface.

I. What warre so cruel, or what siege so sore,
As that which strong affections doe apply
Against the forte of reason evermore,
To bring the sowle into captivity?
Their force is fiercer through infirmity
Of the fraile flesh, relenting to their rage,
And exercise most bitter tyranny
Upon the partes brought into their bondage:
No wretchednesse is like to sinfull vellenage.

II. But in a body which doth freely yeeld
His partes to reasons rule obedient,
And letteth her that ought the scepter weeld,
All happy peace and goodly government
Is setled there in sure establishment.
There Alma, like a virgin Queene most bright,
Doth florish in all beautie excellent;
And to her guestes doth bounteous banket dight,
Attempred goodly well for health and for delight.

III. Early, before the Morne with cremosin ray
The windowes of bright heaven opened had,
Through which into the world the dawning day
Might looke, that maketh every creature glad,
Uprose Sir Guyon, in bright armour clad,
And to his purposd journey him prepar'd:
With him the Palmer eke in habit sad
Him selfe addrest to that adventure hard:
So to the rivers syde they both together far'd:

IV. Where them awaited ready at the ford
The Ferriman, as Alma had behight,
With his well-rigged bote: They goe abord,

And he eftsoones gan launch his barke forthright.
Ere long they rowed were quite out of sight,
And fast the land behynd them fled away.
But let them pas, whiles wind and wether right
Doe serve their turnes: here I a while must stay,
To see a cruell fight doen by the prince this day.

v. For all so soone as Guyon thence was gon
Upon his voyage with his trustie guyde,
That wicked band of villeins fresh begon
That castle to assaile on every side,
And lay strong siege about it far and wyde.
So huge and infinite their numbers were,
That all the land they under them did hyde;
So fowle and ugly, that exceeding feare
Their visages imprest when they approched neare.

vi. Them in twelve troupes their Captein did dispart,
And round about in fittest steades did place,
Where each might best offend his proper part,
And his contrary object most deface,
As every one seem'd meetest in that cace.
Seven of the same against the Castle gate
In strong entrenchments he did closely place,
Which with incessaunt force and endlesse hate
They battred day and night, and entraunce did awate.

vii. The other five five sondry wayes he sett
Against the five great Bulwarkes of that pyle,
And unto each a Bulwarke did arrett,
T' assayle with open force or hidden guyle,
In hope thereof to win victorious spoile.
They all that charge did fervently apply
With greedie malice and import ne toyle,
And planted there their huge artillery,
With which they dayly made most dreadfull battery.

viii. The first troupe was a monstrous rablement
Of fowle misshapen wightes, of which some were
Headed like Owles, with beckes uncomely bent;
Others like Dogs; others like Gryphons dreare;
And some had wings, and some had clawes to teare:
And every one of them had Lynces eyes;

And every one did bow and arrowes beare.
All those were lawlesse lustes, currupt envyes,
And covetous aspects, all cruell enimyes.

IX. Those same against the bulwarke of the Sight
Did lay strong siege and battailous assault,
Ne once did yield it respitt day nor night;
But soone as Titan gan his head exault,
And soone againe as he his light withhault,
Their wicked engins they against it bent;
That is, each thing by which the eyes may fault
But two then all more huge and violent,
Beautie and Money, they that Bulwarke sorely rent.

X. The second Bulwarke was the Hearing sence,
Gainst which the second troupe assignment makes;
Deformed creatures, in straunge difference,
Some having heads like Harts, some like to Snakes,
Some like wilde Bores late rouzd out of the brakes:
Slaunderous reproches, and fowle infamies.
Leasinges, backbytinges, and vain-glorious crakes,
Bad counsels, prayses, and false flatteries:
All those against that fort did bend their batteries.

XI. Likewise that same third Fort, that is the Smell,
Of that third troupe was cruelly assayd;
Whose hideous shapes were like to feendes of hell,
Some like to houndes, some like to Apes, disma,
Some like to Puttockes, all in plumes arayd;
All shap't according their conditions:
For by those ugly formes weren pourtrayd
Foolish delights, and fond abusions,
Which doe that sence besiege with light illusions.

XII. And that fourth band which cruell battry bent
Against the fourth Bulwarke, that is the Taste,
Was, as the rest, a grysie rablement;
Some mouth'd like greedy Oystriges; some faste
Like loathly Toades; some fashioned in the waste
Like swine: for so deformd is luxury,
Surfeat, misdiet, and unthriftie waste,
Vaine feastes, and ydle superfluity:
All those this sences Fort assayle incessantly.

XIII. But the fift troupe, most horrible of hew
    And ferce of force, is dreadfull to report;
    For some like Snailes, some did like spyders shew,
    And some like ugly Urchins thick and short:
    Cruelly they assaged that fift Fort,
    Armed with dartes of sensuall Delight,
    With stinges of carnall lust, and strong effort
    Of feeling pleasures, with which day and night
    Against that same fift bulwarke they continued fight.

XIV. Thus these twelve troupes with dreadfull puissaunce
    Against that Castle restlesse siege did lay,
    And evermore their hideous Ordinaunce
    Upon the Bulwarkes cruelly did play,
    That now it gan to threaten neare decay:
    And evermore their wicked Capitayn
    Provoked them the breaches to assay,
    Sometimes with threats, sometimes with hope of gayn,
    Which by the ransack of that peece they should attayn.

XV. On th' other syde, th' assieged Castles ward
    Their stedfast stonds did mightily maintaine,
    And many bold repulse and many hard
    Atchievement wrought, with perill and with payne,
    That goodly frame from ruine to sustaine:
    And those two brethren Gyauntes did defend
    The walles so stoutly with their sturdie mayne,
    That never entraunce any durst pretend,
    But they to direfull death their groning ghosts did send.

XVI. The noble Virgin, Ladie of the Place,
    Was much dismayed with that dreadful sight,
    For never was she in so evill cace,
    Till that the Prince, seeing her wofull plight,
    Gan her recomfort from so sad affright,
    Offring his service, and his dearest life
    For her defence against that Carle to fight,
    Which was their chiefe and th' authour of that strife:
    She him remercied as the Patrone of her life.

XVII. Eftsoones himselfe in glitterand armes he dight,
    And his well proved weapons to him hent;
    So, taking courteous congé, he behight

Those gates to be unbar'd, and forth he went.
Fayre mote he thee, the prowest and most gent,
That ever brandished bright steele on hye!
Whome soone as that unruly rablement
With his gay Squyre issewing did espye,
They reard a most outrageous dreadfull yelling cry:

XVIII. And therewithall attonce at him let fly
Their fluttring arrowes, thicke as flakes of snow,
And round about him flocke impetuously,
Like a great water flood, that tombling low
From the high mountaines, threates to overflow
With suddein fury all the fertile playne,
And the sad husbandmans long hope doth throw
Adowne the streame, and all his vowes make vayne;
Nor bounds nor banks his headlong ruine may sustayne.

XIX. Upon his shield their heaped hayle he bore,
And with his sword disperst the raskall flockes,
Which fled asonder, and him fell before;
As withered leaves drop from their dryed stockes,
When the wroth Western wind does reave their locks:
And underneath him his courageous steed,
The fierce Spumador, trode them downe like docks;
The fierce Spumador, borne of heavenly seed,
Such as Laomedon of Phœbus race did breed.

XX. Which suddeine horrour and confused cry
When as their Capteine heard, in haste he yode
The cause to weet, and fault to remedy:
Upon a Tygre swift and fierce he rode,
That as the winde ran underneath his lode,
Whiles his long legs nigh raught unto the ground.
Full large he was of limbe, and shoulders brode,
But of such subtile substance and unsound,
That like a ghost he seem'd whose grave-clothes were
    unbound:

XXI. And in his hand a bended bow was seene,
And many arrowes under his right side,
All deadly daungerous, all cruell keene,
Headed with flint, and fethers bloody dide;
Such as the Indians in their quivers hide:
Those could he well direct and streight as line,

And bid them strike the marke which he had eyde;
Ne was there salve, ne was there medicine,
That mote recure their wounds; so inly they did tine.

XXII. As pale and wan as ashes was his looke,
His body leane and meagre as a rake,
And skin all withered like a dryed rooke;
Thereto as cold and drery as a snake,
That seemd to tremble evermore and quake;
All in a canvas thin he was bedight,
And girded with a belt of twisted brake:
Upon his head he wore an Helmet light,
Made of a dead mans skull, that seemd a ghastly sight.

XXIII. Maleger was his name; and after him
There follow'd fast at hand two wicked Hags,
With hoary lockes all loose, and visage grim;
Their feet unshod, their bodies wrapt in rags,
And both as swift on foot as chased Stags;
And yet the one her other legge had lame,
Which with a staffe, all full of litle snags,
She did support, and Impotence her name.
But th' other was Impatience, arm'd with raging flame.

XXIV. Soone as the Carle from far the Prince espyde
Glistring in armes and warlike ornament,
His Beast he felly prickt on either syde,
And his mischievous bow full readie bent,
With which at him a cruell shaft he sent:
But he was warie, and it warded well
Upon his shield, that it no further went,
But to the ground the idle quarrell fell:
Then he another and another did expell.

XXV. Which to prevent the Prince his mortall speare
Soone to him raught, and fierce at him did ride,
To be avenged of that shot whyleare;
But he was not so hardy to abide
That bitter stownd, but turning quicke aside
His light-foot beast, fled fast away for feare:
Whom to poursue the Infant after hide
So fast as his good Courser could him beare;
But labour lost it was to weene approch him neare.

XXVI. For as the winged wind his Tigre fled,
That vew of eye could scarse him overtake,
Ne scarse his feet on ground were seene to tred:
Through hils and dales he speedy way did make,
Ne hedge ne ditch his readie passage brake;
And in his flight the villein turn'd his face
(As wonts the Tartar by the Caspian lake,
Whenas the Russian him in fight does chace)
Unto his Tygres taile, and shot at him apace.

XXVII. Apace he shot, and yet he fled apace,
Still as the greedy knight nigh to him drew;
And oftentimes he would relent his pace,
That him his foe more fiercely should poursew:
But when his uncouth manner he did vew,
He gan avize to follow him no more,
But keepe his standing, and his shaftes eschew,
Untill he quite had spent his perlous store,
And then assayle him fresh, ere he could shift for more.

XXVIII. But that lame Hag, still as abroad he strew
His wicked arrowes, gathered them againe,
And to him brought, fresh batteill to renew;
Which he espying cast her to restraine
From yielding succour to that cursed Swaine,
And her attaching thought her hands to tye;
But soone as him dismounted on the plaine
That other Hag did far away espye
Binding her sister, she to him ran hastily;

XXIX. And catching hold of him, as downe he lent,
Him backeward overthrew, and downe him stayd
With their rude handes and gryesly graplement;
Till that the villein, comming to their ayd,
Upon him fell, and lode upon him layd:
Full litle wanted but he had him slaine,
And of the battell balefull end had made,
Had not his gentle Squire beheld his paine,
And commen to his reskew, ere his bitter bane.

XXX. So greatest and most glorious thing on ground
May often need the helpe of weaker hand;
So feeble is mans state, and life unsound,

That in assuraunce it may never stand,
Till it dissolved be from earthly band.
Proofe be thou, Prince, the prowest man alyve,
And noblest borne of all in Britayne land;
Yet thee fierce Fortune did so nearely drive,
That, had not grace thee blest, thou shouldest not
    survive.

XXXI. The Squyre arriving fiercely in his armes
    Snatcht first the one, and then the other Jade,
    His chiefest letts and authors of his harmes,
    And them perforce withheld with threatned blade,
    Least that his Lord they should behinde invade;
    The whiles the Prince, prickt with reprochful shame,
    As one awakte out of long slombring shade,
    Revivyng thought of glory and of fame,
    United all his powres to purge him selfe from blame.

XXXII. Like as a fire, the which in hollow cave
    Hath long bene underkept and down supprest,
    With murmurous disdayne doth inly rave,
    And grudge in so streight prison to be prest,
    At last breakes forth with furious unrest,
    And strives to mount unto his native seat;
    All that did earst it hinder and molest,
    Yt now devoures with flames and scorching heat,
    And carries into smoake with rage and horror great.

XXXIII. So mightely the Briton Prince him rouzd
    Out of his holde, and broke his caytive bands;
    And as a Beare, whom angry curres have touzd,
    Having off-shakt them and escapt their hands,
    Becomes more fell, and all that him withstands
    Treads down and overthrowes.   Now had the Carle
    Alighted from his Tigre, and his hands
    Discharged of his bow and deadly quar'le,
    To seize upon his foe flatt lying on the marle.

XXXIV. Which now him turnd to disavantage deare;
    For neither can he fly, nor other harme,
    But trust unto his strength and manhood meare,
    Sith now he is far from his monstrous swarme,
    And of his weapons did himselfe disarme.
    The knight, yet wrothfull for his late disgrace,

Fiercely advaunst his valorous right arme,
And him so sore smott with his yron mace,
That groveling to the ground he fell, and fild his place.

XXXV. Wel weened hee that field was then his owne,
And all his labor brought to happy end;
When suddein up the villeine overthrowne
Out of his swowne arose, fresh to contend,
And gan him selfe to second battaill bend,
As hurt he had not beene.   Thereby there lay
An huge great stone, which stood upon one end,
And had not bene removed many a day;
Some land-marke seemd to bee, or signe of sundry way:

XXXVI. The same he snatcht, and with exceeding sway
Threw at his foe, whe was right well aware
To shonne the engin of his meant decay;
It booted not to thinke that throw to beare,
But grownd he gave, and lightly lept areare:
Eft fierce retourning, as a faulcon fayre,
That once hath failed of her souse full neare,
Remounts againe into the open ayre,
And unto better fortune doth her selfe prepayre.

XXXVII. So brave retourning, with his brandisht blade
He to the Carle him selfe agayn addrest,
And strooke at him so sternely, that he made
An open passage through his riven brest,
That halfe the steele behind his backe did rest;
Which drawing backe, he looked evermore
When the hart blood should gush out of his chest,
Or his dead corse should fall upon the flore;
But his dead corse upon the flore fell nathemore.

XXXVIII. Ne drop of blood appeared shed to bee,
All were the wownd so wide and wonderous
That through his carcas one might playnly see.
Halfe in amaze with horror hideous,
And halfe in rage to be deluded thus,
Again through both the sides he strooke him quight,
That made his spright to grone full piteous;
Yet nathemore forth fled his groning spright,
But freshly, as at first, prepared himselfe to fight.

XXXIX. Thereat he smitten was with great affright,
And trembling terror did his hart apall;
Ne wist he what to thinke of that same sight,
Ne what to say, ne what to doe at all:
He doubted least it were some magicall
Illusion that did beguile his sense,
Or wandring ghost that wanted funerall,
Or aery spirite under false pretence,
Or hellish feend raysd up through divelish science.

XL. His wonder far exceeded reasons reach,
That he began to doubt his dazeled sight,
And oft of error did himselfe appeach:
Flesh without blood, a person without spright,
Wounds without hurt, a body without might,
That could doe harme, yet could not harmed bee,
That could not die, yet seemd a mortall wight,
That was most strong in most infirmitee;
Like did he never heare, like did he never see.

XLI. Awhile he stood in this astonishment,
Yet would he not for all his great dismay
Give over to effect his first intent,
And th' utmost meanes of victory assay,
Or th' utmost yssew of his owne decay.
His owne good sword Mordure, that never fayld
At need till now, he lightly threw away,
And his bright shield that nought him now avayld;
And with his naked hands him forcibly assayld.

XLII. Twixt his two mighty armes him up he snatcht,
And crusht his carcas so against his brest,
That the disdainfull sowle he thence dispatcht,
And th' ydle breath all utterly exprest.
Tho, when he felt him dead, adowne he kest
The lumpish corse unto the sencelesse grownd;
Adowne he kest it with so puissant wrest,
That backe againe it did alofte rebownd,
And gave against his mother earth a gronefull sownd.

XLIII. As when Joves harnesse-bearing Bird from hye
Stoupes at a flying heron with proud disdayne,
The stone-dead quarrey falls so forciblye,

That yt rebownds against the lowly playne,
A second fall redoubling backe agayne.
Then thought the Prince all peril sure was past,
And that he victor onely did remayne;
No sooner thought, then that the Carle as fast
Gan heap huge strokes on him, as ere he down was cast.

XLIV. Nigh his wits end then woxe th' amazed knight,
And thought his labour lost, and travell vayne,
Against this lifelesse shadow so to fight:
Yet life he saw, and felt his mighty mayne,
That, whiles he marveild still, did still him payne;
Forthy he gan some other wayes advize,
How to take life from that dead-living swayne,
Whom still he marked freshly to arize
From th' earth, and from her womb new spirits to reprize.

XLV. He then remembered well, that had bene sayd,
How th' Earth his mother was, and first him bore;
She eke, so often as his life decayd,
Did life with usury to him restore,
And reysd him up much stronger than before,
So soone as he unto her wombe did fall:
Therefore to grownd he would him cast no more,
Ne him committ to grave terrestriall,
But beare him farre from hope of succour usuall.

XLVI. Tho up he caught him twixt his puissant hands,
And having scruzd out of his carrion corse
The lothfull life, now loosd from sinfull bands,
Upon his shoulders carried him perforse
Above three furlongs, taking his full course
Until he came unto a standing lake;
Him thereinto he threw without remorse,
Ne stird, till hope of life did him forsake:
So end of that Carles dayes and his owne paynes did
make.

XLVII. Which when those wicked Hags from far did spye,
Like two mad dogs they ran about the lands,
And th' one of them with dreadfull yelling crye,
Throwing away her broken chaines and bands,
And having quencht her burning fier-brands,

Hedlong her selfe did cast into that lake;
But Impotençe with her owne wilfull hands
One of Malegers cursed darts did take,
So ryv'd her trembling hart, and wicked end did make.

XLVIII. Thus now alone he conquerour remaines:
Tho, cumming to his Squyre that kept his steed,
Thought to have mounted; but his feeble vaines
Him faild thereto, and served not his need,
Through losse of blood which from his wounds did bleed,
That he began to faint, and life decay:
But his good Squyre, him helping up with speed,
With stedfast hand upon his horse did stay,
And led him to the Castle by the beaten way.

XLIX. Where many Groomes and Squyres ready were
To take him from his steed full tenderly;
And eke the fayrest Alma mett him there
With balme, and wine, and costly spicery,
To comfort him in his infirmity.
Eftesoones shee causd him up to be convayd,
And of his armes despoyled easily
In sumptuous bed shee made him to be layd;
And al the while his wounds were dressing by him stayd.

CANTO XII

Guyon, by Palmers governaunce,
Passing through perilles great,
Doth overthrow the Bowre of blis,
And Acrasy defeat.

I. Now ginnes that goodly frame of Temperaunce
Fayrely to rise, and her adorned hed
To pricke of highest prayse forth to advaunce,
Formerly grounded and fast setteled
On firme foundation of true bountyhed:
And this brave knight, that for this vertue fightes,
Now comes to point of that same perilous sted,
Where Pleasure dwelles in sensuall delights,
Mongst thousand dangers, and ten thousand Magick mights.

II. Two dayes now in that sea he sayled has,
Ne ever land beheld, ne living wight,
Ne ought save perill still as he did pas:
Tho, when appeared the third Morrow bright
Upon the waves to spred her trembling light,
An hideous roring far away they heard,
That all their sences filled with affright;
And streight they saw the raging surges reard
Up to the skyes, that them of drowning made affeard.

III. Said then the Boteman, " Palmer, stere aright.
And keepe an even course; for yonder way
We needes must pas (God doe us well acquight!)
That is the Gulfe of Greedinesse, they say,
That deepe engorgeth all this worldes pray;
Which having swallowd up excessively,
He soone in vomit up againe doth lay,
And belcheth forth his superfluity,
That all the seas for feare doe seeme away to fly.

IV. " On thother syde an hideous Rocke is pight
Of mightie Magnes stone, whose craggie clift
Depending from on high, dreadfull to sight,

Over the waves his rugged armes doth lift,
And threatneth downe to throw his ragged rift
On whoso cometh nigh; yet nigh it drawes
All passengers, that none from it can shift:
For, whiles they fly that Gulfes devouring jawes,
They on this rock are rent, and sunck in helples wawes."

v. Forward they passe, and strongly he them rowes,
Untill they nigh unto that Gulfe arryve,
Where streame more violent and greedy growes:
Then he with all his puisaunce doth stryve
To strike his oares, and mightily doth drive
The hollow vessell through the threatfull wave;
Which, gaping wide to swallow them alyve
In th' huge abysse of his engulfing grave,
Doth rore at them in vaine, and with great terrour rave.

vi. They, passing by, that grisely mouth did see
Sucking the seas into his entralles deepe,
That seemd more horrible then hell to bee,
Or that darke dreadfull hole of Tartare steepe
Through which the damned ghosts doen often creepe
Backe to the world, bad livers to torment:
But nought that falles into this direfull deepe
Ne that approcheth nigh the wyde descent,
May backe retourne, but is condemned to be drent.

vii. On thother side they saw that perilous Rocke,
Threatning it selfe on them to ruinate,
On whose sharp cliftes the ribs of vessels broke;
And shivered ships, which had beene wrecked late,
Yet stuck with carkases exanimate
Of such, as having all their substance spent
In wanton joyes and lustes intemperate,
Did afterwards make shipwrack violent
Both of their life and fame, for ever fowly blent.

viii. Forthy this hight The Rocke of vile Reproch,
A daungerous and detestable place,
To which nor fish nor fowle did once approch,
But yelling Meawes, with Seagulles hoars and bace,
And Cormoyraunts, with birds of ravenous race,
Which still sat waiting on that wastfull clift

For spoile of wretches, whose unhappy cace,
After lost credit and consumed thrift,
At last them driven hath to this despairefull drift.

IX. The Palmer, seeing them in safetie past,
    Thus saide; " Behold th' ensamples in our sights
    Of lustfull luxurie and thriftlessse wast.
    What now is left of miserable wightes,
    Which spent their looser daies in leud delightes,
    But shame and sad reproch, here to be red
    By these rent reliques, speaking their ill plightes?
    Let all that live hereby be counselled
    To shunne Rocke of Reproch, and it as death to dred! "

X. So forth they rowed; and that Ferryman
   With his stiffe oares did brush the sea so strong,
   That the hoare waters from his frigot ran,
   And the light bubles daunced all along,
   Whiles the salt brine out of the billowes sprong.
   At last far off they many Islandes spy
   On every side floting the floodes emong:
   Then said the knight; " Lo! I the land descry;
   Therefore, old Syre, thy course doe thereunto apply."

XI. " That may not bee," said then the Ferryman,
    " Least wee unweeting hap to be fordonne;
    For those same Islands, seeming now and than,
    Are not firme land, nor any certein wonne,
    But stragling plots which to and fro doe ronne
    In the wide waters: therefore are they hight
    The Wandring Islands. Therefore doe them shonne;
    For they have ofte drawne many a wandring wight
    Into most deadly daunger and distressed plight.

XII. " Yet well they seeme to him, that farre doth vew,
     Both faire and fruitfull, and the grownd dispred
     With grassy greene of delectable hew;
     And the tall trees with leaves appareled
     Are deckt with blossoms dyde in white and red,
     That mote the passengers thereto allure;
     But whosoever once hath fastened
     His foot thereon, may never it recure,
     But wandreth evermore uncertain and unsure.

XIII. " As th' Isle of Delos whylome, men report,
    Amid th' Aegæan sea long time did stray,
    Ne made for shipping any certeine port,
    Till that Latona traveiling that way,
    Flying from Junoes wrath and hard assay,
    Of her fayre twins was there delivered,
    Which afterwards did rule the night and day:
    Thenceforth it firmely was established,
    And for Apolloes temple highly herried."

XIV. They to him hearken, as beseemeth meete,
    And passe on forward: so their way does ly,
    That one of those same Islands, which doe fleet
    In the wide sea, they needes must passen by,
    Which seemd so sweet and pleasaunt to the eye,
    That it would tempt a man to touchen there:
    Upon the banck they sitting did espy
    A daintie damsell dressing of her heare,
    By whom a little skippet floting did appeare.

XV. She, them espying, loud to them can call,
    Bidding them nigher draw unto the shore,
    For she had cause to busie them withall;
    And therewith lowdly laught: But nathemore
    Would they once turne, but kept on as afore:
    Which when she saw, she left her lockes undight,
    And running to her boat withouten ore,
    From the departing land it launched light,
    And after them did drive with all her power and might.

XVI. Whom overtaking, she in merry sort
    Them gan to bord, and purpose diversly;
    Now faining dalliaunce and wanton sport,
    Now throwing forth lewd wordes immodestly;
    Till that the Palmer gan full bitterly
    Her to rebuke for being loose and light:
    Which not abiding, but more scornfully
    Scoffing at him that did her justly wite,
    She turnd her bote about, and from them rowed quite.

XVII. That was the wanton Phædria, which late
    Did ferry him over the Idle lake:
    Whom nought regarding they kept on their gate,

And all her vaine allurements did forsake;
When them the wary Boteman thus bespake:
" Here now behoveth us well to avyse,
And of our safety good heede to take;
For here before a perlous passage lyes,
Where many Mermayds haunt making false melodies:

XVIII. " But by the way there is a great Quicksand,
And a whirlpoole of hidden jeopardy;
Therefore, Sir Palmer, keepe an even hand.
For twixt them both the narrow way doth ly."
Scarse had he saide, when hard at hand they spy
That quicksand nigh with water covered;
But by the checked wave they did descry
It plaine, and by the sea discoloured:
It called was the quickesand of Unthriftyhed.

XIX. They, passing by, a goodly Ship did see
Laden from far with precious merchandize,
And bravely furnished as ship might bee,
Which through great disaventure, or mesprize,
Her selfe had ronne into that hazardize;
Whose mariners and merchants with much toyle
Labour'd in vaine to have recur'd their prize,
And the rich wares to save from pitteous spoyle;
But neither toyle nor traveill might her backe recoyle.

XX. On th' other side they see that perilous Poole,
That called was the Whirlepoole of decay;
In which full many had with haplesse doole
Beene suncke, of whom no memorie did stay:
Whose circled waters rapt with whirling sway,
Like to a restlesse wheele, still ronning round,
Did covet, as they passed by that way,
To draw their bote within the utmost bound
Of his wide Labyrinth, and then to have them dround.

XXI. But th' heedful Boteman strongly forth did stretch
His brawnie armes, and all his bodie straine,
That th' utmost sandy breach they shortly fetch,
Whiles the dredd daunger does behind remaine.
Suddeine they see from midst of all the Maine
The surging waters like a mountaine rise,

And the great sea, puft up with proud disdaine,
To swell above the measure of his guise,
As threatning to devoure all that his powre despise.

XXII. The waves come rolling, and the billowes rore
Outragiously, as they enraged were,
Or wrathfull Neptune did them drive before
His whirling charet for exceeding feare;
For not one puffe of winde there did appeare,
That all the three thereat woxe much afrayd,
Unweeting what such horrour straunge did reare.
Eftsoones they saw an hideous hoast arrayd
Of huge Sea monsters, such as living sence dismayd:

XXIII. Most ugly shapes and horrible aspects,
Such as Dame Nature selfe mote feare to see,
Or shame that ever should so fowle defects
From her most cunning hand escaped bee;
All dreadfull pourtraicts of deformitee:
Spring-headed Hydres; and sea-shouldring Whales;
Great whirlpooles which all fishes make to flee;
Bright Scolopendraes arm'd with silver scales;
Mighty Monoceroses with immeasured tayles.

XXIV. The dreadful Fish that hath deserv'd the name
Of Death, and like him lookes in dreadfull hew;
The griesly Wasserman, that makes his game
The flying ships with swiftnes to pursew:
The horrible Sea-satyre, that doth shew
His fearefull face in time of greatest storme;
Huge Ziffius, whom Mariners eschew
No lesse then rockes, (as travellers informe)
And greedy Rosmarines with visages deforme.

XXV. All these, and thousand thousands many more,
And more deformed Monsters thousand fold,
With dreadfull noise and hollow rombling rore
Came rushing, in the fomy waves enrold,
Which seem'd to fly for feare them to behold,
Ne wonder, if these did the knight appall;
For all that here on earth we dreadfull hold,
Be but as bugs to fearen babes withall,
Compared to the creatures in the seas entrall.

XXVI. " Feare nought," then saide the Palmer well aviz'd,
    " For these same Monsters are not these in deed,
    But are into these fearefull shapes disguiz'd
    By that same witch, to worke us dreed,
    And draw from on this journey to proceed."
    Tho lifting up his vertuous staffe on hye,
    He smote the sea, which calmed was with speed,
    And all that dreadfull Armie fast gan flye
    Into great Tethys bosome, where they hidden lye.

XXVII. Quit from that danger forth their course they kept;
    And as they went they heard a ruefull cry
    Of one that wayld and pittifully wept,
    That through the sea resounding plaints did fly:
    At last they in an Island did espy
    A seemely Maiden sitting by the shore,
    That with great sorrow and sad agony
    Seemed some great misfortune to deplore,
    And lowd to them for succour called evermore.

XXVIII. Which Guyon hearing streight his Palmer bad
    To stere the bote towards that dolefull Mayd,
    That he might know and ease her sorrow sad;
    Who, him avizing better, to him sayd:
    " Faire Sir, be not displeasd if disobayd:
    For ill it were to hearken to her cry,
    For she is inly nothing ill apayd;
    But onely womanish fine forgery,
    Your stubborne hart t'affect with fraile infirmity.

XXIX. " To which when she your courage hath inclind
    Through foolish pitty, then her guilefull bayt
    She will embosome deeper in your mind,
    And for your ruine at the last awayt."
    The Knight was ruled, and the Boteman strayt
    Held on his course with stayed stedfastnesse,
    Ne ever shroncke, ne ever sought to bayt
    His tyred armes for toylesome wearinesse,
    But with his oares did sweepe the watry wildernesse.

XXX. And now they nigh approched to the sted
    Whereas those Mermayds dwelt: it was a still
    And calmy bay, on th' one side sheltered

With the brode shadow of an hoarie hill;
On th'other side an high rocke toured still,
That twixt them both a pleasaunt port they made,
And did like an halfe Theatre fulfill:
There those five sisters had continuall trade,
And usd to bath themselves in that deceiptfull shade.

XXXI. They were faire Ladies, till they fondly striv'd
With th' Heliconian maides for maystery;
Of whom they, over-comen, were depriv'd
Of their proud beautie, and th' one moyity
Transformd to fish for their bold surquedry;
But th' upper halfe their hew retayned still,
And their sweet skill in wonted melody;
Which ever after they abusd to ill,
T' allure weake traveillers, whom gotten they did kill.

XXXII. So now to Guyon, as he passed by,
Their pleasaunt tunes they sweetly thus applyde:
" O thou fayre sonne of gentle Faery,
That art in mightie armes most magnifyde
Above all knights that ever batteill tryde,
O! turne thy rudder hitherward awhile
Here may thy storme-bett vessell safely ryde,
This is the Port of rest from troublous toyle,
The worldes sweet In from paine and wearisome
    turmoyle."

XXXIII. With that the rolling sea, resounding soft,
In his big base them fitly answered;
And on the rocke the waves breaking aloft
A solemne Meane unto them measured;
The whiles sweet Zephyrus lowd whisteled
His treble, a straunge kinde of harmony,
Which Guyons senses softly tickeled,
That he the boteman bad row easily,
And let him heare some part of their rare melody.

XXXIV. But him the Palmer from that vanity
With temperate advice discounselled,
That they it past, and shortly gan descry
The land to which their course they leveled;
When suddeinly a grosse fog over-spred
With his dull vapour all that desert has,

And heavens chearefull face enveloped,
That all things one, and one as nothing was,
And this great Universe seemd one confused mas.

XXXV. Thereat they greatly were dismayd, ne wist
How to direct theyr way in darkenes wide,
But feard to wander in that wastefull mist,
For tombling into mischiefe unespide:
Worse is the daunger hidden then descride.
Suddeinly an innumerable flight
Of harmefull fowles about them fluttering cride,
And with their wicked wings them ofte did smight,
And sore annoyed, groping in that griesly night.

XXXVI. Even all the nation of unfortunate
And fatall birds about them flocked were,
Such as by nature men abhorre and hate;
The ill-faste Owle, deaths dreadfull messengere;
The hoars Night-raven, trump of dolefull drere;
The lether-winged Batt, dayes enimy;
The ruefull Strich, still waiting on the bere;
The whistler shrill, that whoso heares doth dy;
The hellish Harpyes, prophets of sad destiny.

XXXVII. All those, and all that els does horror breed,
About them flew, and fild their sayles with feare:
Yet stayd they not, but forward did proceed,
Whiles th' one did row, and th' other stifly steare;
Till that at last the weather gan to cleare,
And the faire land it selfe did playnly sheow.
Said then the Palmer; "Lo! where does appeare
The sacred soile where all our perills grow.
Therfore, Sir knight, your ready arms about you throw."

XXXVIII. He hearkned, and his armes about him tooke,
The whiles the nimble bote so well her sped,
That with her crooked keele the land she strooke:
Then forth the noble Guyon sallied,
And his sage Palmer that him governed;
But th' other by his bote behind did stay.
They marched fayrly forth, of nought ydred.
Both firmely armd for every hard assay,
With constancy and care, gainst daunger and dismay.

XXXIX. Ere long they heard an hideous bellowing
Of many beasts, that roard outrageously,
As if that hungers poynt or Venus sting
Had them enraged with fell surquedry:
Yet nought they feard, but past on hardily,
Untill they came in vew of those wilde beasts,
Who all attonce, gaping full greedily,
And rearing fercely their upstaring crests,
Ran towards to devoure those unexpected guests.

XL. But soone as they approcht with deadly threat,
The Palmer over them his staffe upheld,
His mighty staffe, that could all charmes defeat.
Eftesoones their stubborne corages were queld,
And high advaunced crests downe meekely feld;
Instead of fraying, they them selves did feare,
And trembled as them passing they beheld:
Such wondrous powre did in that staffe appeare,
All monsters to subdew to him that did it beare.

XLI. Of that same wood it fram'd was cunningly,
Of which Caduceus whilome was made,
Caduceus, the rod of Mercury,
With which he wonts the Stygian realmes invade
Through ghastly horror and eternall shade:
Th' infernall feends with it he can asswage,
And Orcus tame, whome nothing can persuade,
And rule the Furyes when they most doe rage.
Such vertue in his staffe had eke this Palmer sage.

XLII. Thence passing forth, they shortly doe arryve
Whereas the Bowre of Blisse was situate;
A place pickt out by choyce of best alyve,
That natures worke by art can imitate:
In which whatever in this worldly state
Is sweete and pleasing unto living sense,
Or that may dayntest fantasy aggrate,
Was poured forth with plentifull dispence,
And made there to abound with lavish affluence.

XLIII. Goodly it was enclosed rownd about,
As well their entred guestes to keep within,
As those unruly beasts to hold without;

Yet was the fence thereof but weake and thin:
Nought feard theyr force that fortilage to win,
But wisedomes powre, and temperaunces might,
By which the mightiest things efforced bin:
And eke the gate was wrought of substaunce light,
Rather for pleasure then for battery or fight.

XLIV. Yt framed was of precious yvory,
That seemd a worke of admirable witt;
And therein all the famous history
Of Jason and Medæa was ywritt;
Her mighty charmes, her furious loving fitt;
His goodly conquest of the golden fleece,
His falsed fayth, and love too lightly flitt;
The wondred Argo, which in venturous peece
First through the Euxine seas bore all the flowr of Greece.

XLV. Ye might have seene the frothy billowes fry
Under the ship as thorough them she went,
That seemd the waves were into yvory,
Or yvory into the waves were sent;
And otherwhere the snowy substaunce sprent
With vermell, like the boyes blood therein shed,
A piteous spectacle did represent;
And otherwhiles, with gold besprinkeled,
Yt seemd thenchaunted flame which did Crëusa wed.

XLVI. All this and more might in that goodly gate
Be red, that ever open stood to all
Which thither came; but in the Porch there sate
A comely personage of stature tall,
And semblaunce pleasing, more then naturall,
That traveilers to him seemd to entize:
His looser garment to the ground did fall,
And flew about his heeles in wanton wize,
Not fitt for speedy pace, or manly exercize.

XLVII. They in that place him Genius did call:
Not that celestiall powre, to whom the care
Of life, and generation of all
That lives, perteines in charge particulare,
Who wondrous things concerning our welfare,
And straunge phantomes doth lett us ofte foresee,

And ofte of secret ill bids us beware:
That is our Selfe, whom though we do not see,
Yet each doth in him selfe it well perceive to bee.

XLVIII. Therefore a God him sage Antiquity
Did wisely make, and good Agdistes call;
But this same was to that quite contrary,
The foe of life, that good envyes to all,
That secretly doth us procure to fall
Through guilefull semblants which he makes us see:
He of this Gardin had the governall,
And Pleasures porter was devizd to bee,
Holding a staffe in hand for mere formalitee.

XLIX. With diverse flowres he daintily was deckt,
And strowed rownd about; and by his side
A mighty Mazer bowle of wine was sett,
As if it had to him bene sacrifide,
Wherewith all new-come guests he gratyfide:
So did he eke Sir Guyon passing by;
But he his ydle curtesie defide,
And overthrew his bowle disdainfully,
And broke his staffe with which he charmed semblants
sly.

L. Thus being entred, they behold arownd
A large and spacious plaine, on every side
Strowed with pleasauns; whose fayre grassy grownd
Mantled with greene, and goodly beautifide
With all the ornaments of Floraes pride,
Wherewith her mother Art, as halfe in scorne
Of niggard Nature, like a pompous bride
Did decke her, and too lavishly adorne,
When forth from virgin bowre she comes in th' early
morne.

LI. Therewith the Heavens alwayes joviall
Lookte on them lovely, still in stedfast state,
Ne suffred storme nor frost on them to fall,
Their tender buds or leaves to violate;
Nor scorching heat, nor cold intemperate,
T' afflict the creatures which therein did dwell;
But the milde ayre with season moderate

Gently attempred, and disposd so well,
That still it breathed forth sweet spirit and holesom
    smell:

LII. More sweet and holesome then the pleasaunt hill
Of Rhodope, on which the Nimphe that bore
A gyaunt babe herselfe for griefe did kill;
Or the Thessalian Tempe, where of yore
Fayre Daphne Phœbus hart with love did gore;
Or Ida, where the Gods lov'd to repayre,
When ever they their heavenly bowres forlore;
Or sweet Parnasse, the haunt of Muses fayre;
Or Eden selfe, if ought with Eden mote compayre.

LIII. Much wondred Guyon at the fayre aspect
Of that sweet place, yet suffred no delight
To sincke into his sence, nor mind affect,
But passed forth, and lookt still forward right,
Brydling his will and maystering his might,
Till that he came unto another gate;
No gate, but like one, being goodly dight
With bowes and braunches, which did broad dilate
Their clasping armes in wanton wreathings intricate:

LIV. So fashioned a Porch with rare device.
Archt over head with an embracing vine,
Whose bounches hanging downe seemd to entice
All passers by to taste their lushious wine,
And did them selves into their hands incline,
As freely offering to be gathered;
Some deepe empurpled as the Hyacine,
Some as the Rubine laughing sweetely red,
Some like faire Emeraudes, not yet well ripened.

LV. And them amongst some were of burnisht gold,
So made by art to beautify the rest,
Which did themselves emongst the leaves enfold,
As lurking from the vew of covetous guest,
That the weake boughes, with so rich load opprest
Did bow adowne as overburdened.
Under that Porch a comely dame did rest
Clad in fayre weedes but fowle disordered,
And garments loose that seemd unmeet for womanhed.

LVI. In her left hand a Cup of gold she held,
And with her right the riper fruit did reach,
Whose sappy liquor, that with fulnesse sweld,
Into her cup she scruzd with daintie breach
Of her fine fingers, without fowle empeach,
That so faire winepresse made the wine more sweet:
Thereof she usd to give to drinke to each,
Whom passing by she happened to meet:
It was her guise all Straungers goodly so to greet.

LVII. So she to Guyon offred it to tast,
Who, taking it out of her tender hond,
The cup to ground did violently cast,
That all in peeces it was broken fond,
And with the liquor stained all the lond:
Whereat Excesse exceedingly was wroth,
Yet no'te the same amend, ne yet withstond,
But suffered him to passe, all were she loth;
Who, nought regarding her displeasure, forward goth.

LVIII. There the most daintie Paradise on ground
It selfe doth offer to his sober eye,
In which all pleasures plenteously abownd,
And none does others happinesse envye;
The painted flowres, the trees upshooting hye,
The dales for shade, the hilles for breathing space,
The trembling groves, the christall running by,
And, that which all faire workes doth most aggrace,
The art which all that wrought appeared in no place.

LIX. One would have thought, (so cunningly the rude
And scorned partes were mingled with the fine)
That nature had for wantonesse ensude
Art, and that Art at nature did repine;
So striving each th' other to undermine,
Each did the others worke more beautify;
So diff'ring both in willes agreed in fine:
So all agreed, through sweet diversity,
This Gardin to adorne with all variety.

LX. And in the midst of all a fountaine stood,
Of richest substance that on earth might bee,
So pure and shiny that the silver flood

Through every channell running one might see;
Most goodly it with curious ymageree
Was overwrought, and shapes of naked boyes,
Of which some seemd with lively jollitee
To fly about, playing their wanton toyes,
Whylest others did them selves embay in liquid joyes.

LXI. And over all of purest gold was spred
A trayle of yvie in his native hew;
For the rich metall was so coloured,
That wight who did not well avis'd it vew
Would surely deeme it to bee yvie trew:
Low his lascivious armes adown did creepe,
That themselves dipping in the silver dew
Their fleecy flowres they fearefully did steepe,
Which drops of Christall seemd for wantones to weep.

LXII. Infinit streames continually did well
Out of this fountaine, sweet and faire to see,
The which into an ample laver fell,
And shortly grew into so great quantitie,
That like a litle lake it seemd to bee;
Whose depth exceeded not three cubits hight,
That through the waves one might the bottom see,
All pav'd beneath with Jaspar shining bright,
That seemd the fountaine in that sea did sayle upright.

LXIII. And all the margent round about was sett
With shady Laurell trees, thence to defend
The sunny beames which on the billowes bett
And those which therein bathed mote offend.
As Guyon hapned by the same to wend,
Two naked Damzelles he therein espyde,
Which therein bathing seemed to contend
And wrestle wantonly, ne car'd to hyde
Their dainty partes from vew of any which them eyd.

LXIV. Sometimes the one would lift the other quight
Above the waters, and then downe againe
Her plong, as over-maystered by might,
Where both awhile would covered remaine,
And each the other from to rise restraine;
The whiles their snowy limbes, as through a vele,

So through the christall waves appeared plaine:
Then suddeinly both would themselves unhele,
And th' amarous sweet spoiles to greedy eyes revele.

LXV. As that faire Starre, the messenger of morne,
His deawy face out of the sea doth reare;
Or as the Cyprian goddesse, newly borne
Of th' Ocean's fruitfull froth, did first appeare:
Such seemed they, and so their yellow heare
Christalline humor dropped downe apace.
Whom such when Guyon saw, he drew him neare,
And somewhat gan relent his earnest pace;
His stubborne brest gan secret pleasaunce to embrace.

LXVI. The wanton Maidens, him espying, stood
Gazing awhile at his unwonted guise;
Then th' one her selfe low ducked in the flood,
Abasht that her a straunger did avise;
But thother rather higher did arise,
And her two lilly paps aloft displayd,
And all that might his melting hart entyse
To her delights she unto him bewrayd;
The rest hidd underneath him more desirous made.

LXVII. With that the other likewise up arose,
And her faire lockes, which formerly were bownd
Up in one knott, she low adowne did lose,
Which flowing low and thick her cloth'd arownd,
And th' yvorie in golden mantle gownd:
So that faire spectacle from him was reft,
Yet that which reft it no lesse faire was fownd.
So hidd in lockes and waves from lookers theft,
Nought but her lovely face she for his looking left.

LXVIII. Withall she laughed, and she blusht withall,
That blushing to her laughter gave more grace,
And laughter to her blushing, as did fall.
Now when they spyde the knight to slacke his pace
Them to behold, and in his sparkling face
The secrete signes of kindled lust appeare,
Their wanton meriments they did encreace,
And to him beckned to approch more neare,
And shewd him many sights that corage cold could
reare.

LXIX. On which when gazing him the Palmer saw,
He much rebukt those wandring eyes of his,
And counseld well him forward thence did draw.
Now are they come nigh to the Bowre of blis,
Of her fond favorites so nam'd amis,
When thus the Palmer: " Now, Sir, well avise;
For here the end of all our traveill is:
Here wonnes Acrasia, whom we must surprise,
Els she will slip away, and all our drift despise."

LXX. Eftsoones they heard a most melodious sound,
Of all that mote delight a daintie eare,
Such as attonce might not on living ground,
Save in this Paradise, be heard elsewhere:
Right hard it was for wight which did it heare,
To read what manner musicke that mote bee;
For all that pleasing is to living eare
Was there consorted in one harmonee;
Birdes, voices, instruments, windes, waters, all agree:

LXXI. The joyous birdes, shrouded in chearefull shade
Their notes unto the voice attempred sweet;
Th' Angelicall soft trembling voyces made
To th' instruments divine respondence meet;
The silver sounding instruments did meet
With the base murmure of the waters fall;
The waters fall with difference discreet,
Now soft, now loud, unto the wind did call;
The gentle warbling wind low answered to all.

LXXII. There, whence that Musick seemed heard to bee,
Was the faire Witch her selfe now solacing
With a new Lover, whom, through sorceree
And witchcraft, she from farre did thither bring:
There she had him now laid aslombering
In secret shade after long wanton joyes;
Whilst round about them pleasauntly did sing
Many faire Ladies and lascivious boyes,
That ever mixt their song with light licentious toyes.

LXXIII. And all that while right over him she hong
With her false eyes fast fixed in his sight,
As seeking medicine whence she was stong,

Or greedily depasturing delight;
And oft inclining downe, with kisses light
For feare of waking him, his lips bedewd,
And through his humid eyes did sucke his spright,
Quite molten into lust and pleasure lewd;
Wherewith she sighed soft, as if his case she rewd.

LXXIV. The whiles some one did chaunt this lovely lay:
Ah! see, whoso fayre thing doest faine to see,
In springing flowre the image of thy day.
Ah! see the Virgin Rose, how sweetly shee
Doth first peepe foorth with bashfull modestee,
That fairer seemes the lesse ye see her may.
Lo! see soone after how more bold and free
Her bared bosome she doth broad display;
Lo! see soone after how she fades and falls away.

LXXV. So passeth, in the passing of a day,
Of mortall life the leafe, the bud, the flowre;
Ne more doth florish after first decay,
That earst was sought to deck both bed and bowre
Of many a lady', and many a Paramowre.
Gather therefore the Rose whilest yet is prime,
For soone comes age that will her pride deflowre;
Gather the Rose of love whilest yet is time,
Whilest loving thou mayst loved be with equall crime.

LXXVI. He ceast; and then gan all the quire of birdes
Their diverse notes t'attune unto his lay,
As in approvaunce of his pleasing wordes,
The constant payre heard all that he did say,
Yet swarved not, but kept their forward way
Through many covert groves and thickets close,
In which they creeping did at last display
That wanton Lady with her lover lose,
Whose sleepie head she in her lap did soft dispose.

LXXVII. Upon a bed of Roses she was layd,
As faint through heat, or dight to pleasant sin;
And was arayd, or rather disarayd,
All in a vele of silke and silver thin,
That hid no whit her alablaster skin,
But rather shewd more white, if more might bee:
More subtile web Arachne cannot spin;

Nor the fine nets, which oft we woven see
Of scorched deaw, do not in th' ayre more lightly flee.

LXXVIII. Her snowy brest was bare to ready spoyle
Of hungry eies, which n'ote therewith be fild;
And yet, through languour of her late sweet toyle,
Few drops, more cleare then Nectar, forth distild,
That like pure Orient perles adowne it trild;
And her faire eyes, sweet smyling in delight,
Moystened their fierie beames, with which she thrild
Fraile harts, yet quenched not; like starry light,
Which, sparckling on the silent waves, does seeme more
   bright.

LXXIX. The young man, sleeping by her, seemd to be
Some goodly swayne of honorable place,
That certes it great pitty was to see
Him his nobility so fowle deface:
A sweet regard and amiable grace,
Mixed with manly sternesse, did appeare,
Yet sleeping, in his well proportiond face;
And on his tender lips the downy heare
Did now but freshly spring, and silken blossoms beare.

LXXX. His warlike Armes, the ydle instruments
Of sleeping praise, were hong upon a tree;
And his brave shield, full of old moniments,
Was fowly ras't, that none the signes might see:
Ne for them ne for honour cared hee,
Ne ought that did to his advauncement tend;
But in lewd loves, and wastfull luxuree,
His dayes, his goods, his bodie, he did spend:
O horrible enchantment, that him so did blend!

LXXXI. The noble Elfe and carefull Palmer drew
So nigh them, minding nought but lustfull game,
That suddein forth they on them rusht, and threw
A subtile net, which only for that same
The skilfull Palmer formally did frame:
So held them under fast; the whiles the rest
Fled all away for feare of fowler shame.
The faire Enchauntresse, so unwares opprest,
Tryde all her arts and all her sleights thence out to
   wrest.

LXXXII. And eke her lover strove, but all in vaine;
For that same net so cunningly was wound,
That neither guile nor force might it distraine.
They tooke them both, and both them strongly bound
In captives bandes, which there they readie found:
But her in chaines of adamant he tyde;
For nothing else might keepe her safe and sound:
But Verdant (so he hight) he soone untyde,
And counsell sage in steed thereof to him applyde.

LXXXIII. But all those pleasaunt bowres, and Pallace brave,
Guyon broke downe with rigour pittilesse;
Ne ought their goodly workmanship might save
Them from the tempest of his wrathfulnesse,
But that their blisse he turn'd to balefulnesse.
Their groves he feld; their gardins did deface;
Their arbers spoyle; their Cabinets suppresse;
Their banket houses burne; their buildings race;
And, of the fayrest late, now made the fowlest place.

LXXXIV. Then led they her away, and eke that knight
They with them led, both sorrowfull and sad.
The way they came, the same retourn'd they right,
Till they arrived where they lately had
Charm'd those wild-beasts that rag'd with furie mad;
Which, now awaking, fierce at them gan fly,
As in their mistresse reskew whom they lad;
But them the Palmer soone did pacify.
Then Guyon askt, what meant those beastes which
     there did ly?

LXXXV. Sayd he; " These seeming beasts are men indeed,
Whom this Enchauntress hath transformed thus;
Whylome her lovers, which her lustes did feed,
Now turned into figures hideous,
According to their mindes like monstruous."
" Sad end," (quoth he) " of life intemperate,
And mourneful meed of joyes delicious!
But, Palmer, if it mote thee so aggrate,
Let them returned be unto their former state."

LXXXVI. Streight way he with his vertuous staffe them strooke,
And streight of beastes they comely men became;

Yet being men they did unmanly looke,
And stared ghastly; some for inward shame,
And some for wrath to see their captive Dame:
But one above the rest in speciall
That had an hog beene late, hight Grylle by name,
Repyned greatly and did him miscall
That had from hoggish forme him brought to naturall.

LXXXVII. Saide Guyon; " See the mind of beastly man,
That hath so soone forgot the excellence
Of his creation, when he life began,
That now he chooseth with vile difference
To be a beast, and lacke intelligence ! "
To whom the Palmer thus: " The donghill kinde
Delightes in filth and fowle incontinence:
Let Gryll be Gryll, and have his hoggish minde;
But let us hence depart whilest wether serves and
winde."

THE THIRD BOOKE

CONTAYNING THE LEGEND OF BRITOMARTIS, OR OF CHASTITY.

I. IT falls me here to write of Chastity,
The fayrest vertue, far above the rest:
For which what needes me fetch from Faery
Forreine ensamples it to have exprest?
Sith it is shrined in my Soveraines brest,
And formd so lively in each perfect part,
That to all Ladies, which have it profest,
Need but behold the pourtraict of her hart;
If pourtrayd it might bee by any living art.

II. But living art may not least part expresse,
Nor life-resembling pencill it can paynt:
All were it Zeuxis or Praxiteles,
His dædale hand would faile and greatly faynt,
And her perfections with his error taynt:
Ne Poets witt, that passeth Painter farre
In picturing the parts of beauty daynt,
So hard a workemanship adventure darre,
For feare, through want of words, her excellence to
marre.

III. How then shall I, Apprentice to the skill
That whilome in divinest wits did rayne,
Presume so high to stretch mine humble quill?
Yet now my lucklesse lott doth me constrayne
Hereto perforce. But, O dredd Soverayne!
Thus far-forth pardon, sith that choicest witt
Cannot your glorious pourtraict figure playne,
That I in colourd showes may shadow itt,
And antique praises unto present persons fitt.

IV. But if in living colours, and right hew,
Thy selfe thou covet to see pictured,
Who can it doe more lively, or more trew,
Then that sweete verse, with Nectar sprinckeled,

307

In which a gracious servaunt pictured
His Cynthia, his heavens fayrest light?
That with his melting sweetnes ravished,
And with the wonder of her beames bright,
My sences lulled are in slomber of delight.

v. But let that same delitious Poet lend
A little leave unto a rusticke Muse
To sing his mistresse prayse; and let him mend.
If ought amis her liking may abuse:
Ne let his fayrest Cynthia refuse
In mirrours more then one her selfe to see;
But either Gloriana let her chuse,
Or in Belphœbe fashioned to bee;
In th' one her rule, in th' other her rare chastitee.

CANTO I

Guyon encountreth Britomart:
Fayre Florimell is chaced:
Duessaes traines and Malecas-
taes champions are defaced.

I. THE famous Briton Prince and Faery knight,
After long wayes and perilous paines endur'd,
Having their weary limbes to perfect plight
Restord, and sory wounds right well recur'd,
Of the faire Alma greatly were procur'd
To make there lenger sojourne and abode;
But when thereto they might not be allur'd,
From seeking praise and deeds of armes abrode,
They courteous congé tooke, and forth together yode.

II. But the captiv'd Acrasia he sent,
Because of traveill long, a nigher way,
With a strong gard, all reskew to prevent,
And her to Faery court safe to convay;
That her for witnes of his hard assay
Unto his Faery Queene he might present:
But he him selfe betooke another way,
To make more triall of his hardiment,
And seek adventures as he with Prince Arthure went.

III. Long so they traveiled through wastefull wayes,
Where daungers dwelt, and perils most did wonne,
To hunt for glory and renowmed prayse.
Full many Countreyes they did overronne,
From the uprising to the setting Sunne,
And many hard adventures did atchieve;
Of all the which they honour ever wonne,
Seeking the weake oppressed to relieve,
And to recover right for such as wrong did grieve.

IV. At last, as through an open plaine they yode,
They spide a knight that towards pricked fayre;
And him beside an aged Squire there rode,

That seemd to couch under his shield three-square,
As if that age badd him that burden spare,
And yield it those that stouter could it wield.
He them espying gan him selfe prepare,
And on his arme addresse his goodly shield
That bore a Lion passant in a golden field.

v. Which seeing, good Sir Guyon deare besought
The Prince of grace to let him ronne that turne.
He graunted: then the Faery quickly raught
His poynant speare, and sharply gan to spurne
His fomy steed, whose fiery feete did burne
The verdant gras as he thereon did tread;
Ne did the other backe his foote returne,
But fiercely forward came withouten dread,
And bent his dreadful speare against the others head.

vi. They beene ymett, and both theyr points arriv'd;
But Guyon drove so furious and fell,
That seemd both shield and plate it would have riv'd;
Nathelesse it bore his foe not from his sell,
But made him stagger, as he were not well:
But Guyon selfe, ere well he was aware,
Nigh a speares length behind his crouper fell;
Yet in his fall so well him selfe he bare,
That mischievous mischaunce his life and limbs did spare.

vii. Great shame and sorrow of that fall he tooke;
For never yet, sith warlike armes he bore
And shivering speare in bloody field first shooke,
He fownd him selfe dishonored so sore.
Ah! gentlest knight, that ever armor bore,
Let not thee grieve dismounted to have beene,
And brought to grownd that never wast before;
For not thy fault, but secret powre unseene:
That speare enchaunted was which layd thee on the greene.

viii. But weenedst thou what wight thee overthrew,
Much greater griefe and shamefuller regrett
For thy hard fortune then thou wouldst renew,
That of a single damzell thou wert mett
On equall plaine, and there so hard besett:
Even the famous Britomart it was,

Whom straunge adventure did from Britayne sett
To seeke her lover (love far sought alas!)
Whose image shee had seene in Venus looking glas.

IX. Full of disdainefull wrath he fierce uprose
For to revenge that fowle reprochefull shame,
And snatching his bright sword began to close
With her on foot, and stoutly forward came:
Dye rather would he then endure that same.
Which when his Palmer saw, he gan to feare
His toward perill, and untoward blame,
Which by that new rencounter he should reare;
For death sate on the point of that enchaunted speare:

X. And hasting towards him gan fayre perswade
Not to provoke misfortune, nor to weene
His speares default to mend with cruell blade;
For by his mightie Science he had seene
The secrete vertue of that weapon keene,
That mortall puissaunce mote not withstond.
Nothing on earth mote alwaies happy beene:
Great hazard were it, and adventure fond,
To loose long gotten honour with one evill hond.

XI. By such good meanes he him discounselled
From prosecuting his revenging rage:
And eke the Prince like treaty handeled,
His wrathfull will with reason to aswage;
And laid the blame, not to his carriage,
But to his starting steed that swarv'd asyde,
And to the ill purveyaunce of his page,
That had his furnitures not firmely tyde.
So is his angry corage fayrly pacifyde.

XII. Thus reconcilement was betweene them knitt,
Through goodly temperaunce and affection chaste;
And either vowd with all their power and witt
To let not others honour be defaste
Of friend or foe, who ever it embaste;
Ne armes to beare against the others syde:
In which accord the Prince was also plaste,
And with that golden chaine of concord tyde.
So goodly all agreed they forth yfere did ryde.

XIII. O! goodly usage of those antique tymes,
    In which the sword was servaunt unto right;
    When not for malice and contentious crymes,
    But all for prayse, and proofe of manly might,
    The martiall brood accustomed to fight:
    Then honour was the meed of victory,
    And yet the vanquished had no despight.
    Let later age that noble use envy,
    Vyle rancor to avoid and cruel surquedry.

XIV. Long they thus traveiled in friendly wise,
    Through countreyes waste, and eke well edifyde,
    Seeking adventures hard, to exercise
    Their puissaunce, whylome full dernly tryde.
    At length they came into a forest wyde,
    Whose hideous horror and sad trembling sownd,
    Full griesly seemd: Therein they long did ryde,
    Yet tract of living creature none they fownd,
    Save Beares, Lyons, and Buls, which romed them arownd.

XV. All suddenly out of the thickest brush,
    Upon a milkwhite Palfrey all alone,
    A goodly Lady did foreby them rush,
    Whose face did seeme as cleare as Christall stone,
    And eke, through feare, as white as whales bone:
    Her garments all were wrought of beaten gold,
    And all her steed with tinsell trappings shone,
    Which fledd so fast that nothing mote him hold,
    And scarse them leasure gave her passing to behold.

XVI. Still as she fledd her eye she backward threw,
    As fearing evill that poursewd her fast;
    And her faire yellow locks behind her flew,
    Loosely disperst with puff of every blast:
    All as a blazing starre doth farre outcast
    His hearie beames, and flaming lockes dispredd,
    At sight whereof the people stand aghast;
    But the sage wisard telles, as he has redd,
    That it importunes death and dolefull dreryhedd.

XVII. So as they gazed after her a whyle,
    Lo! where a griesly foster forth did rush,
    Breathing out beastly lust her to defyle:

His tyreling Jade he fiersly forth did push
Through thicke and thin, both over banck and bush,
In hope her to attaine by hooke or crooke,
That from his gory sydes the blood did gush.
Large were his limbes, and terrible his looke,
And in his clownish hand a sharp bore speare he shooke.

XVIII. Which outrage when those gentle knights did see,
Full of great envy and fell gealosy
They stayd not to avise who first should bee,
But all spurd after, fast as they mote fly,
To reskew her from shamefull villany.
The Prince and Guyon equally bylive
Her selfe pursewd, in hope to win thereby
Most goodly meede, the fairest Dame alive:
But after the foule foster Timias did strive.

XIX. The whiles faire Britomart, whose constant mind
Would not so lightly follow beauties chace,
Ne reckt of Ladies Love, did stay behynd,
And them awayted there a certaine space,
To weet if they would turne backe to that place;
But when she saw them gone she forward went,
As lay her journey, through that perlous Pace,
With stedfast corage and stout hardiment:
Ne evil thing she feard, ne evill thing she ment.

XX. At last, as nigh out of the wood she came,
A stately Castle far away she spyde,
To which her steps directly she did frame.
That Castle was most goodly edifyde,
And plaste for pleasure nigh that forrest syde:
But faire before the gate a spatious playne,
Mantled with greene, it selfe did spredden wyde,
On which she saw six knights, that did darrayne
Fiers battaill against one with cruell might and mayne.

XXI. Mainely they all attonce upon him laid,
And sore beset on every side arownd,
That nigh he breathlesse grew, yet nought dismaid,
Ne ever to them yielded foot of grownd,
All had he lost much blood through many a wownd,
But stoutly dealt his blowes, and every way,

To which he turned in his wrathfull stownd,
Made them recoile, and fly from dredd decay,
That none of all the six before him durst assay.

XXII. Like dastard Curres that, having at a bay
The salvage beast embost in wearie chace,
Dare not adventure on the stubborne pray,
Ne byte before, but rome from place to place
To get a snatch when turned is his face.
In such distresse and doubtfull jeopardy
When Britomart him saw, she ran apace
Unto his reskew, and with earnest cry
Badd those same six forbeare that single enimy.

XXIII. But to her cry they list not lenden eare,
Ne ought the more their mightie strokes surceasse.
But gathering him rownd about more neare,
Their direfull rancour rather did encreasse;
Till that she rushing through the thickest preasse
Perforce disparted their compacted gyre,
And soone compeld to hearken unto peace.
Tho gan she myldly of them to inquyre
The cause of their dissention and outrageous yre.

XXIV. Whereto that single knight did answere frame:
" These six would me enforce by oddes of might
To chaunge my liefe, and love another Dame;
That death me liefer were then such despight,
So unto wrong to yield my wrested right:
For I love one, the truest one on grownd,
Ne list me chaunge; she th' Errant Damzell hight;
For whose deare sake full many a bitter stownd
I have endurd, and tasted many a bloody wownd."

XXV. " Certes," (said she) " then beene ye sixe to blame,
To weene your wrong by force to justify;
For knight to leave his Lady were great shame
That faithfull is, and better were to dy.
All losse is lesse, and lesse the infamy,
Then losse of love to him that loves but one:
Ne may love be compeld by maistery;
For soone as maistery comes sweet Love anone
Taketh his nimble winges, and soone away is gone."

XXVI. Then spake one of those six; " There dwelleth here
    Within this castle wall a Lady fayre,
    Whose soveraine beautie hath no living pere;
    Thereto so bounteous and so debonayre,
    That never any mote with her compayre:
    She hath ordaind this law, which we approve,
    That every knight which doth this way repayre,
    In case he have no Lady nor no love,
    Shall doe unto her service, never to remove:

XXVII. " But if he have a Lady or a Love,
    Then must he her forgoe with fowle defame,
    Or els with us by dint of sword approve,
    That she is fairer then our fairest Dame;
    As did this knight, before ye hither came."
    " Perdy," (said Britomart) " the choise is hard;
    But what reward had he that overcame?"
    " He should advaunced bee to high regard,"
    (Said they) " and have our Ladies love for his reward.

XXVIII. " Therefore aread, Sir, if thou have a love."
    " Love hath I sure," (quoth she) " but Lady none;
    Yet will I not fro mine own love remove,
    Ne to your Lady will I service done,
    But wreake your wronges wrought to this knight alone,
    And prove his cause."   With that, her mortall speare
    She mightily aventred towards one,
    And downe him smot ere well aware he weare;
    Then to the next she rode, and downe the next did
      beare.

XXIX. Ne did she stay till three on ground she layd
    That none of them himselfe could reare againe:
    The fourth was by that other knight dismayd,
    All were he wearie of his former paine;
    That now there do but two of six remaine,
    Which two did yield before she did them smight.
    " Ah!" (said she then) " now may ye all see plaine,
    That truth is strong, and trew love most of might,
    That for his trusty servaunts doth so strongly fight."

XXX. " Too well we see," (saide they) " and prove too well
    Our faulty weakenes, and your matchlesse might:
    Forthy, faire Sir, yours be the Damozell,

Which by her owne law to your lot doth light,
And we your liegemen faith unto you plight."
So underneath her feet their swords they mard,
And, after, her besought, well as they might,
To enter in and reape the dew reward.
She graunted; and then in they all together far'd.

XXXI. Long were it to describe the goodly frame,
And stately port of Castle Joyeous,
(For so that Castle hight by commun name)
Where they were entertaynd with courteous
And comely glee.of many gratious
Faire Ladies, and of many a gentle knight,
Who, through a Chamber long and spacious,
Eftsoones them brought unto their Ladies sight,
That of them cleeped was the Lady of Delight.

XXXII. But for to tell the sumptuous aray
Of that great chamber should be labour lost;
For living wit, I weene, cannot display
The roiall riches and exceeding cost
Of every pillour and of every post,
Which all of purest bullion framed were,
And with great perles and pretious stones embost;
That the bright glister of their beames cleare
Did sparckle forth great light, and glorious did appeare.

XXXIII. These stranger knights, through passing, forth were led
Into an inner rowme, whose royaltee
And rich purveyance might uneath be red;
Mote Princes place be seeme so deckt to bee.
Which stately manner whenas they did see,
The image of superfluous riotize,
Exceeding much the state of meane degree,
They greatly wondred whence so sumptuous guize
Might be maintaynd, and each gan diversely devize.

XXXIV. The wals were round about appareiled
With costly clothes of Arras and of Toure;
In which with cunning hand was pourtrahed
The love of Venus and her Paramoure,
The fayre Adonis, turned to a flowre;
A worke of rare device and wondrous wit.

First did it shew the bitter balefull stowre,
Which her essayd with many a fervent fit,
When first her tender hart was with his beautie smit.

xxxv. Then with what sleights and sweet allurements she
Entyst the Boy, as well that art she knew,
And wooed him her Paramoure to bee;
Now making girlonds of each flowre that grew,
To crowne his golden lockes with honour dew;
Now leading him into a secret shade
From his Beauperes, and from bright heavens vew,
Where him to sleepe she gently would perswade,
Or bathe him in a fountaine by some covert glade:

xxxvi. And whilst he slept she over him would spred
Her mantle, colour'd like the starry skyes,
And her soft arme lay underneath his hed,
And with ambrosiall kisses bathe his eyes;
And whilst he bath'd with her two crafty spyes
She secretly would search each daintie lim,
And throw into the well sweet Rosemaryes,
And fragrant violets, and Paunces trim;
And ever with sweet Nectar she did sprinkle him.

xxxvii. So did she steale his heedelesse hart away,
And joyd his love in secret unespyde:
But for she saw him bent to cruell play,
To hunt the salvage beast in forrest wyde,
Dreadfull of daunger that mote him betyde,
She oft and oft adviz'd him to refraine
From chase of greater beastes, whose brutish pryde
Mote breede him scath unwares: but all in vaine;
For who can shun the chance that dest'ny doth
ordaine?

xxxviii. Lo! where beyond he lyeth languishing,
Deadly engored of a great wilde Bore;
And by his side the Goddesse groveling
Makes for him endlesse mone, and evermore
With her soft garment wipes away the gore
Which staynes his snowy skin with hatefull hew:
But, when she saw no helpe might him restore,
Him to a dainty flowre she did transmew,
Which in that cloth was wrought as if it lively grew.

XXXIX. So was that chamber clad in goodly wize:
And rownd about it many beds were dight,
As whylome was the antique worldes guize,
Some for untimely ease, some for delight,
As pleased them to use that use it might;
And all was full of Damzels and of Squyres,
Dauncing and reveling both day and night,
And swimming deepe in sensuall desyres;
And Cupid still emongest them kindled lustfull fyres.

XL. And all the while sweet Musicke did divide
Her looser notes with Lydian harmony;
And all the while sweet birdes thereto applide
Their daintie layes and dulcet melody,
Ay caroling of love and jollity,
That wonder was to heare their trim consort.
Which when those knights beheld, with scornefull eye
They sdeigned such lascivious disport,
And loath'd the loose demeanure of that wanton sort.

XLI. Thence they were brought to that great Ladies vew,
Whom they found sitting on a sumptuous bed
That glistred all with gold and glorious shew,
As the proud Persian Queenes accustomed.
She seemd a woman of great bountihed,
And of rare beautie, saving that askaunce
Her wanton eyes, ill signes of womanhed,
Did roll too lightly, and too often glaunce,
Without regard of grace or comely amenaunce.

XLII. Long worke it were, and needlesse, to devize
Their goodly entertainement and great glee.
She caused them be led in courteous wize
Into a bowre, disarmed for to be,
And cheared well with wine and spiceree:
The Redcrosse Knight was soon disarmed there;
But the brave Mayd would not disarmed bee,
But onely vented up her umbriere,
And so did let her goodly visage to appere.

XLIII. As when fayre Cynthia, in darkesome night,
Is in a noyous cloud enveloped,
Where she may finde the substance thin and light,

Breakes forth her silver beames, and her bright hed
Discovers to the world discomfited:
Of the poore traveiler that went astray
With thousand blessings she is heried.
Such was the beautie and the shining ray,
With which fayre Britomart gave light unto the day.

XLIV. And eke those six, which lately with her fought,
Now were disarmd, and did them selves present
Unto her vew, and company unsought;
For they all seemed courteous and gent,
And all sixe brethren, borne of one parent,
Which had them traynd in all civilitee,
And goodly taught to tilt and turnament:
Now were they liegmen to this Ladie free,
And her knights service ought, to hold of her in fee.

XLV. The first of them by name Gardantè hight,
A jolly person, and of comely vew;
The second was Parlantè, a bold knight;
And next to him Jocantè did ensew;
Basciantè did him selfe most courteous shew;
But fierce Bacchantè seemd too fell and keene;
And yett in armes Noctantè greater grew:
All were faire knights, and goodly well beseene;
But to faire Britomart they all but shadowes beene.

XLVI. For shee was full of amiable grace
And manly terror mixed therewithall;
That as the one stird up affections bace,
So th' other did mens rash desires apall,
And hold them backe that would in error fall:
As hee that hath espide a vermeill Rose,
To which sharp thornes and breres the way forstall,
Dare not for dread his hardy hand expose,
But wishing it far off his ydle wish doth lose.

XLVII. Whom when the Lady saw so faire a wight,
All ignorant of her contrary sex,
(For shee her weend a fresh and lusty knight,)
Shee greatly gan enamoured to wex
And with vaine thoughts her falsed fancy vex:
Her fickle hart conceived hasty fyre,

Like sparkes of fire which fall in sclender flex,
That shortly brent into extreme desyre,
And ransackt all her veines with passion entyre.

XLVIII. Eftsoones shee grew to great impatience,
And into termes of open outrage brust,
That plaine discovered her incontinence;
Ne reckt shee who her meaning did mistrust,
For she was given all to fleshly lust,
And poured forth in sensuall delight,
That all regard of shame she had discust,
And meet respect of honor putt to flight:
So shamelesse beauty soone becomes a loathly sight.

XLIX. Faire Ladies, that to love captived arre,
And chaste desires doe nourish in your mind,
Let not her fault your sweete affections marre,
Ne blott the bounty of all womankind,
'Mongst thousands good one wanton Dame to find:
Emongst the Roses grow some wicked weeds:
For this was not to love, but lust, inclind;
For love does alwaies bring forth bounteous deeds,
And in each gentle hart desire of honor breeds.

L. Nought so of love this looser Dame did skill,
But as a cole to kindle fleshly flame,
Giving the bridle to her wanton will,
And treading under foote her honest name:
Such love is hate, and such desire is shame.
Still did she rove at her with crafty glaunce
Of her false eies, that at her hart did ayme,
And told her meaning in her countenaunce;
But Britomart dissembled it with ignoraunce.

LI. Supper was shortly dight, and downe they satt;
Where they were served with all sumptuous fare,
Whiles fruitfull Ceres and Lyæus fatt
Pourd out their plenty without spight or spare.
Nought wanted there that dainty was and rare,
And aye the cups their bancks did overflow;
And aye betweene the cups she did prepare
Way to her love, and secret darts did throw;
But Britomart would not such guilfull message know.

LII. So, when they slaked had the fervent heat
Of appetite with meates of every sort,
The Lady did faire Britomart entreat
Her to disarme, and with delightfull sport
To loose her warlike limbs and strong effort;
But when shee mote not thereunto be wonne,
(For shee her sexe under that straunge purport
Did use to hide, and plaine apparaunce shonne)
In playner wise to tell her grievaunce she begonne.

LIII. And all attonce discovered her desire
With sighes, and sobs, and plaints, and piteous griefe,
The outward sparkes of her inburning fire;
Which spent in vaine, at last she told her briefe,
That but if she did lend her short reliefe
And doe her comfort, she mote algates dye:
But the chaste damzell, that had never priefe
Of such malengine and fine forgerye,
Did easely beleeve her strong extremitye.

LIV. Full easy was for her to have beliefe,
Who by self-feeling of her feeble sexe,
And by long triall of the inward griefe
Wherewith imperious love her hart did vexe,
Could judge what paines doe loving harts perplexe.
Who meanes no guile be guiled soonest shall,
And to faire semblaunce doth light faith annexe:
The bird that knowes not the false fowlers call,
Into his hidden nett full easely doth fall.

LV. Forthy she would not in discourteise wise
Scorne the faire offer of good will profest;
For great rebuke it is love to despise,
Or rudely sdeigne a gentle harts request;
But with faire countenaunce, as beseemed best,
Her entertaynd: nath'lesse shee inly deemd
Her love too light, to wooe a wandring guest;
Which she misconstruing, thereby esteemd
That from like inward fire that outward smoke had steemd.

LVI. Therewith a while she her flit fancy fedd,
Till she mote winne fit time for her desire;
But yet her wound still inward freshly bledd,

And through her bones the false instilled fire
Did spred it selfe, and venime close inspire,
Tho were the tables taken all away;
And every knight, and every gentle Squire,
Gan choose his Dame with *Bascimano* gay,
With whom he ment to make his sport and courtly play.

LVII. Some fell to daunce, some fel to hazardry,
Some to make love, some to make meryment,
As diverse witts to diverse things apply;
And all the while faire Malecasta bent
Her crafty engins to her close intent.
By this th' eternall lampes, wherewith high Jove
Doth light the lower world, were halfe yspent,
And the moist daughters of huge Atlas strove
Into the Ocean deepe to drive their weary drove,

LVIII. High time it seemed then for everie wight
Them to betake unto their kindly rest:
Eftesoones long waxen torches weren light
Unto their bowres to guyden every guest.
Tho, when the Britonesse saw all the rest
Avoided quite, she gan her selfe despoile,
And safe committ to her soft fethered nest,
Wher through long watch, and late daies weary toile,
She soundly slept, and carefull thoughts did quite assoile,

LIX. Now whenas all the world in silence deepe
Yshrowded was, and every mortall wight
Was drowned in the depth of deadly sleepe;
Faire Malecasta, whose engrieved spright
Could find no rest in such perplexed plight,
Lightly arose out of her wearie bed,
And, under the blacke vele of guilty Night,
Her with a scarlott mantle covered
That was with gold and Ermines faire enveloped,

LX. Then panting softe, and trembling every joynt,
Her fearfull feete towards the bowre she mov'd,
Where she for secret purpose did appoynt
To lodge the warlike maide, unwisely loov'd;
And, to her bed approching, first she proov'd
Whether she slept or wakte: with her softe hand

She softely felt if any member moov'd,
And lent her wary eare to understand
If any puffe of breath or signe of sence shee fond.

LXI. Which whenas none she fond, with easy shifte,
For feare least her unwares she should abrayd,
Th' embroder'd quilt she lightly up did lifte,
And by her side her selfe she softly layd,
Of every finest fingers touch affrayd;
Ne any noise she made, ne word she spake,
But inly sigh'd.   At last the royall Mayd
Out of her quiet slomber did awake,
And chaunged her weary side the better ease to take.

LXII. Where feeling one close couched by her side,
She lightly lept out of her filed bedd,
And to her weapon ran, in minde to gride
The loathed leachour.   But the Dame, halfe dedd
Through suddein feare and ghastly drerihedd,
Did shrieke alowd, that through the hous it rong,
And the whole family, therewith adredd,
Rashly out of their rouzed couches sprong,
And to the troubled chamber all in armes did throng.

LXIII. And those six knights, that ladies Champions
And eke the Redcrosse knight ran to the stownd.
Half armd and halfe unarmd, with them attons:
Where when confusedly they came, they fownd
Their lady lying on the sencelesse grownd:
On thother side they saw the warlike Mayd
Al in her snow-white smocke, with locks unbownd,
Threatning the point of her avenging blaed;
That with so troublous terror they were all dismayd.

LXIV. About their Ladye first they flockt arownd;
Whom having laid in comfortable couch,
Shortly they reard out of her frosen swownd;
And afterwardes they gan with fowle reproch
To stirre up strife, and troublous contecke broch:
But by ensample of the last dayes losse,
None of them rashly durst to her approch,
Ne in so glorious spoile themselves embosse:
Her succourd eke the Champion of the bloody Crosse.

LXV. But one of those sixe knights, Gardantè hight,
Drew out a deadly bow and arrow keene,
Which forth he sent, with felonous despight
And fell intent, against the virgin sheene:
The mortall steele stayd not till it was seene
To gore her side; yet was the wound not deepe,
But lightly rased her soft silken skin,
That drops of purple blood thereout did weepe,
Which did her lilly smock with staines of vermeil steep.

LXVI. Wherewith enrag'd she fiercely at them flew,
And with her flaming sword about her layd,
That none of them foule mischiefe could eschew,
But with her dreadfull strokes were all dismayd:
Here, there, and every where, about her swayd
Her wrathfull steele, that none mote it abyde;
And eke the Redcrosse knight gave her good ayd,
Ay joyning foot to foot, and syde to syde;
That in short space their foes they have quite terrifyde.

LXVII. Tho, whenas all were put to shamefull flight,
The noble Britomartis her arayd,
And her bright armes about her body dight.
For nothing would she lenger there be stayd,
Where so loose life, and so ungentle trade,
Was usd of knightes and Ladies seeming gent:
So earely, ere the grosse Earthes gryesy shade
Was all disperst out of the firmament,
They tooke their steeds, and forth upon their journey
went.

[In canto ii Britomart talks with the Red Crosse knight about
Artegall—the knight of Justice of Book V—with whom she is in
love. Stanzas 17–27 describe in flashback how she first saw him in
Merlin's magic mirror, and the rest of the canto concerns Brito-
mart's love-melancholy and arguments with her nurse Glaucè
over her condition. In canto iii Merlin, sought out by Britomart
and her nurse, reveals the 'famous Progenee', springing from
'auncient Trojan blood' (st. 22) and culminating in Elizabeth,
that will derive from her union with Artegall. At the end of the
canto Britomart sets out on her quest dressed in the recently-
captured armour of 'Angela, the Saxon Queene' (st. 58) and
accompanied by Glaucè as her squire.]

CANTO IV

Bold Marinell of Britomart
Is throwne on the Rich Strond
Faire Florimell of Arthure is
Long followed, but not fond.

I. WHERE is the Antique glory now become,
That whylome wont in wemen to appeare?
Where be the brave atchievements doen by some?
Where be the batteilles, where the shield and speare,
And all the conquests which them high did reare,
That matter made for famous Poets verse,
And boastfull men so oft abasht to heare?
Beene they all dead, and laide in dolefull herse,
Or doen they onely sleepe, and shall againe reverse?

II. If they be dead, then woe is me therefore;
But if they sleepe, O let them soone awake!
For all too long I burne with envy sore
To heare the warlike feates which Homere spake
Of bold Penthesilee, which made a lake
Of Greekish blood so ofte in Trojan plaine;
But when I reade, how stout Debora strake
Proud Sisera, and how Camill' hath slaine
The huge Orsilochus, I swell with great disdaine.

III. Yet these, and all that els had puissaunce,
Cannot with noble Britomart compare,
As well for glorie of great valiaunce,
As for pure chastitee and vertue rare,
That all her goodly deedes doe well declare.
Well worthie stock, from which the branches sprong
That in late yeares so faire a blossome bare,
As thee, O Queene! the matter of my song,
Whose lignage from this Lady I derive along.

IV. Who when, through speaches with the Redcrosse Knight,
She learned had th' estate of Arthegall,
And in each point her selfe informd aright,

A friendly league of love perpetuall
She with him bound, and Congé tooke withall:
Then he forth on his journey did proceede,
To seeke adventures which mote him befall,
And win him worship through his warlike deed,
Which alwaies of his paines he made the chiefest meed.

v. But Britomart kept on her former course,
Ne ever dofte her armes, but all the way
Grew pensive through that amarous discourse,
By which the Redcrosse knight did earst display
Her lovers shape and chevalrous aray:
A thousand thoughts she fashiond in her mind,
And in her feigning fancie did pourtray
Him such as fittest she for love could find,
Wise, warlike, personable, courteous, and kind.

vi. With such selfe-pleasing thoughts her wound she fedd,
And thought so to beguile her grievous smart;
But so her smart was much more grievous bredd,
And the deepe wound more deep engord her hart,
That nought but death her dolour mote depart.
So forth she rode, without repose or rest,
Searching all lands and each remotest part,
Following the guydance of her blinded guest,
Till that to the sea-coast at length she her addrest.

vii. There she alighted from her light-foot beast,
And sitting downe upon the rocky shore,
Badd her old Squyre unlace her lofty creast:
Tho having vewd awhile the surges hore
That gainst the craggy clifts did loudly rore,
And in their raging surquedry disdaynd
That the fast earth affronted them so sore,
And their devouring covetize restraynd;
Thereat she sighed deepe, and after thus complaynd.

viii. " Huge sea of sorrow and tempestuous griefe,
Wherein my feeble barke is tossed long
Far from the hoped haven of reliefe,
Why doe thy cruell billowes beat so strong,
And thy moyst mountaines each on others throng,
Threatning to swallow up my fearefull lyfe?

O! doe thy cruell wrath and spightfull wrong
At length allay, and stint thy stormy strife,
Which in thy troubled bowels raignes and rageth **ryfe.**

IX. " For els my feeble vessell, crazd and crackt
Through thy strong buffets and outrageous **blowes,**
Cannot endure, but needes it must be wrackt
On the rough rocks, or on the sandy shallowes,
The whiles that love it steres, and fortune rowes:
Love, my lewd Pilott, hath a restlesse minde;
And fortune, Boteswaine, no assurance knowes;
But saile withouten starres against tyde and winde:
How can they other doe, sith both are bold and blinde?

X. " Thou God of windes, that raignest in the **seas,**
That raignest also in the Continent.
At last blow up some gentle gale of ease,
The which may bring my ship, ere it be **rent,**
Unto the gladsome port of her intent.
Then, when I shall my selfe in safety see,
A table, for eternall moniment
Of thy great grace and my great jeopardee,
Great Neptune, I avow to hallow unto thee! "

XI. Then sighing softly sore, and inly deepe,
She shut up all her plaint in privy griefe
For her great courage would not let her weepe,
Till that old Glaucè gan with sharpe repriefe
Her to restraine, and give her good reliefe
Through hope of those, which Merlin had her to¹
Should of her name and nation be chiefe,
And fetch their being from the sacred mould
Of her immortall womb, to be in heaven enrold.

XII. Thus as she her recomforted, she spyde
Where far away one, all in armour bright,
With hasty gallop towards her did ryde.
Her dolour soone she ceast, and on her dight
Her Helmet, to her Courser mounting light:
Her former sorrow into suddein wrath,
Both coosen passions of distroubled spright,
Converting, forth she beates the dusty path:
Love and despight attonce her courage kindled hath.

XIII. As, when a foggy mist hath overcast
The face of heven, and the cleare ayre engroste,
The world in darkenes dwels; till that at last
The watry Southwinde, from the seabord coste
Upblowing, doth disperse the vapour lo'ste,
And poures it selfe forth in a stormy showre:
So the fayre Britomart, having disclo'ste
Her clowdy care into a wrathfull stowre,
The mist of griefe dissolv'd did into vengeance powre.

XIV. Eftsoones, her goodly shield addressing fayre,
That mortall speare she in her hand did take,
And unto battaill did her selfe prepayre.
The knight, approching, sternely her bespake:
" Sir knight, that doest thy voyage rashly make
By this forbidden way in my despight,
Ne doest by others death ensample take,
I read thee soone retyre, whiles thou hast might,
Least afterwards it be too late to take thy flight."

XV. Ythrild with deepe disdaine of his proud threat,
She shortly thus: " Fly they, that need to fly;
Wordes fearen babes.   I meane not thee entreat
To passe, but maugre thee will passe or dy."
Ne lenger stayd for th' other to reply,
But with sharpe speare the rest made dearly knowne.
Strongly the straunge knight ran, and sturdily
Strooke her full on the brest, that made her downe
Decline her head, and touch her crouper with her crown.

XVI. But she againe him in the shield did smite
With so fierce furie and great puissaunce,
That, through his three-square scuchin percing quite
And through his mayled hauberque, by mischaunce
The wicked steele through his left side did glaunce.
Him so transfixed she before her bore
Beyond his croupe, the length of all her launce;
Till, sadly soucing on the sandy shore,
He tombled on an heape, and wallowd in his gore.

XVII. Like as the sacred Oxe that carelesse stands,
With gilden hornes and flowry girlonds crownd,
Proud of his dying honor and deare bandes,

Whiles th' altars fume with frankincense arownd,
All suddeinly, with mortall stroke astownd,
Doth groveling fall, and with his streaming gore
Distaines the pillours and the holy grownd,
And the faire flowres that decked him afore:
So fell proud Marinell upon the pretious shore.

xviii. The martiall Mayd stayd not him to lament,
But forward rode, and kept her ready way
Along the strond; which, as she over-went,
She saw bestrowed all with rich aray
Of pearles and pretious stones of great assay,
And all the gravell mixt with golden owre:
Whereat she wondred much, but would not stay
For gold, or perles, or pretious stones, an howre,
But them despised all; for all was in her powre.

xix. Whiles thus he lay in deadly stonishment,
Tydings hereof came to his mothers eare:
His mother was the blacke-browd Cymoënt,
The daughter of great Nereus, which did beare
This warlike sonne unto an earthly peare,
The famous Dumarin; who, on a day
Finding the Nymph asleepe in secret wheare,
As he by chaunce did wander that same way,
Was taken with her love, and by her closely lay.

xx. There he this knight of her begot, whom borne
She, of his father, Marinell did name;
And in a rocky cave, as wight forlorne,
Long time she fostred up, till he became
A mighty man at armes, and mickle fame
Did get through great adventures by him donne:
For never man he suffred by that same
Rich strond to travell, whereas he did wonne,
But that he must do battail with the Sea-nymphes sonne.

xxi. An hundred knights of honorable name
He had subdew'd, and them his vassals made
That through all Faerie lond his noble fame
Now blazed was, and feare did all invade,
That none durst passen through that perilous glade:
And to advaunce his name and glory more,

Her Sea-god syre she dearely did perswade
T' endow her sonne with threasure and rich store
Bove all the sonnes that were of earthly wombes ybore.

XXII. The God did graunt his daughters deare demaund,
To doen his Nephew in all riches flow;
Eftsoones his heaped waves he did commaund
Out of their hollow bosome forth to throw
All the huge threasure, which the sea below
Had in his greedy gulfe devoured deepe,
And him enriched through the overthrow
And wreckes of many wretches, which did weepe
And often wayle their wealth, which he from them did keepe.

XXIII. Shortly upon that shore there heaped was
Exceeding riches and all pretious things,
The spoyle of all the world; that it did pas
The wealth of th' East, and pompe of Persian kings:
Gold, ambre, yvorie, perles, owches, rings,
And all that els was pretious and deare,
The sea unto him voluntary brings;
That shortly he a great Lord did appeare,
As was in all the lond of Faery, or else wheare.

XXIV. Thereto he was a doughty dreaded knight,
Tryde often to the scath of many Deare,
That none in equall armes him matchen might:
The which his mother seeing gan to feare
Least his too haughtie hardines might reare
Some hard mishap in hazard of his life.
Forthy she oft him counseld to forbeare
The bloody batteill and to stirre up strife,
But after all his warre to rest his wearie knife.

XXV. And, for his more assuraunce, she inquir'd
One day of Proteus by his mighty spell
(For Proteus was with prophecy inspir'd)
Her deare sonnes destiny to her to tell,
And the sad end of her sweet Marinell:
Who, through foresight of his eternall skill,
Bad her from womankind to keepe him well,
For of a woman he should have much ill;
A virgin straunge and stout him should dismay or kill.

XXVI. Forthy she gave him warning every day
The love of women not to entertaine;
A lesson too too hard for living clay
From love in course of nature to refraine.
Yet he his mothers lore did well retaine,
And ever from fayre Ladies love did fly;
Yet many Ladies fayre did oft complaine,
That they for love of him would algates dy:
Dy, who so list for him, he was loves enimy.

XXVII. But ah! who can deceive his destiny,
Or weene by warning to avoyd his fate?
That, when he sleepes in most security
And safest seemes, him soonest doth amate,
And findeth dew effect or soone or late;
So feeble is the powre of fleshly arme.
His mother bad him wemens love to hate,
For she of womans force did feare no harme;
So, weening to have arm'd him, she did quite disarme.

XXVIII. This was that woman, this that deadly wownd,
That Proteus prophecide should him dismay;
The which his mother vainely did expownd
To be hart-wownding love, which should assay
To bring her sonne unto his last decay.
So ticle be the termes of mortall state,
And full of subtile sophismes, which doe play
With double sences, and with false debate,
T' approve the unknowen purpose of eternall fate.

XXIX. Too trew the famous Marinell it fownd,
Who, through late triall, on that wealthy Strond
Inglorious now lies in sencelesse swownd,
Through heavy stroke of Britomartis hond.
Which when his mother deare did understond,
And heavy tidings heard, whereas she playd
Amongst her watry sisters by a pond,
Gathering sweete daffadillyes, to have made
Gay girlonds from the Sun their forheads fayr to shade;

XXX. Eftesoones both flowres and girlonds far away
Shee flong, and her faire deawy lockes yrent;
To sorrow huge she turnd her former play,

And gamesom merth to grievous dreriment:
Shee threw her selfe downe on the Continent,
Ne word did speake, but lay as in a swowne,
Whiles all her sisters did for her lament
With yelling outcries, and with shrieking sowne;
And every one did teare her girlond from her crowne.

XXXI. Soone as shee up out of her deadly fitt
Arose, shee bad her charett to be brought;
And all her sisters that with her did sitt
Bad eke attonce their charetts to be sought:
Tho, full of bitter griefe and pensife thought,
She to her wagon clombe; clombe all the rest,
And forth together went with sorrow fraught.
The waves, obedient to theyr beheast,
Them yielded ready passage, and their rage surceast.

XXXII. Great Neptune stoode amazed at their sight,
Whiles on his broad rownd backe they softly slid,
And eke him selfe mournd at their mournful plight,
Yet wist not what their wailing ment; yet did,
For great compassion of their sorrow, bid
His mighty waters to them buxome bee:
Eftesoones the roaring billowes still abid,
And all the griesly Monsters of the See
Stood gaping at their gate, and wondred them to see.

XXXIII. A teme of Dolphins raunged in aray
Drew the smooth charett of sad Cymoënt:
They were all taught by Triton to obay
To the long raynes at her commaundement:
As swifte as swallowes on the waves they went,
That their brode flaggy finnes no fome did reare,
Ne bubling rowndell they behinde them sent.
The rest, of other fishes drawen weare,
Which with their finny oars the swelling sea did sheare.

XXXIV. Soone as they bene arriv'd upon the brim
Of the Rich Strond, their charets they forlore,
And let their temed fishes softly swim
Along the margent of the fomy shore,
Least they their finnes should bruze, and surbate sore
Their tender feete upon the stony grownd:

And comming to the place, where all in gore
And cruddy blood enwallowed they fownd
The lucklesse Marinell lying in deadly swownd,

xxxv. His mother swowned thrise, and the third time
Could scarce recovered bee out of her paine:
Had she not beene devoide of mortall slime,
Shee should not then have bene relyv'd againe;
But, soone as life recovered had the raine,
Shee made so piteous mone and deare wayment,
That the hard rocks could scarse from tears refraine;
And all her sister Nymphes with one consent
Supplide her sobbing breaches with sad complement.

xxxvi. " Deare image of my selfe," (she sayd) " that is
The wretched sonne of wretched mother borne,
Is this thine high advauncement?   O! is this
Th' immortall name, with which thee, yet unborne,
Thy Grandsire Nereus promist to adorne?
Now lyest thou of life and honor refte;
Now lyest thou a lumpe of earth forlorne;
Ne of thy late life memory is lefte,
Ne can thy irrevocable desteny bee wefte.

xxxvii. " Fond Proteus, father of false prophecis!
And they more fond that credit to thee give!
Not this the worke of womans hand ywis,
That so deepe wound through these deare members
    drive.
I feared love; but they that love doe live,
But they that dye doe nether love nor hate:
Nath'lesse to thee thy folly I forgive;
And to my selfe, and to accursed fate,
The guilt I doe ascribe: deare wisedom bought too late!

xxxviii. " O! what availes it of immortall seed
To beene ybredd and never borne to dye?
Farre better I it deeme to die with speed
Then waste in woe and waylfull miserye:
Who dyes, the utmost dolor doth abye;
But who that lives is lefte to waile his losse:
So life is losse, and death felicity:
Sad life worse then glad death; and greater crosse
To see frends grave, then dead the grave self to engrosse.

XXXIX. " But if the heavens did his dayes envie,
  And my short blis maligne, yet mote they well
  Thus much afford me, ere that he did die,
  That the dim eies of my deare Marinell
  I mote have closed, and him bed farewell,
  Sith other offices for mother meet
  They would not graunt——
  Yett, maulgre them, farewell, my sweetest sweet!
  Farewell, my sweetest sonne, sith we no more shall
    meet! "

 XL. Thus when they all had sorowed their fill,
  They softly gan to search his griesly wownd:
  And, that they might him handle more at will,
  They him disarmd; ano, spredding on the grownd
  Their watchet mantles frindgd with silver rownd,
  They softly wipt away the gelly blood
  From th' orifice; which having well upbownd,
  They pour in soveraine balme and Nectar good,
  Good both for erthly med'cine and for hevenly food.

 XLI. Tho when the lilly handed Liagore
  (This Liagore whilome had learned skill
  In leaches craft, by great Apolloes lore,
  Sith her whilome upon high Pindus hill
  He loved, and at last her wombe did fill
  With hevenly seed, whereof wise Pæon sprong)
  Did feele his pulse, shee knew there staied still
  Some litle life his feeble sprites emong;
  Which to his mother told, despeyre she from her flong.

 XLII. Tho, up him taking in their tender hands,
  They easely unto her charett beare:
  Her teme at her commaundement quiet stands,
  Whiles they the corse into her wagon reare,
  And strowe with flowres the lamentable beare.
  Then all the rest into their coches clim,
  And through the brackish waves their passage sheare;
  Upon great Neptunes necke they softly swim,
  And to her watry chamber swiftly carry him.

 XLIII. Deepe in the bottome of the sea her bowre
  Is built of hollow billowes heaped hye,

Like to thicke clouds that threat a stormy showre,
And vauted all within, like to the Skye,
In which the Gods doe dwell eternally;
There they him laide in easy couch well dight,
And sent in haste for Tryphon, to apply
Salves to his wounds, and medicines of might;
For Tryphon of sea gods the soveraine leach is hight.

XLIV. The whiles the Nymphes sitt all about him rownd,
Lamenting his mishap and heavy plight;
And ofte his mother, vewing his wide wownd,
Cursed the hand that did so deadly smight
Her dearest sonne, her dearest harts delight:
But none of all those curses overtooke
The warlike Maide, th' ensample of that might;
But fairely well shee thryvd, and well did brooke
Her noble deeds, ne her right course for ought forsooke.

XLV. Yet did false Archimage her still pursew,
To bring to passe his mischievous intent,
Now that he had her singled from the crew
Of courteous knights, the Prince and Faery gent,
Whom late in chace of beauty excellent
Shee lefte, pursewing that same foster strong,
Of whose fowle outrage they impatient,
And full of firy zele, him followed long,
To reskew her from shame, and to revenge her wrong.

XLVI. Through thick and thin, through mountains and
        through playns,
Those two great champions did attonce pursew
The fearefull damzell with incessant payns;
Who from them fled, as light-foot hare from vew
Of hunter swifte and scent of howndes trew.
At last they came unto a double way;
Where, doubtfull which to take, her to reskew,
Themselves they did dispart, each to assay
Whether more happy were to win so goodly prav.

XLVII. But Timias, the Princes gentle Squyre,
That Ladies love unto his Lord forlent,
And with proud envy and indignant yre
After that wicked foster fiercely went:

So beene they three three sondry wayes ybent;
But fayrest fortune to the Prince befell,
Whose chaunce it was, that sonne he did repent,
To take that way in which that Damozell
Was fledd afore, affraid of him as feend of hell.

XLVIII. At last of her far off he gained vew.
Then gan he freshly pricke his fomy steed,
And ever as he nigher to her drew,
So evermore he did increase his speed,
And of each turning still kept wary heed:
Alowd to her he oftentimes did call,
To doe away vaine doubt and needlesse dreed:
Full myld to her he spake, and oft let fall
Many meeke wordes to stay and comfort her withall.

XLIX. But nothing might relent her hasty flight,
So deepe the deadly feare of that foule swaine
Was earst impressed in her gentle spright.
Like as a fearefull Dove, which through the raine
Of the wide ayre her way does cut amaine,
Having farre off espyde a Tassell gent,
Which after her his nimble winges doth straine,
Doubleth her hast for feare to bee for-hent,
And with her pineons cleaves the liquid firmament.

L. With no lesse hast, and eke with no lesse dreed,
That fearefull Ladie fledd from him, that ment
To her no evill thought nor evill deed;
Yet former feare of being fowly shent
Carried her forward with her first intent:
And though, oft looking backward, well she vewde
Her selfe freed from that foster insolent,
And that it was a knight which now her sewde,
Yet she no lesse the knight feard then that villein rude.

LI. His uncouth shield and straunge armes her dismayd,
Whose like in Faery lond were seldom seene,
That fast she from him fledd, no lesse afrayd
Then of wilde beastes if she had chased beene:
Yet he her followd still with corage keene
So long, that now the golden Hesperus
Was mounted high in top of heaven sheene,

And warnd his other brethren joyeous
To light their blessed lamps in Joves eternall hous.

LII. All suddeinly dim wox the dampish ayre,
And griesly shadowes covered heaven bright,
That now with thousand starres was decked fayre:
Which when the Prince beheld, a lothfull sight,
And that perforce, for want of lenger light,
He mote surceasse his suit, and lose the hope
Of his long labour, he gan fowly wyte
His wicked fortune that had turnd aslope,
And cursed night that reft from him so goodly scope.

LIII. Tho, when her wayes he could no more descry,
But to and fro at disaventure strayd;
Like as a ship, whose Lodestar suddeinly
Covered with cloudes her Pilott hath dismayd;
His wearisome pursuit perforce he stayd,
And from his loftie steed dismounting low
Did let him forage.   Downe himselfe he layd
Upon the grassy ground to sleepe a throw:
The cold earth was his couch, the hard steele his pillow.

LIV. But gentle Sleepe envyde him any rest:
In stead thereof sad sorow and disdaine
Of his hard hap did vexe his noble brest,
And thousand Fancies bett his ydle brayne
With their light wings, the sights of semblants vaine.
Oft did he wish that Lady faire mote bee
His Faery Queene, for whom he did complaine,
Or that his Faery Queene were such as shee;
And ever hasty Night he blamed bitterlie.

LV. " Night! thou foule Mother of annoyaunce sad,
Sister of heavie death, and nourse of woe,
Which wast begot in heaven, but for thy bad
And brutish shape thrust downe to hell below,
Where, by the grim floud of Cocytus slow,
Thy dwelling is in Herebus black hous,
(Black Herebus, thy husband, is the foe
Of all the Gods,) where thou ungratious
Halfe of thy dayes doest lead in horrour hideous.

LVI. " What had th' eternall Maker need of thee
The world in his continuall course to keepe,
That doest all thinges deface, ne lettest see
The beautie of his worke?   Indeed, in sleepe
The slouthfull body that doth love to steepe
His lustlesse limbes, and drowne his baser mind,
Doth praise thee oft, and oft from Stygian deepe
Calles thee his goddesse, in his errour blind,
And great Dame Natures handmaide chearing every
     kind.

LVII. " But well I wote, that to an heavy hart
Thou art the roote and nourse of bitter cares,
Breeder of new, renewer of old smarts:
Instead of rest thou lendest rayling teares;
Instead of sleepe thou sendest troublous feares
And dreadfull visions, in the which alive
The dreary image of sad death appeares:
So from the wearie spirit thou doest drive
Desired rest, and men of happinesse deprive.

LVIII. " Under thy mantle black there hidden lye
Light-shonning thefte, and traiterous intent,
Abhorred bloodshed, and vile felony,
Shamefull deceipt, and daunger imminent,
Fowle horror, and eke hellish dreriment:
All these, I wote, in thy protection bee,
And light doe shonne for feare of being shent;
For light ylike is loth'd of them and thee;
And all that lewdnesse love doe hate the light to see.

LIX. " For day discovers all dishonest wayes,
And sheweth each thing as it is in deed:
The prayses of high God he faire displayes,
And his large bountie rightly doth areed:
Dayes dearest children be the blessed seed
Which darknesse shall subdue and heaven win:
Truth is his daughter; he her first did breed
Most sacred virgin without spot of sinne.
Our life is day, but death with darknesse doth begin.

LX. " O! when will day then turne to me againe,
And bring with him his long expected light?

O Titan! hast to reare thy joyous waine;
Speed thee to spred abroad thy beames bright,
And chace away this too long lingring night;
Chace her away, from whence she came, to hell:
She, she it is, that hath me done despight:
There let her with the damned spirits dwell,
And yield her rowme to day that can it governe well."

LXI. Thus did the Prince that wearie night outweare
In restlesse anguish and unquiet paine;
And earely, ere the morrow did upreare
His deawy head out of the Ocean maine,
He up arose, as halfe in great disdaine,
And clombe unto his steed.   So forth he went
With heavy look and lumpish pace, that plaine
In him bewraid great grudge and maltalent:
His steed eke seemd t' apply his steps to his intent.

CANTO V

Prince Arthur heares of Florimell:
Three fosters' Timias wound;
Belphebe findes him almost dead,
And reareth out of sownd.

I. WONDER it is to see in diverse mindes
   How diversly love doth his pageaunts play,
   And shewes his powre in variable kindes:
   The baser wit, whose ydle thoughts alway
   Are wont to cleave unto the lowly clay,
   It stirreth up to sensuall desire,
   And in lewd slouth to wast his carelesse day;
   But in brave sprite it kindles goodly fire,
   That to all high desert and honour doth aspire.

II. Ne suffereth it uncomely idlenesse
    In his free thought to build her sluggish nest,
    Ne suffereth it thought of ungentlenesse
    Ever to creepe into his noble brest;
    But to the highest and the worthiest
    Lifteth it up that els would lowly fall:
    It lettes not fall, it lettes it not to rest;
    It lettes not scarse this Prince to breath at all,
    But to his first poursuit him forward still doth call.

III. Who long time wandred through the forest wyde
     To finde some issue thence; till that at last
     He met a Dwarfe that seemed terrifyde
     With some late perill which he hardly past,
     Or other accident which him aghast;
     Of whom he asked, whence he lately came,
     And whither now he traveiled so fast?
     For sore he swat, and, ronning through that same
     Thicke forest, was bescracht and both his feet nigh lame.

IV. Panting for breath, and almost out of hart,
    The Dwarfe him answerd; "Sir, ill mote I stay
    To tell the same: I lately did depart

From Faery court, where I have many a day
Served a gentle Lady of great sway
And high accompt through out all Elfin land,
Who lately left the same, and tooke this way.
Her now I seeke; and if ye understand
Which way she fared hath, good Sir, tell out of hand."

v. " What mister wight," (saide he) " and how arayd? "
" Royally clad " (quoth he) " in cloth of gold,
As meetest may beseeme a noble mayd:
Her faire lockes in rich circlet be enrold,
A fayrer wight did never Sunne behold;
And on a Palfrey rydes more white then snow,
Yet she her selfe is whiter manifold.
The surest signe, whereby ye may her know,
Is that she is the fairest wight alive, I trow."

vi. " Now certes, swaine," (saide he) " such one, I weene,
Fast flying through this forest from her fo,
A foule ill-favoured foster, I have seene:
Her selfe, well as I might, I reskewd tho,
But could not stay, so fast she did foregoe,
Carried away with wings of speedy feare."
" Ah, dearest God! " (quoth he) " that is great woe,
And wondrous ruth to all that shall it heare:
But can ye read, Sir, how I may her finde, or where? "

vii. " Perdy, me lever were to weeten that,"
(Saide he) " then ransome of the richest knight,
Or all the good that ever yet I gat:
But froward fortune, and too forward Night,
Such happinesse did, maulgre, to me spight,
And fro me reft both life and light attone.
But, Dwarfe, aread what is that Lady bright
That through this forest wandreth thus alone?
For of her errour straunge I have great ruth and mone."

viii. " That Ladie is," (quoth he) " where so she bee,
The bountiest virgin and most debonaire
That ever living eye, I weene, did see.
Lives none this day that may with her compare
In stedfast chastitie and vertue rare,
The goodly ornaments of beautie bright;

And is ycleped Florimell the fayre,
Faire Florimell belov'd of many a knight,
Yet she loves none but one, that Marinell is hight.

IX. " A Sea-nymphes sonne, that Marinell is hight,
Of my deare Dame is loved dearely well:
In other none, but him, she sets delight;
All her delight is set on Marinell,
But he sets nought at all by Florimell;
For Ladies love his mother long ygoe
Did him, they say, forwarne through sacred spell:
But fame now flies, that of a forreine foe
He is yslaine, which is the ground of all our woe.

X. " Five daies there be since he (they say) was slaine,
And fowre since Florimell the Court forwent,
And vowed never to returne againe,
Till him alive or dead she did invent.
Therefore, faire Sir, for love of knighthood gent,
And honour of trew Ladies, if ye may
By your good counsell, or bold hardiment,
Or succour her, or me direct the way,
Do one or other good, I you most humbly pray.

XI. " So may ye gaine to you full great renowme
Of all good Ladies through the worlde so wide,
And haply in her hart finde highest rowme
Of whom ye seeke to be most magnifide;
At least eternall meede shall you abide."
To whom the Prince: " Dwarfe, comfort to thee take,
For, till thou tidings learne what her betide,
I here avow thee never to forsake.
Ill weares he armes, that nill them use for Ladies sake."

XII. So with the Dwarfe he back retourn'd againe,
To seeke his Lady where he mote her finde;
But by the way he greatly gan complaine
The want of his good Squire late lefte behinde,
For whom he wondrous pensive grew in minde,
For doubt of daunger which mote him betide;
For him he loved above all mankinde,
Having him trew and faithfull ever tride,
And bold, as ever Squyre that waited by knights side:

XIII. Who all this while full hardly was assayd
    Of deadly daunger, which to him betidd;
    For, whiles his Lord pursewd that noble Mayd,
    After that foster fowle he fiercely ridd
    To bene avenged of the shame he did
    To that faire Damzell: Him he chaced long
    Through the thicke woods wherein he would have hid
    His shamefull head from his avengement strong,
    And oft him threatned death for his outrageous wrong.

XIV. Nathlesse the villein sped himselfe so well,
    Whether through swiftnesse of his speedie beast,
    Or knowledge of those woods where he did dwell,
    That shortly he from daunger was releast,
    And out of sight escaped at the least:
    Yet not escaped from the dew reward
    Of his bad deedes, which daily he increast,
    Ne ceased not, till him oppressed hard
    The heavie plague that for such leachours is prepard.

XV. For soone as he was vanisht out of sight,
    His coward courage gan emboldned bee,
    And cast t' avenge him of that fowle despight
    Which he had borne of his bold enimee:
    Tho to his brethren came, for they were three
    Ungratious children of one gracelesse syre,
    And unto them complayned how that he
    Had used beene of that foolehardie Squyre:
    So them with bitter words he stird to bloodie yre.

XVI. Forthwith themselves with their sad instruments
    Of spoyle and murder they gan arme bylive,
    And with him foorth into the forest went
    To wreake the wrath, which he did earst revive
    In their sterne brests, on him which late did drive
    Their brother to reproch and shamefull flight;
    For they had vow'd that never he alive
    Out of that forest should escape their might:
    Vile rancour their rude harts had fild with such despight.

XVII. Within that wood there was a covert glade,
    Foreby a narrow foord, to them well knowne,
    Through which it was uneath for wight to wade;

And now by fortune it was overflowne.
By that same way they knew that Squyre unknowne
Mote algates passe: forthy themselves they set
There in await with thicke woods overgrowne,
And all the while their malice they did whet
With cruell threats his passage through the ford to let.

XVIII. It fortuned, as they devised had:
The gentle Squyre came ryding that same way,
Unweeting of their wile and treason bad,
And through the ford to passen did assay;
But that fierce foster, which late fled away,
Stoutly foorth stepping on the further shore,
Him boldly bad his passage there to stay,
Till he had made amends, and full restore
For all the damage which he had him doen afore.

XIX. With that at him a quiv'ring dart he threw,
With so fell force, and villeinous despite,
That through his haberjeon the forkehead flew,
And through the linked mayles empierced quite,
But had no powre in his soft flesh to bite.
That stroke the hardy Squire did sore displease,
But more that him he could not come to smite;
For by no meanes the high banke he could sease,
But labour'd long in that deepe ford with vaine disease.

XX. And still the foster with his long bore-speare
Him kept from landing at his wished will.
Anone one sent out of the thicket neare
A cruell shaft, headed with deadly ill,
And fethered with an unlucky quill:
The wicked steele stayd not till it did light
In his left thigh, and deepely did it thrill:
Exceeding griefe that wound in him empight,
But more that with his foes he could not come to fight.

XXI. At last, through wrath and vengeaunce making way,
He on the bancke arryvd with mickle payne,
Where the third brother him did sore assay,
And drove at him with all his might and mayne
A forest-bill, which both his hands did strayne;
But warily he did avoide the blow,

And with his speare requited him againe,
That both his sides were thrilled with the throw,
And a large streame of blood out of the wound did flow.

XXII. He, tombling downe, with gnashing teeth did bite
The bitter earth, and bad to lett him in
Into the balefull house of endlesse night,
Where wicked ghosts doe waile their former sin.
Tho gan the battaile freshly to begin;
For nathemore for that spectacle bad
Did th' other two their cruell vengeaunce blin,
But both attonce on both sides him bestad,
And load upon him layd his life for to have had.

XXIII. Tho when that villayn he aviz'd, which late
Affrighted had the fairest Florimell,
Full of fiers fury and indignant hate
To him he turned, and with rigor fell
Smote him so rudely on the Pannikell,
That to the chin he clefte his head in twaine.
Downe on the ground his carkas groveling fell:
His sinfull sowle with desperate disdaine
Out of her fleshly ferme fled to the place of paine.

XXIV. That seeing, now the only last of three
Who with that wicked shafte him wounded had,
Trembling with horror, as that did foresee
The fearefull end of his avengement sad,
Through which he follow should his brethren bad,
His bootelesse bow in feeble hand upcaught,
And therewith shott an arrow at the lad;
Which, fayntly fluttering, scarce his helmet raught,
And glauncing fel to ground, but him annoyed naught.

XXV. With that he would have fled into the wood;
But Timias him lightly overhent,
Right as he entring was into the flood,
And strooke at him with force so violent,
That headlesse him into the foord he sent:
The carcas with the streame was carried downe.
But th' head fell backeward on the Continent;
So mischief fel upon the meaners crowne.
They three be dead with shame, the Squire lives with
   renowne.

XXVI. He lives, but takes small joy of his renowne;
For of that cruell wound he bled so sore,
That from his steed he fell in deadly swowne:
Yet still the blood forth gusht in so great store,
That he lay wallowd all in his owne gore.
Now God thee keepe, thou gentlest squire alive,
Els shall thy loving Lord thee see no more;
But both of comfort him thou shalt deprive,
And eke thy selfe of honor which thou didst atchive.

XXVII. Providence hevenly passeth living thought,
And doth for wretched mens reliefe make way;
For loe! great grace or fortune thither brought
Comfort to him that comfortlesse now lay.
In those same woods ye well remember may
How that a noble hunteresse did wonne,
Shee, that base Braggadochio did affray,
And make him fast out of the forest ronne;
Belphœbe was her name, as faire as Phœbus sunne.

XXVIII. She on a day, as shee pursewd the chace
Of some wilde beast, which with her arrowes keene
She wounded had, the same along did trace
By tract of blood, which she had freshly seene
To have besprinckled all the grassy greene:
By the great persue which she there perceav'd,
Well hoped shee the beast engor'd had beene,
And made more haste the life to have bereav'd;
But ah! her expectation greatly was deceav'd.

XXIX. Shortly she came whereas that wofull Squire,
With blood deformed, lay in deadly swownd;
In whose faire eyes, like lamps of quenched fire,
The Christall humor stood congealed rownd;
His locks, like faded leaves fallen to grownd,
Knotted with blood in bounches rudely ran;
And his sweete lips, on which before that stownd
The bud of youth to blossome faire began,
Spoild of their rosy red were woxen pale and wan.

XXX. Saw never living eie more heavy sight,
That could have made a rocke of stone to rew,
Or rive in twaine: which when that Lady bright,

Besides all hope, with melting eies did vew,
All suddeinly abasht shee chaunged hew,
And with sterne horror backward gan to start;
But when shee better him beheld shee grew
Full of soft passion and unwonted smart:
The point of pity perced through her tender hart.

XXXI. Meekely shee bowed downe, to weete if life
Yett in his frosen members did remaine;
And, feeling by his pulses beating rife
That the weake sowle her seat did yett retaine,
She cast to comfort him with busie paine.
His double folded necke she reard upright,
And rubd his temples and each trembling vaine;
His mayled haberjeon she did undight,
And from his head his heavy burganet did light.

XXXII. Into the woods thenceforth in haste shee went,
To seeke for hearbes that mote him remedy;
For shee of herbes had great intendiment,
Taught of the Nymphe which from her infancy
Her nourced had in trew Nobility:
There, whether yt divine Tobacco were,
Or Panachæa, or Polygony,
Shee fownd, and brought it to her patient deare,
Who al this while lay bleeding out his hartblood neare.

XXXIII. The soveraine weede betwixt two marbles plaine
Shee pownded small, and did in peeces bruze;
And then atweene her lilly handes twaine
Into his wound the juice thereof did scruze;
And round about, as she could well it uze,
The flesh therewith shee suppled and did steepe,
T' abate all spasme, and soke the swelling bruze;
And, after having searcht the intuse deepe,
She with her scarf did bind the wound from cold to
keepe.

XXXIV. By this he had sweet life recur'd agayne,
And, groning inly deepe, at last his eies,
His watry eies drizling like deawy rayne,
He up gan lifte toward the azure skies,
From whence descend all hopelesse remedies:
Therewith he sigh'd; and, turning him aside,

The goodly Maide, ful of divinities
And gifts of heavenly grace, he by him spide,
Her bow and gilden quiver lying him beside.

xxxv. " Mercy, deare Lord! " (said he) " what grace is this
That thou hast shewed to me sinfull wight,
To send thine Angell from her bowre of blis
To comfort me in my distressed plight.
Angell, or Goddesse doe I call thee right?
What service may I doe unto thee meete,
That hast from darkenes me returnd to light,
And with thy hevenly salves and med'cines sweete
Hast drest my sinfull wounds? I kisse thy blessed
feete."

xxxvi. Thereat she blushing said; " Ah! gentle Squire,
Nor Goddesse I, nor Angell; but the Mayd
And daughter of a woody Nymphe, desire
No service but thy safety and ayd;
Which if thou gaine, I shal be well apayd.
Wee mortall wights, whose lives and fortunes bee
To commun accidents stil open layd,
Are bownd with commun bond of fraïltee,
To succor wretched wights whom we captived see."

xxxvii. By this her Damzells, which the former chace
Had undertaken after her, arryv'd,
As did Belphœbe, in the bloody place,
And thereby deemd the beast had bene depriv'd
Of life, whom late their ladies arrow ryv'd:
Forthy the bloody tract they followd fast,
And every one to ronne the swiftest stryv'd;
But two of them the rest far overpast,
And where their Lady was arrived at the last.

xxxviii. Where when they saw that goodly boy with blood
Defowled, and their Lady dresse his wownd,
They wondred much; and shortly understood
How him in deadly cace theyr Lady fownd,
And reskewed out of the heavy stownd.
Eftsoones his warlike courser, which was strayd
Farre in the woodes whiles that he lay in swownd,
She made those Damzels search; which being stayd,
They did him set thereon, and forth with them convayd.

xxxix. Into that forest farre they thence him led,
     Where was their dwelling, in a pleasant glade
     With mountaines rownd about environed,
     And mightie woodes which did the valley shade
     And like a stately Theatre it made,
     Spreading it selfe into a spatious plaine:
     And in the midst a little river plaide
     Emongst the pumy stones, which seemd to plaine
     With gentle murmure that his cours they did restraine.

xl. Beside the same a dainty place there lay,
     Planted with mirtle trees and laurells greene,
     In which the birds song many a lovely lay
     Of Gods high praise, and of their loves sweet teene,
     As it an earthly Paradize had beene:
     In whose enclosed shadow there was pight
     A faire Pavilion, scarcely to bee seene,
     The which was al within most richly dight,
     That greatest Princes liking it mote well delight.

xli. Thither they brought that wounded Squyre, and layd
     In easie couch his feeble limbes to rest.
     He rested him awhile; and then the Mayd
     His readie wound with better salves new drest:
     Daily she dressed him, and did the best
     His grievous hurt to guarish, that she might;
     That shortly she his dolour hath redrest,
     And his foule sore reduced to faire plight:
     It she reduced, but himselfe destroyed quight.

xlii. O foolish physick, and unfruitfull paine,
     That heales up one, and makes another wound!
     She his hurt thigh to him recurd againe,
     But hurt his hart, the which before was sound,
     Through an unwary dart, which did rebownd
     From her faire eyes and gratious countenaunce.
     What bootes it him from death to be unbownd,
     To be captived in endlesse duraunce
     Of sorrow and despeyre without aleggeaunce!

xliii. Still as his wound did gather, and grow hole,
     So still his hart woxe sore, and health decayd:
     Madnesse to save a part, and lose the whole!

Still whenas he beheld the heavenly Mayd,
Whiles dayly playsters to his wownd she layd,
So still his Malady the more increast,
The whiles her matchlesse beautie him dismayd,
Ah God! what other could he do at least,
But love so fayre a Lady that his life releast?

XLIV. Long while he strove in his corageous brest
With reason dew the passion to subdew,
And love for to dislodge out of his nest:
Still when her excellencies he did vew,
Her soveraine bountie and celestiall hew,
The same to love he strongly was constraynd;
But when his meane estate he did revew,
He from such hardy boldnesse was restraynd,
And of his lucklesse lott and cruell love thus playnd:

XLV. " Unthankfull wretch," (said he) " is this the meed,
With which her soverain mercy thou doest quight?
Thy life she saved by her gratious deed;
But thou doest weene with villeinous despight
To blott her honour, and her heavenly light.
Dye rather, dye, then so disloyally
Deeme of her high desert, or seeme so light:
Fayre death it is, to shonne more shame, to dy:
Dye rather, dy, then ever love disloyally.

XLVI. " But if to love disloyalty it bee,
Shall I then hate her that from deathes dore
Me brought? ah, farre be such reproch fro mee!
What can I lesse doe then her love therefore,
Sith I her dew reward cannot restore?
Dye rather, dye, and dying doe her serve;
Dying her serve, and living her adore;
Thy life she gave, thy life she doth deserve:
Dye rather, dye, then ever from her service swerve.

XLVII. " But, foolish boy, what bootes thy service bace
To her to whom the hevens doe serve and sew?
Thou, a meane Squyre of meeke and lowly place;
She, hevenly borne and of celestiall hew.
How then? of all love taketh equall vew;
And doth not highest God vouchsafe to take

The love and service of the basest crew?
If she will not, dye meekly for her sake:
Dye rather, dye, then ever so faire love forsake!"

XLVIII. Thus warreid he long time against his will;
Till that through weaknesse he was forst at last
To yield himselfe unto the mightie ill,
Which, as a victour proud, gan ransack fast
His inward partes, and all his entrayles wast,
That neither blood in face nor life in hart
It left, but both did quite drye up and blast;
As percing levin, which the inner part
Of every thing consumes, and calcineth by art.

XLIX. Which seeing fayre Belphœbe gan to feare,
Least that his wound were inly well not heald,
Or that the wicked steele empoysned were:
Litle shee weend that love he close conceald.
Yet still he wasted, as the snow congeald
When the bright sunne his beams theron doth beat:
Yet never he his hart to her reveald;
But rather chose to dye for sorow great,
Then with dishonorable termes her to entreat.

L. She, gracious Lady, yet no paines did spare
To doe him ease, or doe him remedy.
Many Restoratives of vertues rare,
And costly Cordialles she did apply,
To mitigate his stubborne malady:
But that sweet Cordiall, which can restore
A love-sick hart, she did to him envy;
To him, and to all th' unworthy world forlore
She did envy that soveraine salve in secret store

LI. That daintie Rose, the daughter of her Morne,
More deare then life she tendered, whose flowre
The girlond of her honour did adorne:
Ne suffred she the Middayes scorching powre,
Ne the sharp Northerne wind thereon to showre;
But lapped up her silken leaves most chayre,
When so the froward skye began to lowre;
But, soone as calmed was the christall ayre,
She did it fayre dispred and let to florish fayre.

LII. Eternall God, in his almightie powre,
   To make ensample of his heavenly grace,
   In Paradize whylome did plant this flowre;
   Whence he it fetcht out of her native place,
   And did in stocke of earthly flesh enrace,
   That mortall men her glory should admyre,
   In gentle Ladies breste and bounteous race
   Of woman kind it fayrest Flowre doth spyre,
   And beareth fruit of honour and all chast desyre,

LIII. Fayre ympes of beautie, whose bright shining beames
   Adorne the world with like to heavenly light,
   And to your willes both royalties and Reames
   Subdew, through conquest of your wondrous might,
   With this fayre flowre your goodly girlonds dight
   Of chastity and vertue virginall,
   That shall embellish more your beautie bright,
   And crowne your heades with heavenly coronall,
   Such as the Angels weare before Gods tribunall!

LIV. To your faire selves a faire ensample frame
   Of this faire virgin, this Belphebe fayre;
   To whom, in perfect love and spotlesse fame
   Of chastitie, none living may compayre:
   Ne poysnous Envy justly can empayre
   The prayse of her fresh flowring Maydenhead;
   Forthy she standeth on the highest stayre
   Of th' honorable stage of womanhead,
   That Ladies all may follow her ensample dead,

LV. In so great prayse of stedfast chastity
   Nathlesse she was so courteous and kynde,
   Tempred with grace and goodly modesty,
   That seemed those two vertues strove to fynd
   The higher place in her Heroick mynd:
   So striving each did other more augment,
   And both encreast the prayse of woman kynde,
   And both encreast her beautie excellent:
   So all did make in her a perfect complement,

CANTO VI

The birth of fayre Belphœbe and
Of Amorett is told:
The Gardins of Adonis fraught
With pleasures manifold.

I. WELL may I weene, faire Ladies, all this while
   Ye wonder how this noble Damozell
   So great perfections did in her compile,
   Sith that in salvage forests she did dwell,
   So farre from court and royall Citadell,
   The great schoolmaistresse of all courtesy:
   Seemeth that such wilde woodes should far expell
   All civile usage and gentility,
   And gentle sprite deforme with rude rusticity.

II. But to this faire Belphœbe in her berth
    The hevens so favorable were and free,
    Looking with myld aspect upon the earth
    In th' Horoscope of her nativitee,
    That all the gifts of grace and chastitee
    On her they poured forth of plenteous horne:
    Jove laught on Venus from his soverayne see,
    And Phœbus with faire beames did her adorne,
    And all the Graces rockt her cradle being borne.

III. Her berth was of the wombe of Morning dew,
     And her conception of the joyous Prime;
     And all her whole creation did her shew
     Pure and unspotted from all loathly crime
     That is ingenerate in fleshly slime.
     So was this virgin borne, so was she bred;
     So was she trayned up from time to time
     In all chaste vertue and true bounti-hed,
     Till to her dew perfection she were ripened.

IV. Her mother was the faire Chrysogonee,
    The daughter of Amphisa, who by race
    A Faerie was, yborne of high degree.

She bore Belphœbe; she bore in like cace
Fayre Amoretta in the second place:
These two were twinnes, and twixt them two did share
The heritage of all celestiall grace;
That all the rest it seemd they robbed bare
Of bounty, and of beautie, and all vertues rare.

v. It were a goodly storie to declare
By what straunge accident faire Chrysogone
Conceiv'd these infants, and how them she bare
In this wilde forrest wandring all alone,
After she had nine moneths fulfild and gone:
For not as other wemens commune brood
They were enwombed in the sacred throne
Of her chaste bodie; nor with commune food,
As other wemens babes, they sucked vitall blood:

vi. But wondrously they were begot and bred
Through influence of th' hevens fruitfull ray.
As it in antique bookes is mentioned.
It was upon a Sommers shinie day,
When Titan faire his beames did display,
In a fresh fountaine, far from all mens vew,
She bath'd her brest the boyling heat t' allay:
She bath'd with roses red and violets blew,
And all the sweetest flowers that in the forrest grew:

vii. Till faint through yrksome warines, adowne
Upon the grassy ground her selfe she layd
To sleepe, the whiles a gentle slombring swowne
Upon her fell, all naked bare displayd.
The sunbeames bright upon her body playd,
Being through former bathing mollifide,
And pierst into her wombe, where they embayd
With so sweete sence and secret powre unspide,
That in her pregnant flesh they shortly fructifide.

viii. Miraculous may seeme to him that reades
So straunge ensample of conception;
But reason teacheth that the fruitfull seades
Of all things living, through impression
Of the sunbeames in moyst complexion,
Doe life conceive and quickned are by kynd:

So, after Nilus inundation,
Infinite shapes of creatures men doe fynd
Informed in the mud on which the Sunne hath shynd.

IX. Great father he of generation
Is rightly cald, th' authour of life and light;
And his faire sister for creation
Ministreth matter fit, which, tempred right
With heate and humour, breedes the living wight.
So sprong these twinnes in womb of Chrysogone;
Yet wist she nought thereof, but sore affright,
Wondred to see her belly so upblone,
Which still increast till she her terme had full outgone.

X. Whereof conceiving shame and foule disgrace,
Albe her guiltlesse conscience her cleard,
She fled into the wildernesse a space,
Till that unweeldy burden she had reard,
And shund dishonor which as death she feard:
Where, wearie of long traveill, downe to rest
Her selfe she set, and comfortably cheard:
There a sad cloud of sleepe her overkest,
And seized every sence with sorrow sore opprest.

XI. It fortuned, faire Venus having lost
Her little sonne, the winged god of love,
Who, for some light displeasure which him crost,
Was from her fled as flit as ayery Dove,
And left her blisfull bowre of joy above:
(So from her often he had fled away,
When she for ought him sharpely did reprove,
And wandred in the world in straunge aray,
Disguiz'd in thousand shapes, that none might him bewray.)

XII. Him for to seeke, she left her heavenly hous,
The house of goodly formes and faire aspect,
Whence all the world derives the glorious
Features of beautie, and all shapes select,
With which high God his workmanship hath deckt;
And searched everie way through which his wings
Had borne him, or his tract she mote detect:
She promist kisses sweet, and sweeter things,
Unto the man that of him tydings to her brings.

XIII. First she him sought in Court, where most he us'd
Whylome to haunt, but there she found him not;
But many there she found which sore accus'd
His falshood, and with fowle infamous blot
His cruell deedes and wicked wyles did spot:
Ladies and Lordes she everywhere mote heare
Complayning, how with his empoysned shot
Their wofull harts he wounded had whyleare
And so had left them languishing twixt hope and feare.

XIV. She then the Cities sought from gate to gate,
And everie one did aske, did he him see?
And everie one her answerd, that too late
He had him seene, and felt the crueltee
Of his sharpe dartes and whot artilleree:
And every one threw forth reproches rife
Of his mischievous deedes, and sayd that hee
Was the disturber of all civill life,
The enimy of peace, and authour of all strife.

XV. Then in the countrey she abroad him sought,
And in the rurall cottages inquir'd;
Where also many plaintes to her were brought,
How he their heedelesse harts with love had fir'd,
And his false venim through their veines inspir'd:
And eke the gentle Shepheard swaynes, which sat
Keeping their fleecy flockes as they were hyr'd,
She sweetly heard complaine, both how and what
Her sonne had to them doen; yet she did smile thereat.

XVI. But when in none of all these she him got,
She gan avize where els he mote him hyde:
At last she her bethought that she had not
Yet sought the salvage woods and forests wyde,
In which full many lovely Nymphes abyde;
Mongst whom might be that he did closely lye,
Or that the love of some of them him tyde:
Forthy she thither cast her course t' apply,
To search the secret haunts of Dianes company.

XVII. Shortly unto the wastefull woods she came,
Whereas she found the Goddesse with her crew,
After late chace of their embrewed game,

Sitting beside a fountaine in a rew;
Some of them washing with the liquid dew
From off their dainty limbs the dusty sweat
And soyle, which did deforme their lively hew;
Others lay shaded from the scorching heat,
The rest upon her person gave attendance great.

XVIII. She, having hong upon a bough on high
Her bow and painted quiver, had unlaste
Her silver buskins from her nimble thigh,
And her lanck loynes ungirt, and brests unbraste,
After her heat the breathing cold to taste:
Her golden lockes, that late in tresses bright
Embreaded were for hindring of her haste,
Now loose about her shoulders hong undight,
And were with sweet Ambrosia all besprinckled light.

XIX. Soone as she Venus saw behinde her backe,
She was asham'd to be so loose surpriz'd;
And woxe halfe wroth against her damzels slacke,
That had not her thereof before aviz'd,
But suffred her so carelessly disguiz'd
Be overtaken.   Soone her garments loose
Upgath'ring, in her bosome she compriz'd
Well as she might, and to the Goddesse rose;
Whiles all her Nymphes did like a girlond her enclose.

XX. Goodly she gan faire Cytherea greet,
And shortly asked her, what cause her brought
Into that wildernesse for her unmeet,
From her sweete bowres, and beds with pleasures fraught?
That suddein chaunge she straunge adventure thought.
To whom halfe weeping she thus answered;
That she her dearest sonne Cupido sought,
Who in his frowardnes from her was fled,
That she repented sore to have him angered.

XXI. Thereat Diana gan to smile, in scorne
Of her vaine playnt, and to her scoffing sayd:
" Great pitty sure that ye be so forlorne
Of your gay sonne, that gives ye so good ayd
To your disports: ill mote ye bene apayd."
But she was more engrieved, and replide;

"Faire sister, ill beseemes it to upbrayd
A dolefull heart with so disdainfull pride:
The like that mine may be your paine another tide.

XXII. "As you in woods and wanton wildernesse
Your glory sett to chace the salvage beasts,
So my delight is all in joyfulnesse,
In beds, in bowres, in banckets, and in feasts:
And ill becomes you, with your lofty creasts,
To scorne the joy that Jove is glad to seeke:
We both are bownd to follow heavens beheasts,
And tend our charges with obeisaunce meeke.
Spare, gentle sister, with reproch my paine to eeke;

XXIII. "And tell me, if that ye my sonne have heard
To lurke emongst your Nimphes in secret wize,
Or keepe their cabins: much I am affeard
Least he like one of them him selfe disguize,
And turne his arrowes to their exercize.
So may he long him selfe full easie hide;
For he is faire and fresh in face and guize
As any Nimphe; (let not it be envide.")
So saying, every Nimph full narrowly shee eide.

XXIV. But Phœbe therewith sore was angered,
And sharply saide: "Goe, Dame; goe, seeke your boy,
Where you him lately lefte, in Mars his bed:
He comes not here; we scorne his foolish joy,
Ne lend we leisure to his idle toy:
But if I catch him in this company,
By Stygian lake I vow, whose sad annoy
The Gods doe dread, he dearly shall abye:
Ile clip his wanton wings, that he no more shall flye."

XXV. Whom whenas Venus saw so sore displeasd,
Shee inly sory was, and gan relent
What shee had said; so her she soone appeasd
With sugred words and gentle blandishment,
Which as a fountaine from her sweete lips went.
And welled goodly forth, that in short space
She was well pleasd, and forth her damzells sent
Through all the woods, to search from place to place,
If any tract of him or tidings they mote trace.

XXVI. To search the God of love her Nimphes she sent
Throughout the wandring forest every where:
And after them her selfe eke with her went
To seeke the fugitive both farre and nere.
So long they sought, till they arrived were
In that same shady covert whereas lay
Faire Crysogone in slombry traunce whilere;
Who in her sleepe (a wondrous thing to say)
Unwares had borne two babes, as faire as springing day.

XXVII. Unwares she them conceivd, unwares she bore:
She bore withouten paine, that she conceiv'd
Withouten pleasure; ne her need implore
Lucinaes aide: which when they both perceiv'd,
They were through wonder nigh of sence berev'd,
And gazing each on other nought bespake.
At last they both agreed her seeming griev'd
Out of her heavie swowne not to awake
But from her loving side the tender babes to take.

XXVIII. Up they them tooke; each one a babe uptooke
And with them carried to be fostered.
Dame Phœbe to a Nymphe her babe betooke
To be brought up in perfect Maydenhed,
And, of her selfe, her name Belphœbe red:
But Venus hers thence far away convayd,
To be upbrought in goodly womanhed;
And, in her litle loves stead, which was strayd,
Her Amoretta cald, to comfort her dismayd.

XXIX. Shee brought her to her joyous Paradize,
Wher most she wonnes when she on earth does dwell;
So faire a place as Nature can devize:
Whether in Paphos, or Cytheron hill,
Or it in Gnidus bee, I wote not well;
But well I wote by triall, that this same
All other pleasaunt places doth excell,
And called is by her lost lovers name,
The Gardin of Adonis, far renowmd by fame.

XXX. In that same Gardin all the goodly flowres,
Wherewith dame Nature doth her beautify,
And decks the girlonds of her Paramoures,

Are fetcht: there is the first seminary
Of all things that are borne to live and dye,
According to their kynds.   Long worke it were
Here to account the endlesse progeny
Of all the weeds that bud and blossome there;
But so much as doth need must needs be counted here,

XXXI. It sited was in fruitfull soyle of old,
'And girt in with two walls on either side;
The one of yron, the other of bright gold,
That none might thorough breake, nor overstride:
And double gates it had which opened wide,
By which both in and out men moten pas:
Th' one faire and fresh, the other old and dride.
Old Genius the porter of them was,
Old Genius, the which a double nature has.

XXXII. He letteth in, he letteth out to wend
All that to come into the world desire:
A thousand thousand naked babes attend
About him day and night, which doe require
That he with fleshly weeds would them attire:
Such as him list, such as eternall fate
Ordained hath, he clothes with sinfull mire,
And sendeth forth to live in mortall state,
Till they agayn returne backe by the hinder gate,

XXXIII. After that they againe retourned beene,
They in that Gardin planted bee agayne,
And grow afresh, as they had never seene
Fleshly corruption, nor mortall payne.
Some thousand yeares so doen they there remayne,
And then of him are clad with other hew,
Or sent into the chaungefull world agayne,
Till thither they retourne where first they grew:
So, like a wheele, arownd they ronne from old to new.

XXXIV. Ne needs there Gardiner to sett or sow,
To plant or prune; for of their owne accord
All things, as they created were, doe grow,
And yet remember well the mighty word
Which first was spoken by th' Almighty Lord,
That bad them to increase and multiply:

Ne doe they need with water of the ford,
Or of the clouds, to moysten their roots dry;
For in themselves eternall moisture they imply.

XXXV. Infinite shapes of creatures there are bred,
And uncouth formes, which none yet ever knew:
And every sort is in a sondry bed
Sett by it selfe, andranckt in comely rew;
Some fitt for reasonable sowles t' indew;
Some made for beasts, some made for birds to weare;
And all the fruitfull spawne of fishes hew
In endlesse rancks along enraunged were,
That seemd the Ocean could not containe them there.

XXXVI. Daily they grow, and daily forth are sent
Into the world, it to replenish more;
Yet is the stocke not lessened nor spent,
But still remaines in everlasting store,
As it at first created was of yore:
For in the wide wombe of the world there lyes,
In hateful darknes and in deepe horrore,
An huge eternall Chaos, which supplyes
The substaunces of natures fruitful progenyes.

XXXVII. All things from thence doe their first being fetch,
And borrow matter whereof they are made;
Which, whenas forme and feature it does ketch,
Becomes a body, and doth then invade
The state of life out of the griesly shade.
That substaunce is eterne, and bideth so;
Ne when the life decayes and forme does fade,
Doth it consume and into nothing goe,
But chaunged is, and often altred to and froe.

XXXVIII. The substaunce is not chaungd nor altered,
But th' only forme and outward fashion;
For every substaunce is conditioned
To chaunge her hew, and sondry formes to don,
Meet for her temper and complexion:
For formes are variable, and decay
By course of kinde and by occasion;
And that faire flowre of beautie fades away,
As doth the lilly fresh before the sunny ray.

XXXIX. Great enimy to it, and to all the rest
  That in the Gardin of Adonis springs,
  Is wicked Tyme; who with his scyth addrest
  Does mow the flowring herbes and goodly things,
  And all their glory to the ground downe flings,
  Where they do wither, and are fowly mard:
  He flyes about, and with his flaggy winges
  Beates downe both leaves and buds without regard,
  Ne ever pitty may relent his malice hard.

XL. Yet pitty often did the gods relent,
  To see so faire thinges mard and spoiled quight;
  And their great mother Venus did lament
  The losse of her deare brood, her deare delight:
  Her hart was pierst with pitty at the sight,
  When walking through the Gardin them she saw,
  Yet no'te she find redresse for such despight:
  For all that lives is subject to that law;
  All things decay in time, and to their end doe draw.

XLI. But were it not that Time their troubler is,
  All that in this delightfull Gardin growes
  Should happy bee, and have immortall blis:
  For here all plenty and all pleasure flowes;
  And sweete love gentle fitts emongst them throwes,
  Without fell rancor or fond gealosy.
  Franckly each Paramor his leman knowes,
  Each bird his mate; ne any does envy
  Their goodly meriment and gay felicity.

XLII. There is continuall Spring, and harvest there
  Continuall, both meeting at one tyme;
  For both the boughes doe laughing blossoms beare,
  And with fresh colours decke the wanton Pryme,
  And eke attonce the heavy trees they clyme,
  Which seeme to labour under their fruites lode:
  The whiles the joyous birdes make their pastyme
  Emongst the shady leaves, their sweet abode,
  And their trew loves without suspition tell abrode.

XLIII. Right in the middest of that Paradise
  There stood a stately Mount, on whose round top
  A gloomy grove of mirtle trees did rise,

Whose shady boughes sharp steele did never lop,
Nor wicked beastes their tender buds did crop,
But like a girlond compassed the hight;
And from their fruitfull sydes sweet gum did drop,
That all the ground, with pretious deaw bedight,
Threw forth most dainty odours and most sweet delight.

XLIV. And in the thickest covert of that shade
There was a pleasaunt Arber, not by art
But of the trees owne inclination made,
Which knitting their rancke braunches, part to part,
With wanton yvie twine entrayld athwart,
And Eglantine and Caprifole emong,
Fashiond above within their inmost part,
That nether Phœbus beams could through them throng,
Nor Aeolus sharp blast could worke them any wrong.

XLV. And all about grew every sort of flowre,
To which sad lovers were transformde of yore;
Fresh Hyacinthus, Phœbus paramoure
And dearest love;
Foolish Narcisse, that likes the watry shore;
Sad Amaranthus, made a flowre but late,
Sad Amaranthus, in whose purple gore
Me seemes I see Amintas wretched fate,
To whom sweete Poets verse hath given endlesse date.

XLVI. There wont fayre Venus often to enjoy
Her deare Adonis joyous company,
And reape sweet pleasure of the wanton boy:
There yet, some say, in secret he does ly,
Lapped in flowres and pretious spycery,
By her hid from the world, and from the skill
Of Stygian Gods, which doe her love envy;
But she her selfe, when ever that she will,
Possesseth him, and of his sweetnesse takes her fill.

XLVII. And sooth, it seemes, they say; for he may not
For ever dye, and ever buried bee
In balefull night, where all thinges are forgot:
All be he subject to mortalitie,
Yet is eterne in mutabilitie,
And by succession made perpetuall,

Transformed oft, and chaunged diverslie;
For him the Father of all formes they call:
Therfore needs mote he live, that living gives to all.

XLVIII. There now he liveth in eternall blis,
Joying his goddesse, and of her enjoyd;
Ne feareth he henceforth that foe of his,
Which with his cruell tuske him deadly cloyd:
For that wilde Bore, the which him once annoyd,
She firmely hath emprisoned for ay,
That her sweet love his malice mote avoyd,
In a strong rocky Cave, which is, they say,
Hewen underneath that Mount, that none him losen may.

XLIX. There now he lives in everlasting joy,
With many of the Gods in company
Which thither haunt, and with the winged boy,
Sporting him selfe in safe felicity:
Who when he hath with spoiles and cruelty
Ransackt the world, and in the wofull harts
Of many wretches set his triumphes hye,
Thither resortes, and, laying his sad dartes
Asyde, with faire Adonis playes his wanton partes.

L. And his trew love faire Psyche with him playes,
Fayre Psyche to him lately reconcyld,
After long troubles and unmeet upbrayes
With which his mother Venus her revyld,
And eke himselfe her cruelly exyld:
But now in stedfast love and happy state
She with him lives, and hath him borne a chyld,
Pleasure, that doth both gods and men aggrate,
Pleasure, the daughter of Cupid and Psyche late.

LI. Hither great Venus brought this infant fayre
The yonger daughter of Chrysogonee,
And unto Psyche with great trust and care
Committed her, yfostered to bee
And trained up in trew feminitee:
Who no lesse carefully her tendered
Then her owne daughter Pleasure, to whom shee
Made her companion, and her lessoned
In all the lore of love, and goodly womanhead.

LII. In which when she to perfect ripenes grew,
Of grace and beautie noble Paragone,
She brought her forth into the worldes vew,
To be th' ensample of true love alone,
And Lodestarre of all chaste affection
To all fayre Ladies that doe live on grownd.
To Faery court she came; where many one
Admyrd her goodly haveour, and fownd
His feeble hart wide launched with loves cruel wownd.

LIII. But she to none of them her love did cast,
Save to the noble knight Sir Scudamore,
To whom her loving hart she linked fast
In faithfull love, t' abide for evermore;
And for his dearest sake endured sore
Sore trouble of an hainous enimy,
Who her would forced have to have forlore
Her former love and stedfast loialty,
As ye may elswhere reade that ruefull history.

LIV. But well I weene, ye first desire to learne
What end unto that fearefull Damozell,
Which fledd so fast from that same foster stearne
Whom with his brethren Timias slew, befell:
That was, to weet, the goodly Florimell;
Who wandring for to seeke her lover deare,
Her lover deare, her dearest Marinell,
Into misfortune fell, as ye did heare,
And from Prince Arthure fled with wings of idle feare.

CANTO VII

The witches sonne loves Florimell:
She flyes; he faines to dy.
Satyrane saves the Squyre of Dames
From Gyaunts tyranny.

I. LIKE as an Hynd forth singled from the heard,
  That hath escaped from a ravenous beast,
  Yet flyes away of her owne feete afeard,
  And every leafe, that shaketh with the least
  Murmure of winde, her terror hath encreast;
  So fledd fayre Florimell from her vaine feare,
  Long after she from perill was releast:
  Each shade she saw, and each noyse she did heare,
  Did seeme to be the same which she escapt whileare.

II. All that same evening she in flying spent,
  And all that night her course continewed;
  Ne did she let dull sleepe once to relent,
  Nor wearinesse to slack her hast, but fled
  Ever alike, as if her former dred
  Were hard behind, her ready to arrest;
  And her white Palfrey, having conquered
  The maistring raines out of her weary wrest,
  Perforce her carried where ever he thought best.

III. So long as breath and hable puissaunce
  Did native corage unto him supply,
  His pace he freshly forward did advaunce,
  And carried her beyond all jeopardy;
  But nought that wanteth rest can long aby:
  He, having through incessant traveill spent
  His force, at last perforce adowne did ly,
  Ne foot could further move.   The Lady gent
  Thereat was suddein strook with great astonishment;

IV. And, forst t' alight, on foote mote algates fare
  A traveiler unwonted to such way:
  Need teacheth her this lesson hard and rare,

That fortune all in equall launce doth sway,
And mortall miseries doth make her play.
So long she traveild, till at length she came
To an hilles side, which did to her bewray
A litle valley subject to the same,
All coverd with thick woodes that quite it overcame.

v. Through the tops of the high trees she did descry
A litle smoke, whose vapour thin and light
Reeking aloft uprolled to the sky:
Which chearefull signe did send unto her sight
That in the same did wonne some living wight.
Eftsoones her steps she thereunto applyd,
And came at last in weary wretched plight
Unto the place, to which her hope did guyde,
To finde some refuge there, and rest her wearie syde.

vi. There in a gloomy hollow glen she found
A little cottage, built of stickes and reedes
In homely wize, and wald with sods around;
In which a witch did dwell, in loathly weedes
And wilfull want, all carelesse of her needes;
So choosing solitarie to abide
Far from all neighbours, that her divelish deedes
And hellish arts from people she might hide,
And hurt far off unknowne whom ever she envide.

vii. The Damzell there arriving entred in;
Where sitting on the flore the Hag she found
Busie (as seem'd) about some wicked gin:
Who, soone as she beheld that suddein stound,
Lightly upstarted from the dustie ground,
And with fell looke and hollow deadly gaze
Stared on her awhile, as one astound,
Ne had one word to speake for great amaze,
But shewd by outward signes that dread her sence did daze.

viii. At last, turning her feare to foolish wrath,
She askt, what devill had her thither brought,
And who she was, and what unwonted path
Had guided her, unwelcomed, unsought?
To which the Damzell, full of doubtfull thought,
Her mildly answer'd: "Beldame, be not wroth

With silly Virgin, by adventure brought
Unto your dwelling, ignorant and loth,
That crave but rowme to rest while tempest overblo'th."

IX. With that adowne out of her christall eyne
Few trickling teares she softly forth let fall,
That like two orient perles did purely shyne
Upon her snowy cheeke; and therewithall
She sighed soft, that none so bestiall
Nor salvage hart, but ruth of her sad plight
Would make to melt, or pitteously appall;
And that vile Hag, all were her whole delight
In mischiefe, was much moved at so pitteous sight;

X. And gan recomfort her in her rude wyse,
With womanish compassion of her plaint,
Wiping the teares from her suffused eyes,
And bidding her sit downe, to rest her faint
And wearie limbes awhile.   She, nothing quaint
Nor 'sdeignfull of so homely fashion,
Sith brought she was now to so hard constraint,
Sate downe upon the dusty ground anon;
As glad of that small rest as Bird of tempest gon.

XI. Tho gan she gather up her garments rent,
And her loose lockes to dight in order dew
With golden wreath and gorgeous ornament;
Whom such whenas the wicked Hag did vew,
She was astonisht at her heavenly hew,
And doubted her to deeme an earthly wight,
But or some Goddesse, or of Dianes crew,
And thought her to adore with humble spright:
T' adore thing so divine as beauty were but right.

XII. This wicked woman had a wicked sonne,
The comfort of her age and weary dayes,
A laesy loord, for nothing good to donne,
But stretched forth in ydlenesse alwayes,
Ne ever cast his mind to covet prayse,
Or ply himselfe to any honest trade,
But all the day before the sunny rayes
He us'd to slug, or sleepe in slothfull shade:
Such laesinesse both lewd and poore attonce him made.

XIII. He, comming home at undertime, there found
    The fayrest creature that he ever saw
    Sitting beside his mother on the ground;
    The sight whereof did greatly him adaw,
    And his base thought with terrour and with **aw**
    So inly smot, that as one, which hath gaz'd
    On the bright Sunne unwares, doth soone withdraw
    His feeble eyne, with too much brightnes daz'd,
    So stared he on her, and stood long while amaz'd.

XIV. Softly at last he gan his mother aske,
    What mister wight that was, and whence deriv'd,
    That in so straunge disguizement there did maske,
    And by what accident she there arriv'd?
    But she, as one nigh of her wits depriv'd,
    With nought but ghastly lookes him answered;
    Like to a ghost, that lately is reviv'd
    From Stygian shores where late it wandered:
    So both at her, and each at other wondered.

XV. But the fayre Virgin was so meeke and myld,
    That she to them vouchsafed to embace
    Her goodly port, and to their senses vyld
    Her gentle speach applyde, that in short space
    She grew familiare in that desert place.
    During which time the Chorle, through her so kind
    And courteise use, conceiv'd affection bace,
    And cast to love her in his brutish mind:
    No love, but brutish lust, that was so beastly tind.

XVI. Closely the wicked flame his bowels brent,
    And shortly grew into outrageous fire;
    Yet had he not the hart, nor hardiment,
    As unto her to utter his desire;
    His caytive thought durst not so high aspire:
    But with soft sighes and lovely semblaunces
    He ween'd that his affection entire
    She should aread; many resemblaunces
    To her he made, and many kinde remembraunces.

XVII. Oft from the forrest wildings he did bring,
    Whose sides empurpled were with smyling red;
    And oft young birds, which he had taught to sing,

His maistresse praises sweetly caroled:
Girlonds of flowres sometimes for her faire hed
He fine would dight; sometimes the squirrell wild
He brought to her in bands, as conquered
To be her thrall, his fellow-servant vild:
All which she of him tooke with countenance meeke
    and mild.

XVIII. But, past a while, when she fit season saw
To leave that desert mansion, she cast
In secret wize herselfe thence to withdraw,
For feare of mischiefe, which she did forecast
Might by the witch or by her sonne compast.
Her wearie Palfrey, closely as she might,
Now well recovered after long repast,
In his proud furnitures she freshly dight,
His late miswandred wayes now to remeasure right.

XIX. And earely, ere the dawning day appear'd,
She forth issewed, and on her journey went:
She went in perill, of each noyse affeard,
And of each shade that did it selfe present;
For still she feared to be overhent
Of that vile hag, or her uncivile sonne;
Who when, too late awaking, well they kent
That their fayre guest was gone, they both begonne
To make exceeding mone, as they had been undonne.

XX. But that lewd lover did the most lament
For her depart, that ever man did heare:
He knockt his brest with desperate intent,
And scratcht his face, and with his teeth did teare
His rugged flesh, and rent his ragged heare;
That his sad mother, seeing his sore plight,
Was greatly woe begon, and gan to feare
Least his fraile senses were emperisht quight,
And love to frenzy turnd, sith love is franticke hight.

XXI. All wayes shee sought him to restore to plight,
With herbs, with charms, with counsel, and with teares;
But tears, nor charms, nor herbs, nor counsell, might
Asswage the fury which his entrails teares:
So strong is passion that no reason heares.
Tho when all other helpes she saw to faile,

She turnd her selfe backe to her wicked leares;
And by her divelish arts thought to prevaile
To bringe her backe againe, or worke her finall bale.

XXII. Eftesoones out of her hidden cave she cald
An hideous beast of horrible aspect,
That could the stoutest corage have appald;
Monstrous, mishapt, and all his backe was spect
With thousand spots of colours queint elect,
Thereto so swifte that it all beasts did pas:
Like never yet did living eie detect;
But likest it to an Hyena was,
That feeds on wemens flesh as others feede on gras.

XXIII. It forth she cald, and gave it streight in charge
Through thicke and thin her to poursew apace,
Ne once to stay to rest, or breath at large,
Till her he had attaind and brought in place,
Or quite devourd her beauties scornefull grace.
The Monster, swifte as word that from her went,
Went forth in haste, and did her footing trace
So sure and swiftly, through his perfect sent
And passing speede, that shortly he her overhent.

XXIV. Whom when the fearefull Damzell nigh espide,
No need to bid her fast away to flie:
That ugly shape so sore her terrifide,
That it she shund no lesse then dread to die;
And her flitt palfrey did so well apply
His nimble feet to her conceived feare,
That whilest his breath did strength to him supply,
From peril free he her away did beare;
But when his force gan faile his pace gan wex areare.

XXV. Which whenas she perceiv'd, she was dismayd
At that same last extremity ful sore,
And of her safety greatly grew afrayd.
And now she gan approch to the sea shore,
As it befell, that she could flie no more,
But yield herselfe to spoile of greedinesse:
Lightly she leaped, as a wight forlore,
From her dull horse, in desperate distresse,
And to her feet betooke her doubtfull sickernesse.

XXVI. Not halfe so fast the wicked Myrrha fled
From dread of her revenging fathers hond;
Nor halfe so fast to save her maydenhed
Fled fearfull Daphne on th' Ægæan strond,
As Florimell fled from that Monster yond,
To reach the sea ere she of him were raught:
For in the sea to drowne herselfe she fond,
Rather then of the tyrant to be caught:
Thereto fear gave her wings, and need her corage taught.

XXVII. It fortuned (high God did so ordaine)
As shee arrived on the roring shore,
In minde to leape into the mighty maine,
A little bote lay hoving her before,
In which there slept a fisher old and pore,
The whiles his nets were drying on the sand.
Into the same shee lept, and with the ore
Did thrust the shallop from the floting strand:
So safety fownd at sea which she fownd not at land.

XXVIII. The Monster, ready on the pray to sease,
Was of his forward hope deceived quight;
Ne durst assay to wade the perlous seas,
But greedily long gaping at the sight,
At last in vaine was forst to turne his flight,
And tell the idle tidings to his Dame:
Yet, to avenge his divelish despight,
He sett upon her Palfrey tired lame,
And slew him cruelly ere any reskew came.

XXIX. And, after having him embowelled
To fill his hellish gorge, it chaunst a knight
To passe that way, as forth he traveiled:
Yt was a goodly Swaine, and of great might,
As ever man that bloody field did fight;
But in vain sheows, that wont yong knights bewitch,
And courtly services, tooke no delight;
But rather joyd to bee then seemen sich,
For both to be and seeme to him was labor lich.

XXX. It was to weete the good Sir Satyrane,
That raunged abrode to seeke adventures wilde,
As was his wont, in forest and in plaine:

He was all armd in rugged steele unfilde,
As in the smoky forge it was compilde,
And in his Scutchin bore a Satyres hedd.
He comming present, where the Monster vilde
Upon that milke-white Palfreyes carcas fedd,
Unto his reskew ran, and greedily him spedd.

XXXI. There well perceivd he that it was the horse
Whereon faire Florimell was wont to ride,
That of that feend was rent without remorse:
Much feared he least ought did ill betide
To that faire Maide, the flowre of wemens pride;
For her he dearely loved, and in all
His famous conquests highly magnifide:
Besides, her golden girdle, which did fall
From her in flight, he fownd, that did him sore apall.

XXXII. Full of sad feare and doubtfull agony
Fiercely he flew upon that wicked feend,
And with huge strokes and cruell battery
Him forst to leave his pray, for to attend
Him selfe from deadly daunger to defend:
Full many wounds in his corrupted flesh
He did engrave, and muchell blood did spend,
Yet might not doe him die: but aie more fresh
And fierce he still appeard, the more he did him thresh,

XXXIII. He wist not how him to despoile of life,
Ne how to win the wished victory,
Sith him he saw still stronger grow through strife,
And him selfe weaker through infirmity.
Greatly he grew enrag'd, and furiously
Hurling his sword away he lightly lept
Upon the beast, that with great cruelty
Rored and raged to be underkept;
Yet he perforce him held, and strokes upon him hept.

XXXIV. As he that strives to stop a suddein flood,
And in strong bancks his violence enclose,
Forceth it swell above his wonted mood,
And largely overflow the fruitfull plaine,
That all the countrey seemes to be a Maine,
And the rich furrowes flote, all quite foidonne:

The wofull husbandman doth lowd complaine
To see his whole yeares labor lost so soone,
For which to God he made so many an idle boone:

XXXV. So him he held, and did through might amate.
So long he held him, and him bett so long,
That at the last his fiercenes gan abate,
And meekely stoup unto the victor strong:
Who, to avenge the implacable wrong
Which he supposed donne to Florimell,
Sought by all meanes his dolor to prolong,
Sith dint of steele his carcas could not quell;
His maker with her charmes had framed him so well.

XXXVI. The golden ribband, which that virgin wore
About her sclender waste, he tooke in hand,
And with it bownd the beast, that lowd did rore
For great despight of that unwonted band,
Yet dared not his victor to withstand,
But trembled like a lambe fled from the pray;
And all the way him followd on the strand,
As he had long bene learned to obay;
Yet never learned he such service till that day.

XXXVII. Thus as he led the Beast along the way,
He spide far off a mighty Giauntesse
Fast flying, on a Courser dapled gray,
From a bold knight that with great hardinesse
Her hard pursewed, and sought for to suppresse.
She bore before her lap a doleful Squire,
Lying athwart her horse in great distresse,
Fast bounden hand and foote with cords of wire,
Whom she did meane to make the thrall of her desire.

XXXVIII. Which whenas Satyrane beheld, in haste
He lefte his captive Beast at liberty,
And crost the nearest way, by which he cast
Her to encounter ere she passed by;
But she the way shund nathemore forthy,
But forward gallopt fast; which when he spyde,
His mighty speare he couched warily,
And at her ran: she, having him descryde,
Her selfe to fight addrest, and threw her lode aside.

XXXIX. Like as a Goshauke, that in foote doth beare
    A trembling Culver, having spide on hight
    An Eagle that with plumy wings doth sheare
    The subtile ayre stouping with all his might,
    The quarry throwes to ground with fell despight,
    And to the batteill doth her selfe prepare:
    So ran the Geauntesse unto the fight;
    Her fyrie eyes with furious sparkes did stare,
    And with blasphemous bannes high God in peeces tare.

XL. She caught in hand an huge great yron mace,
    Wherewith she many had of life depriv'd;
    But, ere the stroke could seize his aymed place,
    His speare amids her sun-brode shield arriv'd:
    Yet nathemore the steele asonder riv'd,
    All were the beame in bignes like a mast,
    Ne her out of the stedfast sadle driv'd;
    But, glauncing on the tempred metall, brast
    In thousand shivers, and so forth beside her past.

XLI. Her Steed did stagger with that puissaunt strooke;
    But she no more was moved with that might
    Then it had lighted on an aged Oke,
    Or on the marble Pillour that is pight
    Upon the top of Mount Olympus hight,
    For the brave youthly Champions to assay
    With burning charet wheeles it nigh to smite;
    But who that smites it mars his joyous play,
    And is the spectacle of ruinous decay.

XLII. Yet, therewith sore enrag'd, with sterne regard
    Her dreadfull weapon she to him addrest,
    Which on his helmet martelled so hard
    That made him low incline his lofty crest,
    And bowd his battred visour to his brest:
    Wherewith he was so stund that he n'ote ryde,
    But reeled to and fro from east to west.
    Which when his cruell enimy espyde,
    She lightly unto him adjoyned syde to syde;

XLIII. And, on his collar laying puissaunt hand,
    Out of his wavering seat him pluckt perforse,
    Perforse him pluckt, unable to withstand

Or helpe himselfe; and laying thwart her horse,
In loathly wise like to a carrion corse,
She bore him fast away.   Which when the knight
That her pursewed saw, with great remorse
He nere was touched in his noble spright,
And gan encrease his speed as she encreast her flight.

XLIV. Whom when as nigh approching she espyde,
She threw away her burden angrily;
For she list not the batteill to abide,
But made her selfe more light away to fly:
Yet her the hardy knight pursewd so nye
That almost in the backe he oft her strake;
But still, when him at hand she did espy,
She turnd, and semblaunce of faire fight did make,
But, when he stayd, to flight againe she did her take.

XLV. By this the good Sir Satyrane gan awake
Out of his dreame that did him long entraunce,
And, seeing none in place, he gan to make
Exceeding mone, and curst that cruell chaunce
Which reft from him so faire a chevisaunce.
At length he spyde whereas that wofull Squyre,
Whom he had reskewed from captivaunce
Of his strong foe, lay tombled in the myre,
Unable to arise, or foote or hand to styre.

XLVI. To whom approching, well he mote perceive
In that fowle plight a comely personage
And lovely face, made fit for to deceive
Fraile Ladies hart with loves consuming rage,
Now in the blossome of his freshest age.
He reard him up and loosd his yron bands,
And after gan inquire his parentage,
And how he fell into the Gyaunts hands,
And who that was which chaced her along the lands.

XLVII. Then trembling yet through feare the Squire bespake:
" That Geauntesse Argantè is behight,
A daughter of the Titans which did make
Warre against heven, and heaped hils on hight
To scale the skyes and put Jove from his right:
Her syre Typhoeus was; who, mad through merth,

And dronke with blood of men slaine by his might,
Through incest her of his owne mother Earth
Whylome begot, being but halfe twin of that berth:

XLVIII. " For at that berth another Babe she bore;
To weet, the mightie Ollyphant, that wrought
Great wreake to many errant knights of yore,
And many hath to foule confusion brought.
These twinnes, men say, (a thing far passing thought)
While in their mothers wombe enclosd they were,
Ere they into the lightsom world were brought,
In fleshly lust were mingled both yfere,
And in that monstrous wise did to the world appere.

XLIX. " So liv'd they ever after in like sin,
Gainst natures law and good behaveoure;
But greatest shame was to that maiden twin,
Who, not content so fowly to devoure
Her native flesh and staine her brothers bowre,
Did wallow in all other fleshly myre,
And suffred beastes her body to deflowre,
So whot she burned in that lustfull fyre;
Yet all that might not slake her sensuall desyre:

L. " But over all the countrie she did raunge
To seeke young men to quench her flaming thrust,
And feed her fancy with delightfull chaunge:
Whom so she fittest findes to serve her lust,
Through her maine strength, in which she most doth trust,
She with her bringes into a secret Ile,
Where in eternall bondage dye he must,
Or be the vassall of her pleasures vile,
And in all shamefull sort him selfe with her defile.

LI. " Me, seely wretch, she so at vauntage caught,
After she long in waite for me did lye,
And meant unto her prison to have brought,
Her lothsom pleasure there to satisfye;
That thousand deathes me lever were to dye
Then breake the vow that to faire Columbell
I plighted have, and yet keepe stedfastly.
As for my name, it mistreth not to tell:
Call me the Squyre of Dames; that me beseemeth well.

LII. " But that bold knight, whom ye pursuing saw
That Geauntesse, is not such as she seemd,
But a faire virgin that in martiall law
And deedes of armes above all Dames is deemd,
And above many knightes is eke esteemd
For her great worth: She Palladine is hight.
She you from death, you me from dread, redeemd;
Ne any may that Monster match in fight,
But she, or such as she, that is so chaste a wight."

LIII. " Her well beseemes that Quest," (quoth Satyrane)
" But read, thou Squyre of Dames, what vow is this,
Which thou upon thy selfe hast lately ta'ne? "
" That shall I you recount," (quoth he) " ywis,
So be ye pleasd to pardon all amis.
That gentle Lady whom I love and serve,
After long suit and wearie servicis,
Did aske me, how I could her love deserve,
And how she might be sure that I would never swerve?

LIV. " I, glad by any meanes her grace to gaine,
Badd her commaund my life to save or spill.
Eftsoones she badd me, with incessaunt paine
To wander through the world abroad at will,
And every where, where with my power or skill
I might doe service unto gentle Dames,
That I the same should faithfully fulfill;
And at the twelve monethes end should bring their names
And pledges, as the spoiles of my victorious games.

LV. " So well I to faire Ladies service did,
And found such favour in their loving hartes,
That ere the yeare his course had compassid,
Thre hundred pledges for my good desartes,
And thrice three hundred thanks for my good partes,
I with me brought, and did to her present:
Which when she saw, more bent to eke my smartes
Then to reward my trusty true intent,
She gan for me devise a grievous punishment

LVI. " To weet, that I my traveill should resume,
And with like labour walke the world arownd,
Ne ever to her presence should presume,

Till I so many other Dames had fownd,
The which, for all the suit I could propownd,
Would me refuse their pledges to afford,
But did abide for ever chaste and sownd."
" Ah! gentle Squyre," (quoth he) " tell at one word,
How many fownd'st thou such to put in thy record? "

LVII. " Indeed, Sir knight," (said he) " one word may tell
All that I ever fownd so wisely stayd,
For onely three they were disposd so well;
And yet three yeares I now abrode have strayd,
To fynd them out." " Mote I," (then laughing sayd
The knight) " inquire of thee what were those three,
The which thy proffred curtesie denayd?
Or ill they seemed sure avizd to bee,
Or brutishly brought up, that nev'r did fashions see."

LVIII. " The first which then refused me," (said hee)
" Certes was but a common Courtisane;
Yet flat refusd to have adoe with mee,
Because I could not give her many a Jane."
(Thereat full hartely laughed Satyrane.)
" The second was an holy Nunne to chose,
Which would not let me be her Chappellane,
Because she knew, she said, I would disclose
Her counsell, if she should her trust in me repose.

LIX. " The third a Damzell was of low degree,
Whom I in countrey cottage fownd by chaunce:
Full litle weened I that chastitee
Had lodging in so meane a maintenaunce;
Yet was she fayre, and in her countenaunce
Dwelt simple truth in seemely fashion.
Long thus I woo'd her with due observaunce,
In hope unto my pleasure to have won;
But was as far at last, as when I first begon.

LX. " Safe her, I never any woman found
That chastity did for it selfe embrace,
But were for other causes firme and sound;
Either for want of handsome time and place,
Or else for feare of shame and fowle disgrace.
Thus am I hopelesse ever to attaine

My Ladies love in such a desperate case,
But all my dayes am like to waste in vaine,
Seeking to match the chaste with th' unchaste Ladies
    traine."

LXI. " Perdy " (sayd Satyrane) " thou Squyre of Dames,
Great labour fondly hast thou hent in hand,
To get small thankes, and therewith many blames,
That may emongst Alcides labours stand."
Thence backe returning to the former land,
Where late he left the Beast he overcame,
He found him not; for he had broke his band,
And was returnd againe unto his Dame,
To tell what tydings of fayre Florimell became.

CANTO VIII

The Witch creates a snowy La-
dy like to Florimell;
  Who wrong'd by Carle, by Proteus sav'd,
Is sought by Paridell.

I. So oft as I this history record,
   My heart doth melt with meere compassion,
   To thinke how causelesse, of her owne accord,
   This gentle Damzell, whom I write upon,
   Should plonged be in such affliction
   Without all hope of comfort or reliefe;
   That sure, I weene, the hardest hart of stone
   Would hardly finde to aggravate her griefe;
   For misery craves rather mercy then repriefe.

II. But that accursed Hag, her hostesse late,
    Had so enranckled her malitious hart,
    That she desyrd th' abridgement of her fate,
    Or long enlargement of her painefull smart.
    Now when the Beast, which by her wicked art
    Late foorth she sent, she backe retourning spyde
    Tyde with her golden girdle; it a part
    Of her rich spoyles whom he had earst destroyd
    She weend, and wondrous gladnes to her hart applyde.

III. And, with it ronning hast'ly to her sonne,
     Thought with that sight him much to have reliv'd
     Who, thereby deeming sure the thing as donne,
     His former griefe with furie fresh reviv'd
     Much more than earst, and would have algates riv'd
     The hart out of his brest: for sith her dedd
     He surely dempt, himselfe he thought depriv'd
     Quite of all hope wherewith he long had fedd
     His foolish malady, and long time had misledd.

IV. With thought whereof exceeding mad he grew,
    And in his rage his mother would have slaine,
    Had she not fled into a secret mew,

Where she was wont her Sprightes to entertaine,
The maisters of her art: there was she faine
To call them all in order to her ayde,
And them conjure, upon eternall paine,
To counsell her, so carefully dismayd,
How she might heale her sonne whose senses were decayd.

v. By their advice, and her owne wicked wit,
She there deviz'd a wondrous worke to frame,
Whose like on earth was never framed yit;
That even Nature selfe envide the same,
And grudg'd to see the counterfet should shame
The thing it selfe: In hand she boldly tooke
To make another like the former Dame,
Another Florimell, in shape and looke
So lively and so like, that many it mistooke.

vi. The substance, whereof she the body made,
Was purest snow in massy mould congeald,
Which she had gathered in a shady glade
Of the Riphœan hils, to her reveald
By errant Sprights, but from all men conceald:
The same she tempred with fine mercury
And virgin wex that never yet was seald,
And mingled them with perfect vermily;
That like a lively sanguine it seemd to the eye.

vii. Instead of eyes two burning lampes she set
In silver sockets, shyning like the skyes,
And a quicke moving Spirit did arret
To stirre and roll them like to womens eyes:
Instead of yellow lockes she did devyse
With golden wyre to weave her curled head;
Yet golden wyre was not so yellow thryse
As Florimells fayre heare: and, in the stead
Of life, she put a Spright to rule the carcas dead;

viii. A wicked Spright, yfraught with fawning guyle
And fayre resemblance above all the rest,
Which with the Prince of Darkenes fell somewhyle
From heavens blis and everlasting rest:
Him needed not instruct which way were best
Him selfe to fashion likest Florimell,

Ne how to speake, ne how to use his gest;
For he in counterfesaunce did excell,
And all the wyles of wemens wits knew passing well.

IX. Him shaped thus she deckt in garments gay,
Which Florimell had left behind her late;
That who so then her saw would surely say
It was her selfe whom it did imitate,
Or fayrer then her selfe, if ought algate
Might fayrer be.   And then she forth her brought
Unto her sonne that lay in feeble state;
Who seeing her gan streight upstart, and thought
She was the Lady selfe whom he so long had sought.

X. Tho fast her clipping twixt his armes twayne,
Extremely joyed in so happy sight,
And soone forgot his former sickely payne:
But she, the more to seeme such as she hight,
Coyly rebutted his embracement light;
Yet still, with gentle countenaunce, retain'd
Enough to hold a foole in vaine delight.
Him long she so with shadowes entertain'd,
As her Creatresse had in charge to her ordain'd.

XI. Till on a day, as he disposed was
To walke the woodes with that his Idole faire,
Her to disport and idle time to pas
In th' open freshnes of the gentle aire,
A knight that way there chaunced to repaire;
Yet knight he was not, but a boastfull swaine
That deedes of armes had ever in despaire,
Proud Braggadocchio, that in vaunting vaine
His glory did repose, and credit did maintaine.

XII. He, seeing with that Chorle so faire a wight,
Decked with many a costly ornament,
Much merveiled thereat, as well he might,
And thought that match a fowle disparagement:
His bloody speare eftesoones he boldly bent
Against the silly clowne, who dead through feare
Fell streight to ground in great astonishment.
"Villein," (sayd he) " this Lady is my deare;
Dy, if thou it gainesay: I will away her beare."

XIII. The fearefull Chorle durst not gainesay nor dooe,
But trembling stood, and yielded him the pray;
Who, finding litle leasure her to wooe
On Tromparts steed her mounted without stay,
And without reskew led her quite away.
Proud man himselfe then Braggadochio deem'd,
And next to none after that happy day,
Being possessed of that spoyle, which seem'd
The fairest wight on ground, and most of men esteem'd.

XIV. But, when hee saw him selfe free from poursute,
He gan make gentle purpose to his Dame
With termes of love and lewdnesse dissolute;
For he could well his glozing speaches frame
To such vaine uses that him best became:
But she thereto would lend but light regard,
As seeming sory that she ever came
Into his powre, that used her so hard
To reave her honor, which she more then life prefard.

XV. Thus as they two of kindnes treated long,
There them by chaunce encountred on the way
An armed knight upon a courser strong,
Whose trampling feete upon the hollow lay
Seemed to thunder, and did nigh affray
That Capons corage: yet he looked grim,
And faynd to cheare his lady in dismay,
Who seemd for feare to quake in every lim,
And her to save from outrage meekely prayed him.

XVI. Fiercely that straunger forward came: and, nigh
Approching, with bold words and bitter threat
Bad that same boaster, as he mote, on high,
To leave to him that lady for excheat,
Or bide him batteill without further treat.
That challenge did too peremptory seeme,
And fild his senses with abashment great;
Yet seeing nigh him jeopardy extreme,
He it dissembled well, and light seemd to esteeme

XVII. Saying, " Thou foolish knight, that weenst with words
To steale away that I with blowes have wonne,
And brought through points of many perilous swords:

But if thee list to see thy Courser ronne,
Or prove thy selfe, this sad encounter shonne,
And seeke els without hazard of thy hedd."
At those prowd words that other knight begonne
To wex exceeding wroth, and him aredd
To turne his steede about, or sure he should be dedd.

XVIII. " Sith then," (said Braggadochio) " needes thou wilt
Thy daies abridge through proofe of puissaunce,
Turne we our steeds; that both in equall tilt
May meete againe, and each take happy chaunce."
This said, they both a furlongs mountenaunce
Retird their steeds, to ronne in even race;
But Braggadochio, with his bloody launce,
Once having turnd, no more returnd his face,
But lefte his love to losse, and fled him selfe apace.

XIX. The knight, him seeing flie, had no regard
Him to poursew, but to the lady rode;
And having her from Trompart lightly reard,
Upon his Courser sett the lovely lode,
And with her fled away without abode.
Well weened he, that fairest Florimell
It was with whom in company he yode,
And so her selfe did alwaies to him tell;
So made him thinke him selfe in heven that was in hell.

XX. But Florimell her selfe was far away,
Driven to great distresse by fortune straunge,
And taught the carefull Mariner to play,
Sith late mischaunce had her compeld to chaunge
The land for sea, at randon there to raunge:
Yett there that cruell Queene avengeresse,
Not satisfyde so far her to estraunge
From courtly blis and wonted happinesse,
Did heape on her new waves of weary wretchednesse.

XXI. For being fled into the fishers bote
For refuge from the Monsters cruelty,
Long so she on the mighty maine did flote,
And with the tide drove forward carelesly;
For th' ayre was milde and cleared was the skie,
And all his windes Dan Aeolus did keepe

From stirring up their stormy enmity,
As pittying to see her waile and weepe:
But all the while the fisher did securely sleepe,

XXII. At last when droncke with drowsinesse he woke,
And saw his drover drive along the streame,
He was dismayd; and thrise his brest he stroke,
For marveill of that accident extreame:
But when he saw that blazing beauties beame,
Which with rare light his bote did beautifye,
He marveild more, and thought he yet did dreame
Not well awakte; or that some extasye
Assotted had his sence, or dazed was his eye.

XXIII. But when her well avizing hee perceiv'd
To be no vision nor fantasticke sight,
Great comfort of her presence he conceiv'd,
And felt in his old corage new delight
To gin awake, and stir his frosen spright:
Tho rudely askte her, how she thither came?
" Ah! " (sayd she) " father, I note read aright
What hard misfortune brought me to this same;
Yet am I glad that here I now in safety ame.

XXIV. " But thou, good man, sith far in sea we bee,
And the great waters gin apace to swell,
That now no more we can the mayn-land see,
Have care, I pray, to guide the cock-bote well,
Least worse on sea then us on land befell."
Thereat th' old man did nought but fondly grin,
And saide his boat the way could wisely tell;
But his deceiptfull eyes did never lin
To looke on her faire face and marke her snowy skin.

XXV. The sight whereof in his congealed flesh
Infixt such secrete sting of greedy lust,
That the drie withered stocke it gan refresh,
And kindled heat that soone in flame forth brust:
The driest wood is soonest burnt to dust.
Rudely to her he lept, and his rough hond
Where ill became him rashly would have thrust;
But she with angry scorne did him withstond,
And shamefully reproved for his rudenes fond.

XXVI. But he, that never good nor maners knew,
      Her sharpe rebuke full litle did esteeme;
      Hard is to teach an old horse amble trew:
      The inward smoke, that did before but steeme,
      Broke into open fire and rage extreme;
      And now he strength gan adde unto his will,
      Forcyng to doe that did him fowle misseeme.
      Beastly he threwe her downe, ne car'd to spill
      Her garments gay with scales of fish that all did fill.

XXVII. The silly virgin strove him to withstand
       All that she might, and him in vaine revild:
       Shee strugled strongly both with foote and hand
       To save her honor from that villaine vilde,
       And cride to heven, from humane help exild.
       O! ye brave knights, that boast this Ladies love,
       Where be ye now, when she is nigh defild
       Of filthy wretch? well may she you reprove
       Of falsehood or of slouth, when most it may behove.

XXVIII. But if that thou, Sir Satyran, didst weete,
        Or thou, Sir Peridure, her sory state,
        How soone would yee assemble many a fleete,
        To fetch from sea that ye at land lost late!
        Towres, citties, kingdomes, ye would ruinate
        In your avengement and despiteous rage,
        Ne ought your burning fury mote abate;
        But if Sir Calidore could it presage,
        No living creature could his cruelty asswage.

XXIX. But sith that none of all her knights is nye,
      See how the heavens, of voluntary grace
      And soveraine favor towards chastity,
      Doe succor send to her distressed cace;
      So much high God doth innocence embrace.
      It fortuned, whilest thus she stifly strove,
      And the wide sea importuned long space
      With shrilling shriekes, Proteus abrode did rove,
      Along the fomy waves driving his finny drove.

XXX. Proteus is Shepheard of the seas of yore,
     And hath the charge of Neptunes mighty heard;
     An aged sire with head all frory hore,

And sprinckled frost upon his deawy beard:
Who when those pittifull outcries he heard
Through all the seas so ruefully resownd,
His charett swifte in hast he thither steard,
Which with a teeme of scaly Phocas bownd
Was drawne upon the waves that fomed him arownd.

XXXI. And comming to that Fishers wandring bote,
That went at will withouten card or sayle,
He therein saw that yrkesome sight, which smote
Deepe indignation and compassion frayle
Into his hart attonce: streight did he hayle
The greedy villein from his hoped pray,
Of which he now did very litle fayle,
And with his staffe, that drives his heard astray,
Him bett so sore, that life and sence did much dismay

XXXII. The whiles the pitteous Lady up did ryse,
Ruffled and fowly raid with filthy soyle,
And blubbred face with teares of her faire eyes:
Her heart nigh broken was with weary toyle,
To save her selfe from that outrageous spoyle;
But when she looked up, to weet what wight
Had her from so infamous fact assoyld,
For shame, but more for feare of his grim sight,
Downe in her lap she hid her face, and lowdly shright.

XXXIII. Her selfe not saved yet from daunger dredd
She thought, but chaung'd from one to other feare:
Like as a fearefull partridge, that is fledd
From the sharpe hauke which her attached neare,
And fals to ground to seeke for succor theare,
Whereas the hungry Spaniells she does spye
With greedy jawes her ready for to teare:
In such distresse and sad perplexity
Was Florimell, when Proteus she did see her by.

XXXIV. But he endevored with speaches milde
Her to recomfort, and accourage bold,
Bidding her feare no more her foemen vilde,
Nor doubt himselfe; and who he was her told:
Yet all that could not from affright her hold,
Ne to recomfort her at all prevayld;

For her faint hart was with the frosen cold
Benumbd so inly, that her wits nigh fayld,
And all her sences with abashment quite were quayld.

xxxv. Her up betwixt his rugged hands he reard,
And with his frory lips full softly kist,
Whiles the cold ysickles from his rough beard
Dropped adowne upon her yvory brest:
Yet he him selfe so busily addrest,
That her out of astonishment he wrought;
And out of that same fishers filthy nest
Removing her, into his charet brought,
And there with many gentle termes her faire besought.

xxxvi. But that old leachour, which with bold assault
That beautie durst presume to violate,
He cast to punish for his hainous fault:
Then tooke he him, yet trembling sith of late,
And tyde behind his charet, to aggrate
The virgin whom he had abusde so sore;
So drag'd him through the waves in scornfull state,
And after cast him up upon the shore;
But Florimell with him unto his bowre he bore.

xxxvii. His bowre is in the bottom of the maine,
Under a mightie rocke, gainst which doe rave
The roring billowes in their proud disdaine,
That with the angry working of the wave
Therein is eaten out an hollow cave,
That seemes rough Masons hand with engines keene
Had long while laboured it to engrave:
There was his wonne; ne living wight was seene
Save one old Nymph, hight Panopè, to keepe it cleane

xxxviii. Thither he brought the sory Florimell,
And entertained her the best he might,
And Panopè her entertaind eke well,
As an immortall mote a mortall wight,
To winne her liking unto his delight:
With flattering wordes he sweetly wooed her,
And offered faire guiftes t' allure her sight;
But she both offers and the offerer
Despysde, and all the fawning of the flatterer.

XXXIX. Dayly he tempted her with this or that,
    And never suffred her to be at rest;
    But evermore she him refused flat,
    And all his fained kindnes did detest,
    So firmely she had sealed up her brest.
    Sometimes he boasted that a God he hight,
    But she a mortall creature loved best:
    Then he would make him selfe a mortall wight;
    But then she said she lov'd none, but a Faery knight.

XL. Then like a Faerie knight him selfe he drest,
    For every shape on him he could endew;
    Then like a king he was to her exprest,
    And offred kingdoms unto her in vew,
    To be his Leman and his Lady trew:
    But when all this he nothing saw prevaile,
    With harder meanes he cast her to subdew,
    And with sharpe threates her often did assayle;
    So thinking for to make her stubborne corage quayle.

XLI. To dreadfull shapes he did him selfe transforme;
    Now like a Gyaunt; now like to a feend;
    Then like a Centaure; then like to a storme
    Raging within the waves: thereby he weend
    Her will to win unto his wished eend;
    But when with feare, nor favour, nor with all
    He els could doe, he saw him selfe esteemd,
    Downe in a Dongeon deepe he let her fall,
    And threatned there to make her his eternall thrall.

XLII. Eternall thraldome was to her more liefe
    Than losse of chastitie, or chaunge of love:
    Dye had she rather in tormenting griefe
    Then any should of falsenesse her reprove,
    Or loosenes, that she lightly did remove.
    Most vertuous virgin! glory be thy meed,
    And crowne of heavenly prayse with Saintes above,
    Where most sweet hymmes of this thy famous deed
    Are still emongst them song, that far my rymes exceed.

XLIII. Fit song of Angels caroled to bee!
    But yet whatso my feeble Muse can frame
    Shal be t' advance thy goodly chastitee

And to enroll thy memorable name
In th' heart of every honourable Dame,
That they thy vertuous deedes may imitate,
And be partakers of thy endlesse fame.
Yt yrkes me leave thee in this wofull state,
To tell of Satyrane where I him left of late.

XLIV. Who having ended with that Squyre of Dames
A long discourse of his adventures vayne,
The which himselfe then Ladies more defames,
And finding not th' Hyena to be slayne,
With that same Squyre retourned back againe
To his first way.   And, as they forward went,
They spyde a knight fayre pricking on the playne,
As if he were on some adventure bent,
And in his port appeared manly hardiment.

XLV. Sir Satyrane him towardes did addresse,
To weet what wight he was, and what his quest;
And, comming nigh, eftsoones he gan to gesse,
Both by the burning hart which on his brest
He bare, and by the colours in his crest,
That Paridell it was.   Tho to him yode,
And him saluting as beseemed best,
Gan first inquire of tydinges farre abrode,
And afterwardes on what adventure now he rode.

XLVI. Who thereto answering said: " The tydinges bad,
Which now in Faery court all men doe tell,
Which turned hath great mirth to mourning sad,
Is the late ruine of proud Marinell,
And suddein parture of faire Florimell
To find him forth: and after her are gone
All the brave knightes that doen in armes excell
To saveguard her ywandred all alone:
Emongst the rest my lott (unworthy') is to be one."

XLVII. " Ah! gentle knight," (said then Sir Satyrane)
" Thy labour all is lost, I greatly dread,
That hast a thanklesse service on thee ta'ne,
And offrest sacrifice unto the dead:
For dead, I surely doubt, thou maist aread
Henceforth for ever Florimell to bee;

That all the noble knights of Maydenhead,
Which her ador'd, may sore repent with mee,
And all faire Ladies may for ever sory bee."

XLVIII. Which wordes when Paridell had heard, his hew
Gan greatly chaunge and seemd dismaid to bee;
Then said: "Fayre Sir, how may I weene it trew,
That ye doe tell in such uncerteintee?
Or speake ye of report, or did ye see
Just cause of dread, that makes ye doubt so sore?
For, perdie, elles how mote it ever bee,
That ever hand should dare for to engore
Her noble blood?   The hevens such crueltie abhore."

XLIX. "These eyes did see that they will ever rew
T' have seene," (quoth he) "when as a monstrous
     beast
The Palfrey whereon she did travell slew,
And of his bowels made his bloody feast:
Which speaking token sheweth at the least
Her certeine losse, if not her sure decay:
Besides, that more suspicion encreast,
I found her golden girdle cast astray,
Distaynd with durt and blood, as relique of the
     pray."

L. "Ay me!" (said Paridell) "the signes be sadd;
And, but God turne the same to good sooth-say.
That Ladies safetie is sore to be dradd.
Yet will I not forsake my forward way,
Till triall doe more certeine truth bewray."
"Faire Sir," (quoth he) "well may it you succeed!
Ne long shall Satyrane behind you stay,
But to the rest, which in this Quest proceed,
My labour adde, and be partaker of their speed."

LI. "Ye noble knights," (said then the Squyre of Dames)
"Well may yee speede in so praiseworthy payne!
But sith the Sunne now ginnes to slake his beames
In deawy vapours of the westerne mayne,
And lose the teme out of his weary wayne,
Mote not mislike you also to abate
Your zealous hast, till morrow next againe

Both light of heven and strength of men relate:
Which if ye please, to yonder castle turne your gate."

LII. That counsell pleased well: so all yfere
Forth marched to a Castle them before;
Where soone arryving they restrained were
Of ready entraunce, which ought evermore
To errant knights be commune: wondrous sore
Thereat displeasd they were, till that young Squyre
Gan them informe the cause, why that same dore
Was shut to all which lodging did desyre:
The which to let you weet will further time requyre.

CANTO IX

Malbecco will no straunge knights host,
For peevish gealousy.
Paridell giusts with Britomart:
Both shew their auncestry.

I. REDOUBTED knights, and honorable Dames,
To whom I levell all my labours end,
Right sore I feare, least with unworthie blames
This odious argument my rymes should shend,
Or ought your goodly patience offend,
Whiles of a wanton Lady I doe write,
Which with her loose incontinence doth blend
The shyning glory of your soveraine light;
And knighthood fowle defaced by a faithlesse knight.

II. But never let th' ensample of the bad
Offend the good; for good, by paragone
Of evill, may more notably be rad,
As white seemes fayrer macht with blacke attone;
Ne all are shamed by the fault of one:
For lo! in heven, whereas all goodnes is,
Emongst the Angels, a whole legione
Of wicked Sprightes did fall from happy blis;
What wonder then if one, of women all, did mis?

III. Then listen, Lordings, if ye list to weet
The cause why Satyrane and Paridell
Mote not be entertaynd, as seemed meet,
Into that Castle, (as that Squyre does tell.)
"Therein a cancred crabbed Carle does dwell,
That has no skill of Court nor courtesie,
Ne cares what men say of him, ill or well;
For all his dayes he drownes in privitie,
Yet has full large to live and spend at libertie.

IV. "But all his minde is set on mucky pelfe,
To hoord up heapes of evill gotten masse,
For which he others wrongs, and wreckes himselfe:

Yet is he lincked to a lovely lasse,
Whose beauty doth her bounty far surpasse;
The which to him both far unequall yeares,
And also far unlike conditions has;
For she does joy to play emongst her peares,
And to be free from hard restraynt and gealous feares.

v. " But he is old, and withered like hay,
Unfit faire Ladies service to supply;
The privie guilt whereof makes him alway
Suspect her truth, and keepe continuall spy
Upon her with his other blincked eye;
Ne suffreth he resort of living wight
Approch to her, ne keepe her company,
But in close bowre her mewes from all mens sight,
Depriv'd of kindly joy and naturall delight.

vi. " Malbecco he, and Hellenore she hight;
Unfitly yokt together in one teeme.
That is the cause why never any knight
Is suffred here to enter, but he seeme
Such as no doubt of him he neede misdeeme."
Thereat Sir Satyrane gan smyle, and say;
" Extremely mad the man I surely deeme,
That weenes with watch and hard restraynt to sta
A womans will, which is disposed to go astray.

vii. " In vaine he feares that which he cannot shonne;
For who wotes not, that womans subtiltyes
Can guylen Argus, when she list misdonne?
It is not yron bandes, nor hundred eyes,
Nor brasen walls, nor many wakefull spyes,
That can withhold her wilfull wandring feet;
But fast goodwill, with gentle courtesyes,
And timely service to her pleasures meet,
May her perhaps containe, that else would algates fleet."

viii. " Then is he not more mad," (sayd Paridell)
" That hath himselfe unto such service sold,
In dolefull thraldome all his dayes to dwell?
For sure a foole I doe him firmely hold,
That loves his fetters, though they were of gold.
But why doe wee devise of others ill,

Whyles thus we suffer this same dotard old
To keepe us out in scorne, of his owne will,
And rather do not ransack all, and him selfe kill? "

IX. " Nay, let us first " (sayd Satyrane) " entreat
The man by gentle meanes to let us in,
And afterwardes affray with cruell threat,
Ere that we to efforce it doe begin:
Then, if all fayle, we will by force it win,
And eke reward the wretch for his mesprise,
As may be worthy of his haynous sin."
That counsell pleasd: then Paridell did rise
And to the Castle gate approcht in quiet wise.

X. Whereat soft knocking entrance he desyrd.
The good man selfe, which then the Porter playd,
Him answered, that all were now retyrd
Unto their rest, and all the keyes convayd
Unto their maister, who in bed was layd,
That none him durst awake out of his dreme;
And therefore them of patience gently prayd.
Then Paridell began to chaunge his theme,
And threatned him with force and punishment extreme:

XI. But all in vaine, for nought mote him relent.
And now so long before the wicket fast
They wayted, that the night was forward spent,
And the faire welkin fowly overcast
Gan blowen up a bitter stormy blast,
With showre and hayle so horrible and dred,
That this faire many were compeld at last
To fly for succour to a little shed,
The which beside the gate for swyne was ordered.

XII. It fortuned, soone after they were gone,
Another knight, whom tempest thither brought,
Came to that Castle, and with earnest mone,
Like as the rest, late entrance deare besought:
But, like so as the rest, he prayd for nought;
For flatly he of entrance was refusd.
Sorely thereat he was displeased, and thought
How to avenge himselfe so sore abusd,
And evermore the Carle of courtesie accusd.

XIII. But, to avoyde th' intollerable stowre,
　　　He was compeld to seeke some refuge neare,
　　　And to that shed, to shrowd him from the showre,
　　　He came, which full of guests he found whyleare,
　　　So as he was not let to enter there:
　　　Whereat he gan to wex exceeding wroth,
　　　And swore that he would lodge with them yfere,
　　　Or them dislodge, all were they liefe or loth;
　　　And so defyde them each, and so defyde them both.

XIV. Both were full loth to leave that needfull tent,
　　　And both full loth in darkenesse to debate;
　　　Yet both full liefe him lodging to have lent,
　　　And both full liefe his boasting to abate:
　　　But chiefely Paridell his hart did grate
　　　To heare him threaten so despightfully,
　　　As if he did a dogge in kenell rate
　　　That durst not barke; and rather had he dy
　　　Then, when he was defyde, in coward corner ly.

XV. Tho hastily remounting to his steed
　　　He forth issew'd: like as a boystrous winde,
　　　Which in th' earthes hollow caves hath long ben hid
　　　And shut up fast within her prisons blind,
　　　Makes the huge element, against her kinde,
　　　To move and tremble as it were aghast,
　　　Untill that it an issew forth may finde:
　　　Then forth it breakes, and with his furious blast
　　　Confounds both land and seas, and skyes doth overcast.

XVI. Their steel-hed speares they strongly coucht, and met
　　　Together with impetuous rage and forse,
　　　That with the terrour of their fierce affret
　　　They rudely drove to ground both man and horse,
　　　That each awhile lay like a sencelesse corse.
　　　But Paridell sore brused with the blow
　　　Could not arise the counterchaunge to scorse,
　　　Till that young Squyre him reared from below;
　　　Then drew he his bright sword, and gan about him throw.

XVII. But Satyrane forth stepping did them stay,
　　　And with faire treaty pacifide their yre.
　　　Then, when they were accorded from the fray,

Against that Castles Lord they gan conspire,
To heape on him dew vengeaunce for his hire.
They beene agreed; and to the gates they goe
To burn the same with unquenchable fire,
And that uncurteous Carle, their commune foe,
To doe fowle death to die, or wrap in grievous woe.

XVIII. Malbecco, seeing them resolvd indeed
To flame the gates, and hearing them to call
For fire in earnest, ran with fearfull speed,
And to them calling from the castle wall,
Besought them humbly him to beare withall,
As ignorant of servants bad abuse
And slacke attendaunce unto straungers call.
The knights were willing all things to excuse,
Though nought belev'd, and entraunce late did not refuse.

XIX. They beene ybrought into a comely bowre,
And servd of all things that mote needfull bee;
Yet secretly their hoste did on them lowre,
And welcomde more for feare then charitee;
But they dissembled what they did not see,
And welcomed themselves.   Each gan undight
Their garments wett, and weary armour free,
To dry them selves by Vulcanes flaming light,
And eke their lately bruzed parts to bring in plight.

XX. And eke that straunger knight emongst the rest
Was for like need enforst to disaray:
Tho, whenas vailed was her lofty crest,
Her golden locks, that were in trammells gay
Upbounden, did them selves adowne display
And raught unto her heeles; like sunny beames,
That in a cloud their light did long time stay,
Their vapour vaded, shewe their golden gleames,
And through the persant aire shoote forth their azure
     streames.

XXI. Shee also dofte her heavy haberjeon,
Which the faire feature of her limbs did hyde;
And her well-plighted frock, which she did won
To tucke about her short when she did ryde,
Shee low let fall, that flowd from her lanck syde
Downe to her foot with carelesse modestee.

Then of them all she plainly was espyde
To be a woman-wight, unwist to bee,
The fairest woman-wight that ever eie did see.

xxii. Like as Bellona (being late returnd
From slaughter of the Giaunts conquered;
Where proud Encelade, whose wide nosethrils burnd
With breathed flames, like to a furnace redd,
Transfixed with her speare downe tombled dedd
From top of Hemus by him heaped hye:)
Hath loosd her helmet from her lofty hedd,
And her Gorgonian shield gins to untye
From her lefte arme, to rest in glorious victorye.

xxiii. Which whenas they beheld, they smitten were
With great amazement of so wondrous sight;
And each on other, and they all on her,
Stood gazing, as if suddein great affright
Had them surprized. At last, avizing right
Her goodly personage and glorious hew,
Which they so much mistooke, they tooke delight
In their first error, and yett still anew
With wonder of her beauty fed their hongry vew.

xxiv. Yet note their hongry vew be satisfide,
But seeing still the more desir'd to see,
And ever firmely fixed did abide
In contemplation of divinitee:
But most they mervaild at her chevalree
And noble prowesse, which they had approv'd,
That much they faynd to know who she mote bee;
Yet none of all them her thereof amov'd
Yet every one her likte, and every one her lov'd.

xxv. And Paridell, though partly discontent
With his late fall and fowle indignity,
Yet was soone wonne his malice to relent,
Through gratious regard of her faire eye,
And knightly worth which he too late did try,
Yet tried did adore. Supper was dight;
Then they Malbecco prayd of courtesy,
That of his lady they might have the sight
And company at meat, to doe them more delight.

XXVI. But he, to shifte their curious request,
Gan causen why she could not come in place;
Her crased helth, her late recourse to rest,
And humid evening ill for sicke folkes cace;
But none of those excuses could take place,
Ne would they eate till she in presence came.
Shee came in presence with right comely grace,
And fairely them saluted, as became,
And shewd her selfe in all a gentle courteous Dame.

XXVII. They sat to meat; and Satyrane his chaunce
Was her before, and Paridell beside;
But he him selfe sate looking still askaunce
Gainst Britomart, and ever closely eide
Sir Satyrane, that glaunces might not glide:
But his blinde eie, that sided Paridell,
All his demeasnure from his sight did hide:
On her faire face so did he feede his fill,
And sent close messages of love to her at will.

XXVIII. And ever and anone, when none was ware,
With speaking lookes, that close embassage bore,
He rov'd at her, and told his secret care
For all that art he learned had of yore;
Ne was she ignoraunt of that leud lore,
But in his eye his meaning wisely redd,
And with the like him aunswerd evermore.
Shee sent at him one fyrie dart, whose hedd
Empoisned was with privy lust and gealous dredd.

XXIX. He from that deadly throw made no defence,
But to the wound his weake heart opened wyde:
The wicked engine through false influence
Past through his eies, and secretly did glyde
Into his heart, which it did sorely gryde.
But nothing new to him was that same paine,
Ne paine at all; for he so ofte had tryde
The powre thereof, and lov'd so oft in vaine,
That thing of course he counted love to entertaine.

XXX. Thenceforth to her he sought to intimate
His inward griefe, by meanes to him well knowne:
Now Bacchus fruit out of the silver plate

He on the table dasht, as overthrowne,
Or of the fruitfull liquor overflowne;
And by the dauncing bubbles did divine,
Or therein write to lett his love be showne;
Which well she redd out of the learned line;
A sacrament prophane in mistery of wine.

XXXI. And, when so of his hand the pledge she raught,
The guilty cup she fained to mistake,
And in her lap did shed her idle draught,
Shewing desire her inward flame to slake.
But such close signes they secret way did make
Unto their wils, and one eies watch escape:
Two eies him needeth, for to watch and wake,
Who lovers will deceive.   Thus was the ape,
By their faire handling, put into Malbeccoes cape.

XXXII. Now, when of meats and drinks they had their fill,
Purpose was moved by that gentle Dame
Unto those knights adventurous, to tell
Of deeds of armes which unto them became,
And every one his kindred and his name.
Then Paridell, in whom a kindly pride
Of gratious speach and skill his words to frame
Abounded, being glad of so fitte tide
Him to commend to her, thus spake, of al well eide.

XXXIII. " Troy, that art now nought but an idle name,
And in thine ashes buried low dost lie,
Though whilome far much greater then thy fame,
Before that angry Gods and cruell skie
Upon thee heapt a direfull destinie;
What boots it boast thy glorious descent,
And fetch from heven thy great genealogie,
Sith all thy worthie prayses being blent
Their ofspring hath embaste, and later glory shent?

XXXIV. " Most famous Worthy of the world, by whome
That warre was kindled which did Troy inflame,
And stately towres of Ilion whilome
Brought unto balefull ruine, was by name
Sir Paris far renowmd through noble fame;
Who, through great prowesse and bold hardinesse,

From Lacedæmon fetcht the fayrest Dame
That ever Greece did boast, or knight possesse,
Whom Venus to him gave for meed of worthinesse;

xxxv. " Fayre Helene, flowre of beautie excellent,
And girlond of the mighty Conquerours,
That madest many Ladies deare lament
The heavie losse of their brave Paramours,
Which they far off beheld from Trojan toures,
And saw the fieldes of faire Scamander strowne
With carcases of noble warrioures
Whose fruitlesse lives were under furrow sowne,
And Xanthus sandy bankes with blood all overflowne.

xxxvi. " From him my linage I derive aright,
Who long before the ten yeares siege of Troy,
Whiles yet on Ida he a shepeheard hight,
On faire Oenone got a lovely boy,
Whom, for remembrance of her passed joy,
She, of his Father, Parius did name;
Who, after Greekes did Priams realme destroy,
Gathred the Trojan reliques sav'd from flame,
And with them sayling thence to th' isle of Paros came.

xxxvii. " That was by him cald Paros, which before
Hight Nausa: there he many yeares did raine,
And built Nausicle by the Pontick shore;
The which he dying lefte next in remaine
To Paridas his sonne,
From whom I Paridell by kin descend:
But, for faire ladies love and glories gaine,
My native soile have lefte, my dayes to spend
In seewing deeds of armes, my lives and labors end.'

xxxviii. Whenas the noble Britomart heard tell
Of Trojan warres and Priams citie sackt,
The ruefull story of Sir Paridell,
She was empassiond at that piteous act,
With zelous envy of Greekes cruell fact
Against that nation, from whose race of old
She heard that she was lineally extract;
For noble Britons sprong from Trojans bold,
And Troynovant was built of old Troyes ashes cold.

XXXIX. Then, sighing soft awhile, at last she thus:
  " O lamentable fall of famous towne!
  Which raignd so many yearés victorious,
  And of all Asie bore the soveraine crowne,
  In one sad night consumd and throwen downe:
  What stony hart, that heares thy haplesse fate,
  Is not empierst with deepe compassiowne,
  And makes ensample of mans wretched state,
  That floures so fresh at morne, and fades at evening
   late?

 XL. " Behold, Sir, how your pitifull complaint
  Hath fownd another partner of your payne;
  For nothing may impresse so deare constraint
  As countries cause, and commune foes disdayne.
  But if it should not grieve you backe agayne
  To turne your course, I would to heare desyre
  What to Aeneas fell; sith that men sayne
  He was not in the cities wofull fyre
  Consum'd, but did him selfe to safety retyre."

 XLI. " Anchyses sonne, begott of Venus fayre,"
  Said he, " out of the flames for safegard fled,
  And with a remnant did to sea repayre;
  Where he through fatall errour long was led
  Full many yeares, and weetlesse wandered
  From shore to shore emongst the Lybick sandes,
  Ere rest he fownd. Much there he suffered,
  And many perilles past in forreine landes,
  To save his people sad from victours vengefull handes.

 XLII. " At last in Latium he did arryve,
  Where he with cruell warre was entertaind
  Of th' inland folke, which sought him backe to drive,
  Till he with old Latinus was constraind
  To contract wedlock, (so the fates ordaind)
  Wedlocke contract in blood, and eke in blood
  Accomplished, that many deare complaind:
  The rivall slaine, the victour, through the flood
  Escaped hardly, hardly praisd his wedlock good.

 XLIII. " Yet, after all, he victour did survive,
  And with Latinus did the kingdom part;

But after, when both nations gan to strive
Into their names the title to convart,
His sonne Iülus did from thence depart
With all the warlike youth of Trojans bloud,
And in long Alba plast his throne apart;
Where faire it florished and long time stoud,
Till Romulus, renewing it, to Rome remoud."

XLIV. " There; there," (said Britomart) " afresh appeard
The glory of the later world to spring,
And Troy againe out of her dust was reard
To sitt in second seat of soveraine king
Of all the world, under her governing.
But a third kingdom yet is to arise
Out of the Trojans scattered ofspring,
That in all glory and great enterprise,
Both first and second Troy shall dare to equalise.

XLV. " It Troynovant is hight, that with the waves
Of wealthy Thamis washed is along,
Upon whose stubborne neck, (whereat he raves
With roring rage, and sore him selfe does throng)
That all men feare to tempt his billowes strong,
She fastned hath her foot; which stands so hy,
That it a wonder of the world is song
In forreine landes; and all which passen by,
Beholding it from farre, doe thinke it threates the skye.

XLVI. " The Trojan Brute did first that citie fownd,
And Hygate made the meare thereof by West,
And Overt gate by North: that is the bownd
Toward the land; two rivers bownd the rest.
So huge a scope at first him seemed best,
To be the compasse of his kingdomes seat:
So huge a mind could not in lesser rest,
Ne in small meares containe his glory great,
That Albion had conquered first by warlike feat."

XLVII. " Ah! fairest Lady knight," (said Paridell)
" Pardon, I pray, my heedlesse oversight,
Who had forgot that whylome I heard tell
From aged Mnemon; for my wits beene light.
Indeed he said, (if I remember right)

That of the antique Trojan stocke there grew
Another plant, that raught to wondrous hight,
And far abroad his mightie braunches threw
Into the utmost Angle of the world he knew.

XLVIII. " For that same Brute, whom much he did advaunce
In all his speach, was Sylvius his sonne,
Whom having slain through luckles arrowes glaunce,
He fled for feare of that he had misdonne,
Or els for shame, so fowle reproch to shonne,
And with him ledd to sea an youthly trayne;
Where wearie wandring they long time did wonne,
And many fortunes prov'd in th' Ocean mayne,
And great adventures found, that now were long to
sayne.

XLIX. " At last by fatall course they driven were
Into an Island spatious and brode,
The furthest North that did to them appeare:
Which, after rest, they, seeking farre abrode,
Found it the fittest soyle for their abode,
Fruitfull of all thinges fitt for living foode,
But wholy waste and void of peoples trode,
Save an huge nation of the Geaunts broode
That fed on living flesh, and dronck mens vitall blood.

L. " Whom he, through wearie wars and labours long,
Subdewd with losse of many Britons bold:
In which the great Goemagot of strong
Corineus, and Coulin of Debon old,
Were overthrowne and laide on th' earth full cold,
Which quaked under their so hideous masse;
A famous history to bee enrold
In everlasting moniments of brasse,
That all the antique Worthies merits far did passe.

LI. " His worke great Troynovant, his worke is eke
Faire Lincolne, both renowmed far away;
That who from East to West will endlong seeke,
Cannot two fairer Cities find this day,
Except Cleopolis: so heard I say
Old Mnemon.   Therefore, Sir, I greet you well
Your countrey kin; and you entyrely pray

Of pardon for the strife, which late befell
Betwixt us both unknowne." So ended Paridell.

LII. But all the while that he these speeches spent,
Upon his lips hong faire Dame Hellenore
With vigilant regard and dew attent,
Fashioning worldes of fancies evermore
In her fraile witt, that now her quite forlore:
The whiles unwares away her wondring eye
And greedy eares her weake hart from her bore;
Which he perceiving, ever privily,
In speaking many false belgardes at her let fly.

LIII. So long these knights discoursed diversly
Of straunge affaires, and noble hardiment,
Which they had past with mickle jeopardy,
That now the humid night was farforth spent,
And hevenly lampes were halfendeale ybrent:
Which th' old man seeing wel, who too long thought
Every discourse, and every argument,
Which by the houres he measured, besought
Them go to rest. So all unto their bowres were brought.

CANTO X

Paridell rapeth Hellenore:
Malbecco her poursewes:
Fynds emongst Satyres, whence with him
To turne she doth refuse.

I. THE morow next, so soone as Phœbus Lamp
Bewrayed had the world with early light,
And fresh Aurora had the shady damp
Out of the goodly heven amoved quight,
Faire Britomart and that same Faery knight
Uprose, forth on their journey for to wend:
But Paridell complaynd, that his late fight
With Britomart so sore did him offend,
That ryde he could not, till his hurts he did amend.

II. So foorth they far'd; but he behind them stayd,
Maulgre his host, who grudged grievously
To house a guest that would be needes obayd,
And of his owne him lefte not liberty:
Might wanting measure moveth surquedry.
Two things he feared, but the third was death;
That fiers youngmans unruly maystery;
His money, which he lov'd as living breath;
And his faire wife, whom honest long he kept uneath.

III. But patience perforce, he must abie
What fortune and his fate on him will lay;
Fond is the feare that findes no remedie:
Yet warily he watcheth every way,
By which he feareth evill happen may;
So th' evill thinkes by watching to prevent:
Ne doth he suffer her, nor night nor day,
Out of his sight her selfe once to absent:
So doth he punish her, and eke him selfe torment.

IV. But Paridell kept better watch then hee,
A fit occasion for his turne to finde.
False love! why do men say thou canst not see,

And in their foolish fancy feigne thee blinde,
That with thy charmes the sharpest sight doest binde,
And to thy will abuse? Thou walkest free,
And seest every secret of the minde;
Thou seest all, yet none at all sees thee:
All that is by the working of thy Deitee.

v. So perfect in that art was Paridell,
That he Malbeccoes halfen eye did wyle;
His halfen eye he wiled wondrous well,
And Hellenors both eyes did eke beguyle,
Both eyes and hart attonce, during the whyle
That he there sojourned his woundes to heale;
That Cupid selfe, it seeing, close did smyle
To weet how he her love away did steale,
And bad that none their joyous treason should reveale.

vi. The learned lover lost no time nor tyde
That least avantage mote to him afford,
Yet bore so faire a sayle, that none espyde
His secret drift, till he her layd abord.
When so in open place and commune bord
He fortun'd her to meet, with commune speach
He courted her; yet bayted every word,
That his ungentle hoste n'ote him appeach
Of vile ungentlenesse, or hospitages breach.

vii. But when apart (if ever her apart)
He found, then his false engins fast he plyde,
And all the sleights unbosomd in his hart:
He sigh'd, he sobd, he swownd, he perdy dyde,
And cast himselfe on ground her fast besyde:
Tho, when againe he him bethought to live,
He wept, and wayld, and false laments belyde,
Saying, but if she Mercie would him give,
That he mote algates dye, yet did his death forgive.

viii. And otherwhyles with amorous delights
And pleasing toyes he would her entertaine;
Now singing sweetly to surprize her sprights,
Now making layes of love and lovers paine,
Bransles, Ballads, virelayes, and verses vaine;
Oft purposes, oft riddles, he devysd,

And thousands like which flowed in his braine,
With which he fed her fancy, and entysd
To take to his new love, and leave her old despysd.

IX. And every where he might, and everie while,
He did her service dewtifull, and sewd
At hand with humble pride and pleasing guile;
So closely yet, that none but she it vewd,
Who well perceived all, and all indewd.
Thus finely did he his false nets dispred,
With which he many weake harts had subdewd
Of yore, and many had ylike misled:
What wonder then, if she were likewise carried?

X. No fort so fensible, no wals so strong,
But that continuall battery will rive,
Or daily siege, through dispurvayaunce long
And lacke of reskewes, will to parley drive;
And Peece, that unto parley eare will give,
Will shortly yield it selfe, and will be made
The vassall of the victors will bylive:
That stratageme had oftentimes assayd
This crafty Paramoure, and now it plaine display'd:

XI. For through his traines he her intrapped hath,
That she her love and hart hath wholy sold
To him, without regard of gaine or scath,
Or care of credite, or of husband old,
Whom she hath vow'd to dub a fayre Cucquold.
Nought wants but time and place, which shortly shee
Devized hath, and to her lover told.
It pleased well: So well they both agree:
So readie rype to ill ill wemens counsels bee!

XII. Darke was the Evening, fit for lovers stealth,
When chaunst Malbecco busie be elsewhere,
She to his closet went, where all his wealth
Lay hid; thereof she countlesse summes did reare,
The which she meant away with her to beare;
The rest she fyr'd, for sport, or for despight:
As Hellene, when she saw aloft appeare
The Trojane flames and reach to hevens hight,
Did clap her hands, and joyed at that dolefull sight.

XIII. This second Helene, fayre Dame Hellenore,
The whiles her husband ran with sory haste
To quench the flames which she had tyn'd before,
Laught at his foolish labour spent in waste,
And ran into her lovers armes right fast;
Where streight embraced she to him did cry
And call alowd for helpe, ere helpe were past;
For lo! that Guest did beare her forcibly,
And meant to ravish her, that rather had to dy.

XIV. The wretched man hearing her call for ayd,
And ready seeing him with her to fly,
In his disquiet mind was much dismayd:
But when againe he backeward cast his eye,
And saw the wicked fire so furiously
Consume his hart, and scorch his Idoles face,
He was therewith distressed diversely,
Ne wist he how to turne, nor to what place:
Was never wretched man in such a wofull cace.

XV. Ay when to him she cryde, to her he turnd,
And left the fire; love money overcame:
But, when he marked how his money burnd,
He left his wife; money did love disclame:
Both was he loth to loose his loved Dame,
And loth to leave his liefest pelfe behinde;
Yet, sith he n'ote save both, he sav'd that same
Which was the dearest to his dounghill minde,
The God of his desire, the joy of misers blinde.

XVI. Thus whilest all things in troublous uprore were,
And all men busie to suppresse the flame,
The loving couple neede no reskew feare,
But leasure had and liberty to frame
Their purpost flight, free from all mens reclame;
And Night, the patronesse of love-stealth fayre,
Gave them safe conduct, till to end they came.
So beene they gone yfere, a wanton payre
Of lovers loosely knit, where list them to repayre.

XVII. Soone as the cruell flames yslaked were,
Malbecco, seeing how his losse did lye,
Out of the flames which he had quencht whylere,

Into huge waves of griefe and gealosye
Full deepe emplonged was, and drowned nye
Twixt inward doole and felonous despight:
He rav'd, he wept, he stampt, he lowd did cry,
And all the passions that in man may light
Did him attonce oppresse, and vex his caytive spright.

XVIII. Long thus he chawd the cud of inward griefe,
And did consume his gall with anguish sore:
Still when he mused on his late mischiefe,
Then still the smart thereof increased more,
And seemd more grievous then it was before.
At last when sorrow he saw booted nought,
Ne griefe might not his love to him restore,
He gan devise how her he reskew mought:
Ten thousand wayes he cast in his confused thought.

XIX. At last resolving, like a Pilgrim pore,
To search her forth where so she might be fond,
And bearing with him treasure in close store,
The rest he leaves in ground: So takes in hond
To seeke her endlong both by sea and lond.
Long he her sought, he sought her far and nere,
And every where that he mote understond
Of knights and ladies any meetings were;
And of each one he mett he tidings did inquere.

XX. But all in vaine: his woman was too wise
Ever to come into his clouch againe,
And hee too simple ever to surprise
The jolly Paridell, for all his paine.
One day, as hee forpassed by the plaine
With weary pace, he far away espide
A couple, seeming well to be his twaine,
Which hoved close under a forest side,
As if they lay in wait, or els them selves did hide.

XXI. Well weened hee that those the same mote bee;
And as he better did their shape avize,
Him seemed more their maner did agree;
For th' one was armed all in warlike wize,
Whom to be Paridell he did devize;
And th' other, al yclad in garments light

Discolourd like to womanish disguise,
He did resemble to his lady bright;
And ever his faint hart much earned at the sight:

XXII. And ever faine he towards them would goe,
But yet durst not for dread approchen nie,
But stood aloofe, unweeting what to doe;
Till that prickt forth with loves extremity
That is the father of fowle gealosy,
He closely nearer crept the truth to weet:
But, as he nigher drew, he easily
Might scerne that it was not his sweetest sweet,
Ne yet her Belamour, the partner of his sheet:

XXIII. But it was scornefull Braggadochio,
That with his servant Trompart hoverd there,
Sith late he fled from his too earnest foe:
Whom such whenas Malbecco spyed clere,
He turned backe, and would have fled arere,
Till Trompart, ronning hastely, him did stay,
And bad before his soveraine Lord appere.
That was him loth, yet durst he not gainesay,
And comming him before low louted on the lay.

XXIV. The boaster at him sternely bent his browe,
As if he could have kild him with his looke,
That to the ground him meekely made to bowe,
And awfull terror deepe into him strooke,
That every member of his body quooke.
Said he, " Thou man of nought, what doest thou here
Unfitly furnisht with thy bag and booke,
Where I expected one with shield and spere
To prove some deeds of armes upon an equall pere? "

XXV. The wretched man at his imperious speach
Was all abasht, and low prostrating said:
" Good Sir, let not my rudenes be no breach
Unto your patience, ne be ill ypaid;
For I unwares this way by fortune straid,
A silly Pilgrim driven to distresse,
That seeke a Lady "—There he suddein staid,
And did the rest with grievous sighes suppresse,
While teares stood in his eies, few drops of bitternesse.

xxvi. "What Lady, man?" (said Trompart) "take good hart,
  And tell thy griefe, if any hidden lye:
  Was never better time to shew thy smart
  Then now that noble succor is thee by,
  That is the whole worlds commune remedy."
  That chearful word his weak heart much did cheare,
  And with vaine hope his spirits faint supply,
  That bold he sayd; "O most redoubted Pere!
  Vouchsafe with mild regard a wretches cace to heare."

xxvii. Then sighing sore, "It is not long," (saide hee)
  "Sith I enjoyd the gentlest Dame alive;
  Of whom a knight, no knight at all perdee,
  But shame of all that doe for honor strive,
  By treacherous deceipt did me deprive:
  Through open outrage he her bore away,
  And with fowle force unto his will did drive;
  Which al good knights, that armes doe bear this day,
  Are bownd for to revenge, and punish if they may.

xxviii. "And you, most noble Lord, that can and dare
  Redresse the wrong of miserable wight,
  Cannot employ your most victorious speare
  In better quarell then defence of right,
  And for a Lady gainst a faithlesse knight:
  So shall your glory bee advaunced much,
  And all faire Ladies magnify your might,
  And eke my selfe, albee I simple such,
  Your worthy paine shall wel reward with guerdon rich."

xxix. With that out of his bouget forth he drew
  Great store of treasure, therewith him to tempt;
  But he on it lookt scornefully askew,
  As much disdeigning to be so misdempt,
  Or a war-monger to be basely nempt;
  And sayd; "Thy offers base I greatly loth,
  And eke thy words uncourteous and unkempt:
  I tread in dust thee and thy money both,
  That, were it not for shame"—So turned from him
    wroth.

xxx. But Trompart, that his maistres humor knew
  In lofty looks to hide an humble minde,
  Was inly tickled with that golden vew.

And in his eare him rownded close behinde:
Yet stoupt he not, but lay still in the winde,
Waiting advauntage on the pray to sease,
Till Trompart, lowly to the grownd inclinde,
Besought him his great corage to appease,
And pardon simple man that rash did him displease.

XXXI. Big looking like a doughty Doucepere,
At last he thus; " Thou clod of vilest clay,
I pardon yield, and with thy rudenes beare;
But weete henceforth, that all that golden pray,
And all that els the vaine world vaunten may,
I loath as doung, ne deeme my dew reward:
Fame is my meed, and glory vertues pay:
But minds of mortall men are muchell mard
And mov'd amisse with massy mucks unmeet regard.

XXXII. " And more: I graunt to thy great misery
Gratious respect; thy wife shall backe be sent:
And that vile knight, who ever that he bee,
Which hath thy lady reft and knighthood shent,
By Sanglamort my sword, whose deadly dent
The blood hath of so many thousands shedd,
I sweare, ere long shall dearely it repent;
Ne he twixt heven and earth shall hide his hedd,
But soone he shal be fownd, and shortly doen be dedd."

XXXIII. The foolish man thereat woxe wondrous blith,
As if the word so spoken were halfe donne,
And humbly thanked him a thousand sith
That had from death to life him newly wonne.
Tho forth the Boaster marching brave begonne
His stolen steed to thunder furiously,
As if he heaven and hell would over-ronne,
And all the world confound with cruelty;
That much Malbecco joyed in his jollity.

XXXIV. Thus long they three together traveiled,
Through many an wood and many an uncouth way,
To seeke his wife that was far wandered:
But those two sought not but the present pray,
To weete, the treasure which he did bewray,
On which their eies and harts were wholly sett,

With purpose how they might it best betray;
For, sith the howre that first he did them lett
The same behold, therwith their keene desires were
        whett.

XXXV. It fortuned, as they together far'd,
They spide where Paridell came pricking fast
Upon the plaine; the which him selfe prepar'd
To guist with that brave straunger knight a cast,
As on adventure by the way he past,
Alone he rode without his Paragone;
For, having filcht her bells, her up he cast
To the wide world, and lett her fly alone:
He nould be clogd.   So had he served many one.

XXXVI. The gentle Lady, loose at randon lefte,
The greene-wood long did walke, and wander wide
At wilde adventure, like a forlorne wefte;
Till on a day the Satyres her espide
Straying alone withouten groome or guide:
Her up they tooke, and with them home her ledd,
With them as housewife ever to abide,
To milk their gotes, and make them cheese and bredd;
And every one as commune good her handeled

XXXVII. That shortly she Malbecco has forgott,
And eke Sir Paridell, all were he deare;
Who from her went to seeke another lott,
And now by fortune was arrived here,
Where those two guilers with Malbecco were.
Soone as the old man saw Sir Paridell,
He fainted, and was almost dead with feare,
Ne word he had to speake his gricfe to tell,
But to him louted low, and greeted goodly well;

XXXVIII. And, after, asked him for Hellenore:
" I take no keepe of her," (sayd Paridell)
" She wonneth in the forrest there before."
So forth he rode as his adventure fell;
The whiles the Boaster from his loftie sell
Faynd to alight, something amisse to mend;
But the fresh Swayne would not his leasure dwell,
But went his way: whom when he passed kend,
He up remounted light, and after faind to wend.

XXXIX. "Perdy, nay," (said Malbecco) " shall ye not;
　　　　But let him passe as lightly as he came:
　　　　For litle good of him is to be got,
　　　　And mickle perill to bee put to shame.
　　　　But let us goe to seeke my dearest Dame,
　　　　Whom he hath left in yonder forest wyld;
　　　　For of her safety in great doubt I ame,
　　　　Least salvage beastes her person have despoyld:
　　　　Then all the world is lost, and we in vaine have toyld."

XL. They all agree, and forward them addresse:
　　　" Ah! but," (said crafty Trompart) " weete ye well,
　　　That yonder in that wastefull wildernesse
　　　Huge monsters haunt, and many dangers dwell;
　　　Dragons, and Minotaures, and feendes of hell,
　　　And many wilde woodmen which robbe and rend
　　　All traveilers: therefore advise ye well
　　　Before ye enterprise that way to wend:
　　　One may his journey bring too soone to evill end."

XLI. Malbecco stopt in great astonishment,
　　　And with pale eyes fast fixed on the rest,
　　　Their counsell crav'd in daunger imminent.
　　　Said Trompart; " You, that are the most opprest
　　　With burdein of great treasure, I thinke best
　　　Here for to stay in safetie behynd:
　　　My Lord and I will search the wide forest."
　　　That counsell pleased not Malbeccoes mynd,
　　　For he was much afraid him selfe alone to fynd.

XLII. " Then is it best," (said he) " that ye doe leave
　　　Your treasure here in some security,
　　　Either fast closed in some hollow greave,
　　　Or buried in the ground from jeopardy,
　　　Till we returne againe in safety:
　　　As for us two, least doubt of us ye have,
　　　Hence farre away we will blyndfolded ly,
　　　Ne privy bee unto your treasures grave."
　　　It pleased; so he did.   Then they march forward brave.

XLIII. Now, when amid the thickest woodes they were,
　　　They heard a noyse of many bagpipes shrill,
　　　And shrieking Hububs them approching nere,
　　　Which all the forest did with horrour fill.

That dreadfull sound the bosters hart did thrill
With such amazment, that in hast he fledd,
Ne ever looked back for good or ill;
And after him eke fearefull Trompart spedd:
The old man could not fly, but fell to ground half dedd.

XLIV. Yet afterwardes, close creeping as he might,
He in a bush did hyde his fearefull hedd.
The jolly Satyres, full of fresh delight,
Came dauncing forth, and with them nimbly ledd
Faire Helenore with girlonds all bespredd,
Whom their May-lady they had newly made:
She, proude of that new honour which they redd,
And of their lovely fellowship full glade,
Daunst lively, and her face did with a Lawrell shade.

XLV. The silly man that in the thickett lay
Saw all this goodly sport, and grieved sore;
Yet durst he not against it doe or say,
But did his hart with bitter thoughts engore,
To see th' unkindnes of his Hellenore.
All day they daunced with great lusty-hedd,
And with their horned feet the greene gras wore,
The whiles their Gotes upon the brouzes fedd,
Till drouping Phœbus gan to hyde his golden hedd.

XLVI. Tho up they gan their mery pypes to trusse,
And all their goodly heardes did gather rownd;
But every Satyre first did give a busse
To Hellenore; so busses did abound.
Now gan the humid vapour shed the grownd
With perly deaw, and th' Earthes gloomy shade
Did dim the brightnesse of the welkin rownd,
That every bird and beast awarned made
To shrowd themselves, whiles sleepe their sences did invade.

XLVII. Which when Malbecco saw, out of the bush
Upon his handes and feete he crept full light,
And like a Gote emongst the Gotes did rush;
That, through the helpe of his faire hornes on hight,
And misty dampe of misconceyving night,
And eke through likenesse of his gotish beard,
He did the better counterfeite aright:
So home he marcht emongst the horned heard,
That none of all the Satyres him espyde or heard.

XLVIII. At night, when all they went to sleepe, he vewd
Whereas his lovely wife emongst them lay,
Embraced of a Satyre rough and rude,
Who all the night did minde his joyous play:
Nine times he heard him come aloft ere day,
That all his hart with gealosy did swell;
But yet that nights ensample did bewray
That not for nought his wife them loved so well,
When one so oft a night did ring his matins bell.

XLIX. So closely as he could he to them crept,
When wearie of their sport to sleepe they fell,
And to his wife, that now full soundly slept,
He whispered in her eare, and did her tell
That it was he which by her side did dwell;
And therefore prayd her wake to heare him plaine.
As one out of a dreame not waked well
She turnd her, and returned back againe;
Yet her for to awake he did the more constraine.

L. At last with irkesom trouble she abrayd;
And then perceiving that it was indeed
Her old Malbecco, which did her upbrayd
With loosenesse of her love and loathly deed,
She was astonisht with exceeding dreed,
And would have wakt the Satyre by her syde;
But he her prayd, for mercy or for meed,
To save his life, ne let him be descryde,
But hearken to his lore, and all his counsell hyde.

LI. Tho gan he her perswade to leave that lewd
And loathsom life, of God and man abhord,
And home returne, where all should be renewd
With perfect peace and bandes of fresh accord,
And she receivd againe to bed and bord,
As if no trespas ever had beene donne:
But she it all refused at one word,
And by no meanes would to his will be wonne,
But chose emongst the jolly Satyres still to wonne.

LII. He wooed her till day-spring he espyde,
But all in vaine; and then turnd to the heard,
Who butted him with hornes on every syde,

And trode downe in the durt, where his hore beard
Was fowly dight, and he of death afeard.
Early, before the heavens fairest light
Out of the ruddy East was fully reard,
The heardes out of their foldes were loosed quight,
And he emongst the rest crept forth in sory plight.

LIII.   So soone as he the Prison-dore did pas,
He ran as fast as both his feet could beare,
And never looked who behind him was,
Ne scarsely who before: like as a Beare,
That creeping close amongst the hives to reare
An hony-combe, the wakefull dogs espy,
And him assayling sore his carkas teare,
That hardly he with life away does fly,
Ne stayes, till safe him selfe he see from jeopardy.

LIV.   Ne stayd he, till he came unto the place
Where late his treasure he entombed had;
Where when he found it not, (for Trompart bace
Had it purloyned for his maister bad)
With extreme fury he became quite mad,
And ran away, ran with him selfe away;
That who so straungely had him seene bestadd,
With upstart haire and staring eyes dismay,
From Limbo lake him late escaped sure would say.

LV.   High over hilles and over dales he fledd,
As if the wind him on his winges had borne;
Ne banck nor bush could stay him, when he spedd
His nimble feet, as treading still on thorne:
Griefe, and despight, and gealosy, and scorne,
Did all the way him follow hard behynd;
And he himselfe himselfe loath'd so forlorne,
So shamefully forlorne of womankynd,
That, as a Snake, still lurked in his wounded mynd.

LVI.   Still fled he forward, looking backward still;
Ne stayd his flight nor fearefull agony,
Till that he came unto a rocky hill
Over the sea suspended dreadfully,
That living creature it would terrify
To looke adowne, or upward to the hight:

From thence he threw him selfe despiteously,
All desperate of his fore-damned spright,
That seemd no help for him was left in living sight.

LVII. But through long anguish and selfe-murdring thought,
He was so wasted and forpined quight,
That all his substance was consum'd to nought,
And nothing left but like an aery Spright,
That on the rockes he fell so flit and light,
That he thereby receiv'd no hurt at all;
But chaunced on a craggy cliff to light,
Whence he with crooked clawes so long did crall,
That at the last he found a cave with entrance small.

LVIII. Into the same he creepes, and thenceforth there
Resolv'd to build his balefull mansion
In drery darkenes and continuall feare
Of that rocks fall, which ever and anon
Threates with huge ruine him to fall upon,
That he dare never sleepe, but that one eye
Still ope he keepes for that occasion;
Ne ever rests he in tranquillity,
The roring billowes beat his bowre so boystrously.

LIX. Ne ever is he wont on ought to feed
But todes and frogs, his pasture poysonous,
Which in his cold complexion doe breed
A filthy blood, or humour rancorous,
Matter of doubt and dread suspitious,
That doth with curelesse care consume the hart,
Corrupts the stomacke with gall vitious,
Cros-cuts the liver with internall smart,
And doth transfixe the soule with deathes eternall dart.

LX. Yet can he never dye, but dying lives,
And doth himselfe with sorrow new sustaine,
That death and life attonce unto him gives,
And painefull pleasure turnes to pleasing paine.
There dwels he ever, miserable swaine,
Hatefull both to him selfe and every wight;
Where he, through privy griefe and horrour vaine,
It woxen so deform'd that he has quight
Forgot he was a man, and Gelosy is hight.

CANTO XI

Britomart chaceth Ollyphant;
Findes Scudamour distrest:
Assayes the house of Busyrane,
Where loves spoyles are exprest.

I. O HATEFULL hellish Snake! what furie furst
Brought thee from balefull house of Proserpine,
Where in her bosome she thee long had nurst,
And fostred up with bitter milke of tine,
Fowle Gealosy! that turnest love divine
To joylesse dread, and mak'st the loving hart
With hatefull thoughts to languish and to pine,
And feed it selfe with selfe-consuming smart?
Of all the passions in the mind thou vilest art!

II. O! let him far be banished away,
And in his stead let Love for ever dwell;
Sweete Love, that doth his golden wings embay
In blessed Nectar and pure Pleasures well,
Untroubled of vile feare or bitter fell.
And ye, faire Ladies, that your kingdomes make
In th' harts of men, them governe wisely well,
And of faire Britomart ensample take,
That was as trew in love as Turtle to her make.

III. Who with Sir Satyrane, as earst ye red,
Forth ryding from Malbeccoes hostlesse hous,
Far off aspyde a young man, the which fled
From an huge Geaunt, that with hideous
And hatefull outrage long him chaced thus;
It was that Ollyphant, the brother deare
Of that Argantè vile and vitious,
From whom the Squyre of Dames was reft whylere
This all as bad as she, and worse, if worse ought were.

IV. For as the sister did in feminine
And filthy lust exceede all womankinde,
So he surpassed his sex masculine,

In beastly use, all that I ever finde:
Whom when as Britomart beheld behinde
The fearefull boy so greedily poursew,
She was emmoved in her noble minde,
T' employ her puissaunce to his reskew,
And pricked fiercely forward where she did him vew.

v. Ne was Sir Satyrane her far behinde,
But with like fiercenesse did ensew the chace.
Whom when the Gyaunt saw, he soone resinde
His former suit, and from them fled apace:
They after both, and boldly bad him bace,
And each did strive the other to outgoe;
But he them both outran a wondrous space,
For he was long, and swift as any Roe,
And now made better speed t' escape his feared foe.

vi. It was not Satyrane, whom he did feare,
But Britomart the flowre of chastity;
For he the powre of chaste hands might not beare,
But alwayes did their dread encounter fly:
And now so fast his feet he did apply,
That he has gotten to a forrest neare,
Where he is shrowded in security.
The wood they enter, and search everie where;
They searched diversely, so both divided were.

vii. Fayre Britomart so long him followed,
That she at last came to a fountaine sheare,
By which there lay a knight all wallowed
Upon the grassy ground, and by him neare
His haberjeon, his helmet, and his speare:
A little off his shield was rudely throwne,
On which the winged boy in colours cleare
Depeincted was, full easie to be knowne,
And he thereby, where ever it in field was showne.

viii. His face upon the grownd did groveling ly,
As if he had beene slombring in the shade;
That the brave Mayd would not for courtesy
Out of his quiet slomber him abrade,
Nor seeme too suddeinly him to invade.
Still as she stood, she heard with grievous throb

Him grone, as if his hart were peeces made,
And with most painefull pangs to sigh and sob,
That pitty did the Virgins hart of patience rob.

IX. At last forth breaking into bitter plaintes
He sayd; " O soverayne Lord! that sit'st on hye
And raignst in blis emongst thy blessed Saintes,
How suffrest thou such shamefull cruelty
So long unwreaked of thine enimy?
Or hast thou, Lord, of good mens cause no heed?
Or doth thy justice sleepe and silent ly?
What booteth then the good and righteous deed,
If goodnesse find no grace, nor righteousnes no meed?

X. " If good find grace, and righteousnes reward,
Why then is Amoret in caytive band,
Sith that more bounteous creature never far'd
On foot upon the face of living land?
Or if that hevenly justice may withstand
The wrongfull outrage of unrighteous men,
Why then is Busirane with wicked hand
Suffred, these seven monethes day, in secret den
My Lady and my love so cruelly to pen!

XI. " My Lady and my love is cruelly pend
In dolefull darkenes from the vew of day,
Whilest deadly torments doe her chast brest rend,
And the sharpe steele doth rive her hart in tway,
All for she Scudamore will not denay.
Yet thou, vile man, vile Scudamore, art sound,
Ne canst her ayde, ne canst her foe dismay;
Unworthy wretch to tread upon the ground,
For whom so faire a Lady feeles so sore a wound!"

XII. There an huge heape of singults did oppresse
His strugling soule, and swelling throbs empeach
His foltring toung with pangs of drerinesse,
Choking the remnant of his plaintife speach,
As if his dayes were come to their last reach:
Which when she heard, and saw the ghastly fit
Threatning into his life to make a breach,
Both with great ruth and terrour she was smit,
Fearing least from her cage the wearie soule would flit.

XIII. Tho stouping downe she him amoved light;
　　　Who, therewith somewhat starting, up gan looke,
　　　And seeing him behind a stranger knight,
　　　Whereas no living creature he mistooke,
　　　With great indignaunce he that sight forsooke,
　　　And, downe againe himselfe disdainfully
　　　Abjecting, th' earth with his faire forhead strooke:
　　　Which the bold Virgin seeing gan apply
　　　Fit medcine to his griefe, and spake thus courtesly:—

XIV. " Ah gentle knight! whose deepe conceived griefe
　　　Well seemes t' exceede the powre of patience,
　　　Yet, if that hevenly grace some goode reliefe
　　　You send, submit you to high providence;
　　　And ever in your noble hart prepense,
　　　That all the sorrow in the world is lesse
　　　Then vertues might and values confidence:
　　　For who nill bide the burden of distresse,
　　　Must not here thinke to live; for life is wretchednesse,

XV. " Therefore, faire Sir, doe comfort to you take,
　　　And freely read what wicked felon so
　　　Hath outrag'd you, and thrald your gentle make,
　　　Perhaps this hand may helpe to ease your woe,
　　　And wreake your sorrow on your cruell foe;
　　　At least it faire endevour will apply."
　　　Those feeling words so neare the quicke did goe,
　　　That up his head he reared easily,
　　　And, leaning on his elbowe, these few words lett fly,

XVI. " What boots it plaine that cannot be redrest,
　　　And sow vaine sorrow in a fruitlesse eare,
　　　Sith powre of hand, nor skill of learned brest,
　　　Ne worldly price, cannot redeeme my deare
　　　Out of her thraldome and continuall feare:
　　　For he, the tyrant, which her hath in ward
　　　By strong enchauntments and blacke Magicke leare,
　　　Hath in a dungeon deepe her close embard,
　　　And many dreadfull feends hath pointed to her gard,

XVII. " There he tormenteth her most te ribly
　　　And day and night afflicts with mortall paine,
　　　Because to yield him love she doth deny,

Once to me yold, not to be yolde againe:
But yet by torture he would her constraine
Love to conceive in her disdainfull brest;
Till so she doe, she must in doole remaine,
Ne may by living meanes be thence relest:
What boots it then to plaine that cannot be redrest?"

XVIII. With this sad hersall of his heavy stresse
The warlike Damzell was empassiond sore,
And sayd; "Sir knight, your cause is nothing lesse
Then is your sorrow certes, if not more;
For nothing so much pitty doth implore
As gentle Ladyes helplesse misery:
But yet, if please ye listen to my lore,
I will, with proofe of last extremity,
Deliver her fro thence, or with her for you dy.

XIX. "Ah! gentlest knight alive," (sayd Scudamore)
"What huge heroicke magnanimity
Dwells in thy bounteous brest! what couldst thou more,
If shee were thine, and thou as now am I?
O! spare thy happy daies, and them apply
To better boot; but let me die that ought:
More is more losse; one is enough to dy."
"Life is not lost," (said she) "for which is bought
Endlesse renowm, that, more then death, is to be sought."

XX. Thus shee at length persuaded him to rise,
And with her wend to see what new successe
Mote him befall upon new enterprise.
His armes, which he had vowed to disprofesse,
She gathered up and did about him dresse,
And his forwandred steed unto him gott:
So forth they forth yfere make their progresse,
And march not past the mountenaunce of a shott,
Till they arriv'd whereas their purpose they did plott.

XXI. There they dismounting drew their weapons bold,
And stoutly came unto the Castle gate,
Whereas no gate they found them to withhold,
Nor ward to waite at morne and evening late;
But in the Porch, that did them sore amate,
A flaming fire, ymixt with smouldry smoke

And stinking sulphure, that with griesly hate
And dreadfull horror did all entraunce choke,
Enforced them their forward footing to revoke.

XXII. Greatly thereat was Britomart dismayd,
Ne in that stownd wist how her selfe to beare;
For daunger vaine it were to have assayd
That cruell element, which all things feare,
Ne none can suffer to approchen neare:
And, turning backe to Scudamour, thus sayd:
" What monstrous enmity provoke we heare?
Foolhardy as th' Earthes children, the which made
Batteill against the Gods, so we a God invade.

XXIII. " Daunger without discretion to attempt
Inglorious, beastlike is: therefore, Sir knight,
Aread what course of you is safest dempt,
And how he with our foe may come to fight."
" This is " (quoth he) " the dolorous despight,
Which earst to you I playnd: for neither may
This fire be quencht by any witt or might,
Ne yet by any meanes remov'd away;
So mighty be th' enchauntments which the same do stay.

XXIV. " What is there ells but cease these fruitlesse paines,
And leave me to my former languishing?
Faire Amorett must dwell in wicked chaines,
And Scudamore here die with sorrowing."
" Perdy not so," (saide shee) " for shameful thing
Yt were t' abandon noble chevisaunce
For shewe of perill, without venturing:
Rather let try extremities of chaunce,
Then enterprised praise for dread to disavaunce."

XXV. Therewith, resolv'd to prove her utmost might,
Her ample shield she threw before her face,
And her swords point directing forward right
Assayld the flame; the which eftesoones gave place,
And did it selfe divide with equall space,
That through she passed, as a thonder bolt
Perceth the yielding ayre, and doth displace
The soring clouds into sad showres ymolt;
So to her yold the flames, and did their force revolt.

XXVI. Whom whenas Scudamour saw past the fire
Safe and untoucht, he likewise gan assay
With greedy will and envious desire,
And bad the stubborne flames to yield him way:
But cruell Mulciber would not obay
His threatfull pride, but did the more augment
His mighty rage, and with imperious sway
Him forst, (maulgre) his fercenes to relent,
And backe retire, all scorcht and pittifully brent.

XXVII. With huge impatience he inly swelt,
More for great sorrow that he could not pas
Then for the burning torment which he felt;
That with fell woodnes he effierced was,
And wilfully him throwing on the gras
Did beat and bounse his head and brest ful sore:
The whiles the Championesse now entred has
The utmost rowme, and past the foremost dore;
The utmost rowme abounding with all precious store:

XXVIII. For round about the walls yclothed were
With goodly arras of great majesty,
Woven with gold and silke, so close and nere
That the rich metall lurked privily,
As faining to be hidd from envious eye;
Yet here, and there, and every where, unwares
It shewd it selfe and shone unwillingly;
Like a discoloured Snake, whose hidden snares
Through the greene gras his long bright burnisht back
    declares.

XXIX. And in those Tapets weren fashioned
Many faire pourtraicts, and many a faire feate;
And all of love, and al of lusty-hed,
As seemed by their semblaunt, did entreat:
And eke all Cupids warres they did repeate,
And cruell battailes, which he whilome fought
Gainst all the Gods to make his empire great;
Besides the huge massacres, which he wrought
On mighty kings and kesars into thraldome brought.

XXX. Therein was writt how often thondring Jove
Had felt the point of his hart-percing dart,
And, leaving heavens kingdome, here did rove

In straunge disguize, to slake his scalding smart;
Now, like a Ram, faire Helle to pervart,
Now, like a Bull, Europa to withdraw:
Ah! how the fearefull Ladies tender hart
Did lively seeme to tremble, when she saw
The huge seas under her t' obay her servaunts law.

XXXI. Soone after that, into a golden showre
Him selfe he chaung'd, faire Danaë to vew;
And through the roofe of her strong brasen towre
Did raine into her lap an hony dew;
The whiles her foolish garde, that litle knew
Of such deceipt, kept th' yron dore fast bard,
And watcht that none should enter nor issew:
Vaine was the watch, and bootlesse all the ward,
Whenas the God to golden hew him selfe transfard.

XXXII. Then was he turnd into a snowy Swan,
To win faire Leda to his lovely trade:
O wondrous skill! and sweet wit of the man,
That her in daffadillies sleeping made
From scorching heat her daintie limbes to shade;
Whiles the proud Bird, ruffing his fethers wyde
And brushing his faire brest, did her invade:
She slept; yet twixt her eielids closely spyde
How towards her he rusht, and smiled at his pryde.

XXXIII. Then shewd it how the Thebane Semelee,
Deceivd of gealous Juno, did require
To see him in his soverayne majestee
Armd with his thunderbolts and lightning fire,
Whens dearely she with death bought her desire.
But faire Alcmena better match did make,
Joying his love in likenes more entire:
Three nights in one, they say, that for her sake
He then did put, her pleasures lenger to partake.

XXXIV. Twise was he seene in soaring Eagles shape,
And with wide winges to beat the buxome ayre:
Once, when he with Asterie did scape;
Againe, when as the Trojane boy so fayre
He snatcht from Ida hill, and with him bare:
Wondrous delight it was there to behould

How the rude Shepheards after him did stare,
Trembling through feare least down he fallen should,
And often to him calling to take surer hould.

xxxv. In Satyres shape Antiopa he snatcht;
And like a fire, when he Aegin' assayd:
A shepeheard, when Mnemosyne he catcht;
And like a Serpent to the Thracian mayd.
Whyles thus on earth great Jove these pageaunts playd,
The winged boy did thrust into his throne,
And scoffing thus unto his mother sayd:
" Lo! now the hevens obey to me alone,
And take me for their Jove, whiles Jove to earth is
gone."

xxxvi. And thou, faire Phœbus, in thy colours bright
Wast there enwoven, and the sad distresse
In which that boy thee plonged, for despight
That thou bewray'dst his mothers wantonnesse,
When she with Mars was meynt in joyfulnesse:
Forthy he thrild thee with a leaden dart
To love faire Daphne, which thee loved lesse;
Lesse she thee lov'd then was thy just desart,
Yet was thy love her death, and her death was thy
smart.

xxxvii. So lovedst thou the lusty Hyacinct;
So lovedst thou the faire Coronis deare;
Yet both are of thy haplesse hand extinct,
Yet both in flowres doe live, and love thee beare,
The one a Paunce, the other a sweet-breare:
For griefe whereof, ye mote have lively seene
The God himselfe rending his golden heare,
And breaking quite his garlond ever greene,
With other signes of sorrow and impatient teene.

xxxviii. Both for those two, and for his owne deare sonne,
The sonne of Climene, he did repent;
Who, bold to guide the charet of the Sunne,
Himselfe in thousand peeces fondly rent,
And all the world with flashing fire brent;
So like, that all the walles did seeme to flame:
Yet cruell Cupid, not herewith content,

Forst him eftsoones to follow other game,
And love a Shephards daughter for his dearest **Dame.**

XXXIX. He loved Isse for his dearest Dame,
And for her sake her cattell fedd awhile,
And for her sake a cowheard vile became
The servant of Admetus, cowheard vile,
Whiles that from heaven he suffered exile.
Long were to tell each other lovely fitt;
Now, like a Lyon hunting after spoile;
Now, like a stag; now, like a faulcon flit:
All which in that faire arras was most lively writ.

XL. Next unto him was Neptune pictured,
In his divine resemblance wondrous lyke:
His face was rugged, and his hoarie hed
Dropped with brackish deaw: his threeforkt Pyke
He stearnly shooke, and therewith fierce did stryke
The raging billowes, that on every syde
They trembling stood, and made a long broad dyke,
That his swift charet might have passage wyde
Which foure great Hippodames did draw in temewise
        tyde.

XLI. His seahorses did seeme to snort amayne,
And from their nosethrilles blow the brynie streame,
That made the sparckling waves to smoke agayne,
And flame with gold; but the white fomy creame
Did shine with silver, and shoot forth his beame.
The God himselfe did pensive seeme and sad,
And hong adowne his head as he did dreame;
For privy love his brest empierced had,
Ne ought but deare Bisaltis ay could make him glad.

XLII. He loved eke Iphimedia deare,
And Aeolus faire daughter, Arnè hight,
For whom he turned him selfe into a Steare,
And fedd on fodder to beguile her sight.
Also to win Deucalions daughter bright,
He turned him selfe into a Dolphin fayre;
And like a winged horse he tooke his flight
To snaky-locke Medusa to repayre,
On whom he got faire Pegasus that flitteth in the ayre.

XLIII. Next Saturne was, (but who would ever weene
That sullein Saturne ever weend to love?
Yet love is sullein, and Saturnlike seene,
As he did for Erigone it prove)
That to a Centaure did him selfe transmove.
So proov'd it eke that gratious God of wine,
When for to compasse Philliras hard love,
He turnd himselfe into a fruitfull vine,
And into her faire bosome made his grapes decline.

XLIV. Long were to tell the amorous assayes,
And gentle pangues, with which he maked meeke
The mightie Mars, to learne his wanton playes;
How oft for Venus, and how often eek
For many other Nymphes, he sore did shreek,
With womanish teares, and with unwarlike smarts,
Privily moystening his horrid cheeke:
There was he painted full of burning dartes,
And many wide woundes launched through his inner partes.

XLV. Ne did he spare (so cruell was the Elfe)
His owne deare mother, (ah! why should he so?)
Ne did he spare sometime to pricke himselfe,
That he might taste the sweet consuming woe,
Which he had wrought to many others moe.
But, to declare the mournfull Tragedyes
And spoiles wherewith he all the ground did strow,
More eath to number with how many eyes
High heven beholdes sad lovers nightly theeveryes.

XLVI. Kings, Queenes, Lords, Ladies, knights, and Damsels gent,
Were heap'd together with the vulgar sort,
And mingled with the raskall rablement,
Without respect of person or of port,
To shew Dan Cupids powre and great effort:
And round about a border was entrayld
Of broken bowes and arrowes shivered short;
And a long bloody river through them rayld,
So lively and so like that living sence it fayld.

XLVII. And at the upper end of that faire rowme
There was an Altar built of pretious stone
Of passing valew and of great renowme,

On which there stood an Image all alone
Of massy gold, which with his owne light shone;
And winges it had with sondry colours dight,
More sondry colours then the proud Pavone
Beares in his boasted fan, or Iris bright,
When her discolourd bow she spreds through hevens hight.

XLVIII. Blyndfold he was; and in his cruell fist
A mortall bow and arrowes keene did hold,
With which he shot at randon, when him list,
Some headed with sad lead, some with pure gold;
(Ah man! beware how thou those dartes behold.)
A wounded Dragon under him did ly,
Whose hideous tayle his lefte foot did enfold, .
And with a shaft was shot through either eye,
That no man forth might draw, ne no man remedye.

XLIX. And underneath his feet was written thus,
Unto the Victor of the Gods this bee :
And all the people in that ample hous
Did to that image bowe their humble knee,
And oft committed fowle Idolatree.
That wondrous sight faire Britomart amazd,
Ne seeing could her wonder satisfie,
But ever more and more upon it gazd,
The whiles the passing brightnes her fraile sences dazd.

L. Tho, as she backward cast her busie eye
To search each secrete of that goodly sted,
Over the dore thus written she did spye,
Bee bold : she oft and oft it over-red,
Yet could not find what sence it figured:
But what so were therein or writ or ment,
She was no whit thereby discouraged
From prosecuting of her first intent,
But forward with bold steps into the next roome went.

LI. Much fayrer then the former was that roome,
And richlier by many partes arayd;
For not with arras made in painefull loome,
But with pure gold it all was overlayd,
Wrought with wilde Antickes, which their follies playd
In the rich metall as they living were.

A thousand monstrous formes therein were made,
Such as false love doth oft upon him weare;
For love in thousand monstrous formes doth oft appeare.

LII. And all about the glistring walles were hong
With warlike spoiles and with victorious prayes
Of mightie Conquerours and Captaines strong,
Which were whilome captived in their dayes
To cruell love, and wrought their owne decayes.
Their swerds and speres were broke, and hauberques rent,
And their proud girlonds of tryumphant bayes
Troden in dust with fury insolent,
To shew the victors might and mercilesse intent.

LIII. The warlike Mayd, beholding earnestly
The goodly ordinaunce of this rich Place,
Did greatly wonder; ne could satisfy
Her greedy eyes with gazing a long space:
But more she mervaild that no footings trace
Nor wight appeard, but wastefull emptinesse
And solemne silence over all that place:
Straunge thing it seem'd, that none was to possesse
So rich purveyaunce, ne them keepe with carefulnesse.

LIV. And, as she lookt about, she did behold
How over that same dore was likewise writ,
Be bolde, be bolde, and every where, *Be bold ;*
That much she muz'd, yet could not construe it
By any ridling skill, or commune wit.
At last she spyde at that rowmes upper end
Another yron dore, on which was writ,
Be not too bold ; whereto though she did bend
Her earnest minde, yet wist not what it might intend.

LV. Thus she there wayted untill eventyde,
Yet living creature none she saw appeare,
And now sad shadowes gan the world to hyde
From mortall vew, and wrap in darkenes dreare;
Yet nould she d'off her weary armes, for feare
Of secret daunger, ne let sleepe oppresse
Her heavy eyes with natures burdein deare,
But drew her selfe aside in sickernesse,
And her wel-pointed wepons did about her dresse.

CANTO XII

The maske of Cupid, and the enchant—
ed Chamber are displayd;
Whence Britomart redeemes faire A-
moret through charmes decayd.

I. Tho, whenas chearelesse Night ycovered had
Fayre heaven with an universall clowd,
That every wight dismayd with darkenes sad
In silence and in sleepe themselves did shrowd,
She heard a shrilling Trompet sound alowd,
Signe of nigh battaill, or got victory:
Nought therewith daunted was her courage prowd,
But rather stird to cruell enmity,
Expecting ever when some foe she might descry.

II. With that an hideous storme of winde arose,
With dreadfull thunder and lightning atwixt,
And an earthquake, as if it streight would lose
The worlds foundations from his centre fixt:
A direfull stench of smoke and sulphure mixt
Ensewd, whose noyaunce fild the fearefull sted
From the fourth howre of night untill the sixt;
Yet the bold Britonesse was nought ydred,
Though much emmov'd, but stedfast still persevered.

III. All suddeinly a stormy whirlwind blew
Throughout the house, that clapped every dore,
With which that yron wicket open flew,
As it with mighty levers had bene tore;
And forth yssewd, as on the readie flore
Of some Theatre, a grave personage
That in his hand a braunch of laurell bore,
With comely haveour and count'nance sage,
Yclad in costly garments fit for tragicke Stage.

IV. Proceeding to the midst he stil did stand,
As if in minde he somewhat had to say;
And to the vulgare beckning with his hand,

In signe of silence, as to heare a play,
By lively actions he gan bewray
Some argument of matter passioned:
Which doen, he backe retyred soft away,
And, passing by, his name discovered,
Ease, on his robe in golden letters cyphered.

v. The noble Mayd still standing all this vewd,
And merveild at his straunge intendiment.
With that a joyous fellowship issewd
Of Minstrales making goodly meriment,
With wanton Bardes, and Rymers impudent;
All which together song full chearefully
A lay of loves delight with sweet concent:
After whom marcht a jolly company,
In manner of a maske, enranged orderly.

vi. The whiles a most delitious harmony
In full straunge notes was sweetly heard to sound,
That the rare sweetnesse of the melody
The feeble sences wholly did confound,
And the frayle soule in deepe delight nigh drownd:
And, when it ceast, shrill trompets lowd did bray,
That their report did far away rebound;
And, when they ceast, it gan againe to play,
The whiles the maskers marched forth in trim aray.

vii. The first was Fansy, like a lovely Boy
Of rare aspect, and beautie without peare,
Matchable ether to that ympe of Troy,
Whom Jove did love and chose his cup to beare;
Or that same daintie lad, which was so deare
To great Alcides, that, when as he dyde,
He wailed womanlike with many a teare,
And every wood and every valley wyde
He filled with Hylas name; the Nymphes eke Hylas cryde.

viii. His garment nether was of silke nor say,
But paynted plumes in goodly order dight,
Like as the sunburnt Indians do aray
Their tawney bodies in their proudest plight:
As those same plumes so seemd he vaine and light,
That by his gate might easily appeare;

For still he far'd as dauncing in delight,
And in his hand a windy fan did beare,
That in 'the ydle ayre he mov'd still here and theare.

IX. And him beside marcht amorous Desyre,
Who seemd of ryper yeares then th' other Swayne,
Yet was that other swayne this elders syre,
And gave him being, commune to them twayne:
His garment was disguysed very vayne,
And his embrodered Bonet sat awry:
Twixt both his hands few sparks he close did strayne,
Which still he blew and kindled busily,
That soone they life conceiv'd, and forth in flames did fly.

X. Next after him went Doubt, who was yclad
In a discolour'd cote of straunge disguyse,
That at his backe a brode Capuccio had,
And sleeves dependaunt Albanese-wyse:
He lookt askew with his mistrustfull eyes,
And nycely trode, as thornes lay in his way,
Or that the flore to shrinke he did avyse;
And on a broken reed he still did stay
His feeble steps, which shrunck when hard thereon he lay.

XI. With him went Daunger, cloth'd in ragged weed
Made of Beares skin, that him more dreadfull made;
Yet his owne face was dreadfull, ne did need
Straunge horrour to deforme his griesly shade:
A net in th' one hand, and a rusty blade
In th' other was; this Mischiefe, that Mishap:
With th' one his foes he threatned to invade,
With th' other he his friends ment to enwrap;
For whom he could not kill he practizd to entrap.

XII. Next him was Feare, all arm'd from top to toe,
Yet thought himselfe not safe enough thereby,
But feard each shadow moving too or froe;
And, his owne armes when glittering he did spy
Or clashing heard, he fast away did fly,
As ashes pale of hew, and winged heeld,
And evermore on Daunger fixt his eye,
Gainst whom he alwayes bent a brasen shield,
Which his right hand unarmed fearefully did wield.

XIII. With him went Hope in rancke, a handsome Mayd,
        Of chearefull looke and lovely to behold:
        In silken samite she was light arayd,
        And her fayre lockes were woven up in gold:
        She alway smyld, and in her hand did hold
        An holy-water-sprinckle, dipt in deowe,
        With which she sprinckled favours manifold
        On whom she list, and did great liking sheowe,
        Great liking unto many, but true love to feowe.

XIV. And after them Dissemblaunce and Suspect
        Marcht in one rancke, yet an unequall paire;
        For she was gentle and of milde aspect,
        Courteous to all and seeming debonaire,
        Goodly adorned and exceeding faire:
        Yet was that all but paynted and pourloynd,
        And her bright browes were deckt with borrowed haire;
        Her deeds were forged, and her words false coynd,
        And alwaies in her hand two clewes of silke she twynd.

XV. But he was fowle, ill favoured, and grim,
        Under his eiebrowes looking still askaunce;
        And ever, as Dissemblaunce laught on him,
        He lowrd on her with daungerous eyeglaunce,
        Shewing his nature in his countenaunce:
        His rolling eies did never rest in place,
        But walkte each where for feare of hid mischaunce,
        Holding a lattis still before his face,
        Through which he stil did peep as forward he did pace.

XVI. Next him went Griefe and Fury, matcht yfere;
        Griefe all in sable sorrowfully clad,
        Downe hanging his dull head with heavy chere,
        Yet inly being more then seeming sad:
        A paire of Pincers in his hand he had,
        With which he pinched people to the hart,
        That from thenceforth a wretched life they ladd,
        In wilfull languor and consuming smart,
        Dying each day with inward wounds of dolours dart.

XVII. But Fury was full ill appareiled
        In rags, that naked nigh she did appeare,
        With ghastly looks and dreadfull drerihed;

And from her backe her garments she did teare,
And from her head ofte rente her snarled heare:
In her right hand a firebrand shee did tosse
About her head, still roming here and there;
As a dismayed Deare. in chace embost,
Forgetfull of his safety, hath his right way lost.

XVIII. After them went Displeasure and Pleasaunce,
He looking lompish and full sullein sad,
And hanging downe his heavy countenaunce;
She chearfull, fresh, and full of joyaunce glad,
As if no sorrow she ne felt ne drad;
That evill matched paire they seemd to bee:
An angry Waspe th' one in a viall had,
Th' other in hers an hony-laden Bee.
Thus marched these six couples forth in faire degree.

XIX. After all these there marcht a most faire Dame,
Led of two grysie Villeins, th' one Despight,
The other cleped Cruelty by name:
She, dolefull Lady, like a dreary Spright
Cald by strong charmes out of eternall night,
Had Deathes owne ymage figurd in her face,
Full of sad signes, fearfull to living sight;
Yet in that horror shewd a seemely grace,
And with her feeble feete did move a comely pace.

XX. Her brest all naked, as nett yvory
Without adorne of gold or silver bright,
Wherewith the Craftesman wonts it beautify,
Of her dew honour was despoyled quight;
And a wide wound therein (O ruefull sight!)
Entrenched deep with knyfe accursed keene,
Yet freshly bleeding forth her fainting spright,
(The worke of cruell hand) was to be seene,
That dyde in sanguine red her skin all snowy cleene.

XXI. At that wide orifice her trembling hart
Was drawne forth, and in silver basin layd,
Quite through transfixed with a deadly dart,
And in her blood yet steeming fresh embayd:
And those two villeins, which her steps upstayd,
When her weake feete could scarcely her sustaine,

And fading vitall powres gan to fade,
Her forward still with torture did constraine,
And evermore encreased her consuming paine.

XXII. Next after her, the winged God him selfe
Came riding on a Lion ravenous,
Taught to obay the menage of that Elfe
That man and beast with powre imperious
Subdeweth to his kingdome tyrannous.
His blindfold eies he bad awhile unbinde,
That his proud spoile of that same dolorous
Faire Dame he might behold in perfect kinde;
Which seene, he much rejoyced in his cruell minde.

XXIII. Of which ful prowd, him selfe up rearing hye
He looked round about with sterne disdayne,
And did survay his goodly company;
And, marshalling the evill-ordered trayne,
With that the darts which his right hand did straine
Full dreadfully he shooke, that all did quake,
And clapt on hye his coulourd winges twaine,
That all his many it affraide did make:
Tho, blinding him againe, his way he forth did take.

XXIV. Behinde him was Reproch, Repentaunce, Shame;
Reproch the first, Shame next, Repent behinde:
Repentaunce feeble, sorrowful, and lame;
Reproch despightfull, carelesse, and unkinde;
Shame most ill-favourd, bestiall, and blinde:
Shame lowrd, Repentaunce sighd, Reproch did scould;
Reproch sharpe stings, Repentaunce whips entwinde,
Shame burning brond-yrons in her hand did hold:
All three to each unlike, yet all made in one mould.

XXV. And after them a rude confused rout
Of persons flockt, whose names is hard to read:
Emongst them was sterne Strife, and Anger stout;
Unquiet Care, and fond Unthriftyhead;
Lewd Losse of Time, and Sorrow seeming dead;
Inconstant Chaunge, and false Disloyalty;
Consuming Riotise, and guilty Dread
Of heavenly vengeaunce; faint Infirmity;
Vile Poverty; and, lastly, Death with infamy.

XXVI. There were full many moe like maladies,
  Whose names and natures I note readen well;
  So many moe, as there be phantasies
  In wavering wemens witt, that none can tell,
  Or paines in love, or punishments in hell:
  All which disguized marcht in masking wise
  About the chamber by the Damozell;
  And then returned, having marched thrise,
  Into the inner rowme from whence they first did rise.

XXVII. So soone as they were in, the dore streightway
  Fast locked, driven with that stormy blast
  Which first it opened, and bore all away.
  Then the brave Maid, which al this while was plast
  In secret shade, and saw both first and last,
  Issewed forth, and went unto the dore
  To enter in, but fownd it locked fast:
  It vaine she thought with rigorous uprore
  For to efforce, when charmes had closed it afore.

XXVIII. Where force might not availe, there sleights and art
  She cast to use, both fitt for hard emprize:
  Forthy from that same rowme not to depart
  Till morrow next shee did her selfe avize,
  When that same Maske againe should forth arize.
  The morrowe nexte appeard with joyous cheare,
  Calling men to their daily exercize:
  Then she, as morrow fresh, her selfe did reare
  Out of her secret stand that day for to outweare.

XXIX. All that day she outwore in wandering
  And gazing on that Chambers ornament,
  Till that againe the second evening
  Her covered with her sable vestiment,
  Wherewith the worlds faire beautie she hath blent:
  Then, when the second watch was almost past,
  That brasen dore flew open, and in went
  Bold Britomart, as she had late forecast,
  Nether of ydle showes, nor of false charmes aghast.

XXX. So soone as she was entred, rownd about
  Shee cast her eies to see what was become
  Of all those persons which she saw without:

But lo! they streight were vanisht all and some;
Ne living wight she saw in all that roome,
Save that same woefull Lady, both whose hands
Were bounden fast, that did her ill become,
And her small waste girt rownd with yron bands
Upon a brasen pillour, by the which she stands.

XXXI. And her before the vile Enchaunter sate,
Figuring straunge characters of his art:
With living blood he those characters wrate,
Dreadfully dropping from her dying hart,
Seeming transfixed with a cruell dart;
And all perforce to make her him to love.
Ah! who can love the worker of her smart?
A thousand charmes he formerly did prove,
Yet thousand charmes could not her stedfast hart
    remove.

XXXII. Soone as that virgin knight he saw in place,
His wicked bookes in hast he overthrew,
Not caring his long labours to deface;
And, fiercely running to that Lady trew,
A murdrous knife out of his pocket drew,
The which he thought, for villeinous despight,
In her tormented bodie to embrew:
But the stout Damzell, to him leaping light,
His cursed hand withheld, and maistered his might.

XXXIII. From her, to whom his fury first he ment,
The wicked weapon rashly he did wrest,
And, turning to herselfe, his fell intent,
Unwares it strooke into her snowie chest,
That litle drops empurpled her faire brest.
Exceeding wroth therewith the virgin grew,
Albe the wound were nothing deepe imprest,
And fiercely forth her mortall blade she drew,
To give him the reward for such vile outrage dew.

XXXIV. So mightily she smote him, that to ground
He fell halfe dead: next stroke him should have slaine,
Had not the Lady, which by him stood bound,
Dernly unto her called to abstaine
From doing him to dy.   For else her paine

Should be remedilesse; sith none but hee
Which wrought it could the same recure againe.
Therewith she stayd her hand, loth stayd to bee;
For life she him envyde, and long'd revenge to see:

XXXV. And to him said: " Thou wicked man, whose meed
For so huge mischiefe and vile villany
Is death, or if that ought doe death exceed;
Be sure that nought may save thee from to dy
But if that thou this Dame do presently
Restore unto her health and former state:
This doe, and live, els dye undoubtedly."
He, glad of life, that lookt for death but late,
Did yield him selfe right willing to prolong his date:

XXXVI. And, rising up, gan streight to over-looke
Those cursed leaves, his charmes back to reverse.
Full dreadfull thinges out of that balefull booke
He red, and measur'd many a sad verse,
That horrour gan the virgins hart to perse,
And her faire locks up stared stiffe on end,
Hearing him those same bloody lynes reherse;
And, all the while he red, she did extend
Her sword high over him, if ought he did offend.

XXXVII. Anon she gan perceive the house to quake,
And all the dores to rattle round about:
Yet all that did not her dismaied make,
Nor slack her threatfull hand for daungers dout:
But still with stedfast eye and courage stout
Abode, to weet what end would come of all.
At last that mightie chaine, which round about
Her tender waste was wound, adowne gan fall,
And that great brasen pillour broke in peeces small.

XXXVIII. The cruell steele, which thrild her dying hart,
Fell softly forth, as of his owne accord,
And the wyde wound, which lately did dispart
Her bleeding brest, and riven bowels gor'd,
Was closed up, as it had not beene bor'd,
And every part to safety full sownd,
As she were never hurt, was soone restord.
Tho, when she felt her selfe to be unbownd
And perfect hole, prostrate she fell unto the grownd.

XXXIX. Before faire Britomart she fell prostrate,
          Saying; " Ah noble knight! what worthy meede
          Can wretched Lady, quitt from wofull state,
          Yield you in lieu of this your gracious deed?
          Your vertue selfe her owne reward shall breed,
          Even immortal prayse and glory wyde,
          Which I your vassall, by your prowesse freed,
          Shall through the world make to be notifyde,
          And goodly well advaunce that goodly well was tryde."

XL. But Britomart, uprearing her from grownd,
       Said: " Gentle Dame, reward enough I weene,
       For many labours more then I have found,
       This, that in safetie now I have you seene,
       And meane of your deliverance have beene.
       Henceforth, faire Lady, comfort to you take,
       And put away remembrance of late teene;
       Insted thereof, know that your loving Make
       Hath no lesse griefe endured for your gentle sake."

XLI. She much was cheard to heare him mentiond,
       Whom of all living wightes she loved best.
       Then laid the noble Championesse strong hond
       Upon th' enchaunter which had her distrest
       So sore, and with foule outrages opprest.
       With that great chaine, wherewith not long ygoe
       He bound that pitteous Lady prisoner, now relest,
       Himselfe she bound, more worthy to be so,
       And captive with her led to wretchednesse and wo.

XLII. Returning back, those goodly rowmes, which erst
        She saw so rich and royally arayd,
        Now vanisht utterly and cleane subverst
        She found, and all their glory quite decayd;
        That sight of such a chaunge her much dismayd
        Thence forth descending to that perlous porch
        Those dreadfull flames she also found delayd
        And quenched quite like a consumed torch,
        That erst all entrers wont so cruelly to scorch.

XLIII. More easie issew now then entrance late
         She found; for now that fained dreadfull flame,
         Which chokt the porch of that enchaunted gate

And passage bard to all that thither came,
Was vanisht quite, as it were not the same,
And gave her leave at pleasure forth to passe.
Th' Enchaunter selfe, which all that fraud did frame
To have efforst the love of that faire lasse,
Seeing his worke now wasted, deepe engrieved was.

XLIV. But when the Victoresse arrived there
Where late she left the pensife Scudamore
With her own trusty Squire, both full of feare,
Neither of them she found where she them lore:
Thereat her noble hart was stonisht sore;
But most faire Amoret, whose gentle spright
Now gan to feede on hope, which she before
Conceived had, to see her own deare knight,
Being thereof beguyld, was fild with new affright.

XLV. But he, sad man, when he had long in drede
Awayted there for Britomarts returne,
Yet saw her not, nor signe of her good speed,
His expectation to despaire did turne,
Misdeeming sure that her those flames did burne;
And therefore gan advize with her old Squire,
Who her deare nourslings losse no lesse did mourne,
Thence to depart for further aide t' enquire:
Where let them wend at will, whilest here I doe respire.

[Book IV is closely linked thematically with the preceding book:
from chaste love Spenser now moves to 'the Legend of Cambel
and Triamond, or of Friendship'. Many of the characters from
Book III have important parts to play in Book IV, and here, in
canto x, Scudamour, still questing for Amoret, tells Sir Claribell,
Britomart, Arthur, and others, how he first won her love. This is
the allegorical core of Book IV and is based on medieval love
allegory, the tradition of the Garden of Pleasure (compare III. vi
and contrast the Bower of Bliss in II. xii), and traditional
descriptions of the temples of the gods. The allegory is largely
psychological in intent, and the hermaphroditic Venus symbolizes
the ideal union of man and woman in marriage as well as having
larger, cosmic, implications.]

CANTO X

Scudamour doth his conquest tell
Of vertuous Amoret:
Great Venus Temple is describ'd;
And lovers life forth set.

I. " TRUE he it said, what ever man it sayd,
That love with gall and hony doth abound;
But if the one be with the other wayd,
For every dram of hony therein found
A pound of gall doth over it redound:
That I too true by triall have approved;
For since the day that first with deadly wound
My heart was launcht, and learned to have loved,
I never joyed howre, but still with care was moved.

II. " And yet such grace is given them from above,
That all the cares and evill which they meet
May nought at all their setled mindes remove,
But seeme, gainst common sence, to them most sweet;
As bosting in their martyrdome unmeet.
So all that ever yet I have endured
I count as naught, and tread downe under feet,
Since of my love at length I rest assured,
That to disloyalty she will not be allured.

III. " Long were to tell the travell and long toile
Through which this shield of love I late have wonne,
And purchased this peerelesse beauties spoile,
That harder may be ended, then begonne:
But since ye so desire, your will be donne.
Then hearke, ye gentle knights and Ladies free,
My hard mishaps that ye may learne to shonne;
For though sweet love to conquer glorious bee,
Yet is the paine thereof much greater then the fee.

IV. " What time the fame of this renowmed prise
Flew first abroad, and all mens eares possest,
I, having armes then taken, gan avise

To winne me honour by some noble gest,
And purchase me some place amongst the best.
I boldly thought, (so young mens thoughts are bold)
That this same brave emprize for me did rest,
And that both shield and she whom I behold
Might be my lucky lot; sith all by lot we hold.

v. " So on that hard adventure forth I went,
And to the place of perill shortly came:
That was a temple faire and auncient,
Which of great mother Venus bare the name,
And farre renowmed through exceeding fame,
Much more then that which was in Paphos built,
Or that in Cyprus, both long since this same,
Though all the pillours of the one were guilt,
And all the others pavement were with yvory spilt.

vi. " And it was seated in an Island strong,
Abounding all with delices most rare,
And wall'd by nature gainst invaders wrong,
That none mote have accesse, nor inward fare,
But by one way that passage did prepare.
It was a bridge ybuilt in goodly wize
With curious Corbes and pendants graven faire,
And, arched all with porches, did arize
On stately pillours fram'd after the Doricke guize.

vii. " And for defence thereof on th' other end
There reared was a castle faire and strong
That warded all which in or out did wend,
And flanckked both the bridges sides along,
Gainst all that would it faine to force or wrong:
And therein wonned twenty valiant Knights,
All twenty tride in warres experience long;
Whose office was against all manner wights
By all meanes to maintaine that castels ancient rights.

viii. " Before that Castle was an open plaine,
And in the midst thereof a piller placed;
On which this shield, of many sought in vaine,
The shield of Love, whose guerdon me hath graced,
Was hangd on high with golden ribbands laced;
And in the marble stone was written this,

With golden letters goodly well enchaced;
Blessed the man that well can use his blis :
Whose ever be the shield, faire Amoret be his.

IX. " Which when I red, my heart did inly earn
And pant with hope of that adventures hap:
Ne stayed further newes thereof to learne,
But with my speare upon the shield did rap,
That all the castle ringed with the clap.
Streight forth issewd a Knight all arm'd to proofe,
And bravely mounted to his most mishap:
Who, staying nought to question from aloofe,
Ran fierce at me that fire glaunst from his horses hoofe.

X. " Whom boldly I encountred (as I could)
And by good fortune shortly him unseated.
Eftsoones outsprung two more of equall mould;
But I them both with equall hap defeated.
So all the twenty I likewise entreated,
And left them groning there upon the plaine:
Then, preacing to the pillour, I repeated
The read thereof for guerdon of my paine,
And taking downe the shield with me did it retaine,

XI. " So forth without impediment I past,
Till to the Bridges utter gate I came;
The which I found sure lockt and chained fast.
I knockt, but no man aunswred me by name;
I cald, but no man answred to my clame:
Yet I persever'd still to knocke and call,
Till at the last I spide within the same
Where one stood peeping through a crevis small,
To whom I cald aloud, halfe angry therewithall.

XII. " That was to weet the Porter of the place,
Unto whose trust the charge thereof was lent:
His name was Doubt, that had a double face,
Th' one forward looking, th' other backeward bent,
Therein resembling Janus auncient
Which hath in charge the ingate of the yeare:
And evermore his eyes about him went,
As if some proved perill he did feare,
Or did misdoubt some ill whose cause did not appeare,

XIII. " On th' one side he, on th' other sate Delay,
 Behinde the gate that none her might espy;
 Whose manner was all passengers to stay
 And entertaine with her occasions sly:
 Through which some lost great hope unheedily,
 Which never they recover might againe;
 And others, quite excluded forth, did ly
 Long languishing there in unpittied paine,
 And seeking often entraunce afterwards in vaine.

XIV. " Me when as he had privily espide
 Bearing the shield which I had conquerd late,
 He kend it streight, and to me opened wide.
 So in I past, and streight he closd the gate:
 But being in, Delay in close awaite
 Caught hold on me, and thought my steps to stay,
 Feigning full many a fond excuse to prate,
 And time to steale, the threasure of mans day,
 Whose smallest minute lost no riches render may.

XV. " But by no meanes my way I would forslow
 For ought that ever she could doe or say;
 But from my lofty steede dismounting low
 Past forth on foote, beholding all the way
 The goodly workes, and stones of rich assay,
 Cast into sundry shapes by wondrous skill,
 That like on earth no where I reckon may:
 And underneath, the river rolling still
 With murmure soft, that seem'd to serve the workmans
  will.

XVI. " Thence forth I passed to the second gate,
 The Gate of Good Desert, whose goodly pride
 And costly frame were long here to relate.
 The same to all stoode alwaies open wide;
 But in the Porch did evermore abide
 An hideous Giant, dreadfull to behold,
 That stopt the entraunce with his spacious stride,
 And with the terrour of his countenance bold
 Full many did affray, that else faine enter would.

XVII. " His name was Daunger, dreaded over-all,
 Who day and night did watch and duely ward
 From fearefull cowards entrance to forstall

And faint-heart-fooles, whom shew of perill hard
Could terrifie from Fortunes faire adward:
For oftentimes faint hearts, at first espiall
Of his grim face, were from approaching scard;
Unworthy they of grace, whom one deniall
Excludes from fairest hope withouten further triall.

XVIII. " Yet many doughty warriours, often tride
In greater perils to be stout and bold,
Durst not the sternnesse of his looke abide;
But, soone as they his countenance did behold,
Began to faint, and feele their corage cold.
Againe, some other, that in hard assaies
Were cowards knowne, and litle count did hold,
Either through gifts, or guile, or such like waies,
Crept in by stouping low, or stealing of the kaies,

XIX. " But I, though meanest man of many moe,
Yet much disdaining unto him to lout,
Or creepe betweene his legs, so in to goe,
Resolv'd him to assault with manhood stout,
And either beat him in, or drive him out.
Eftsoones, advauncing that enchaunted shield,
With all my might I gan to lay about:
Which when he saw, the glaive which he did wield
He gan forthwith t' avale, and way unto me yield.

XX. " So, as I entred, I did backeward looke,
For feare of harme that might lie hidden there;
And loe! his hindparts, whereof heed I tooke,
Much more deformed fearefull, ugly were,
Then all his former parts did earst appere:
For hatred, murther, treason, and despight,
With many moe lay in ambushment there,
Awayting to entrap the warelesse wight
Which did not them prevent with vigilant foresight.

XXI. " Thus having past all perill, I was come
Within the compasse of that Islands space;
The which did seeme, unto my simple doome,
The only pleasant and delightfull place
That ever troden was of footings trace:
For all that nature by her mother-wit

Could frame in earth, and forme of substance base,
Was there; and all that nature did omit,
Art, playing second natures part, supplyed it.

XXII. " No tree, that is of count, in greenewood growes,
From lowest Juniper to Ceder tall,
No flowre in field, that daintie odour throwes,
And deckes his branch with blossomes over all,
But there was planted, or grew naturall:
Nor sense of man so coy and curious nice,
But there mote find to please it selfe withall;
Nor hart could wish for any queint device,
But there it present was, and did fraile sense entice.

XXIII. " In such luxurious plentie of all pleasure,
It seem'd a second paradise to ghesse,
So lavishly enricht with Natures threasure,
That if the happie soules, which doe possesse
Th' Elysian fields and live in lasting blesse,
Should happen this with living eye to see,
They soone would loath their lesser happinesse,
And wish to life return'd againe to bee,
That in this joyous place they mote have joyance free.

XXIV. " Fresh shadowes, fit to shroud from sunny ray;
Faire lawnds, to take the sunne in season dew;
Sweet springs, in which a thousand Nymphs did play;
Soft rombling brookes, that gentle slomber drew;
High reared mounts, the lands about to vew;
Low looking dales, disloignd from common gaze;
Delightfull bowres, to solace lovers trew;
False Labyrinthes, fond runners eyes to daze;
All which by nature made did nature selfe amaze.

XXV. " And all without were walkes and alleyes dight
With divers trees enrang'd in even rankes;
And here and there were pleasant arbors pight,
And shadie seates, and sundry flowring bankes,
To sit and rest the walkers wearie shankes:
And therein thousand payres of lovers walkt,
Praysing their god, and yeelding him great thankes,
Ne ever ought but of their true loves talkt,
Ne ever for rebuke or blame of any balkt.

xxvi. " All these together by themselves did sport
          Their spotlesse pleasures and sweet loves content.
          But, farre away from these, another sort
          Of lovers lincked in true harts consent,
          Which loved not as these for like intent,
          But on chast vertue grounded their desire,
          Farre from all fraud or fayned blandishment;
          Which, in their spirits kindling zealous fire,
          Brave thoughts and noble deedes did evermore aspire.

xxvii. " Such were great Hercules and Hyllus deare
          Trew Jonathan and David trustie tryde
          Stout Theseus and Pirithous his feare
          Pylades and Orestes by his syde;
          Myld Titus and Gesippus without pryde;
          Damon and Pythias, whom death could not sever:
          All these, and all that ever had bene tyde
          In bands of friendship, there did live for ever;
          Whose lives although decay'd, yet loves decayed never.

xxviii. " Which when as I, that never tasted blis
          Nor happie howre, beheld with gazefull eye,
          I thought there was none other heaven then this;
          And gan their endlesse happinesse envye,
          That being free from feare and gealosye
          Might frankely there their loves desire possesse;
          Whilest I, through paines and perlous jeopardie,
          Was forst to seeke my lifes deare patronnesse:
          Much dearer be the things which come through hard
                    distresse.

xxix. " Yet all those sights, and all that else I saw,
          Might not my steps withhold, but that forthright
          Unto that purposed place I did me draw,
          Where as my love was lodged day and night,
          The temple of great Venus, that is hight
          The Queene of beautie, and of love the mother,
          There worshipped of every living wight;
          Whose goodly workmanship farre past all other
          That ever were on earth, all were they set together.

xxx. " Not that same famous Temple of Diane,
          Whose hight all Ephesus did oversee,
          And which all Asia sought with vowes prophane,

One of the worlds seven wonders sayd to bee,
M ght match with this by many a degree:
Nor that which that wise King of Jurie framed
With endlesse cost to be th' Almighties see;
Nor all, that else through all the world is named
To all the heathen Gods, might like to this be clamed.

XXXI. " I, much admyring that so goodly frame,
Unto the porch approcht which open stood;
But therein sate an amiable Dame,
That seem'd to be of very sober mood,
And in her semblant shew'd great womanhood:
Strange was her tyre; for on her head a crowne
She wore, much like unto a Danisk hood,
Poudred with pearle and stone; and all her gowne
Enwoven was with gold, that raught full low adowne.

XXXII. On either side of her two young men stood,
Both strongly arm'd, as fearing one another;
Yet were they brethren both of halfe the blood,
Begotten by two fathers of one mother,
Though of contrarie natures each to other:
The one of them hight Love, the other Hate.
Hate was the elder, Love the younger brother;
Yet was the younger stronger in his state
Then th' elder, and him maystred still in all debate.

XXXIII. " Nathlesse that Dame so well them tempred both,
That she them forced hand to joyne in hand,
Albe that Hatred was thereto full loth,
And turn'd his face away, as he did stand,
Unwilling to behold that lovely band.
Yet she was of such grace and vertuous might,
That her commaundment he could not withstand,
But bit his lip for felonous despight,
And gnasht his yron tuskes at that displeasing sight.

XXXIV. " Concord she cleeped was in common reed,
Mother of blessed Peace and Friendship trew;
They both her twins, both borne of heavenly seed,
And she her selfe likewise divinely grew;
The which right well her workes divine did shew:
For strength and wealth and happinesse she lends

And strife and warre and anger does subdew:
Of litle much, of foes she maketh friends,
And to afflicted minds sweet rest and quiet sends.

xxxv. " By her the heaven is in his course contained.
And all the world in state unmoved stands,
As their Almightie maker first ordained,
And bound them with inviolable bands;
Else would the waters overflow the lands,
And fire devoure the ayre, and hell them quight,
But that she holds them with her blessed hands.
She is the nourse of pleasure and delight,
And unto Venus grace the gate doth open right.

xxxvi. " By her I entring half dismayed was;
But she in gentle wise me entertayned,
And twixt her selfe and Love did let me pas;
But Hatred would my entrance have restrayned,
And with his club me threatned to have brayned,
Had not the Ladie with her powrefull speach
Him from his wicked will uneath refrayned;
And th' other eke his malice did empeach,
Till I was throughly past the perill of his reach.

xxxvii. " Into the inmost Temple thus I came,
Which fuming all with frankensence I found
And odours rising from the altars flame.
Upon an hundred marble pillors round
The roofe up high was reared from the ground,
All deckt with crownes, and chaynes, and girlands gay,
And thousand pretious gifts worth many a pound,
The which sad lovers for their vowes did pay;
And all the ground was strow'd with flowres as fresh
as May.

xxxviii. " An hundred Altars round about were set,
All flaming with their sacrifices fire,
That with the steme thereof the Temple swet,
Which rould in clouds to heaven did aspire,
And in them bore true lovers vowes entire:
And eke an hundred brasen caudrons bright,
To bath in joy and amorous desire,
Every of which was to a damzell hight;
For all the Priests were damzels in soft linnen dight.

XXXIX. " Right in the midst the Goddesse selfe did stand
　　　　　Upon an altar of some costly masse,
　　　　　Whose substance was uneath to understand:
　　　　　For neither pretious stone, nor durefull brasse,
　　　　　Nor shining gold, nor mouldring clay it was;
　　　　　But much more rare and pretious to esteeme,
　　　　　Pure in aspect, and like to christall glasse,
　　　　　Yet glasse was not, if one did rightly deeme;
　　　　　But, being faire and brickle, likest glasse did seeme.

XL. " But it in shape and beautie did excell
　　　　All other Idoles which the heathen adore,
　　　　Farre passing that, which by surpassing skill
　　　　Phidias did make in Paphos Isle of yore,
　　　　With which that wretched Greeke, that life forlore,
　　　　Did fall in love: yet this much fairer shined,
　　　　But covered with a slender veile afore;
　　　　And both her feete and legs together twyned
　　　　Were with a snake, whose head and tail were fast
　　　　　combyned.

XLI. " The cause why she was covered with a vele
　　　　Was hard to know, for that her Priests the same
　　　　From peoples knowledge labour'd to concele:
　　　　But sooth it was not sure for womanish shame,
　　　　Nor any blemish which the worke mote blame;
　　　　But for, they say, she hath both kinds in one,
　　　　Both male and female, both under one name:
　　　　She syre and mother is her selfe alone,
　　　　Begets and eke conceives, ne needeth other none.

XLII. " And all about her necke and shoulders flew
　　　　A flocke of litle loves, and sports, and joyes,
　　　　With nimble wings of gold and purple hew;
　　　　Whose shapes seem'd not like to terrestriall boyes,
　　　　But like to Angels playing heavenly toyes,
　　　　The whilest their eldest brother was away,
　　　　Cupid their eldest brother; he enjoyes
　　　　The wide kingdome of love with lordly sway,
　　　　And to his law compels all creatures to obay.

XLIII. " And all about her altar scattered lay
　　　　Great sorts of lovers piteously complayning,
　　　　Some of their losse, some of their loves delay,

Some of their pride, some paragons disdayning,
Some fearing fraud, some fraudulently fayning,
As every one had cause of good or ill.
Amongst the rest some one, through Loves constrayning
Tormented sore, could not containe it still,
But thus break forth, that all the temple it did fill.

XLIV. "'Great Venus! Queene of beautie and of grace,
The joy of Gods and men, that under skie
Doest fayrest shine, and most adorne thy place;
That with thy smyling looke doest peaifie
The raging seas, and makst the stormes to flie;
Thee, goddesse, thee the winds, the clouds doe feare,
And, when thou spredst thy mantle forth on hie,
The waters play, and pleasant lands appeare,
And heavens laugh, and al the world shews joyous cheare.

XLV. "'Then doth the dædale earth throw forth to thee
Out of her fruitfull lap aboundant flowres;
And then all living wights, soone as they see
The spring breake forth out of his lusty bowres,
They all doe learne to play the Paramours;
First doe the merry birds, thy prety pages,
Privily pricked with thy lustfull powres,
Chirpe loud to thee out of their leavy cages,
And thee their mother call to coole their kindly rages.

XLVI. "'Then doe the salvage beasts begin to play
Their pleasant friskes, and loath their wonted food:
The Lyons rore; the Tygres loudly bray;
The raging Buls rebellow through the wood,
And breaking forth dare tempt the deepest flood
To come where thou doest draw them with desire.
So all things else, that nourish vitall blood,
Soone as with fury thou doest them inspire,
In generation seeke to quench their inward fire.

XLVII. "'So all the world by thee at first was made,
And dayly yet thou doest the same repayre;
Ne ought on earth that merry is and glad,
Ne ought on earth that lovely is and fayre,
But thou the same for pleasure didst prepayre:
Thou art the root of all that joyous is:

Great God of men and women, queen of th' ayre,
Mother of laughter, and welspring of blisse,
O graunt that of my love at last I may not misse!'

XLVIII. " So did he say: but I with murmure soft,
That none might heare the sorrow of my hart,
Yet inly groning deepe and sighing oft,
Besought her to graunt ease unto my smart,
And to my wound her gratious help impart.
Whilest thus I spake, behold! with happy eye
I spyde where at the Idoles feet apart
A bevie of fayre damzels close did lye,
Wayting when as the Antheme should be sung on hye.

XLIX. " The first of them did seeme of ryper years
And graver countenance then all the rest;
Yet all the rest were eke her equall peares.
Yet unto her obayed all the best.
Her name was Womanhood; that she exprest
By her sad semblant and demeanure wyse:
For stedfast still her eyes did fixed rest,
Ne rov'd at randon, after gazers guyse,
Whose luring baytes oftimes doe heedlesse harts entyse.

L. " And next to her sate goody Shamefastnesse,
Ne ever durst her eyes from ground upreare,
Ne ever once did looke up from her desse,
As if some blame of evill she did feare,
That in her cheekes made roses oft appeare:
And her against sweet Cherefulnesse was placed,
Whose eyes, like twinkling stars in evening cleare,
Were deckt with smyles that all sad humors chaced,
And darted forth delights the which her goodly graced.

LI. " And next to her sate sober Modestie,
Holding her hand upon her gentle hart;
And her against sate comely Curtesie,
That unto every person knew her part;
And her before was seated overthwart
Soft Silence, and submisse Obedience,
Both linckt together never to dispart;
Both gifts of God, not gotten but from thence,
Both girlonds of his Saints against their foes offence.

LII. " Thus sate they all around in seemely rate:
    And in the midst of them a goodly mayd
    Even in the lap of Womanhood there sate,
    The which was all in lilly white arayd,
    With silver streames amongst the linnen stray'd;
    Like to the Morne, when first her shyning face
    Hath to the gloomy world itselfe bewray'd:
    That same was fayrest Amoret in place,
    Shyning with beauties light and heavenly vertues grace.

LIII. " Whom soone as I beheld, my hart gan throb
    And wade in doubt what best were to be donne;
    For sacrilege me seem'd the Church to rob,
    And folly seem'd to leave the thing undonne
    Which with so strong attempt I had begonne.
    Tho, shaking off all doubt and shamefast feare
    Which Ladies love, I heard, had never wonne
    Mongst men of worth, I to her stepped neare,
    And by the lilly hand her labour'd up to reare.

LIV. " Thereat that formost matrone me did blame,
    And sharpe rebuke for being over bold;
    Saying, it was to Knight unseemely shame
    Upon a recluse Virgin to lay hold,
    That unto Venus services was sold.
    To whom I thus: ' Nay, but it fitteth best
    For Cupids man with Venus mayd to hold,
    For ill your goddesse services are drest
    By virgins, and her sacrifices let to rest.'

LV. " With that my shield I forth to her did show,
    Which all that while I closely had conceld;
    On which when Cupid, with his killing bow
    And cruell shafts, emblazond she beheld,
    At sight thereof she was with terror queld,
    And said no more: but I, which all that while
    The pledge of faith, her hand, engaged held,
    Like warie Hynd within the weedie soyle,
    For no intreatie would forgoe so glorious spoyle.

LVI. " And evermore upon the Goddesse face
    Mine eye was fixt, for feare of her offence;
    Whom when I saw with amiable grace

To laugh at me, and favour my pretence,
I was emboldned with more confidence;
And nought for nicenesse nor for envy sparing,
In presence of them all forth led her thence
All looking on, and like astonisht staring,
Yet to lay hand on her not one of all them daring.

LVII. " She often prayd, and often me besought,
Sometime with tender teares to let her goe,
Sometime with witching smyles; but yet, for nought
That ever she to me could say or doe,
Could she her wished freedome fro me wooe:
But forth I led her through the Temple gate,
By which I hardly past with much adoe:
But that same Ladie, which me friended late
In entrance, did me also friend in my retrate.

LVIII. " No lesse did Daunger threaten me with dread,
Whenas he saw me, maugre all his powre,
That glorious spoyle of beautie with me lead,
Then Cerberus, when Orpheus did recoure
His Leman from the Stygian Princes boure:
But evermore my shield did me defend
Against the storme of every dreadfull stoure:
Thus safely with my love I thence did wend."
So ended he his tale, where I this Canto end.

[In Book V Spenser considers Justice, a virtue at once subtly
different from and yet traditionally including the friendship and
concord that have been the themes of the preceding Book IV.
Justice is Equity—not now so much in the individual soul (that,
after all, is the meaning of its complementary cardinal virtue
Temperance, the subject of Book II) but in the world at large,
and especially the world of politics. It expresses God's 'soveraine
powre' that on earth is delegated to princes (Proem to Book V,
stanzas 10, 11). Artegall is the knight of Justice in the book, and
his executive agent is the iron man Talus. Their task is to destroy
the giant Grantorto (Great Wrong) and restore Irena (Peace,
Ireland) to her kingdom; but it is a task that can be accomplished
only after Artegall has learned the meaning of Equity (in part the
subject of Britomart's vision in canto vii). Much of the book is
topical: the pagan 'Souldan' of canto viii is Philip, King of Spain,
and his defeat is the defeat of the Armada; in canto ix Elizabeth

as Mercilla tries Duessa, and here the reference is to the trial and execution of Mary Queen of Scots in 1586–7; while other concerns are Elizabethan policies in the Netherlands and Ireland. It is a book that, as a whole, does not have a ready appeal for the modern reader (the story is repetitive, the allegory a bit thin and monothematic), and this, together with considerations of available space, is why no excerpt from it is included in this selection.

Book VI contains 'the Legend of Sir Calidore, or Courtesie'. In this core canto to the book, Calidore, who has fallen in love with 'the faire Pastorell' (VI. ix. 46) and abandoned his knightly quest for the Blatant Beast, catches a glimpse of Colin Clout and Venus's Graces. The episode is discussed in the Introduction.]

CANTO X

Calidore sees the Graces daunce
To Colins melody;
The whiles his Pastorell is led
Into captivity.

I. Who now does follow the foule Blatant Beast,
Whilest Calidore does follow that faire Mayd,
Unmyndfull of his vow, and high beheast
Which by the Faery Queene was on him layd,
That he should never leave, nor be delayd
From chacing him, till he had it attchieved?
But now, entrapt of love, which him betrayd,
He mindeth more how he may be relieved
With grace from her, whose love his heart hath sore
    engrieved.

II. That from henceforth he meanes no more to sew
His former quest, so full of toile and paine:
Another quest, another game in vew
He hath, the guerdon of his love to gaine;
With whom he myndes for ever to remaine,
And set his rest amongst the rusticke sort,
Rather then hunt still after shadowes vaine
Of courtly favour, fed with light report
Of every blaste, and sayling alwaies in the port,

III. Ne certes mote he greatly blamed be
From so high step to stoupe unto so low;
For who had tasted once (as oft did he)
The happy peace which there doth overflow,
And prov'd the perfect pleasures which doe grow
Amongst poore hyndes, in hils, in woods, in dales,
Would never more delight in painted show
Of such false blisse, as there is set for stales
T' entrap unwary fooles in their eternall bales,

IV. For what hath all that goodly glorious gaze
Like to one sight which Calidore did vew?
The glaunce whereof their dimmed eies would daze,

That never more they should endure the shew
Of that sunne-shine that makes them looke askew:
Ne ought, in all that world of beauties rare,
(Save onely Glorianaes heavenly hew,
To which what can compare?) can it compare;
The which, as commeth now by course, I will declare.

v. One day, as he did raunge the fields abroad,
Whilest his faire Pastorella was elsewhere,
He chaunst to come, far from all peoples troad,
Unto a place whose pleasaunce did appere
To passe all others on the earth which were:
For all that ever was by natures skill
Devized to worke delight was gathered there,
And there by her were poured forth at fill,
As if, this to adorne, she all the rest did pill.

vi. It was an hill plaste in an open plaine,
That round about was bordered with a wood
Of matchlesse hight, that seem'd th' earth to disdaine;
In which all trees of honour stately stood,
And did all winter as in summer bud,
Spredding pavilions for the birds to bowre,
Which in their lower braunches sung aloud;
And in their tops the soring hauke did towre,
Sitting like King of fowles in majesty and powre:

vii. And at the foote thereof a gentle flud
His silver waves did softly tumble downe,
Unmard with ragged mosse or filthy mud;
Ne mote wylde beastes, ne mote the ruder clowne,
Thereto approch; ne filth mote therein drowne:
But Nymphes and Faeries by the bancks did sit
In the woods shade which did the waters crowne,
Keeping all noysome things away from it,
And to the waters fall tuning their accents fit.

viii. And on the top thereof a spacious plaine
Did spred it selfe, to serve to all delight,
Either to daunce, when they to daunce would faine,
Or else to course about their bases light;
Ne ought there wanted which for pleasure might
Desired be, or thence to banish bale,

So pleasauntly the hill with equall hight
Did seeme to overlooke the lowly vale;
Therefore it rightly cleeped was mount Acidale.

IX. They say that Venus, when she did´dispose
Her selfe to pleasaunce, used to resort
Unto this place, and therein to repose
And rest her selfe as in a gladsome port,
Or with the Graces there to play and sport:
That even her owne Cytheron, though it in
She used most to keepe her royall court,
And in her soveraine Majesty to sit,
She in regard hereof refusde and thought unfit.

X. Unto this place when as the Elfin Knight
Approcht, him seemed that the merry sound
Of a shrill pipe he playing heard on hight,
And many feete fast thumping th' hollow ground,
That through the woods their Eccho did rebound.
He nigher drew to weete what mote it be:
There he a troupe of Ladies dauncing found
Full merrily, and making gladfull glee,
And in the midst a Shepheard piping he did see.

XI. He durst not enter into th' open greene,
For dread of them unwares to be descryde,
For breaking of their daunce, if he were seene;
But in the covert of the wood did byde,
Beholding all, yet of them unespyde.
There he did see that pleased much his sight,
That even he him selfe his eyes envyde,
An hundred naked maidens lilly white
All raunged in a ring and dauncing in delight.

XII. All they without were raunged in a ring,
And daunced round; but in the midst of them
Three other Ladies did both daunce and sing,
The whilest the rest them round about did hemme,
And like a girlond did in compasse stemme:
And in the middest of those same three was placed
Another Damzell, as a precious gemme
Amidst a ring most richly well enchaced,
That with her goodly presence all the rest much graced.

XIII. Looke! how the crowne, which Ariadne wore
Upon her yvory forehead, that same day
That Theseus her unto his bridale bore,
When the bold Centaures made that bloudy fray
With the fierce Lapithes which did them dismay,
Being now placed in the firmament,
Through the bright heaven doth her beams display,
And is unto the starres an ornament,
Which round about her move in order excellent.

XIV. Such was the beauty of this goodly band,
Whose sundry parts were here too long to tell;
But she that in the midst of them did stand
Seem'd all the rest in beauty to excell,
Crownd with a rosie girlond that right well
Did her beseeme: And ever, as the crew
About her daunst, sweet flowres that far did smell
And fragrant odours they uppon her threw;
But most of all those three did her with gifts endew.

XV. Those were the Graces, daughters of delight,
Handmaides of Venus, which are wont to haunt
Uppon this hill, and daunce there day and night:
Those three to men all gifts of grace do graunt;
And all that Venus in her selfe doth vaunt
Is borrowed of them.   But that faire one,
That in the midst was placed paravaunt,
Was she to whom that shepheard pypt alone;
That made him pipe so merrily, as never none.

XVI. She was, to weete, that jolly Shepheards lasse,
Which piped there unto that merry rout;
That jolly shepheard, which there piped, was
Poore Colin Clout, (who knowes not Colin Clout?)
He pypt apace, whilest they him daunst about.
Pype, jolly shepheard, pype thou now apace
Unto thy love that made thee low to lout:
Thy love is present there with thee in place;
Thy love is there advaunst to be another Grace.

XVII. Much wondred Calidore at this straunge sight,
Whose like before his eye had never seene;
And standing long astonished in spright,

And rapt with pleasaunce, wist not what to weene;
Whether it were the traine of beauties Queene,
Or Nymphes, or Faeries, or enchaunted show,
With which his eyes mote have deluded beene.
Therefore, resolving what it was to know,
Out of the wood he rose, and toward them did go.

XVIII. But, soone as he appeared to their vew,
They vanisht all away out of his sight,
And cleane were gone, which way he never knew:
All save the shepheard, who, for fell despight
Of that displeasure, broke his bag-pipe quight,
And made great mone for that unhappy turne:
But Calidore, though no lesse sory wight
For that mishap, yet seeing him to mourne,
Drew neare, that he the truth of all by him mote learne.

XIX. And, first him greeting, thus unto him spake:
" Haile, jolly shepheard, which thy joyous dayes
Here leadest in this goodly merry-make,
Frequented of these gentle Nymphes alwayes,
Which to thee flocke to heare thy lovely layes!
Tell me, what mote these dainty Damzels be,
Which here with thee doe make their pleasant playes?
Right happy thou that mayst them freely see!
But why, when I them saw, fled they away from me? "

XX. " Not I so happy," answered then that swaine,
" As thou unhappy, which them thence didst chace,
Whom by no meanes thou canst recall againe;
For, being gone, none can them bring in place,
But whom they of them selves list so to grace."
" Right sory I," (saide then Sir Calidore)
" That my ill fortune did them hence displace;
But since things passed none may now restore,
Tell me what were they all, whose lacke thee grieves
so sore? "

XXI. Tho gan that shepheard thus for to dilate:
" Then wote, thou shepheard, whatsoever thou bee,
That all those Ladies, which thou sawest late,
Are Venus Damzels, all within her fee,
But differing in honour and degree:
They all are Graces which on her depend,

Besides a thousand more which ready bee
Her to adorne, when so she forth doth wend
But those three in the midst doe chiefe on her attend.

XXII. " They are the daughters of sky-ruling Jove,
By him begot of faire Eurynome,
The Oceans daughter, in this pleasant grove,
As he, this way comming from feastfull glee
Of Thetis wedding with Æacidee,
In sommers shade him selfe here rested weary:
The first of them hight mylde Euphrosyne,
Next faire Aglaia, last Thalia merry;
Sweete Goddesses all three, which me in mirth do cherry!

XXIII. " These three on men all gracious gifts bestow,
Which decke the body or adorne the mynde,
To make them lovely or well-favoured show;
As comely carriage, entertainement kynde,
Sweete semblaunt, friendly offices that bynde,
And all the complements of curtesie:
They teach us how to each degree and kynde
We should our selves demeane, to low, to hie,
To friends, to foes; which skill men call Civility.

XXIV. " Therefore they alwaies smoothly seeme to smile,
That we likewise should mylde and gentle be;
And also naked are, that without guile
Or false dissemblaunce all them plaine may see,
Simple and true, from covert malice free;
And eeke them selves so in their daunce they bore,
That two of them still froward seem'd to bee,
But one still towards shew'd her selfe afore;
That good should from us goe, then come, in greater store.

XXV. " Such were those Goddesses which ye did see;
But that fourth Mayd, which there amidst them traced,
Who can aread what creature mote she bee,
Whether a creature, or a goddesse graced
With heavenly gifts from heven first enraced?
But what so sure she was, she worthy was
To be the fourth with those three other placed:
Yet was she certes but a countrey lasse;
Yet she all other countrey lasses farre did passe:

XXVI. " So farre, as doth the daughter of the day
All other lesser lights in light excell;
So farre doth she in beautyfull array
Above all other lasses beare the bell;
Ne lesse in vertue that beseemes her well
Doth she exceede the rest of all her race;
For which the Graces, that here wont to dwell,
Have for more honor brought her to this place,
And graced her so much to be another Grace.

XXVII. " Another Grace she well deserves to be,
In whom so many Graces gathered are,
Excelling much the meane of her degree;
Divine resemblaunce, beauty soveraine rare,
Firme Chastity, that spight ne blemish dare:
All which she with such courtesie doth grace,
That all her peres cannot with her compare,
But quite are dimmed when she is in place:
She made me often pipe, and now to pipe apace.

XXVIII. " Sunne of the world, great glory of the sky,
That all the earth doest lighten with thy rayes,
Great Gloriana, greatest Majesty!
Pardon thy shepheard, mongst so many layes
As he hath sung of thee in all his dayes,
To make one minime of thy poore handmayd,
And underneath thy feete to place her prayse;
That when thy glory shall be farre displayd
To future age, of her this mention may be made! "

XXIX. When thus that shepheard ended had his speach
Sayd Calidore: " Now sure it yrketh mee,
That to thy blisse I made this luckelesse breach,
As now the author of thy bale to be,
Thus to bereave thy loves deare sight from thee:
But, gentle Shepheard, pardon thou my shame,
Who rashly sought that which I mote not see."
Thus did the courteous Knight excuse his blame,
And to recomfort him all comely meanes did frame.

XXX. In such discourses they together spent
Long time, as fit occasion forth them led;
With which the Knight him selfe did much content,

And with delight his greedy fancy fed
Both of his words, which he with reason red,
And also of the place, whose pleasures rare
With such regard his sences ravished,
That thence he had no will away to fare,
But wisht that with that shepheard he mote dwelling
      share.

XXXI. But that envenimd sting, the which of yore
His poysnous point deepe fixed in his hart
Had left, now gan afresh to rancle sore,
And to renue the rigour of his smart;
Which to recure no skill of Leaches art
Mote him availe, but to returne againe
To his wounds worker, that with lovely dart
Dinting his brest had bred his restlesse paine;
Like as the wounded Whale to shore flies from the
      maine.

XXXII. So, taking leave of that same gentle Swaine,
He backe returned to his rusticke wonne,
Where his faire Pastorella did remaine:
To whome, in sort as he at first begonne,
He daily did apply him selfe to donne
All dewfull service, voide of thoughts impure;
Ne any paines ne perill did he shonne,
By which he might her to his love allure,
And liking in her yet untamed heart procure.

XXXIII. And evermore the shepheard Coridon,
What ever thing he did her to aggrate,
Did strive to match with strong contention,
And all his paines did closely emulate;
Whether it were to caroll, as they sate
Keeping their sheepe, or games to exercize,
Or to present her with their labours late;
Through which if any grace chaunst to arize
To him, the Shepheard streight with jealousie did frize.

XXXIV. One day, as they all three together went
To the greene wood to gather strawberies
There chaunst to them a dangerous accident:
A Tigre forth out of the wood did rise,

That with fell clawes full of fierce gourmandize,
And greedy mouth wide gaping like hell-gate,
Did runne at Pastorell her to surprize;
Whom she beholding, now all desolate,
Gan cry to them aloud to helpe her all too late.

xxxv. Which Coridon first hearing ran in hast
To reskue her; but, when he saw the feend,
Through cowherd feare he fled away as fast,
Ne durst abide the daunger of the end:
His life he steemed dearer then his frend:
But Calidore soone comming to her ayde,
When he the beast saw ready now to rend
His loves deare spoile, in which his heart was prayde
He ran at him enraged, instead of being frayde.

xxxvi. He had no weapon but his shepheards hooke
To serve the vengeaunce of his wrathfull will;
With which so sternely he the monster strooke,
That to the ground astonished he fell;
Whence, ere he could recou'r, he did him quell,
And, hewing off his head, he it presented
Before the feete of the faire Pastorell;
Who, scarcely yet from former feare exempted,
A thousand times him thankt that had her death
prevented.

xxxvii. From that day forth she gan him to affect,
And daily more her favour to augment;
But Coridon for cowherdize reject,
Fit to keepe sheepe, unfit for loves content:
The gentle heart scornes base disparagement.
Yet Calidore did not despise him quight,
But usde him friendly for further intent,
That by his fellowship he colour might
Both his estate and love from skill of any wight.

xxxviii. So well he wood her, and so well he wrought her,
With humble service, and with daily sute,
That at the last unto his will he brought her;
Which he so wisely well did prosecute,
That of his love he reapt the timely frute,
And joyed long in close felicity,

Till fortune, fraught with malice, blinde and brute,
That envies lovers long prosperity,
Blew up a bitter storme of foule adversity.

XXXIX. It fortuned one day, when Calidore
Was hunting in the woods, (as was his trade)
A lawlesse people, Brigants hight of yore,
That never usde to live by plough nor spade,
But fed on spoile and booty, which they made
Upon their neighbours which did nigh them border,
The dwelling of these shepheards did invade,
And spoyld their houses, and them selves did murder,
And drove away their flocks; with other much disorder.

XL. Amongst the rest, the which they then did pray,
They spoyld old Melibee of all he had,
And all his people captive led away;
Mongst which this lucklesse mayd away was lad,
Faire Pastorella, sorrowfull and sad,
Most sorrowfull, most sad, that ever sight,
Now made the spoile of theeves and Brigants bad,
Which was the conquest of the gentlest Knight
That ever liv'd, and th' onely glory of his might,

XLI. With them also was taken Coridon,
And carried captive by those theeves away;
Who in the covert of the night, that none
Mote them descry, nor reskue from their pray,
Unto their dwelling did them close convay.
Their dwelling in a little Island was,
Covered with shrubby woods, in which no way
Appeared for people in nor out to pas,
Nor any footing fynde for overgrowen gras:

XLII. For underneath the ground their way was made
Through hollow caves, that no man mote discover
For the thicke shrubs, which did them alwaies shade
From view of living wight and covered over;
But darkenesse dred and daily night did hover
Through all the inner parts, wherein they dwelt;
Ne lightned was with window, nor with lover,
But with continuall candle-light, which delt
A doubtfull sense of things, not so well seene as felt,

XLIII. Hither those Brigants brought their present pray,
      And kept them with continuall watch and ward;
      Meaning, so soone as they convenient may,
      For slaves to sell them for no small reward
      To Merchants, which them kept in bondage hard,
      Or sold againe.   Now when faire Pastorell
      Into this place was brought, and kept with gard
      Of griesly theeves, she thought her self in hell,
      Where with such damned fiends she should in darknesse
          dwell.

XLIV. But for to tell the dolefull dreriment
      And pittifull complaints which there she made,
      Where day and night she nought did but lament
      Her wretched life shut up in deadly shade,
      And waste her goodly beauty, which did fade
      Like to a flowre that feeles no heate of sunne,
      Which way her feeble leaves with comfort glade—
      And what befell her in that theevish wonne,
      Will in another Canto better be begonne.

p. 470

[The Mutability Cantos were probably going to be the core cantos of Book VII. Their concern is that of Ovid's *Metamorphoses*, Petrarch's *Trionfi*, Theseus' speech at the end of Chaucer's *Knight's Tale*, and many other works; and their argument is the relationship of flux to ordered development, process to eternity, and the classical versus the Christian view of time and history.]

TWO CANTOS OF

MUTABILITIE

WHICH, BOTH FOR FORME AND MATTER, APPEARE TO BE
PARCELL OF SOME FOLLOWING BOOKE OF

THE FAERIE QUEENE

UNDER

THE LEGEND OF CONSTANCIE

CANTO VI

Proud Change (not pleasd in mortall things
Beneath the Moone to raigne)
Pretends as well of Gods as Men
To be the Soveraine.

I. WHAT man that sees the ever-whirling wheele,
Of Change, the which all mortall things doth sway,
But that therby doth find, and plainly feele,
How MUTABILITY in them doth play
Her cruell sports to many mens decay?
Which that to all may better yet appeare,
I will rehearse that whylome I heard say,
How she at first her selfe began to reare
Gainst all the Gods, and th' empire sought from them
     to beare.

II. But first, here falleth fittest to unfold
Her antique race and linage ancient,
As I have found it registred of old
In Faery Land mongst records permanent,
She was, to weet, a daughter by descent
Of those old Titans that did whylome strive
With Saturnes sonne for heavens regiment;
Whom though high Jove of kingdome did deprive,
Yet many of their stemme long after did survive:

471

III. And many of them afterwards obtain'd
Great power of Jove, and high authority:
As Hecaté, in whose almighty hand
He plac't all rule and principalitie,
To be by her disposed diversly
To Gods and men, as she them list divide;
And drad Bellona, that doth sound on hie
Warres and allarums unto Nations wide,
That makes both heaven and earth to tremble at her pride.

IV. So likewise did this Titanesse aspire
Rule and dominion to her selfe to gaine;
That as a Goddesse men might her admire,
And heavenly honors yield, as to them twaine:
And first, on earth she sought it to obtaine;
Where shee such proofe and sad examples shewed
Of her great power, to many ones great paine,
That not men onely (whom she soone subdewed)
But eke all other creatures her bad dooings rewed.

V. For she the face of earthly things so changed,
That all which Nature had establisht first
In good estate, and in meet order ranged,
She did pervert, and all their statutes burst:
And all the worlds faire frame (which none yet durst
Of Gods or men to alter or misguide)
She alter'd quite; and made them all accurst
That God had blest, and did at first provide
In that still happy state for ever to abide.

VI. Ne shee the lawes of Nature onely brake,
But eke of Justice, and of Policie;
And wrong of right, and bad of good did make
And death for life exchanged foolishlie:
Since which all living wights have learn'd to die,
And all this world is woxen daily worse.
O pittious worke of MUTABILITY,
By which we all are subject to that curse,
And death, instead of life, have sucked from our Nurse!

VII. And now, when all the earth she thus had brought
To her behest, and thralled to her might,
She gan to cast in her ambitious thought

T' attempt the empire of the heavens hight,
And Jove himselfe to shoulder from his right.
At first, she past the region of the ayre
And of the fire, whose substance thin and slight
Made no resistance, ne could her contraire,
But ready passage to her pleasure did prepaire.

VIII. Thence to the Circle of the Moone she clambe,
Where Cynthia raignes in everlasting glory,
To whose bright shining palace straight she came,
All fairely deckt with heavens goodly storie;
Whose silver gates (by which there sate an hory
Old aged Sire, with hower-glasse in hand,
Hight Time,) she entred, were he liefe or sory;
Ne staide till she the highest stage had scand,
Where Cynthia did sit, that never still did stand.

IX. Her sitting on an Ivory throne shee found,
Drawne of two steeds, th' one black, the other white,
Environd with tenne thousand starres around
That duly her attended day and night;
And by her side there ran her Page, that hight
Vesper, whom we the Evening-starre intend;
That with his Torche, still twinkling like twylight,
Her lightened all the way where she should wend,
And joy to weary wandring travailers did lend:

X. That when the hardy Titanesse beheld
The goodly building of her Palace bright,
Made of the heavens substance, and up-held
With thousand Crystall pillors of huge hight,
She gan to burne in her ambitious spright,
And t' envie her that in such glory raigned.
Eftsoones she cast by force and tortious might
Her to displace, and to her selfe to have gained
The kingdome of the Night, and waters by her wained.

XI. Boldly she bid the Goddesse downe descend,
And let her selfe into that Ivory throne;
For she her selfe more worthy thereof wend,
And better able it to guide alone;
Whether to men, whose falls she did bemone,
Or unto Gods, whose state she did maligne,

Or to th' infernall Powers her need give lone
Of her faire light and bounty most benigne,
Her selfe of all that rule she deemed most condigne.

XII. But she, that had to her that soveraigne seat
By highest Jove assign'd, therein to beare
Nights burning lamp, regarded not her threat,
Ne yielded ought for favour or for feare;
But with sterne count'naunce and disdainfull cheare,
Bending her horned browes, did put her back;
And, boldly blaming her for comming there,
Bade her attonce from heavens coast to pack,
Or at her perill bide the wrathfull Thunders wrack.

XIII. Yet nathemore the Giantesse forbare,
But boldly preacing-on raught forth her hand
To pluck her downe perforce from off her chaire;
And, there-with lifting up her golden wand,
Threatned to strike her if she did with-stand:
Where-at the starres, which round about her blazed,
And eke the Moones bright wagon still did stand,
All beeing with so bold attempt amazed,
And on her uncouth habit and sterne looke still gazed.

XIV. Mean-while the lower World, which nothing knew
Of all that chaunced heere, was darkned quite;
And eke the heavens, and all the heavenly crew
Of happy wights, now unpurvaid of light,
Were much afraid, and wondred at that sight;
Fearing least Chaos broken had his chaine,
And brought againe on them eternall night;
But chiefely Mercury, that next doth raigne,
Ran forth in haste unto the king of Gods to plaine.

XV. All ran together with a great out-cry
To Joves faire palace fixt in heavens hight;
And, beating at his gates full earnestly,
Gan call to him aloud with all their might
To know what meant that suddaine lacke of light.
The father of the Gods, when this he heard,
Was troubled much at their so strange affright,
Doubting least Typhon were againe uprear'd,
Or other his old foes that once him sorely fear'd.

XVI. Eftsoones the sonne of Maia forth he sent
Downe to the Circle of the Moone, to knowe
The cause of this so strange astonishment,
And why she did her wonted course forslowe;
And if that any were on earth belowe
That did with charmes or Magick her molest,
Him to attache, and downe to hell to throwe;
But if from heaven it were, then to arrest
The Author, and him bring before his presence prest.

XVII. The wingd-foot God so fast his plumes did beat,
That soone he came where-as the Titanesse
Was striving with faire Cynthia for her seat;
At whose strange sight and haughty hardinesse
He wondred much, and feared her no lesse:
Yet laying feare aside to doe his charge,
At last he bade her (with bold stedfastnesse)
Ceasse to molest the Moone to walke at large,
Or come before high Jove her dooings to discharge.

XVIII. And there-with-all he on her shoulder laid
His snaky-wreathed Mace, whose awfull power
Doth make both Gods and hellish fiends affraid:
Where-at the Titanesse did sternly lower,
And stoutly answer'd, that in evill hower
He from his Jove such message to her brought,
To bid her leave faire Cynthia's silver bower;
Sith shee his Jove and him esteemed nought,
No more then Cynthia's selfe; but all their kingdoms
          sought.

XIX. The Heavens Herald staid not to reply,
But past away, his doings to relate
Unto his Lord; who now, in th' highest sky,
Was placed in his principall Estate,
With all the Gods about him congregate:
To whom when Hermes had his message told,
It did them all exceedingly amate,
Save Jove; who, changing nought his count'nance bold,
Did unto them at length these speeches wise unfold;

XX. "Harken to mee awhile, yee heavenly Powers!
Ye may remember since th' Earths cursed seed
Sought to assaile the heavens eternall towers,

And to us all exceeding feare did breed,
But, how we then defeated all their deed,
Yee all do knowe, and them destroyed quite;
Yet not so quite, but that there did succeed
An off-spring of their bloud, which did alite
Upon the fruitfull earth, which doth us yet despite.

XXI. " Of that bad seed is this bold woman bred,
That now with bold presumption doth aspire
To thrust faire Phœbe from her silver bed,
And eke our selves from heavens high Empire,
If that her might were match to her desire.
Wherefore it now behoves us to advise
What way is best to drive her to retire,
Whether by open force, or counsell wise:
Areed, ye soones of God, as best ye can devise."

XXII. So having said, he ceast; and with his brow
(His black eye-brow, whose doomefull dreaded beck
Is wont to wield the world unto his vow,
And even the highest Powers of heaven to check)
Made signe to them in their degrees to speake,
Who straight gan cast their counsell grave and wise.
Mean-while th' Earths daughter, thogh she nought did reck
Of Hermes message, yet gan now advise
What course were best to take in this hot bold emprize.

XXIII. Eftsoones she thus resolv'd; that whil'st the Gods
(After returne of Hermes Embassie)
Were troubled, and amongst themselves at ods,
Before they could new counsels re-allie,
To set upon them in that extasie,
And take what fortune, time, and place would lend.
So forth she rose, and through the purest sky
To Joves high Palace straight cast to ascend,
To prosecute her plot. Good on-set boads good end.

XXIV. Shee there arriving boldly in did pass;
Where all the Gods she found in counsell close,
All quite unarm'd, as then their manner was.
At sight of her they suddaine all arose
In great amaze, ne wist what way to chose:
But Jove, all fearlesse, forc't them to aby;

And in his soveraine throne gan straight dispose
Himselfe, more full of grace and Majestie,
That mote encheare his friends, and foes mote terrifie.

xxv. That when the haughty Titanesse beheld,
All were she fraught with pride and impudence,
Yet with the sight thereof was almost queld;
And, inly quaking, seem'd as reft of sense
And voyd of speech in that drad audience,
Until that Jove himselfe her selfe bespake:
" Speake, thou fraile woman, speake with confidence;
Whence art thou, and what doost thou here now make?
What idle errand hast thou earths mansion to forsake?"

xxvi. She, halfe confused with his great commaund,
Yet gathering spirit of her natures pride,
Him boldly answer'd thus to his demaund:
" I am a daughter, by the mothers side,
Of her that is Grand-mother magnifide
Of all the Gods, great Earth, great Chaos child;
But by the fathers, (be it not envide)
I greater am in bloud (whereon I build)
Then all the Gods, though wrongfully from heaven exil'd.

xxvii. " For Titan (as ye all acknowledge must)
Was Saturnes elder brother by birth-right,
Both sonnes of Uranus; but by unjust
And guilefull meanes, through Corybantes slight,
The younger thrust the elder from his right:
Since which thou, Jove, injuriously hast held
The Heavens rule from Titans sonnes by might,
And them to hellish dungeons downe hast feld.
Witnesse, ye Heavens, the truth of all that I have teld!"

xxviii. Whil'st she thus spake, the Gods, that gave good eare
To her bold words, and marked well her grace,
(Beeing of stature tall as any there
Of all the Gods, and beautifull of face
As any of the Goddesses in place,)
Stood all astonied; like a sort of steeres,
Mongst whom some beast of strange and forraine race
Unwares is chaunc't, far straying from his peeres:
So did their ghastly gaze bewray their hidden feares.

XXIX. Till, having pauz'd awhile, Jove thus bespake:
" Will never mortall thoughts ceasse to aspire
In this bold sort to Heaven claime to make,
And touch celestiall seats with earthly mire?
I would have thought that bold Procrustes hire,
Or Typhons fall, or proud Ixions paine,
Or great Prometheus tasting of our ire,
Would have suffiz'd the rest for to restraine,
And warn'd all men by their example to refraine.

XXX. " But now this off-scum of that cursed fry
Dare to renew the like bold enterprize,
And chalenge th'heritage of this our skie;
Whom what should hinder, but that we likewise
Should handle as the rest of her allies,
And thunder-drive to hell? "   With that, he shooke
His Nectar-deawed locks, with which the skyes
And all the world beneath for terror quooke,
And eft his burning levin-brond in hand he tooke.

XXXI. But when he looked on her lovely face,
In which faire beames of beauty did appeare
That could the greatest wrath soone turne to grace,
(Such sway doth beauty even in Heaven beare)
He staid his hand; and, having chang'd his cheare,
He thus againe in milder wise began:
" But ah! if Gods should strive with flesh yfere,
Then shortly should the progeny of man
Be rooted out, if Jove should do still what he can.

XXXII. " But thee, faire Titans child, I rather weene,
Through some vaine errour, or inducement light,
To see that mortall eyes have never seene;
Or through ensample of thy sisters might,
Bellona, whose great glory thou doost spight,
Since thou hast seene her dreadfull power belowe,
Mongst wretched men (dismaide with her affright)
To bandie Crownes, and Kingdoms to bestowe:
And sure thy worth no lesse then hers doth seem to
showe.

XXXIII. " But wote thou this, thou hardy Titanesse,
That not the worth of any living wight

May challenge ought in Heavens interesse;
Much lesse the Title of old Titans Right:
For we by conquest, of our soveraine might,
And by eternal doome of Fates decree,
Have wonne the Empire of the Heavens bright;
Which to our selves we hold, and to whom wee
Shall worthy deeme partakers of our blisse to bee.

xxxiv. " Then ceasse thy idle claime, thou foolish gerle;
And seeke by grace and goodnesse to obtaine
That place, from which by folly Titan fell:
There to thou maist perhaps, if so thou faine
Have Jove thy gracious Lord and Soveraine."
So having said, she thus to him replide:
" Ceasse, Saturnes sonne, to seeke by proffers vaine
Of idle hopes t'allure me to thy side,
For to betray my Right before I have it tride.

xxxv. " But thee, O Jove! no equall Judge I deeme
Of my desert, or of my dewfull Right;
That in thine owne behalfe maist partiall seeme:
But to the highest him, that is behight
Father of Gods and men by equall might,
To weet, the God of Nature, I appeale."
There-at Jove wexed wroth, and in his spright
Did inly grudge, yet did it well conceale;
And bade Dan Phœbus scribe her Appellation seale.

xxxvi. Eftsoones the time and place appointed were,
Where all, both heavenly Powers and earthly wights,
Before great Natures presence should appeare,
For triall of their Titles and best Rights:
That was, to weet, upon the highest hights
Of Arlo-hill (Who knowes not Arlo-hill?)
That is the highest head (in all mens sights)
Of my old father MOLE, whom Shepheards quill
Renowmed hath with hymnes fit for a rurall skill.

xxxvii. And, were it not ill fitting for this file
To sing of hilles and woods mongst warres and Knights,
I would abate the sternenesse of my stile,
Mongst these sterne stounds to mingle soft delights;
And tell how Arlo, through Dianaes spights,

(Beeing of old the best and fairest Hill
That was in all this holy Islands hights)
Was made the most unpleasant and most ill:
Meane-while, O Clio! lend Calliope thy quill.

XXXVIII. Whylome when IRELAND florished in fame
Of wealths and goodnesse, far above the rest
Of all that beare the British Islands name,
The gods then us'd (for pleasure and for rest)
Oft to resort there-to, when seem'd them best,
But none of all there-in more pleasure found
Then Cynthia, that is soveraine Queene profest
Of woods and forrests which therein abound,
Sprinkled with wholsom waters more then most on
ground:

XXXIX. But mongst them all, as fittest for her game,
Eyther for chace of beasts with hound or boawe,
Or for to shrowde in shade from Phœbus flame,
Or bathe in fountaines that do freshly flowe
Or from high hilles or from the dales belowe,
She chose this Arlo; where she did resort
With all her Nymphes enranged on a rowe,
With whom the woody Gods did oft consort,
For with the Nymphes the Satyres love to play and
sport.

XL. Amongst the which there was a Nymph that hight
Molanna; daughter of old Father Mole,
And sister unto Mulla faire and bright,
Unto whose bed false Bregog whylome stole,
That Shepheard Colin dearely did condole,
And made her lucklesse loves well knowne to be:
But this Molanna, were she not so shole,
Were no lesse faire and beautifull then shee;
Yet, as she is, a fayrer flood may no man see.

XLI. For, first, she springs out of two marble Rocks,
On which a grove of Oakes high-mounted growes,
That as a girlond seemes to deck the locks
Of som faire Bride, brought forth with pompous showes
Out of her bowre, that many flowers strowes:
So through the flowry Dales she tumbling downe

Through many woods and shady coverts flowes,
(That on each side her silver channell crowne)
Till to the Plaine she come, whose Valleyes she doth
  drowne.

XLII. In her sweet streames Diana used oft
  (After her sweaty chace and toylesome play)
  To bathe her selfe; and, after, on the soft
  And downy grass her dainty limbes to lay
  In covert shade, where none behold her may;
  For much she hated sight of living eye.
  Foolish god Faunus, though full many a day
  He saw her clad, yet longed foolishly
  To see her naked mongst her Nymphes in privity.

XLIII. No way he found to compasse his desire,
  But to corrupt Molanna, this her maid,
  Her to discover for some secret hire:
  So her with flattering words he first assaid;
  And after, pleasing gifts for her purvaid,
  Queene-apples, and red Cherries from the tree,
  With which he her allured, and betrayd
  To tell what time he might her Lady see
  When she her selfe did bathe, that he might secret bee.

XLIV. There-to he promist, if shee would him pleasure
  With this small boone, to quit her with a better;
  To weet, that where-as shee had out of measure
  Long lov'd the Fanchin, who by nought did set her,
  That he would undertake for this to get her
  To be his Love, and of him liked well:
  Besides all which, he vow'd to be her debter
  For many moe good turnes then he would tell,
  The least of which this little pleasure should excell.

XLV. The simple mayd did yield to him anone;
  And eft him placed where he close might view
  That never any saw, save onely one,
  Who, for his hire to so foole-hardy dew,
  Was of his hounds devour'd in Hunters hew.
  Tho, as her manner was on sunny day,
  Diana, with her Nymphes about her, drew
  To this sweet spring; where, doffing her array,
  She bath'd her lovely limbes, for Jove a likely pray.

XLVI. There Faunus saw that pleased much his eye,
And made his hart to tickle in his brest,
That, for great joy of some-what he did spy,
He could him not containe in silent rest;
But, breaking forth in laughter, loud profest
His foolish thought: A Foolish Faune indeed,
That couldst not hold thy selfe so hidden blest,
But wouldest needs thine owne conceit areed!
Babblers unworthy been of so divine a meed.

XLVII. The Goddesse, all abashed with that noise,
In haste forth started from the guilty brooke;
And, running straight where-as she heard his voice,
Enclos'd the bush about, and there him tooke,
Like darred Larke, not daring up to looke
On her whose sight before so much he sought.
Thence forth they drew him by the hornes, and shooke
Nigh all to peeces, that they left him nought;
And then into the open light they forth him brought.

XLVIII. Like as an huswife, that with busie care
Thinks of her Dairy to make wondrous gaine,
Finding where-as some wicked beast unware
That breakes into her Dayr' house, there doth draine
Her creaming pannes, and frustrate all her paine,
Hath, in some snare or gin set close behind,
Entrapped him, and caught into her traine;
Then thinkes what punishment were best assign'd,
And thousand deathes deviseth in her vengefull mind.

XLIX. So did Diana and her maydens all
Use silly Faunus, now within their baile:
They mocke and scorne him, and him foule miscall;
Some by the nose him pluckt, some by the taile,
And by his goatish beard some did him haile:
Yet he (poore soule!) with patience all did beare;
For nought against their wils might countervaile:
Ne ought he said, what ever he did heare,
But, hanging downe his head, did like a Mome appeare.

L. At length, when they had flouted him their fill,
They gan to cast what penaunce him to give.
Some would have gelt him; but that same would spill

The Wood-gods breed, which must for ever live:
Others would through the river him have drive
And ducked deepe; but that seem'd penaunce light:
But most agreed, and did this sentence give,
Him in Deares skin to clad; and in that plight
To hunt him with their hounds, him selfe save how hee
    might.

LI. But Cynthia's selfe, more angry then the rest,
Thought not enough to punish him in sport,
And of her shame to make a gamesome jest;
But gan examine him in straighter sort,
Which of her Nymphes, or other close consort,
Him thither brought, and her to him betraid?
He, much affeard, to her confessed short
That 'twas Molanna which her so bewraid.
Then all attonce their hands upon Molanna laid.

LII. But him (according as they had decreed)
With a Deeres-skin they covered, and then chast
With all their hounds that after him did speed;
But he, more speedy, from them fled more fast
Then any Deere, so sore him dread aghast.
They after follow'd all with shrill out-cry,
Shouting as they the heavens would have brast;
That all the woods and dales, where he did flie,
Did ring againe, and loud re-eccho to the skie.

LIII. So they him follow'd till they weary were;
When, back returning to Molann' againe,
They, by commaund'ment of Diana, there
Her whelm'd with stones. Yet Faunus (for her paine)
Of her beloved Fanchin did obtaine,
That her he would receive unto his bed:
So now her waves passe through a pleasant Plaine,
Till with the Fanchin she her selfe do wed,
And (both combin'd) themselves in one faire river spred.

LIV. Nath'lesse Diana, full of indignation,
Thence-forth abandond her delicious brooke,
In whose sweet streame, before that bad occasion,
So much delight to bathe her limbes she tooke:
Ne onely her, but also quite forsooke

All those faire forrests about Arlo hid;
And all that Mountaine, which doth over-looke
The richest champain that may else be rid;
And the faire Shure, in which are thousand Salmons bred.

LV. Them all, and all that she so deare did way,
Thence-forth she left; and, parting from the place,
There-on an heavy haplesse curse did lay;
To weet, that Wolves, where she was wont to space,
Should harbour'd be and all those Woods deface,
And Thieves should rob and spoile that Coast around:
Since which, those Woods, and all that goodly Chase
Doth to this day with Wolves and Thieves abound:
Which too-too true that lands in-dwellers since have found.

CANTO VII

Pealing from Jove to Nature's bar,
Bold Alteration pleades
Large Evidence: but Nature soone
Her righteous Doome areads.

I. Aн! whither doost thou now, thou greater Muse,
Me from these woods and pleasing forrests bring,
And my fraile spirit, (that dooth oft refuse
This too high flight, unfit for her weake wing)
Lift up aloft, to tell of heavens King
(Thy soveraine Sire) his fortunate successe;
And victory in bigger notes to sing
Which he obtain'd against that Titanesse,
That him of heavens Empire sought to dispossesse?

II. Yet, sith I needs must follow thy behest,
Do thou my weaker wit with skill inspire,
Fit for this turne; and in my feeble brest
Kindle fresh sparks of that immortall fire
Which learned minds inflameth with desire
Of heavenly things: for who, but thou alone
That art yborne of heaven and heavenly Sire,
Can tell things doen in heaven so long ygone,
So farre past memory of man that may be knowne?

III. Now, at the time that was before agreed,
The gods assembled all on Arlo Hill;
As well those that are sprung of heavenly seed
As those that all the other world do fill,
And rule both sea and land unto their will:
Onely th' infernall Powers might not appeare;
As well for horror of their count'naunce ill,
As for th' unruly fiends which they did feare;
Yet Pluto and Proserpina were present there.

IV. And thither also came all other creatures,
What-ever life or motion do retaine,
According to their sundry kinds of features,

That Arlo scarsly could them all containe,
So full they filled every hill and Plaine;
And had not Natures Sergeant (that is Order)
Them well disposed by his busie paine,
And raunged farre abroad in every border,
They would have caused much confusion and disorder.

v. Then forth issewed (great goddesse) great dame Nature
With goodly port and gracious Majesty,
Being far greater and more tall of stature
Then any of the gods or Powers on hie:
Yet certes by her face and physnomy,
Whether she man or woman inly were,
That could not any creature well descry;
For with a veile, that wimpled every where,
Her head and face was hid that mote to none appeare.

vi. That, some do say, was so by skill devized,
To hide the terror of her uncouth hew
From mortall eyes that should be sore agrized;
For that her face did like a Lion shew,
That eye of wight could not indure to view:
But others tell that it so beautious was,
And round about such beames of splendor threw,
That it the Sunne a thousand times did pass,
Ne could be seene but like an image in a glass.

vii. That well may seemen true; for well I weene,
That this same day when she on Arlo sat,
Her garment was so bright and wondrous sheene,
That my fraile wit cannot devize to what
It to compare, nor finde like stuffe to that:
As those three sacred Saints, though else most wise,
Yet on mount Thabor quite their wits forgat,
When they their glorious Lord in strange disguise
Transfigur'd sawe; his garments so did daze their eyes.

viii. In a fayre Plaine upon an equall Hill
She placed was in a pavilion;
Not such as Craftes-men by their idle skill
Are wont for Princes states to fashion;
But th' Earth herselfe, of her owne motion,
Out of her fruitfull bosome made to growe

Most dainty trees, that, shooting up anon,
Did seeme to bow their bloosming heads full lowe
For homage unto her, and like a throne did showe,

IX. So hard it is for any living wight
All her array and vestiments to tell,
That old Dan Geffrey (in whose gentle spright,
The pure well head of Poesie did dwell)
In his *Foules parley* durst not with it mel,
But it transferd to Alane, who he thought
Had in his *Plaint of kinde* describ'd it well:
Which who will read set forth so as it ought,
Go seeke he out that Alane where he may be sought,

X. And all the earth far underneath her feete
Was dight with flowers that voluntary grew
Out of the ground, and sent forth odours sweet;
Tenne thousand mores of sundry sent and hew,
That might delight the smell, or please the view,
The which the Nymphes from all the brooks thereby
Had gathered, they at her foot-stoole threw;
That richer seem'd then any tapestry,
That Princes bowres adorne with painted imagery,

XI. And Mole himselfe, to honour her the more,
Did deck himselfe in freshest faire attire;
And his high head, that seemeth alwayes hore
With hardned frosts of former winters ire,
He with an Oaken girlond now did tire,
As if the love of some new Nymph, late seene,
Had in him kindled youthfull fresh desire,
And made him change his gray attire to greene:
Ah, gentle Mole! such joyance hath the well beseene,

XII. Was never so great joyance since the day
That all the gods whylome assembled were
On Hæmus hill in their divine array,
To celebrate the solemne bridall cheare
Twixt Peleus and Dame Thetis pointed there;
Where Phœbus selfe, that god of Poets hight,
They say, did sing the spousall hymne full cleere,
That all the gods were ravisht with delight
Of his celestiall song, and Musicks wondrous might,

XIII. This great Grandmother of all creatures bred,
Great Nature, ever young, yet full of eld;
Still mooving, yet unmoved from her sted;
Unseene of any, yet of all beheld;
Thus sitting in her throne, as I have teld,
Before her came dame Mutability;
And, being lowe before her presence feld
With meek obaysance and humilitie,
Thus gan her plaintif Plea with words to amplifie:

XIV. " To thee, O greatest Goddesse, onely great!
An humble suppliant loe! I lowely fly,
Seeking for Right, which I of thee entreat,
Who Right to all dost deale indifferently,
Damning all Wrong and tortious Injurie,
Which any of thy creatures do to other
(Oppressing them with power unequally,)
Sith of them all thou art the equall mother,
And knittest each to each, as brother unto brother.

XV. " To thee therefore of this same Jove I plaine,
And of his fellow gods that faine to be,
That challenge to themselves the whole worlds raign,
Of which the greatest part is due to me,
And heaven it selfe by heritage in Fee:
For heaven and earth I both alike do deeme,
Sith heaven and earth are both alike to thee,
And gods no more then men thou doest esteeme;
For even the gods to thee, as men to gods, do seeme.

XVI. " Then weigh, O soveraigne goddesse! by what right
These gods do claime the worlds whole soveraynty,
And that is onely dew unto thy might
Arrogate to themselves ambitiously:
As for the gods owne principality,
Which Jove usurpes unjustly, that to be
My heritage Jove's selfe cannot denie,
From my great Grandsire Titan unto mee
Deriv'd by dew descent; as is well knowen to thee.

XVII. " Yet mauger Jove, and all his gods beside,
I do possesse the worlds most regiment;
As if ye please it into parts divide,

And every parts inholders to convent,
Shall to your eyes appeare incontinent.
And, first, the Earth (great mother of us all)
That only seemes unmov'd and permanent,
And unto Mutabilitie not thrall,
Yet is she chang'd in part, and eeke in generall:

XVIII. " For all that from her springs, and is ybredde,
How-ever faire it flourish for a time,
Yet see we soone decay; and, being dead,
To turne againe unto their earthly slime:
Yet, out of their decay and mortall crime,
We daily see new creatures to arize,
And of their Winter spring another Prime,
Unlike in forme, and chang'd by strange disguise:
So turne they still about, and change in restlesse wise,

XIX. " As for her tenants, that is, man and beasts,
The beasts we daily see massacred dy
As thralls and vassals unto mens beheasts;
And men themselves do change continually,
From youth to eld, from wealth to poverty,
From good to bad, from bad to worst of all:
Ne doe their bodies only flit and fly,
But eeke their minds (which they immortall call)
Still change and vary thoughts, as new occasions fall,

XX. " Ne is the water in more constant case,
Whether those same on high, or these belowe;
For th' Ocean moveth still from place to place,
And every River still doth ebbe and flowe;
Ne any Lake, that seems most still and slowe,
Ne Poole so small, that can his smoothnesse holde
When any winde doth under heaven blowe;
With which the clouds are also tost and roll'd,
Now like great Hills, and streight like sluces them unfold,

XXI. " So likewise are all watry living wights
Still tost and turned with continuall change,
Never abiding in their stedfast plights:
The fish, still floting, doe at random range,
And never rest, but evermore exchange
Their dwelling places, as the streames them carrie:

Ne have the watry foules a certaine grange
Wherein to rest, ne in one stead do tarry;
But flitting still doe flie, and still their places vary.

XXII. " Next is the Ayre; which who feeles not by sense
(For of all sense it is the middle meane)
To flit still, and with subtill influence
Of his thin spirit all creatures to maintaine
In state of life? O weake life! that does leane
On thing so tickle as th' unsteady ayre,
Which every howre is chang'd and altred cleane
With every blast that bloweth, fowle or faire:
The faire doth it prolong: the fowle doth it impaire,

XXIII. " Therein the changes infinite beholde,
Which to her creatures every minute chaunce;
Now boyling hot, streight friezing deadly cold;
Now faire sun-shine, that makes all skip and daunce;
Streight bitter stormes, and balefull countenance
That makes them all to shiver and to shake:
Rayne, haile, and snowe do pay them sad penance,
And dreadfull thunder-claps (that make them quake)
With flames and flashing lights that thousand changes
make.

XXIV. " Last is the fire; which, though it live for ever,
Ne can be quenched quite, yet every day
We see his parts, so soone as they do sever,
To lose their heat and shortly to decay;
So makes himself his owne consuming pray;
Ne any living creatures doth he breed,
But all that are of others bredd doth slay;
And with their death his cruell life dooth feed;
Nought leaving but their barren ashes without seede,

XXV. " Thus all these fower (the which the groundwork bee
Of all the world and of all living wights)
To thousand sorts of Change we subject see:
Yet are they chang'd (by other wondrous slights)
Into themselves, and lose their native mights;
The Fire to Ayre, and th' Ayre to Water sheere,
And Water into Earth; yet Water fights
With Fire, and Ayre with Earth, approaching neere:
Yet all are in one body, and as one appeare.

XXVI. " So in them all raignes Mutabilitie;
How-ever these, that Gods themselves do call,
Of them do claime the rule and soverainty;
As Vesta, of the fire æthereall;
Vulcan, of this with us so usuall;
Ops, of the earth; and Juno, of the ayre;
Neptune, of seas; and Nymphes, of Rivers all:
For all those Rivers to me subject are,
And all the rest, which they usurp, be all my share.

XXVII. " Which to approven true, as I have told,
Vouchsafe, O Goddesse! to thy presence call
The rest which doe the world in being hold;
As times and seasons of the yeare that fall:
Of all the which demand in generall,
Or judge thyselfe, by verdit of thine eye,
Whether to me they are not subject all."
Nature did yeeld thereto; and by-and-by
Bade Order call them all before her Majesty.

XXVIII. So forth issew'd the Seasons of the yeare.
First, lusty Spring, all dight in leaves of flowres
That freshly budded and new bloosmes did beare,
(In which a thousand birds had built their bowres
That sweetly sung to call forth Paramours)
And in his hand a javelin he did beare,
And on his head (as fit for warlike stoures)
A guilt engraven morion he did weare;
That as some did him love, so others did him feare.

XXIX. Then came the jolly Sommer, being dight
In a thin silken cassock coloured greene,
That was unlyned all, to be more light;
And on his head a girlond well beseene
He wore, from which, as he had chauffed been,
The sweat did drop; and in his hand he bore
A boawe and shaftes, as he in forrest greene
Had hunted late the Libbard or the Bore,
And now would bathe his limbes with labor heated sore.

XXX. Then came the Autumne all in yellow clad,
As though he joyed in his plentious store,
Laden with fruits that made him laugh, full glad

That he had banisht hunger, which to-fore
Had by the belly oft him pinched sore:
Upon his head a wreath, that was enroll
With ears of corne of every sort, he bore;
And in his hand a sickle he did holde,
To reape the ripened fruits the which the earth had yold.

XXXI. Lastly, came Winter cloathed all in frize,
Chattering his teeth for cold that did him chill;
Whil'st on his hoary beard his breath did freese,
And the dull drops, that from his purpled bill
As from a limbeck did adown distill.
In his right hand a tipped staffe he held,
With which his feeble steps he stayed still;
For he was faint with cold, and weak with eld,
That scarse his loosed limbes he hable was to weld.

XXXII. These, marching softly, thus in order went;
And after them the Monthes all riding came.
First, sturdy March, with brows full sternly bent
And armed strongly, rode upon a Ram,
The same which over Hellespontus swam;
Yet in his hand a spade he also hent,
And in a bag all sorts of seeds ysame,
Which on the earth he strowed as he went,
And fild her wombe with fruitfull hope of nourishment.

XXXIII. Next came fresh Aprill, full of lustyhed,
And wanton as a Kid whose horne new buds:
Upon a Bull he rode, the same which led
Europa floting through th' Argolick fluds:
His hornes were gilden all with golden studs,
And garnished with garlonds goodly dight
Of all the fairest flowres and freshest buds
Which th' earth brings forth; and wet he seem'd in sight
With waves, through which he waded for his loves
delight.

XXXIV. Then came faire May, the fayrest mayd on ground,
Deckt all with dainties of her seasons pryde,
And throwing flowres out of her lap around:
Upon two brethrens shoulders she did ride,
The twinnes of Leda; which on eyther side
Supported her like to their soveraigne Queene:

Lord! how all creatures laught when her they spide
And leapt and daunc't as they had ravisht beene!
And Cupid selfe about her fluttred all in greene.

xxxv. And after her came jolly June, arrayd
All in greene leaves, as he a Player were;
Yet in his time he wrought as well as playd,
That by his plough-yrons mote right well appeare.
Upon a Crab he rode, that him did beare
With crooked crawling steps an uncouth pase,
And backward yode, as Bargeman wont to fare
Bending their force contrary to their face;
Like that ungracious crew which faines demurest grace.

xxxvi. Then came hot July boyling like to fire,
That all his garments he had cast away.
Upon a Lyon raging yet with ire
He boldly rode, and made him to obay:
It was the beast that whylome did forray
The Nemæan forrest, till th' Amphytrionide
Him slew, and with his hide did him array.
Behinde his back a sithe, and by his side
Under his belt he bore a sickle circling wide.

xxxvii. The sixt was August, being rich arrayd
In garment all of gold downe to the ground;
Yet rode he not, but led a lovely Mayd
Forth by the lilly hand, the which was cround
With eares of corne, and full her hand was found:
That was the righteous Virgin, which of old
Liv'd here on earth, and plenty made abound;
But after Wrong was lov'd, and Justice solde,
She left th' unrighteous world, and was to heaven extold.

xxxviii. Next him September marched, eeke on foote,
Yet was he heavy laden with the spoyle
Of harvests riches, which he made his boot,
And him enricht with bounty of the soyle:
In his one hand, as fit for harvests toyle,
He held a knife-hook; and in th' other hand
A paire of waights, with which he did assoyle
Both more and lesse, where it in doubt did stand,
And equall gave to each as Justice duly scann'd.

XXXIX. Then came October full of merry glee;
    For yet his noule was totty of the must,
    Which he was treading in the wine-fats see,
    And of the joyous oyle, whose gentle gust
    Made him so frollick and so full of lust:
    Upon a dreadfull Scorpion he did ride,
    The same which by Dianaes doom unjust
    Slew great Orion; and eeke by his side
    He had his ploughing-share and coulter ready tyde.

XL. Next was November; he full grosse and fat
    As fed with lard, and that right well might seeme;
    For he had been a fatting hogs of late,
    That yet his browes with sweat did reek and steem,
    And yet the season was full sharp and breem:
    In planting eeke he took no small delight.
    Whereon he rode not easie was to deeme;
    For it a dreadfull Centaure was in sight,
    The seed of Saturne and faire Nais, Chiron hight.

XLI. And after him came next the chill December:
    Yet he, through merry feasting which he made
    And great bonfires, did not the cold remember;
    His Saviour's birth his mind so much did glad.
    Upon a shaggy-bearded Goat he rode,
    The same wherewith Dan Jove in tender yeares,
    They say, was nourisht by th' Idæan mayd;
    And in his hand a broad deepe boawle he beares,
    Of which he freely drinks an health to all his peeres.

XLII. Then came old January, wrapped well
    In many weeds to keep the cold away;
    Yet did he quake and quiver, like to quell,
    And blowe his nayles to warme them if he may;
    For they were numbd with holding all the day
    An hatchet keene, with which he felled wood
    And from the trees did lop the needlesse spray:
    Upon an huge great Earth-pot steane he stood,
    From whose wide mouth there flowed forth the Romane
        Flood.

XLIII. And lastly came cold February, sitting
    In an old wagon, for he could not ride,
    Drawne of two fishes, for the season fitting,

Which through the flood before did softly slyde
And swim away: yet had he by his side
His plough and harnesse fit to till the ground,
And tooles to prune the trees, before the pride
Of hasting Prime did make them burgein round.
So past the twelve Months forth, and their dew places
     found.

XLIV. And after these there came the Day and Night,
Riding together both with equall pase,
Th' one on a Palfrey blacke, the other white;
But Night had covered her uncomely face
With a blacke veile, and held in hand a mace,
On top whereof the moon and stars were pight;
And sleep and darknesse round about did trace:
But Day did beare upon his scepters hight
The goodly Sun encompast all with beames bright.

XLV. Then came the Howres, faire daughters of high Jove
And timely Night; the which were all endewed
With wondrous beauty fit to kindle love;
But they were virgins all, and love eschewed
That might forslack the charge to them foreshewed
By mighty Jove; who did them porters make
Of heavens gate (whence all the gods issued)
Which they did daily watch, and nightly wake
By even turnes, ne ever did their charge forsake.

XLVI. And after all came Life, and lastly Death;
Death with most grim and griesly visage seene,
Yet is he nought but parting of the breath;
Ne ought to see, but like a shade to weene,
Unbodied, unsoul'd, unheard, unseene:
But Life was like a faire young lusty boy,
Such as they faine Dan Cupid to have beene,
Full of delightfull health and lively joy,
Deckt all with flowres, and wings of gold fit to employ.

XLVII. When these were past, thus gan the Titanesse:
" Lo! mighty mother, now be judge, and say
Whether in all thy creatures more or lesse
CHANGE doth not raign and bear the greatest sway;
For who sees not that Time on all doth pray?
But Times do change and move continually:

So nothing heere long standeth in one stay:
Wherefore this lower world who can deny
But to be subject still to Mutability? "

XLVIII. Then thus gan Jove: " Right true it is, that these
And all things else that under heaven dwell
Are chaung'd of Time, who doth them all disseise
Of being: But who is it (to me tell)
That Time himselfe doth move, and still compell
To keepe his course? Is not that namely wee
Which poure that vertue from our heavenly cell
That moves them all, and makes them changed be?
So them we gods do rule, and in them also thee.

XLIX. To whom thus Mutability: " The things,
Which we see not how they are mov'd and swayd
Ye may attribute to your selves as Kings,
And say, they by your secret powre are made:
But what we see not, who shall us perswade?
But were they so, as ye them faine to be,
Mov'd by your might and ordered by your ayde,
Yet what if I can prove, that even yee
Your selves are likewise chang'd, and subject unto mee?

L. " And first, concerning her that is the first,
Even you, faire Cynthia; whom so much ye make
Joves dearest darling, she was bred and nurst
On Cynthus hill, whence she her name did take;
Then is she mortall borne, how-so ye crake:
Besides, her face and countenance every day
We changed see and sundry formes partake,
Now hornd, now round, now bright, now browne and gray;
So that " as changefull as the Moone " men use to say.

LI. " Next Mercury; who though he lesse appeare
To change his hew, and alwayes seeme as one,
Yet he his course doth alter every yeare,
And is of late far out of order gone.
So Venus eeke, that goodly Paragone,
Though faire all night, yet is she darke all day:
And Phœbus selfe, who lightsome is alone,
Yet is he oft eclipsed by the way,
And fills the darkned world with terror and dismay.

LII. " Now Mars, that valiant man, is changed most;
　　 For he sometimes so far runnes out of square,
　　 That he his way doth seem quite to have lost,
　　 And cleane without his usuall spheere to fare;
　　 That even these Star-gazers stonisht are
　　 At sight thereof, and damne their lying bookes:
　　 So likewise grim Sir Saturne oft doth spare
　　 His sterne aspect, and calme his crabbed lookes.
　　 So many turning cranks these have, so many crookes.

LIII. " But you, Dan Jove, that only constant are,
　　 And King of all the rest, as ye doe clame,
　　 Are you not subject eeke to this misfare?
　　 Then, let me aske you this withouten blame;
　　 Where were ye borne?   Some say in Crete by name,
　　 Others in Thebes, and others other-where;
　　 But, wheresoever they comment the same,
　　 They all consent that ye begotten were
　　 And borne here in this world; ne other can appeare.

LIV. " Then are ye mortall borne, and thrall to me
　　 Unlesse the kingdome of the sky yee make
　　 Immortall and unchangeable to be:
　　 Besides, that power and vertue which ye spake,
　　 That ye here worke, doth many changes take,
　　 And your owne natures change; for each of you,
　　 That vertue have or this or that to make,
　　 Is checkt and changed from his nature trew,
　　 By others opposition or obliquid view.

LV. " Besides, the sundry motions of your Spheares,
　　 So sundry wayes and fashions as clerkes faine,
　　 Some in short space, and some in longer yeares,
　　 What is the same but alteration plaine?
　　 Onely the starry skie doth still remaine:
　　 Yet do the Starres and Signes therein still move,
　　 And even itselfe is mov'd, as wizards saine:
　　 But all that moveth doth mutation love;
　　 Therefore both you and them to me I subject prove.

LVI. " Then, since within this wide great Universe
　　 Nothing doth firme and permanent appeare,
　　 But all things tost and turned by transverse,

What then should let, but I aloft should reare
My Trophee, and from all the triumph beare?
Now judge then, (O thou greatest goddesse trew)
According as thy selfe doest see and heare,
And unto me addoom that is my dew;
That is, the rule of all, all being rul'd by you."

LVII. So having ended, silence long ensewed;
Ne Nature to or fro spake for a space,
But with firme eyes affixt the ground still viewed,
Meane-while all creatures, looking in her face,
Expecting th' end of this so doubtful case,
Did hang in long suspence what would ensew,
To whether side should fall the soveraine place:
At length she, looking up with chearefull view,
The silence brake, and gave her doome in speeches few,

LVIII. "I well consider all that ye have said,
And find that all things stedfastnesse do hate
And changed be; yet, being rightly wayd,
They are not changed from their first estate;
But by their change their being do dilate,
And turning to themselves at length againe,
Do worke their owne perfection so by fate:
Then over them Change doth not rule and raigne,
But they raigne over Change, and do their states maintaine,

LIX. "Cease therefore, daughter, further to aspire,
And thee content thus to be rul'd by mee,
For thy decay thou seekst by thy desire;
But time shall come that all shall changed bee,
And from thenceforth none no more change shal see."
So was the Titanesse put downe and whist,
And Jove confirm'd in his imperiall see.
Then was that whole assembly quite dismist,
And Natur's selfe did vanish, whither no man wist,

THE VIII. CANTO

UNPERFITE

I. When I bethinke me on that speech whyleare
  Of Mutabilitie, and well it way!
  Me seemes, that though she all unworthy were
  Of the Heav'ns Rule; yet, very sooth to say,
  In all things else she beares the greatest sway:
  Which makes me loath this state of life so tickle,
  And love of things so vaine to cast away;
  Whose flowring pride, so fading and so fickle,
  Short Time shall soon cut down with his consuming sickle.

II. Then gin I thinke on that which Nature sayd,
  Of that same time when no more Change shall be,
  But stedfast rest of all things, firmely stayd
  Upon the pillours of Eternity,
  That is contrayr to Mutabilitie;
  For all that moveth doth in Change delight:
  But thence-forth all shall rest eternally
  With Him that is the God of Sabaoth hight:
  O! that great Saboath God, grant me that Sabaoths sight.

GLOSSARY

Abace, abase, to lower, to hang down.

Aband, to abandon.

Abashment, fear.

Abeare, to behave, conduct.

Abet, abett, to aid, support, maintain, asserting falsely.

Abid, abode, remained.

Abie, aby, abye, to pay the penalty of, to atone for, suffer for, abide by.

Abject, to throw or cast down.

Abode, remained, a delay, stay.

Abolish, to wipe out.

Aborde, harbour.

Abouts, about.

Abrade, to rouse, wake up.

Abray (pret. *abrayde*), to start up suddenly, to awake, to quake with sudden fear.

Abusion, abuse, deceit, fraud.

Accloye, to clog up, choke, encumber, hinder.

Accoasting, skimming along near the ground.

Accorage, to encourage.

Accord, to grant, to agree, to reconcile, an agreement.

According, agreeably to, according to, accordingly.

Accoste, to go side by side, to adjoin, border.

Accourting, entertaining (courteously).

Accoy, to coy, caress.

Accoyl, to assemble, gather together.

Accrew, to increase.

Achates (*Acates*), purchased provisions, cates.

Acquight, acquit, acquite, to deliver, release, acquitted, free.

Adamants, chrystals.

Adaw, to adaunt, tame, moderate.

Addeeme, to adjudge.

Addoom, to adjudge.

Address, to prepare, adjust, direct, clothe, arm.

Addrest, ready.

Adjoyne, to approach, join.

Admiraunce, admiration.

Admire, to wonder at.

Adore, to adorn.

Adorne, ornament.

Adowne, down.

Adrad, adred, adredde, afraid, terrified.

Adrad, to be frightened.

Advaunce, to extol.

Adventure, chance, opportunity, to attempt.

Adview, to view.

Advize, advise, to consider, perceive, take thought of, bethink.

Advizement, consideration.

Adward, an award, to award.

Æmuling, emulating, rivalling (æmuled).

Afeard, afraid.

Affear, to frighten.

Affect, affection.

Affection, passion.

Affide, affyde, betrothed, intrusted.

Afflicted, low, humble.

Afford, to consent.

Affrap, to strike, to strike down, to encounter, to assault.

Affray, to terrify, fray, terror.

Affrende, to make friends.

Affret, encounter.

Affront, to confront, encounter, oppose.

Affy, to betroth, espouse, entrust.

Affyaunce, betrothal.

Afore, in front, before.

Aggrace, favour, kindness, goodwill, to make gracious.

Aggrate, to please, delight, charm, treat politely.

Aglet, point, tag.

Agree, to settle, to cause to agree.

Agreeably, alike, in a manner to agree.

Agrise, agrize, agryse, agryze, to cause to shudder, to terrify, to make disgusted.

Agryz'd, having a terrible look, disfigured.

Aguise, aguize, to deck, adorn, fashion, accoutre, to disguise.

501

Alablaster, alabaster.
Albee, although.
Aleggeaunce, alleviation.
Alew, howling.
Algate, algates, altogether, wholly, by all means, in all ways, at all events.
All, although.
Almes, a free allowance, alms.
Alone (only), without compulsion.
Alow, downwards.
Als, also.
Amaine, violently, by force.
Amate, to daunt, subdue, to stupefy, terrify, to keep company with.
Amaze, amazement.
Amenage, to manage, handle.
Amenaunce, carriage, behaviour.
Amis, amice, a priestly vestment.
Amount, to mount up, ascend.
Amove, to move, remove.
Andvile, anvil.
Annoy, annoyance, grief, hurt.
Antickes, antiques, ancient or fantastic figures.
Apace, fast, copiously.
Appall, to falter, to weaken.
Appay, apay (præt. and p. p. *appay'd, appaid*), to please, satisfy, pay.
Appeach, to impeach, accuse.
Appease, to cease from.
Appele, to accuse, to offer.
Appellation, appeal.
Apply, to attend to, to bend one's steps to.
Approvaunce, approval.
Approven, to put to the proof, to prove.
Arborett, little grove.
Aread, areed (p. p. *ared*), to tell, say, declare, describe, inform, teach, interpret, explain, appoint, detect.
Arear, areare, arere, arreare, to the rear, backward, aback.
Aret, arret, to allot, entrust, adjudge.
Arew, in a row, in order.
Arguments, signs, indications.
Arights, rightly.
Arke, box, chest.
Arras, tapestry of Arras.
Arraught (pret. of *arreach*), seized forcibly.
As, as if.
Askaunce, sideways.
Aslake, to slake, abate, appease.
Aslope, on the slope, aside.

Assay, to try, attempt, assail, attack, an attempt, trial, value.
Asseige, to besiege.
Assignment, design.
Assoil, assoyl, to absolve, determine, set free, let loose, renew, remove.
Assott, to befool, to beguile, bewilder.
Assure, to promise, assert confidently.
Asswage, to grow mild.
Assyn, to mark or point out.
Astart, to start up suddenly.
Astond, astound, astonished, stunned.
Astonish, to stun.
Astonying, confounding.
Attach, to seize, take prisoner (*attack*).
Attaine, attayne, to find, reach, fall in with.
Attaint, to stain, obscure.
Attempt, to tempt.
Attendement, intent.
Attent, attention.
Attone (*atone*), at one, together, reconciled.
Attone, attons, at once, together.
Attrapt, dressed.
Atween, atweene, between.
Atwixt, between, at intervals.
Aumayl, to enamel.
Avale, to fall, sink, lower, descend, bow down.
Avaunt, depart.
Avauntage, advantage.
Avaunting, advancing (boastfully).
Avenge, revenge.
Avengement, revenge.
Aventred, thrust forward (at a venture).
Aventring, pushing forward.
Avize, avyze, to perceive, consider, regard, view, take note of, reflect, bethink, advise.
Avizefull, observant.
Avoid, to depart, go out.
Avoure, "to make avoure" = to justify, maintain.
Awarned, made, was made aware.
Awayte, to wait for, watch.
Awhape, to terrify, frighten.
Aygulets (*aglets*), tags, points of gold.
Aym, direction.

Bace, low.
Bace, " bad *bace* " = challenged.

Baffuld, disgraced (as a recreant knight).

Baile, to deliver, custody.

Bains, banns (of marriage).

Bale, grief, sorrow, affliction, trouble, *bales*, ruins, *baleful*, full of bale, destructive, deadly, *balefulnesse*, ruin.

Balke, to disappoint, to deal at cross purposes, a ridge between two furrows.

Ban, banne, to curse (*band*, cursed).

Band, forbid, banish, assemble.

Bane, death, destruction.

Banket, banquet.

Bannerall, a standard (shaped like a swallow's tail).

Barbe, equipments of a horse, horse armour.

Barbican, a watch-tower.

Bard, ornamented with *bars* (ornaments of a girdle).

Base, low, the lower part.

Baseness, a low humble condition.

Bases, armour for the legs.

Bash, to be abashed.

Bastard, base, lowborn.

Basted, sewed slightly.

Bate, did bite.

Bate, to bait, attack.

Battailous, ready for battle, in order for battle.

Battill (properly to *fatten*), to be of good flavour.

Batton, stick, club.

Bauldricke, belt.

Bay, a standstill, a position in which one is kept at bay.

Baye, to bathe.

Bayes (*baies*), laurels.

Bayt, bait, artifice, to bait (a bull), to cause to abate, to let rest.

Beades, prayers.

Beadroll, a list.

Beare, bier.

Beath'd, plunged.

Beauperes, fair companions.

Beckes, beaks.

Become, to come to, go to, to suit, to happen.

Bed, bad.

Bedight, dressed, equipped, decked, adorned, "ill-bedight," disfigured.

Beduck, to dive, dip.

Befell, was fitting, proper.

Beginne, beginning.

Begord, stained with gore.

Behave, to employ, use.

Beheast; behest, command.

Behight, call, name, address, pronounce, promise, command, adjudged, entrusted.

Behoofe, profit.

Behote, to promise, *behott*, promised.

Belaccoyle, kind salutation or greeting.

Belamoure, belamy, a lover.

Belay, adorn.

Beldame, fair lady.

Belgard, fair (or kind) looks.

Belyde, counterfeited.

Ben, (*bene, been*), are.

Bend, band.

Bent, long stalks of (*bent*) grass.

Beraft, bereft.

Bere, to bear, bier.

Beseeke, beseech.

Beseene, "well-beseen," of good appearance, comely.

Beseme, beseeme, to be seemly, to seem fit, to suit, fit, become, appear.

Besitting, befitting.

Bespeake, to address.

Bespredd, adorned.

Bestad, (*bested, bestedded*), situated, placed, placed in peril, treated, attended, beset, "ill-bested "= in a bad plight.

Bestaine, to stain.

Bestow, to place.

Bestrad, bestrided.

Bet, did beat.

Betake, (pret. *betooke*), to take (into), to deliver, bestow, betake one's self.

Beteeme, to deliver, give.

Bethinke, to make up one's mind.

Bethrall, to take captive.

Betide, betyde, to befall, to happen to, *betid*, befall, befallen.

Bever, the front part of a helmet (covering the mouth).

Bevy, company (of ladies).

Bewaile, to choose, select.

Bewray, to reveal, betray, accuse.

Bickerment, bickering, strife.

Bid, to pray.

Bide, to bid, offer.

Bilive, bylive, blive, forthwith, quickly.

Bils, battle-axes.

Blame, to blemish; injury, hurt.

Blanckt, confounded, put out of countenance.

Blast, to wither.

Blaze, to blazon forth, proclaim.

Blemishment, a blemish.

Blend, (pret. and p. part. *blent*),

to mix, confuse, confound, defile, blemish, stain, obscure, *Blent*, blinded, obscured, blotted.

Bless, to preserve, deliver, **to** brandish.

Blesse, bliss.

Blin, to cease.

Blincked, dimmed.

Blind, dark.

Blist, wounded, struck.

Blist, blessed.

Bloosme, blossom, bloom.

Blot, blotten, to defame, blemish.

Blubbred, wet or stained with tears.

Boads, bodes, portends.

Bode, abode.

Bollet, bullet.

Bond, bound.

Boone, prayer, petition.

Boord, bord, to accost, to address, talk with, conversation, go side by side.

Boot, to avail, profit; booty, gain.

Booting, availing.

Bore, borne.

Borde, coast.

Bordraging (pl. *bordrags*), border ravaging, border raid.

Bosse, middle of shield.

Bouget, budget.

Bought, fold.

Boult, to sift, bolt.

Bounse, to beat.

Bountie, bounty, goodness, *Bounteous*, generous, good; *bountyhed*, generosity.

Bourne, boundary.

Bout, about.

Bouzing-can, a drinking-can.

Bownd, to lead (by a direct course).

Bowre, chamber, inner room, to lodge, shelter.

Bowrs, muscles (of the shoulder).

Boy, a term of reproach.

Boystrous, rough, rude (as applied to a club).

Brame, sharp passion (cf. O.E. *breme*, severe, sharp).

Bransles, dances, brawls.

Brast, burst.

Brave, fair, beautiful.

Bravely, gallantly, splendidly.

Brawned, muscular, brawny.

Bray, (*braie*), to cry out suddenly, cry aloud, utter aloud, gasp out.

Braynepan, skull.

Breaded, braided, embroidered.

Breare, brere, briar.

Breech, breeches.

Breede, work, produce.

Breem, boisterous, rough, sharp.

Brenne, to burn.

Brent, burnt.

Brickle, brittle.

Brim, margin of the horizon.

Broch, to commence, broach.

Brode, abroad.

Brond, sword.

Brondiron, sword.

Bronds, embers, *brands*.

Brood, a brooding-place (? an error for *bood* = O.E. *bood* or *abood*, an abode, resting-place; cf. *bode*).

Brooke, to endure, bear *brook*.

Brouzes, twigs.

Brunt, assault.

Brust, burst.

Brutenesse, brutishnesse, brutality, brute-like state.

Bryze, gadfly.

Buckle to, make ready.

Buff (pl. *buffes*), a blow.

Bug, apparition, bugbear, goblin.

Buegle, wild ox.

Bullion, pure gold.

Burdenous, heavy.

Burganet, headpiece, helmet.

Burgein, burgeon, bud.

Busse, kiss.

But-if, unless.

Buxom, obedient, yielding, tractable.

By-and-by, one by one, singly.

Byde, abide; *byding*, abiding, remaining.

Bylive, quickly, also active, **see** *Blive, belive*.

Bynempt, named, appointed.

Cabinet, cottage, little cabin.

Caitive, caytive, subject, captive, vile, base, menial, rascal.

Call, caul, cowl, cap.

Camis, camus, a light loose robe of some light material (as silk, etc.), chemise.

Can or *Gan* (an auxiliary of the past tense), did.

Cancred, cankerd, corrupt.

Canon bitt, a smooth round bit (for horses).

Capitayn, captain.

Caprifole, woodbine.

Captivaunce, captivity.

Captived, taken captive, enslaved.

Capuccio, hood (of a cloak), capuchin.

Card, chart.

Care, sorrow, grief, injury; *care-*

ful, sorrowful; *careless*, free from care, uncared for.

Carke, care, sorrow, grief.

Carl, carle, an old man, churl.

Carriage, burden.

Cast, to consider, plot, resolve, purpose, time, period, oppor-. tunity, " *nere their utmost cast*," =almost dead; a couple.

Castory, colour (red or pink).

Caudron, caldron.

Causen, to assign a cause or reason, explain.

Caved, made hollow.

Centonel, a sentinel.

Certes, certainly.

Cesse, to cease.

Cesure, a breaking off, stop.

Chaffar, to chaffer, exchange.

Chalenge, to claim, to track, follow, accusation.

Chamelot water, camlet watered.

Champain, champian, champion, open country, plain.

Championesse, a female warrior.

Character, image.

Charge, assault, attack.

Charget, chariot.

Chauff, chaufe, to become warm, to be irritated, to *chafe*, rage.

Chaunticleer, the cock.

Chaw, jaw, to chew.

Chayre, chary.

Cheare, chere, countenance, favour, cheer; *chearen*, to cheer up.

Checked, chequered.

Checklaton (O.E. *ciclaton*), a rich kind of cloth.

Cherry, to cherish.

Chevisaunce, enterprise, undertaking, performance, bargain.

Chickens (faithlesse), heathen brood.

Childed, gave birth to a child.

Chimney, fireplace.

Chine, back.

Chorle, churl.

Chynd, cut, divided.

Clarkes, scholars.

Clove, cleft, did cleave.

Cleane, Cleene, clene, pure; *clean*, entirely.

Cleep, to call.

Clemence, clemency.

Clew, plot, purpose (properly a hank of thread).

Clift, cliff.

Clombe, climbed, mounted.

Close, secret, *closely*, secretly.

Clouches, clutches.

Cloyd, wounded.

Coast, to approach.

Coch, coach.

Cognizaunce, knowledge, recollection.

Colled, embraced, fondled.

Colour, to hide.

Combrous, laborious, troublesome.

Commen, common, to commune, discourse.

Comment, to relate (falsely).

Commodity, advantage.

Commonly, in common, equally.

Compacte, (?) compacted, concerted.

Compacted, close; *compacture*, a close knitting together.

Companie, companion.

Compare, to collect, procure.

Compasse, circuit.

Compast, contrived; *compast creast*, the round part of the helmet.

Compel, to cite, call to aid.

Complement, perfection (of character), union.

Complish, to accomplish.

Comportaunce, behaviour.

Compound, to agree.

Comprize, to comprehend, understand.

Comprovinciall, to be contained in the same province with.

Compyle, to heap up, frame, settle, reconcile.

Conceiptful, thoughtful.

Concent, to harmonize.

Concert, harmony.

Concrew, to grow together.

Condign, worthy.

Conditions, qualities.

Conduct, conductor, guide, management.

Congé, leave.

Conjure, to conspire.

Consort, company, companion, concert; to combine, unite (in harmony).

Constraint, distress, uneasiness.

Containe, to restraine, control.

Contrive, to wear out, spend.

Controverse, debate, controversy.

Convent, to convene, summon.

Convert, to turn.

Convince, to conquer, overthrow.

Coosen, kindred.

Coportion, an equal portion.

Corage, heart, mind, wrath.

Corbe, corbel, a projecting piece of wood, stone, or iron, placed so as to support a weight of material.

Cordwayne, cordovan leather.

Coronall, a wreath, garland.
Corse, a body, bulk, frame.
Corsive, corrosive.
Cott, a little abode.
Couched, bent, laid (in order).
Could, knew.
Count, an object of interest or account.
Countenance, to make a show of.
Countercast, counterplot.
Counterchaunge, return of a blow.
Counterfesaunce, a counterfeiting.
Counterpoys, to counterbalance.
Countervayle, to oppose, resist.
Couplement, couple.
Coure, to cover, protect.
Courst, chaced.
Couth, could.
Covert, concealed.
Covetise, covetize, covetousness.
Craggy, knotty.
Crake, to boast, boast, boasting.
Crank, a winding.
Crapples, grapples, claws.
Crased helth, impaired health.
Creasted, crested, tufted.
Cremosin, crimson.
Crime, accusation, reproach, fault.
Crisped, curly (hair).
Crooke (cross), gibbet.
Croslet, a little cross.
Cros-cut, to pierce or cut across.
Cruddy, curdled.
Cuffing (or *cuffling*), striking.
Culver, dove.
Culvering, culverin, a sort of cannon.
Cumbrous, troublesome.
Curats, curiets, cuirasses.
Curelesse, hard to be cured, incurable.
Curtaxe, cutlass.

Dædale, skilful.
Daint, daynt, dainty; (superl. *dayntest*), *dainty*, rare, valuable.
Dallie, to trifle; *dalliaunce*, idle talk, trifling.
Dame, lady.
Damnify, to injure, damage.
Damozel, damsel.
Danisk, Danish.
Darrayne, to prepare, get ready, for battle.
Darred, dazzled, frightened ("a *darred* lark" is generally explained as a lark caught (? frightened) by means of a looking-glass).
Dayesman, a judge, arbitrator.

Daze, to dazzle, dim, to confound.
Dead-doing, death-dealing.
Deaded, deadened.
Dealth, bestows.
Deare, valuable, precious.
Deare, hurt, injury, sore, sad, sorely.
Dearling, darling.
Deaw, to bedew.
Debate, to contend, strive, battle, strife; *Debatement*, debate.
Debonaire, gracious, courteous.
Decay, to destroy, perish, relax, destruction, ruin, death.
Deceaved, taken by deceit.
Decesse, decease.
Decreed, determined on.
Decrewed, decreased.
Deeme (pret. *dempst*), to judge, deem, " *deeme his payne* "=adjudge his punishment.
Deering-dooers, doers of daring deeds.
Deface, to defeat.
Defame, disgrace, dishonour.
Defaste, defaced, destroyed.
Defeasaunce, defeat.
Defeature, defeat.
Defend, to keep or ward off.
Define, to settle, decide.
Deforme, shapeless, deformed.
Defray, to avert (by a proper settlement), appease.
Degendered, degenerated.
Delay, to temper, stop, remove.
Delices, delights. *Delightsome*, delightful.
Delve, dell, hole, cave.
Demayne, demeane, demeasnure, demeanour, bearing, treatment.
Dempt. See *Deeme*.
Denay, to deny.
Dent, dint, blow.
Depainted, depicted.
Depart, to divide, separate, re move, departure.
Depend, to hang down.
Deprave, to defame.
Dernly, secretly, grievously, severely.
Der-doing = performance of daring deeds.
Derring-doe, daring deeds, warlike deeds.
Derth, scarcity.
Deryve, to draw away, transfer.
Descrie, descry, to perceive, discover, reveal.
Descrive, to describe.

Desine, to denote.
Despairefull drift, hopeless cause.
Desperate, despairing.
Despight, anger, malice, a scornful defiance.
Despightful, despiteous, malicious.
Despoyl, to unrobe, undress.
Desse, dais.
Desynde, directed.
Detaine, detention.
Devicefull, full of devices (as masques, triumphs, etc.).
Devise, devize, to guess at, purpose, to describe, talk; *devized,* painted; *devized of,* reflected on.
Dew, due, *Dewfull,* due.
Diapase, diapason.
Difference, choice.
Diffused, scattered.
Dight, to order, to arrange, prepare, dress, deck, mark.
Dilate, to spread abroad, enlarge upon.
Dinting, striking.
Dint, scar, dent.
Disaray, disorder.
Disaccord, to withhold consent.
Disadvaunce, to lower, to draw back.
Disaventrous, unfortunate, unsuccessful, unhappy. *Disaventure,* mishap, misfortune.
Disburden, to unburden.
Discharge, to acquit oneself of, account for.
Discide, to cut in two.
Disciple, to discipline.
Disclaim, to expel.
Disclose (pret. *discloste*), to unfold, transform, set free, disengage.
Discoloured, many-coloured.
Discomfited, disconcerted.
Discommend, to speak disparagingly of.
Discounsell, to dissuade.
Discoure, discure, to discover.
Discourse, shifting.
Discourteise, discourteous.
Discreet, differing.
Discust, thrown or shook of.
Disease, to distress, uneasiness, *Diseased,* ill at ease, afflicted.
Disentrayle, to draw forth, to cause to flow.
Disgrace, deformity.
Disguizement, disguise.
Dishable, to disparage.
Disleall (disloyal), perfidious.
Dislikeful, disagreeable.
Disloignd, separated.

Dismall, fatal.
Dismay, to subdue, defeat, grieve, disquiet, defeat, ruin. *Dismayfull,* terrifying.
Dismayd = mismade, deformed.
Dismayl, to take off a coat of mail.
Dispairful, despairing. See *Despairefull.*
Disparage, disparagement.
Dispart, to divide.
Dispence, to pay for, expense, abundance.
Dispiteous, cruel.
Display, to spread out, discover.
Disple, to discipline.
Displeasance, displeasaunce, displeasure.
Disport, play, sport.
Disprad, dispred, spread abroad.
Dispraize, to disparage.
Dispredden (pl.), spread out.
Disprofesse, to abandon.
Dispurvayaunce, want of provisions.
Disseise, disseize, to dispossess.
Disshivered, shivered to pieces.
Dissolute, weak.
Distayne, to defile.
Distent, beaten out.
Disthronize, to dethrone.
Distinct, marked.
Distraine, to rend.
Distraught, distracted, drawn apart, separated.
Distroubled, greatly troubled.
Dite, dighte, to make ready.
Ditt, ditty, song.
Diverse, distracting, diverting.
Diverst, diverged, turned off.
Divide, to play a florid passage in music.
Divorced, separated by force.
Doale = dole, destruction.
Documents, instructions.
Doe, to cause.
Doffe, to put off.
Dole, doole, sorrow, grief. *Doolefull,* sorrowful.
Dolor (dolour), grief.
Dome, doome, doom, judgment, censure.
Don, to put on.
Done, donne, to do, " of well to donne " = of well-doing. *Doen,* to cause.
Doomefull, threatening doom.
Dortours, sleeping apartments.
Doted, foolish.
Doubt, fear (also to fear), a matter of doubt, *Doubtfull,* fearful.

Drad, dred, dread, dreaded, feared, an object of reverence. *Dreddest,* most dread.

Draft, drift, aim, purpose.

Drapet, cloth.

Draught (= *draft*), stratagem, aim.

Dread, fury, *Dreadful,* fearful.

Dreare, Drere, (*Dreriment*), grief, sorrow, dreadful force. *Drerihed, drearyhood, dryrihed,* dreariness, affliction.

Drent, drowned.

Dresse, to dispose, adorn.

Drevill, a slave.

Droome, a drum.

Droupe, to droop.

Drousy-hed, drowsiness.

Drouth, drought.

Drover, a boat.

Drugs, dregs.

Dumpish, heavy.

Duraunce, bondage.

Durefull, enduring.

Duresse, confinement.

Dye, lot, destiny.

Earne, to yearn, to be grieved.

Earst, erst, first, soonest, previously, *at earst,* at length.

Easterlings, men of the East (Norwegians, Danes, etc.).

Eath, ethe, easy.

Edge, to sharpen.

Edifye, to build, inhabit.

Eek, eke, to increase.

Effierced, made fierce, inflamed.

Efforce, to oppose.

Efforced, efforst, forced, constrained, compelled (to yield).

Effraid, scared.

Eft, afterwards, again, forthwith, moreover.

Eftsoones, soon after, forthwith.

Eide, seen.

Eld, age, old age.

Elfe, fairy.

Els (*elles*), else, elsewhere, otherwise.

Embace, embase, to bring or cast down, humiliate. *Embaste,* debased, dishonoured.

Embar, to guard, confine.

Embassage, embassy, message.

Embatteil, to arm for battle.

Embaulm, to anoint.

Embay, to bathe.

Embayl, to bind up.

Embosome, to foster.

Emboss, to overwhelm, press hard, to surround, enclose.

Embosse, to adorn, ornament, array.

Embow, to arch over, to curve, bend.

Embowell, to take out the bowels.

Emboyl, to boil (with anger). *Emboyled,* heated.

Embrace, to brace, to fasten, or bind, to protect.

Embracement, an embrace.

Embrave, to decorate.

Embreade, embroder, to embroider.

Embrewe, to stain with blood.

Embusied, occupied.

Eme, uncle.

Emeraud, emerald.

Emmove, to move.

Emong, among. *Emongest,* amongst.

Empare, empair, to diminish, impair, hurt.

Emparlaunce, treaty.

Empart, assign.

Empassioned, empassionate, moved or touched with passion, feeling.

Empeach, to hinder, prevent, hindrance.

Empeopled, dwelt.

Emperce, empierce, to pierce through (pret. *emperst, empierst*).

Emperill, to endanger.

Empight, fixed, settled.

Emplonged, plunged.

Empoysoned, poisoned.

Emprise, emprize, enterprise, attempt.

Empurpled, purple-dyed.

Embosome, to fix firmly.

Enchace, enchase, to adorn, embellish, to honour with befitting terms, engrave, dart.

Encheason, reason, cause, occasion.

Encomberment, hindrance.

Endamage, to damage, do harm.

Endangerment, danger.

Endew, to endow.

Endite, to censure.

Endlong, from end to end, continuously.

Endosse, write on the back, endorse.

Endure, to harden.

Enfelon'd, made fell or fierce.

Enfested. See *Infest.*

Enfierce, to make fierce.

Enforme, to fashion.

Enfouldred, hurled out like thunder and lightning.

Engin, wiles, deceit, contrivance.

Englut, to glut, fill.

Engore, to gore, wound.
Engorge, to devour, glut.
Engraffed, engraft, implanted, fixed.
Engrasp, to grasp.
Engrave, to bury, to cut, to pierce.
Engreeve, engrieve, to grieve, to be vexed.
Engroste, made thick.
Enhaunse, to lift up, raise.
Enlargen, enlarge, to set at large, deliver.
Enlumine, to illumine.
Enmove, to move. See *Emmove.*
Enrace, to implant.
Enraunge, to range.
Enraunged, ranged in order.
Enrold, encircled.
Enseames, encloses.
Ensew, ensue, to follow after, pursue. *Ensuing,* following.
Ensnarle, to ensnare, entangle.
Entayle, to carve, inlay, (sb.) carving.
Enterdeale, negotiation.
Enterpris, to undertake.
Enterprize, to entertain, take in hand.
Entertain, take, receive (pay). *Entertayne, entertainment,* hospitality.
Entertake, to entertain.
Entire, inward, internal, *Entyrely,* earnestly, entirely.
Entraile, entrayl, to twist, entwine, interlace.
Entraile, twisting, entanglement.
Entrall, the lowest part, depth (bowels).
Entreat, to treat of, treat.
Enure, to use, practise. *Enured,* accustomed, committed habitually.
Envy, to be angry, indignant; to emulate.
Enwallowe, roll about.
Enwombed, pregnant.
Enwrap, to wrap up.
Equipage, array, equipment, to array, equip.
Ermelin, an ermine.
Ermine, skin of the ermine.
Erne, to yearn.
Errant, wandering.
Errour, wandering.
Eschew, escape.
Esloyne, to withdraw.
Espiall, sight, appearance, observation.
Essoyne, to excuse.

Estate, state, rank.
Eterne, eternal. *Eternize,* to make eternal.
Ethe, easy.
Eugh, yew. *Ewghen,* of yew.
Evangely, gospel.
Evill, poor, unskilful.
Exanimate, lifeless.
Excheat, gain, profit, escheet.
Expire, breathe out, to fulfil a term, put an end to.
Express, to press out.
Extasie, surprise.
Extent, stretched out.
Extirpe, to root out.
Extort, extorted.
Extract, descended.
Extreate, extraction.
Ewfts, efts.
Eyas, newly-fledged young.
Eyne, eyes.

Face, to carry a false appearance.
Fact, feat, deed.
Fail, fayl, to deceive, to cause to fail.
Fain, fayne, glad, eager, *fayned,* desired, *faynes,* delights.
Fain, fayne, to feign, dissemble, to mistake, imagine; "*fained* dreadful*" = apparently dreadful.
Faitour, faytour, cheat, deceiver, vagabond, villain.
Falsed, falsified, deceived, insecure, weak. *Falses,* falsehoods. *Falser,* a liar.
Faltring, faltering.
Fantasy, fantazy, fancy, apprehension.
Fare, to go, proceed, act, deal.
Farforth, very far.
Faste, having a face.
Fastnesse, stronghold.
Fate, destined term of life. *Fatal,* ordained by fate.
Fault, to offend, be in error.
Favour, feature.
Favourlesse, not showing favour.
Fay, a fairy, faith.
Fear, feare, companion, *to fear,* together.
Fear, fearen, to frighten, "*feard —— of,*" alarmed by.
Fearfull, timid.
Feastfull, festival.
Feature, fashion, form, character.
Fee, tenure, pay, service, property.
Feeble, enfeebled. *Feblesse,* feebleness.

Feeld (golden), an emblazoned field (of a knight's shield).

Feend, fiend, devil.

Feld, let fall, thrown down.

Fell, befell, gall.

Fell, fierce, cruel. *Felly*, cruelly. *Fellonest*, most fell. *Fellonous*, wicked, fell. *Fellnesse*, cruelty, fierceness.

Feminitee, womanhood.

Feood, feud, enmity.

Fensible, fit for defence, defensible.

Fere, companion, husband.

Ferme, lodging.

Ferry, a ferry boat.

Fett, to fetch, fetched (rescued).

Fleur-de-luce, the iris. See *Delice*.

Feutre, fewtre, to place the spear in the rest, to prepare for battle.

File, to defile.

File, to polish, smoothe.

Fine, end.

Firm, to fix firmly.

Fit, to be fitting. " Of loves were ' fitted ' " =were suited, furnished with lovers.

Fit, fitt, emotion, passion, grief, a musical strain.

Flaggy, loose.

Flake, a flash.

Flamed, inflamed.

Flatling, flatwise, with the flat side (of the sword).

Flaw, a gust of wind.

Fleet, to sail, float; to flit.

Flex, flax.

Flit, fleet, swift, changing, unsubstantial, light.

Flit, flitte, to move, change, flee. *Flitting*, fleeting, yielding.

Flore, ground, spot.

Flout, to mock, deride.

Flushing, rapidly flowing.

Fodder, grass.

Foen, foes.

Foile, a leaf (of metal).

Folkmote, a meeting, assembly.

Fond, foolish, doting; *fondling*, fool.

Fondly, foolishly.

Fond, found, tried.

Fone, foes.

Food, feud.

Foolhappie, undesigned.

Foolhardise, foolhardiness, folly.

For, notwithstanding.

Fordo, to destroy. *Fordonne*, utterly undone, ruined, overcome.

Foreby, forby, hard by, near, with, past.

Forecast, previously determined.

Foredamned, utterly damned.

Forelay, to lay before, or over.

Forelent, given up entirely.

Forelifting, lifting up in front.

Forepast, gone by.

Foreshewed, previously instructed.

Foreside, the side to the fore, external covering.

Forespent, forspent, utterly wasted.

Forestall, to take previous possession of, to hinder, obstruct.

Foretaught, previously taught.

Forged, false.

Forgery, fiction, deceit, a counterfeit or assumed character.

Forgive, to give up.

Forbent, overtaken.

Forhent, gave up.

Forlore, forlorn, utterly lost, abandoned; *forlore* (pret.), deserted, lost (to sense of propriety).

Formally, expressly.

Formerlie, beforehand.

Forpassed, past by or through.

Forpined, pined away.

Forray, to ravage, prey on, a raid.

Forsake, to avoid, renounce.

Forslacke, forsloe, forslow, to delay, waste in sloth, neglect, omit.

Forthink, to repent, be sorry for, to give up.

Forthright, straightway.

Forthy, therefore, because.

Fortilage, a little fortress.

Fortune, to happen.

Fortunize, to make happy.

Fortuneless, unfortunate.

Forwandre, to stray away.

Forwasted, utterly wasted.

Forwearie (*forwearied*), utterly wearie, worn out.

Forwent, left.

Forworne, much worne.

Foster, forester.

Fouldring, thundering.

Found, established.

Foundring, toppling, falling.

Foy, allegiance, faith.

Foyle, repulse, defeat; to defeat, ruin, overthrow.

Foyne, to thrust, push.

Frame, to make, form, support, prepare, direct; to put in shape for motion.

Franchisement, deliverance.

Franck, free, forward.

Francklin, freeman, freeholder.
Franion, a loose woman.
Fray, to frighten, terrify, alarm, affray.
Fret, ornamental border. *Fretted*, ornamented with fret-work.
Frett, to consume.
Friend, to befriend.
Frigot, a little boat.
Friskes, gambols.
Frize, to freeze.
Fro, from.
Frolicke, "fained her to *frolicke*" = desired her to be cheerful.
Fronts, foreheads.
Frory, frosty, frozen.
Frounce, to fold, plait.
Froward = fromward, at a distance from.
Fry, swarms (of young children).
Fry, to foam.
Fulmined, fulminated.
Funerall, death.
Furniment, furnishing.
Furniture, gear, equipment.
Fylde, felt.
Fyle, to polish.
Fyled, kept in files, registered.

Gage, pledge.
Gain, against (as in *gain*strive).
Gainsay, denial.
Gail, bile.
Gamesome, pleasant.
Gan (can), began, did.
Gard, safeguard, protection.
Garre, to cause, make.
Gate, way, procession.
Gazement, gaze.
Gealosy, *gelosy*, jealousy.
Geare, *gere*, *gear*, dress, equipment, matter, affair.
Geare, to jeer, scoff.
Geason, rare, uncommon.
Gelly, clotted.
Gelt, bribed with gold.
Gelt. This word has been variously explained—by some as a gelding, by others as a *guilty* person. Professor Child explains it as a wild Irishman, *Celt*.
Gelt, castrated.
Gent, gentle, kind, accomplished.
Gere. See *Geare*.
German, brother.
Gerne, to grin.
Gesse, to deem, think, *guess*.
Gest, deed of arms, gesture, deportment, bearing.

Ghastly, terrible, *Ghastlinesse*, terribleness.
Ghess, to guess, deem.
Ghost, spirit, soul.
Giambeux, leggings, greaves.
Gin, engine (of torture), plot, contrivance, snare.
Gin, *ginne*, to begin.
Giust, tournaments, tilts, to joust, tilt.
Glade, valley, dale.
Glade, to gladden.
Glaive, *glave*, *glayve*, a sword.
Glee, pleasure? fee property.
Glib, a thick bush of hair overhanging the eyes.
Glims, glimpse, indistinct light.
Glinne, glen.
Glitterand, glittering.
Glister, to glitter, shine.
Glode, glided.
Glory, vainglory, boasting.
Glozing, deceitful.
Gnarre, growl, snarl.
Gobbeline, goblin.
Gobbet, morsel, piece.
Gondelay, gondola.
Goodlihed, *goodlihead*, goodness; goodly appearance.
Gooldes, marigolds.
Gore, to pierce, wound.
Gore-blood, clotted blood.
Gorge, throat.
Gorget, armour for the throat.
Goshawke, a large kind of hawk.
Gossib, kinsman.
Gourmandize, greediness.
Governall, government.
Governaunce, government.
Government, control.
Grace, favour, kindness; to give favour to.
Graile, gravel.
Graine, dye (scarlet).
Grammercy, many thanks.
Grange, dwelling, place.
Graple, to tug.
Graplement, grasp, clutch.
Graste, graced, favoured.
Grate, to scorn.
Grayle, gravel.
Grayle, the holy vessel said to have been used at Our Saviour's Last Supper.
Greave, grove.
Gree, favour, goodwill.
Greete, to congratulate, praise, to assign with praise.
Gren, to grin, snarl.
Grenning, grinning.

Griefull, grievous.

Griesie, thick, sluggish.

Grieslie, grisely, horrible.

Grieved, hurt.

Grin, to gnash the teeth.

Gripe, to grasp.

Griple, gripe, grasp; grasping, greedy.

Gronefull, full of groans.

Groome, man, a young man, a servant.

Grosse, heavy.

Groundhold, ground - tackle (as cables, anchors).

Groveling, with face flat to the ground.

Groynd, growled.

Grudge, grutch, to murmur, growl.

Gryde, cut, pierce through.

Gryesy, grysie, squalid, foggy, moist.

Grufon, gryphon, griffin (a fabulous animal), perhaps used for vulture, eagle.

Grypt, "*through grypt*" =*through-gyrd*, pierced through.

Guarish, to heal.

Guerdon, reward.

Guilen, to beguile.

Guiler, guyler, deceiver.

Guilt, guilded.

Guize, manner, mode (of life), custom.

Gust, taste.

Gyeld, guild, courthouse.

Gyre, circle, course.

Gyvd, fettered.

Habergeon, haberjeon, a small coat of mail, armour for the neck and breast.

Habiliment, clothing.

Habitaunce, habitation.

Hable, able, fit.

Hacqueton, a jacket worn under armour.

Hagard, wild, untamed.

Haile, hayl, to drag, haul.

Halfendeale, half part.

Halfen-eye = half ordinary sight, *i.e.* one eye

Hand, "out of *hand*"=at once, "nigh *hand*" =near.

Handsell, price, reward.

Hap, to happen, fortune, lot.

Happily, haply, by chance.

Happy, successful.

Hard, heard.

Hardiment, hardihood, boldness.

Hardnesse, rudeness.

Hardyhed, hardihood.

Harnesse, weapons.

Harrow, an exclamation of distress, a call for help.

Hartned, encouraged.

Hartlesse, timid.

Haubergh, hauberk, hauberque, hawberk, a coat of mail.

Haught, high, august.

Hault, haughty.

Haulst, embraced.

Haveour, deportment, behaviour.

Hayle, to drag.

Hazardize, danger.

Hazardry, hazard, risk, gaming.

Heard, a keeper of cattle.

Heare, hair. *Hearie*, hairy.

Heast, hest, command, behest, name, office (of one who had *taken vows*).

Heben, ebony, of ebony wood.

Hedstall, that part of the bridle which is put on the horse's head.

Heedinesse, heedfulness.

Hefte, raised, threw.

Hell, to cover.

Helme, helmet.

Hend, to seize, grasp.

Henge, hinge.

Hent, took, seized.

Herbars, herbs.

Herneshaw, heron.

Herried, heried, praised, worshipped, honoured.

Hersall, rehearsal.

Herse, ceremonial.

Hether, hither.

Hew, shape, form.

Hew, hacking.

Hide, hastened. See *Hye*.

Hie, to hasten.

Hight, called, named, entrusted, directed, pronounce worthy, hence determine, choose, appointed.

Hight, "on *hight*" =aloud.

Hild, held.

Hippodames, sea-horses.

Hole, whole.

Holpen (pp.), helped.

Hond, hand.

Hong, hung.

Honycrock, pot of honey.

Hood, state, manner.

Hopelesse, unexpected.

Hore, hoary.

Horrid, rough.

Hospitage, hospitality.

Hospitale, a place of rest.

Hoste, to entertain, lodge.

Hostlesse, inhospitable.
Hostry, lodging.
Hot, hote, was called.
Housling, sacramental.
Hove, rise, float, hover.
Howre, time; " *good houre* " = good fortune.
Howres, devotional exercises.
Hoye, vessel, ship.
Hububs, shouts, din.
Humblesse, humility, humbleness.
Hurlyburly, noise of battle.
Hurtle, to rush, dash, hurl, attack, brandish, crowd.
Hurtlesse, innocent.
Husband, farmer.
Hyacine, hyacinth.
Hye, to hasten.
Hylding, base, vile.
Hynde, a servant.

Idle, causeless.
Idole, image.
Ill-faste, having an ill-look. *Ill-hedded*, disturbed in the head.
Imbrast, embraced.
Immeasured, unmeasured.
Imp, child, scion, shoot.
Impacable, unappeasible.
Imperceable, not able to be pierced.
Implore, entreaty.
Imply, to enfold, entangle, envelop.
Importable, intolerable.
Importune, violent, savage, full of trouble, to threaten, to solicit.
Importunely, with importunity.
Impresse, to make an impression.
Improvided, unprovided, unlooked for.
In, inne, dwelling, lodging.
In, " *in . . . lyte* " = fall upon.
Incontinent, forthwith, immediately.
Indew, to put on.
Indifferent, impartial. *Indifferently*, impartially.
Indignaunce, indignation.
Indigne, unworthy.
Indignify, to treat with indignity.
Inferd, offered.
Infest, to make fierce or hostile, hostile.
Influence, the power of the stars.
Informed, formed imperfectly.
Ingate, entrance.
Ingowe, ingot.
Inholder, inhabitant.
Inly, inwardly.

Inquest, quest, adventure.
Inquire, to call.
Insolent, rude.
Inspyre, to breathe.
Insu'th = *ensu'th*, follows.
Intend, to stretch out, to denote, name, direct one's course.
Intendiment, intention, knowledge.
Intent, purpose.
Interesse, interest.
Interlace, to intermingle, interweave.
Intermedle, to intermix.
Intimate, to communicate.
Intreat, to prevail upon.
Intuse, contusion.
Invade, to come into.
Invent, to find out.
Invest, to put on.
Irkes, wearies.
Irkesome, tired, weary.
Irrenowmed, inglorious.

Jacob's staffe, a pilgrim's staff.
Jade, a horse, a scolding woman.
Jarre, quarrel, variance.
Jeopardie, jeopardy, danger.
Jesses, strips of leather tied round the legs of hawks, with which they are held upon the fist.
Jollie, jolly, handsome, pretty, lively.
Jolliment, jollitee, jollity, joyfulness, prettiness, liveliness.
Jollyhead, jollity.
Jott, speck, small piece.
Journall, diurnal.
Jovial, bright, sunny.
Joy, to rejoice, be glad, enjoy.
Joyaunce, joyfulness, merriment.
Juncates, junkets.

Kaies, keys.
Keepe, heed, care, charge, to take care, protect, " *heedie keepe* " = watchful care.
Keight, caught.
Kemd, combed.
Ken, kend, kent, knew, perceived, known.
Kerve, to cut.
Kesar, emperor.
Kest, cast.
Kestrell-kynd, base nature.
Kind, nature, sex, occupation. *Kindly*, natural.
Kirtle, a coat fastened at the waist.
Knee, projection of rocks.
Knife, a sword, dagger.

Kond, knew.
Kynded, begotten.

Lackey, to follow as a servant.
Lad, led.
Lade, to load.
Laid, attacked.
Laire, plain.
Lamping, shining.
Lanck loynes, slender waist.
Langurous, languid.
Lap, lappe, to enfold, entangle.
Lare, pasture.
Large, bountiful.
Launce, balance.
Launch, to pierce.
Laver, a basin.
Lay, field, lea, plain.
Lay, cry.
Lay, to throw up.
Lay, law.
Laystall, a dunghill, a place for the deposit of filth.
Lazar, leper.
Leach, a physician.
Leachcraft, medical skill.
Leake, leaky.
Leare, lore, counsel. *Leares*, lessons.
Leasing, lying, falsehood.
Least, lest.
Leave, to raise.
Ledden, dialect, speech.
Lee, river.
Lefte, lifted.
Legierdemain, sleight of hand.
Leke, leaky.
Leman, a lover.
Lend, to give, provide.
Lenger, longer.
Lessoned, instructed.
Lest, to listen.
Let, to hinder; "*let be*" = away with, hindrance.
Level, to direct one's course.
Levin, lightning. *Levin brond*, thunderbolt.
Lewdly, foolishly.
Lewdnesse, wickedness.
Libbard, leopard.
Lich, like.
Lief, liefe, dear, beloved, willing; "*liefe or sory*" = willing or unwilling = *lief* or *loth*, (comp.) *liefer*; (superl.) *liefest*, "*liefest liefe*" = dearest loved one.
Liege, lord, master—one to whom faith has been pledged. *Liege-man*, a vassal, one who owes homage to a liege lord.

Liful, living, full of life.
Lig, to lie.
Light, easy, ready, to lighten, befall.
Lignage, lynage, lineage.
Like, to please.
Like as, as if.
Likelynesse, likeness.
Lill, to put out the tongue.
Limbeck, retort.
Limehound, a bloodhound, limer.
Lin, to cease.
List, to desire, like; (impers.) please. *Listful*, attentive.
Lite, lyte, alight, befall.
Livelod, livelood, livelihood.
Lively, lifelike, living.
Livelyhed, livelyhead, livelihood, living original, motion of a living being.
Liverey, delivery.
Loathly, loathsome.
Loft, height.
Lome, clay, loam.
Lompish, dull, slow.
Long, to belong.
Loord, lout.
Loos, fame.
Loose, to solve.
Lore, learning, teaching, fashion, speech.
Lore, lorn, left, deserted, lost sight of.
Loring, learning.
Losell, lozell, a loose idle fellow.
Lose, to loosen.
Losen, to set loose. *Los'te* = loosed, dissolved.
Lot, fate, share.
Lothfull, unwilling, unpleasant, loathsome.
Loup, loop.
Lout, lowt, to bow, to do obeisance.
Lovely, loving, lovingly; *lovely* of love.
Lover, an opening in the roof to let out the smoke.
Lug, a perch or rod of land.
Luskishnesse, sluggishness.
Lust, pleasure, desire, to desire, please.
Luster, a glittering, sheen.
Lustlesse, feeble, listless.
Lusty-hedd, pleasure.
Lynage, lineage.
Lyte, to alight, light, befall.

Mace, sceptre.
Mage, magician.

Magnes-stone, the magnet.
Mail, *mayl*, *male*, armour.
Maine, *mayne*, force, ocean. *Mainely*, *maynly*, strongly, violently.
Mainsheat, mainsail.
Maintenaunce, condition.
Maisterdome, *maistery*, mastery, superiority.
Maistring, superior, controlling.
Make, companion, mate.
Malengine, ill intent, deceit, guile.
Malice (pret. *malist*), regarded with malice, bore ill-will to.
Maligne, to grudge.
Mall, club, mallet, to maul.
Maltalent, ill-will.
Mand, blocked up with men.
Manie, *many*, company, multitude.
Manner, kind of.
Mantle, to rest with outspread wings.
Mard, spoilt, injured, dishonour.
Marge, margin, bank.
Margent, margin.
Marle, ground, soil.
Marishes, marshes.
Martelled, hammered.
Martyr, to afflict, torment.
Maske, to conceal oneself by means of a mask (as at a masquerade).
Masse, wealth, material.
Massy, massive.
Mate, to stupefy, confound, *amate*.
Matchlesse, not to be matched.
Maugre, *maulgre*, in spite of, a curse on! unwillingly.
Maysterdome, superiority.
Mazed, amazed, confounded.
Mazer, a kind of hard wood (probably the maple).
Me, "he cast *me* down" (ethic dative).
Mealth, melteth.
Mean, middle, moderate, moderation, means, "by *meanes*," because.
Meanesse, humble birth.
Meare, pure, boundary.
Measure, moderation.
Medewart, meadow-wort.
Measured, sang.
Medling, mixing.
Mell, to intermeddle.
Melling, meddling.
Menage, to manage, guide (a horse); to wield (arms); management.
Mendes, amends.
Mene, means.

Ment, purposed, meant.
Ment, joined, united.
Mercie, *mercy*, thanks, favour, thank you.
Mercify, to pity.
Merimake, *meryment*, merry-making, sport.
Mery, pleasant, cheerful.
Mesprise, *mesprize*, contempt, insolence, mistake.
Mew, to confine, secrete, prison, den.
Mickle, much, great.
Middest, midst, midmost.
Mieve, to move.
Mincing, affected.
Mind, to call to mind.
Mindlesse, unmindful.
Minime, a trifling song, but properly a musical note.
Miniments, trifles, toys.
Mineon, a favourite.
Minisht, diminished.
Mirkesome, dark.
Mis, to sin, err.
Misavized, ill-advised, misinformed.
Misaymed, ill-aimed.
Miscall, to abuse.
Mischalenge, false challenge.
Misconceipt, mistake.
Miscreant, unbeliever.
Miscreated, ill-formed.
Miscreaunce, false faith, misbelief.
Misdeem, to deem amiss, misjudge. *Misdeeming*, misleading. *Misdempt*, misjudged, misweened.
Misdesert, crime.
Misdid, failed.
Misdiet, over-eating.
Misdight, ill-dressed.
Misdonne, to misdo.
Misdoubting, fearing sadly.
Miser, wretch.
Misfeign, to feign wrongfully.
Misfare, misfortune.
Misfaring, misfortune.
Misguyde, trespass.
Mishappen, happen amiss.
Mishapt, misshaped.
Misleeke, to dislike.
Misregard, misconstruction.
Missay, to say to no purpose, uselessly, abuse, speak ill of.
Misseem, to be unseemly, to misbecome.
Misseeming, unseemly, wrong, deceit.

Misshape, deformity.
Misshapen, deformed.
Mister, sort of, manner of.
Misthought, mistake.
Mistooke, suspected.
Mistrayne, to mislead.
Mistreth, signifies, matters.
Misweene, to think amiss.
Mo, moe, more.
Mold, mole, spot.
Molt, melted.
Mome, blockhead.
Moniment, mark, stamp, record.
Monoceros, sea-unicorn (? sword-fish).
Morish, marshy.
Moralize, to cause to be moral.
More, root, plant.
Morion, helmet.
Morrow, morning.
Mortall, deadly.
Mortality, the estate of mortal man.
Most, greatest.
Mot, mote (pl. *moten*), may, must, might.
Mould, to moulder.
Mountenaunce, space, distance.
Mowes, insulting grimaces, *mouths.*
Moyity, half.
Muckell, much, great.
Muck, wealth.
Mucky, sordid, vile.
Munificence (munifience), fortification, defence.
Mured, walled, enclosed.
Muse, to wonder, wonderment.
Must, new wine.
Myndes, resolves.

Namely, especially.
Napron, apron.
Native, natural.
Nathlesse, nathless, none the less, never the less.
Nathemoe, nathemore, none the more, never the more.
Ne, nor.
Neat, cattle.
Nempt, named.
Nephewes, descendants, grandchildren.
Net, nett, pure, clean.
Nigardise, niggardliness, miserliness.
Nill, will not, *will* or *nill*, willing or unwilling; "*nilled*," unwilling.
Nimblesse, nimbleness.
Nobilesse, noblesse, nobleness, nobility.

Nominate, to name, affirm.
Noriture, norture, nurture, bringing up.
Norveyses, Norwegians.
Not, note, wot not, know not, knows not. (It sometimes seems to stand for *ne mote =* could not).
Nothing, not at all.
Notifye, to proclaim.
Nought, not, of no value.
Nould, would not.
Noule, the head, pate.
Noursle, nousle, to nurse, foster, rear.
Nousling, nestling, burrowing.
Noyance, noyaunce, annoyance.
Noyd, noyed, annoyed.
Noyes, noise.
Noyous, annoying, disagreeable, injurious.
Noysome, hurtful.
Nycely, carefully.

Obliquid, oblique.
Obsequy, funeral rite.
Oddes, advantage.
Of, upon, by; *of all*, above all.
Offal, that which falls off.
Offend, to harm, hurt.
Ofnew, recently.
Ofspring, origin.
Onely, chief, especial.
Ope, open.
Opprest, taken captive.
Ordain, to set (the battle) in order.
Order, to arrange, rank (of army).
Ordinaunce, arrangement, ordinance, artillery.
Origane, bastard, marjoram.
Other, left.
Otherwise, elsewhere.
Otherwhiles, sometimes.
Ought, owned.
Ouibarre, to arrest.
Outgo, to surpass.
Outhyred, let out for hire.
Out-learn, to learn from.
Outrage, violence, outburst.
Outweave, wear out, pass, spend.
Outwell, to gush or well out.
Outwin, to get out.
Outwind (= *outwin*), to get out.
Outwrest, wrest out, discover.
Outwrought, completed, passed.
Overall, everywhere, all over.
Overbore, overthrew.
Overcame, overspread.
Overcaught, overtook.
Overcraw, to crow over, insult.

Overdight, decked over, covered over, overspread.

Overgive, to give over.

Overgo, to overpower, surpass.

Overhent overtook, overtaken.

Overkest, overcast.

Overlade, to overwhelm.

Overplast, overhanging.

Over-raught, overtook.

Over-red, read over.

Overpasse, pass over, alleviate.

Overren, to over-run, oppress.

Oversee, to overlook.

Oversight, escape (through having overlooked a danger).

Overswim, to swim over.

Overbore, overthrow.

Overthwart, opposite.

Owe, to own. See *Ought*.

Owch, a socket of gold to hold precious stones, a jewel.

Owre, ore.

Oystrige, ostrich.

Pace, pase, step, pass, passage.

Packe, to pack off, a burden.

Paine, payne, labour, pains, punishment, " *did him paine* "=took pains, exerted himself.

Paire, to impaire.

Paled, " *pinckt* upon gold, and *paled part per part*," = " adorned with golden points or eyelets, and regularly intersected with stripes." In heraldry a shield is said to be *parted per pale* when it is longitudinally divided by a pale or broad bar.

Paled, fenced off.

Pall, to subdue, moderate.

Pall, a cloak of rich material.

Panachœa, panacea.

Pannikell, skull, crown.

Paragon, paragone, companion, equal, rivalry.

Paravaunt, first, beforehand, in front.

Parbreake, vomit.

Pardale, panther.

Parentage, parent.

Part, party, depart.

Partake, to share.

Parture, departure.

Pas, passe (*passing*, surpassing), to surpass, exceed.

Passion, suffering. *Passioned*, affected with feeling, be grieved. *Passionate*, to express feelingly.

Patronage, defence. *Patronesse*, a female defender.

Paunce, pansy.

Pavone, peacock.

Payne, to take pains, exert.

Payse, to poise, balance.

Pealing, appealing.

Peare, pere, equal.

Peasant knight, base knight.

Peaze, blow.

Peece, fabric, fortified place, as a castle, ship, etc.

Peise, to pose, weigh.

Pen, to confine, restrain.

Pendants, ornaments (of wood or stone) hanging down from a Gothic roof.

Penne, feather.

Penurie, want of food.

Percen, to pierce.

Perdu, perdy, pardieu, truly.

Perforce, of necessity.

Perlous, perilous.

Persant, persaunt, piercing.

Persant, piercing.

Personage, personal appearance.

Persue, a track.

Perveyaunce, provision. See *Purveyaunce*.

Pesaunt, a peasant.

Physnomy, countenance.

Pictural, a picture.

Pight, fixed, placed, fastened.

Pill, to spoil, plunder.

Pine, pyne, sorrow, grief, to waste away through torment; " *pined ghost*," a spirit wasted away (through torment); *done to pine*, caused to die.

Pinnoed, pinioned.

Pitteous, compassionate, tenderhearted.

Place, " *of place*," of rank.

Plaine, playne, to complain.

Plaintiffe, plaintive.

Platane, plane tree.

Pleasaunce, pleasure, delight, objects affording pleasure.

Pled, pleaded.

Plesh, a shallow pool, plash.

Plight (p. p. *plight*), weave, plait, fold; a plait, fold, condition.

Ply, to move.

Poise, poyse, weight, force.

Point, poynt, to appoint; a whit, " *to poynt* " = exactly.

Poke, a pouch.

Poll, to plunder.

Pollicie, statecraft.

Port, portance, portaunce, demeanour, bearing.

Portesse, breviary.

Possesse, to accomplish.

Potshares = *potshards*, fragments of broken vessels.

Pouldred, powdered, spotted.

Pounce, claws, talons.

Pound, weight, balance. "*new in pound*" = anew in the balance.

Pourtrahed, drawn.

Pourtraict, *pourtraiture*, portrait, image.

Poynant, piercing, sharp.

Poyse, weight, force.

Practic, *practicke*, treacherous, deceitful, skilful.

Prancke, to trim, deck, adorn, adjust, a malicious trick.

Praunce, to prance.

Pray, to be the prey of, to make a prey of.

Preace, *prease*, to press, a press, crowd.

Prefard, preferred.

Prefixt, fixed beforehand.

Prejudize, foresight.

Prepense, to consider.

Presage, to tell or point out, foresee.

Presence, reception-room.

President, precedent.

Prest ready, prepared.

Pretend, to attempt, to stretch out (or over), offer.

Prevent, anticipate.

Price, to pay the price of, atone for, value.

Prick, to ride hard, to spur on quickly; point, centre of target.

Prief, *priefe*, proof, trial, experiment.

Prieve, to prave.

Prime, *pryme*, spring time, morning.

Principle, beginning.

Prise, adventure.

Privitee, *privitie*, private life, intimate relation.

Procure, to arrange, entreat.

Prodigious, ominous.

Professe, to present the appearance of.

Project, to throw forward.

Prolong, to postpone.

Prone, subjected.

Proper, own, peculiar; *proper good*, own property.

Protense, a stretching out.

Prove, to experience, try, feel.

Provokement, a provoking.

Prow, brave; (superl.) *prowest*; *prowes*, prowess.

Pryse, to pay for. See *Price*.

Puissant, powerful.

Pumy stones, pumice stones.

Purchase, to obtain, to get, win (honestly or otherwise).

Purchas, *purchase*, property, booty, robbery.

Purfled, embroidered on the edge.

Purport, disguise.

Purpos, *purpose*, conversation, discourse; "*to purpose*," to the purpose, to speak as "*purpose diversly*" = to speak of various things.

Purvay, to provide.

Purveyaunce, provision, management, function.

Puttocke, a kite.

Pyne, pain (of hunger), torment.

Pyoning, diggings, work of pioneers.

Quaile, to cast down, defeat, conquer.

Quaint, nice, fastidious.

Qualify, to ease, sooth.

Quarle, *quarrel*, a square-headed arrow.

Quarrie, *quarry*, prey, game.

Quart, quarter.

Quayd, *quailed*, quelled, subdued.

Queane, a worthless woman.

"*Queint elect*," oddly chosen.

Queint, quenched.

Quell, to kill, to subdue, to perish, to disconcert, frighten.

Quest, expedition, pursuit.

Quick, alive.

Quich, to stir, move,

Quietage, quietness.

Quight, to set free, to requite,

Quilted, padded.

Quib, to sneer at, taunt.

Quire, company.

Quit, *quite*, *quyte*, to set free, to requite, repay, to return (a salute), freed, removed; "*quite clame*," to release.

Quooke, quaked.

Rablement, a rabble, troop.

Race, to raze, to cut; *raced*, erazed.

Rad, rode.

Rad, perceived. See *Read*.

Raft, bereft.

Ragged, rugged.

Raile, *rayle*, to flow, pour down.

Rain, *rayne*, to reign, kingdom.

Rakehell, loose, worthless.

Ramp, tear, attack, leap.

Ranck, fiercely.

Randon, random.

Ranke, fiercely.

Rape, rapine.

Rascal, raskall, low, base, worthless.

Rase (pret. *rast*), to erase.

Rash, to tear violently, hack. *Rashly*, hastily, suddenly. *Rash*, quick.

Rate, to scold.

Rate, allowance, order, state.

Rath, early, soon.

Raught, reached, extended, took.

Ravin, ravine, plunder, prey.

Ravishment, ecstasy.

Ray, to defile, soil.

Ray, array.

Rayle, to flow. See *Raile*.

Rayle, abuse.

Rayne, kingdom.

Read, reede, advice, motto, prophecy.

Read, reed (pret. *rad, red*), to know, declare, explain or advise, discover, perceive, suppose, regard.

Readifye, to rebuild.

Reallie, to reform.

Reames, realms.

Reare, to raise, take up or away, steal, excite, to rouse.

Reason, proportion.

Reave (pret. *reft, raft*), to bereave, take away (forcibly).

Rebuke, conduct deserving of reproof, rudeness.

Rebutte, to cause to recoil.

Reclayme, to call back.

Recorde, to remember, to call to mind.

Recoure, recower, recure, to recover.

Recourse, to recur, return; "had recourse" = did recur, return.

Recoyle, to retire, retreat.

Recuile, recule, to recoil.

Red, redd, declared, described, perceived, saw. See *Read*.

Redisbourse, to repay.

Redoubted, doughty.

Redound, to overflow, flow, be redundant.

Redress, to reunite, remake, to rest.

Reed, to deem. *Reede, read*, to advise.

Reek, to smoke.

Reele, to roll.

Refection, refreshment.

Reft, bereft, taken violently away. See *Reave*.

Regalitie, rights of royalty.

Regarde, a subject demanding consideration or attention, value.

Regiment, government, command.

Relate, to bring back.

Release, to break loose from, to give up.

Relent, to give way, to slacken, relax, soften.

Relide, to ally, join.

Relieve, to recover, **revive, live** again.

Remeasure, to retrace.

Remedilesse, without hope of rescue.

Remercy, to thank.

Remorse, pity.

Rencounter, to encounter, meet in battle.

Renfierced (renfierst), made more fierce or = *renforst* = reinforced.

Renforst, reinforced, enforced, made fresh effort.

Renverse, to reverse, overturn.

Repent, repentance, to grieve.

Repining, a failing (of courage).

Replevie, a law term signifying to take possession of goods claimed, giving security at the same time to submit the question of property to a legal tribunal within a given time.

Report, to carry off.

Reprief, reproof, shame.

Reprive, to deprive of, **take away.**

Reprive, reprieve.

Reprize, to retake.

Requere, to require, demand.

Request, demand.

Requit, requited, returned.

Reseize, to reinstate, to be repossessed of.

Resemble, to compare.

Resemblaunce, look, regard.

Resiant, resident.

Respect, care, caution.

Respondence, correspondence, **reply** (in music).

Respyre, to breathe again.

Restlesse, resistless.

Restore, restitution.

Resty, restive.

Retourn, to turn (the eyes) back.

Retraite, picture, portrait.

Retrate, a retreat.

Retyre, retirement.

Revel, a feast,

Revengement, revenge.

Reverse, to return, **to cause to** return.

Revest, to reclothe.

Revilement, a reviling, abuse.

Revoke, to recall, withdraw.

Revolt, to roll back.

Reu, rue, to pity, to be sorry for, to lament over, repent.

Rew, row.

Ribauld, rybauld, a loose impure person, ribald.

Richesse, riches.

Ridling, skill, skill in explaining riddles.

Rife, ryfe, abundant, abundantly, much, frequent.

Rift, split, broken, gap, fissure, fragment.

Rigor, force. *Rigorous,* violent.

Ring, to encircle.

Riotise, riotize, riot, extravagance.

Rivage, bank.

Rive, to split, tear.

Rize, to come to.

Rocke, distaff.

Rode, raid, incursion.

Rode, roadstead, anchorage for ships.

Rong, rang.

Roode, a cross, crucifix.

Rosiere, a rose tree.

Rosmarine, a sea-monster that was supposed to feed on the dew on the tops of the sea rocks.

Rote, a lyre, harp.

Roules, rolls, records.

Rout, crowd, troop.

Rove, to shoot (with a sort of arrow called a rover).

Rowel, the ring of a bit—any small movable ring.

Rowme, place, space.

Rownded, whispered.

Rowndell, a round bubble (of foam).

Rowze, rouze, to shake up.

Royne, to mutter.

Rubin, Rubine, the ruby.

Rue, to grieve.

Ruffed, ruffled. *Ruffin,* disordered. *Ruffing,* ruffling.

Ruinate, to ruin.

Ruing, pitying.

Ruth, pity.

Ryve, to pierce.

Sacrament, oath of purgation taken by an accused party.

Sacred, accursed.

Sad, firm, heavy, grave.

Saine, to say (pl. *suy*).

Sake, cause.

Salew, to salute.

Saliaunce, onslaught.

Salied, leapt, sallied.

Sallows, willows.

Salvage, savage, wild.

Salute, to salute.

Salve, to heal, save, remedy.

Salving, salvation, restoration.

Sam, together.

Samite, silk stuff.

Sanguine, blood-colour.

Sardonian, sardonic.

Saufgard, guard, defence. *Savegard,* to protect.

Say, a thin stuff (for cloaks).

Say, assay, proof.

Scald, scabby.

Scand, climbed.

Scarmoges, skirmishes.

Scath, hurt, harm, damage, ruin.

Scatter, to let drop.

Scatterling, a vagrant.

Scerne, to discern.

Schuchin, scutchin, escutcheon, shield, device on a shield.

Scolopendra, a fish resembling a centipede.

Scope, dimension; " aymed scope," a mark aimed at.

Scorse, to exchange.

Scorse, to chase.

Scould, scowled.

Scriene, scrine, scryne, skreene, a cabinet for papers, a writing desk; entrance of a hall.

Scrike, shriek.

Scruze, to squeeze, crush.

Scryde, descried.

Sdeigne, to disdain.

Sea-shouldring, having shoulders that displace the sea.

Sear, to burn, burning.

Sease, to fasten on, seize.

See. seat.

Seelde, seldom, rare.

Seely, simple, innocent.

Seeming, apparently.

Seemlesse, unseemly.

Seemly, in a seemly manner, comely, apparent.

Seemlyhed, a seemly appearance.

Seene, skilled, experienced.

Seew, to pursue.

Seised, taken possession of.

Seisin, possession.

Selcouth, seldom known, rare, strange.

Sell, seat, saddle.

Semblaunce, semblaunt, semblant, likeness, appearance, phantom, cheer, entertainment.

Sence, feeling.

Seneschall, governor, steward.

Sens, since.

Sensefull, sensible.

Sent, scent, perception.
Serve, to bring to bear upon.
Set by, to esteem.
Severall, diverse.
Sew, to follow, to solicit.
Shade, to shadow, represent.
Shalloh, aloop.
Shame, to feel shame, to be ashamed.
Shamefast, modest.
Shamefastnesse, modesty.
Shard, division, boundary, cut.
Share, portion, piece, to cut.
Shayres, shires.
Sheare, to cut, divide.
Sheare, shere, bright, clear.
Sheares, wings.
Shed, to spill life blood, to kill.
Sheene, shene, bright, shining, clear.
Shend (pret. *shent*), to disgrace, defile, abuse, reproach, shame.
Shere, to cleave, divide.
Shere, bright, clear.
Shew, mark, track.
Shine, shyne, a bright light, bright.
Shiver, to quiver.
Shole, shallow.
Shonne, to shun.
Shope, shaped, framed.
Shot, advanced (in years).
Shriech, shriek.
Shrieve, to question (shrive).
Shright, a shriek, to shriek.
Shrill, to give out a ringing, shrill sound.
Shrilling, shrill.
Sib, sibbe, akin, related.
Sich, such.
Sickernesse, security, safety.
Siege, seat.
Sield, cieled.
Sient, scion.
Sight, sighed.
Sign, watchword, representation, picture.
Silly, simple, innocent.
Sin, since.
Singults, sighs.
Sinke, hoard, deposit.
Sited, placed, situated.
Sith, sithe, sythe, time, since.
Sithens, since, since that time.
Sithes, times.
Sits, is becoming.
Skill, to signify, to be a matter of importance.
Skippet, a little boat.
Slacke, slow.
Slake, to slack.
Slaver, slobber.

Slight, sleight, device, trick.
Slombry, sleepy.
Slug, to live idle.
Sly, subtle, clever.
Smit, smote, smitten.
Smouldry, smouldring, suffocating.
Snag, a knot.
Snaggy, knotted, covered with knots.
Snags, knots.
Snaky - wreathed = (?) *snake-ywreathed,* snake-entwined.
Snar, to snarl.
Snarled, twisted.
Snub, knob (of a club).
Sold, pay, remuneration.
Solemnize, a solemn rite.
Song, sang.
Sooth, truly.
Soothly, soothlich, truly, indeed.
Soothsay, prediction, omen.
Sort, company.
Sort, " *in sort,*" inasmuch as.
Souce, souse, sowse, to swoop on, as a bird does upon his prey, strike, attack, the swoop (of a hawk), blow.
Souse, to immerse.
Southsay, soothsay. *Southsayer,* soothsayer.
Sovenaunce, remembrance.
Sownd, to wield. *Sownd = swound,* swoon.
Sowne, a sound.
Sowst, struck.
Soyle, prey.
Space, to walk, roam.
Spalles, the shoulders.
Spangs, spangles.
Sparckle forth, to cause to sparkle.
Spare, sparing, niggardliness, to save.
Sparre, bolt, bar.
Speed, " *evill speed,*" misfortune.
Sperre, to bolt, shut.
Sperse, to disperse, scatter.
Spies, spyes, keen glances, eyes.
Spight, displeasure, grudge.
Spill, to ravage, destroy.
Spilt, pieced, inlaid.
Spoil, to ravage, carry off.
Sponned, flowed out quickly.
Spot, to blame.
Spoused, espoused, betrothed.
Sprad, spread.
Spray, branch.
Spred, spredden, to spread over, to cover.
Sprent, sprinkled.
Spright, spirit.

Springal, a youth, stripling.
Spring-headed, having heads that spring afresh.
Sprong, sprang.
Spurne, to spur.
Spyall, spy.
Spyre, to shoot forth.
Squire, a square, a rule, a carpenter's measure.
Stadle, a staff, prop.
Stale, decoy, bait.
Stalk, a stride.
Stare, to shine.
Stared, " *up stared*," stood up stiffly.
Stark, strong, stiff.
Star-read, knowledge of the stars.
Stay, to hold, hold up, support.
Stayd, caused to stay.
Stayed, constant.
Stayne, to dim, deface.
Stayre, a step.
Stead, *sted*, *stedd*, station, place, situation.
Stead, to help, avail, bestead.
Steale, stale, handle.
Steane, a stone (vessel).
Steare, a steer.
Sted, place, condition, steed horse. See *Stead*.
Steedy, steady.
Steely = *steelen*, of steel.
Steemed, esteemed.
Steep, to bathe, stain.
Steliths, thefts.
Steme, to exhale.
Stemme, to rush against.
Stent, to cease, stop.
Sterve, to die.
Stew, a hot steaming place.
Stie, to ascend.
Still, to drop, flow, trickle.
Stint, to stop, cease.
Stir, *styre*, to stir, move, incite, provoke, to direct, steer.
Stole, a long robe.
Stomachous, angry.
Stomacke, temper.
Stond, attach.
Stonied, astonished, alarmed.
Stound, *stownd*, *stond*, a moment of time (a time of) trouble, peril, alarm, assault, a stunning influence, a blow, amazement, stunned.
Stoup, to swoop.
Stout, stubborn, bold.
Stoure, *stowre*, tumult, disturbance, battle, passion, fit, paroxysm, danger, peril.

Straine, race, lineage.
Straine, *strayne*, to stretch out.
Straint, grasp, strain.
Strake, strook, a streak.
Straunge, foreign, borrowed.
Strayne, to wield.
Strayt, a street.
Streight, narrow, strait, strict, close.
Streightly, straitly, closely.
Streightnesse, straitness.
Strene, strain, race.
Stresse, distress.
Strich, the screech-owl.
Strif-ful, *stryfull*, contentious.
Stroken, struck.
Strond, strand.
Stub, stock of a tree.
Sty, to ascend, mount.
Subject, lying beneath.
Submisse, submissive.
Subtile, fin-spun.
Subverst, subverted.
Succeed, to approach.
Successe, succession.
Sue, solicit. See *Sew*.
Sufferaunce, patience, endurance.
Suffised, satisfied.
Sugred, sweet.
Supple, to make supple.
Suppress, to overcome, keep down.
Surbate, to batter.
Surbet, bruised, wearied.
Surcease, to leave off, utterly to cease.
Surcharge, to attack with renewed vigour.
Surcharged, heavily laden.
Surmount, to surpass.
Surplusage, excess.
Surprise, to seize suddenly.
Surquedray, pride, insolence, presumption.
Suspect, suspicion.
Swain, *swayn*, a labourer, youth, person.
Swart, black.
Swarve, to swerve, retreat.
Swat, did sweat.
Sway, to swing, brandish, wield (arms), force, a rapid motion.
Sweard, sword.
Sweath-bands, swaddling-bands.
Swelt, fainted, swooned, burnt (? swelled).
Swinck, labour, toil.
Swinge, to singe.
Swound, swoon.

Table, a picture.

Tackle (pl. *tackles*), rigging.
Talaunts, talons.
Tare, tore.
Targe, target.
Tarras, terrace.
Tassal gent, the tiersel, or male gosshawk.
Teade, a torch.
Teene (*tene*), grief, sorrow, pain, affliction. See *Tine*.
Teene (?*leene*, lend, give), to bestow.
Tell, to count. *Teld*, told.
Temed, yoked in a team.
Temewise, like a team.
Tempring, controlling, governing.
Tend, to wait on.
Tender, to tend, attend to.
Thee, to prosper, thrive.
Theeveryes, thefts.
Then, than.
Thereto, besides.
Thether, thither.
Thewed, behaved, mannered.
Thewes, qualities, manners.
Thick, a thicket.
Thirst, to thirst, thirst.
Tho, *thoe*, then.
Thorough, through.
Thother, that other, the other.
Thrall, to take captive, enslave, bring into subjection, constrain, a slave, enslaved.
Threat, to threaten, *Threatfull*, threatening.
Thresher, a flail.
Thrid, a thread.
Thrill, to pierce. *Thrillant*, piercing.
Thristy, thirsty.
Throughly, thoroughly.
Throw, time, while.
Throw, throe, pang, thrust, attack.
Thrust, to thirst, thirst.
Thwart, athwart.
Tickle, uncertain, insecure.
Tide, *tyde*, time, season, opportunity.
Tight, tied.
Timbered, massive (like timbers).
Tine, affliction.
Tine, to light, kindle, inflame.
Tine or *teen*, sorrow, grief, pain.
Tire, rank, train.
Tire, *tyre*, attire, dress.
To=for (as in *to frend*).
Tofore, before.
Toole, weapon.
Top, head.
To-rent, rent asunder.
Tort, wrong, injury.

Tortious, injurious, wrongful.
Tossen, to brandish, toss.
Totty, tottering, unsteady.
To-torne, torn to pieces.
Tourney, to tilt, joust.
Touze, to tease, worry.
Toward, favourable, approaching, near at hand.
To-worne, worn out.
Toy, pastime, sport.
Trace, to walk, track, tract.
Tract, trace, to trace.
Trade, footstep, tread, occupation, conduct.
Traduction, transfer.
Traine, *trayne*, to drag along, trail, to allure, wile, deceit, snare, trap, track, assembly.
Tramell, a net for the hair, tresses.
Transfard, transformed.
Transmew, to transmute, transform.
Transmove, to transpose.
Trap, to adorn (with trappings).
Traveiled, toiled.
Travell, toil.
Trayled, interwoven, adorned.
Treachour, *treachetour*, a traitor.
Treague, truce.
Treat, to discourse, hold parley with.
Treen, of trees.
Trenchand, *trenchant*, cutting.
Trentals, services of 30 masses, which were usually celebrated upon as many different days, for the dead.
Trild, flowed.
Trim, neat, well-formed, pleasing.
Trinall, threefold.
Triplicity, quality of being threefold.
Trode, path, footstep.
Troncheon, a headless spear.
Troth, truth.
Troublous, restless.
Trow, to believe.
Truncked, truncated, having the head cut off.
Trusse, to pack up, carry off.
Tryde, proved, essayed.
Trye, tried, purified.
Turmoild, troubled.
Turney, an encounter.
Turribant, turban.
Tway, twain, two.
Twight, to twit.
Twyfold, twofold.
Tynde, kindled.
Tyne, grief, pain. See *Tine*, *Teen*.

Tyne, to come to grief, to perish.
Tyrannesse, a female tyrant.
Tyranning, acting like a tyrant.
Tyre, to dress, attire.
Tyreling (?) weary.

Ugly, horrible.
Umbriere, the visor of a helmet.
Unacquainted, unusual, strange.
Unbid, without a prayer.
Unblest, unwounded.
Unbrace, to unfasten.
Uncivile, wild, uncivilised.
Uncouth, unusual, strange.
Undefide, unchallenged.
Underfong, to surprise, circumvent.
Underhand, secretly.
Understand, to learn the cause of (or perhaps to take in hand for purpose of arbitration).
Undertake, to perceive, hear.
Undertime, time of the mid-day meal.
Undight, to undress, take off ornaments, unloose.
Uneasy, disturbed.
Uneath, unneath unneathes, uneth, scarcely, with difficulty, uneasily.
Unespyde, unseen.
Unfilde, unpolished.
Ungentle, uncourteous.
Ungentlenesse, base conduct.
Unguilty, not conscious of guilt.
Unhible, incapable.
Unhappie paine, unsuccessful labours (because there was no heir to reap the benefit of their pains).
Unhappy, unfortunate.
Unhastie, slow.
Unheale, unhele, to expose, uncover.
Unheedy, unwary; *Unheedily,* unheedingly.
Unherst, "took from the herse or temporary monument where the knights' arms were hung."
Unkempt, uncombed, rude.
Unkend, unknown.
U kind, unnatural.
Unkindly, unnatural.
Unlast, unlaced.
Unlich, unlike.
Unlike, not likely.
Unmannurd, not cultivated.
Unmard, uninjured.
Unmeet, unfit.
Unpurvaide of, unprovided with.

Unred, untold.
Unredrest, without redress, unrescued.
Unreproved, blameless.
Unshed, unparted.
Unspidie, unseen.
Unstayd, unsteady.
Unthrifty, wicked.
Unthriftyhead, unthrift.
Untill, unto.
Untimely, unfortunately.
Unwary, unwary, unexpected.
Unware, unwares, unawares, unexpectedly, unknown.
Unweeting, not knowing, unconscious.
Unweldy, unwieldy.
Unwist, unknown.
Unworthy, undeserved.
Unwreaked, unrevenged.
Upbraide, upbraiding, reproach, abuse.
Upbrast, burst open.
Upbray, to upbraid, an upbraiding.
Uphild, upheld.
Upreare, to raise up.
Upstare, to stand up erect.
Up-start, start up.
Upstay, to support.
Uptyde, tied up.
Upwound, knotted.
Urchin, hedgehog.
Usage, behaviour.
Usaunce, usage.
Use, to practise, habits.
Utmost, uttermost, outmost, last.
Utter, outer.

Vade, to go, to vanish.
Vaile, to lay down.
Vaine, frail.
Valew, value, valour, courage.
Valiaunce, valour.
Variable, various.
Vauncing, advancing.
Vaunt, to display.
Vauntage, advantage, opportunity.
Vaut, a vault.
Vauted, vaulted.
Vele, a veil.
Vellanage, villinage, slavery.
Venery, hunting.
Vengeable, revengeful, deserving of revenge.
Vengement, revenge.
Venger, avenger.
Ventayle, the place of the helmet.
Vented, lifted up the visor.
Ventre, to venture.

Ventrous, venturous, bold, adventurous.

Vere, to veer.

Vermeil, vermeill, vermell, vermily, vermilion.

Vertuous, possessing virtue or power.

Vestiment, vestment.

Vild, vile.

Vildly, vilely.

Villein, base-born, low.

Virginal, pertaining to a virgin.

Visnomie, visage.

Vitall, life-giving.

Voide, to avoid, turn aside, to remove.

Voided, cleared.

Wade, to walk, go.

Wag, to move (the limbs).

Wage, a pledge, to pledge.

Waide, weighed, proved.

Waift, a waif, an article found and not claimed by an owner.

Waite, to watch.

Wakefull, watchful.

Walke, to rolle, wag.

Wallowed, groveling.

Wan, gained, took.

Wan, pale, faint.

Wand, branch of a tree.

Wanton, wild.

Ward, to guard.

Ware, wary, cautious.

Wareless, unaware, unexpected, heedless.

War-hable, fit for war.

Wariment, caution.

Warke, work.

War-monger, a mercenary warrior.

Warray, warrey, to make war on, to lay waste.

Warre, worse.

Wasserman, a sea monster in shape like a man.

Wast, to desolate, lay waste.

Wastfull, barren, uninhabited, wild.

Wastness, wilderness.

Water-sprinckle, waterpot.

Wawes, waves.

Wax, wex, to grow.

Way, to weigh, esteem.

Wayd, went on their way, weighed, determined.

Waylfull, lamentable.

Wayment, to lament, lamentation.

Wayne, chariot.

Weare, to pass, spend (the time).

Wearish, mischievous, evil-disposed.

Weasand-pipe, windpipe.

Weather, to expose to the weather.

Weaved, waved, floated.

Weed, clothes, dress.

Weeke, wick.

Weeldelesse, unwieldy.

Ween (pret. *weend*), to suppose, expect, think.

Weet, weeten, to know, learn, understand, perceive. *To weet* = to wit.

Weeting, knowledge.

Weetingly, knowingly.

Weetlesse, unconscious, ignorant.

Weft, a waif.

Wefte, was wafted, avoided, a waif, a thing cast adrift.

Weld, to wield, govern.

Welke, to wane.

Welkin, sky, heavens.

Well, weal, very (*well affectionate*).

Well, to pour. *Well-head,* fountain head.

Well-away, an exclamation of great sorrow, alas!

Well-seene, experienced.

Wend, to turn, go.

Went, journey, course.

Wesand, weasand, windpipe.

Wex, to grow, increase, become.

Wex, wax.

Whally, marked with streaks.

What, a thing — *homely what,* homely fare.

Wheare, where, place.

Whelm, to overwhelm.

Whether, which of two.

Whileare, whilere = erewhile, formerly, lately.

Whiles, whilest, whilst.

Whimpled, covered with a wimple.

Whirlpool, a kind of whale.

Whist, silenced.

Whot, hot.

Whylome, formerly.

Wicked, vile (chains).

Wide, round-about.

Wight, person, being.

Wimple, to gather, plait, fold, a covering for the neck, veil.

Win (out), get (out), come up to.

Wisard, wizard, wise man.

Wise, wize, mode, manner, guise.

Wist, wiste, knew.

Witch, to bewitch.

Wite, witen, wyte, to blame, twit, reprove.

With-hault, withheld.

Withouten, without.

Witt, mind, intelligence. *Wittily*, wisely, sensibly.
Wo, woe, sad.
Womanhood, womanly feeling.
Won (*did won*), be wont.
Won, *wonne* (*wonning*), dwelling-place, abode, to dwell.
Wondred, marvellous.
Wont, to be accustomed.
Wood, mad, frantic, furious.
Woodnes, madness.
Word, motto.
Wore, passed or spent the time.
Worshippe, honour, reverence.
Worth, to be.
Wot, *wote*, know, knows.
Wotes, knows. *Wotest*, knowest.
Wowed, wooed.
Woxe, *woxen*, become, grown.
Wracke, wreck, destruction, violence, to take vengeance. *Wrackfull*, avenging.
Wrast, to wrest.
Wrate, did write.
Wrawling, mewing like a cat.
Wreak, vengeance, ruin, to avenge, take vengeance.
Wreakfull, avenging.
Wreath, to turn.
Wreck, destruction.
Wrest, to wrench, twist, a wrenching, over-turning.
Wrest, the wrist.
Wrethe, to twist.
Writ (pl. *writtes*), writing, a written paper.
Wroke, *wroken*, avenged.
Wyde, turned away (cf. *wide* of the mark).
Wyte, to blame.

Y, as a prefix of the past participle, is frequently employed by Spenser, as *Y-clad*, clothed, *Y-fraught*, filled, etc.
Ybent, turned, gone.
Ybet, beaten.
Yblent, blinded, dazzled.
Ybore, born.
Yclad, clad.
Ycleped, called, named.
Ydle, empty.
Ydlesse, idleness.
Ydrad, *ydred*, dreaded, feared.
Yead, *yede*, *yeed*, to go (properly a preterite tense).
Yearne, to earn.
Yfere, together, in company with.
Yfretted, adorned.
Ygo, *ygoe*, gone, ago.
Yglaunst, glanced, glided.
Yilde, yield.
Yirks, jirks, lashes.
Ylike, alike.
Ymolt, melted.
Ympe, youth. See *Imp*.
Ympt, joined.
Ynd, India.
Yod, *bode*, went.
Yold, yielded.
Yond, yonder.
Yond, outrageous, terrible.
Youngling, young of man or beast.
Younker, a youth.
Youthly, youthful.
Yplight, plighted.
Yrkes, wearies.
Yron-braced, sinewed, like iron (of the arm).
Ysame, together.
Ywis, certainly, truly.
Ywrake, *ywroke*, *ywroken*, avenged, revenged.